Rebels Against Tyranny

Rebels Against Tyranny

Civil War in the Crusader States

Helena P. Schrader

Published by Wheatmark®
2030 East Speedway Boulevard, Suite 106
Tucson, Arizona 85719 USA
www.wheatmark.com

ISBN: 978-1-62787-624-7 (paperback)
ISBN: 978-1-62787-625-4 (ebook)
LCCN: 2018946096

Contents

Introduction and Acknowledgments

NOT MUCH HISTORICAL FICTION HAS BEEN written about the crusades of the 13th century, much less life in the crusader states during this period. The Sixth Crusade, if mentioned at all, is usually condensed to the bloodless return of Jerusalem to Christian control. The inherent flaws in Frederick II's treaty—the short duration of the truce, the prohibitions on Christian fortifications, the legal impediments to the treaty—are ignored or glossed over. Likewise, Frederick II Hohenstaufen is more often depicted as a monarch ahead of his time, even as a "genius" and a man of "exceptional tolerance," without acknowledging that many of his contemporaries considered him a tyrant.

From the 15th to the early 20th century, popular adulation of absolutism and central authority transformed Frederick into the embodiment of "good government;" the fact that he ran roughshod over the law and arbitrarily exercised his authority was largely ignored or justified. Contempt for feudalism (a dogma of the Enlightenment) and hatred of the papacy (a dogma of the Reformation) combined to discredit Frederick's opponents in the eyes of historians. Particularly German scholars of the 19th and early 20th century sought to create a glorious "German Emperor" to incarnate all the Germanic virtues then in vogue.

While Frederick's struggle with the papacy is legendary, his defeat at the hands of his own barons in the crusader kingdoms of Jerusalem and Cyprus is familiar only to historians of the 13[th]century Latin East. Yet the history of the baronial revolt against Frederick II offers all the ingredients of first-rate historical fiction. On the one side there is the legendary and colorful Emperor—the man who called himself "the Wonder of the World"—and on the other side a cast of rebels, who were also scholars and intellectuals, poets and patrons of the arts.

The men of Outremer who opposed Frederick II left an impressive legacy of *intellectual* accomplishments. They were the authors of histories, poetry, and works of philosophy, although they are most famous today for their outstanding contributions to medieval jurisprudence. The renowned crusades historian Jonathan Riley-Smith goes so far as to claim: "Perhaps the greatest monument to the western settlers in Palestine, finer even than the cathedrals and castles still dominating the landscape, is the law-book of John of Jaffa, which…is one of the great works of thirteenth-century thought." (Riley-Smith, Jonathan. *The Feudal Nobility and the Kingdom of Jerusalem 1174 – 1277*. Macmillan Press, 1973, p. 230.)

Furthermore, the issues at stake remain relevant today: how much central power is necessary for the good of a state? Does "raison d'etat" justify dishonor and treachery? When does a citizen have the right to defend himself against tyranny? At what point is forgiveness and reconciliation the wisest action— regardless of the crimes committed? When is trust constructive—and when is it dangerously naïve?

After deciding to write a novel (or more) about this fascinating chapter in human history, the question became which of a large cast of historical figures should I put at the center of my fictional work. Three major historical personalities offered themselves.

- **John d'Ibelin, the "Old" Lord of Beirut**: the original leader of the baronial opposition. A man of moderation and wisdom, Beirut enjoyed huge respect among his contemporaries. He was, furthermore, the youthful hero of *The Last Crusader Kingdom*. However, he died before the final victory of the baronial revolt. Furthermore, as a wise and elderly widower, even at the start of the revolt, he wasn't ideal for developing drama and romance.

- **John d'Ibelin, Count of Jaffa**: the author of the book praised so highly by Riley-Smith (see above). In the later 13th century, Jaffa was an important personality, who took part in King Louis' crusade, rebuilt Jaffa from ruins, and was a prolific writer. A colorful character who carried on a notorious, illicit love affair later in life, he had all the qualities of a great fictional hero, but unfortunately, he was born a little too late to be a major actor in the early phases of the baronial revolt at the heart of my novel(s).

- **Philip de Novare: the author of the most detailed contemporary account of the revolt**, *The Wars of Frederick II against the Ibelins in Syria and Cyprus*. Philip was a vassal of the Ibelins and unabashedly biased in favor of his patrons. He was a poet, singer, historian, and jurist as well—and this was what disqualified him for my hero: he left a far too comprehensive legacy to give me sufficient leeway as a novelist to mold him to my purposes.

So, rather than choosing any of the above for my central protagonist, I chose a character at the very center of the revolt, a man whose adult life spanned the entire crisis, his knighting (coming of age) and death bracketing the historical events depicted. He is a man who, according to Novare, distinguished himself in the fighting, defied an archbishop and his father to marry the woman he loved and won the final victory against the Emperor. Yet, almost the exception among his peers, he did not leave a written legacy that reveals his character, attitudes, and temperament. In short, he was enough of a blank page—despite the intriguing hints left by Novare—to be malleable for literary purposes. The only serious disadvantage to making him my central protagonist was that he bears the same name (indeed was named for) the hero of my Jerusalem Trilogy: Balian d'Ibelin. He was the eldest son and heir of the "Old Lord of Beirut," a grandson of the defender of Jerusalem, and succeeded to the title of Lord of Beirut on his father's death.

Having selected my male hero, the heroine was predetermined by history: she could only be the woman that Balian II defied the church and his father to marry. Even less is known about her than about Balian II. We know her family heritage, that she was widowed early, and that she actively, at one point decisively, took part in the baronial revolt. That seemed enough material, however, to give me a strong character.

Around these two central characters are grouped the rest of the historical cast: Frederick Hohenstaufen and his five deputies (the baillies of Cyprus), King Henry of Cyprus, Balian's father, brothers, sister and cousins, and Philip of Novare himself. I hope that you will find them an appealing, intriguing, and compelling cast of characters, some delightful and some despicable, but all believable and complex.

I wish to take this opportunity to thank my editor Christopher Cervelloni for his sensitive and meticulous editing of my sometimes erratic text, and Mikhail Greuli for his magnificent cover. To meet my demands for a cover that looked like something from a medieval manuscript, Mikhail had to develop an entirely new style, for which I am sincerely grateful.

Addis Ababa,
April 28, 2018

Royal House of Cyprus
(Royalty in Bold)

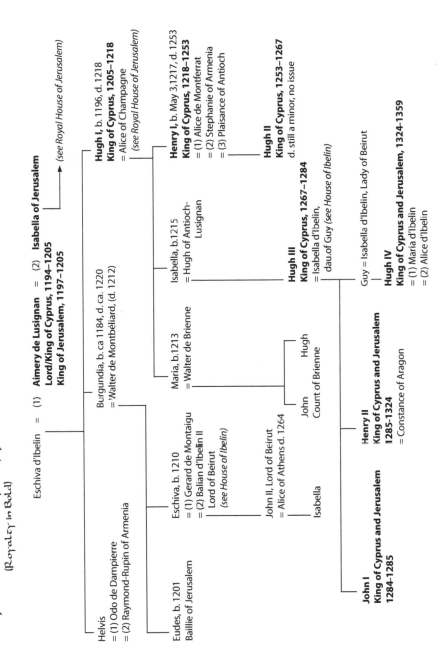

Eschiva d'Ibelin = (1) **Aimery de Lusignan** = (2) **Isabella of Jerusalem**
Lord/King of Cyprus, 1194–1205
King of Jerusalem, 1197–1205

(see Royal House of Jerusalem)

Helvis
= (1) Odo de Dampierre
= (2) Raymond-Rupin of Armenia

Burgundia, b. ca 1184, d. ca. 1220
= Walter de Montbéliard, (d. 1212)

Hugh I, b. 1196, d. 1218
King of Cyprus, 1205–1218
= Alice of Champagne
(see Royal House of Jerusalem)

Eudes, b. 1201
Baillie of Jerusalem

Eschiva, b. 1210
= (1) Gerard de Montaigu
= (2) Balian d'Ibelin II
Lord of Beirut
(see House of Ibelin)

Maria, b. 1213
= Walter de Brienne

Isabella, b. 1215
= Hugh of Antioch-
Lusignan

Henry I, b. May 3, 1217, d. 1253
King of Cyprus, 1218–1253
= (1) Alice de Montferrat
= (2) Stephanie of Armenia
= (3) Plaisance of Antioch

John II, Lord of Beirut
= Alice of Athens d. 1264

John   Hugh
Count of Brienne

Hugh III
King of Cyprus, 1267–1284
= Isabella d'Ibelin,
dau. of Guy (see House of Ibelin)

Hugh II
King of Cyprus, 1253–1267
d. still a minor, no issue

Isabella

Henry II
King of Cyprus and Jerusalem
1285-1324
= Constance of Aragon

Guy = Isabella d'Ibelin, Lady of Beirut

Hugh IV
King of Cyprus and Jerusalem, 1324-1359
= (1) Maria d'Ibelin
= (2) Alice d'Ibelin

John I
King of Cyprus and Jerusalem
1284-1285

House of Jerusalem
in the Early 13th Century
(Reigning Monarchs in bold)

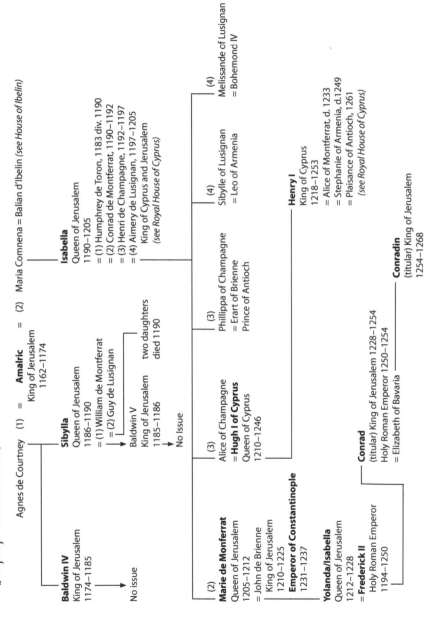

Agnes de Courtney (1) = **Amalric** = (2) Maria Comnena = Balian d'Ibelin *(see House of Ibelin)*
King of Jerusalem
1162–1174

Baldwin IV
King of Jerusalem
1174–1185

No issue

Sibylla
Queen of Jerusalem
1186–1190
= (1) William de Montferrat
= (2) Guy de Lusignan

Baldwin V
King of Jerusalem
1185–1186

No Issue

two daughters
died 1190

Isabella
Queen of Jerusalem
1190–1205
= (1) Humphrey de Toron, 1183 div. 1190
= (2) Conrad de Montferrat, 1190–1192
= (3) Henri de Champagne, 1192–1197
= (4) Aimery de Lusignan, 1197–1205
King of Cyprus and Jerusalem
(see Royal House of Cyprus)

(2)
Marie de Monferrat
Queen of Jerusalem
1205–1212
= John de Brienne
King of Jerusalem
1210–1225

Emperor of Constantinople
1231–1237

(3)
Alice of Champagne
= **Hugh I of Cyprus**
Queen of Cyprus
1210–1246

(3)
Phillippa of Champagne
= Erart of Brienne
Prince of Antioch

(4)
Sibylle of Lusignan
= Leo of Armenia

(4)
Melissande of Lusignan
= Bohemond IV

Henry I
King of Cyprus
1218–1253
= Alice of Montferrat, d. 1233
= Stephanie of Armenia, d.1249
= Plaisance of Antioch, 1261
(see Royal House of Cyprus)

Yolanda/Isabella
Queen of Jerusalem
1212–1228
= **Frederick II**
Holy Roman Emperor
1194–1250

Conrad
(titular) King of Jerusalem 1228–1254
Holy Roman Emperor 1250–1254
= Elizabeth of Bavaria

Conradin
(titular) King of Jerusalem
1254–1268

The House of Ibelin in the 12th Century

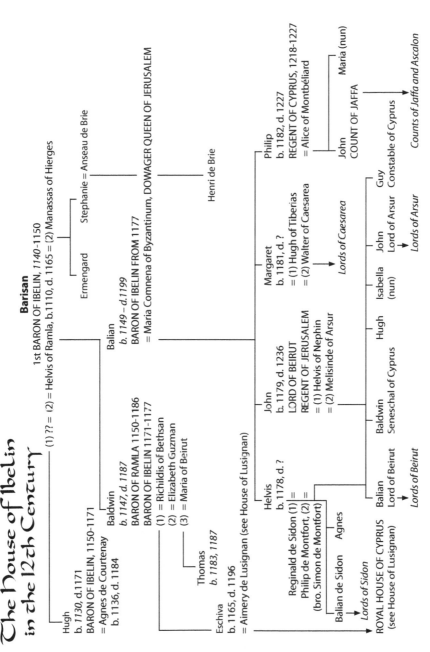

Barisan
1st BARON OF IBELIN, *1140*-1150
(1) ?? = (2) = Helvis of Ramla, b.1110, d. 1165 = (2) Manasses of Hierges

Hugh
b. 1130, d.1171
BARON OF IBELIN, 1150-1171
= Agnes de Courtenay

Baldwin
b. 1147, d. 1187
BARON OF RAMLA 1150-1186
BARON OF IBELIN 1171-1177
(1) = Richildis of Bethsan
(2) = Elizabeth Guzman
(3) = Maria of Beirut

Ermengard

Stephanie = Anseau de Brie

Balian
b. 1149 – d.1199
BARON OF IBELIN FROM 1177
= Maria Comnena of Byzantinum, DOWAGER QUEEN OF JERUSALEM

Henri de Brie

Philip
b. 1182, d. 1227
REGENT OF CYPRUS, 1218-1227
= Alice of Montbéliard

Maria (nun)

John
COUNT OF JAFFA

Counts of Jaffa and Ascalon

Margaret
b. 1181, d. ?
= (1) Hugh of Tiberias
= (2) Walter of Caesarea

Lords of Caesarea

Guy
Constable of Cyprus

John
Lord of Arsur

Lords of Arsur

Isabella
(nun)

Hugh
Seneschal of Cyprus

John
b. 1179, d. 1236
LORD OF BEIRUT
REGENT OF JERUSALEM
= (1) Helvis of Nephin
= (2) Melisinde of Arsur

Baldwin
Seneschal of Cyprus

Balian
Lord of Beirut

Lords of Beirut

Thomas
b. 1183, 1187

Eschiva
b. 1165, d. 1196
= Aimery de Lusignan (see House of Lusignan)

Helvis
b. 1178, d. ?
Reginald de Sidon (1) =
Philip de Montfort, (2) =
(bro. Simon de Montfort)

Agnes

Balian de Sidon

Lords of Sidon

ROYAL HOUSE OF CYPRUS
(see House of Lusignan)

Philip de Montfort,
(bro. Simon de Mortfort)

The House of Ibelin
in the Early 13th Century
(Royalty in bold)

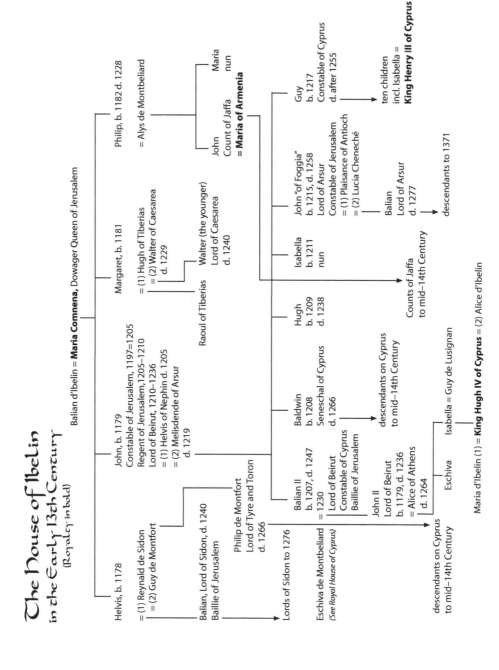

Balian d'Ibelin = **Maria Comnena**, Dowager Queen of Jerusalem

Helvis, b. 1178
= (1) Reynald de Sidon
= (2) Guy de Montfort

John, b. 1179
Constable of Jerusalem, 1197=1205
Regent of Jerusalem, 1205–1210
Lord of Beirut, 1210–1236
= (1) Helvis of Nephin d. 1205
= (2) Melisdende of Arsur
d. 1219

Margaret, b. 1181
= (1) Hugh of Tiberias
= (2) Walter of Caesarea
d. 1229

Philip, b. 1182 d. 1228
= Alys de Montbeliard

Balian, Lord of Sidon, d. 1240
Baillie of Jerusalem

Philip de Montfort
Lord of Tyre and Toron
d. 1266

Lords of Sidon to 1276

Raoul of Tiberias

Walter (the younger)
Lord of Caesarea
d. 1240

John
Count of Jaffa
= **Maria of Armenia**

Maria
nun

Balian II
b. 1207, d. 1247
= 1230
Lord of Beirut
Constable of Cyprus
Baillie of Jerusalem

Baldwin
b. 1208
Seneschal of Cyprus
d. 1266

Hugh
b. 1209
d. 1238

Isabella
b. 1211
nun

John "of Foggia"
b. 1215, d. 1258
Lord of Arsur
Constable of Jerusalem
= (1) Plaisance of Antioch
= (2) Lucia Cheneché

Guy
b. 1217
Constable of Cyprus
d. after 1255

John II
Lord of Beirut
b. 1179, d. 1236
= Alice of Athens
d. 1264

descendants on Cyprus
to mid–14th Century

Counts of Jaffa
to mid–14th Century

Balian
Lord of Arsur
d. 1277

ten children
incl. Isabella =
King Henry III of Cyprus

Eschiva de Montbeliard
(See Royal House of Cyprus)

descendants on Cyprus
to mid–14th Century

Eschiva

Isabella = Guy de Lusignan

descendants to 1371

Maria d'Ibelin (1) = **King Hugh IV of Cyprus** = (2) Alice d'Ibelin

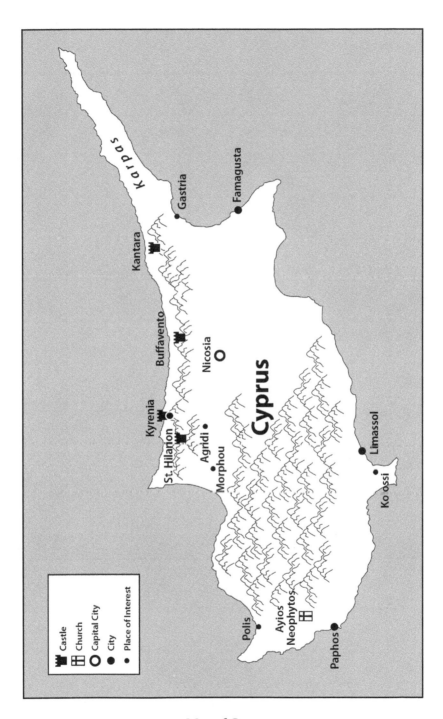

Map of Cyprus

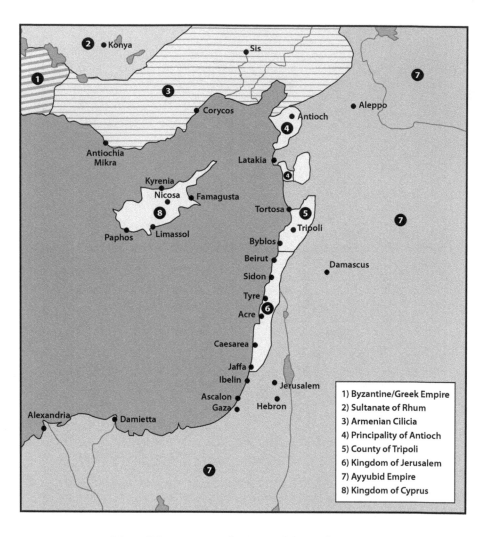

Map of Outremer at the Start of the 13th Century

1) Byzantine/Greek Empire
2) Sultanate of Rhum
3) Armenian Cilicia
4) Principality of Antioch
5) County of Tripoli
6) Kingdom of Jerusalem
7) Ayyubid Empire
8) Kingdom of Cyprus

Cast of Characters

Historical figures are in **bold**;
characters who appear twice are marked by an *;
dates in italics are estimates.

House of Ibelin

John, Lord of Beirut, formerly Constable and Regent of the Kingdom of Jerusalem, b. 1179, son of Balian d'Ibelin and Maria Comnena, Dowager Queen of Jerusalem.

Balian II, Beirut's eldest son and heir, *b.1207*

Baldwin, Beirut's second son, *b. 1208*

Hugh, Beirut's third son, *b. 1209*

Isabella "Bella," Beirut's only daughter, *b.1211*

John "Johnny," Beirut's fourth son, *b. 1215*

Guy, Beirut's fifth son, *b. 1217*

Philip, Beirut's brother, Regent of Cyprus 1218-1228, *b. 1182*

Alys de Montbéliard, Philip's wife, sister of Walter de Montbéliard (Regent of Cyprus from 1205-1210).

John "Jacques" son of Philip and Alys, *b. 1215*.

Maria, daughter of Philip d'Ibelin and Alys de Montbéliard, *b. 1217*

Marguerite "Meg,"* Lady of Caesarea (2nd marriage), formerly Lady of Tiberias, sister of John (the elder) and Philip d'Ibelin, *b. 1181*.

Royalty

Frederick II Hohenstaufen, "The Wonder of the World" or "Stupor Mundi," Holy Roman Emperor, King of the Romans, King of Sicily, son of Henry VI Hohenstaufen and grandson of Frederick "Barbarossa," husband to Yolanda of Jerusalem, and through her King of Jerusalem, 1225-1228, b. 1194.

Henry I, King of Cyprus 1218–1253, son of Hugh I and his wife Alice de Champagne, b. May 3, 1218.

Yolanda (also Isabella II), Queen of Jerusalem, daughter of John de Brienne and Marie de Montferrat, born November 1212, wife of Frederick Hohen-staufen and through him Empress of the Holy Roman Empire.

The Imperial Baillies of Cyprus

Amaury Barlais, son of Reynald Barlais, one of the five baillies of Cyprus appointed by Frederick II.

Gauvain de Cheneché, son of Galganus de Cheneché, one of the five baillies of Cyprus appointed by Frederick II.

Amaury "Grimbert" de Bethsan, son of Walter de Bethsan, one of the five baillies of Cyprus appointed by Frederick II; the name "Grimbert" was given him by Novare in his songs, and to avoid two Amaurys (both baillies of Cyprus at the same time) I have substituted "Grimbert" for "Amaury" throughout.

William de Rivet, son of Amaury de Rivet, one of the five baillies of Cyprus appointed by Frederick II.

Hugh de Gibelet, one of the five baillies of Cyprus appointed by Frederick II. (Sometimes also referred to as Hugh de Jubail.)

Other Barons and Ladies of Outremer

Eudes de Montbéliard, Constable and Baillie of Jerusalem, son of Walter de Montbéliard the former Regent of Cyprus and Burgundia de Lusignan the sister of King Hugh I, b. 1201.

Eschiva de Montbéliard, sister of Eudes, daughter of Walter de Montbéliard and Burgundia of Lusignan, first cousin to King Henry I, b.1210.

Balian de Sidon, Lord of Sidon, son of Reginald de Sidon and Helvis d'Ibelin, Beirut's elder sister, b. 1195. Renowned jurist, Baillie of the Kingdom of Jerusalem for Frederick Hohenstaufen.

Walter "the elder" of Caesarea, Lord of Caesarea, Constable of Cyprus, second husband of Margaret d'Ibelin, Beirut's sister.

Marguerite "Meg" d'Ibelin*, his wife and Beirut's sister, *b.1181.*

Walter "the younger" of Caesarea, eldest son and heir to the Lord of Caesarea, son of Walter and Meg d'Ibelin.

Anseau de Brie, "the Lion (or Leopard) of Karpas," *b. 1184,* a grandson of Balian I's half-sister—either Ermengard or Stephanie—and so a cousin of Beirut

Gerard de Montaigu, nephew of the Masters of the Temple and Hospital and the Archbishop of Nicosia.

Philip de Novare, a vassal of the Ibelins, friend of Balian II, later chronicler, historian and legal expert.

Lords of the Church

Pedro de Montaigu, Master of Knights Templar, 1219-1230

Guerin de Montaigu, Master of the Knights Hospitaller (brother of Pedro), 1207–1236.

Eustace de Montaigu, Archbishop of Nicosia 1217-1250, brother of Pedro and Guerin.

Herman von Salza, Master of the Deutsche Ritter Orden, 1210-1239

Gunther von Falkenhayn, Marshal of the Deutsche Ritter Orden, 1228-1230 (Only his first name is recorded, I have added the Falkenhayn)

Iago, Archbishop of Capua

Ibelin Household

Denis, Seneschal of Beirut Citadel

Denise, his daughter

"Rob" de Maumeni, Balian's squire, later Sir Robert de Maumeni

Eudes "Lucas" de la Fierté, Balian's squire

Genoese

Hugh di Ferrario, Consul of the Genoese of Cyprus

Paulo, his son

Florio Sanuto, Consul of the Genoese Commune in Acre

Giovanni Gabriele, a spice merchant in Acre

Cecilia, his only daughter

Captain Maurizio di Domenico, Captain of the *Rose of Acre*

Others

André, Philip de Novare's squire
Ullrich von Alvensleben, a Templar of German origin
Gebhard von Salder, a Templar of German origin
Sir Rohard, Seneschal of the Lusignan manor at Vouno
Father Ernesius, a Templar priest

Part 1

The Seeds of Civil War

Chapter One
A Fateful Fall

Limassol, Cyprus
May 18, 1224

"PHILIP, ARE YOU ALL RIGHT?" a young, male voice called out anxiously.

Sir Philip of Novare couldn't see the owner of the voice because his squire was trying to pry his misshapen great helm off his head—without taking half his face off with it. Philip had just lost a "friendly" joust. Although his opponent had used only a blunted mace, he'd still managed to bash in the side of Philip's helm.

Philip was sweating profusely, as much from increasing panic as the heat of a Cypriot summer day. The air inside the helm seemed to grow thinner and thinner as his squire Andre twisted the metal pot to try to maneuver it past Philip's chin. The pounding of his blood in his temples and the rasping of his breath seemed to echo inside the helmet, blotting out most other sounds. He could barely hear Andre answer the newcomer in an anxious, frightened voice. "I can't get the helm off, sir."

"Let me try," the voice answered, coming nearer. "It's me. Balian."

"I can hardly breathe anymore, Bal," Philip gasped.

Firm hands grasped the helmet, and a moment later the air flooded back into Philip's lungs like a fresh breeze. Balian had twisted the helm so that both the eye slit and breathing holes were in position again. Their eyes met, and Philip could see the concern and question in Balian's eyes.

"I'm fine—if I could just get this damned thing off!" Philip assured his friend.

Balian and he had just spent the last three years earning their spurs together. Yesterday, in an extravagant ceremony, they had been knighted by Balian's father, the powerful Lord of Beirut, along with Balian's younger brother Baldwin and five other youths. Today's jousting was part of the three-day celebration, which would culminate in a full-scale melee pitting the barons and knights of Syria against those of Cyprus.

Balian was already seventeen and had long felt ready for the accolade of knighthood. Philip knew that Balian was both wounded and resentful that his father had delayed his knighting so long—and then knighted his fourteen-month-younger brother at the same time. Being so close in age, the brothers had always been rivals, but the intensity of their competition was aggravated by the fact that they were very different in temperament. Baldwin was like water to Balian's fire—and took pleasure in dousing Balian's enthusiasm and pride. Balian's need to prove himself better than Baldwin in front of all the peers of the realm had provoked him into taking stupid risks this morning. Fortunately, he'd gotten away with them and ridden undefeated from the lists.

Under the circumstances, Philip thought, he might have been forgiven for basking in his hard-won glory and gloating a bit instead of coming down into the dusty tent-city to find out what had happened to his friend. After all, in addition to practically every baron and knight of Outremer, there were scores of ladies and maidens in the stands. Balian had the kind of good looks that appealed to women. By the way the maidens had been biting their fingernails at Balian's near falls and cheering his successes, Philip could imagine all too vividly the way Balian would be adulated and adored by blushing young beauties the moment he joined the spectators. Instead, Balian hadn't even taken the time to change out of his sweat-soaked gambeson and dusty surcoat.

"I think I better fetch an armorer, Philip," Balian told Philip after a moment of inspection.

"He'll want to cut it open!" Philip protested with a new kind of panic. Unlike Balian who was heir to the lordship of Beirut, son of one of the richest men in both Syria and Cyprus, Philip was an orphan. His father, a knight from Lombardy, had died during the first siege of Damietta when he was only twelve. A Cypriot, Sir Peter Chappe, had taken Philip under his wing, letting him serve as his page until Philip's skill at reading earned him the patronage of a more powerful lord, Sir Ralph of Tiberias. The latter had been nearing death, however, and Philip had soon found himself without a lord, let alone a fief. Balian's father had rescued him by bestowing a small Cypriot fief upon him and sending him to serve as a squire in his brother's household, where he had met and befriended Balian. Philip had spent all the cash he could raise from his one fief just to outfit himself—and now his expensive helm was in risk of being ruined beyond repair.

"Very probably," Balian agreed calmly, and Philip knew his friend just *couldn't* understand. Balian's armor had cost twice as much in the first place, and he wouldn't have given a thought to replacing it on a whim. Balian didn't hesitate to wear silk surcoats on the tiltyard either or buy a sword with an enameled pommel or a saddle with ivory inlays.

"Balian! I can't *afford* a new helmet!" Philip protested in exasperation.

"You can't exactly spend the rest of your life wearing that one either," Balian retorted practically. "You can't drink or eat in it for a start. I'm going to fetch the armorer. Andre?" He turned to his friend's young, inexperienced and frightened squire.

"Yes, my lord?"

"Draw a cold bath for Sir Philip. When we get him out of that thing, he's going to need to cool off. He very likely got a concussion and doesn't even know it yet."

"Yes, my lord."

"I'll be right back, Philip," Balian assured his friend, and ducked under the partially opened tent flap.

Outside Philip's tent, Balian was in a city of canvas. Literally, hundreds of lords and knights had pitched their tents on the plain west of Limassol to take part in this sporting event. Tournaments had been popular in France and Flanders for nearly a century, but for most of that time, the knights and lords of Outremer had been engaged in too much real warfare against the Saracens to seek mock combat. The last decades, however, had been comparatively settled due to squabbling between the heirs of al-Adil. With the Ayyubids fighting among themselves, the Franks had been given a respite from war, and their appetite for sport had grown commensurately.

Although the actual lists were a couple hundred yards away, the dust churned up by the jousting wafted on the wind across the tent city, turning the air a murky beige and the sound of cheering and shouting was only slightly dampened. Clearly, the current joust was exciting the crowd because the shouts and collective groans seemed particularly intense. Balian, however, only glanced in the direction of the lists, knowing that the matches scheduled for this afternoon did not include any of his friends or family. Instead, he tried to decide the best way through the rows of tents to the armorers who had set up shops along the far periphery.

He had only gone a few steps when a new roar of agitation rose from the bleachers. People seemed to be shouting, "Stop! Stop!"

Balian paused to look in the direction of the lists and saw a little man come storming out on foot. It was Sir Amaury Barlais. He was covered with sand, evidently from a tumble, but that was hardly unusual. What was striking was that he was beet red with fury as he cursed and gestured. "I'll kill him! I swear! I'll kill him! He was *cheating*! It was obvious! If they refuse to see that, they're all cheats and liars!"

Two other knights were running after him, his cousin Sir Grimbert de Bethsan and Sir Gauvain de Cheveché. "Amaury, you might be right that Sir Toringuel was cheating, but it does you no good to accuse the baillie of being in cahoots with him—"

"Why shouldn't I? Damn it! Toringuel is Ibelin's knight. If he was cheating, it was with his knowledge and consent!"

Balian flinched at such an accusation. Aside from being baillie, his uncle was an Ibelin, and he had been raised to believe that all Ibelins had an obligation to live by the very highest standards of chivalry. From the time he was a little boy, it had been beaten into him that as an Ibelin he had to be *more* honest, *more* charitable, *more* loyal, *more* diligent, *more* persistent, *more* courageous, *more* compassionate—in short more *noble* than other men. That he didn't always live up to that ideal was obvious, but he had never expected to hear anyone impute that his *uncle* fell short of the highest standards. People might not like all of his policies, but Balian had never before heard anyone accuse his uncle of anything dishonorable.

Sir Grimbert made a second attempt to calm Barlais. "You don't know that, Amaury. If you're so sure Sir Toringuel was cheating, then demand an inspection of his weapons, but don't lash out at the judges! That only makes them disinclined to support you!"

"They're all a bunch of bastards!" Barlais insisted, his rage so intense that his veins were pulsing in his temples as he tore off his coif and arming cap. He was in his mid-thirties and his hair was thinning over angular features that made Balian's friend Philip de Novare compare him to a weasel. The latter image was reinforced because he wore his short, brown hair slicked back away from his sharp face. He ducked back into a tent like a rodent going to earth, but as Balian passed by he was still raging, "I'll kill him! I swear, I'll kill him!"

Limassol, Cyprus
May 19, 1224

Philip d'Ibelin, baillie of Cyprus for the seven-year-old King Henry I, had built a palace in Limassol. It did not rival his brother's palace in Beirut because the latter was set above the mighty walls of the citadel of Beirut, giving it spectacular views in all directions, but Philip's palace at Limassol was pleasant and impressive in its own way. It sat beside the shore, offering views of the Mediterranean, and contained three large interior courtyards.

One of these enclosed a formal garden with a fountain at the center like the cloisters of a monastery. Here sunlight was angling through the encircling arcade, casting golden arches on the green-and-cream tiles paving the walkway. The columns supporting the arches were polished marble and the capitals were elaborately carved with foliage and beasts. A light breeze off the sea gently swayed the tips of the tall cypress trees at the four corners of the garden, and birds twittered in the oleander bushes.

"I think you can be pleased with the way things have gone so far," Philip d'Ibelin remarked to his elder brother John as they strolled under the arcade. The individual contests were over now, and everyone had returned to their lodgings to rest, bathe and dress for tonight's feast and festivities. Tomorrow there would be the melee and then theater followed by a feast with more singing, dancing and poetry contests.

John d'Ibelin, Lord of Beirut, was 45 years old, two years older than his host. He was tall, like all Ibelins, and being a vigorous man (he would lead his own troop in the melee tomorrow), he had a sleek, almost slender figure despite his age. His brown hair was bleached and his face tanned by too much exposure to the Syrian sun. Although a good-looking man, he was sober and serious by nature, something reflected in the lines on his face. He frowned now, too. "Balian was flirting with every single damsel of the kingdom—and half the ladies too! It was embarrassing!"

"Don't be so hard on him, John," Philip answered with a smile. "I was no different at his age."

"And I was ashamed of you too!" John quipped back, making them both laugh.

"But you shouldn't have been," Philip countered in a gentle voice when the laughter faded. "The bolder maidens all but threw themselves at him, and the shyer ones were breathless just watching him."

"It will go to his head!" John grumbled.

"For a day or two," the younger Ibelin conceded.

John eyed his brother reproachfully, and with a laugh, Philip revised his statement. "All right. For a month or two, maybe even a year or two, but eventually he'll realize it isn't worth much. Don't forget he's been with me these past three years. I've had ample opportunity to watch him mature. Yes, he's a bit full of himself at the moment, but what do you expect after the festival *you* organized for him, John? Balian enjoys life. If he's happy and having fun, he embraces the whole world. That doesn't mean he can't be serious and determined when he needs to be. He had a terrible time with the crossbow for some reason, but rather than saying it was a 'common' weapon as many another noble youth has done, he put in extra time trying to master it, practicing—literally—until his fingers bled."

John looked hard at his brother. "I *want* to believe you. He's my heir. I want him to be worthy of our father's name."

"That's a heavy burden, John. Can you say without hesitation that *we* have lived up to our father's expectations?"

John smiled at that, but it was a sad smile accompanied by a sigh. "His expectations? Certainly. But only because his humility extended to us as well as to himself. 'We can only be what God has made us,' he said again and again. 'Be the best you can be, but do not strive to be that which God has not given you the means to achieve.'" The Lord of Beirut fell silent, remembering his father's words.

Philip gave his brother a moment to reflect before asking gently, "And you think that Balian is in some way *able* but *unwilling* to fulfill his role in life?"

John answered with a sigh.

Philip pressed him. "In what way is Balian unworthy of his name? He is bright. Sharp as a whip, actually, even if he doesn't have a scholarly bone in his body. He's courageous almost to a fault. He's a superb horseman and an outstanding swordsman—even if he's less good with a lance and I wouldn't want to trust my life to his archery. He's generous and, for a seventeen-year-old, devout. True, he enjoys his wine, but he doesn't get belligerent when he drinks too much, just mellow and sleepy." Philip fell silent running out of things to say.

"He's too emotional," John answered, looking Philip straight in the eye. "He's ruled by his emotions rather than his reason. He feels before he thinks. *That* is dangerous."

Philip thought about this a moment and then remarked softly. "He's more like me in that regard too, but emotions aren't *bad*, John—only acting upon them without reflecting first. He'll learn to do that. Just give him time."

"Hmm," John grunted ambiguously, but then pointed out, "Acting without reflecting is certainly what our niece Alice did when she married Antioch. She would appear to have let her passion run away with her completely. As I understand it, she didn't so much as *inform* the High Court of Cyprus, much less ask permission. Not to mention she abandoned her children as if they meant no more to her than a pair of old shoes!" Beirut's indignation sharpened his words.

The brothers were in accord on this subject. The Dowager Queen of Cyprus, Alice of Champagne, was their niece. She was the daughter of their late half-sister Queen Isabella of Jerusalem. She had been betrothed to King Hugh of Cyprus when they were both infants, married to him at the age of fifteen, and widowed at the age of 23. Unlike her mother Isabella of Jerusalem, Alice of Champagne had never taken an interest in actually ruling her kingdom. Her husband had commended his kingdom to Philip d'Ibelin on his deathbed, and the High Court of Cyprus had confirmed and legalized their dead king's wish by electing Philip d'Ibelin baillie of Cyprus. Alice had willingly turned over the burdens of government to her Uncle Philip—on the condition she retained the better part of the revenues. The barons and knights of Cyprus had taken oaths to Philip d'Ibelin as their liege "until King Henry came of age."

Alice of Champagne was now 29, however, and she had remarried—without the consent of either her uncles or her barons—a man of her own choosing: Bohemond, Prince Antioch. No one objected to a dowager queen remarrying. John and Philip d'Ibelin were the children of such a union. In the case of Alice of Champagne, however, the High Court was angry and outraged because they mistrusted Antioch.

Philip expressed these fears bluntly. "If Antioch sets foot on this island, I wouldn't give poor Henry a year to live!" Philip had been the young king's surrogate father ever since he assumed the *bailliage* when Henry was just nine months old. "Antioch wants this island for his own. He wants to see *his* sons inherit it. If Antioch comes to Cyprus, he will find a way to remove Henry and, bitch that Alice is, she'll probably aid and abet him in it!"

"I *do* presume you are talking about a different Alice," a female voice surprised the brothers.

They turned sharply to face the speaker. John bowed deeply to his sister-in-law, Alys de Montbéliard, while Philip raised her hand to his lips and assured her, "we were talking of the queen."

"In that case," she agreed with a mischievous smile, "'bitch' is almost too good a word—or rather an insult to female dogs."

Alys de Montbéliard was not a beauty and never had been. The sister of the man who had ruled Cyprus during the late King Hugh's minority, her marriage to Philip d'Ibelin had been entirely political. The Montbéliards and Ibelins had frequently been at odds, and Beirut had accused Alys' brother Walter of plun-

dering the royal Cypriot treasury. Alys' marriage to Philip had been arranged as
a grand reconciliation between the families, and neither party had been particularly keen about it at the time. In the subsequent twelve years, however, they had
become increasingly fond of one another.

"May I join you?" she asked the brothers, "or was this an exclusively Ibelin
affair?"

"You are always welcome, my dear," Philip assured her.

Alys sank down on a marble bench in the shade, her silk skirts and long bell
sleeves falling gracefully about her as she looked up at them expectantly. "You
were speaking of the Queen Mother, I believe," she prompted.

"Yes, we were saying that should Antioch come to Cyprus, we would fear
for the King's life."

"And rightly so. Alice of Champagne, as I was saying, has less affection for
her children than a mother dog. She is, as far as I can see, completely vain and
avaricious. What Bohemond sees in her I will never know, but then men are
often blinded by a pretty face—present company excluded, of course."

"What he more likely sees in her is Cyprus itself. Antioch is rich, but it
is vulnerable to Saracen attack. Cyprus is both wealthy and secure," Beirut
answered soberly.

Alys nodded agreement. "You are probably right. Have you thought of
crowning Henry king? It won't prevent outright murder, of course, but it is
considerably more difficult to set aside a crowned and anointed king than a boy
who *should* be king."

"He's only seven!" Philip protested.

His wife shrugged and looked at her brother-in-law. John looked more
thoughtful. "There's some truth to what you say," he remarked cautiously.
"Perhaps equally important, it would bind the barons of Cyprus directly to
Henry. Men are more unwilling to break an oath of fealty, particularly if their
liege gives them no cause. We should give it serious thought."

"What about the Holy Roman Emperor?" Philip asked back. "As Henry's
overlord, he might raise objections to Henry being crowned as a child."

"I don't see why," John countered. "The subordination of Cyprus to the
Holy Roman Empire has always been nominal. Richard of England took the
island and the Lusignans have held it. The Holy Roman Emperors have done
nothing but graciously accept Lusignan homage. Besides, if rumors are to be
believed, King John of Jerusalem is close to betrothing his daughter Yolanda to
Frederick Hohenstaufen."

"What?" Philip and Alys asked in unison.

"Hadn't you heard? He's been exchanging ambassadors with the Hohenstaufen for months now. Frederick has twice taken the cross but seems singularly reluctant to actually act upon it. He let the entire expedition to Egypt languish three years ago, at great expense and tragic loss of life. I'm told that King John thinks that if the Hohenstaufen had a *material* interest in the Holy Land, he might be more ready and willing to fulfill his crusader vows."

"Material interest meaning the entire kingdom?" Alys asked sourly before her husband could get a word out.

"Exactly," Beirut confirmed.

Alys and Philip looked at one another. The thought of a powerful monarch like Frederick Hohenstaufen being so near was not particularly welcome. The Lusignans had done homage to his father for the sake of raising their island lordship to a kingdom, but they had never expected to have a Holy Roman Emperor on their doorstep—or not for more than a short interlude of campaigning against the Saracens. A *King* of Jerusalem who was *also* a Holy Roman Emperor sounded ominous.

But not as ominous as the shouting coming from inside the palace. Someone was asking loudly for "My lord Philip," and another young voice asked even more urgently, "Where's my uncle?" Behind them were other voices—men calling, arguing, and apparently screaming at each other.

A moment later, Beirut's second son Baldwin burst out of the passageway leading from the central courtyard. "My lord! Father! Come quick! Amaury Barlais and his friends waylaid Sir Toringuel in an alley and damn near killed him. In fact, there's no surety he will survive. We managed to intervene at the last moment, but he's badly wounded. We just managed to apprehend Barlais as he tried to flee the scene."

For a stunned second the Ibelin brothers gaped at Baldwin, but then Philip asked urgently, "Where are they?"

"In the main court, my lord!"

Philip plunged down the passageway with his brother and nephew close on his heels. The main courtyard was a scene of apparent chaos. At least two dozen men had gathered, some holding a still struggling Barlais and three of his men-at-arms. On the stairs leading up to the gallery, a man soaked in his own blood was being laid down. Several men had stripped off their surcoats and bunched them under his head as an improvised pillow. A young and frightened squire was pressing his own surcoat into the wounds in his knight's gut, but the blood had already saturated the cloth and was glistening on his hands.

At the sight of the baillie of Cyprus, men drew back to let him through, and he went straight to the wounded man. One look was enough to see that it would be a miracle if he survived. Philip shouted over his shoulder, "Sir Baldwin, fetch a priest!" He then bent over the wounded knight and gently touched his face. "Sir Tor, who did this to you?"

"Barlais!" the man gasped out. "Barlais and his henchmen, so help me God!"

Philip spun around and saw Barlais restrained by two knights. When Philip's eyes fell on him, he stopped struggling and stared at the baillie with a defiant expression. "Sir Tor *cheated* yesterday, and no one would even *listen* to me. I took the matter into my own hands!"

"He cheated at *sport*, and you think that gives you the right to kill him?" Philip d'Ibelin asked in disbelief. "You think you have the *right* to commit murder in the streets of Limassol over a stupid joust?" His voice was rising in volume and pitch as his outrage boiled up. "Who the hell do you think you are?" He shouted. "I'll show you who you are! Son of an illiterate mercenary! And now a murderer!" He flung himself at Barlais, his sword singing as he drew.

It was all Beirut could do to grab his brother from behind and hold him back. For two seconds the brothers wrestled with one another as Philip struggled to break free of his brother's iron embrace.

"A second murder will not right the first!" Beirut shouted. "Don't dishonor yourself, Philip! Barlais must answer before a court!"

At this critical moment, the physician arrived in his black cap and robes. He spared the Ibelin brothers barely a glance and pushed the squire aside to inspect the wounds.

"Put him in the dungeon in chains!" Philip screamed at his knights. "Or better yet, in the pillory!" Then he knocked his brother angrily aside as he turned to go to his injured knight.

Beirut nodded to the knights holding Barlais, and they hastened to manhandle him out of the courtyard. As he was dragged away, Barlais shouted: "You have no right to arrest me! He *deserved* what he got! He cheated and could have killed me yesterday! Why is his life more valuable than mine?"

Limassol, Cyprus
May 30, 1224

It was the humiliation of the pillory that hurt Barlais most. The pillory was where they put common criminals—people accused of pick-pocketing and fraud, sorcery and slander, adultery and wife-beating. Knights and noblemen were not put in the stocks. They defended themselves in judicial combat—or were imprisoned, tortured in unforgiving chambers of unnamed dungeons, or hung, drawn and quartered in public—but they were not put in a pillory and subjected to *public* scorn and ridicule.

Putting him in the pillory, even if only for a few hours, was a calculated insult. It was meant to remind him that his father had never been knighted. They still saw it as his shame rather than theirs. Yet it was *their* shame because his father *should* have been knighted. No man had fought longer, harder, or more fervently for the Lusignans than Reynald Barlais. His only fault was that he'd been born unfree. He had run away to become a soldier and eventually a sergeant. He'd been freed by Geoffrey de Lusignan after proving his worth in the endless and ignoble struggle with the Plantagenets. His worth was in his willingness to do whatever the Lusignans needed done—no matter how distasteful. Reynald Barlais had been the man the Lusignans turned to whenever they needed a man with no scruples and a strong stomach. Reynald had never failed them, which was why the crusade appealed to him. A man with so much on his conscience needed absolution. More than once. So he'd stayed in the Holy Land.

Geoffrey de Lusignan had returned to France in disgust when the so-called "Lionheart" abandoned his brother Guy and recognized Conrad de Montferrat as King of Jerusalem. But Reynald Barlais stood by Guy and had come with him to Cyprus, where they had started all over again. Reynald played the same role for Guy that once he played for the French Lusignans. Reynald Barlais, more than anyone, had put Guy de Lusignan in power on Cyprus. He'd been prepared to do what the squeamish Ibelins would not—use brute force against the Greek rebels. He was prepared to hit them where it hurt—by sacking their monasteries and arresting their priests. He was willing to take sins on his conscience for the sake of securing Lusignan rule on Cyprus.

But no one wanted to remember that now—least of all the pampered son and grandson of the first Lusignan king. The second generation, King Hugh, had not liked being reminded that his House had come to power by the force of the sword. He had preferred to think of himself as a "legitimate" king.

Barlais hated him for it—and even more for the fact that because he didn't want to remember how much he owed the elder Barlais, he had never knighted him. Amaury Barlais was sure King Hugh had *known* that knighthood was the one honor his father had coveted more than all the riches they had given him. His father had wanted to die a knight—and King Hugh had denied that to him.

It was because King Hugh failed to knight his father before his death that

Amaury Barlais had seduced Hugh's widow. Alice de Champagne was pretty enough, but she was a vain and silly woman. Barlais had not found her particularly attractive—except for the fact she was Hugh de Lusignan's widow. Of course, it would have given him more satisfaction to actually cuckold that spoilt Lusignan brat, but at least he had brought Alice to the point where she swore to him in her passion-raw voice "You're so much better than Hugh ever was! So much harder, and oh—oh—oh—" The memories of Alice gasping those words in his ear kept him sane in the pillory. He was better than a king. It didn't matter that they treated him like a peasant, he was better than a king…

But then he'd been transferred to the Templar dungeon and chained to the wall. The dungeon was dark, dank, and filled with ghosts.

"Is this what I suffered for all those years?" His father snarled from the darkest corner. "Did I put up with so much shit so you could end your days in a dungeon?" The rough voice was getting nearer and it made Amaury shiver.

"Why did I pay good money so you could learn to read—like I never could? Not to mention learn to play fucking instruments, and write fucking poetry?" Reynald demanded, breathing grave-cold breath over Amaury's face.

A moment later, Amaury felt his father's fists raining blows to his head, and then, as Reynald liked to do, he delivered a kick to the groin. Amaury cried out in protest and tried to avoid that famous kick. He cracked his head against the walls of the dungeon and woke up from the nightmare.

His father was dead and buried. His father would never hurt him again.

He forced himself to concentrate; it was Ibelins who had put him here. The Lusignans preferred to *forget* the debt they owed Barlais, but the Ibelins had *usurped* Barlais' rightful place. They conveniently forgot (and had contrived to make Hugh's son and heir, Henry, forget) that *their* father had been a bitter enemy of Guy de Lusignan. They liked to forget that their father had been a landless knight too—until he wormed his way into the bed of a dowager queen! That was the basis of all their puffed up status: a seduction, a bedroom conquest.

Yet all because of that bedroom conquest, the Ibelins had been half-brothers to Queen Isabella of Jerusalem, and, through her, uncles to both Queen Maria of Jerusalem and Queen Alice of Cyprus.

Dear Alice detested her uncles John and Philip d'Ibelin because they accused her of being extravagant and egotistical. They had driven her mad with their admonishments about "thinking of her poor people" and reminding her of her "duty of charity." Amaury had enjoyed watching and then exploiting her tantrums (she was a particularly wild lover after she'd been in a rage) when she got a lecture from her baillie Philip d'Ibelin criticizing one expense or another.

The more Philip d'Ibelin urged "restraint" or "responsibility," the more Alice wanted Amaury's services.

Until one day after a particularly violent clash with her baillie, she tried to set him aside. The High Court replied that they had taken an oath to Philip "until King Henry came of age." Of course, that only made Alice angrier, so angry that (after a memorable night with Amaury) she started looking for a new husband. She wanted a man willing and able to defend her "rights." Barlais, no matter how good he was in bed, couldn't do that, so she'd lost interest in him.

He was getting bored with her anyway, Amaury reminded himself. His father was dead. He'd inherited. It had been time to marry. He'd found a rich and docile maiden, and she'd given him a litter of little girls. Just girls. So far. She was only twenty-six. There was time for a son. If he ever got out of here....

He looked about his dungeon again and tried to calculate his chances of release. Why was he here? For taking his revenge upon a cheater? That couldn't be the real reason. Surely. But they would pretend it was the reason.

So how long could they keep him locked up for attempted murder? Or even successful murder. Even if Toringuel was really dead, he was nothing but a household knight of Italian extraction. Who cared if Toringuel lived or died? The Ibelins apparently.

But they were notoriously legalistic. They couldn't just let him rot in here as his father would have done to any of his enemies. They would have to put him on trial for murder. They had to bring charges, and when they did he would demand trial-by-combat. They could not deny that to him. He was a knight. He'd been knighted by Walter de Montbéliard during King Hugh's minority. The thought of demanding trial-by-combat was comforting.

But how long had he been here already? There was no way to tell time in a dungeon. There was no day or night. Food and water were delivered irregularly. Sometimes he waited so long for food that he began to think they intended to starve him to death. Then the food came before he could finish the last portion. Not knowing the time was a form of torture, Amaury concluded.

And for what? For defending himself against a cheater! It was ridiculous.

Still, he should not have let Toringuel upset him so much. His friends had tried to calm him down. He should have listened to them. Toringuel had cheated and he deserved humiliation, but trying to kill him had been unnecessary. There would have been other ways to put him in his place, to show him up for the cheater he was. Trying to kill him had given the Ibelins the excuse they needed to humiliate him. They were his enemies, not Toringuel. It was the Ibelins who had usurped his rightful place.

"I'll kill them!" He raged at the darkness. "I'll kill them all! I'll have my revenge!"

But when the echoes of his words died away in the darkness, Amaury was still alone in the dungeon with one wrist and one ankle clasped in iron manacles that connected him to the wall.

Because he'd defended himself against a cheater? No, because they didn't want to be reminded of the fact that his father alone had done more for the Lusignans than the whole pack of Ibelins put together! Because they wanted everyone to forget that Sir Amaury Barlais should be baillie of Cyprus for the Lusignan boy-king. That was what was at issue here, and he stupidly played into their hands by attacking Toringuel.

He *had* to get his temper under control. Grimbert had told him that, and William and Gauvain, too, in different ways. They were good men. They were his friends. They were giving him good advice. Amaury was determined to follow it. From now on he would not show his fury. He would disguise his feelings behind a façade of friendship.

He got to his feet to pace. The chain was only three feet long and he could walk only in a semi-circle with the leg chains scraping as they dragged on the floor. The stones were scratched and worn by countless prisoners that had paced back and forth at the limits of that chain. The sound almost drowned out the grating of the key in the lock. Only as the door was already being pushed open did Amaury pause to stare at the door.

The light of the lantern made him squint after so long in the darkness, but his ears were sharper than ever. He registered that there were several voices and tensed just as the man with the lantern pushed into the room and stepped to one side.

Amaury stared at the second man who ducked through the low doorway. It was Beirut's whelp, pretty-boy Balian, dressed as always in his foppish clothes with embroidered trim. It was too dim to see the colors exactly, but after days in the stench of the dungeon, boy-Balian wore the scent of pine balsam from a recent bath that made Amaury want to puke. It was all he could do not to spit in his pretty face. He hated boy-Balian more than he hated his father or uncle simply because the boy was so worthless. He was nothing but a spoiled brat, the heir to a barony, the favorite nephew of a regent, rich beyond measure and pretty to boot.

But Amaury had promised himself he would not show his anger. He had decided to pretend docility and friendship instead. He forced a smile on his lips.

"Sir Amaury," boy-Balian opened in a voice Amaury presumed was supposed to sound serious but seemed like mockery in one so young and worthless. "Sir Toringuel has made an astonishing recovery. The physician says he is no longer in mortal danger and will live. Your attempted murder failed, and the lord regent has ordered your release. I am here to see that order carried out."

Amaury gaped at him. He had focused so much on demanding trial-by-combat, that he was slightly disoriented by this turn of events. He had not expected to simply walk out of the dungeon a free man.

Meanwhile, boy-Balian had gestured for a Templar sergeant with a huge ring of keys to come forward. While the Templar tried one key after another in the shackles, Amaury's squire Thomas slipped into the cell with a sheepish expression.

Amaury felt sorry for him. Thomas wasn't the brightest boy, but he was loyal as a spaniel, and he was clearly torn between relief at his master's release and shock at the state he was in. "I've brought you a change of clothes, sir, and Sirs Gauvain, Grimbert and William are waiting outside with your horse, arms, and armor. I packed the other things you like to travel with."

"Good boy, Tom. Thank you." But why was he talking about travel? Why should he go anywhere, if all charges had been dropped? Turning to boy-Balian he asked, "Have all charges have been dropped? I am a free man?"

"Yes," the Ibelin confirmed, adding, "However, Sir Toringuel has friends who are not as forgiving as my uncle. You might find it better to leave Cyprus until tempers cool."

Amaury nodded ambiguously. He was not going to *let* his temper cool—he was going to stoke it and cherish it for future use. For the moment, however, he chose to keep it hidden. Pretend to be docile! He reminded himself.

The Templar had at last found the right key and released Amaury from the manacles around his wrist and ankle. Freed of the restraints, Amaury pulled his filthy shirt off over his head and then tugged to release the cords of his braies. They dropped to the floor, and he stepped out of them. Tom handed him a clean pair and then helped him into the hose and shoes he'd brought. Next came a clean shirt and finally a surcoat. It wasn't perfect, but Amaury was grateful to his squire for bringing at least this much.

Boy-Balian led him out of the dungeon, up the narrow stairs to the courtyard of the Temple, and here he found Sirs Gauvain de Chenéché, William de Rivet, and his cousin Grimbert de Bethsan. Sir Gauvain and he had been squires almost two decades ago and friends ever since. His face broke into a smile of relief when he saw Amaury emerge from the Templar Commandery. Sirs William and Grimbert also closed around him, both inspecting him with their eyes. "Are you alright, Amaury?" Rivet asked with concern.

Barlais nodded, biting down the bitter remark he wanted to make.

"We're here to see you are unharmed and will gladly stay with you wherever you wish to go," Chenéché spoke for all of them, "but we recommend leaving Cyprus for a while. If you need a place—"

"Thank you, but I know where I'm going," Amaury interrupted his friend, laying his hand on his arm. Although it was a spontaneous decision, the idea had been ripening unconsciously as long as he'd been in the dungeon: it was time to pay a visit to dear Alice and her new husband. Alice hated the Ibelins, while her new husband wanted the weak, little Lusignan boy out of the way. What would be sweeter revenge, Amaury thought to himself, than for Antioch to depose the Lusignan brat (really just a puppet of the Ibelins) and in so doing destroy the power-base of Ibelins? If Reynald Barlais had put the Lusignans on this throne, there was no reason why Amaury Barlais couldn't put Antioch there instead.

"We've brought your traveling household," Rivet indicated several servants standing in an awkward group beside a loaded cart. They nodded to him as his eyes fell on them, and he nodded back.

"Then let's go directly to the port and see if there is a ship bound for Tripoli," Amaury announced. No reason to let boy-Balian know his true destination. He signaled for the groom to bring forward his palfrey.

While the others turned to mount their waiting horses, Chenéché caught Amaury by the arm and pressed a purse into his hand. "You can pay me back later," he murmured.

Amaury felt a surge of gratitude and flung his free arm over Chenéché's shoulder to give him a quick hug of thanks. They had always helped one another in times of need as far back as Amaury could remember.

Rivet noted simply. "If you need more, let me know."

"I won't, but my lady and daughters might. Can I count on you to see to their welfare, while I am away?"

"Of course, Amaury," Rivet assured him.

In a small cavalcade, Amaury rode from the Templar Commandery to the busy harbor. Here a few inquiries established that the next ship leaving the harbor eastbound was making for Tyre, but that was good enough for Amaury. He was in a hurry to be gone, anxious to set his plan into action. He agreed to take passage on her and paid for passage for himself, his squire and servants. He opted to leave his horse behind, however, turning it over to Chenéché. "Look after him for me. I won't be gone for long."

Amaury was already buoyed up by the thought of this new alliance with Antioch. He liked the thought of tossing the ungrateful Lusignan's from the throne of Cyprus and dealing with the Ibelins at the same time. Alice might be King Henry's mother, but she was not very motherly. She would sacrifice him for her new husband and their joint children.

With the ship making ready to sail and a stiff breeze turning the surface of the little harbor rough, Amaury felt as if the air of the dungeon had been utterly blown away. He really *was* free, and he would not return until he had the means of avenging the humiliations he had suffered. Like the fluttering bright bunting on the ship he was about to board, he felt uplifted and victorious already.

Turning to his Ibelin escort, he flung an arm over Sir Balian's shoulders and declared, "Now that we are all friends again, I hope you won't mind a word of advice... from a friend."

Sir Balian seemed to hesitate before agreeing. "Of course not."

"Don't waste your time on serving wenches, lover boy. Aim higher! Follow in your grandfather's footsteps and seduce a high-born lady. That will get you much farther than you could ever otherwise go!" Amaury burst into a laugh and punched Balian on the arm in a man-to-man gesture.

Still laughing at his own joke, Amaury jumped energetically aboard the gangway and nimbly down into the waist of the ship. He turned to wave to his friends before following the sailor that led him to his cabin.

The four men on the quay stood awkwardly side-by-side for a moment, and then Chenéché turned on Sir Balian. "Your uncle did well to reconcile with Sir Amaury. He was ill-treated and humiliated."

"He tried to kill a man!" Balian shot back indignantly.

"Oh, don't get on your high-horse, Ibelin! It was a matter of honor between Sir Amaury and Sir Toringuel. Your family had no right to interfere!"

"My uncle is baillie," Balian corrected. "It is his *duty* to uphold the laws of Cyprus! If Sir Amaury felt it was a matter of honor, then he should have challenged Sir Toringuel face to face—not trapped him, four to one, in an alley from behind!"

"Sir Toringuel didn't play by the rules either!" Sir Gauvain snapped as he turned his back on Sir Balian.

Sir William just nodded and likewise turned to mount. Sir Grimalt hesitated, and then admitted, "My cousin was wrong to attack Sir Toringuel in an alley, but your uncle should not have humiliated him the way he did. His father may not have been a knight, but he helped put the Lusignans on the throne. Sir Amaury is an intelligent and diligent knight. He deserves to hold a high office. It is not right that your family holds Cyprus like a personal fief." He then mounted his horse and rode away leading Sir Amaury's horse.

Balian watched Sir Amaury's friends ride away and then turned back towards the ship. His father had entrusted him with seeing that Barlais left Cyprus, so he waited on the quay while the crew made ready to cast off. They were already starting to hoist the sails when Barlais came back on deck.

Seeing Balian still standing on the quay, Barlais started visibly, but then a smile spread across his face. He raised his hand to wave and shouted across the distance, "Don't forget my advice, lover boy!"

Balian could feel his anger boiling inside and he wanted to lash out, but his father's words were ringing in his ears. "Don't disgrace me! I'm entrusting you with your first assignment as my son and heir. Treat Sir Amaury with impeccable courtesy and amity, as if he was indeed a dear friend. I don't care what you really think of him. A good diplomat can always disguise his feelings."

Balian forced himself to smile and wave back at Barlais. As the ship started to fall away from the quay, Balian shouted across the increasing distance, "Never, Sir Amaury! I will never forget what you said!"

Chapter Two
Of Alliances and Liaisons

Acre
August 1225

YOLANDA, THE HEIRESS TO THE KINGDOM of Jerusalem, took after her father John de Brienne more than her beautiful mother, Marie de Montferrat. Most of her life that hadn't mattered. Her mother had died giving her birth, and she had been doted on and spoiled by her father, her nurses, the palace servants, her father's knights and just about everyone else—until she was six that is.

At that point in her life, her stepmother Stephanie of Armenia sent her to the Convent of St. Anne in Acre to learn her letters, Latin, Greek, theology, rhetoric, mathematics, history, astronomy—and her manners. With the good sisters, Yolanda dressed exactly like all the other boarders in a pale blue cotton gown and sleeveless, linen surcoat. Her hair was braided and kept modestly under a white gauze veil. She was not addressed as "my lady" by the nuns or her fellow pupils, only as Yolanda. She was not permitted any privileges, not even a pet, and she had been subject to the same discipline as all the others.

The news that she was to be married to the Holy Roman Emperor had burst into her secluded world like an earthquake. Suddenly she was yanked out of the schoolroom, returned to the royal palace and placed at the center of frantic efforts to finish wedding robes, coronation robes, a trousseau of clothes for herself and her household, bed and table furnishings, and gifts for high and low.

Yolanda's father was still in the West, where he had been for the last five years, trying to recruit lords and knights for a new crusade. While there, he had not only arranged this marriage but taken a third wife himself, his Armenian wife having since died. It was, therefore, her father's baillie and constable, Eudes de Montbéliard, who summoned Yolanda to explain what was expected of her.

Eudes de Montbéliard was a young man, 24 years old, of average height and frail of frame. He did not look like the kind of man who excelled at sport, and he dressed in silks rather than chainmail. He was long in the face, a feature exaggerated by hair so pale and thin that his brow didn't seem to end, and he had the annoying habit of speaking with his eyes wholly or partially closed. When Yolanda presented herself to him still in the habit of a convent boarder, he lifted his head and talked down his long nose to her with his eyelids so low over his eyes that she could not see his pupils.

Yolanda had been excited to learn she was betrothed to the Holy Roman Emperor, but when Montbéliard announced that she was to be married by proxy within the week, excitement had turned to terror. Furthermore, immediately following her wedding she was to be crowned and then travel "forthwith" in the company of the Archbishop Capua, who was to be the Emperor's proxy at the wedding, to the Kingdom of Sicily, where she was to wed her bridegroom again in person. The speed at which her life was to be transformed left Yolanda's head spinning. In less than a month, she would be married, crowned and leave the only home she'd ever known to marry a man who was already legendary.

Frederick of Hohenstaufen liked to be called the "Wonder of the World." He had vast power, a history of political victories, and was reputedly a man of great learning. Like Yolanda herself, he had succeeded to his titles and claims as an infant. Frederick's father had died when he was two, he'd been crowned King of Sicily at age three, and lost his mother just six months later. For the next ten years, he was more pawn than king, an excuse for various factions to pursue one policy or another in his Kingdom of Sicily, while his father's title of Holy Roman Emperor was snatched away by the Welfs with the coronation of Otto IV. Yet no sooner had he come of age, than he had—almost without a fight— vanquished his enemies. He had been greeted as a savior in Northern Italy and Germany and elected King of the Germans. He had been crowned in Mainz before he reached his 20th birthday. On that same day, Yolanda had been told many times since the announcement of her impending wedding, he took the cross and vowed to deliver Jerusalem from the Saracens. This was the romantic vision that Yolanda clung too. She was determined not to dwell on the fact that Frederick's crusader vow had been made more than eleven years ago and he was yet to come East—despite the fact he had re-affirmed his vow at his coronation as Holy Roman Emperor in 1220.

Montbéliard had pedantically explained that her marriage to the Holy Roman Emperor, King of the Germans and King of Sicily, would make him

King of Jerusalem too. The acquisition of this additional title and kingdom was supposed to ensure that Frederick would at last lead a great crusade for the liberation of Jerusalem. Such a great monarch, Montbéliard lectured, would achieve what even the legendary Richard the Lionheart had failed to do: he would retake Jerusalem and with it Bethlehem and Nazareth and all the holy sites that had once been—and *should* again be—part of Yolanda's kingdom.

Yolanda was very willing to believe that, but she was still three months shy of her 13th birthday. The very things Montbéliard found most appealing about the Emperor—his power and successes—made him seem very intimidating to Yolanda. How was she supposed to please "the Wonder of the World," Yolanda asked herself with a look in her mirror.

The nuns, of course, discouraged all vanity. The girls had not been allowed mirrors, and any trace of rouge on lips or cheeks had been punished with a night at prayer. Yet that did not stop the girls from peering in pools of still water or looking at their reflection on the surface of the silver collection plate at Mass. Nor could the nuns prevent the youth of Acre from whistling or calling out as the convent boarders passed in the streets. It had not escaped Yolanda's notice that she never attracted much attention. She had inherited her father's height and big-bones, but what was admired in a fighting man was disliked in a girl. Her hair was brown, rather than blond or black. Her eyes were hazel, rather than blue or green. Her nose was rather too prominent, her lips too thin, and her skin was blemished with pimples along her hairline. Yolanda concluded that she needed *both* prayer and rouge if she was going to please a husband—any husband, much less a great monarch eighteen years older than she was.

The bevy of girls who were to be Yolanda's bridesmaids descended upon her like a gaggle of geese, all talking at once. The Lady of Sidon, who was in charge of preparing Yolanda for her proxy wedding, had a plethora of other things to do. She admonished the bridesmaids to see Yolanda properly dressed, adding, "I've left some rouge, kohl, and paints on the table there. Do make her look as pretty as you can, but don't be late. She's only giving her vows to the Archbishop of Capua, and he's not likely to care much what she looks like."

As the Lady of Sidon withdrew, the six bridesmaids, all daughters of barons, swooped down on Yolanda, giggling and cackling to one another. Two went immediately to the bed where her wedding gown was spread out. They started admiring it with words and hands.

"It must be Greek silk, don't you think?" one asked the other. "Oh, and the dyes! Red weft and blue weave to give such a rich purple! I must remember to order something like this!"

Another girl went to look at the glass bottles on the table, removing the glass or cork stoppers to sniff at them.

Another discovered the jewelry laid out on the chest by the bed. She started trying it on herself, calling to the girl sniffing at the perfumes, "Melissa! Look! Do you think Sir Balian would notice me in these?"

"Oh, you're going to need a lot more than *jewels*—or rather *less*!—to get Sir Balian's attention!" Her friend quipped back with a giggle.

"Didn't he look *gorgeous*?" Her friend countered, unfazed as she put the jewelry back on the chest. "I *loved* the way he wore hose of the opposite colors to this parti-colored surcoat. Did you notice that? A copper leg under the olive side of the surcoat and an olive leg under the copper side. He's got such a sense of style and color!"

"Who are you talking about?"

"Sir Balian d'Ibelin!" the two girls answered in unison. "Didn't you notice? Beirut, after being absent from Acre for *years*, arrived with his three eldest sons."

"Sir Baldwin isn't bad looking either."

"And Sir Hugh's cute too!"

"Sir Balian isn't married yet, is he?"

"Not even betrothed."

The only girl who had hung back up to now stepped up beside Yolanda and bending down looked her deeply in the eyes. "Are you alright, my lady? Shall I dry your hair and comb it out?"

Yolanda had bathed before her bridesmaids came to dress her, and her hair was still wrapped in a towel. "Yes, please," she whispered with a look of gratitude to this girl who looked vaguely familiar. "Do I know you?"

"I was at St. Anne's with you," the girl answered with a smile, "only two classes ahead of you." At the convent school, the girls did most things by class and contact with older or younger girls was restricted to meals and Mass for the most part. Yolanda's twelve-year-old companions, however, were deemed too young to serve her at an official occasion such as this. "I'm Eschiva de Montbéliard," the girl continued.

"Lord Eudes' sister?" Yolanda asked surprised. She hadn't liked Lord Eudes, much less the way he talked down to her with his eyes half-closed, but she liked this girl.

Eschiva nodded. "He's nine years older than me, and I don't know him very well. He's been too busy being baillie while your father was away to pay any attention to his little sister."

Yolanda nodded while Eschiva's firm fingers rubbed not only the towel and hair but her scalp as well. It felt good, and she looked up gratefully at Eschiva, noting that although she was blond and blue-eyed like her brother, she had skin problems too. "Can you help me cover these pimples?" Yolanda asked spontaneously.

Eschiva smiled at her. "Of course! I've had plenty of practice. Don't worry. No one will notice in the church, least of all the Archbishop of Capua."

"Have you met him?" Yolanda asked anxiously.

"Yes, I was introduced yesterday," Eschiva replied.

"And?" Yolanda pressed her.

Eschiva shrugged. "He's a prelate. Prim and pompous. But he's *not* who you're marrying. Frederick Hohenstaufen is very different. My brother tells me he loves hawking and horses. I'm sure he's vigorous and comely."

"But nothing to Sir Balian," one of the others added with a sigh.

Eschiva and Yolanda just ignored her and her silly chatter; they had more important things and people to worry about.

Tyre
August 1225

"It's good to see you, Uncle John, cousins." The Baron of Sidon crossed the quay to greet the Lord of Beirut and his three eldest sons. Sidon was preparing to embark on the Imperial dromond as part of Queen Yolanda's escort to Sicily. For the last fifteen days, there had been feasting and celebration across the kingdom for the coronation of their young queen. Now the festivities were over, the tide high and the winds favorable. Sidon was anxious to set sail.

Beirut and his three sons dismounted, and Beirut set the tone by offering his hand to Sidon. The Lord of Sidon was his nephew, the son of his deceased elder sister Helvis, but there was only a fifteen-year age difference between them. Sidon was now 31, a vigorous and well-built man, although he did not have the Ibelin's famed height. More important, he had already acquired a reputation, fast approaching Beirut's own, of judicial knowledge and wisdom. In almost any legal dispute, the advice of one of these two men was sought. More than once, they had argued against one another before the High Court or one of the lesser courts. They respected each other profoundly, but their relationship had cooled markedly ever since King John de Brienne's arrival.

Beirut had been regent of the Kingdom of Jerusalem for his niece Marie de Montferrat, the daughter of his sister Queen Isabella. He had naturally surrendered his position as soon as she was crowned and married to John de Brienne.

Since King John was from Champagne and had little experience in Outremer, however, Beirut had expected to serve the new king as a close advisor. Instead, the two men had quickly clashed over a variety of minor issues, and Brienne had favored men from his native Champagne over advisors from Outremer.

It had particularly offended Beirut that Brienne had welcomed his kinsman Walter de Montbéliard to his kingdom after the latter was expelled from Cyprus by King Hugh. King Hugh accused Montbéliard of massive embezzlement of royal funds during his tenure as regent during Hugh's minority. When Hugh came of age, Montbéliard had become *persona non grata* in Cyprus, while the king turned to Philip d'Ibelin, Beirut's younger brother, as his closest advisor. The Montbéliards blamed the Ibelins for Walter's loss of influence on Cyprus.

Although Sidon was not involved in either of these disputes, he had profited from Beirut's fall from royal favor. He had been the local baron to whom Brienne turned when he wanted advice about local conditions, customs or laws. Further-more, unlike Beirut, he had gotten along well with Walter de Montbéliard, and when Walter died in 1212 he had taken Walter's young son Eudes under his wing. Sidon had groomed Eudes for the position of baillie to King John, a position he assumed when King John went first on crusade in Egypt and then opted not to return to his kingdom but instead to go to the West to try to raise funds and manpower for a new crusade.

"I hope you are not offended that you were not included among the digni-taries escorting Queen Yolanda to Brindisi," Sidon opened.

"No, not at all," Beirut assured him less than honestly, adding, "Although I would have liked to send my son Sir Hugh with you as a gesture of loyalty to our young queen." He indicated his third son, now sixteen, whom he had only recently knighted in Beirut.

Hugh nodded to Sidon with a winning smile. "I don't take up much room, my lord, and I eat less than either of my brothers here."

It was a speech well designed to elicit a laugh from his cousin. Sidon nodded agreement at once. "Of course, Sir Hugh. You are very welcome to join us as long as you don't delay our sailing. Hurry and get your things aboard, for we sail within the hour—assuming the Queen arrives on time." Sidon twisted to glance in the direction of the street that led down to the harbor from the citadel.

Hugh glanced at his father, who consented with a nod and a "Go with God." Grinning, Sir Hugh eagerly led his horse toward the gangway, calling to the sailors that he was sailing with them before he even reached the side of the ship. His excitement to be going west was patent, and both his brothers followed him with envious eyes.

Sidon turned back to Beirut to assure him. "No one doubts your loyalty to our queen, Uncle John. Your absence from court has been regretted sincerely, not viewed as disloyalty."

"I'm relieved to hear that," Beirut noted, adding, "Have I been correctly informed that *both* you and Montbéliard plan to travel with the Queen?"

"Yes, that is correct."

"And the Archbishop of Tyre and Bishop of Acre as well?"

"Yes, exactly."

"But what of the Kingdom? Who is baillie in Montbéliard's place?"

"Ah." Sidon had the grace to look embarrassed. "The Emperor sent Count Thomas of Acerra out with the Archbishop of Capua. Capua acted as his proxy at the wedding, as you know, but the Count of Acerra is to serve as his baillie until he arrives in person."

"I thought he was not planning to come on crusade until August of 1227?" Beirut protested, revealing that he already knew about the agreement reached between the Holy Roman Emperor, the Pope and King John of Jerusalem at Ferentino this past summer.

"That is the latest date by which he *must* depart to avoid excommunication. We all hope he will come sooner, perhaps as early as next year."

"And in the meantime, we are to be ruled by an outsider with little understanding of our circumstances, our enemies or our laws," Beirut concluded pointedly.

"Give Acerra a chance, Uncle. He took part in the last crusade—"

"Hardly a recommendation," Beirut noted, "given the deplorable behavior and idiotic decisions of the leadership."

Sidon sighed and repeated, "Give him a chance."

"Of course. The queen must be nearly here."

Cheering from the city marked the progress of the queen toward the harbor. They all turned to watch and shortly afterward, the queen's party emerged. Yolanda was riding on a very pretty, dish-faced white palfrey decked out in a saddlecloth with the arms of Jerusalem on it. She herself wore a practical russet gown, but over this, a surcoat of white silk "dusted" with gold crosses. Her head was encased in a white, gauze wimple to mark her status as a married woman, despite the fact she was still a maiden.

The cheering of her people made the girl-queen blush with embarrassment, but it also made her smile and wave. Beirut's heart went out to her. She was still so very young. Indeed, she was the same age as his only daughter, Bella. He couldn't have borne the thought of sending his little girl across the water to an utter stranger, and he found his dislike of John de Brienne hardening.

Despite the death of his wife, Brienne continued to claim the crown of Jeru-

salem, dubiously Beirut thought, because of Yolanda. Yet he hadn't bothered to
visit her in five years. And while Beirut recognized the advantages of Yolanda's
marriage to the Holy Roman Emperor, he was also a father. He loved his six
children more than his own life, and sometimes more than Jerusalem. Based on
what he had heard, he would not have sent his daughter Bella to marry Frederick Hohenstaufen—not for all the gold in Constantinople.

Queen Yolanda approached, flanked on one side by Eudes de Montbéliard
and on the other by a young woman Beirut did not recognize. "Who is the
young lady with the Queen?" Beirut asked Sidon.

"Ah, that is Eudes' sister Eschiva. The Queen *asked* her to join her household," Sidon hastened to explain, anticipating Beirut's objections to the
"parvenu" Montbéliards again successfully positioning themselves close to the
crown.

To Sidon's surprise, Beirut nodded with approval. Now that they were nearer,
he recognized the girl as the most sensible of all the maidens in attendance on
the Queen over the past three weeks. He had noticed and approved of the way
she had kept to the background while the other girls preened and flirted—all
too often with his son Balian. More important, it had been this girl who repeatedly calmed or encouraged an uncertain and nervous Yolanda. He simply had
not realized that she was Montbéliard's daughter. Now that Sidon identified
her, however, he noticed that she shared a family resemblance with her brother
from the bright blond hair and blue eyes to the long face and nose. Unlike her
brother, however, she smiled and chattered excitedly with the Queen. Like his
son Hugh, she seemed delighted to be going West, something that would surely
help the Queen overcome her obvious foreboding.

As the Queen reached the gangway to the Imperial dromond, she drew up.
At once, a knight from her entourage sprang down to hold her off-stirrup. As
she touched the ground, a groom came forward to lead her horse away. Meanwhile, the ship's captain descended the gangway to bend his knee, his hand on
his heart, before her. Beirut was glad she was traveling on an Imperial ship commanded by a Sicilian captain because there had been some very unseemly squabbling between the Pisans, Genoese and Venetian communities of Outremer
about who should have the honor of transporting the Queen and her party.

Before the captain could lead Yolanda aboard his ship, however, Beirut
stepped forward. "My lady queen!"

Yolanda turned, startled, in the direction of his voice. She looked at Beirut
uncertainly, unsure who he was.

"John d'Ibelin, Lord of Beirut, my lady." Beirut helped her out of her
dilemma, and she broke into a wide smile.

"Of course, my lord. I should have remembered you, but I've met so many new people these last few weeks."

"I understand entirely, my lady. I have come to see you off, and give you a little gift—more for your voyage than your marriage." As he spoke he gestured to his sons, and Balian at once opened his father's saddlebag to remove an object wrapped in painted leather. He handed this to his father, and Beirut unwrapped the leader cover to withdraw a book. This he held out to Queen Yolanda.

Eschiva de Montbéliard had come to stand behind her queen. At the sight of the book, she let out a little gasp of delight.

Beirut cast the Montbéliard girl a smile before addressing the Queen again. "This was your great-grandmother's book. She would have wanted you to have it."

Queen Yolanda looked up at him frowning slightly as she tried to work it out. "My great-grandmother? Queen Maria Comnena? Your mother?" Yolanda might not have recognized him, but she had learned the lessons about her dynasty well.

"Exactly." Beirut lovingly opened the ivory cover of the book to reveal the interior, eliciting another appreciative gasp from the Montbéliard girl. "It is, I am afraid, in Greek, but I was told you were taught Greek." It was as much a question as a statement.

The Queen nodded vigorously, going on tip-toe to see the book better. Beirut at once lowered his hands to make it easier for her to see and explained. "It is the story of a Greek sailor trying to return home after a long war in what is now the Empire of Nicaea. Along the way, he suffers many adventures and hardships that take him all across the Mediterranean. Although the journey is embellished with many fanciful beasts and mythical adventures, still I think you will find it a lively and informative companion on your journey. At least I hope you do." Beirut bowed deeply and handed the book to his Queen.

Yolanda took it from him and held it to her still flat chest. "It is very, very kind of you, my lord! I can't wait to read it!" For an instant, she was a little girl again rather than a queen and bride.

Beirut bowed again. "I hope it will always bring you pleasure—and remind you of your home and your heritage."

Yolanda seemed to want to say more, but Eudes de Montbéliard was moving from foot to foot to indicate his impatience. He cleared his throat and admonished, "We do not want to miss the tide, my lady." He always managed to sound as if he thought he knew better than everyone else, Beirut thought.

Yolanda responded as if she had been guilty of some misdeed and hastened to do as Montbéliard urged. She started for the ship, but then she stopped to say over her shoulder with heartfelt emphasis, "Thank you again, my lord! *I love books!*"

Montbéliard shooed his queen and his sister aboard the ship, giving her no chance to stay on deck to watch them cast off. They are prisoners already, Beirut thought—not entirely logically. Yolanda was on her way to be crowned Holy Roman Empress—arguably the most powerful woman on earth. So why did he feel so sorry for her, and so sad?

Beirut, December 1225

"It's pissing rain out there," Novare told his friend Balian. "Let's have another round, and you can give me a chance to win back my losses."

The friends had been dicing with the off-duty sergeants at a tavern just below the citadel of Beirut. Because of its proximity to the castle, the tavern was popular with the garrison of Beirut, and many of the younger knights, like Sirs Balian and Philip, frequented it as well. The cook here was a Syrian Christian, a genuine master of Outremer cuisine, who knew how to blend the spices of Arabia with the fruits of Byzantium and the meats of the West. Meals were served with flat-bread, rolls or rice, and the wine was decent, plentiful and affordable.

"I could do with another drink," Balian agreed, looking over his shoulder for the proprietor or one of the serving girls, "but I'm done dicing with you, Philip. I might keep winning!"

"Come on! My luck is bound to change!" Novare countered. While he recognized that Balian meant well, he simply couldn't *stop* gambling. He was on the brink of winning. He could feel it in his bones. Winning and losing always came in streaks, and he'd been losing for days now. His fortunes *must* be about to change.

"Play something on your lute instead," Balian countered, jerking his head toward the instrument that Novare carried around with him the way other men carried a hat. He had a talent for putting rhyming couplets, usually disrespectful and slightly off-color, to music to make easy-to-sing ditties.

Philip didn't have to be asked twice. About the only thing he liked more than gambling and women of easy virtue was music. He removed his lute from its leather case and was just tuning it when the door banged open and the cold, wet air blew in.

The man in the door shoved his lined, chainmail coif off his head and searched the room as his eyes adjusted to the dark.

"Shit!" Balian muttered as he recognized his brother Baldwin. A moment later Baldwin found him.

"You are in trouble up to your eyeballs, Balian!"

"Well, don't sound so sorry about it!" Balian shot back.

Baldwin just shook his head. "I'm not kidding. This time you're in shit so deep, I don't think Hercules could dig you out! Come with me!"

"What is it?" Balian asked frowning but getting to his feet and collecting his cloak.

"I'm not at liberty to talk about it here," Baldwin answered primly.

That was bad, and Balian knew it. He absently removed a coin and laid it on the table in front of Novare. "Pay my bill, will you?" It was not a question, and Novare noted that it was more than twice what he owed; a subsidy from Balian to his ever-out-of-pocket friend.

Outside in the rain, Baldwin lit into his brother. "I've never in my life seen our father so furious. Absolutely white with suppressed rage. I wouldn't be surprised if he flogged you in front of the entire garrison!"

"What is this about?" Balian asked. They again started together for the citadel that loomed over them, a darker grey against the dull grey of the rainy day.

"Oh, don't play innocent! This is one thing you can't pretend you didn't do!"

"When have I ever pretended not to do something I did?" Balian shot back. "I'm not some stinking coward, who doesn't own up to what he does!"

"So sorry! I forgot you were a paragon of chivalry! Except for when you're sniffing around some bitch's skirts!"

"Don't be such an ass! As if you didn't drop your braies whenever you get the chance!"

"Except, I'm not *stupid* enough to do it with the kind of girl who can point a finger!"

"What do you mean?"

"Does the name Denise strike a bell?"

"What?!"

They had already crossed the bridge over the fosse and reached the barbican. Baldwin called up to the watch to let them in through the postern. The Ibelin brothers slipped sideways through the door held only half-open for them; the men on watch didn't want to let in too much wind and rain. In the presence of the other men, the brothers suspended their conversation and did not resume it until they were out of hearing.

"Denise?" Balian asked. "You mean the seneschal's daughter?"

"Yes, that's the one."

"What about her?"

"She's pregnant."

Balian didn't answer.

Baldwin led at a fast pace up interior stairs that by-passed the large double hall and opened in the hallway of the residential tract behind the solar. Baldwin did not give his brother time to catch his breath before pounding on the back door to the solar and announcing in a loud voice. "It's me, father! I've found Balian."

"Come in!" Beirut answered, and Baldwin opened the door to usher Balian in ahead of him.

"You may go, Baldwin," their father intoned, and from the look on Baldwin's face, Balian knew his brother was disappointed.

Beirut waited until his younger son had closed the door, and then jerked his head to his heir to come deeper into the room. His face was so immobile, it might as well have been carved out of stone. The expression petrified upon it was harsh and forbidding. Balian looked quickly about and to his horror saw the seneschal standing beside the fireplace.

This man went by name of Denis of Paris. He had joined the crusade of 1203 but had been one of the many men who abandoned that adventure when it lost papal sanction because it was diverted to Constantinople. He had instead attached himself to Simon and Guy de Montfort and come with them to Syria. While Simon returned to the West to lead the crusade against the Albigensian heresy, Guy de Montfort remained in Syria, where he married the widow of Reginald de Sidon, Helvis d'Ibelin, the now deceased elder sister of the Lord of Beirut.

Denis himself had risen fast and high in Montfort's service until an obscure quarrel had ended in manslaughter. Although released from prison after serving his sentence, he held a grudge against Montfort and quit his service. Shortly afterward he had come to Beirut seeking employment. So far he had not disappointed them. He was ambitious almost to a fault, but that brought with it diligence and a willingness to make enemies for the sake of discipline. He had also married a native woman and had four daughters, the eldest of which was named after him.

"Come here," Beirut ordered his eldest son.

Balian moved closer to the fire so that he stood opposite Denis of Paris. The seneschal avoided his eyes, preferring to look down at his feet. He was a big man with the broad shoulders of an archer and large knotty joints. His face was flat, his hair thinning, and his fingers were fleshy and stubby.

Balian's insides were in turmoil.

"The good seneschal has come to me in a matter touching upon the honor of our House," Beirut opened, and Balian knew this was going to be hotter than hell itself.

"He tells me," Beirut continued ominously, "that his beloved firstborn, his little girl Denise, who has grown up almost like a sister to you, is pregnant out of wedlock."

Balian was no longer breathing, let alone prepared to speak.

"She has named you as the father of her unborn child." Beirut paused, looking at his son with his immobile, harsh face. When Balian still said nothing, he demanded in a sharp tone, "Is that true?"

"I was not aware that she was pregnant, my lord."

"That's not the point. The question is whether you knew Denise carnally and *could* be the father of her child."

Balian was burning from the inside. Of course, he had "known her carnally." She had been one of the most aggressive, eager and demanding lovers he had ever known in his not very celibate life so far. But he could hardly say that with her father standing five feet away from him.

"Well?" His father snapped.

"Yes, my lord. Denise and I have been lovers."

"I told you so!" The seneschal lifted his head for the first time to glare belligerently at Balian. "Your son has dishonored my daughter, and I demand recompense."

Beirut turned his stony face to his eldest son and remarked in a voice so low it was almost inaudible. "You have dishonored me and, above all, the name you carry. Your grandfather would never, never have brought shame on his house by taking advantage of the daughter of a member of his household."

Balian felt cornered and humiliated. He hated the constant comparisons to a grandfather he had never known and could never equal. His grandfather wasn't a person anymore; he was a family saint. He could *never* live up to his grandfather's example. He lashed out with the only weapon he had: impudence. In an insolent tone, Balian remarked, "Well, let's not forget that he seduced a dowager queen and Aunt Helvis was conceived out of wedlock!"

Beirut hit his son so hard and so fast that Balian reeled. Indeed, he staggered backward, and as he recovered his balance, his eyes locked with his father's. His chin was pulsing from the blow of a hardened fighting man, and his face flushed with the blood of rage. Bluntly Beirut warned, "If you ever insult your grandfather again, I'll do more than hit you. I'll kill you! Now get out of my sight. I can't stand to look at you a second longer. One of your bothers will let you know when I'm ready to lay eyes on you again."

Balian's blood was pounding in his temples, and his heart was hammering at the inside of his chest, but he managed to bow stiffly as he spat out, "My lord!" Then he stalked out of the solar, a volcano on the brink of explosion.

The door crashed shut behind him, and Beirut looked back at his seneschal. "I—What can I say? I am ashamed of him. I apologize for him. What can I do to make this right?"

"He should marry her," Denis declared, thrusting his chin forward. "If he marries her, he will make it right."

Beirut froze. The *heir* to Beirut marry the daughter of a commoner? An Ibelin marry the daughter of a man without a fief or a last name? Make the little hussy Denise *Lady* of Beirut? The idea was so ludicrous that it sobered Beirut as completely as ice water in his veins. That this man could voice such an absurd idea put Beirut instantly on his guard. To his shame, he realized that he had made the cardinal mistake of not weighing both sides of a case before coming to a decision. He had been so angry that a son of his might abuse his position that he had not stopped to think that the seneschal might be manipulating the situation.

The seneschal was ambitious and ingratiating. Montfort had warned him he could be pushy as well. He appeared to be shamelessly exploiting his daughter's behavior for his own benefit.

"Sir Balian took away her virtue. Only marriage will restore it!" the seneschal declared stubbornly. "I demand that he marry her."

"You have no right to demand anything," Beirut replied coldly. There was no anger in his voice. He was not even defensive. He was stating facts. "Your daughter has foolishly squandered her virtue."

"Your son forced himself on her!" The seneschal barked, frowning more darkly than ever.

"*That*," Beirut replied pointedly, "I do not believe. My son has no need to use force on anyone, much less your daughter."

The seneschal didn't answer, but he wouldn't meet Beirut's eyes, just lowered his chin and grumbled inarticulately to himself.

Beirut decided he needed to hear no more. "Do not treat me like an idiot. I have seen, perhaps too indulgently in retrospect, the way Denise flirts with the whole garrison. I would not be surprised if Sir Balian was not alone in enjoying her favors. If that is the case, it would be impossible to know whether he is the father of her child or not."

"No! That's not true! I swear she has slept with no one but Sir Balian."

"Shall I call my senior sergeants here and question them on this point one at a time?"

The seneschal looked down at his feet, his fists clenching and unclenching, but after a moment he shook his head.

"Good. Then we understand one another. My son's behavior was reprehensible, but it does not absolve your daughter of her share of the guilt. I am prepared to pay you ten gold bezants so your daughter can go away and have her child someplace else. I will donate another 20 bezants as a dowry so that you will have an easier time finding her a suitable husband." He stressed the word 'suitable' only slightly, but sufficiently to make his point.

The seneschal did not answer. He stood looking at the ground and smoldering for several seconds more before mumbling, "Yes, my lord." He then barged out of the solar without a backward glance.

"Balian? Are you here?" Hugh's voice echoed in the cave church and he shivered slightly as he searched the darkness of the interior. Candles were lit before the icons opposite the door, making the silver halos gleam, but there was no one in sight. Looking deeper into the cave, he saw the Eucharist candle flickering before the ancient, wooden screens, but still, he didn't see his brother. Then something moved to his right, the curtain to a confessional carved out of the rock was shoved aside and Balian emerged.

"Hugh? Where did you come from? I thought you'd stay in Sicily at least until the spring sailing season."

"That's what I'd planned to do, but it's colder than the grave in Sicily this time of year, and rains are worse than here. Besides, I wanted to get word to our father about what happened in Brindisi. That's why Father has sent for you. He wants you to come back at once so we can discuss the situation as a family. Baldwin's out scouring the taverns of Beirut—"

"As if that's where I spend all my time!" Balian bristled at once.

"Well, he won't find you there, will he? I have to admit, though, this wasn't exactly the first place I looked either." Hugh looked around at the narrow church painted with frescoes that could hardly be seen in the dark. They were ancient and Greek in style, darkened by centuries of candle smoke. This had been a hermit's cave back before the Muslim conquest, and the Maronites had built the church in it centuries ago. Hugh hadn't a clue why Balian liked it so much, but he had remembered that his brother did sometimes come here when he needed to calm himself down.

Balian stood with his hands on his hips, gazing at him. "I'm glad you're back, Hugh, but I'm not sure I'm ready to face our father just yet. I'm still too furious with him! Do you know what he did?"

"Well, not exactly. Baldwin said you're in trouble for seducing the sene-schal's daughter."

"He confronted me *in front of* her father! He didn't give me a chance to tell my side of the story! Just insulted me then and there—hit me—and sent me away!"

"What did he hit you for?" Hugh asked startled.

"For reminding him that our grandparents had an illicit affair before their marriage and that Aunt Helvis was conceived out of wedlock."

Hugh gasped. "You didn't!" But then he shook his head in admiration and bemusement at his brother's audacity. He could remember the day the boys had accidentally stumbled over their aunt's baptismal records and Baldwin had said, "What? May 1178? But—"

Balian had jumped in at once. "Wait, Father always claimed they were allowed to marry because of our grandfather's prowess at Montgisard!"

"That was in November 1177," Hugh had added to show he knew. They had all looked at each other, counting the months mentally, and then burst out laughing together. "He seduced a dowager queen!" They had chortled in delight. It had made their "perfect" grandfather so much more likable.

"Maybe I shouldn't have said it," Balian admitted, "but he cornered me—confronted me with Denise's pregnancy in front of her father. If he'd talked to me in private first, I could have told him how she came into my room and literally locked the door behind her before she started stripping. Christ! No man could withstand temptation like that! My confessor didn't have any trouble absolving me! If Father had given me a chance to explain, I could have made him understand!"

"Hm," Hugh answered ambiguously.

Balian frowned at him. "Don't tell me *you* would have sent her away!"

"Hell, no! I wish she *had* come to me! Honestly. I've always been a little attracted to her. She's got something, you know, something that makes my lower body parts get all excited."

Balian laughed at that, and the laugh echoed in the vault of the narrow church.

"But, you see," Hugh spoke up more soberly as the echoes died away, "Father *would* have turned her away, even though he's desperately lonely." Hugh's voice was deep with sympathy.

That too seemed to get magnified in the church, giving Balian pause. He stopped to reflect on his father for a moment and when he spoke it was with reluctant empathy. "He needs a lady," Balian admitted. "I don't understand why he never married again after our mother died. It's been six years."

"You really don't know why?" Hugh asked surprised, and then answered himself, "No, I suppose as his heir, you've never thought about it."

"What do you mean?"

Hugh shrugged, "Just that, as he told me once, he can't risk having more sons. He says it's going to be hard enough providing for the five of us."

Balian looked at his brother dumbfounded. It was true, he had never thought about it. Beirut was a rich inheritance, but it went to the first born and heir, Balian himself. The lordship of Arsuf came from their mother and would presumably go to Baldwin—unless their father chose to give him their holdings on Cyprus and keep Arsur for Hugh. But they had two more brothers: Johnny and Guy, now aged ten and eight respectively. If they lived to adulthood, they would have to make their way in the world as landless knights.

"He had five sons by his first wife too, you know," Hugh said into the stillness and chill of the little church. "They all died as infants. Then he had five sons by mother. So it's only natural that he fears he'll sire more sons if he marries again. Only he's got neither land nor titles left to give Johnny and Guy as it is, let alone any new sons."

"He could break up our Cypriot estates," Balian suggested exasperated. "Having a lady would make him less judgmental and prudish!"

"Oh, come on, Bal! He's not a prude. He doesn't object to you having *fun*. It's the scandal he detests. He wants the Ibelin name to be above reproach. You and I know Denise is a bit of a tart. Still, because of her father's position of trust, a liaison with her is viewed as dishonorable."

"I didn't sleep with her more than a dozen times!" Balian protested. "That's hardly a liaison."

"But a bit more than a single night too. I don't think you should mention that to father."

Balian snorted ambiguously.

"Shall we go back now? I'm getting cold."

Balian, having known where he was going when he set out, was wearing a wolf-lined leather cloak; Hugh was in nothing but his leather gambeson and a comparatively light wool cloak.

Balian drew a deep breath. "He sent for me?"

"Yes, and not to give you a piece of his mind either. In fact, he seemed quite anxious to make up with you. He was visibly distressed to discover you were nowhere in the castle."

Balian said nothing, but he looked down at his signet ring, thinking of his father.

"The seneschal didn't look very happy either, I must say. He was busy preparing to send Denise off to Tyre, and he was very short-tempered. Whatever father said to him after you left wasn't to his liking."

Balian raised his eyebrows, but then nodded and, taking Hugh's arm, led them back out of the church into the fading winter afternoon. At least the rain had stopped. He untied his grazing palfrey, as did Hugh, and they mounted.

As they started along the narrow rocky trail that led back down to the shore, Balian asked, "So what is the news from Brindisi that brought you back here when you could have spent the whole winter enjoying yourself in Sicily?"

"You aren't going to believe it: no sooner had Frederick Hohenstaufen married Yolanda than he demanded all the barons who had accompanied her to do homage to him as King of Jerusalem."

"I thought the agreement was for John de Brienne to remain king for the rest of his life?" Balian asked puzzled.

"That's what we *all* thought—first and foremost King John himself, the Pope and the Master of the Teutonic Knights, who had negotiated the marriage contract! There was a terrible scene. The Teutonic Master was almost as furious as King John, and he kept admonishing the Emperor that he was disgracing him. King John, however, was threatening outright war. It didn't help that, according to Yolanda's women, Fredrick spent his wedding night in the harem with one of his slaves, leaving his little bride to cry herself to sleep."

"What?!" Balian could hardly believe his ears. "Are you sure about that?"

"As sure as anyone can be who wasn't in the bedchamber! Let's put it this way, Frederick really *does* have a harem tract in the palace at Palermo, complete with eunuchs as servants and a troop of Muslim guards. No one is allowed inside, of course, but I was told by men in his household that he has twenty-three harem slaves locked up in there. The queen's apartments are directly adjacent to the harem and guarded by the same troop of Muslim soldiers."

"That's unchristian!" Balian protested indignantly.

"It is rather, but Father's more upset about the fact that Frederick has broken his agreement with Brienne. We all know Father doesn't like Brienne much, but for him, a contract is a contract, and a man, much less a lord, is bound by his word. He's shaken by the fact that the greatest Christian monarch on earth is indifferent to his own signed promises."

Balian nodded. He agreed with his father on this. Then he thought to ask, "Did any of the lords of Jerusalem take the oath of homage?"

"They *all* did! Eudes de Montbéliard first and foremost, but Sidon too."

"What about you?"

"I didn't want to make a scene," the affable Hugh admitted, rationalizing. "Besides, my oath doesn't count for much. I'm just a young, landless knight. I thought that if father didn't like what I did, he could always disown me." Hugh shrugged and laughed lightly as he spoke, evidently not so certain of himself after all.

"He'd never do that, Hugh," Balian remarked with a wan smile. "He loves you."

"Yes, and you too, Balian. You do know that, don't you? If he's hard on you, it's because he wants so much for you."

"Yes, I know," Balian admitted with a deep sigh. "Nor do I want to disappoint him. Yet sometimes I wish he'd let me be *me* rather than trying to force me into the image of our grandfather—or rather the image of our grandfather that *he* carries around in his head."

Hugh nodded sympathetically. He had often been thankful he was neither the firstborn nor named Balian. He had learned early that he could get away with more than Balian could. His misadventures were more likely to be met by a laugh than a rebuke.

They had reached a small sandy beach at the head of a cove and now started climbing the steep, stony path that led up to the plain above. Darkness was falling fast, and the horses were eager for their feed and the warmth of the barn. They strained up the slope, their riders standing in the stirrups to help them. As they reached the top, Hugh drew up beside his brother. "Balian?"

"Yes?"

"In your shoes, I'd try to stay away from women for a bit."

Balian just laughed and put his heels to his horse to start racing for home.

Chapter Three

Rival Regents
for a Crowned King

Nicosia, Cyprus
January 1226

KING HENRY I OF CYPRUS WAS just eight years old and the coronation, anointing, and subsequent mass had exhausted him. Normally, he enjoyed riding around surrounded by lords and knights and hearing people cheer for him, but it had been too long a day. All he wanted to do was get out of his stiff, heavy and uncomfortable ceremonial robes, and curl up in bed with a big fire going.

Lord Philip, his baillie, seemed to understand that. He personally helped Henry down from his pony, and put his arm over his shoulders with the words, "I'll bet you're ready for some peace and quiet and a soft bed."

"Yes, my lord, I am," Henry admitted.

"Well, you've earned it. Here's Lady Alys now," Lord Philip nodded toward his wife, coming down the stairs toward Henry. "She'll see you to your chamber while I take care of the dignitaries."

"So I don't have to come to the banquet?" Henry asked hopefully.

"No, you don't. Go upstairs with Lady Alys. There's a surprise waiting for you in your room. A little present from me on the day of your coronation."

"Oh, what is it?" Henry asked, excited at once. "Is it something for my menagerie?"

Henry loved nothing more than his menagerie of wild beasts. He had lions, an antelope, ostriches, and gazelles, peacocks and crocodiles.

"No, not quite," Lord Philip admitted. "The zebra I ordered from the Nubian traders hasn't arrived yet—if it ever does. This isn't quite so exotic, but I think you'll like it."

Henry, his mind on his surprise, willingly took Lady Alys' hand and let her lead him up the stairs to his suite of rooms that overlooked an interior courtyard with orange and lemon trees. Smiling at his eagerness, Lady Alys knocked on the door to warn his nanny they had arrived. The door opened and the Greek woman, who had nursed Henry as an infant and looked after his person ever since, backed up, smiling to reveal a magnificent subtlety: painted marzipan lions, leopards, horses, antelopes and crocodiles held up a marzipan crown. "It's wonderful!" Henry exclaimed in delight, his exhaustion completely forgotten.

He ran forward to admire the confectioner's creation, turning it around to see each of the animals. Sniffing, he reached out and broke off the cross at the top of the crown and popped it into his mouth. "It's my crown," he told the two women as if expecting reprimands, "and I can eat it if I want to!"

They laughed. Then Lady Alys assured him, "Yes, you can eat it all—but hopefully not all at once. Here, let's get you out of those heavy robes." His coronation robes were embroidered with gold thread and studded with jewels. While Henry stood still, the two women carefully removed the jeweled brooch that held the heavy cloak together at his neck, then helped him out of the stiff surcoat underneath, and finally untied the cords of his shirt and the laces on his sleeves so he could squirm out of this as well. It was damp from sweating under the heavy outer-clothes. He was now wearing nothing but his braies with the hose attached. His nurse brought a fresh nightshirt from the adjoining bed-chamber and pulled it over his head. She then urged him to sit on a chair while she removed his shoes, his hose, and finally his braies. While she took the dirty underclothes to put them in a laundry hamper in the bedchamber, Lady Alys folded the ceremonial robes together.

Henry, left alone for a moment, went back to break another piece of marzipan off his crown. Lady Alys remarked over her shoulder, "Leave some for tomorrow, Henry. If you eat it all tonight, you'll get a stomach ache." Then turning to the nurse she ordered, "Pour some water for Henry, so he can wash his face and brush his teeth, while I take these robes to the treasury. I'll be right back to say Henry's prayers with him." The robes of state with their gold and jewels were kept locked in a chest in the treasury.

Henry hastened to break off another piece of marzipan, while his nurse went into the bedchamber to pour the water into a glazed bowl and lay out his washcloth and the boar-hair toothbrush. The knock at the door startled him, and he said, "Come in!" without thinking. Henry was in his own palace and had not learned fear. With all his nobles, bishops and foreign diplomats at the banquet, however, he hadn't expected anyone to disturb him.

The door opened and a strange man entered. Although he was dressed like a high nobleman in velvet robes with wide bands of embroidery, he was slight of stature, with sharp features, receding hairline, and a smile that made Henry's skin creep.

"Sir!" The nurse, coming from the bedchamber, exclaimed, astonished by the intrusion of a stranger on the king when he was almost ready for bed.

"Go away, woman!" The man dismissed her irritably. "I am Sir Amaury Barlais, and I bring a letter to the king from his mother, Queen Alice of Champagne."

At the mention of his mother, Henry's fear receded and he eagerly held out his hands. "Oh, that's wonderful! Give it to me!"

Barlais did not comply, but staring at the Greek serving woman ordered a second time. "Leave us, woman! I come directly from the Queen Mother!"

The nurse looked in alarm at her charge, at the intruder, and then back to Henry for guidance.

"She's my nurse, why can't she stay?" Henry asked Barlais.

Barlais started, and then with a smile conceded. "You're right, my lord. Why not? But I am ever so thirsty and I'm sure you must be too after all that marzipan." He glanced at the diminished marzipan crown. "Would you be so kind as to fetch us wine, woman?"

The nurse was of humble birth and she knew her place. She did not speak very much French, her language with Henry being her native Greek. She did not have any interest in politics and did not know the names of most of Henry's vassals. Her world revolved around keeping Henry happy and healthy, making sure he ate, washed and said his prayers. She did not know who Sir Amaury Barlais was, nor whether it was credible that he had a letter from the Queen Mother. It seemed odd, however, that he came now as if he had been lurking in wait for Lady Alys to leave the chamber. Her maternal instincts screamed that this man meant Henry harm, but what was a Greek peasant woman supposed to say to a Frankish lord when he asked for wine?

She bobbed a curtsey and darted out the door. Outside she started running down the corridor. Her mind was fixed on one thing: she had to fetch Lady Alys immediately. Henry was in danger, even if the man had not been armed—or didn't appear to be. He might, she realized in horror, have a dagger hidden somewhere in the skirts or sleeves of his fine robes. Or he might have poison. Or maybe he had come to kidnap Henry, and hold him for ransom? She had heard tell that the old king, Henry's father, had been seized by pirates when he was a little boy and taken to the land of the Armenians.

Henry's nanny was not an old woman, but her life of luxury in the royal palace with a child king who loved sweets had made her fat. She was not used to running, and she was soon out of breath. Even as she gasped for breath, the thought of Henry alone with that man frightened her forward. She burst into the treasury, babbling in Greek, rendered incomprehensible by her breathlessness.

"Good heavens!" Lady Alys exclaimed, shocked and alarmed to have someone burst into the treasury when she was alone there. If it had been an armed man, she would have been utterly helpless to defend the royal treasure. As it was, the sight of the nurse set off other alarms. The woman was bright red, panting, sweating and wailing in Greek, "Come quick, come quick! Man with Henry! Bad man! Hurry! Hurry!"

Lady Alys barely took the time to close the lock on the chest before she followed the nanny out the door. She took a step before remembering to return and turn the key in the door of the treasury. She replaced the key on the ring tied to her belt, and the keys jingled and clacked as she hastened down the hall. Although the king's apartments were only on the far side of the interior court-yard, it seemed to take forever for the two women to reach the royal suite. The nanny was so out of breath she could not keep up with Lady Alys, and the wife of the baillie burst into the king's apartment alone exclaiming, "My lord king! Sir!"

The room was empty.

"Henry?"

No answer.

Lady Alys stood stalk still inside the door, her eyes scanning the room before her. The marzipan subtlety stood on the table, the broken crown still held up by the various animals of the king's menagerie. Nothing seemed amiss, and there was not a soul in the room. She looked toward the adjoining bedchamber, and her heart missed a beat. The bed covers had been torn off and tossed on the floor. She moved cautiously forward. "Henry?"

The covers shrugged and a sob reached her ears. Alys ran to the bed and pulled back the sheets to find King Henry curled up with his hands over his face.

"Henry? What's happened? What's wrong?"

Henry came into her arms at once and he turned his tear-covered face into her breast, but he didn't say anything articulate. Lady Alys folded her arms around her eight-year-old king and held him as his nanny hobbled breathlessly into the room and sat on the bed beside her.

"What's happened, pet?" The nanny asked in Greek, stroking Henry's shoulder.

"Sir Amaury," Henry gasped out at last.

"Which Sir Amaury?" Lady Alys asked.

"Barlais," Henry answered between sobs, and Lady Alys stiffened at once.

"He—he said—he had—a letter—from my mother!"

Lady Alys was holding her breath, remembering all the rumors from years ago of Barlais' affair with the Queen Mother. If he had gotten to her…. If he had managed to sweet-talk her….

"But—it wasn't even for me!" Henry broke down into miserable sobs again, and Lady Alys held him closer, while his nanny clucked and cooed to him sympathetically. Why the boy should care this much about the worthless bitch who had borne him, Lady Alys would never know. The Queen Mother had never taken much interest in him, and six months ago she'd abandoned him with hardly a farewell to marry Bohemond of Antioch.

Henry suddenly drew back so he could look her in the face, his own face red, puffy, and wet from crying. "It was a letter from my mother naming Barlais as my baillie!" Henry wailed. "He says he's—he's in charge now—and I have to do whatever he says! I don't like him, Lady Alys!" Henry declared with the simplicity of childhood. "I don't like him. I don't *want* to do what he says! I want Lord Philip to be my baillie like he's always been!"

Lady Alys pulled Henry back into her arms and stroked his back. "That's what Lord Philip wants too, Henry. We will have to look into this."

Henry had pulled away again to speak to her, his eyes fixed on hers and a frown furrowing his forehead. "But Barlais says my mother is my regent and she appoints my baillie and he had a paper to prove it. He had a letter with my mother's seal and he showed it to me. It named *him* my baillie!"

"We'll see about that, Henry. It's true your mother is your regent, but she named Lord Philip your baillie. The entire High Court took an oath to obey him until you came of age. You may have been crowned today, but you haven't come of age yet. I'm quite sure the High Court will have something to say about this."

"Then Barlais isn't right?" Henry asked hopefully.

"Let's just say the High Court will have to rule on what is right. Now, will you be alright, while I go tell Lord Philip about this?" She asked earnestly.

Henry nodded with a glance at his nanny.

Lady Alys extricated herself from his embrace. She stood, kissed him on his forehead, and admonished his nanny to bar the door behind her. "Don't let anyone in, unless you recognize the voice as myself, my lord, or Father Vasilius." The latter was Henry's confessor. "I'll send the good father to say your prayers with you, Henry. It's important that I tell Lord Philip about Barlais and his letter right away."

"Uncle Philip, what happened?" Balian had been sent by his impatient father to find out where Philip was. The High Court of Cyprus had gathered in the choir of the Cathedral of Saint Sophia to hear Barlais' claim to be baillie of Cyprus. As the man appointed baillie nine years earlier, Philip d'Ibelin's presence was absolutely essential. Yet he had been conspicuously absent.

Balian had found his uncle lying on the flagstone floor of the cloisters. As he went down on his heels beside his uncle, Lord Philip stirred with a groan. "What happened?" Balian repeated with concern, looking over his shoulders for an assassin, and then at his uncle for some wound.

"I don't know," Lord Philip admitted, trying to right himself and feeling his forehead with his fingers. A lump was already forming there. "I—I just suddenly felt dizzy and crashed down so hard that I must have knocked myself out."

Balian was still inspecting him for blood, but he found none. "The High Court is waiting for you so they can convene."

Philip nodded and held out his hand to Balian so the younger man could help him to his feet. Together they dusted him off, and Balian collected the documents his uncle had evidently been carrying. "The seal of Cyprus, Balian. It has to be somewhere here!" Lord Philip sounded slightly panicked.

Balian started searching around the stairs up into the nave. Not finding it there, his eyes scanned the paved walkway of the cloisters. The bright sunlight pouring through the elegantly carved arches created dark shadows and it was several minutes before Balian found the seal that had rolled almost two yards. Meanwhile, his uncle had composed himself somewhat and with a nod of thanks took the seal back into his hand and continued into the still unfinished nave of the cathedral.

The cornerstone for this Latin cathedral had been laid some eighteen years earlier. Although the choir enclosing the high altar was complete and usable, work on the nave had been halted several years back due to lack of finances. Balian knew that his uncle was anxious to re-start work, but the crusade in Egypt had left a huge gap in the royal treasury. So the nave remained unroofed and open to the sky.

"How many knights and lords have assembled?" Lord Philip asked his nephew as they made their way toward the screens. These were closed provisionally with wooden walls between the arches until the nave was finished.

"We counted 138. All barons are represented, either personally, by a relative or a senior household official. There is a quorum," Balian assured him.

Lord Philip nodded and absently felt the swelling on his forehead where his head had hit the flagstone.

Balian asked earnestly, "Are you sure you're alright?"

"I don't know. I still feel a little faint. Stay close by me."

Balian opened the provisional door into the choir and, with apologies to the many younger men standing there, led his uncle through the crowd of bystanders and between the wooden choir stools to the seat opposite the bishop's throne with a baldachin bearing the arms of Lusignan. This was the king's seat, and it was traditionally occupied by the regent or baillie during the king's minority.

Amaury Barlais stood beside this seat and as soon as Philip approached, he stepped in front of it, blocking Philip d'Ibelin's way. As he did so, he declared in a loud voice, "My lords, sirs! I have been appointed baillie by Queen Alice de Champagne, and hereby claim the right to chair this session of the High Court!" His voice was amplified by the acoustics of the choir designed to project the words of priests saying Mass.

"Let us first ask the Lord's blessing on this assembly, as is traditional, my lord!" The Archbishop of Nicosia admonished reproachfully. He was dressed in his full ecclesiastical regalia, and his words were met with a murmur of approval from the men gathered. As he raised his hands for silence, anyone who had been sitting or slouching in the choir stalls righted themselves. They all bowed their heads. A stillness settled over the choir.

The Archbishop of Nicosia raised his voice to the Lord, requesting blessings, wisdom, and grace, ending with: "Guide us, oh Lord, to do *Thy* Will!" Then he transitioned into the Lord's Prayer, and the men of the High Court, as well as the observers like Balian, joined in. Only after the last ragged "Amen" ended did the Archbishop turn pointedly to Barlais and order more than ask, "Present your case, Sir Amaury."

Barlais did not need to be asked twice. Taking a scrolled parchment from his sleeve he held it up so that it unraveled from the weight of the heavy seal attached to it. "Behold!" He intoned. "This is a letter signed and sealed by our regent, the Dowager Queen Alice, naming *me*, Sir Amaury Barlais, her baillie! I will pass it around so that all of you can see it for yourselves!" He handed the document to the man sitting in the front row of the choir stall to his right.

In doing so, he pointedly avoided giving it to Lord Philip, who was standing right in front of him. Balian, who was still standing close but a little behind his uncle, noticed that his uncle was holding his own documents to his chest with both arms. He looked very strange, semi-absent, and wore an unnaturally twisted expression on his face as he watched the reaction of the Lord of Caesarea, who had been the first recipient of the document Barlais was passing around.

Caesarea was the brother-in-law of both Ibelin brothers; the husband of their sister Marguerite, known in the family as Meg. Caesarea read the document with an impassive face and passed it to the man beside him, Sir Anseau de Brie. Brie was a big, fair-haired man with a flat nose and splotched skin, known for his prowess at arms. His father had been one of the original supports of Guy de Lusignan and had received the large Cypriot barony of Karpas for his unwavering support. His father, however, had also earned a reputation for ruthlessness and brutality, and his memory was still widely hated by the local inhabitants. There were rumors that Sir Anseau had been implicated in some of his father's atrocities, but no one knew for sure. Nevertheless, for his courage he had earned the moniker "Lion" (or sometimes because of his splotched skin "Leopard") of Karpas."

Brie skimmed over Barlais' document and snorted loud enough for everyone to hear before passing it on the next man in the front row. This happened to be Sir William Rivet, a good friend of Barlais, he nodded vigorously while reading the letter, and reminded those present, "We should not forget the service Sir Amaury's father gave the crown, and with so little reward. It is only right that a Barlais be recognized at last."

As the document made its way from man to man, restlessness seized the spectators by the screens. "Surely we have enough witnesses that it says what Sir Amaury claims," someone suggested out loud.

Beirut silenced them. "Let every member of the Court see for himself," he insisted.

"We'll take your word on the legality of it, Beirut," one of the back-benchers, a rear-vassal with only a small fief, called out.

Beirut didn't answer directly, but when it eventually reached him, he read it very carefully and nodded. For the room, he declared, "The document is exactly what Sir Amaury claims. It is signed and sealed by the Dowager Queen and witnessed by Prince Bohemond of Antioch, the Patriarch of Antioch, the Masters of the Temple, Hospital and Teutonic Knights in Antioch, as well as a number of lesser men."

"Then it's settled," Sir Amaury announced. Grinning triumphantly, he moved toward the royal chair to take his place.

Balian felt his uncle stiffen, but he said nothing. It was Beirut that spoke up. "Not so fast, Sir Amaury. While the letter is all you claim, there is an impediment to its authority."

"What?" Barlais demanded, frowning with irritation. His tone was peremptory, yet Balian was close enough to see that Barlais had broken out into a sweat. Like every other man in the room, he knew Beirut's reputation as a legal scholar. It was never good to dispute with Beirut on a legal matter.

"At the time of good King Hugh's death, the High Court met and, having done homage to Queen Alice as Regent, urged the Queen to respect the dying wishes of her late lord and husband and appoint my brother, Sir Philip d'Ibelin, baillie of Cyprus. Queen Alice readily agreed, and forthwith requested that all her liegemen do homage to my brother as baillie until the majority of her son Henry."

"Yes, of course. We all know that. But Queen Alice has changed her mind about who she wants as her baillie. She has named *me* to *replace* Lord Philip," Barlais answered irritably. His fingers were nervously clasping and unclasping.

"The Queen may have changed her mind," Beirut replied patiently, "but that does not release us from our oaths."

"You must swear new oaths to me!" Barlais countered, visibly and audibly irritated. "It's really that simple, Beirut."

"But the oath we took was *until King Henry came of age*," Beirut reminded Barlais calmly. "King Henry was crowned yesterday, but he is only eight years old. He will not come of age until May 3, 1232."

"I don't see how that is at all relevant," Barlais countered with a dismissive flick of his hand. His face had become more pinched than ever, as if he had just bit into something sour. "No one questions that Queen Alice is the rightful regent. She appoints a baillie to act for her because, as a woman, she cannot lead the feudal levee. She is free to appoint whoever she likes, and she has chosen me!"

"It's not that simple, because we all—including you, Sir Amaury—took a binding oath to another man." Beirut stood his ground.

"That oath is obsolete in the face of the Queen's wish for a new baillie!" Sir Amaury insisted.

"No, it's not!" Sir Anseau de Brie lost his patience and boomed out in his deep voice, making the choir hum.

His words also provoked a chorus of "Hear! Hear!"

"Furthermore," Brie continued in his loud, blunt voice, "you knew damned well that we were all bound to Lord Philip when you went crawling to Queen Alice in the first place."

Barlais reddened, and his fists started to clench.

"While I wonder what the Prince of Antioch was doing while you resumed your liaison with his wife—"

"How dare you!" Barlais flung himself at Brie.

Balian and Rivet both instinctively stepped between Barlais and Brie, but Balian was closer. Before he knew what was happening, a knife sliced right through his sleeve and cut deep into his forearm. Luckily for him, the point had been aimed at Brie. Balian was bigger and stronger than Barlais, and when he realized that Barlais was armed, he re-doubled his efforts to hold him back. Around him, others leapt up, and it seemed like everyone started shouting.

The Archbishop of Nicosia was forbidding bloodshed before the high altar, while others shouted various things like, "Have you gone mad?" or "Control your temper!" Or just "Stop! Stop!"

Brie sprang forward and slapped Barlais across the face with the back of his hand, knocking the knife away almost as a second thought. "You are a *traitor*, Sir Amaury! You know damn well Lord Philip is baillie until King Henry comes of age! You *know* you had no business putting poisoned suggestions into the ears of our impressionable queen. You are the architect of this appointment, not Queen Alice, and in plotting it and securing that signed document you are in violation of your oath to Lord Philip! I hereby charge you with High Treason, and offer my body to prove it!"

Sir Amaury was struggling so violently in Balian's arms that the younger man was having a hard time staying upright. It didn't help that his own blood was making his grip and the tiles at his feet slippery. He glanced to his uncle for assistance, but Lord Philip remained strangely lamed.

Before anyone else could assist Balian, Barlais twisted free of Balian's arms and flung a fist into Balian's face. With his hands still around Barlais trying to hold him, Balian could only turn his head aside. Barlais' fist hit him in the side of his neck, and the shock of it made him lose both his breath and his hold on Barlais.

In a flash, Barlais was free of his grip and ran to the high altar. "Anyone who dares lay a hand on me defiles this altar!" He screamed out. "I claim right of sanctuary!"

"Are you admitting your treason then?" Brie barked out.

"No! I'll meet you on the field of honor, Brie! God is my witness! I am the rightful baillie of Cyprus! *You* are the traitors! Ignoring the wishes of our regent and queen! I'll prove it before God!" He was breathing hard, his face was red, and his eyes darted around the room like a trapped animal.

"Then so be it," Beirut announced in a voice that was calming in its very definitiveness. "You have no need to claim sanctuary, Sir Amaury, nor hold on to the altar. No man here will hurt you. You were the one to bring a weapon into a church and the one to attack." Then with a nod to the Archbishop, Beirut turned to the knights and barons collected in the choir and called, "I move to adjourn this session of the High Court."

"Amen! Amen!" "Adjourn!" many voices seconded, and men started to disperse, pouring out into the nave or the surrounding ambulatory, all talking at once in agitation.

Surgeon Jocelyn d'Auber removed the bandages around Balian's wound carefully, frowning the whole time. He didn't like what he saw or smelled. Leaning closer, he sniffed the wound directly and shook his head. "It was a clean wound and we treated it almost immediately. It shouldn't be festering like this. It makes me wonder if Sir Amaury's blade was contaminated in some way."

"Contaminated?"

"Had some substance on it designed to make wounds more deadly."

"You mean poisoned?"

The surgeon weighed his head from side to side. "In a manner of speaking."

Balian looked at him mutely in stunned horror before asking, "What if it was?"

"I'm going to remove the sutures, clean the wound again, and bind it together anew," the surgeon looked at his patient from under his eyebrows. "Do you want something to dull the pain?"

"No, just get it over with," Balian urged.

D'Auber nodded and turned to limp over to the satchel with his instruments. The surgeon had broken his ankle in a fall as a youth, completely snapping the tendons and ligaments at the same time. He was lucky to walk at all, and his ankles still bore the scars of the hours-long surgery that had partially restored use of the limb. The incident had made him determined to learn all he could about wound treatment. He had been in the service of the Ibelins longer than Balian had been alive.

A knock on the door surprised both doctor and patient, and Balian called out warily, "Who is it?" He didn't want a witness to his discomfort and possible fainting, swearing or screaming during what promised to be a very unpleasant treatment.

His brother Hugh poked his head around the edge of the door. "It's me, Balian. May I come in?"

Balian was relieved. Hugh wasn't just his brother; he was his friend. "Master Auber's just about to tear everything open again and douse the wound with things that make it hurt like hell. So, by all means, come join the laughs," Balian answered in an attempt at levity.

Hugh sat down on the chest under the window beside Balian's bed. "I thought you'd be interested to hear that Barlais has fled Cyprus."

"Again?" Balian asked.

"Last time he was *invited* to leave; this time he ran away in the dark of night."

"What did you expect? For him to seriously face Karpas—of all men!—in the lists? It's obvious to everyone that Karpas can beat Barlais with one hand tied behind his back. Look what happened when Barlais fought Sir Toringuel— he charged Toringuel with cheating and turned everything on its head! Barlais doesn't expect to win, he wants to find a means to declare himself the winner without winning at all!"

Hugh looked at him a little suspiciously. "That sounds pretty far-fetched to me. How could he risk judicial combat with someone so much better at arms than he is? It would be crazy. Father is relieved he's gone. He says the important thing is that Barlais can't stir up any more trouble here."

"True enough, but *where* has he gone? Last time he went whining to the Queen Mother and that's what got us to where we are *now*," Balian noted with an edge to his voice and a hostile look at the surgeon. Auber approached the bed and started laying out his instruments. Balian's squire Rob had meanwhile brought a pitcher of clean water from the courtyard on the surgeon's orders.

The surgeon smiled faintly and gestured for Balian to give him his arm. With little scissors, he neatly clipped the sutures in two and then ordered Balian. "Just keep talking to your brother."

"If the reports we've had are correct, he took a ship heading west," Hugh obligingly picked up the conversation.

"So not back to Antioch and Queen Alice?"

"No. The harbormaster says the ship he sailed on—"

Balian barked in pain as the surgeon expertly yanked the first suture out. He turned a resentful eye to Auber, but the surgeon answered, "That came out nice and clean. Keep talking."

"As I was saying," Hugh continued amiably, "the harbormaster at Kyrenia says he shipped aboard a Pisan vessel bound for Taranto."

"So—aagh!" Balian cast the surgeon a look of hatred, and then spat out, "The Holy Roman Empire. He sailed for the Holy Roman Empire."

"It would seem so," Hugh replied evenly as his brother braced for the next suture to be drawn. There were, thank God, only four of them. "You know that's where Cheneché washed up?"

Balian was having a hard time concentrating. "What?"

"Don't you remember? Not long after you and Baldwin were knighted, Sir William de la Tour accused Sir Gauvain de Cheneché of breaking into his home, killing one of his servants and injuring him. They exchanged gages and agreed to trial by combat, but just when—" He paused while Balian shouted in pain. By now the bleeding had started again and the arm was pulsing with pain. Balian looked again at the surgeon, down at his arm, and then gritted his teeth. "Get on with it!"

"Just relax, sir. Sir Hugh was telling you about Sir Gauvain."

"Yes," Hugh agreed calmly, ignoring his brother's situation. "Just when Sir Gauvain was down and about to be killed, Uncle Philip stopped him. Sir Gauvain was allowed his life in exchange for paying a huge fine, having Masses said for the servant killed, and—"

Balian roared one last time as the last suture came out, but already the surgeon was wrapping a clean, freshly pressed linen around his arm to staunch the bleeding. "Hold that tight over your arm for the moment." Balian did so mutely, as Hugh continued.

"Sir Gauvain agreed as long as Sir William's sword was pointed at his throat, but by the very next day, he was refusing to pay the fine, claiming it wasn't fair, and that Sir William had no proof, even that he hadn't agreed to the settlement. Uncle Philip was furious and gave him thirty days to pay the fine or face arrest."

"And Sir Gauvain chose to break his word and just disappear," Balian finished the story.

"Well, that's just it. He *didn't* exactly 'disappear.' He was at the Emperor's court when I arrived last fall with Queen Yolanda."

"Do you think the Emperor knew he was a felon fleeing justice?"

Hugh shrugged. "All I know is that he rode right beside the Emperor both times the court went hawking. I was told by members of the Emperor's household that the Emperor 'honored him' because of his great wisdom concerning birds of prey."

"So knowing something about birds is more important to the Holy Roman Emperor than whether a man is a scoundrel and oath-breaker?" Balian retorted incredulously.

Hugh shrugged his shoulders awkwardly. "I'm only telling you what I heard, Balian. I suppose it's possible that the Emperor doesn't know that he ran away from his sentence."

"Possible but not likely. Emperors are notorious for their networks of spies." Balian paused to eye the surgeon warily as he took the pitcher of water from Rob and poured from it into a bowl. He then added vinegar and soaked a sponge in the mixture.

"Remove the linen and put your arm in the water," the surgeon instructed. Balian dutifully complied. The blood from his arm flowed into the water, swirling and slowly dying it red.

"There's something else you should know," Hugh said, his eyes fixed on the swirls of red in the basin of water.

"Yes?" Balian prompted.

"Uncle Philip isn't well. He had a second fall and complains of seeing double. His right hand has gone limp, and he can't hold a pen firmly enough to write. He told our father that he doesn't feel well enough to be baillie anymore."

Balian flinched, splashing water from the bowl, and cursed his own clumsiness. The surgeon set the bowl aside, patted the arm dry with a towel and started applying the sponge to the wound. Balian yelped in pain but then adjusted to the stinging and simply clenched his teeth while the surgeon proceeded with his treatment.

"Father said it would not be a good thing to resign now. Barlais would come back in an instant and most people don't trust him."

"With good reason! Auber says the knife might well have been poisoned."

"We have no proof of that," the surgeon cautioned.

"I don't like him either," Hugh agreed, "but you have to feel a little sorry for the man. Think how frightened and insecure he must have felt facing the whole High Court and knowing most of them don't want him to be baillie. It was fear that made him bring a knife with him. Remember how he clung to the altar when he realized his letter wasn't going to be accepted?"

"Whose side are you on?" Balian demanded offended by his brother's sympathy for his assailant.

"I'm on our side, Balian, and I always will be, but we mustn't forget that Barlais has friends and supporters too. Many men, like Rivet and Bethsan, think his father did not get his just rewards. They argue that Barlais deserves a greater say in the affairs of the kingdom. So, Father really doesn't want it to come to a vote before the High Court."

Balian only frowned in answer, and Hugh continued, "He's talked Uncle Philip into remaining baillie, but to rest more."

"How is he supposed to do that? The demands of the kingdom won't slow down just because he's sick," Balian pointed out, squirming as the surgeon pressed hard, sealing the wound shut with his hand.

"Uncle Philip has asked you to stay with him," Hugh replied as if that solved everything.

Balian looked at his brother. "What did Father say?"

"He said it was up to you."

"You can go tell them both that I'm happy to stay with Uncle Philip," Balian agreed at once. His father might have made no further mention of Denise, but he hadn't apologized either and their relationship was strained. Meanwhile, Baldwin missed no chance to put Balian in a bad light, constantly asking about his gambling, his drinking, and his conquests. It would be good to get away from Beirut, and especially Baldwin. Besides, Balian had always gotten on well with Uncle Philip. No doubt Novare would be happy to return to Cyprus too since this was where his one fief was. The only one he would miss was Hugh. Spontaneously he asked, "Do you want to stay with me, Hugh?"

"May I?"

"If Father agrees."

"I'll go ask!" Hugh was already on his feet and out the door.

Balian turned his attention back to the surgeon, who now started to wrap a bandage around his arm deftly.

"No new sutures?"

"No, let's see if we can get it to heal without."

Part II

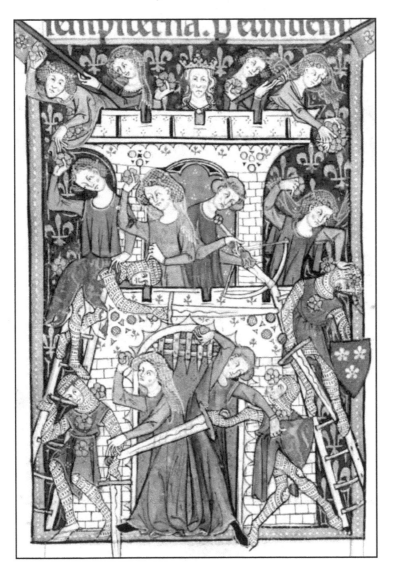

The Women of Outremer

Chapter Four

Death of an Empress

Andria, Apulia, Kingdom of Sicily
May 5, 1228

"The Queen, my lord, is dead." Eschiva de Montbéliard stood in front of Queen Yolanda's chamber confronting the Holy Roman Emperor. It was less than three years since Yolanda and Eschiva had left their native Palestine to travel to Sicily. They had been twelve and fourteen respectively, full of trepidation, excitement, and hope. Three years at Frederick's court, confined in the harem tract, had left Eschiva looking older than her seventeen years—and Yolanda dead.

Eschiva had not had a chance to dye any of her dresses black, but she was soberly dressed and wore her hair completely covered by a white wimple. Her face was marked by chapped lips, dark circles under her eyes, and teenage acne at the base of her nose and corner of her mouth.

"And our son?" The new widower asked without a flicker of emotion.

Eschiva was not prepared for that question. She stumbled over her answer, "He—he's with the wet-nurse, my lord. I presume he is well."

"Presume?" The Emperor raised his eyebrows ever so slightly. He was not a handsome man. He was stocky rather than tall, and his waist was thick. His arms and shoulders were no longer muscular. He had bright red hair, and a ruddy complexion that burned easily in the sun, testimony to his mother's Norman ancestry. He had a soft, fleshy chin under full lips and a small nose. The dominant feature in his face was his pale blue eyes. These bore into Eschiva like blue flames.

"The queen died of—of milk—milk-fever, my lord," Eschiva stammered in her dazed effort to explain. "It is not—a—a contagious condition. There is no reason to think your son is ill. He is with the wet-nurse," she repeated.

"Good," The Emperor answered.

Good? What was good? Eschiva was too numbed to understand anything beyond Frederick Hohenstaufen's apparent indifference to the death of his wife, queen and empress. The death of her only friend.

The Emperor nodded once, but it was more to himself than to Eschiva. He turned his back on her to depart.

Eschiva was confused—by his reaction and by his departure. "Have you no instructions for me, my lord?" She'd been struggling to keep Yolanda alive for ten days, watching her slowly fade from life in delirium and despair. Now she was left with a corpse that reminded her of her best friend but was cold and admonishing—as if she had done something wrong. What could she have done differently? What was she supposed to do now? She didn't have a clue. For three years, her life had revolved about Yolanda, and now Yolanda was gone.

"Prepare the corpse for lying in state and the funeral, of course," the Emperor answered in a tone that suggested he was annoyed with the question and a look that expressed his contempt for the questioner. His eyes dismissed her as an idiot, beneath conversation for someone as intelligent as himself.

Eschiva dared not ask more and dropped her eyes as the Emperor again turned to leave. The eunuch door-keeper bowed deeply and opened the door for the Emperor. Abruptly the Hohenstaufen turned back to censure Eschiva in a low, even voice. "The proper form of address from someone of your station is not 'my lord' but 'your magnificence.' We would have expected you to know that by now. Be sure you do not make the same mistake again." Then he was gone.

The eunuch cast her a disgusted look, his lips pressed together in disapproval before he slipped out the open door to take up his position on the outside. The door clunked shut. Eschiva heard the bolt clack, locking her inside. With a corpse that had been her only friend.

For ten days she had resisted crying. She had fought down her own emotions to show a brave, encouraging and comforting face to Yolanda. To the very last, she had told Yolanda she would be fine. She had promised her she would recover. She had lied. Intuitively she had known Yolanda was dying. The whole time, she had been terrified of what was happening. She had just never dared admit it out loud.

The doctors had been no help. Most spoke only the perverted Italian of Sicily. Not that Eschiva understood the Italian of Venice or Genoa either. They had come and gone, consulting among themselves and giving her only the barest of instructions through the eunuch. Do this, do that, don't do this, don't do that. No one had ever tried to explain anything to her, much less address her own distress—except the Arabic-speaking Jewish doctor who'd come twice.

Eschiva spoke fluent Arabic, as did most natives of Outremer. Arabic had been the language of her nurses, both good Syrian Christian women, of the grooms in the stable, the laundry women, the shopkeepers in the market, the traveling tradesmen, and just about everyone else of the working class.

The Jewish doctor had been the only one to show the slightest sympathy for either the patient or her waiting woman. He had shaken his head and muttered about the strain put on a "child's" body to give birth at fourteen (Yolanda's first pregnancy that ended in a still-birth) and now again, just thirteen months later, at fifteen. He had also taken the time to explain what some of the medicines were and what effect they would have. He had, at one point, pressed a powder into Eschiva's hand and suggested she put a pinch of it into her own wine. "It is very powerful," he warned, "and it will help you sleep. You need to sleep," he added kindly, "or you will not have the strength to help our dear Empress."

He had been right. A little of the powder had helped her sleep, and the next day she had been far more effective—better able to pretend cheerfulness to ease Yolanda's fear.

But that strength had died with Yolanda.

Eschiva sank down on the thick oriental carpets paving the floor and sobbed miserably. She didn't have the strength to go back into the queen's chamber and deal with the cold, pale, inanimate *thing* that had once been her friend. Hugging herself, because there was no one else in the world to hug her, Eschiva sobbed for Yolanda. She had endured a miserable marriage only to end like this. An unloved corpse.

She sobbed too for her faded dreams of life at a great court filled with great scholars, poets, musicians, and brave knights. Frederick's court, along with its scholars, poets, musicians, and knights, had been for men only. Like a Muslim Sultan, he kept his women, including his empress, at the back of his palace, guarded by a eunuch and a troop of Muslim guards.

Although indignant at first and discouraged with time, Eschiva and Yolanda had come to terms with being isolated from world affairs. They had each other for company. They had musical instruments and books. The harem tracts of all Frederick's palaces were luxurious. They had glazed tiles and rich carpets, fresh fountains and gracious gardens. They did not lack for comfort in their gilded cage.

Yet there had been little joy because Yolanda had suffered miserably from her husband's indifference. From the day they met at their wedding, Frederick had never shown a flicker of affection for his little bride. Even on their wedding night, he walked past his wife's chamber to sleep with one of his slaves, leaving Yolanda to sob herself to sleep in Eschiva's arms.

When he did deign to consummate his marriage, it had been between other appointments and on a schedule that left him no time to take her feelings into account. When his thirteen-year-old bride cried out in pain, he had told her "not to make a fuss," and Eschiva had been the one to pick up the pieces.

No, there hadn't been a day of joy in this marriage. Not at the celebration, the consummation, or the two pregnancies that ended with the death of the child in the first instance and the death of the mother in the second. Frederick had offered his bride and empress nothing resembling joy, affection, partnership, or respect.

So Eschiva had comforted her friend with books. The girls had read aloud to one another until Yolanda discovered that Eschiva had a talent for sketching and painting. After that, Yolanda had insisted that Eschiva capture favorite scenes in illustrations, while Yolanda translated the texts from French into Arabic so they could share their creations with the harem slaves.

They were friends with the harem slaves because they shared the space with them, and the imprisonment. The other girls had had even less to say about their fate than Yolanda and Eschiva. They had been sold by fathers and brothers, taken captive in wars, or were simply the product of the streets. A fair face, a delicate waist, bulbous breasts or bombastic buttocks—anything that caught the fancy of a jaded monarch could land them here. It did no good to indignantly declaim that they were mere slaves while Yolanda was a queen in her own right.

Yet as her sobbing subsided, Frederick's parting remark rang in Eschiva's ear: the proper term of address for someone of her station was "Your magnificence." That was what the harem slaves called him. Surely, he didn't mean that she, the grand-daughter of a king, the sister of the baillie and Constable of Jerusalem, was no better than a slave? Did he?

Eschiva felt a shiver run down her spine, and she looked around the queen's apartment. What *was* her station, now that her reason for being here was dead? What was her future?

Surely, Frederick would send her home to her brother.

Eschiva had never been close to her brother. He had left the care of their mother to start training as squire to King John de Brienne when Eschiva had been only three or four years old. After that, she had seen him only at holidays. When her mother died and she had been sent to the convent of St. Anne, they had seen even less of one another. He had traveled with them to Brindisi, of course, but he'd spared little time for his little sister.

No doubt he would have little time for her now, either, but he was still her brother, the only member of her immediate family still alive. Where else should she go, but back to him? She couldn't stay here. She had no place here anymore. No reason for staying. No desire to stay.

But how was she supposed to leave, when the door was locked from the outside and guarded by fifty Mamelukes?

What was she thinking about? Yolanda's corpse was lying in the next room. They needed to prepare it for a state funeral. They ought to be saying Masses for her soul!

Who did she mean by "they"? There was no one but herself.

Eschiva pulled herself together. She took a deep breath and walked to the door. "Omar?"

"What?" The eunuch growled from the far side of the door.

"You must send Father Yohannes to me. He must help me prepare the queen's corpse." Eschiva interpreted the answering grumble as assent and returned back to face the corpse. She could, she supposed, call to the harem girls to help her, but that would be cowardice. Yolanda deserved better. Yolanda's mother had died giving her birth. Her father was too busy fighting for her kingdom and marrying two new brides in succession to be a father to her. Her baillies had delivered her into the hands of Frederick Hohenstaufen. And he, her husband, had treated her like a distasteful duty. The only one in the whole world who had ever loved Yolanda was Eschiva.

With tears streaming down her face, Eschiva made herself return to the bedroom to wash and dress her friend's corpse.

Chapter Five

A Messenger from Cyprus

Andria, Apulia, Kingdom of Sicily
May 7, 1228

IT WAS THE TIME OF DAY Frederick liked best, the time when he dismissed the supplicants, ambassadors, ministers, and courtiers and retired to his private apartments for a discussion with scholars and scientists on the nature of the universe itself. Today he had with him Moses ben Samuel, who was working on a translation of Aristotle from Arabic into Italian, Brother Angelo, Master of Novices for the Augustinian Order, and Michael Scott, astrologer, alchemist, and magician all-in-one.

Frederick entered his library, a room lined with shelves for both books and scrolls, paved with mosaics, and lit only by glass lanterns. The three scholars bowed deeply, murmuring greetings in their most familiar tongue. Frederick waved their expressions of humility aside graciously. With these men, he liked to pretend he was among equals, conscious that too much reverence for his person and his office would interfere with intellectual debate. Instead, he clapped his hands and ordered refreshments for everyone from the servant who appeared, bowed and withdrew. Then indicating a small table surrounded by elaborately carved armed chairs, he gestured for the learned men to join him there.

On entering, he had overheard Moses and Michael speaking in Arabic. They had first met at the Court in Toledo and seemed to enjoy keeping their Arabic active by speaking it to one another. The third man in the room, however, was not conversant in the tongue, so Frederick pointedly opened the conversation in Latin by turning to Father Angelo first. "So, tell us, how is our experiment going? The boy must surely have started speaking by now?"

The Augustine canon shook his head and his lips narrowed. "I deeply regret to inform you, Your Excellency, that the boy remains as mute as his attendants."

The child born to a repentant prostitute on the doorstep of Brother Angelo's monastery had been taken in by the monks as an act of charity. Frederick had heard of the incident and immediately assumed the costs of the child's care on the condition that the boy be raised without hearing the human voice. Because Frederick had been exposed to so many different languages in his life, they fascinated him. He wanted to know what language God spoke. The Jews, of course, claimed it was Hebrew, but Arab scholars argued that Hebrew was the language of the Fallen, while the Garden of Eden was surely in the Arabian Peninsula and so Arabic was the language of God, as the Koran proved. While most children learned the language of their parents or nurses, Frederick reasoned that if a child did not hear any language spoken around him, then he would learn language directly from God. He was not pleased to learn that his experimental child, although old enough to speak, was still silent. "Is there something wrong with his vocal chords?" he asked.

"He screams lustily, evidently trying to make his wishes known to his nurses, but his shouts, snarls, and grunts remain inarticulate."

"How old is he?"

"He is now 26 months old."

Frederick frowned and insisted, "He should be speaking by now."

"Indeed, Your Excellency, but I must report that he is often morose and lethargic."

"Has a physician examined him?"

"Yes. He ordered blood-letting to reduce ill-humors but to no evident effect. The boy appears to have no interest in life, and often lies or sits about staring at nothing."

Frederick frowned, and glanced at the other two scholars. "If he is not physically ill, then he should be encouraged to do something."

"But how, Your Excellency? Without speaking to him? It is one thing to beat a child for doing something, but to beat him for doing nothing?" Father Angelo asked, eyebrows raised. When Frederick did not answer, he continued, "We have been forced to replace no less than three women. Each claimed they could not bear to care for the boy without being able to play games with him or sing him lullabies. The woman we have now is herself little more than an idiot and mute, so even if tempted to talk to him, she cannot. Still, I must in honesty report that the boy is doing more poorly under her care, though she is very correct about feeding and cleaning him."

Frederick detected unspoken disapproval despite the monk's cautious and apparently neutral tone. That irritated him, and he declared firmly, "We will continue the experiment."

Father Angelo bowed his head, "As you wish, Your Excellency."

Annoyed both by the lack of results and the monk's greater concern for the well-being of a whore's bastard than the scientific value of his experiment, Frederick dismissed the monk. He turned to Michael Scott instead. "My good man, I hope you have more enlightening thoughts!"

Scott smiled and launched into a lengthy description of some observations he had made of birds of prey. Frederick was pleased both by the topic, as he loved falconry, and Scott's astuteness in choosing the topic to cheer him up. It was the Scotsman's ability to judge his mood so accurately and respond to it—whatever it was—so sensitively that made him such a good companion.

"...but it does make me wonder," Scott noted in that voice with which he approached particularly knotty questions, "whether rest or activity is the best means of stimulating digestion. You know, Your Excellency, in many parts of the world, people are told to lie down and rest after a heavy meal, and certainly, we see that in the case of large animals like lions, and yet, this does not seem to be the case with great birds of prey."

"We should experiment!" Frederick concluded with enthusiasm.

"Yes? How?" Scott waited expectantly.

"Well," Frederick thought about it a minute, "we could feed two men of roughly the same age and build the same large meal, then chain one to a bed so he cannot move and chase the other around and around until he drops. Then we kill them both and immediately open their stomachs to see which has digested more!" Frederick was excited by the prospect and surprised that his two companions failed to share his enthusiasm. In fact, they both looked shocked.

"We'll use criminals already condemned to death, of course," Frederick explained, surmising the cause of their shock.

Scott recovered first, nodding agreement. "Yes, of course, that would be— uh—reasonable. But the Church prohibits the dissection of a Christian body."

"Then we'll use Muslim or Jewish criminals in the experiment," Frederick answered irritably. "Surely you see how important this is? If we know—"

A knock on the door interrupted him, and Frederick turned in his chair to call out crossly. "Who is it and what do you want?"

"Your Excellency." The voice answering was muffled by the heavy door. "A

Cypriot ship has docked and all aboard are dressed in mourning. A knight disembarked and is seeking an audience with you."

Frederick digested this news. His father had granted a crown to Aimery de Lusignan in exchange for the latter's homage, making Cyprus a vassal kingdom of the Holy Roman Empire. In the impending crusade, which Frederick intended to initiate this summer, he expected Cyprus to provide knights, sergeants, and archers. More important, he expected Cyprus to help defray a large part of his expenses. He had not expected any problems with that, since King Henry, a grandson of Aimery de Lusignan, was only a boy of eleven. A child monarch was easily manipulated and exploited—as Frederick knew from first-hand experience. The boy king of Cyprus would not be able to prevent him taking command of Cyprus' human and financial resources.

If the boy was dead, of course, that would make things even easier. The boy had no direct heirs, so Frederick would be in the ideal position to exploit the inevitable rival claimants to the throne to his own advantage. Anyone who wanted the crown of Cyprus would need his support as the kingdom's overlord, and that would give him the leverage to demand significant concessions and financial contributions to the Imperial treasury. Yes, this could be a very good turn indeed, he concluded and called toward the door. "We will receive him in the audience chamber in half an hour." Then turning to his scholarly friends, he excused himself and withdrew.

The main audience chamber of his residence in Andrea was not as well decorated as his palace in Palermo, but it was large. It also echoed badly when it was not filled with hundreds of people for a banquet, reception or another state occasion. The footsteps of the approaching emissary from Cyprus seemed very loud in consequence, and even the scraping of his spurs on the tiled floor was audible.

Frederick had not bothered calling together his court or even his council for this meeting. It was better, he thought, to have a head-start over everyone else in learning about dynastic changes in Cyprus. That would enable him to be a step ahead of everyone else in suggesting any action. He was attended, therefore, only by his legal counsel, Piero della Vigna, and two secretaries to take down a transcript of the encounter.

The distance from the entrance to the raised throne was nearly thirty yards, giving Frederick time to watch the emissary as he approached. Unfortunately, Frederick's eyes, never very good, were deteriorating. It was not until the emissary bowed deeply before him and stood upright a few feet away that

Frederick realized how very young the man was. Far from being a grey-haired cleric, or even a seasoned vassal in his prime, the man before him was little more than a youth. He was slender but so tall that standing three steps lower than the Emperor he stood eye-to-eye with the seated Emperor. Frederick hated tall men!

"My lord," the young man said as he straightened, making Frederick grimace inwardly. That was the second time in as many days that someone had dared to address him in so demeaning a manner. "I come to inform you," (again Frederick noted the rude directness of his speech; the young man had less understanding of protocol than a donkey-driver!) "that the good Philip d'Ibelin, baillie of Cyprus, is dead."

"The baillie?" Frederick asked astonished. He had been so focused on the prospect of King Henry himself being dead, that he found the news of the regent's death both anti-climactic and confusing. "The King is well?"

"King Henry is in the best of health—beyond his natural, deep grief for his beloved baillie."

Idiot, Frederick thought to himself, no king mourns the death of his regent! Regents were parasites that drained royal treasuries into the hands of grasping inferiors. A king always hated his regents.

He focused his attention on the messenger again, squinting to see better. The young man was dressed in black, but it was black composed of beautifully brushed suede boots, a surcoat of black linen trimmed with satin, and a black silk shirt. In addition to the expensive fabrics tailored to perfection, the young man wore a gold cross paté and a signet ring, both set with red stones. His spurs were gold with red enamel as well. No low-born messenger, Frederick surmised, despite his evident ignorance of court protocol. So a provincial, it seemed, from Cyprus. "Who are you?" Frederick asked.

"I am Sir Balian d'Ibelin, my lord," the young man answered directly, without the slightest hint that he was unimportant, his name irrelevant.

Curiously, the name did sound vaguely familiar to Frederick, but it was inconceivable that this puppy had done anything to earn the attention of the Holy Roman Emperor. Irritated, Frederick admitted, "We've heard the name, but we can't place it."

"You will have heard of my grandfather of the same name," the emissary responded as if this was a common remark. "He defended Jerusalem against Salah ad-Din in 1187."

"He *surrendered* Jerusalem to Salah ad-Din," Frederick corrected the impudent young man. While it was understandable that the descendants of the man who surrendered the Holiest City in Christendom to the Saracens preferred not to mention that disgrace, it was nevertheless disingenuous, in Frederick's eyes, to speak of "defense" as if it had been successful.

The young emissary seemed to flinch at the correction, as if he did not expect it. Well, it was time he learned his lesson—and more manners. At the moment, however, it was more important to understand his relationship to the deceased regent, who was also an Ibelin. So Frederick asked, "You are Philip d'Ibelin's son?"

"No, his nephew," Balian answered.

"Near enough," Frederick answered. "We want you to know that we are extremely displeased with your uncle, who *called* himself baillie of Cyprus, although he was never appointed by *us*. Furthermore, we were outraged to learn that he had King Henry crowned when he was only eight, which was not proper, as we should have crowned our vassal ourselves—when we were ready. The coronation was an act of calculated insubordination and disrespect that we have neither forgotten nor forgiven. Furthermore, we have heard in great detail from men dear to us about the abuse of power and the sham-courts over which your uncle presided. Last but not least, we know all-too-well what regents do during the reigns of minor kings: they plunder! They steal from the royal treasury to enrich themselves, and they put their grasping hands into every possible source of royal revenue. They grant themselves liberties and properties. They use royal resources to build themselves castles and palaces. They are, in short, little better than pirates and bandits."

Fredrick noted with contempt that Sir Balian was so simple that his shock and disbelief were written all over his face. Idiot, Frederick thought before continuing: "So don't expect us to show great sorrow at the death of your uncle. And don't expect us to forget his crimes either—just because he had the good fortune to die before we had the opportunity to come to Cyprus in person to deliver justice. When we *do* come to Cyprus, which will be later this year, we will expect a reckoning from your uncle's nearest adult kin. Who, if I remember correctly, was his brother John, was it not?"

"Yes. That is my father, the Lord of Beirut."

It surprised Frederick that Sir Balian spoke with so much obvious pride, but then it further confirmed his low opinion of his intelligence. After an imperial threat of retribution, an intelligent man would have distanced himself from the dead man's kin as much as possible. Out loud, Frederick merely observed, "Beirut is in the Kingdom of Jerusalem."

"Yes, most of the lords of Cyprus hold fiefs in both Cyprus and Syria," Sir Balian remarked—as if he thought he had the right to educate his overlord.

"Maybe not for long," Frederick warned ominously, only to receive a look of such utter confusion that he dismissed this young man as too stupid to be worthy of further conversation. "You may go!" He announced with a wave of his hand.

Sir Balian took a step back, bowed deeply and then turned and walked back down the length of the great audience chamber. He had only made it part way when Frederick remembered that Beirut had been the Regent of Jerusalem for his wife's mother, suggesting there was some blood relationship with his late wife. "Wait!"

Sir Balian stopped and turned back toward the Emperor expectantly.

"Your father was great-uncle to the late Empress, Yolanda of Jerusalem. You must be her cousin, no?"

Sir Balian gasped audibly. "The Queen is dead?"

"Yes, the day before yesterday. Answer the question: are you her cousin?"

"Yes, of course," Balian stammered out, still stunned by the unexpected news.

"Good. Then you will represent her family at the funeral the day after tomorrow."

"But, my lord—" Balian intercepted Frederick's look and snapped his mouth shut as he again bowed deeply, before striding out of the hall.

Chapter Six
Escape from the Harem

Andria, Apulia, Kingdom of Sicily
May 10, 1228

FROM THE "EMPRESS' BALCONY," ESCHIVA FOLLOWED the entire funeral
Mass in privacy. When the pallbearers moved forward to surround the coffin,
Eschiva stood and pressed up against the latticework of the wooden screen to get
a final glimpse of Yolanda. Her friend lay dressed in her coronation robes of white
satin stitched with the gold crosses of Jerusalem, and someone had scattered red
rose petals over her. She looked beautiful and peaceful—until the jostling of the
coffin as the pallbearers hefted it onto their shoulders displaced one of Yolanda's
arms. It fell from her breast in a gesture so life-like that Eschiva gasped.

The man standing closest to the coffin glanced up in the direction of the
sound. He looked straight at Eschiva, and she caught her breath. He was young,
dark-haired, and a stranger—yet strangely familiar. Eschiva pressed closer to the
screen to see him better, but he looked down again, unable to see through the
screen. Despite looking straight at her, he had not seen her.

Eschiva watched Yolanda disappear from sight. Even after the coffin was
no longer visible, she remained to listen to the echo of voices. Only when the
last whispers had died away did she pull herself together and leave the balcony.
Yolanda was gone from her life forever. She now had to see to her own future.

Her requests to speak to Frederick Hohenstaufen had been rebuffed. The
Holy Roman Emperor had more important things to do. Her request to Yolanda's secretary that he transmit a letter to Eudes had been dismissed as impracti-
cal; he was heading in the other direction to meet with King John of Brienne.

Her request to her confessor, Father Yohannes, to undertake the same mission had been turned down on the ground that he was too old for the journey back to Outremer and planned to join a Cistercian monastery to prepare for the hereafter. From the harem, she had no other access to the outside world, and so she had hoped to use the funeral as an opportunity to mingle with others who might be willing and able to take a message back to the Kingdom of Jerusalem for her.

Instead, she had been made to feel that it was an act of great generosity that Omar agreed to escort her to the screened balcony to hear the funeral Mass. Now, as Mass ended, Omar was waiting to escort her back to the harem. He cast her a reproachful look—as if he knew she had drafted a letter to Eudes, folded it very small, and had it in her purse. Certainly, he led her through the back passageways of the palace, ensuring she could not encounter any of the other mourners, or clergy from the royal chapel. Back at the harem tract, Omar shooed her inside and bolted the door from the outside.

Eschiva listened to his footsteps retreating, and, discouraged, took her precious letter from inside the leather purse that hung, more decoratively than purposefully, from her belt. She returned it to the wall niche beside the queen's bed, and carefully locked the wooden doors over the niche, before slipping the key into her purse.

She looked around the chamber. Yolanda's beautiful gowns still hung in the wardrobe, her needlework waited beside her favorite chair, and on the table was parchment, paints, and brushes—abandoned thoughtlessly two weeks ago when Yolanda's water broke and Eschiva had rushed to call the midwife. She had not given her work a thought since. She walked to the table and looked down at the unfinished illustration. It depicted Yvain killing the dragon who had a lion by the tail. Yolanda loved the tale of Yvain and the lion, and Eschiva had promised to illustrate the entire book for her.

Seeing her work after such a long break, Eschiva was startled by the resemblance between the dragon and Frederick Hohenstaufen. They had the same pale blue, cold-blooded eyes. The lion, in contrast, looked back at her so sadly, that she couldn't bear to resume her work. No knight had come to rescue Yolanda from Frederick Hohenstaufen. He had killed her. And no knight could rescue her either since no one even knew she was here!

She snatched the unfinished illustration from the table, crumpled it up and tossed it in the cold fireplace. Then she moved quickly out of the grimly silent apartment of the deceased Empress-Queen and stepped into the bright courtyard of the harem.

Here the sun glinted off the gently bubbling fountain and from the shade of the arcade opposite came the tinkling laughter of some of the harem slaves. They were playing some kind of game together. One of the older women, more nurse to the others than an object of the Emperor's desire, caught sight of Eschiva and came to slip her arm around her waist. Her embrace was light but warm as she brushed her lips to Eschiva's forehead. "Come, little one," she urged. "Come, join us and forget your loss for a little bit. Life can and does go on."

Eschiva drew a deep breath and nodded. Much as she wanted to go home, she was here now, and she needed friends. She crossed the courtyard and joined the circle of girls until Omar called that the "fruit lady" had come. The coming of the "fruit lady" was always a major event in the harem. She brought fresh fruits and, more important, sweets, which she sold to the girls.

Leaping up, the girls rushed across the courtyard to cluster around the fruit lady with her little handcart. She had fresh oranges and lemons, dried dates and figs, and a tray with little pistachio tarts, honey cakes, and candied quince. At once the bargaining began, but the fruit lady was nearly as well-loved for her gossip as her wares. Once the harem girls had chosen and taken what they wanted, the fruit lady settled herself without invitation on a bench and smugly announced. "I saw the funeral of the Empress today!"

The harem girls gathered around, sitting at her feet, except for the older slave and Eschiva, who sat on either side of her on the bench she had commandeered. She continued, "You have never seen anything like it! So many fine nobles on black horses, and priests and bishops in a long procession! They had flute players too and drums that beat slowly. The Sultana's coffin was open all the way to the Cathedral, and many people placed roses or other little trinkets in the coffin as she passed.

"The Emperor looked very magnificent and somber, all in black with black pearls on his robes. His buttons and dagger were made of Toledo goldwork. He was followed by a dashing, young man leading the Queen's mare, all caparisoned with white feathers and gold ribbons, but with the empty saddle, of course. He was so tall, his head was as high as the mare's! They said he was some Cypriot relative of the dead Queen. Her cousin, I think."

That was surely the man she had seen in the choir, Eschiva registered with a start, and if he was Yolanda's cousin from Cyprus, then he must be a relation of her mother Marie de Montferrat. She didn't have time to work it out because the fruit lady was continuing.

"When they got to the Cathedral, beside the open grave, the Emperor put a huge bouquet of red roses into the coffin and then signaled for it to be closed."

Hypocrite! Eschiva thought to herself.

"But tell us more of the cousin of the Queen!" One of the other girls asked with a giggle. "Was he handsome?"

The fruit lady knew her customers well, and now she smiled broadly. "Oh, yes, he was very handsome, Tahra, and by his clothes and the sword at his hip and the spurs of gold, very rich as well."

"How was he related to the Queen?" Eschiva asked. She realized he might be a means of her getting a message home to Eudes.

"I don't know," the fruit lady answered with a slight frown. "All I know is that he arrived on that Cypriot ship, the one where even the sailors were dressed in mourning."

"But how could they know already that the Queen was dead?" Eschiva protested. The news could hardly have reached Cyprus yet!

"Oh, they didn't," the fruit lady answered with a dismissive gesture of her hand. "They were in mourning for the Regent of Cyprus, who apparently died this past winter."

"Philip d'Ibelin?" Eschiva gasped out.

The others looked at her blankly.

"Philip d'Ibelin is—was—my uncle," she stammered. "He's married to my aunt Alys."

"Oh, I'm sorry," the fruit lady responded perfunctorily without a trace of feeling, but the elder slave woman looked suitably stricken as Eschiva jumped up and ran to the Queen's apartment. "Poor Eschiva!" she exclaimed. "First the Sultana and now her uncle."

Eschiva fled to the Queen's bedchamber and closed the door behind her. It wasn't that she was *close* to her Uncle Philip. On the contrary, he was an Ibelin and the Ibelins and Montbéliards had been rivals more than allies for as long as she could remember. The Ibelins had been behind the accusations of malfeasance leveled against her father when *he* had been regent of Cyprus for King Henry's father.

But in an attempt to heal the breach between the two families, her father's sister, Alys, had been married to Philip d'Ibelin. She had then moved to Cyprus and Eschiva had seen little of either of them. She certainly did not know his son, who presumably was the mysterious young Cypriot knight who had accompanied the funeral cortege. But the relationship would explain why he had looked vaguely familiar: he looked like a younger version of the Lord of Beirut, who had come down to the quay to see Yolanda off to her wedding, and like young Hugh d'Ibelin, who had traveled with them all the way to Brindisi. Furthermore, he was her cousin and he was here with a Cypriot ship. He was, in short, the ideal messenger to take her letter back to Eudes. The only question was how to get it to him.

There was a light knock on the door.

Eschiva spun around, trying to compose herself, and called, "Who is it?"

"It's me. Amira." As she spoke, the Arab woman peered around the door. "Are you alright?"

"Yes, yes. But I—I would like to be alone for a bit. Oh—but—please, could you send the fruit lady to me first? I would like to buy something from her."

"Of course," Amira smiled and withdrew.

A moment later, the fruit lady put her head in the door. "Can't bring the cart. Tell me what you want."

"Oranges," Eschiva replied. "Four oranges. How much will that be?"

"Half a dirhem," the fruit lady answered, her eyes caressing briefly the luxury of the queen's apartment.

Eschiva crossed to the wall-niche beside the bed and opened it with the little key. She removed her sealed letter and took two dirhems from her purse. When the fruit lady returned, she was ready for her. With a smile, she pressed the letter and the two coins into her calloused hand. "Here, please take this to my cousin, the Cypriot knight who was in the procession. It is a letter of condolence to my aunt."

The fruit lady looked down at the sealed message and the coins. Then she looked up again with slightly narrowed eyes, as if she was thinking of asking for more money.

Should she offer more? Eschiva wondered in a near panic. This service was *worth* much more, but if she offered more that might arouse the woman's suspicions?

Fortunately, the fruit lady smiled and nodded. "I'll see that he gets it, my lady," she answered as she withdrew.

Eschiva did not return to the others. Instead, she took a clean sheet of parchment and sat down to paint. Painting had always been her escape from the world, from reality, but she couldn't even decide on a new motif for wondering how long it would take for her message to reach Eudes. At this time of year, the winds in the Mediterranean were erratic. They could fade away altogether, or suddenly rouse themselves to a short, summer gale. She must certainly reckon with three weeks, she told herself, more likely four—in both directions, of course. That meant no reply would reach her before the end of July. But, no, it would be longer than that. If her cousin was bound for Cyprus, he would need to find another messenger to take her letter to Eudes in Acre. That, or he might deliver it to her Aunt Alys.

She tried to remember her Aunt Alys. She had always been viewed vaguely as a traitor because she sided with her husband's family rather than her own. Although, Eschiva wondered, what choice women had in such things. Marriage alliances were supposed to bring families together, to bridge differences and end strife. Yet they rarely did, Eschiva decided with the wisdom of seventeen, reminded of her friend Yolanda.

Yolanda had not seen her father since the week of her marriage. She had been completely isolated here at Frederick's court. Nothing Yolanda said or did had the slightest impact on the breach between her father and her husband—and they had not been enemies to begin with.

With a sigh, Eschiva recognized she did not have the concentration she needed in order to paint. Besides, she needed a motif. She needed inspiration. She went to the book cabinet and took down one book after another: a beautiful book on the Life of St. Helena, a book of psalms, the New Testament, a wonderfully illustrated copy of *Eric et Enid* by Chrétien de Troyes, and the dogeared copy of *Yvain*.

Eschiva shied away from the familiar book. Instead, her hand fell on the least familiar: a copy of the *Odyssey* in Greek. Since the voyage out, she had not looked at this book, yet Eschiva felt a thrill as she took it in her hand. This book had belonged to the Lord of Beirut. He had presented it to Yolanda on the quay at Tyre as a parting gift. Yolanda had been delighted and grateful, and she had read it aloud to Eschiva on the long voyage to Brindisi. Together they had delighted in the adventures of the brave Ulysses and speculated about whether the places they stopped were the places mythically described in the book. It had made the long journey much more interesting, but the book had been forgotten in all the things that had happened since.

Eschiva sank down in a chair and reverently opened the book. Although Yolanda had learned to read and write in Greek, Eschiva's education had been less rigorous and, while she spoke Greek, she could not read it. Greek letters, however, appealed to her artistic sense. They were graceful and fluent, like the waves of the sea, rather than square and harsh like the Latin alphabet. The illustrations were distinctly Greek in character as well, something that intrigued Eschiva. Although she had learned the fundamentals of illumination at the convent of St. Anne in Acre and later had been tutored by one of the canons of the Holy Sepulcher, she had not been exposed to other schools of illumination.

In this copy of the Odyssey, she noted with excitement, the colors were rich and vivid as if made of real lapis and jade. Certainly, real gold had been used extensively. The more she focused, the more she realized that this was a very, very expensive book. Of course! The Lord of Beirut said it had belonged to his mother, and she had been a Greek princess—before she became Queen of Jerusalem. When he gave the book to Yolanda, he made it sound like he was only giving her what rightfully hers, saying, "This was your great-grandmother's book. She would have wanted you to have it."

And yet something about the way his long fingers had lingered over the book even after he had handed it to Yolanda suggested that he found it hard to part with it. No doubt he had loved his mother well, Eschiva reflected. And what a contrast to Frederick Hohenstaufen, who could not show even kindness toward his child bride. Eschiva's bitterness was so intense she could taste it in her mouth. The Wonder of the World indeed! A short, balding, flabby man with fading eyesight and pale skin that turned bright red when he was angry.

So he must be very angry, she registered, as she got to her feet and put the book behind her back to help her stand straighter as she faced him.

The Holy Roman Emperor had entered his wife's apartment so silently that Eschiva had not realized he was here until he was glowering over her and hissed: "How dare you?" His voice was almost inaudible from chocking fury.

"How dare I what, my lo—your magnificence?" She stammered out. She could hardly hear her own words over the sound of her heart hammering in her ears.

Frederick answered by flinging her letter in her face, the seal broken and the parchment unfolded.

"How dare you go behind my back!"

"I—I—" The fruit lady. She had betrayed her. Apparently, the woman had guessed the letter was in some way surreptitious, and surmised she could sell it to someone in the palace—maybe just Omar, who took it directly to Frederick. "I—didn't mean to—to—I just—"

Frederick lashed out hard and fast, slapping her face so forcefully that it whipped her head to the side and left her neck aching as well as her cheek burning. "You are a liar as well as a deceitful bitch! We have tolerated your arrogance, impudence, and pride for the sake of our consort, but we will tolerate it no longer! We warned you not to mistake your position, but you are evidently too stupid to understand hints. We will speak plainly: you are in our power and we will dispose of you as we please. Don't *flatter* yourself that it would please us to lie with you! You are too cold, boring and plain to arouse our interest! But we expect your brother to support us generously on our crusade, and he will assuredly do that more willingly if he thereby secures your, shall we say, well-being? If you ever, ever cross us again—much less write drivel as is in that scrap," he gestured toward the letter on the floor between them, "we will give your brother a *good* reason to pay a *fortune* for your freedom."

Their eyes were locked. His were like a serpent's, burning her with his contempt and yet by their very intensity making her afraid to break eye contact. In those eyes was the promise of punishment, of pain and humiliation. He hated her, she registered with surprise. It surprised her because she was so far beneath him that she thought he took no note of her at all. She had been nothing but a witness, a silent witness, to all he had done to Yolanda.

But maybe that was enough to make him hate her? Maybe she reminded him of his own injustice? Or did he hate her simply because he sensed *her* hatred of him?

Whatever his reason, his hatred was very, very dangerous. Eschiva crumpled into a deep curtsy, and managed to squeak out, "You will have no reason for complaint, your magnificence." Eschiva spoke to her discarded letter and the toes of his black shoes.

Frederick turned on heel and stalked out, slamming the door behind him.

Only very slowly did Eschiva unbend, pushing herself upright again. No terror she had ever known before equaled what she felt now. This threat, this hint of dark dungeons, pillories, floggings or starvation, was terrifying precisely because it was so vague. It was open-ended and unfathomable. Hadn't he heated an iron crown to a glowing red and then nailed it to the head of a defeated enemy?

He was not a man of mercy, Yolanda had remarked once. Just that: not a man of mercy. Another time she had complained, "He is vindictive. He bears a grudge forever, but in silence and hidden under sweet words—until he chooses to take his revenge."

Eschiva discovered to her surprise that she was still clinging to the *Odyssey*. Indeed, she was clinging to it so firmly that her fingers were hurting. She forced them to relax, but she hugged the book to her chest. It was a memory, a talisman, from a better time and place. From home.

She started. The Odyssey. Ulysses had been driven off course, endured horrible and wonderful adventures, lost all his companions, but in the end, he returned home. And there was a ship in the harbor at this very moment, which would soon set sail for Cyprus. A ship on which her cousin, stranger though he was, would sail. She had thought to send a message by him, but since that had failed, somehow, somehow—Mary have mercy on me!—somehow, Eschiva told herself, she had to be aboard that ship herself.

She didn't have a moment to lose. The funeral was over. Her cousin would undoubtedly sail with the morning tide, anxious to bring word to Yolanda's vassals and subjects that she was dead. Good God! The High Court of Jerusalem would need to elect a baillie for Yolanda's infant son Conrad.

Eschiva started pacing the little chamber in an effort to calm her nerves and stimulate her brain. Like a captive lion, she moved back-and-forth on silent feet, her eyes searching and searching for something. She stopped. She was staring at Yolanda's dressing table. On it was the little glass bottle with the sleeping powder the Jewish doctor had given her. "Use only a very little," he had warned. "No more than a pinch in a glass of wine. It is very powerful. Too much, and you will sleep like the dead. A little more, and you *will* be dead."

She had to get some of that powder into something Omar drank.

Of course! The wine!

Omar was Muslim, but he had a weakness for wine. To maintain his image and authority among his co-religionists, he publicly abhorred and condemned wine. He drank in secret. In the Queen's anteroom. Because no one dared follow him inside, and the harem girls did not enter the Queen's apartment either, it was the perfect place. Yolanda had encouraged him in this vice, because, of course, she used it as a means to coerce him into little favors. "If you don't do this, I'll tell the Imam that you drink...." He had had no wine since Yolanda died.

Eschiva nodded to herself, confident that she could invite him in and give him wine with a hefty dose of the sleeping powder already mixed in. She would then retreat to the bedchamber and loudly lock the door from the inside, as if she wanted nothing to do with him. When he was asleep, she would be able to come out, remove the keys to the outer door, leave the harem, and bolt it from the outside. No one would suspect anything was amiss until the next morning when Ahmed came to bring Omar his breakfast as he washed, changed and prayed.

Eschiva's mind turned immediately to what she would take with her and how to dress herself to attract minimal attention. She would take the Odyssey, she decided, placing the book at the end of the bed as she started to collect everything else she needed: her box of brushes and pens for illumination and paper—her most precious possessions—and all the paintings she had made for Yolanda. They were a tie between them that could live beyond the grave. She'd also take the Queen's seal and jewels, not for herself but to preserve them for the Kingdom. On the practical side, she would need several changes of underwear and stockings, but two gowns and three surcoats ought to be enough. She would wear practical, everyday shoes. She would bring a little bag of toiletries: her comb, hand mirror, hairpins, a tiny pot of rouge for her lips and cheeks, a bar of lavender soap, a washcloth, toothpicks, and toothbrush. Oh, and a nail-file. And some cream for her hands and face. And she mustn't forget her eating knife and spoon, both of carved ivory.

The pile was getting much too large. She wouldn't be able to carry all that under her cloak. She started over, reducing her articles of clothing and then, on second thought, experimenting with ways to fold it up very small and tight. It *had* to all fit inside just one of the five leather bags she had used on her journey west. She brought one of the bags over and packed and re-packed it, but it was impossible to fit everything in. She would either have to go without clothes or give up the box with her illustrations. Her heart clung to the illustrations, but her mind won out. She would have to leave the illustrations here and hope that someday, somehow she would be able to recover them. Without the bulky box, with the illustrations, she was at last able to pack the bag with the rest of her things and it was still light enough for her to carry.

It was now dusk and nearing the time of dinner. She forced herself to join the harem girls for dinner. She deflected their questions. Yes, she was feeling better, but she was very tired. She would take a little of the sleeping potion so she could get a good night's sleep. No doubt she would sleep in later than usual. They should not wonder if she did not join them for breakfast. But for lunch. She would join them for lunch, and they must teach her the game they had been playing yesterday.

After dinner, she withdrew again into the Queen's apartment. Gradually silence descended over the harem. At last.

She drew a flask of wine from the barrel that lay on its side in the anteroom, awaiting the Queen's pleasure. She had drawn wine for Yolanda hundreds of times during their time together. She used the same flask as always and took it to the little bedside table. Here she set the flask down and removed the cork from the bottle with the sleeping powder. She poured the powder into the palm of her hand, and took first one, then two, and finally four pinches of the power and dropped them into the wine. Was that enough? She didn't want to kill Omar, but he was a big man, and fat. He would need more than she did. She added two more pinches of powder and used her spoon to stir it all together. She licked the spoon clean to see if the wine tasted funny. A little bitter maybe, but not much. She returned the spoon to her leather bag.

Her heart tight in her chest and her hand sweating cold sweat, Eschiva went to the outer door, the flask in her hand, and called, "Omar?"

An annoyed grunt answered her.

"Don't you want some wine?"

"What?"

"The Sultana always had me give you wine before retiring. Don't you want it?" Dear Jesus, Mary, and Joseph, don't let him say no!

A growl answered, but then he shoved back the bolt, cracked the door, and scowled at her.

Eschiva held up the flask, to show it to him, and then set it down on the table just inside the door next to a pair of silver goblets. She turned her back on him to return to the bedroom. She was so tense, she felt as if she might explode as she waited to hear what he would do next. The door clunked shut behind her, but was Omar inside or out?

She strained to hear the bolt go into place. It did not.

She reached the bedroom door, entered, and closed it behind her. She spun about, bent down and looked through the key-hole. Omar had seated himself in one of the cushioned chairs and was smugly pouring himself wine from the flask into a silver goblet. She let out a sigh of relief and sat down on the end of the bed to wait for the potion to work.

Omar contentedly poured himself a second and then a third glass of wine without any apparent impairment. Eschiva started to think she had put too little powder in the wine. Now what?

And then, in slow motion, Omar's arm went limp, flopped down, and the silver goblet slid from his slack fingers, spilling the remaining contents onto the carpet and staining it red.

With all her pent-up nervous energy, Eschiva grabbed her cloak, flung it over her shoulders and closed it with a heavy, silver brooch. She picked up the packed, leather bag, and slowly cracked open the bedroom door.

Omar was slumped in the chair, his head hanging to one side, his mouth open, his jaw slack. He didn't twitch as Eschiva tiptoed across the anteroom. As she passed him, she registered that his breath was foul and, most unusual, he smelled as if he'd soiled himself with his own shit. She screwed up her face in distaste and put her hand on the door handle. Casting a last prayer to the Virgin, she pressed down and pushed. The door opened easily before her. Eschiva slipped through the door and closed it firmly behind her, throwing the bolt.

She now stood in Omar's guard chamber. Eschiva stepped to the lantern and blew it out. Darkness was her ally. She stopped and listened.

All was quiet.

When she had accompanied Yolanda to Mass or some state function, they turned left toward the front of the palace, but to the right was a passage that led to the service entrance by which the peddlers and cleaners came and went. Eschiva turned right and followed it, moving slowly because of the dark and to make as little noise as possible. The passage had a couple stairs, and it twisted a few times, but it brought her to a door with a large iron key stuck in it.

Eschiva reached for the key and turned it. The click it made was so loud she startled, and still, the door didn't open. With rising panic, she turned the key again. If the door didn't open, should she look for another door or just return to the Queen's apartment and give up?

The door gave way to her weight and she almost fell into the alleyway. This was nearly as dark as the inside passageway but smelled worse. Eschiva had not spent much of her life in back alleyways and had no idea how much rubbish accumulated in them. It didn't matter. She closed the door firmly but softly behind her and then froze.

What now? She was alone in a city full of thieves and cutthroats. The only women who walked alone at night in Andria were whores. Worse, she hadn't a clue how to get to the port!

She fought down her panic and set out blindly. Somewhere, she would surely find a familiar landmark.

Once she reached the wider street at the end of the alleyway, she could indeed orient herself. She turned toward the harbor and started hurrying. She had to put as much distance between herself and the palace as possible. Besides, the faster and more purposefully she walked, the less likely she was to be accosted.

The district around the palace was nearly deserted, but as she approached the port, the city came to life. Here, many establishments were open. They spilled light and the sound of voices, sometimes fragments of singing or arguing, into the street. Eschiva was getting very tired. She did not usually walk this far, much less carry anything as heavy as her leather bag. But fear and hope drove her forward.

She reached the harbor at last, and was at once confronted with a new dilemma: Which was her cousin's ship? More than a dozen of ships were tied up at the quay. In the darkness, their bunting and their banners furled, they all looked much the same. It didn't help that at this time of night most of the crews were either below deck or in a tavern somewhere.

Cautiously, Eschiva approached the first ship on the quay and gazed up at it trying to see *something* that would indicate its nationality: a name, a home port, a coat-of-arms. "Hey! Senorita! Want a quick one? Come on board!" The man gestured vigorously for her to come on the ship.

Eschiva turned and hurried away while the sailor shouted after her in a mix of languages, both cajoling, and insulting. Although he did not follow her, his shouts drew the attention of a gaggle of men pouring out of a dockside tavern. "Hey! Hey!" They called out to her. "Don't run away! Come with us! We'll buy you wine!"

Eschiva fled even faster down the quay, but this only brought her into a direct collision with yet another group of sailors. These men blocked her way. And one of them hitched up his long-legged braies with an all too obvious smirk as another grabbed her arm. "Here, give us a kiss!" He ordered pulling her toward him.

"NO!" Eschiva yanked her arm free. "Let me pass!"

"Not until you've paid the toll!" The sailor answered, and pulled her into his arms to smother his mouth over hers.

Eschiva kicked his shins with the strength of panic and managed to break free. "NO!" she shouted breathlessly as she backed away. "I'm looking for my cousin!"

"Sure you are!" They all laughed together, crowding in closer, slowly herding her against the side of the tavern as she kept trying to back away from them. "But I'm as good as he is. I'll show you! Right here against the wall."

"LET GO OF ME!" Eschiva shouted, kicking out again. "LET GO OF ME! I'm Eschiva de Montbéliard! If you harm me, you'll have hell to pay!" Unfortunately, the name Montbéliard meant nothing to sailors in Andria.

They had her pinned against the wall, and the biggest of them pressed her shoulders against the wall and again lowered his mouth over hers. His tongue forced its way between her lips although she kept her teeth clenched as she yanked her head from side to side to try to escape him. Another one was groping her from behind his colleague. If only she could scream!

The scream came from one of the sailors instead. And then another, while the others scattered. The man who had been groping her crashed down at her feet with a groan as he puked all over her gown. The man pinning her shoulders to the wall dropped his hold as he doubled up and crashed down with a horrible grunt, blood spurting from his neck.

Eschiva was left trembling like a leaf in a gale as she stared at the bloody sword that had felled her assailants. The little, dark man who had wielded it bowed to her. "Mademoiselle de Montbéliard, Philip de Novare, at your service."

Chapter Seven

Cousins

Andria, Apulia, Kingdom of Sicily
May 11, 1228

BALIAN WAS TRYING TO SLEEP, BUT the many impressions of the last few days tormented him. To be sure, the Hohenstaufen had been courteous and friendly on the surface over the last few days, yet his gentle and apparently reasonable demeanor tasted foul in Balian's mouth. It was like the alluring, graceful moves of a snake awaiting the opportunity to strike. Nothing the Emperor had said or done had eradicated the memory of that first interview. Balian was convinced to the marrow of his bones that Frederick II Hohenstaufen was irreversibly hostile to the Ibelins.

What he couldn't grasp was why. Balian dismissed the possibility that Uncle Philip had done anything wrong. If anything, he had been too forgiving, too generous, too easily talked into pardons and second chances. To call him a pirate and bandit was so ridiculous that Balian couldn't even get angry about it. But *why* would the Hohenstaufen do it?

Was it really just the influence of Barlais and Cheneché? When Balian had asked some of the courtiers about them, he'd been told they had been "well received" at the Emperor's court. Several testified particularly to Cheneché's popularity with the Emperor. But would the Holy Roman Emperor really allow a couple of troublemakers and discontents to color his judgment? To sway his policies against men he had not met? Balian didn't want to believe that. Besides, he had not seen either Barlais and Cheneché during his short stay, nor could anyone tell him where they were.

Balian tried to reconstruct that fateful first interview with the Holy Roman Emperor in his mind again. The problem was that he'd been so blindsided by the Hohenstaufen's hostility that he could remember only fragments—like the Emperor calling Uncle Philip a pirate and bandit. That wasn't going to be good enough for his father.

Balian turned over in his bunk and punched the pillow in frustration. His father was a meticulous jurist. He wanted evidence. He wanted exact and precise reports and verbatim quotes. Most of all he wanted logical thinking, and Balian could see nothing logical in the Emperor's inexplicable threats of "revenge" for crimes not committed. He kept having conversations in his head with his father in which he tried to convince him that the Emperor was their enemy, and they all ended badly. Balian knew his father wasn't going to believe him.

Balian sat up in frustration. He couldn't possibly sleep, despite being exhausted by the funeral, burial, and subsequent court festivities. Maybe he should have gone with Novare on a drinking spree after all? But he had vowed not to do that ever again after the last incident ended with him losing a small fortune at the gaming tables. Not to mention that he'd promised his father he would behave like a sober diplomat throughout the voyage. He had promised both his father and himself that he would give his father no grounds for disappointment, much less reproach on this trip.

Balian ruffled his hair in frustration. His father was a sober man. A man without vices. A man of self-restraint and self-discipline. He did not understand going out on a binge or doing something stupid on the spur of the moment, or simply getting carried away by emotions and circumstances. He believed that a man should always be in control of himself, and always behave rationally. He loathed emotion. But Balian had—and knew he had—an excess of temperament and passion.

Maybe he should have another cup of wine here in his cabin? The worst that could happen here, he rationalized, was that he'd fall into a drugged sleep.

Balian swung his legs over the edge of the bunk and dropped to the floor of the compact cabin. It was the best cabin aboard and stretched across the stern, but it was barely six feet deep. The bunk was built along the port side, parallel to the hull with the foot to the bows, and Balian had to lie at a slight diagonal to accommodate his six-foot, two-inch frame. His squire Rob, on the other hand, had no trouble in the bunk opposite, Balian noted enviously; Rob was sleeping so soundly he snored.

Below each bunk, the passengers stowed their chests and beneath Balian's was also a commode with a glazed pottery bowl that could be used for washing— or as a toilet if one was squeamish about hanging over the side of the ship. To the right along the stern of the ship was a chest of drawers for charts, log, and manifest because, when not carrying high-born passengers, this cabin belonged to the captain. Over the chest, two windows looked out over the stern. At present they offered only a dingy view of the bow of the next ship at the quay. At sea, the windows let in good fresh air, now they let in the stench of a stagnant harbor filled with waste and rubbish.

Because Balian expected to sail in the morning, he had already packed away his chainmail hauberk and his court dress of silk shirts, hose, and surcoats, as well as his suede gambeson, boots, and spurs. For the voyage home, he planned to dress in loose cotton shirts and footless, cotton hose that allowed him to go barefoot like the sailors. Because it was stuffy below deck, he wore only his cotton braies at the moment.

Balian stepped out of his cabin into the windowless, central cabin, where passengers and officers took their meals. He inched his way around the table bolted down in the center toward the entrance to the galley opposite. Abruptly shouting and thudding feet directly overhead made him freeze.

He looked up. The officer of the watch always walked the afterdeck, which was also the roof of the cabins. He recognized the voice of the Second Mate, Julio, shouting. "Stop right there! You know the rules, sir! No women allowed on board! Take your whore—"

"She's not a whore!" Novare answered from much farther away. "She's—"

"No women allowed on board!" Julio bellowed emphatically, while Balian shook his head in bemusement. Leave it to Novare to try to bring a whore back with him.

"She's my lord's cousin! The Lady Eschiva de Montbéliard!" Novare insisted manfully.

Jesus God! Balian started toward the ladder to the afterdeck, remembered he was wearing only his braies and ducked back into his cabin to pull on a shirt and tunic. By the time he emerged on deck, half the crew was standing about enjoying the entertainment. Novare stood on the quay, a cloaked woman hanging on his arm, and Julio was standing stubbornly at the ship-end of the gangway, blocking Novare from coming aboard.

The shouting, however, had aroused Captain di Domenico as well. Before Balian could say a word, he told Julio to stand down. Together Balian and Domenico converged on the gangway, while Philip de Novare helped the woman onto the other end of the precarious bridge between ship and shore.

"What is this all about, sir?" Domenico demanded in a low but hostile tone.

"I have rescued a damsel in distress," Novare declared, grinning as he spread his arms dramatically. "The lady was assaulted by drunken sailors, and I—"

"No *lady* walks around a port at this time of night!" Domenico snapped. "Just because you're too drunk to know the difference between a whore and a—"

"I am Eschiva de Montbéliard," a frail, female voice interrupted him. "I was a lady to Queen Yolanda, and I beg you to let me speak with my cousin of Ibelin."

Before Domenico could answer, Balian laid a restraining hand on the captain's arm and murmured. "Let her come on board, Maurizio. If she is who she says she is, she is the sister of the baillie of Jerusalem, cousin of King Henry of Cyprus, and indeed my cousin. If she's not, we'll have no trouble putting her back ashore." Then moving past the captain, he offered his hand to the young woman to help her down from the gangway onto the deck.

The hand offered him was small and trembling so violently that Balian felt a surge of protectiveness rush through his veins despite his skepticism about her identity. He instinctively closed his own hand over hers in a gesture that was sincere yet more intimate than would normally have been considered polite—presuming she was who she said she was. The woman had averted her eyes in apparent embarrassment, but he could still see the smooth curve of her cheek and her neck. Whoever she was, she was young, and her teeth were chattering. In this heat, that could only come from deep shock. The whiff of vomit and blood drew his attention to her skirts, and although it was too dark to distinguish either substance, the smells and soils were obvious. Something terrible must just have occurred.

Novare, meanwhile, had swung himself onto the railing and jumped down nimbly in Balian's path with a large leather bag in one hand. He grinned. "I'm not exaggerating, Bal! She was surrounded by five sailors who had—"

"You can tell me later, Philip," Balian cut him off. The girl was clinging to his hand as if he were a lifeline. Her hand did not hurt his. He was used to controlling full-blooded stallions, sword, and lance. Yet her grip expressed desperation; it was an inarticulate but powerful plea that overwhelmed him. Never in his short life had anyone looked to him for help with such intensity as this strange young woman—whether she was his cousin or not. It made him feel mature, strong, and important. He realized that he had the power to help—or not. The thought was more intoxicating than wine. "My lady, let me take you below," he suggested, offering her his elbow.

"Are you my cousin? The son of Philip d'Ibelin?" The girl asked in an almost inaudible voice. Although she did not take his arm, she turned her face to him at last. Her eyes were huge in her pale face and her cheek streaked with tear stains.

Balian bowed to her, "Philip d'Ibelin was my uncle, Mademoiselle. I am Sir Balian d'Ibelin, son and heir to the Lord of Beirut."

"Oh!" She caught her breath, then in a rush, she put into words what her hand had already told him. "My lord, even if we are not first cousins, I beg your assistance. I am in need of—your protection."

"It is yours, Mademoiselle," Balian answered without hesitation, adding just as thoughtlessly. "Whatever your distress, I promise upon my life and soul that I will help you."

"Ha! You're stealing my lines!" Novare protested.

Balian ignored his friend and again offered his arm to Lady Eschiva. This time she took it and let him lead her to aft. Balian led her directly from the main deck into the galley and through it to the salon beyond. Here he gestured for her to sit on the wooden bench that surrounded the fixed table before he ducked back into the galley. He found the cook already there, roused by the commotion. The cook gestured for Balian to go back to the salon, adding, "I'll bring wine and water."

Balian returned to the salon to find Captain di Domenico standing at the foot of the ladder, and Novare sitting opposite Lady Eschiva grinning inanely as he clutched her large leather bag on his lap.

Maurizio di Domenico was a weathered and experienced captain of the ripe old age of 31. He had been going to sea since the age of six, his skin was leathery, his body wiry, his face rugged and his eyes sharp. They shifted from Lady Eschiva to Sir Balian to Sir Philip and back again. Then without another word, he started lighting lanterns, first the one that hung over the table in the salon, then others, which he placed at each end of the table.

The light revealed the face of a pale young woman with patches of acne on her face, tear stains, and trembling hands. But they were manicured hands, and by the light of the lanterns, it was obvious that her cloak was of very fine cotton and beautifully stitched, her veils silk, and the brooch at her neck worth a small fortune by itself. Domenico shook his head in incomprehension and muttered. "What were you doing alone in a port like Andria in the middle of the night, Mademoiselle? Surely you know how dangerous it is?"

Balian had seen all that Domenico had, and more. Obviously, something terrible had driven this gentle maiden out in the middle of the night. "That's enough, Maurizio," Balian admonished, adding, "Leave us."

Domenico shook his head and then grabbed the handrails and pulled himself up the ladder in a fluid motion.

The door from the galley banged open and the cook pushed his way into the salon. "The wine and water, my lord," he announced, clunking them down on the table with a curious glance at Lady Eschiva before withdrawing.

Balian called after him, "Bring cups!"

The door opened again, and four pottery mugs, the cheap kind that can easily be replaced, were plunked down on the table.

Balian reached forward, and filled a glass halfway, paused, and asked Lady Eschiva, "Straight or cut with water?"

"Pure, please."

Balian obliged.

Lady Eschiva took the mug in both hands and brought it to her lips to sip very carefully. She was still trembling, but not as severely as before, more in spasms. After a few swallows, she set the mug down and looked at Balian to whisper, "The captain is right. I—I underestimated the danger, and..." she shifted her gaze to Philip of Novare, "I am unspeakably grateful to you, Monsieur." The sincerity in her eyes and voice was patent, and Balian was jealous of his friend. If only he had not kept his promise to his father, he might have been the one to rescue her from the sailors!

Novare set her leather bag aside so he could jump up and bow more dramatically as he assured her, "The pleasure was entirely mine, Mademoiselle. Rarely have I had the opportunity to put my sword to better purpose."

Balian stiffened. "You didn't actually kill anyone did you, Novare?"

"I believe I did," Philip answered with a look of surprised satisfaction on his face. "They were not paying attention to anything but their poor victim, so I was able to get in two clean thrusts. I'm sure I gutted the first man, and the second—"

"Two men?" Balian gasped, stiffening with alarm. This was what came of hanging out in seaside taverns! Just as his father had warned him. "Were they alone?"

"No, no! I told you. There were five altogether, but the other three fled when they saw the blade of my sword."

"Jesu!" Balian exclaimed. It was very dangerous to kill men like this, not in battle or judicial combat but in the dark, in anger. It would be Sir Philip and Lady Eschiva's word against that of the sailors. And the Emperor was already ill-disposed to the Ibelins—not to mention what Barlais and Cheneché would make of it, given the chance. The Emperor could easily use this as an excuse to arrest them, at the very least impound the ship, and demand an inquiry. They could be trapped here for days, weeks, months, subject to less than certain justice.

Yet, he could hardly fault Novare for coming to the rescue of a lady, his cousin, this fragile and frightened maiden! He would certainly have done so himself. Indeed, he *wished* he had done so.

Still, they were in trouble. He jumped up and called up the ladder.

"Maurizio? Sir Philip just killed two sailors. You better increase the watch. Or better still, prepare to put to sea."

A growl answered him.

Balian returned to the table and sat down. He had no idea that he was flushed and that his nervous energy gave him an aura of decisiveness and courage. As his eyes met those of Lady Eschiva, he was again overwhelmed by the appeal, awe, and fear in them.

She appeared to be coming out of her state of shock. "I'm so sorry," she gasped. "I didn't mean to—I had no idea—I didn't think things through properly." She clasped her hands together on the table in front of her and stared at him, pleading for understanding and forgiveness.

Balian reached out and laid his hand on her shoulder very lightly. "My lady, cousin, I am sure that only something very serious would have driven you out into the night. Can you at least tell us what it was and what you want of us?"

Eschiva took a deep breath, but her eyes filled with tears. "I tried to send you a letter, but the Emperor intercepted it and threw it in my face. He has kept me locked in the harem—"

"The harem?!" Novare reared up. "Surely not—"

"Shhh!" Balian hissed. "Let her finish."

"No," she assured Sir Philip, "he has not dishonored me *physically*, but he has threatened to use me as a hostage for my brother's good behavior."

Balian and Philip looked at each other. "Your brother? The baillie?" Turning back to Lady Eschiva, Balian asked. "But why should the Emperor think that necessary?"

Lady Eschiva was shaking her head. "I don't know, but if you could have seen—seen the way he treated our Queen Yolanda." Her bitterness slipped into her voice as she said this, and Balian could hear her indignation even before she continued, "All he cared about was her crown. She was never a *person* to him. Never…" She broke off, her eyes searching for understanding.

"Then Hugh was right and John de Brienne wasn't lying," Balian concluded soberly after a moment.

Lady Eschiva shook her head vigorously.

With a loud thump Captain di Domenico was back in the salon. "We're ready to cast off except for two missing crewmen. Do you want me to look for them or cast off at once?"

"Should they be back by now?" Balian asked.

"Certainly. No one had shore leave tonight. Both men violated my orders."

"Then," Balian spoke with his eyes on Eschiva, "I think we better leave

without them because—unless I misunderstood you, cousin—Lady Eschiva
came to us to escape the Holy Roman Emperor."

Lady Eschiva was trembling again as she answered in a tight, soft voice.
"Yes, I—I want to go home. I—thought you would be sailing in the morning.
I thought I had—no time to lose. And I—I can't go back. God knows what he
will do to me if he finds out I ran away, drugged the harem eunuch—"

"You did what?" Novare asked in astonishment.

"I gave a large dose of sleeping powder to—"

"It doesn't matter," Balian cut off the side conversation to lean forward and
ask Lady Eschiva earnestly, "Let me be absolutely sure I understand you. You
have run away from the harem of the Holy Roman Emperor and wish to escape
all the way to Acre?"

Lady Eschiva swallowed. In her face dawned understanding of the gravity
of her transgressions and the magnitude of her demands. What right had she to
ask this of *anyone*, much less a stranger?

Captain di Domenico started swearing in Italian, then swung about and
clattered up the ladder to start issuing orders to the crew. The patter of feet
overhead was followed by the thump of lines being flung onto the deck. The
ship, freed of the shore, started to sway and dip slightly.

Even as the bows started to swing out, angry shouting in Italian reached
them. Domenico answered by shouting more loudly and furiously at his crew.
The sound of the oars being run out followed. They rasped and squeaked in the
oarlocks. The ship lurched forward, banged loudly into something, provoking
an eruption of more shouting. Then they sheared off and surged forward again.

The shouting came from the stern now, louder and more emphatic than
ever. "…under arrest for murder!"

"Stroke!" Julio shouted. "Stroke!"

The ship surged and glided, sped and slowed. The overhead lantern in the
salon swayed in rhythm. Water gurgled along the side of the hull drowning out
most of the sounds from the quay. The last thing they heard was a very faint "…
in the name of the Holy Roman Emperor…"

Chapter Eight
The Island of Calypso

Kythera
May 1228

FROM OVERHEAD CAME SHOUTING AND THE pounding of feet as the ship swung onto a new course. It was a familiar pattern and did not worry Eschiva. She had traveled to Brindisi with Yolanda by ship, and this voyage home had lasted ten days already.

But then she heard seagulls.

After the first frightful days, when they sailed along the Italian coast in constant fear of interception by the Holy Roman Emperor's fleet, they had not been in sight of land. Seagulls had been rare.

Eschiva uncurled herself, threw back the covers and crossed barefoot to the stern windows to look out. All she could see was the sky and the wake of the ship on the turquoise sea—and a flock of at least a dozen seagulls riding the wind. There was a fresh, following breeze, and the ship was gracefully rising and falling on the swells. At moments like this, Eschiva wished the voyage would never end.

What fate could her dour yet pompous brother offer her to equal this peace, beauty, and freedom?

And what the ship lacked in luxury, it made up for in privacy. As the only woman on board, she had been given the "stateroom" and had it completely to herself. She had been ordered to stay in this cabin because they did not want anyone, whether from the shore or from a passing vessel, to see her, Sir Balian explained. Better the Emperor's men think they were fleeing only a murder charge from a dockside brawl, than spiriting away a valuable hostage. Furthermore, Captain di Domenico explained, the crew didn't like having women on board. It was bad luck. As long as the weather held and she stayed out of sight, he thought they might forget—or at least forgive—her presence, rather than mutiny.

Eschiva had not protested. Although she had no serving woman to look after her, the cabin boy emptied her commode morning and night and washed and dried her clothes in a bucket on deck for her. The cook brought her meals. All that mattered was escaping the wrath of the emperor, the oppression of the harem, and the memories of Yolanda's misery.

Eschiva had always been a solitary child, a girl who preferred to retreat into a book rather than chatter with friends. She had lost her mother by the time she was ten. In the convent, she had been befriended by the nuns more than the other boarders. Yolanda had been her first, best, and only close friend. And she was dead.

The time alone at sea had been a balm to her soul. Time to remember, time to grieve, time to reflect on what had been. Most important: she had her brushes, ink, and paper, and Eschiva had long since discovered that her thoughts came easiest when she painted. They came unbidden and unformulated, but they took form on paper, and as she worked thoughts and feelings fell into place.

So as the galley sailed eastwards, she had spent her days creating images. At first, they were focused on the things Yolanda had loved—cats and flowers. She had painted Yolanda sitting in a garden with a cat curled in her lap and surrounded by flowers and angels. She had cried as she painted, but in the end, a sense of peace settled over her too. Yolanda was in heaven. And Frederick Hohenstaufen, Eschiva thought with bitter triumph, would surely go to hell!

At the start of her second week at sea, the pictures began to change. It was as if the sea itself, or her utter freedom, had unleashed her imagination, and with it came the awakening of a creative talent dormant up to now. When she sat down to paint, she rarely knew what image would come to mind, and it was exciting to discover what was in her subconscious. She found herself painting curling fish, and fire-breathing sea monsters, ships riding waves shaped like horse's heads with whitecap manes, billowing sails forming the letter "b" and seagull's wings that embraced an "m." She was happy, lost in this dreamy world of beautiful colors and creatures that required no explanation to anyone.

But the seagulls reminded her that the voyage would end. At some point, she would have to re-emerge and face the others—and her brother. Eschiva was embarrassed by how much she owed Sirs Philip and Balian for her escape from the sailors and the Emperor. The embarrassment made her very reluctant to face either of them—certainly not in her poorly washed and un-pressed clothes.

There was simply no way she or her brother could ever thank them enough, much less repay them, for all they had done for her.

Assuming her brother was inclined to reward them. Eschiva was no longer certain how Eudes would respond. Would he be indignant about the way she had been treated? Or would he think she had undermined his position? The Emperor was hardly going to be pleased with her behavior, and her brother might be the one to pay the price.

When she wasn't lost in her art, her thoughts ran in the same vicious circle. She recognized that her flight represented an insult to the Holy Roman Emperor, but what choice had she had? Should she really have stayed in the harem like a lamb for the slaughter, a ready victim whenever he wanted to punish her or her brother? When she thought back to those terrible days following Yolanda's death, she felt the same sense of panic, the same desperation to escape. But when she thought of facing her brother, she felt trepidation and uncertainty. What if Eudes was *really* angry? What if he sent her back?

A knock on the door was so unexpected that she caught her breath and held it as she turned toward the door. "Yes?"

"We're putting into Cerigo for fresh water," Domenico answered. "If you'd like a chance to go ashore, this is it."

Cerigo? Where was that? It sounded Italian. A Venetian outpost perhaps? The Venetians were no friends of the Holy Roman Emperor, but Captain di Domenico was Genoese and they were hardly on good terms with the Venetians either. "That would be wonderful, Captain. May I come on deck before we make port?"

"Yes. We've only just made landfall. It will be another hour or two before we actually dock, but the coastline is pretty. I think you would enjoy it."

"I'll be there shortly!" Eschiva was already removing her shift. A moment later, she plunged a sponge into a bucket of sea water that stood ready beside the commode. She washed herself off and dressed in the one gown and surcoat that had not been soiled with blood on that first night. She combed out her hair and plaited it as best she could into a long, single braid hanging down her back. She covered her head with a veil, leaving her neck exposed, and held it in place with a flat, crown-like hat. The latter had been badly crushed in her leather bag during her escape, but once on her head, she hoped it looked alright. If only she'd had a mirror, but the one she'd brought had shattered when she dropped her bag during the assault. She tried to see her reflection in the water of the pitcher, but the ship was moving too much. At least her acne had largely cleared up in the last several days.

As she set the pitcher down, her flurry of preparations finished, she was brought back to earth; she was deluding herself if she thought she could make herself look pretty. How had Frederick worded it? Cold, boring and plain.

From overhead came shouted orders followed by pounding footfalls, the crack of canvas and the whine of hemp. They appeared to be handing sail, and the sound of the oars being run out confirmed her assessment.

Eschiva drew a deep breath and squared her shoulders. She might be plain, but the Emperor was wrong to call her cold and boring. She would show them that. They must surely think her a silly goose for the way she'd allowed herself to be trapped by the sailors and her near hysterical plea for help. Today she must show them that she was not a hysterical or vain female.

She opened the cabin door, slipped into the salon and, grabbing a handful of skirt, lifted it so she could climb up the ladder to the after deck. As she emerged, Captain di Domenico came over to help her out. The sun was so bright she had to squint, and then she let out a cry of shock and amazement as she registered that they were sailing close alongside a sheer cliff three times as high as their masts. She gaped upwards, while the captain laughed. "Cerigo," he told her, "or Kythera in Greek. The island of Aphrodite, the place where Helen and Paris spent their first night together. And if I had my way," he added with an inner smile and a glint in his eye, "where *I* would spend my wedding night with my little Cecilia—instead of Acre with her father holding his ear to the door of the bedroom!" He laughed.

Eschiva was embarrassed by this talk of a wedding night, so she protested instead. "But there's nowhere to land! No harbor or—"

The captain nodded toward the bow. "The harbor is up ahead, beyond that headland and a few more, but you're right. This is no coast to be caught on in a gale."

Eschiva looked again at the cliffs towering over them and shuddered. They were sheer rock, without a blade of grass much less a bush or tree, and the rock was jagged and sharp, the kind of rocks that would tear open the planking of a ship as surely as the claws of bear could tear open a human belly. Yet they were dramatically beautiful too. As the water neared the shore it turned from bright cobalt blue to vivid turquoise and finally a brilliant aqua. A sea turtle paddled along between them and the shore. Little coves were formed by the rock and there were large grottos as well.

"Does anyone live on this island?" Eschiva asked in disbelief, although when she lifted her eyes from the cliffs to the rugged hills behind them, she could make out some scrub brush that might support a few sheep.

"Oh, yes, there is quite a large population. Mostly farmers and fishermen."

"Farmers? They must be desperately poor!" Eschiva noted with sympathy, unable to imagine how anyone could eke out a living on such a barren rock.

Captain di Domenico laughed. "No, they are quite rich. Further inland, the island is heavily forested and fertile. The fertile land lies like a bowl, or rather a series of bowls, behind the forbidding coastline. Since the age of the *Iliad*, the barren coast has discouraged pirates and invaders, leaving the residents to prosper in peace."

Eschiva looked at him disbelieving, but he laughed and pointed to the bow. A wide bay had opened up and at the far side a headland gradually sloped down from the mountain to the shoreline. Opposite this was a dramatic island that reared up straight out of the sea like a three-sided pyramid.

Domenico pointed in the direction of the island. "Kitra. No one can live there, but there is large grotto on the backside. It's where our skiff is heading." Now that he pointed it out, Eschiva could see a small sailboat bouncing on the waves that hardly disturbed the larger ship. The skiff was heeling sharply over in the wind.

"Why did you send the skiff there?" Eschiva asked.

"I didn't. Your cousin insisted on seeing the grotto," Domenico explained. "It goes deep under the island. It is quite shallow in places, making it ideal for fishing, but treacherous. If the wind gets up, the waves fill the chambers of the grotto and anyone inside drowns."

Eschiva looked at him in horror, and the captain laughed. "Nothing to worry about today. There! You can start to see the Venetian fortress—well, the watchtower, and on the saddle of the mountain behind you can see a church and a few houses."

A stone tower sat perched upon the top of one of the cliffs, and crouched behind it, a few white-painted houses. It looked like a poor settlement from here, but they had spectacular views of the surrounding seascape.

For all that she liked her art, Eschiva discovered that she was starved for human contact after the solitude of her cabin. She ventured another question. "Did I understand you are to be married soon, Captain?"

"As soon as my feet touch the quay at Acre, my lady!" Domenico answered readily, smiling again at the thought. "I have persuaded Signore Gabrieli to let me take his precious daughter Cecilia to wife as soon as I deliver your cousin safely back at Beirut. Do you know the Gabrielis, mademoiselle? They have a lovely house on the corner of South Street and St. Joseph's—about halfway between the shore and the Ibelin palace and the Palace of Genoa in Acre."

"Gabrieli? Is he not a merchant of spices and apothecary goods?"

"Exactly the man, mademoiselle. The family has been merchants in Acre for a century now. They lost everything to Saladin in 1187 and the old man took part in the siege alongside Richard the Lionheart to regain his property in Acre. He is now over seventy and my Cecilia is the late child of his second marriage. He dotes on her insanely—but then so do I! She is pretty as a rosebud or a summer sunset or—or—" he searched for words and images that would do justice to the girl he loved and concluded with a laugh and an expansive gesture "—or Kythera on a sunny day!"

The ship steadily made its way along the coast, rounded the headland and slipped into a nearly round natural harbor that sat at the foot of the headland on which the Venetian tower sat. A large stone cistern sat at the foot of a gorge at the back of the harbor, and Domenico explained that it sat over a natural spring and also collected rainwater. Beyond the stone building, a peninsula stretched around to enclose the other half of the harbor. Pines occupied the lower slopes, but behind them, sheer cliffs reared up. Here, clinging to the face of the reddish limestone like a barnacle, was the white-painted entrance to a Greek Orthodox church carved into the rock. At the foot of the pine-clad hills was a sandy beach that cuddled on the inside of an arm of rock that protected the cove from the sea to the north and east. A wooden pier ran out from a shack on the sandy beach, and a few fishing vessels were drawn upon the sand.

They tied up to the pier, and while Captain di Domenico negotiated with the "harbor master" in the hut, his crew started to roll the empty water barrels off the ship and down to the foot of the pier. Eschiva was on her own. She went ashore, prepared for the sensation of unsteadiness from her earlier sea voyage. Her eyes feasted on the spectacular panorama of shifting shades of aqua, blue and turquoise in the harbor and the dozens of tiny blue, purple and white flowers growing along the edge of the beach.

Eschiva loved color. It was colors that had drawn her to book illuminations, but color also attracted her to markets full of fruit, or shops with fresh dyed yarn, and the workshops of weavers. She had come to love embroidery almost as much as illumination because of the vivid silk threads she could use. She loved working the colors together into designs and images that imitated the richness of nature—like here. The captain was right, she thought to herself, this island was a hidden treasure.

It must surely be in the *Odyssey*, she thought with excitement. Captain di Domenico said it had been where Helen and Paris spent their first night together, which meant it was mentioned in the *Iliad*. But surely Ulysses had been here too? Maybe it was the island of Calypso? If only she could read Greek. Maybe she could ask Sir Balian to read to her? It had been his father's book and the Lord of Beirut had been able to read it. But she doubted she would have the courage to ask Sir Balian to read to her.

Eschiva removed her shoes and stockings, hitched up her skirts and waded into the shallows. The water was chilly at first, but soon her feet adjusted to the temperature, countering the heat of the sun that made her head sweat under her hat and veils. The stones and shells glistened under the clear water, and schools of minnows darted back and forth casting shadows on the sand underneath.

Good-natured shouting drew Eschiva's attention back toward the entrance of the harbor. The little skiff was entering the cove, leaning far over under the pressure of the wind. Then, as Eschiva watched, the little boat righted herself as it sailed into the lee of the high cliffs behind her. Still it raced toward the shore, and just when Eschiva was certain it was about to collide with the land, a shout went up, the boat pivoted into the wind, and the sail flapped and fluttered. An anchor was thrown into the bay, and while a crewman handed the sail, she caught a glimpse of Sirs Balian and Philip as they dove overboard to swim ashore. They were both stark naked.

Eschiva started slightly, although she knew they had no idea she was watching them. They appeared to be racing one another, completely carefree. It was a glimpse of a world women never knew, she thought, a world of adventures and freedom from manners, propriety and even clothes. They reached the shore and staggered out. The two knights seemed as lean and perfect as the Greek athletes and warriors she had seen on statues in the Holy Roman Emperor's palaces. Then, embarrassed by her own interest, she looked away and concentrated on the fish around her feet again.

Eschiva did not consider herself rebellious in any way, but she was reminded that when she was growing up she had wanted to do so many things. She had wanted to discover the markets of Acre, to ride a camel, to race her pony, to sail in one of the fishing boats. She had resisted wearing so many clothes, resisted sitting still, resisted needlework, until she discovered the beauty of silk thread. She had even resisted reading, until she discovered that the books allowed her to do all those things—at least in her head.

Voices reached her across the water from the pier. She looked over and saw Captain di Domenico gesturing to her. Apparently, he wanted her to return to the ship. She left the water, sat on a large rock and brushed the sand from her feet. Even so, her feet were too damp for stockings, so she slipped her bare feet into her low shoes and returned to the ship carrying her stockings.

When she arrived, she found the cook with the help of two youths had set up a table on the afterdeck, shaded by a canvas awning. Watermelon had already been sliced and divided up, while on an open grill a huge fish sizzled.

"Dinner!" The captain indicated she should sit down on a bench beside the improvised table, and at once a youth came over with a shy smile and offered her a beaker full of cool water. "I'm Rob," he murmured, "Sir Balian's squire, and that's Andre, Sir Philip's squire."

A moment later, Sirs Philip and Balian emerged from below deck. Their hair was wet, and they were both dressed like sailors in footless hose and loose shirts with the arms rolled up to the elbows. They were deeply tanned, and exuded health, youth and strength. At the sight of Eschiva, they both broke into smiles.

Sir Philip was first off the mark, coming to bow over her hand. "What a pleasure to see you again at last, my lady," he opened. "I was beginning to think you were a mere figment of my imagination, that that entire encounter on the quay at Andria was nothing but a dream, a fantasy, a fairytale—"

Sir Balian gently cut him off by nudging him aside to bow to her in turn. He was much more serious. His eyes searched her face. "Are you well, cousin? I was much concerned, but Captain di Domenico assured me you were in the best of health and spirits."

"Thank you, cousin. I have been well ever since you granted me your protection. In fact, I wish this voyage would never end at all, or that I could stay here on Kythera," (the Greek name for the island came to her more readily than the Italian one) "forever."

Sir Balian laughed and then looked over his shoulder. "It is enchanted, isn't it? I'm sure it's in the *Odyssey* somewhere. If only I had a copy."

"*I* have a copy!" Eschiva answered excited by this shared interest. "Your grandmother's copy!" She remembered.

Sir Balian stared at her astonished. "How?"

"Your father gave it to Queen Yolanda as a wedding gift, on the quay at Tyre. Don't you remember? I did not want to leave it behind in Andria."

"No wonder your bag was so heavy!" Sir Philip groaned, "I thought it was full of jewels and gold."

"But this is the greatest jewel of all!" Eschiva answered, so caught up in her delight for the book, the island, and Sir Balian's interest that she quite forgot herself. "It has the most beautiful illustrations you've ever seen. I'll go get it!" She jumped up and disappeared down the companionway.

When she returned, book in hand, the squires had brought chilled white wine and a pitcher full of spring water just collected on the island itself. They all preferred the water to the wine, but while Philip turned his attention to the food, going over to "help" the cook and squires at the grill, Sir Balian beckoned Eschiva to his side.

She sat down, acutely aware of the smell of his tanned skin and the warmth he exuded. Embarrassed, she moved a little farther away and placed the book on the table in front of them.

"It *is* Grandma's book!" Sir Balian exclaimed as if he had not believed her, reaching out to take it into his own hands.

"Can you read it?" Eschiva asked hopefully.

"Not as well as my father can," Sir Balian prevaricated. "I learned Greek growing up and can still remember speaking it with my grandmother, but I haven't really kept it up. Let's see." He opened the book and scanned down the page, looking for something he recognized.

Eschiva couldn't wait, confiding in excitement: "I was thinking, maybe this is the island of Calypso."

Sir Balian looked up and their eyes met. He looked straight at her without seeing that she was plain, and there was excitement in his voice as he exclaimed "I thought the same thing! Or, not exactly, but the island out there," he pointed to the steep, triangular island they had passed earlier. "It has an amazing grotto— just the kind of place poor, shipwrecked Ulysses would have washed up. In fact, there's nowhere *else* on the island to wash up. But once he was inside the grotto, he could have been driven deeper and deeper into the rooms that stretch *under* the island. Once inside, he might not have been able to find his way out again. It's absolutely perfect."

"Dinner!" Philip interrupted, dropping two plates laden with large slabs of fish in front of them. With a gasp Eschiva seized the precious book before any of the sizzling fat could damage it.

"You don't want the fish to get cold!" Philip told her, as the squires came with pans of grilled carrots and eggplant in his wake.

"Take it below," Sir Balian seconded Eschiva's sentiments regarding the precious book. "We can read it together later when there is less going on."

Eschiva hugged the book to her chest with one arm as she returned down the ladder to stow the book safely away. She knew already that when she returned on deck the mood would be different, but nothing could take away that moment of shared excitement—or that look of delight empty of any acknowledgement that she was plain.

Balian had borrowed the *Odyssey* from Eschiva and sat at the salon table trying to read it by the light of a hurricane lamp. He desperately wanted to read it, so he could entertain Eschiva with it in the morning, but although he could read the letters, sound out the words, and occasionally even make out whole phrases, it wasn't good enough. He could not read an entire stanza of verse, much less a page or an episode.

Tiring, he flipped through the pages half-heartedly hoping something he could understand would catch his eye. Instead, he was distracted by the beautiful illustrations. They were powerful, colorful, and evocative. They reminded him of the tales in the book, and he remembered lying on his belly on the cool tiles of his father's palace in Beirut while his grandmother read to him in Greek.

She had been very old by then and she dressed in old-fashioned robes. She didn't wear black like some widows; she permitted herself royal purple, dark blues and greens as well. Her voice was old too, but melodic. When she read the *Odyssey*, Balian had heard the waves of the sea carrying him away.

As he turned another page he was startled to find a piece of paper folded inside. Puzzled, he removed it and caught his breath. It was covered with beautiful illuminated letters. They were cast haphazardly across the page, forming no single word, just letters decorated with fishes and ships, gulls and sea monsters. He glanced toward the closed door of the aft cabin. Eschiva.

"What? Are you still up?" Philip asked in surprise, squinting in the unexpected light as he emerged from his cabin with the evident intent of going on deck to relieve himself.

"I was just reading—well, trying to read," Balian admitted, hastily returning the sheet with the beautiful letters and glancing anxiously toward the door of the cabin where Eschiva slept. He didn't want her to know he'd been up all night for nothing.

"Why?" Philip asked, still confused.

"I wanted to read it for Eschiva."

"Wait. I'll be back in a moment." Philip disappeared to take care of his business, and when he returned he plopped himself down next to Balian. "Now," he opened, addressing his friend seriously. "What is this about? You aren't, you know—I mean she's your cousin."

"Yes, I know," Balian answered sharply, an annoyed frown creasing his face.

"Well, so, you can't seduce her, right?"

"No! Of course not!"

"And you can't be serious about her either. I mean, if nothing else, you could do a lot better."

"Her father, like mine, was regent of a kingdom. She's the granddaughter of a king, while I'm the grandson of a queen. I think that makes us remarkably well suited in rank, don't you?" Balian noted tartly.

"Yes, well, true, but—though I hate to admit it—you're not bad-looking, so, as well as being an Ibelin, you can have any maid you want."

Balian shrugged uncomfortably. He knew that. It had gotten him in enough trouble already. "I've had a lot of girls, Novare, and I've chased more. The prettier, the more conceited, I've found."

Novare snorted. There was truth to that, but that didn't stop him dreaming about the perfect maid: sweet-tempered, cheerful, biddable, rich, full-bodied, hot-blooded, breathtakingly beautiful, and virtuous—at least until he came along. Bringing his thoughts back to his friend, he asked. "So you really like her?"

"Yes, don't you?"

Novare shrugged. "She's not my type. Too—I don't know—boring."

"Boring? How many maids do you know could drug a guard and escape by night through a city to run away from the most powerful monarch on earth?"

"Well, she *did* have a little help," Novare reminded his friend immodestly.

"Once she reached the port, yes, but she had to get there first. I think that took tremendous courage."

Novare raised his hands in surrender. "No question, Bal. She must have spunk, I just don't see…."

"Beyond her plain face," Balian finished for him.

"Maybe you're right. If her skin clears up more and she put on a little weight, she wouldn't be half-bad."

Balian nodded and looked down at the book on the table in front of him. "It's not as though I've lost my heart to her, Novare. I would just have liked to entertain her a little. She must be terribly lonely, all alone in the world except for Eudes."

Novare rolled his eyes at the mention of Eudes de Montbéliard, whom neither of them liked.

"It must also be very boring cooped up in the cabin all day and night," Balian continued.

"No doubt, but—if you'll forgive me for saying so—a little, meaningless kindness on your part could be quite misinterpreted. She's probably never had any man pay her much attention. A few of your smiles could turn her head. You don't want to break her heart when she finds out it all meant nothing to you, do you?"

"Of course not," Balian dismissed the suggestion. "Don't worry. I'm not going to trifle with her feelings. Go back to bed."

Balian looked down again and his eyes fell on the first illustration. It showed Helen being led away by Paris. Helen had long golden hair and white skin;

Paris was dark and dressed in armor. In the background, a king with a crown on his head slept in a bed with a baldachin. Helen of Troy had been the greatest beauty on earth and what had it gotten her husband? Ten years of bloody war. Penelope, on the other hand.... Balian shrugged and carefully closed the book.

Chapter Nine

Return to Beirut

Beirut, Kingdom of Jerusalem
June 2, 1228

ISABELLA "BELLA" OF IBELIN WAS AT the postern of Beirut castle distributing alms to the poor when a shout went up from the lookout platform of the southwestern tower. She glanced up briefly, but then resumed giving out yesterday's bread, trying to ensure that no one pushed anyone else aside or took more than their share.

A moment later, however, the sergeant on the roof of the barbican called down to her, "Lady Isabella! Your brother's ship just cleared the headland!"

This time Isabella looked up, shielding her eyes against the bright sunlight. The sergeant was silhouetted and she couldn't see him properly, but she recognized the voice of one of their senior sergeants, "Are you sure, Gautier?"

"As sure as one can be, my lady!" He answered cheerfully. Bella was a favorite with the entire garrison. Their lord's only daughter, she might have been spoilt and haughty, but Bella was just the opposite. Growing up with five brothers, she had been a tomboy as a child, and even now at seventeen, she was plump and practical rather than self-important. "It's a Genoese galley flying the Ibelin arms from the masthead," Gautier explained.

Bella nodded and waved, then hurried to complete her alms-giving. Balian had been away two months and didn't know yet that Barlais had dared to return to Cyprus and take up Karpas' gage. The judicial combat was set for just over a week from now. They had been afraid he might not return in time to stand by his father at the trial. She was relieved that he was back, and anxious to tell him all the news.

At last, her burlap sack empty, she dismissed the beggars with the assurance, "There will be more again tomorrow." Then she folded the bag over her arm and started up the paved slope of the outer bailey toward the inner wall.

She was just about to pass through the inner gate when her brothers Baldwin, Hugh, and Johnny burst out of it. "Balian's ship has rounded the headland and is making for the harbor!" Baldwin announced importantly.

"We're going down to meet the ship!" Thirteen-year-old Johnny added excitedly.

"Do you want to come?" Hugh asked Bella with a smile.

Bella hesitated, for a moment tempted to join her brothers. Yet she was also seriously considering a life in the church. As a nun, she reminded herself, she wouldn't be free to gallop about on a whim, so she shook her head. "No, I'll go make sure the kitchen has something ready for him. Does Father know?"

"Yes, he's in the solar."

Bella nodded and waved her brothers off. She continued through the inner gate and across the cobbled inner ward to the large kitchen tract carved out of the bedrock of the cliff on which the upper castle sat. This precipice fell sharply, well over a hundred feet, to the sea below. Bella put her head into the kitchen and asked if they'd heard the news about Balian's return. Indeed, they had! Everyone was feverishly at work to put together a meal with as many of Balian's favorites as possible. Bella laughed to herself. Baldwin always complained that Balian got preferential treatment because he was the heir, but it had far more to do with the fact that Balian took the time to come down to the kitchens now and again. It was often to pinch an extra bite to eat—but he took the time to praise and flatter as well. As a result, the kitchen staff *knew* what Balian liked best and *wanted* to please him.

She continued to the walled garden set in the northwest corner of the inner ward. This had almond, pomegranate, lemon and orange trees planted amidst lavender, hibiscus and oleander bushes. Paths of crushed marble meandered through the garden and surrounded a gurgling marble fountain. It was one of Bella's favorite places. She often came here to read or do needlework.

Now, however, she took the exterior stairs that led from the back of the garden up along the outside of the western wall to the great hall. The hall sat nearly 150 feet above the sea, and the six west-facing windows offered spectacular views of the Mediterranean. The six east-facing windows, on the other hand, looked across the inner ward to the meadows, orchards and the snow-capped mountains beyond.

The hall itself was paved with white marble with black veins that wiggled the same way sand did on the floor of the sea. Although Bella had grown up here, she still felt like she was wading in shallow water when she walked across the cool surface toward the fountain at the center of the room. The marble fountain, carved like a sea-dragon, spewed water into a round marble basin. The interior was inlaid with colored marble flowers so that as the water cascaded down making the water shiver, the marble flowers appeared to be swaying in a light breeze. The run-off from the fountain was drained out to the garden in the inner ward, keeping it green regardless of the season.

Bella continued to the dais paved with mosaics depicting the Garden of Eden, including the snake, and passed through the door at the back into the solar. Sitting at the junction of the western and northern walls, the solar windows pierced the west and northern walls, and doors gave access to the hall to the south and the residential tract to the east. Gilding highlighted the ribs of the cross-vaulted ceiling, while the panels in between were painted with the constellations of the night sky.

The Lord of Beirut was already in the solar, peering out of the western window toward the harbor. He was dressed for his ease in the summer heat but in mourning for his brother in a long black kaftan, tied at the waist by a red-and-gold cord. With pride, Bella noted that although he was nearly half a century old he was slender and unbent. The only hint of his age was a streak of grey in his dark brown hair, and grey eyebrows.

At the sight of his daughter, he smiled and opened an arm. "Balian's back!"

"So I heard," Bella answered stepping up beside her father in the window niche and kissing his cheek before following his gaze. The harbor was crammed with ships off-loading cotton from Egypt, wheat from Cyprus and pottery from Antioch, or loading the exports of Beirut: the famous red-glass, and the equally precious purple and scarlet silks, and the more necessary nails and horseshoes. These were Beirut's most important exports and the source of the Lord of Beirut's wealth. Amidst all that, Bella could just barely see the tip of a mast bearing (when the wind blew enough to make it lift and flap) a marigold pennant with a red cross on it. It had apparently tied-up at the quay.

"I'm relieved," Beirut admitted to his daughter, "that Balian's back. This way we can all go to Cyprus together. I don't know what Barlais is up to exactly, but I honestly don't believe he's going to face Karpas in judicial combat. I expect some kind of trick, and I want your brothers with me—well, Balian, Baldwin, and Hugh. Have you decided if you'll join us or stay here?"

"I'd like to come," Bella acknowledged. "I'm worried about Aunt Alys. She was very despondent in her last letter."

Beirut tightened his hold around Bella's shoulders for a second and brushed his lips to the top of her head as he muttered, "I should have known you'd be thinking of others rather than yourself. Your Aunt Alys retired from court to one of her manors. Would you like to spend a few weeks with her perhaps?"

Bella nodded. "I was thinking of that, yes. If you don't mind—"

The sound of a door crashing open startled them both, and they spun about to see Baldwin burst into the solar, still breathing hard from running all the way up from the stables. "My lord! Queen Yolanda is dead!" he exclaimed.

"What?" Beirut dropped his arm from his daughter's shoulders and stepped down from the window niche. "How? When?"

Bella was stunned; Yolanda was several months *younger* than she was!

"Early May, of milk fever," Baldwin answered his father.

"She was delivered of a child?"

"A son. He was still alive when Balian set sail, but God knows how long he'll live."

Beirut frowned. "Don't be so callous, Baldwin. This infant is your sovereign liege."

"I know, I know, but there's something else you need to know. Balian returned with a young lady aboard. He claims she is our cousin Eschiva de Montbéliard."

"Eschiva de Montbéliard was Queen Yolanda's waiting-woman, and traveled with her to Brindisi. It is understandable that she would wish to return home after the Queen's death," Beirut commented.

"Yes, but *alone*—and with only one gown? Balian wants Bella to send her a change of clothes." Baldwin re-directed his gaze to his sister.

Beirut frowned. "You don't think…. *Surely* he's learned his lesson! His own cousin? No, I refuse to believe it of him. Bella?"

"Yes, Father, I'll find something suitable at once and take it down to her."

"Please."

"She's a little thing, about half your size, Bella," Baldwin flung after her helpfully.

Bella just continued. Baldwin was fond of teasing her for her bulk, but she didn't need to be reminded that her girth was greater than that of most girls her own age. Besides, a girl who had been serving at court wouldn't want her simple, nun-like gowns and surcoats anyway. In her chamber, Bella opened the chest in which she stored the gowns left by her mother and grandmother. She found a practical, but not drab, mustard-colored linen gown and a green, cotton surcoat. She rolled these together with a pair of silk stockings and a green silk veil. Stuffing these into a little bag, she set off to the stables. Here she found her palfrey already tacked and waiting for her on Baldwin's instructions. She was told to go to the bath-house in the silk quarter, where, Baldwin said, their unexpected guest had gone.

At the bath-house, attendants took her bundle and disappeared inside. Shortly afterward, a young woman emerged wearing the clothes she'd brought. She had beautiful long blond hair, and wide-set, deep blue eyes. Bella supposed her nose was too long and her mouth too wide to qualify as a great beauty, but Bella liked her intuitively. Her expression, furthermore, was one of wary apprehension rather than arrogance or self-importance as one might have expected of an empress' lady.

Bella moved forward with a smile and kissed her on both cheeks. "Welcome to Beirut, Cousin! I'm Isabella d'Ibelin, but everyone calls me Bella."

"Thank you so much for the clothes. I'm sorry to impose. You must think it very odd that I didn't have a change of clothes," Eschiva stammered out.

Sensing her nervousness, Bella smiled and stroked Eschiva's arm. "I'm sure you had a good reason. Let's sit here on the wall while we wait for my brothers. I was told they would meet us here when Balian was finished."

Bella led her cousin to sit on a low wall enclosing the grounds of the bath-house. Sitting side-by-side, Bella coaxed the story of what had happened in Andria out of Eschiva, and by the time Balian, Hugh, and Rob rode up, Bella had taken Eschiva into her heart.

Bella had a sixth sense for people's feelings, and she felt Eschiva's acute loneliness. Eschiva had built defenses against her loneliness, Bella recognized. She had her books and her painting and she had given her heart to Yolanda. But books cannot put their arms around you, nor dry your tears, and her love of Yolanda had ended in heartbreak.

Not that Eschiva wallowed in self-pity. On the contrary, Eschiva was at pains to convince Bella that she was in control of her destiny. She was returning to her brother's care. She was an heiress. She was the cousin of the King of Cyprus. She would not lack for noble suitors. Bella just wasn't entirely convinced.

Beirut received Eschiva graciously, offering his sincere condolences on the loss of the Queen. He listened to her tale patiently and assured her his house was hers as long as she wished. However, the moment she left to go with Bella to be shown her new "home," Balian was left facing his father. The disapproval in the air was palpable.

Beirut remained calm, as he always did, and he gestured for Balian to sit down opposite him. Balian was not deceived.

The Lord of Beirut opened with, "I don't know what to say, Balian. I concede, you were placed in an awkward situation. I assume the poor girl was quite hysterical after being assaulted by sailors and only rescued at the price of watching two men killed. Still," he paused, sighed deeply, and then continued, "still, I am flabbergasted that you could be so irresponsible and hot-headed. It makes me regret entrusting you with this mission. Your brother Baldwin would certainly have behaved more rationally and responsibly."

"What do you mean?" Balian answered defensively. "What have I done wrong now?"

"Honestly, Balian!" Baldwin exclaimed in an exasperated tone. "How could you be so stupid? God knows what really happened! You can't seriously believe that a noblewoman was kept in a harem like a slave, or that the Holy Roman Emperor would make threats against one of his most loyal vassals. The girl is obviously unstable—"

The Lord of Beirut gestured for his second son to be silent, admonishing in a stern but restrained tone. "There is no need to cast aspersions on your cousin, Baldwin." Turning back to Balian, he continued, "I would have expected my son and heir to be more circumspect and cautious in a delicate situation like this."

"Just what the hell did you expect me to do?" Balian burst out.

"There's no need to swear," his father reminded him sternly.

Balian drew a deep breath. "Just what would *you* have had me do? Lady Eschiva arrived in a bloodstained gown and *begged* for my protection. Was I supposed to turn her away?"

"No. Of course not. The only thing you could do initially was to take her in, give her comfort, help her calm down, and ensure her immediate safety. *However*, you should *not* have set sail with her on board until you had sent word to the Emperor. As it is, it appears to all the world that you fled criminal charges of murder against Novare *and* kidnapped a woman of the Imperial household. In doing so, you have succeeded, no doubt, in making an enemy of the most powerful monarch on earth, the rightful regent of the Kingdom of Jerusalem, and your overlord."

Balian squirmed in his chair because, of course, they *had* fled charges against Novare. "Father, you have to understand something. Barlais and Cheneché have been at the Imperial court for months, *and* they were well received. They have turned the Emperor against us. The Emperor is—" How could he possibly word this in a way to make his father understand? "I need to tell you about my first audience with the Hohenstaufen," he announced. "Please! Hear me out."

His father bowed his head in agreement.

"When I was admitted to see Emperor Frederick and told him that Uncle Philip was dead, he didn't so much as blink. He didn't offer a word of condolence or express an ounce of regret. Instead, he just asked about King Henry."

"Well, that's natural," the Lord of Beirut defended the Emperor. "He must have feared there had been an accident or illness that threatened them both."

"Maybe, but when he learned my name he said something insulting about grandfather *surrendering* Jerusalem." His father stiffened slightly. Taking advantage of his father's temporary sympathy, Balian plunged ahead with his defense, "and the next thing he did was inform me that he was extremely angry that Uncle Philip had crowned King Henry without his permission. He called him a bandit and a pirate."

"I don't believe that! You're making it up!" Baldwin dismissed his brother's account.

"Why would I do that?" Balian snapped back at his brother. "Barlais and Cheneché have been at the Hohenstaufen's court telling him God-knows-what lies."

Beirut frowned and gestured for his second son to be still. Then he looked hard at Balian. "Go on."

"Frederick implied Uncle Philip had robbed him, and said he would demand a reckoning from you as his next-of-kin. Later, when I referred to you as Lord of Beirut, he said, 'maybe not for long.'"

"What's that supposed to mean?" Baldwin asked impatiently.

Balian ignored him and continued to meet his father's eyes as he added, "Have you forgotten that he promised John of Brienne he would remain king even after Yolanda's marriage, only to break his word the moment the vows were exchanged?"

His father's eyes narrowed slightly, and Balian sensed that his father was not as blind to the Emperor's deviousness as he pretended. He pressed ahead. "After this encounter, I had no difficulty believing that he had also threatened to use cousin Eschiva as a hostage."

Beirut nodded slowly in acknowledgment not agreement, but he did not speak for several minutes. At last, he nodded once and declared, "I see that you have formed an ill opinion of our king, which is not wise or useful, and I fear that your actions will have given him good reason to view us as insubordinate and hot-headed, not to say rebellious—regardless of what he thought of us before. It will not be easy to reassure him of our loyalty."

Balian wanted to protest, to insist that the Emperor had been hostile to them *before* he'd ever set foot on Sicily, but it was hard to argue with the fact that giving Eschiva refuge and running from the murder on the dock at Andria had made things worse. The contradiction between instinctively feeling he was in the right while objectively being in the wrong created an almost unbearable tension. Balian felt like he was going to explode, but knew that if he did it would make things worse.

"I think we've said enough on this for now. Eschiva is now our guest, and we will not speak of this with her. She is not blameless, obviously, but I think under the circumstances that she cannot be held accountable. I don't know what her brother will think. He was dismissed as baillie before this episode, and I have no idea what was behind that. There are things going on here about which we know too little. We will have to be alert and tread warily. First, however, we must deal with Barlais and his trial for treason."

"What trial?" Balian asked, inwardly still tied in knots by his father's reaction and his inability to explain himself. He spoke with a tight jaw, pretending an interest in the Barlais case that he only partially felt.

"Barlais returned to Cyprus and told King Henry he was willing to defend himself in judicial combat. King Henry set Monday of next week as the day of the trial, and summoned the entire High Court of Cyprus to be present. As baillie, I must preside. We sail this Friday."

"Good," Balian agreed willingly.

"One more thing, oh—" Beirut interrupted himself and turned to his second son. "Baldwin, would you fetch me the garrison roster? I need to make some adjustments before we depart."

Baldwin nodded, and dutifully departed, while Beirut laid a hand on his eldest son's arm to detain him. Only after the door had closed behind Baldwin, did Beirut look over at his firstborn. "Balian, I want you to tell me the truth. Did anything unchaste transpire between you and Lady Eschiva?"

"God in heaven!" Balian exploded. "What do you take me for? I'd never laid eyes on her before Novare brought her to the ship in a traumatized state! Captain di Domenico kept her locked in her cabin all the way to Kythera, claiming the crew might mutiny because we had a woman on board! I'm not a beast that can't leave women alone! Nor am I so base that I would take advantage of a noble maiden in distress! How can you think this of me? I'm your flesh and blood, for God's sake!"

Beirut did not answer. He just considered his raging son with a sense of deep disappointment—not because he didn't believe what he was saying, but because he was offended by such a passionate outburst. He did not understand where Balian came by his temper. It was not an Ibelin trait. It had to come from his mother's side of the family, he concluded with a sigh.

Balian meanwhile had fallen silent, conscious that his outburst had only further damaged his standing with his father. He waited sullenly for his reaction.

"I accept your assurances of good conduct, Balian," Beirut told him solemnly. "I trust that you will give me no grounds to doubt you again. Now, let's lay this conversation to rest."

Balian bowed stiffly, and resentfully departed the hall.

Chapter Ten

Aphrodite in Acre

Acre, Kingdom of Jerusalem
June 5, 1228

GIOVANNI GABRIELI COULD NOT REMEMBER BEING so nervous at either of his own weddings. As the groom, things were different. You were either eager and excited, looking forward to the new adventure, or apprehensive and reluctant. Either way, you were fundamentally incapable of imagining that you could be found wanting in any way.

But for the father of the bride, a wedding was completely different. First of all, of course, it was *his* wedding in the sense that the whole Genoese Commune of Acre would judge him by how beautiful, how tasteful yet exceptional, and how expensive it was. The rumors of his financial difficulties would be common knowledge. Giovanni suspected people whispered about them behind closed doors. He feared that some of his many creditors had dropped hints about his impending insolvency. He was certain that everyone would be looking for signs of him saving money, sparing this expense or the other. He could not afford to feed the rumors of his impending ruin.

Not to mention that he was determined to shield his precious little Cecilia from any hint of scandal or hardship. She deserved everything her heart desired on this most important day of her life. If she wanted more expensive roses rather than locally abundant hibiscus, then there would be nothing but roses for the table bouquets, the garlands decorating the hall, and for her hair. If she wanted a dress of woven gold from Constantinople, then she would have a gown of cloth-of-gold studded with flowers formed by rolled rubies. Giovanni had pawned all his silver plate to pay for the dress—on the condition that he could use the place settings for the wedding itself.

The Genoese merchants and bankers of Acre knew him well, of course. They were his friends. None of them wanted to see him bankrupt—they just didn't trust his promises anymore. He had been forced to deal with the Templars to raise the money for the wedding feast. The Templars might be men of God, but they were not sentimental when it came to finances. At times they seemed hardly better than the Jews. Still, in the end, they had advanced him the sum necessary in exchange for him writing over a deed to his house that would come into effect if he failed to repay the borrowed sum within one year. Giovanni was willing to sign the deal because his future son-in-law, Maurizio di Domenico, had promised to be back within half that time.

Maurizio was his savior. He was the son Giovanni had always dreamed about but never had. He was all that Giovanni had hoped for it—and more. He came from an noble Genoese family. He was healthy, good-looking, and charming. He was educated and fluent in multiple languages. He had a solid reputation as a first-rate seaman. Most important, he just launched a new ship, reputed the fastest merchant dromond ever seen. In fact, some argued she shouldn't be called a dromond at all because she had sacrificed considerable cargo space for a longer, sleeker hull. Yet it was enough space for the small, lightweight spices and drugs that Giovanni was entrusting to him.

Giovanni had turned over to Maurizio nearly his entire warehouse of goods, particularly his stores of mandrake and Egyptian opium, as well as saffron, cinnamon and cumin. Maurizio had promised to take them all the way to London. Most ships leaving the ports of the Levant travelled only to the cities of Italy or at most to Marseilles or Barcelona. The goods then travelled overland to destinations in the Holy Roman Empire, France, Flanders and on to England, Scotland and Denmark. Maurizio had convinced Giovanni, however, that with his new ship he could sail all the way to England where the coveted drugs and spices would sell at twice the price they commanded in Barcelona. Furthermore, he was confident his fast dromond could make the journey in a single season.

Giovanni could not resist the offer. If he could sell his goods at twice the price they commanded in Mediterranean ports *and* paid no transport because Maurizio was willing to waive the shipping charge in exchange for Cecilia, then he would be able to completely clear his debts. Indeed, he would have cash left over to purchase more goods and send Maurizio out next year again—maybe to Antwerp or Hamburg.

The prospects were tantalizing. He had been as excited as a schoolboy when Maurizio took him down to the ship yesterday morning to see his precious cargo stowed and stashed in every conceivable nook and cranny of the ship. Giovanni's entire life savings, except for his house and furnishings, were aboard Maurizio's ship, named in honor of his bride-to-be, the *Rose of Acre*.

Giovanni was aware that men cynically accused him of selling his daughter for the price of shipping his cargo to London, but Giovanni had no qualms about what he was doing. He had only to look at Cecilia's glowing face and her dazzling smile as she came down the stairs from her chamber. The look she gave him as he took her hand and tucked it into his elbow was one of sheer gratitude and boundless joy. "Do I look alright, Papa?" she asked in an excited whisper.

He laughed at her, then bent to kiss her on her forehead before lowering the shimmering silk veil of stiff orange and gold silk over her face. He led her down the stairs to the ground floor, where the household was assembled to escort them to the Church of St. Lawrence. While the household clapped and shouted out their approval, Giovanni ushered Cecilia into the street and helped her aboard a garlanded litter. The household fell in around them, a groom took hold of the bridle of the front horse to lead them on the short journey to the church.

Cecilia and Maurizio had fallen in love with each other at first sight. At least, Maurizio had bedazzled his little girl at their first meeting more than a year ago at the Sanuto wedding. At the time he had noted with disapproval that the seaman dominated Cecilia's company, arranging himself so that he held her hand in every dance, and seating himself beside her at the table. He had also noted that Cecilia had been transformed by Maurizio's attention, and he had been concerned. She had been only fourteen at the time, and had not been much in public. So the next day he had summoned her to his office to chastise her for her "wanton" behavior, warning her to stay away from "cads and seducers."

"Oh, but Maurizio, I mean *Capitaine di Domenico*, isn't like that at all, Papa!" she had assured him breathlessly, her face blushing at the mention of his name. "He's a perfect gentleman, a man of honor—as chivalrous as a knight of the round table!"

Giovanni had snorted and muttered something about many real knights being little better than rogues before sending his daughter to her room. He had then sent for Maurizio. The captain had surprised him by ardently declaring his honorable intentions and swearing he wanted no other woman in the world except Cecilia Gabrieli. This was a great honor since the Domenicos were resident in Genoa, not settlers to Outremer, like the Gabrielis. They had been ship owners for generations and were now nobles.

As the wedding party approached the Church of St. Lawrence, Maurizio stood out at the head of his large party of friends and colleagues, more by the breadth of his smile than his clothes or stature. He was, Giovanni reflected, no more than average in height and he dressed conservatively in low leather shoes that were not too pointed, hose of a solid blue color (not particolored like the silly squires of the court), a loose and wide-sleeved surcoat the color of the sea belted at the waist with a broad belt studded with brass. The long-sleeved inner tunic was sky blue and had beautifully embroidered cuffs. All in all, he looked affluent and respectable, neither gaudy nor extravagant, the perfect backdrop for his shimmering, golden Cecilia.

Giovanni dismounted from his side of the litter and went around to help Cecilia out, but before he could reach his daughter's side, Maurizio had sprung forward and offered his own hand. Shameless hussy that his daughter was, she handed her little, gloved hand to her future husband and slipped down to the pavement in a rustle of silk. Whispers erupted from the wedding guests, but Giovanni was relieved to see that Cecilia at least had the modesty to keep her eyes down, and Maurizio surrendered her hand to her father as soon as the older man, with an admonishing frown, nudged him aside.

The priest was waiting in the doorway of the Church, and Giovanni waited with Cecilia at the foot of the steps until Maurizio, taking them two at a time, repositioned himself. Then Giovanni and Cecilia mounted the steps at a decorous pace. Here, Giovanni officially surrendered Cecilia's hand to Maurizio and took a step back. The priest called out to the crowd that they were assembled to witness the marriage of Cecilia Gabrieli to Captain Maurizio di Domenico and asked if anyone knew of any reason why these two Christian souls could not be legally bound together in holy matrimony.

After a dramatic pause that allowed an objection to be made, the priest proceeded to ask the parties if they wished to be married to one another. Maurizio answered in a voice that could have been heard to the harbor, Giovanni thought. Cecilia, in contrast, spoke in a whisper so faint that even the priest seemed to have trouble hearing her. "Did you say 'yes,' my dear?" he asked her a little anxiously.

Cecilia lifted her head and said loudly and firmly, "*Sì! Sì! Sì!*"

That brought an approving ripple of laughter from the crowd. As soon as the chuckles died down, the priest presided over the exchange of the marriage vows and blessed the couple. Only after the blessing did he indicate with a nod to Maurizio that he could lift Cecilia's veil. Maurizio's eagerness again elicited a little laughter, but when he bent to kiss his bride and she went on tip-toe to meet him, the crowd "aahhed" with approval. Then they all filed inside the church for Mass.

The bells rang joyously as the wedding party exited St. Lawrence and started the short trip back to the Gabrieli residence in a procession behind the litter in which Maurizio now sat with Cecilia. Giovanni had paid for three street musicians to accompany them, playing their instruments and singing as they trailed behind the litter. The bells and the musicians attracted the attention of residents and travelers, peddlers, passers-by and street urchins. The sight of Cecilia, shining in her cloth-of-gold gown, her bright blond hair cascading about her shoulders for the last time in her life, brought shouts and whistles of approval. Cecilia seemed embarrassed by the bold attention and kept her eyes down, her cheeks flushed to a bright red. Then again, Giovanni thought with mixed feelings, maybe she blushed because Maurizio had his arm around her waist already and kept bending to whisper in her ear.

On arrival at the Gabrieli residence, Giovanni was far too distracted by the need to give last minute instructions to his staff to relax even for a moment. He became flustered when the Genoese Consul of Acre, Signor Sanuto, sent his excuses. This meant that the visiting Vice Consul from Cyprus, Signor Orto was the most senior guest and needed to be placed at the head table. But he was accompanied by the eldest son and heir of the Cypriot Consul, a certain Paulo di Ferrario. Did the boy rank a seat at the high table or not? With a look of disapproval for his foppish dress, Gionvanni decided he did not and sent him to a lower table. Then just after everyone was seated, Signor Sanuto appeared after all. Giovanni, unable to send the venerable Orto away, had his staff squeeze in another place at the head table for Sanuto.

Meanwhile, there was a mishap with one of the sauces (that curdled), and a cask of wine that sprang a leak, and a hundred other little things that seemed to be going wrong. The feast was already over before Giovanni could focus on his guests. By then the young people had moved aside the lower tables and started dancing, led by Cecilia and Maurizio. The bridal couple was like a bright light of happiness that swept everyone around them into a spell of joy and brightness with them. The young foppish Cypriot Paulo di Ferrario apparently more than anyone, Giovanni thought with amusement; the young man kept dancing around the bridal couple like a moth around a candle.

Beyond the reach of their happiness, however, the older women clustered together to gossip, while the older men sat together at the tables in earnest discussion. As he joined the other members of the Genoese community, Giovanni heard Sanuto intone, "The death of Queen Yolanda is an unmitigated disaster!"

"Her death? Her *marriage* to the Hohenstaufen was the disaster! This is actually an improvement!" Orto countered emphatically.

"If she had died without leaving an heir, I would agree with you, but her son is a Hohenstaufen! That arrogant pig Frederick is bound to claim the regency for his son!"

"Of course he will, but that is better than him being the *reigning* king-consort of our queen! We must consult a legal counsel, the Lord of Beirut would know, but I believe a regent must be resident in the kingdom, which means that as soon as the Hohenstaufen sails for home, he will need to appoint someone else in his place—unless he plans to stay here forever, which I doubt."

"In the long run you may be right, but at last report, he was preparing to sail any day now. He could be here within weeks."

"But he's excommunicate! I have that on the highest authority—a message direct from our man in the Papal Curia."

"As he deserves!"

"The point is the Pope has forbidden him from embarking on this crusade."

"And? Is that going to stop him? Of course not! The Pisans are already preparing to welcome him with processions, feasts, gifts and honors to curry favor from him!"

"That's the real danger! If we don't watch out, they'll have secured new privileges that muscle us out of Outremer. Mind my words! The Pisans will try to get a monopoly on the most lucrative trades like ivory, incense and opium."

Giovanni stiffened at the mention of opium. It was his most important export. Several of the others cast him a glance.

It was now late in the afternoon. As the sun sank low over the Mediterranean, the golden light flooded through the tall, peaked windows of his upstairs hall and bathed his guests and servants in mellow light. The sunlight glinted off Cecilia's golden gown, made the rubies gleam, and seemed to create a halo around her perfectly oval face. Giovanni was so enchanted, he hardly noticed the way Florio Sanuto leered.

Cecilia's flushed face seemed to her father like a freshly opened rose. She was more beautiful than any mortal had a right to be, Giovanni thought to himself, in awe that she was his own flesh and blood. Seeing his awe reflected in Maurizio's eyes, reassured him. Maurizio would cherish her as much as he had done and long after he was gone to the grave. Besides, for the next six to eight months Maurizio would be at sea and Cecilia would remain with him just as before, his joy and comfort, as beautiful, gentle and cheerful as an angel.

"But why *can't* I come with you?" Cecilia asked her husband of only twelve hours. They lay naked side by side as the sun streamed into the bridal bower in which their clothes still lay strewn across the floor amidst the broken garlands of roses. They had left the bed only very briefly to fetch refreshment and breakfast from the waiting sideboard, and Maurizio was half entangled in Cecilia's hair.

"Because, *mi amore*, it will be a very long and arduous journey, and I will be driving the crew mercilessly so that I can return to you as soon as possible." Maurizio ended this statement with a kiss.

Cecilia coquettishly evaded his lips to answer brightly, "But you wouldn't have to rush back, dearest husband, if I was *with you* the *whole time.*"

"The ship is crammed to the very gills, little one—"

"Are you saying I am too *fat* to find a place in your ship?" she asked, provocatively drawing the covers back to reveal her still slim and nubile body.

"*Deo mio!*" Maurizio gasped, and he started feverishly kissing her belly, setting off a delighted fit of giggling from Cecilia. Soon they were engaged in a mock struggle in which Cecilia pretended to ward Maurizio off, while he pursued her all the more ardently, while imitating the growling of a wild beast. This game ended, as it must, in their fourth coupling of the wedding night. Maurizio had never in his life enjoyed such virility, and Cecilia had discovered only ecstasy in her marriage bed.

As their breathing settled again, however, Maurizio realized that the sun was halfway up the sky and he drew a deep breath to explain. "I've filled even the accommodations with your father's wares, Cecilia mine. I'll be sharing my mate's cabin as we alternate on duty. There is nowhere for you to sleep or spend your time, and I would not want you exposed to the rude eyes and comments of my crew or the elements and the risks. Your father and I agreed long ago that you would stay right here with him in the safety of his lovely home while I make this first voyage to London. If all goes well, you can come with me next time. I promise."

"But, Maurizio," she looked up at him with tears in her eyes, "how can I live so long without you?"

Chapter Eleven

Trial by Combat

Nicosia, Kingdom of Cyprus
June 10, 1228

THE LISTS HAD BEEN ERECTED OUTSIDE of the city walls on a level stretch often used for tournaments or horse markets. Banners fluttered from each of the tall poles surrounding them, bearing the colors of all the nobles of the kingdom. Bleachers for spectators lined both sides of the narrow, sandy tiltyard. Teams of carpenters were busy erecting blue and gold striped canvas awnings to provide shade, and hanging the curtains of the royal box. Outside of the railing, crowds of vendors collected along with opportunistic blacksmiths, armorers, barbers, surgeons and undertakers. The most avid spectators were already collecting in a bid to get a place on the rail at either end of the yard, where there were no seats.

The arrival of the challenger, the Lord of Karpas, with his entourage of squires, grooms, a priest and a herald caused a minor sensation. Karpas rode a heavy, black destrier at a controlled trot to the far end of the lists, and then jumped down to allow his squires to arm him fully while the grooms watered the horse. He then knelt and confessed to the priest before remounting and starting to warm up the destrier.

Meanwhile, some of the members of the High Court, their families and retainers began to arrive. The least important arrived first as they did not have reserved seats. Unlike most tournaments, where the seats were occupied primarily by ladies because their men were participating, men far outnumbered women for this judicial duel, and the bleachers were rapidly filling up.

A quarter of an hour before the designated start of the trial, King Henry arrived with a large retinue. Henry was now ten years old. He was solemn, cognizant of his dignity and afraid of making a mistake. Flanking him were his constable, Walter of Caesarea, and his new baillie, the Lord of Beirut. Behind him flocked other knights and nobles, all in armor and colorful surcoats sporting their coat of arms.

Beirut and Caesarea guided their young king to the royal box hung with white and gold curtains and sat him in the large, high-backed chair in the middle, then took seats on either side of him. Henry looked decidedly nervous, conscious of the solemn significance of a judicial combat to the death.

"You don't have to let it run to the end, my lord," Caesarea assured him. "It is your right to stop the combat at any point."

"But it says 'to the death,'" Henry protested, looking from constable to baillie and back again uncertainly.

"It does, but you can intervene at any time and try to persuade the combatants to accept a judgement short of death," Caesarea explained. "Don't you remember? That's what Lord Philip did in the combat between Sir Gauvain of Cheneché and Sir William de la Tor."

Henry frowned. He didn't remember because they hadn't let him come to that combat. Instead, he pointed out, "But that wouldn't be the verdict of God. Isn't that the whole point of trial by combat? To see the judgement of God?"

"Yes, indeed." Beirut agreed. "If you don't stop the combat, then the judgement is the Lord's. However, if you stop a trial by combat, and convince the participants to accept your sentence instead of fighting to the end, then it is your judgement as their liege lord."

"And the High Court wouldn't have anything to say?" Henry asked, sounding skeptical yet a little excited too. He had been raised to understand and respect the important role of the High Court played in helping him rule his kingdom.

"No, at that point the agreement is only between you, as liege, and the combatants," Beirut confirmed.

Henry liked that idea and sat up a little straighter. Unfortunately, the chair they had brought for him was too large and his feet dangled.

Meanwhile, the arrival of several ladies was causing a slight disruption. Although they were comparatively late, people made way for them, so they could climb to the top of the bleachers. "I should have known Meg wouldn't miss a joust even if it was mortal combat," Beirut remarked, shaking his head as if in disapproval, but his expression betrayed him. Meg was his younger sister, Walter of Caesarea's wife, and Beirut had always been indulgent to her.

"Meg wouldn't have missed this for the world!" Caesarea confirmed, shaking his head at the peculiarities of his wife.

"I don't think I recognize the fourth lady," Beirut admitted, glancing at his brother-in-law. Meg was accompanied by his daughter Bella and Eschiva de Montbéliard, both of whom had come with him from Cyprus, but another young lady was with them. She was wearing the veils of a married woman yet hardly looked older than his Bella.

"That's Yvonne de Hebron, Sir Anseaus' new wife, the Lady of Karpas."

"Sir Anseau remarried?" Beirut asked, turning a somewhat horrified look at his brother-in-law. Karpas was a valuable vassal, but he was not the kind of man Beirut would have entrusted a maiden to—much less one as pretty and fragile-looking as the creature that had now taken a seat in front of him. Besides, Karpas had two sons and a daughter by his first wife. He was the kind of man more commonly found on the tiltyard or building siege engines than dancing or courting.

"Yes, quite suddenly, and he took her penniless. Quite the talk of the town this past winter. The grizzled old lion appears to be completely smitten by her, although it's hard to imagine her returning his affection in equal measure, given his looks and the fact that he's old enough to be her father. Her grandfather was constable of Hebron before Hattin, and lost everything there. After halfway recovering over the last quarter century, her father lost everything again when Brienne was so unceremoniously dismissed by the Emperor."

Beirut nodded. "Yes, now I remember." He understood her father's dilemma, but was still moved to pity for the girl herself. It was a hard fate to be bartered to an older man with an unsavory reputation simply because her father did not have the means to hold out for better suitors.

"Ah!" Caesarea interrupted his thoughts, "Here comes Barlais now."

They all turned to look as the defendant rode into the lists surrounded by four other knights, as well as sundry squires and grooms. Sir Amaury Barlais rode an exceptionally tall horse that was covered from the tips of his ears to his fetlocks by a brightly colored trapper. "Is that chainmail under the trapper?" Caesarea asked over the king's head to his brother-in-law.

"Looks like it to me."

Caesarea raised his eyebrows.

"What's so strange?" The young king asked, catching the looks between his advisors but not understanding them.

"Good war horses, my lord, are extremely expensive and it makes sense to try to protect them, particularly against the arrows the Saracens use. The Saracens often direct their fire more at our horses than our knights precisely because chainmail can only be pierced at close range. In single combat with a fellow Frank, however, putting so much mail on a horse seems counter-productive. No Frank would intentionally attack a horse—not least because the winner of any joust takes the horse as a prize and so has a selfish interest in keeping it healthy. The chainmail, however, weighs down the destrier, making him slower, less agile and sure to tire faster."

"Oh," Henry answered, looking back at the horse with the heavy trapper.

"Is that Sir Gauvain de Cheneché?" Beirut burst out in surprise. "He broke the terms of his sentence, and my brother promised to arrest him if he ever set foot on Cyprus again. I thought he fled to Sicily?"

"You're right," Caesarea answered. "It is Sir Gauvain, he did break his word, and he did flee to the Emperor's court."

"When did he return? Have you pardoned him?" Beirut looked to the king and then back at the constable.

"Hardly, but he acts as if we had—and damned sure of himself, too."

Beirut looked back at the man flanking Barlais and saw him smile in the direction of the royal box. It was a sneering, triumphant smile—and was clearly not directed at the young king. An odd shudder went down Beirut's spine. How and why could a man who'd fled Cyprus in disgrace after breaking the terms of judicial combat dare to look at his baillie like that?

Balian leaned forward from the row behind and muttered in his father's ear, "Remember what I told you, Father: Sir Gauvain was very thick with the Emperor. He shares the Emperor's passion for hawking, which earned him much favor."

Beirut turned to glance at his son. He remembered now that Hugh had reported this too, but a shared interest in birds hardly put him above the law. He could not pursue his thoughts, however, because already Caesarea was pointing out, "and that's Sir Grimbert de Bethsan, Sir William de Rivet, and Sir Hugh de Gibelet with them."

Beirut turned to look again at the men with Barlais. Bethsan was Barlais cousin and loyal to him, while Rivet and Gibelet were troublemakers in their own ways, men who constantly complained and quarreled. Before his death, his brother Philip had warned him that they resented the fact that the Ibelins held the bailliage. All three men believed they better deserved the honor merely because their families had been loyal to the Lusignans before the Ibelins. It was a facile and false argument to Beirut's ears because, while it was true his father had steadfastly opposed *Guy* de Lusignan, he had just as vigorously supported *Aimery* de Lusignan. Indeed, his father had been instrumental in putting Aimery on the throne of both Cyprus and Jerusalem. It infuriated him that men could forget—or intentionally try to obscure—that fact.

The heralds of the combatants came forward to stand before the royal box.

Their lords sat fully armored and mounted behind them. While Barlais was wearing one of the new "great helms" that completely enclosed his face with only a horizontal slit for vision and holes punched in the lower half of the face for air, Karpas had opted for an old-fashioned helmet with a separate visor that was now lowered. With trumpet fanfare, the chatter was silenced. All eyes turned to the four men waiting before the king. Karpas' herald raised his voice to be heard at both ends of the lists and repeated the charge against Barlais. Barlais' herald answered by declaring Karpas a liar.

"Now?" King Henry whispered to Caesarea, and the latter nodded.

King Henry got to his feet and raised his childish voice to speak as loudly as possible. "Are you ready to prove the truth of what you say with your bodies before God?"

"Aye, my lord!" the heralds answered in unison, while the knights nodded silently.

"Then—" King Henry looked sharply at Caesarea.

Caesarea whispered, "Take your positions, in the name of God."

King Henry repeated the phrase and the knights turned their backs on one another to canter to opposite ends of the lists. The heralds took up their positions behind the barriers watching carefully for deeds they could later relate in poem and song. The contestants turned to face each other. Lances were passed up to them. A tense silence fell.

"Give the signal, my lord," Caesarea murmured to Henry, and the boy king raised his hand, held it up for a moment, and then let it drop sharply. A trumpet sounded the advance. The two knights thundered down the lists toward one another.

As Caesarea had predicted, Barlais' horse was slower, encumbered as he was by his heavy armor. The knights clashed not at mid-point but closer to Barlais' starting point. Karpas' lance hit Barlais' shield squarely and splintered from the force of the blow. Barlais was flung against the cantle of his saddle, and failed to land a blow with his lance at all, although he was not flung down.

In a normal joust, this would have been viewed as a 'win' for Karpas. Yet this was not a friendly tournament, but rather a no-holds-barred duel to the death.

As Barlais righted himself, he shifted the hold on his still intact lance to just four feet behind the head, and pivoting his horse around, he flung himself at Karpas. With a communal intake of breath, the spectators recognized that Barlais had anticipated his opponent's "success" and planned this unconventional attack.

Karpas drew his sword and swung at his opponent, delivering a hefty blow to Barlais' shoulder and then his side that looked crippling.

Yet Barlais not only withstood the blows, he crouched low over his saddle and continued straight at Sir Anseau, his arm lifted. A split second later, he plunged the lance downwards.

To gasps of horror from the spectators, Karpas' visor was torn off by the first blow. The lance tip had found its way into the vulnerable crack between the helmet and visor. The next blow hit flesh and blood gushed from Karpas' face.

Yvonne de Hebron clapped both hands over her face in horror, and Bella flung her arm over her shoulders to comfort her.

Barlais delivered a second blow to Karpas' face, whose sword appeared to have no effect on Barlais. Then in stunned shock, the spectators watched Barlais strike a third time at Karpas' unprotected face. The spectators held their breath in horrified anticipation of a fatal blow.

Instead, Karpas flung his sword aside, reached up, and grasped the lance directly behind the steel tip. With an audible roar, he wrenched the lance to one side. Still roaring he urged his horse forward.

Barlais' horse staggered and sidestepped. His rider clung to the lance as if for life, but inexorably the saddle moved out from under him. With a loud thud, Barlais landed in the sand. His head cracked down after him so hard that many people in the stands winced instinctively. Others sprang to their feet in surprise and excitement.

Barlais was not dead. Slowly, swaying, he rolled to one side and got a knee under himself. He shoved himself up, staggered, fell again to his knees. For a moment his head sank down as if the weight of the great helm was too much for him. Then, the thunder of hooves penetrated his armor, and he jerked his head back up. Karpas had collected a lance from his squires and was galloping back to finish Barlais off. With superhuman effort, Barlais forced himself to his feet and started running toward the grandstands below the king's box.

It was obvious that Barlais didn't have a chance. He was armored, on foot and already injured. Karpas bore down on him, hunched over the lance like the angel of death. The big black horse consumed two yards of tiltyard with each stride.

Abruptly Barlais' horse put his head down and bolted after his master. He placed his armored body between the attacking Karpas and the defenseless Barlais.

Everyone jumped to their feet a second time. Meg dragged the near unconscious Lady Yvonne with her, while Bella and Eschiva clung to each other.

The horse protected his rider all the way to the side of the lists, where Barlais drew his sword and stood with his back against the wooden fence. The horse, snorting and prancing intercepted each attempt by Karpas to get around him. One minute he kicked out with his hind feet, the next he tried to tear the face off Karpas' horse with his teeth. Within minutes he had thoroughly intimidated Karpas' stallion, despite the infuriated kicks Karpas landed on his flanks drawing more and more blood.

Frustrated by his inability to come to grips with his opponent, Karpas grasped his lance half way down the shaft and tried to thrust it across Barlais' loyal horse at the man pinned to the railing. While these efforts yielded little at first, bit by bit the heavy armor was wearing down the spirited stallion. He was breathing so heavily it could be heard in the grandstands, and his turns started to become clumsy, his head started to droop. His will to protect his master was undiminished, but his ability was fading fast.

Barlais too was in trouble. Sheer terror had enabled him to run, but now the injuries of his fall were catching up with him. He could not stand upright, apparently having injured his right hip. The shoulder above it also hung awkwardly. He was unable to lift his sword above shoulder height in self-defense.

Karpas, blood streaming from the wounds to his face, flung the lance aside, and turned his horse around to cross to the center of the lists to retrieve his sword.

"This is the moment to stop the contest, my lord," Beirut murmured in the young king's ear.

Henry looked up at him astonished. "But—"

"Barlais is finished and his horse nearly so. God has favored the Lord of Karpas. Give Barlais his life, and he should be grateful to you."

"What do I do?"

"Stand up and call on Karpas to desist."

The look King Henry gave Beirut said it all, but the baillie insisted, "Caesarea and I will enforce your command."

King Henry took a deep breath and stood up. "Enough! Stop! Sir Anseau! My Lord of Karpas! Stop!"

The people in the stands turned to gape at the young king, but the Lord of Karpas had hold of his sword and was already re-mounting.

"Walter! Boys!" Beirut called out, and then plunged down the bleachers. He leapt with easy grace over the railing of the lists, his brother-in-law and sons behind him.

"See to Sir Amaury!" Beirut hissed to his sons, while he and the constable continued toward Sir Anseau. The latter tried to spur forward past the regent and constable, perfectly aware that they had come to rob him of his victory. Beirut reached up and grabbed the Lord of Karpas' bridle as he tried to ride past, and Caesarea did the same on the other side.

"Damn you! Let me finish him off!" The Lord of Karpas shouted furiously. His face was a sheen of red. Blood still flooding from his open wounds was mixed with sweat, making it thin.

"The King has ordered an end," Beirut responded.

"The hell he has!" The Lord of Karpas flung back at him. "This was *your* idea, Beirut! Don't think I don't know that you want peace! But there will be none as long as that weasel lives! Let me put an end to this!"

"No!"

The Lord of Karpas brutally put spurs to his horse, who reared up and tried to break free. Caesarea, who was shorter than Beirut, was lifted clear off the ground for a second, but between them, Beirut and Caesarea held the horse from moving forward. The Lord of Karpas started cursing Beirut in a colorful stream of invective, but the combat was over.

Bella was getting worried about Eschiva. She had been closeted with her brother Eudes for more than an hour. While his reception of his sister the day before had not been particularly warm, Bella had attributed it to the fact that he was by nature a cold fish. He had seemed surprised rather than pleased to see her, but had been too preoccupied with the upcoming session of the High Court to focus on her. He'd dismissed Eschiva's efforts to explain herself, saying they could talk tomorrow, and asking Beirut if he had made arrangements for her accommodation since he was quite unprepared for a sister. Beirut had replied that she was welcome to stay with his daughter in the Ibelin palace, which she had done, coming with the Ibelins to the judicial combat. As they were leaving the lists following the combat, however, Eudes had come over and ordered his sister to come back with him to the royal palace. The Ibelins had returned to their own residence to change before the banquet, and on arrival at the royal palace, Bella found Eschiva was still closeted with her brother in his chamber.

Bella had lurked about in the hallway for half an hour, straining to hear what was going on inside, but her Aunt Meg had just ordered her to go to the Lady of Karpas. "She's completely distraught."

Bella could understand that and wanted to help, but how could she just leave Eschiva here?

An inner voice answered her: the Lady of Karpas and Eschiva had been pupils at St. Anne's together! She had the perfect excuse for knocking at the door.

Eudes opened it so rapidly, Bella was taken aback and found herself stammering, "I—I'm—sorry, my lord, but I was wondering if you could spare your sister for a few minutes? My Lady of Karpas is very distraught and my lady of Caesarea asked me to see if Lady Eschiva would mind coming to help her."

Eudes raised his eyebrows and turned his head to look at his sister who was standing deeper inside the room. "If I may, Eudes?" she squeaked out in answer to his stare.

Eudes stepped back to let his sister exit, and then stood in the door and watched as Bella took her by the elbow and led her along the paved walkway around the inner courtyard. Only after they had turned the bend, did he close the door, and Bella spun on her new friend. "Are you alright?"

Eschiva stood very still, very composed, and yet she looked as if she would shatter if you blew on her too hard.

"Oh, Eschiva! What did he say?" Bella reached out and took both her hands.

"He said I should have stayed in the harem. He said I behaved like a 'hysterical fool' and that I had 'fewer brains than a peahen' and 'less sense than a canary.'"

"That's outrageous!" Bella declared indignantly, casting a glance through the arches of the arcade in the direction of the closed door. "Come, we must sit for a minute or two. Yvonne can wait!"

Eschiva seemed to have no will of her own, so Bella led her down a flight of stairs leading to the walled garden with the menagerie. There was a marble bench against the back wall of the palace, and here Bella sat herself down and pulled Eschiva beside her, putting her arm around Eschiva's waist as she did so.

"He's so angry with me, I think he would beat me if he was that sort of man," Eschiva declared unbidden. "He says I've made an enemy of the most powerful man on earth, that I've ruined his future, warning that we will both pay a heavy price."

"With no thought of what might have happened to you if you'd stayed? Is he utterly heartless?" Bella demanded rhetorically.

Eschiva responded as if the question had been serious. "I wonder that sometimes too. He seemed particularly outraged that I took passage on your brother's ship. This stupid old quarrel between the Montbéliards and the Ibelins!" Eschiva exclaimed indignantly while Bella caught her breath. She suspected that Eudes would have been less distressed if it had Beirut's ship, or even Baldwin's or Hugh's. It was probably Balian's reputation with women that distressed Eudes. Eschiva was innocently continuing, "He told me I was not to mention that to anyone. In fact, he told me I was not to breathe a word about my escape at all. I am to tell everyone that I returned because *he* sent for me, that I returned as a paying passenger on the next pilgrim ship."

Bella nodded and took a deep breath. "I suppose that is just as well. There is no need for anyone to know the danger you were in, or how you had to flee in the dark of night. Other people might react like your brother and see your flight as foolish rather than courageous."

Eschiva nodded numbly.

Bella took her hands. "Dear Eschiva, don't look so sad! The important thing is you are now *safe*, and we have become friends. Maybe you can come with me to visit our shared aunt, Aunt Alys? Wouldn't that be fun? I'm sure it would cheer her up to see her Ibelin and Montbéliard nieces are friends, don't you think?"

Ecshiva smiled faintly at that. "Yes, I suppose it would, although I hardly know her really."

"You'll like her!" Bella promised confidently, "but now we better hurry to poor Yvonne. Aunt Meg says she is in a terrible state after sitting with her husband through his surgery."

Eschiva nodded, and they got to their feet to hurry to the Lady of Karpas' chamber.

Yvonne had stripped out of her bloodstained surcoat and gown and sat in an armed chair wearing nothing but her shift. She started at the approach of the two maidens and hastened to wipe the tears away from her face. "I'm sorry, I'm sorry," she whispered in agitation.

"What are you sorry for?" Bella asked. "We just came to help you."

"I don't know," Yvonne gasped, looking about helplessly. "The Lady of Caesarea says I must come to the banquet, but I—I just—how can I be gracious and cheerful? Anseau will be scarred for life! The surgeon says one of the wounds came very close to taking out his eye. And he lost three teeth as well. He is in terrible pain. The surgeon had to give him opium."

Bella sank onto the floor at Yvonne's feet and laid her arms on her lap in a gesture that exuded sympathy and acceptance. When she spoke, her voice was like a lullaby, soft, melodic and soothing. "Your husband fought for Our Lord this day, and like all servants of the Lord he was tested before he was granted grace."

"He'll be scarred for life!" Yvonne repeated with a little sob.

"I know," Bella stroked her knee slowly. "And he wasn't very handsome to begin with. God *is* asking a lot of you." There was no reproach in Bella's voice.

"I *want* to be a good wife," Yvonne protested. "I *want* to love him. But—" she put her hands to her face, "if you had seen him."

"But it will get better." Eschiva, encouraged by Bella's example, stepped closer and laid a hand on Yvonne's shoulder. Bella smiled up at her in thanks. Eschiva assured Yvonne softly, "The stitches will help the skin heal in place."

Yvonne took an unsteady breath and lowered her hands. She looked from

Bella to Eschiva and back. "Thank you." She took a deep breath. "Thank you for listening to my tantrum. I know I should be grateful that I have such a powerful, rich and honorable husband. I shouldn't worry about how he *looks*."

"But that's only human!" Bella countered cheerfully. "God *made* beauty. He made it to give us joy, and he wants us to value it. The trick is in *seeing* beauty where it is hidden. I'm sure you will find Anseau attractive—if he gives you reason to."

"He's been very good to me," Yvonne hastened to assure them. "He's not the monster people say he is. He's always been very gentle with me." That sounded suspiciously defensive to Eschiva—the way Yolanda used to defend the Emperor Frederick.

A sharp knocking on the door made them all jump. "Girls?" It was the voice of the Lady of Caesarea. "Aren't you ready yet? It's time to go down to the hall."

Yvonne guiltily tried to rise, but Bella held her down. "Yvonne's not feeling well, Aunt Meg. I think she should stay here."

"No, Bella. Precisely because the Lord of Karpas cannot accept the honors himself, his lady must represent him. Hurry and help her to dress. I'm going ahead."

"It's alright," Yvonne assured the two maidens. "I can manage, particularly if you stay near me."

"Of course we will," Bella and Eschiva answered in unison.

By the time they made it down to the hall, the first course had already been served in a room overflowing with guests. Although musicians were playing from a gallery, they could hardly be heard over the thousand conversations of the diners. Pages and squires were having difficulty squeezing between the benches to replace empty pitchers of wine and water. Even on the dais, the chairs were so close together the squires could barely pour the wine over the guests' shoulders.

King Henry sat in the middle, of course, with the Lady of Caesarea on one side of him and an empty chair on the other. Beirut sat next to the empty chair, while Caesarea was beside his wife. On the far ends of the table sat the two elected baillies of Jerusalem: Balian de Sidon, Beirut's nephew by his other sister, and Eudes de Montbéliard, Eschiva's brother. Between the ballies in a quartet around the king were the Masters of the Temple and Hospital, the Archbishop of Nicosia, and the Bishop of Limassol. Such a battery of churchmen would have been intimidating under any circumstances, but these four men also looked uncannily similar.

"The Montaigu brothers," Bella commented with a sigh. "It's rare to see them all together in one place."

"Unlike your brothers," Eschiva noted, her eyes quickly locating the four Ibelin brothers at one of the lower tables.

The Lady of Caesarea was gesturing the girls forward. Yvonne quailed. "There's an empty seat between the Lord of Beirut and the king. You don't think...."

"I'm afraid so. It's the seat of honor, meant for your husband, but you will have to fill it," Bella concluded.

Yvonne knew she had no choice. She continued forward, but her misery dulled her natural beauty. "Don't worry," Bella whispered, squeezing her hand in encouragement. "King Henry's great fun. He's just as unhappy about being up there with the dour Montaigus as you are. Makes jokes about them and you'll have a friend for life."

Yvonne looked at Bella scandalized.

"I'm serious. King Henry will be grateful to you, and you never know when a king's gratitude may come in useful."

They reached the foot of the dais, and Yvonne mounted the steps as if she were mounting a scaffold to her execution.

"I *do* feel sorry for her," Bella murmured to Eschiva.

"So do I," Eschiva answered, and then found Sir Hugh d'Ibelin at her elbow.

"We've been looking all over for you!" he told them in an exasperated tone. "We've practically had to *kill* people to keep your seats free. Come this way!" He pulled her toward the table with his brothers.

As they approached, Sir Philip de Novare jumped up and, with a dramatic bow, gestured for Eschiva to step over the bench to sit beside Sir Balian. Bella went around to the other side to sit between her brothers Baldwin and Johnny.

No sooner had Eschiva's seat touched the bench than Sir Balian was offering her a goblet of wine. Their eyes met over the rim of the silver chalice, and Eschiva inexplicably felt herself blushing. "Turquoise is your color," she heard him say despite all the noise around them. "It brings out the blue in your eyes."

Bella frowned at her brother and hissed, "Balian! Stop it!" in a reproving tone.

Eschiva stammered in embarrassment, "It was your grandmother's dress." His scrutiny was making her very nervous. He was bound to find all her faults, she thought, looking down and straightening her skirts.

"She was a great beauty, you know. Even in her old age, she was beautiful."

"Why do you men always stress beauty over everything else?" Bella chided from the other side of the table. "Grandma's beauty wasn't what made her admirable, but her political acumen, her financial savvy, and her unwavering loyalty to grandpa."

Balian laughed. "You're right, as always, Bella, but beauty never hurts." He cast a conspiratorial glance at Eschiva as he spoke—as if he found her beautiful. Before Eschiva had decided what to make of this remark, Balian matter-of-factly turned his attention to the slab of meat on his plate, sawed it in half, and stabbed a large portion with the tip of his knife to shift it to Eschiva's plate. "Here!" he remarked, "you missed the first serving, and it could be hours before the next course arrives."

"And what about me?" Bella asked, looking from Baldwin to Johnny.

"Oh, you're fat enough already," Johnny told her bluntly, before shoveling another chunk of meat into his own mouth.

"Johnny!" His elder brothers exclaimed in unison. Baldwin added, "Mind your manners!" Hugh warned, "You don't *say* things like that to ladies."

"Bella's not a lady, she's my sister," Johnny defended himself.

Balian glanced at Eschiva to see her reaction and when their eyes met they burst out laughing.

Annoyed by his brother's laughter, Johnny added, "Besides, she's going to be a nun, so she doesn't care about her looks. At least that's what she *says*."

"No, I don't care about my *looks*, but I *am* hungry," Bella retorted, evidently not at all offended. She took her own knife, stabbed the largest piece of meat on Johnny's plate, and pulled it on to her own—provoking a squawk of protests from her youngest brother and laughs from the others.

"You see, that's what I like in a woman," Balian declared still laughing, "courage and initiative. I think passive women are boring." He glanced significantly at Eschiva, only to receive a kick under the table from Bella. Eschiva understood what was going on: Balian was 'charming her' the way he did all the ladies, and Bella was trying to protect her from disappointment by warning off her brother.

They were interrupted by the arrival of the next course, platters loaded with sizzling mushrooms and artichokes with melted cheese on top. Balian quickly cut away a portion for Eschiva, and then himself before his siblings had a chance. Hugh graciously served Bella, while Baldwin noticed the wine pitcher was empty and held it up to signal to one of the squires.

His gesture drew attention away from their immediate circle for a moment, and Eschiva noted that her brother was glaring at them. As Eschiva watched, the Archbishop of Nicosia leaned over and addressed Eudes earnestly, drawing his attention away from the Ibelins. The Archbishop was intent on introducing another man, who had mounted the dais, to Eudes.

Balian had followed Eschiva's gaze and now asked generally, "Who's that?"

Novare could be trusted to know everyone. "Gerard de Montaigu," he identified him readily. Adding, "the mysterious nephew of the Formidable Four."

"What do you mean 'mysterious'?" Baldwin challenged Novare at once. "There's nothing mysterious about him. He's the son of their elder brother, recently arrived from Aragon."

"Yes, but that's *exactly* what's mysterious!" Novare countered. "As the son of the elder brother he stands to inherit the family estates in Aragon, surely?"

"Maybe he's the second son," Baldwin countered.

"Why is he wearing black?" Eschiva asked, as always sensitive to color.

"For his wife, the mother of the small son he brought with him."

"Did his wife die in childbed?" Bella asked quickly.

"Apparently not, but there was something fishy about what happened. He's come out under a cloud of some sort."

"He certainly looks as sour as the rest of the clan," Hugh concluded.

"A man who's just lost his wife has the right to look sober, I think," Bella reminded her brothers.

"Sober, yes, but not like he just swallowed a lemon whole! I ran into him earlier and you would think he'd invented piety," Hugh defended himself.

"Maybe he's come to atone for some sin?" Johnny suggested. "A lot of people come out here to do that, although I don't know *why*, since Jerusalem is in Saracen hands."

"You can still travel there as a pilgrim," Baldwin pointed out.

"Unarmed and with a Saracen escort?" Johnny asked, incredulous. "Who'd want to do that?!"

"Lots of people do it," Baldwin reminded him.

"Idiots!" Johnny scoffed, then brightened as he turned to Eschiva and asked, "Did you see the Emperor's army? Do you think it's big enough to re-capture Jerusalem?"

His elder brothers jumped on him at once, with Balian saying size wasn't the only thing that mattered, and Hugh pointing out it hadn't assembled before Eschiva departed.

The wine they had ordered arrived, and shortly afterward the next course. The conversation turned to the judicial combat and the terms the Lord of Beirut had extracted from the participants. Barlais, Balian reported, had been fined heavily, "but the thing that offended him most, I think, was that he had to forfeit his loyal destrier."

"But that's normal," Johnny remarked to show off his understanding of these things.

"Forfeiture may be normal, but that was no normal destrier. I think it may have been unwise to insist on it," Balian noted. "Father would have let Barlais substitute a cash payment, but the Lord of Karpas absolutely refused. He'd lost so much blood by that point that he was swaying on his feet and about to swoon, but he refused to end the combat unless he had the horse. Father gave in so Karpas could be treated by the surgeon."

"Barlais didn't look particularly grateful for his life," Hugh remarked.

"Where is he now?" Baldwin asked, looking around the room superficially; there were far too many people to see everyone.

"He's fled again, of course!" Johnny answered, pleased to know more than his elder brothers. "Cheneché and Bethsan helped him on another horse, and with Gibelet and Rivet in tow, they rode out of Nicosia for Kyrenia."

"No doubt he is going to try to intercept the Emperor and fill his ear with complaints against our father—again," Balian concluded bitterly.

"But Father stopped Karpas from killing him! He'd be dead if Father hadn't intervened," Johnny protested.

"That's not the point," Novare tried to explain. "The Emperor is looking for excuses to discredit your father."

"That's what Balian has been saying," Baldwin retorted, "but it doesn't make sense."

"It doesn't have to make sense!" Balian flared, provoked by Baldwin's tone. "I heard him threaten us with my own ears!"

"You have an overactive imagination, Bal! If I—"

"Don't fight!" Bella admonished. "Father is looking our way!"

Balian and Baldwin composed themselves instantly. Baldwin even turned in his seat to wave to their father. The Lord of Beirut nodded his head in acknowledgement and then resumed his conversation with the Templar Master.

Unfortunately, Eudes' attention had also been drawn to them, and this time he excused himself to descend from the dais and came straight to Eschiva. He reached her side, took her elbow and bowed to the others as he announced, "You will forgive me. I must introduce my sister to the good Gerard de Montaigu." As he spoke, he pulled her up by the elbow.

Eschiva, taken by surprise, had a hard time getting to her feet. Both Balian and Novare jumped up to help her climb over the bench. Her eyes met Balian's for only a second. He seemed alarmed for her, but there was nothing he could do.

Eudes was hurrying her away. "Have you no shame?" he hissed in her ear. "It's bad enough that you took ship with Sir Balian! There's no need for you to throw yourself at him in public. He's a known seducer. If I find out you have slept with him, I'll see you locked away for the rest of your life! How can you disgrace me like this! Not to mention our father's memory."

Eschiva stopped in her tracks and jerked her arm free. "I have *not* slept with Sir Balian! How dare you insult *me*!"

"I've been watching you make public love to him all evening!"

They stared at one another. Eschiva felt the fury of the helpless. She had not so much as kissed Sir Balian, yet she would have been lying to say she had not fallen in love with him. Anything she said in her defense, however, would be held against her. To say he had offered her refuge when she needed it most would only provoke her brother into reminding her that she should not have fled from the harem in the first place. To say he had been hospitable since, would surely make her brother impute base motives to Sir Balian.

Eudes took her silence for either submission or an admission of guilt. Lifting his head and closing his eyes he announced, "I hope you now understand. I have been talking to the good Archbishop of Nicosia and we are agreed that you would make an admirable wife for his bereaved nephew."

"What?" Eschiva gasped. Things were happening too fast.

"His nephew is a widower with a sickly son. He needs a wife," Eudes intoned pompously, taking Eschiva by the elbow again, and guiding her through the crowds. Around them people laughed, chatted, argued and continued to enjoy the feast, oblivious to the private drama of the Montbéliards.

As they squeezed between the rows of revelers, Eudes hissed into Eschiva's ear, "*I* need the support of the Montaigus. Do you understand me? *You* marry Gerard, and *I* get the backing of *both* the Hospitallers and the Templars. It's the best, maybe the only, way to ensure your *stupidity* back in Andria does not hurt my position here."

Part III

The Curious Crusade of
Frederick Hohenstaufen
1228-1229

Chapter Twelve
The Overlord of Cyprus

Nicosia, Kingdom of Cyprus
July 18, 1228

"Balian! Hurry!" Philip de Novare called to his friend from the steps leading up from the stable courtyard at the back of the Royal Palace at Nicosia.

Balian jumped down from his lathered stallion and flung the reins over the neck to hand them off to a royal groom with the words, "Walk him out for at least twenty minutes before you water him. I've ridden him hard all the way from Limassol. My squire wasn't able to keep up, but should be here soon." Then he bounded up the stairs two at a time to reach Novare.

As Balian reached Philip, the latter exclaimed, "Your father has called the barons and leading knights together for a meeting with the King. He said he couldn't wait for you to arrive. The Cypriot feudal levees have been flooding in. We're only missing a score or two of the full five hundred knights. Your father has been asking about you every half hour."

"I was in Limassol when the Emperor arrived. He came with just over twenty ships," Balian explained in agitation, adding with disgusted anger, "and most were filled with clerics, scholars and—"

"Come! Tell your father! The Emperor sent a personal letter, which is why he's called this meeting. He—"

"Philip, listen to me!" Balian stopped. He was breathing hard from the ride and bounding up the steps. "There were not more than 200 knights with him! Instead of fighting men, he brought four archbishops, scores of bookworms, and—you wouldn't believe it—Barlais, Cheneché and Gibelet!"

"We'd suspected that was where they went when they fled Cyprus," Philip agreed with a shrug.

"Philip, I don't mean they are just taking part in this crusade, I mean they were with the *Emperor*. Personally. They travelled on his ship and when I saw them they were immediately beside him. Barlais was still limping a little, but he was speaking into the Emperor's ear, commenting on every man who met the Emperor on the quay. I swear to you—"

"You don't have to convince *me* of anything, Bal. Come and tell your father." Philip took Balian by his elbow and pulled him up the final stairs and through one of the back doors. Both men were familiar with the palace and made their way with ease through the maze of corridors from the stable courtyard toward the large representational rooms at the front. Built originally by the Greek despot Isaac Comnenus, the palace had been expanded and modernized in the last two decades by the Lusignans. Visitors from the West were particularly awed by the many clocks, the extensive baths, the exotic plants both in pots and in the gardens, and by the menagerie, the latter a project undertaken by Philip d'Ibelin largely because it delighted his child king so much. Novare and Sir Balian, however, had seen it all before and had no time to notice the marble facing the walls or the bright tiles they trod heavily with their spurred boots.

"They're in the council chamber," Novare explained, turning away from the massive doors that gave access to the official throne room in which the King of Cyprus received foreign dignitaries, dispensed justice or met with the High Court. They continued down the hall to the next door and entered without knocking.

The council chamber was a square room with a high, rib-vaulted ceiling and a large table in the center. The King sat in a slightly higher chair with a baldachin bearing the arms of Cyprus over it; it faced a balcony overlooking the main street below. On a hot day like this, the balcony doors had been opened to let in the light breeze, and the air carried the sound of traffic and street vendors from the street below.

The council chamber was crowded. In addition to the King, his baillie and constable, the Archbishop of Nicosia and two of his suffragan bishops sat at the table along with a dozen Cypriot barons. As a result, all the chairs were full and the younger men stood against the wall. Balian's attention was drawn briefly to the Lord of Karpas, whose face was still swollen and discolored from the wounds he had sustained in the judicial combat. Although the stitches had been removed, the skin along the edge of the gashes was slightly inflamed. He next noted his brothers Baldwin and Hugh, who were both standing along with their cousin, Walter of Caesarea the younger. Baldwin cast him a reproachful and Hugh a relieved glance.

The Lord of Beirut interrupted himself at the sight of his eldest son and nodded to him. "I'm glad you made it, Sir Balian. Perhaps, before I continue you would be so kind as to report on the Emperor's arrival at Limassol?"

"Yes, my lord." Balian could sense his father's tension although it was well disguised under an apparently calm exterior. He endeavored to deliver a clear, concise and sober report, knowing this was what his father expected. "The Emperor put into Limassol with just 23 ships, less than half of which were galleys. I was told, but cannot confirm, that a larger number of ships under the command of his Marshal, a certain Richard Filangeri, the Teutonic Knights under their Master Herman von Salza, and a number of German nobles proceeded direct to Acre. If true, his total fleet still does not exceed seventy ships. I was told that the part of the fleet that went to Acre included the bulk of his horse transports, while four ships belonging to Demetrius de Montferrat, King of Salonica, and another two belonging to Manfred II, Marquis of Lancia joined the Imperial fleet and are now in Acre."

This brought a murmur from the men gathered around the table; some seemed satisfied, others less so.

"Of the men travelling with the emperor," Balian continued anxiously, "the majority—seriously—are from the Emperor's personal household. I couldn't count more than 200, maybe 250 knights, and about 1,000 archers. Instead of fighting men, the Emperor brought *four* archbishops—all Sicilians, the archbishops of Palermo, Capua, Bari and Reggio."

"And all in violation of the Pope's express command!" The Archbishop of Nicosia pointed out.

"Even four archbishops don't take up more than four ships!" the Lord of Karpas protested. "What else did he have with him?"

Balian smiled at the "leopard," grateful for the question. "The Emperor appears to be accompanied by a large number of scholars, masters of various sciences, his falconers, of course, and Sirs Gauvain de Cheneché and Amaury Barlais—"

The Lord of Karpas reared up in his seat with an outraged growl. "HOW DARE HE!" He spun on Beirut. "I warned you, my lord! I warned you! That man will never be reconciled. He covets control of Cyprus for himself."

"My lord of Karpas, please," Beirut answered with a calming gesture. "The Emperor of the Romans has mustered an army to re-capture Jerusalem. We can hardly blame Barlais for wanting to join in such a great and holy undertaking."

"Barlais doesn't give a tinker's damn about Jerusalem!" Karpas snarled back.

"My lords, listen to me," Balian pleaded. "When I saw Barlais, he was directly beside the Emperor providing a running commentary as men came forward to be introduced. That's not the action of a man intent on fighting for the Holy Land, but rather of a man intent on poisoning the Emperor's mind."

"What did I tell you?" Karpas insisted with a grateful nod to Balian.

Beirut ignored Karpas and looked at his son instead. Their eyes locked. Balian was sure there was a conspiracy against them and that Barlais was behind it, but his father refused to see the danger. The look his father gave him, however, was more probing than he had expected. It was almost as if his father was beginning to understand.

"My lords." Beirut broke eye contact with his son and addressed the others around the table. "I wish to share with you a letter I received from the Holy Roman Emperor by herald earlier today. May I, my lord?" Beirut turned to the King for permission to proceed.

King Henry nodded impatiently, and answered, "Of course!"

Beirut unfolded a letter that had lain before him on the table. He smoothed it unnecessarily, and began to read in a studiously monotone and emotionless voice:

"From the feared Caesar, Roman Emperor, King of Germany, Lombardy, Tuscany, Calabria, Sicily and Jerusalem—"

"Not any more, he's not!" Karpas protested.

Beirut gestured for the grizzled baron to calm down and tried to find his place.

"Frederick. Greetings my lord and very honored Uncle. The present will serve to inform you of our arrival at Limassol in passing on our way to Palestine, for the purpose of assisting the servitors of Jesus Christ, and to tell you that before our departure for that country we desire to have the satisfaction of seeing you with the king." Beirut paused to bow his head to King Henry. *"And your children, all our dear and well beloved cousins, that we may have the pleasure of embracing you—"*

"In a death-grip!" Karpas threw in with a snort.

Beirut frowned at him, and continued,

"and of knowing you personally. We desire moreover to consult with you as to the conduct which we should pursue for the recovery of the Holy Land, esteeming infinitely your advice and the counsels of a man so sage and experienced—"

"I'm going to puke," Karpas growled.

This brought a flurry of rebukes from several men, who insisted that the Emperor was only saying what they all knew to be true.

"That's not the point!" Karpas protested. "This is false flattery and it stinks!"

"My lord of Karpas is right, my lord," Balian jumped in, thankful for the big man's bluntness. "You always told us to beware of anyone who praised us to our face. You said, 'when people start telling you how clever or how brave you are, don't listen; they want something from you.'"

"Balian's right," Hugh chimed in. "You taught us that flatterers insult our intelligence."

Beirut's eyes shifted from one son to the other, and then with a nod and a faint smile, he remarked, "Well said. Both of you. Now let me continue reading the Emperor's letter. Where was I? Ah, yes, here:

> '... so sage and experienced as you, and persuaded that the alliance which exists between us should make you take part in the happy success of our enterprise. It is for this that we pray you come at once to Limassol, since the urgency of our affairs does not permit us to make a prolonged sojourn here. Your very affectionate nephew, Frederick, Emperor."

The Lord of Beruit laid the letter back onto the table in front of him and again smoothed it with his hand. There was stunned silence around the table, and several of the barons looked at each other with frowns of confusion, but no one knew exactly what was expected of them or what to say.

It was the young king who broke the awkward silence. "It seems a very nice letter. Isn't it?" King Henry sensed from the reactions of the others that something was wrong with the letter, he just couldn't tell what it was.

"Indeed, it is polite in tone," Beirut agreed solemnly to his king, adding "but I would have been much happier if it had been addressed to you."

"Lies! Flattery and lies!" Karpas interrupted in alarm.

Caesarea too felt it was necessary to warn, "John, be careful! This wouldn't be the first time the Hohenstaufen has put fine words to paper while behaving quite differently. Have you forgotten the promises he made to King John? The marriage contract was explicit about John remaining King for his lifetime, with full powers of action and access to the royal treasury. The Hohenstaufen didn't even wait for the marriage to be consummated before he dismissed Brienne—an anointed king—as if he were nothing better than a stable boy!"

To Balian's relief, several at the table nodded and agreed. The Archbishop of Nicosia added, "And don't forget the man is excommunicate! We should not be 'embracing him' in joy!"

"Just what do you suppose Barlais and Cheneché have been telling the Emperor since they joined his household?" Caesarea asked. "We know they left Cyprus after the judicial duel in a state of belligerent resentment. Barlais was heard insisting that he could still have won, if only you had not interceded."

"Damned lying fool!" Karpas bellowed furiously, his face so red with fury that his unhealed wounds looked ready to burst open again.

"No one is suggesting he's right," Caesarea assured the outraged combatant. "I'm only trying to picture what he's been telling the Emperor."

"It's not just that." Balian felt that since the others had spoken out against the Emperor that he too could risk it. Directing himself to the king, Balian reported, "Even before Barlais and Cheneché reached him, the Emperor accused Lord Philip of embezzling from the royal treasury, my lord."

"That's a lie!" King Henry blurted out, tears flooding his eyes. He loved Lord Philip and missed him terribly. Beirut was nice, but not the same. Lord Philip had been his friend.

"As I was about to tell you, my lord, before being interrupted," Beirut glanced reproachfully at the Lord of Karpas, "not all things are what they seem. I have summoned your principal barons and the worthy bishops to hear their advice. Shall we see what they say?"

King Henry nodded vigorously, swallowing down his tears and trying to get his emotions in hand.

Beirut turned back to the men collected around the table. "Is there any among you here who thinks I should follow the emperor's summons, taking my sons and my sovereign with me to meet him in Limassol?"

Dead silence answered him, until Nicosia repeated, "The man is excommunicate, my lord. We should all keep our distance from him."

"And what of Jerusalem?" Beirut retorted.

"We could proceed independently," someone from the lower end of the table ventured. Balian looked over too late to see who had made this sensible suggestion, but it received a rumble of approval from around the table—except from his father.

Silence fell again as men registered that Beirut remained mute. They waited perplexed. Beirut was usually a decisive man; now he sat staring at the letter.

The Lord of Karpas lost patience first. "Damn it, Beirut! You know the Emperor can't be trusted! You know Barlais is a conniving weasel trying to wrench the regency out of your hands! If this were about the crusade, the Hohenstaufen would have told King Henry where to muster his troops for a joint campaign, and been done with it. That letter—" he gestured toward it contemptuously "— is nothing but a transparent attempt to get you off your guard so he can throw you in the nearest dungeon and seize control of the king and the royal treasury for his own purposes."

A buzz of anxious discussion greeted this statement. While not all those present shared Karpas' harsh assessment, they agreed that it *was* odd the Emperor had not addressed King Henry, and it *was* odd that the Hohenstaufen was more intent on 'embracing his cousins' than mustering his troops. Something, they agreed, wasn't right about that letter—precisely because of its slimy tone of flattery. Gradually, Balian noted with relief, consensus formed around a "polite but evasive answer" that avoided actually attending on the emperor in Limassol.

"We could say we've mustered our troops and transports in Kyrenia," Caesarea pointed out. "It's true enough. Tell the Emperor that we will join him in Palestine—without King Henry." He bowed to the King as he added this. "We want you to stay safe here, my lord," he explained.

This suggestion met with a rumble of approval, and Balian was about to heave a sigh of relief when he noticed his father was shaking his head and lifting his hand for silence.

"I appreciate that all of you advised me loyally," he looked significantly at Caesarea, Karpas and Balian, "and with concern for my welfare, but I would rather be arrested or even slain than for someone to say that I placed more value on my personal safety than on the cause of Christ. I do not want men to say of me that 'the Emperor of the Romans came from across the sea with a great host and would have freed the Holy Land—but the Lord of Beirut loved the Saracens better than the Christians.' I do not want it said that because I was not willing to serve the Emperor of the Romans, the sites of Christ's passion could not be recovered." He paused and looked at the men gathered around the table one after the other. "Is there any among you who would risk that being said of *you?*"

"Damn it, Beirut," Karpas started, but he stopped himself. He met Beirut's eyes, and recognized he had no hope of changing Beirut's mind. He shook his head and warned instead. "You're going to regret this!" He then cast a significant glance at Balian as if urging him to speak up.

Beirut also looked to his eldest son, and in his eyes was a sharp warning to keep his mouth shut. Balian recognized the look. His father was demanding his absolute and unconditional support. From the time he was old enough to speak, he had learned to respect that look. The rules of the family were simple: they could disagree among themselves and even with their father in private, but not in public. Balian clamped his jaw together and held his thoughts inside.

"So." Beirut turned to his king. "My lord, I recommend that we proceed with all our knights, sergeants and archers to Limassol to join the Emperor's host. Are you agreed?"

King Henry looked to Caesarea and then to Karpas and finally to Balian, as if looking for contradiction. When none came, he nodded with evident uncertainty. "If you really think that is best, my lord."

"There is no risk to you, my lord. The anger of Barlais and Cheneché is directed at me and mine. Any action will be against my house, not yours."

King Henry sat straighter in his over-sized chair and lifted his chin. "Lord Philip was the closest thing to a father that I ever knew, my lord. I will not let his memory be sullied!" His tone, although meant to be firm and decisive, sounded somewhat petulant in someone so young.

Beirut met his king's eyes and told him solemnly. "That means more to me than I can say, my lord. I thank you."

"We will all go to Limassol," King Henry declared, "but we will not set aside our mourning for Lord Philip, and I won't let anyone treat me like a puppet or a pawn."

"Won't any of you support me in this?" Balian demanded of his siblings furiously as soon as they were alone together. "The Emperor intends to humiliate and ruin our father! He told me to my face that he would hold him accountable for Uncle Philip 'plundering' the royal Cypriot treasury—and that was *before* Barlais started filling his ear with further lies."

"That's what you keep saying, but the Emperor's letter spoke a very different message," Baldwin pointed out in an annoyed tone.

"Didn't you hear what everyone in there was saying?" Balian countered incredulously. "*Everyone* agreed the letter was suspicious! The Emperor's letters have more often been filled with lies than truth! He lied to King John, he lied to the Pope, he lied to the Lombard League, he lied to the German princes! His reign is a catalogue of broken promises. Starting with a crusading vow that he's deferred so many times I lost track! The Patriarch of Jerusalem warned against any association with the Hohenstaufen."

"Don't let yourself get dragged into Church affairs, Bal," Hugh advised. "The Emperor's dispute with the papacy has nothing to do with us. The Pope tried to stop this crusade even though it's the best chance we've had of regaining Jerusalem since Richard the Lionheart went home."

"That's not the point," Balian argued. "You've got to understand how often

Frederick has *said* one thing and *done* the opposite! If this is supposed to be a crusade, why the hell did the Holy Roman Emperor bring more scholars and clerics than fighting men? Why did he bring his harem?"

"Oh, come on!" Baldwin rolled his eyes. "You don't have to lower yourself to repeating convent-girl gossip!"

"Damn it, Baldwin!" Balian lashed out at his brother furiously. "I *saw* them with my own eyes!"

"Really? Harem girls?" Hugh pricked up his ears and looked like a bird-dog ready to pounce. "*I'd* like to see them."

"They were veiled, of course," Balian tossed at Hugh, deflating his interest a little, "but there were about a dozen of them. Furthermore, they were escorted off one of Fredrick's ships by a score of *Mamlukes*—probably eunuchs—in turbans and Saracen sashes. I could hardly believe my eyes so I asked one of the sailors about them. He told me they were Sicilian Muslims who served the Emperor as his personal bodyguard—and the body guard of his harem it seems—just like our cousin Eschiva tried to tell us. This is *not* a man who is the least bit serious about a crusade! He's here for no other purpose than to exert his authority over us—the lords of Cyprus and Jerusalem! You've got to believe me!" Balian was starting to feel desperate.

"*I* agree with you, Balian," Bella spoke up, startling her brothers. "Frederick isn't much of a fighter, but he's obsessed with his power and position."

"Just what makes *you*, of all people, an expert on the Holy Roman Emperor?" Baldwin wanted to know.

"I'm the one who talked to cousin Eschiva most, and *she* spent three years at his court." Bella told him bluntly, staring him down.

"Eschiva? You should have heard the way her brother talked about her! She's not a reliable witness," Baldwin said dismissively, earning the immediate ire of both Balian and Bella.

Balian rose to Eschiva's defense "She's a far more reliable witness than Eudes is! Eudes is so wrapped up in his own importance and self-interest he wouldn't be able to see a rabid dog if it was standing three feet in front of him."

Bella insisted belligerently, "Eschiva is very perceptive and intelligent, and she saw the callous and cold-blooded way Frederick treated his *bride*—which is why all that talk about 'dear and well beloved cousins,' and 'affectionate' feelings for Papa is fake. Think about it, Baldwin! Why on earth would the Emperor want Papa to bring 'his children' with him on crusade? He seemed far more interested in us than in the King—which is very suspicious."

"We happen to be some of the best knights—" Hugh started to point out.

"Spare me!" Bella cut him off. "The Emperor didn't say 'adult sons' or 'knighted sons,' he said 'your children,'—which, by the way, included Johnny and Guy and me!"

"And *you* will stay right here in Nicosia with the King's sisters," John of Beirut ordered firmly, coming into the room and bringing his sons to their feet respectfully.

"Father, we need to talk," Balian declared at once, only to break off when his father shook his head.

"Balian, I know what you think and feel. You've told me often enough already."

"Father, listen to me! Frederick is surrounded by Muslims and Jews."

"And four archbishops," his father reminded him.

"Four *Sicilian* Archbishops, who are about as spirited as donkeys!"

"Balian! Please! I don't like to hear you talk that way about princes of the Church. Calm down, and listen to me instead. We don't need to discuss it again because this letter gave your suspicions more credence than anything more you could say. Bella, sharp as she is," Beirut smiled at his daughter with genuine pride, "put her finger on it. This insistence on me bringing my children is alarming. You and Hugh are also right: the letter reeks of nauseating flattery. His assurances of affection for the 'uncle' of a bride he treated hardly better than a slave girl ring very hollow indeed. I do not believe for a moment that the Emperor intends to seek my advice much less honor me in any way." He paused to let his words sink in, and Balian was humbled by his father's clear understanding of the situation.

"That said, I was not being melodramatic when I said I would rather die than be accused of undermining this crusade. Your grandfather spent his entire life in the service of Jerusalem. He gave *everything* for Jerusalem—offering his own freedom to ransom the poor. I, in contrast, have done nothing but enrich myself. I have rebuilt a city and built a splendid palace. By the grace of God, I have six fine children, and have seen them educated and outfitted in the most lavish manner possible. I am one of the wealthiest and most powerful men this side of the sea. Many men in Outremer follow my lead and my example. If I fail to respond to the Emperor's summons, then men will be right to say that I am nothing but a wealthy, ambitious and self-serving man."

"But he's hardly brought any troops himself!" Balian protested again.

"All the more reason that we must come with our full strength," his father countered. "You," he looked to Balian, but then included Bella and Hugh, "however, are right that there is good reason to doubt the Emperor's intentions. So we must all be on the alert, but the men of the House of Ibelin will go to meet the Emperor, while Bella remains here. Understood?" He looked from one child to the other, receiving a "Yes, my lord," from all his children.

Limassol, Kingdom of Cyprus
July 21, 1228

Frederick Hohenstaufen made himself as comfortable as possible in the Cypriot throne. Although they had closed the shutters over the windows facing the sun, the heat still beat against that side of the building and the air hardly stirred. It didn't help that the audience chamber was full of people already. Frederick sweated beneath his robes of state and wished himself in a cool bath with one of his slave girls languidly lying half in and half out. He was glad he'd brought his harem with him. They were a very useful distraction from all the tedious—

"Gerard de Montaigu," the herald announced.

Frederick sat up a little straighter and narrowed his eyes. "Any relative of the Grand Masters of the Temple and Hospital?" he asked Amaury Barlais without turning his head. Barlais stood directly behind him along with two trusted advisors, the Archbishops of Palermo and Capua.

"Yes, Your Excellency, a nephew. He also recently wed the sister of the baillie of Jerusalem, Eudes de Montbéliard."

Frederick raised his eyebrows and twisted in the throne to look squarely at Barlais. The Cypriot seemed oblivious to the fact that the little bitch had openly defied him and left Cyprus without his permission—not to mention poisoning the harem eunuch. Had she run away because she wanted to marry this man? He turned back to watch her husband approach the throne.

The solemn man hardly seemed like the type to capture a maiden's heart, Frederick thought. He was dressed in black with a large silver cross around his neck. Frederick judged him to be about forty with dark, thinning hair, a thin face with a fringe beard, and not a trace of a smile as he bowed deeply. Although dressed in black armor, he seemed frailer than most knights. A bookish man, Frederick judged, or perhaps a religious fanatic? "Your excellency," Montagu dutifully addressed the Emperor.

"Monsieur de Montaigu, we understand that you are to be congratulated on a recent marriage," Frederick remarked with a leering smile. "The bride was in the service of our late Empress. We have vague memories of her, although, we confess, she did not impress us overly much. A mousy creature of ordinary appearance, if we are not mistaken."

"Indeed, your excellency. The description fits her well."

"Were you betrothed long?"

"No, Your Excellency. I only recently arrived in the East to join your crusade."

"We welcome your support, Monsieur. Do you have many men under your banner?"

"I hope to raise a number of knights, sergeants and archers from my wife's estates."

"Excellent." Frederick nodded his head in dismissal, and Montaigu backed away.

"Eudes de Montbéliard," the herald intoned.

Frederick raised his eyebrows. He had met Montbéliard already at the quay when he landed. He had been decidedly nervous then and seemed downright agitated now. The baillie hastened through the crowd to go down on one knee. "Your Excellency! I just wanted to warn you." He lifted his head and spoke in the direction of the Emperor with his eyes shielded by his lids. Frederick could see his eyeballs shifting about under the skin of his eyelids nervously. A very strange affectation, Frederick thought, surely indicative of profound inner insecurity. "The King of Cyprus, surrounded by Ibelins and their friends, has just ridden in," Montbéliard announced. "They will be here shortly."

"Excellent," Frederick answered sitting up straighter. He was looking forward to this confrontation.

"Do you wish me to stand near you?" Montbéliard asked.

Frederick glanced at Barlais and dismissed him with a flick of his fingers. "Leave us, Sir Amaury. Montbéliard will take your place for this interview."

Barlais drew a deep breath as if to protest, but bowed instead and dutifully withdrew with a murmured, "Your Excellency."

Montbéliard took his place just in time. With a fanfare, the King of Cyprus was announced.

The young king, dressed completely in black but wearing his crown, entered the throne room. As he advanced up the length of the room, people successively went down on one knee like a wave rolling along a beach. Eventually, everyone was kneeling except the men of his entourage in his wake, and the Holy Roman Emperor. The latter was standing politely.

Henry de Lusignan was a pretty, blond boy, neither fat nor thin, and not particularly tall but poised beyond his years. Poised or passive? Frederick concluded that Barlais was right: the boy was a puppet of the men behind him—Beirut and Caesarea. The latter two men were of similar age, both in armor, but rather than wearing surcoats with their arms so he could distinguish between them, they were dressed in black mourning surcoats. The fact that they, by chance or intent, walked in step underlined the fact that they were kinsmen and allies. Frederick frowned and hissed to Montbéliard, "Which one is Beirut?"

"On your left, your excellency, the King's right."

Frederick focused on Beirut. He had been suspicious of Ibelin ambitions ever since they crowned King Henry at the age of eight in an obvious ploy to undermine his authority as overlord of Cyprus. The stories Barlais and Cheneché had told him since, however, had reinforced his low opinion. This man was grasping, overweening and unscrupulous. He was the kind of nobleman who undermined royal authority and tried to build up his own clients and power-base. Indeed, he was the kind of nobleman who denied the divine source of royal power altogether and saw kings as little more than "first among equals." Frederick hated him for that. Noblemen such as these were his worst enemies among the German princes, too.

Frederick also noted that Beirut was tall, robust, yet sleek, like an athlete. His hair was thick and dark with dramatic accents of grey in his eyebrows and sideburns. His hair was cut comparatively short, and the baron was clean shaven. Altogether he was strikingly handsome for a mature man, with eyes that met Frederick's unflinchingly. Surprisingly, however, he was modestly dressed. Frederick had not expected that. In his experience, men puffed up with their own importance tended toward extravagance of dress. Take 'his Holiness' Gregory IX, for example, Frederick thought sourly. He wore rings on all eight fingers and both thumbs as well. He also favored gold brocade robes and reeked of perfume. A thoroughly disgusting man!

Beirut, Frederick reluctantly admitted, was impressive. It wasn't just his imposing figure, but his brother-in-law and three adult sons. They followed him dressed in the same severe black as the young King. They looked lethal in black, he conceded—even that stupid little ass who'd come to Andria with the news of Philip d'Ibelin's death.

Frederick narrowed his eyes and he bit down on his teeth as he temporarily focused on Sir Balian. He would have liked to arrest that cad here and now for the murder of two sailors in Andria harbor, but aside from the fact that he had no evidence, it would only disrupt his more important plans.

Frederick forced his lips into a smile and stepped down from the dais to embrace King Henry. "Beloved brother!" he exclaimed. "What a pleasure to embrace you at last!"

King Henry flushed and tried to look over his shoulder at his puppet-master, but Frederick held him too firmly. "Come sit beside us," Frederick urged, pulling him onto the dais to sit in the somewhat smaller chair beside his own, usually reserved for the Queen.

Henry managed to glance over his shoulder as he mounted the dais steps, and Frederick intercepted the little nod from Beirut. He took this opportunity to gesture for King Henry to continue while he turned back to address the men behind the King.

They all dutifully went down on one knee when he faced them, and Frederick went forward to raise them up and demonstrably embrace first Beirut and then Caesarea. "Dearest uncle!" he addressed Beirut. "We are *overjoyed* to see you. Why all the mourning?"

"My brother, the good Lord Philip, late baillie of Cyprus, has not been in the grave a year yet, my lord."

There it was again, Frederick noted, 'my lord' as if the Emperor was no better than any other lord. This man's son had used the same demeaning form of address, Frederick remembered, and indeed that little bitch Eschiva had too. They were all self-important and disrespectful. They would soon learn better manners.

Aloud he remarked in apparent astonishment, "True, true, but we would have expected that your joy at our coming would outweigh your sorrow at the loss of your brother, noble and good as he undoubtedly was." He paused to let the rebuke sink in, and then made a great show of forgiveness. "We will set things right. Allow us to give you new robes and tomorrow we will dine together to celebrate this great campaign against the infidel that we shall undertake together."

"My lord, we are here to offer you our bodies and all our riches in the service of Christ and for the sake of regaining Jerusalem."

"Truly?" Frederick asked, lifting his head as if delighted, while noting what a bunch of hypocrites they all were.

The Lord of Beirut dropped again to his knee, crossed himself and intoned with the hypocritical solemnity of a papal envoy that he was at the Emperor's service. His brother-in-law and sons echoed his gesture and words like a flock of mindless choirboys. Frederick disguised his contempt behind an even broader smile as he raised the Lord of Beirut up and kissed him on both cheeks. "Uncle, we shall reward you richly for your service."

Limassol, Kingdom of Cyprus
July 22, 1228

The next day Balian found himself feeling ridiculous dressed in scarlet velvet. The robes provided by the Emperor were long, voluminous and inhibiting because of their weight, wide sleeves and long skirts. They were also oppressively hot not only because they were of velvet but because the Emperor had insisted that he and Baldwin wear a doublet over these "as was the usage and law in the Empire." "The Empire," Balian fumed inwardly, was located north of the Alps in some of the coldest places on earth, and they were on the shore of Mediterranean at the height of summer! Yet, that was not the worst of it. Balian boiled not only physically but emotionally because he had been assigned the "honor" of serving the Emperor at table.

The request had been made at the last minute: Balian was to fill the Emperor's cup, Baldwin his bowl, and their cousin Walter the Younger of Caesarea and the Lord of Karpas were to carve the Emperor's meat throughout the feast—all dressed up in these ridiculous, almost feminine, clothes. The Emperor's butler, who had delivered the request, made much about the "great honor" the Emperor was showing "such untried young men."

Significantly and surprisingly, Beirut had bristled at the request. As soon as the butler was gone, he apologized to his sons, saying the request had taken him completely by surprise; he had been unable to think of an excuse for declining fast enough. "What credible reason do we have for rejecting such an honor? Yet I do not like even a symbolic attempt to impose the customs of the Holy Roman Empire on the Kingdom of Cyprus! Still, while I do not trust this apparent amiability, we must not be the ones to disrupt it. I beg you both to put a good face on it and appear as pleased and attentive as humanly possible."

Balian and Baldwin assured their father he could count on them, and had taken up their duties diligently. Baldwin was at great pains to show himself better at this game than his rival Balian. The latter made that easy by showing his resentment far too obviously by the stiffness of his gestures and his sour face.

The feast was arranged so that the Emperor sat at a short table flanked by Beirut and Caesarea looking down the length of a long hall at which three tables stretched. The King of Cyprus and Salonika sat at the head of the middle table, followed by all the other ranking nobles from the Emperor's party and Cyprus. The two flanking tables were headed by the four archbishops and filled with the lower ranking yet prominent knights of Cyprus. Altogether there were over 500 men collected here, all in festive robes, although the Emperor's scarlet gifts highlighted the Cypriots of Beirut's party.

During the first several courses, the Emperor kept up a gracious, superficial conversation with his neighbors, while scrupulously ignoring Balian and Baldwin as if they were indeed imperial servants. Balian was surprised when the Emperor turned to him as the fifth course was cleared away to ask in a honeyed voice, "Do tell me about your *dear* cousin Eschiva. We understand you are, shall we say, quite *close*?"

Alarm set Balian's pulse to racing, but he maintained the appearance of calm as he asked back, "Are you referring to my Aunt Helvis' daughter? I haven't seen her since my Uncle Philip's funeral. I believe she is in a convent school in Tripoli."

The Emperor's jaw tightened with anger, but he too retained outward calm. "No, I was referring to Eschiva de Montbéliard."

"Oh. Her. I hardly know her. Her father and mine were not always on the best terms. I believe she recently married."

Although the Emperor glared, he said no more as the next course had arrived. No sooner had this course been consumed, than the Emperor signaled for more wine. As Balian leaned forward to refill the Emperor's goblet, the Emperor remarked condescendingly, "We understand you enjoyed the brothels of Andria when you visited this past spring."

Balian viewed this as a calculated insult and found it impossible to retain a friendly expression and tone. His words came out tense and short, earning a look of warning from his father. "You were misinformed, my lord. I did not— and *do* not—visit bawdy houses. Ever."

"Really?" The Emperor's tone was disbelieving. "But you *did* kill two sailors on the quay over some whore, didn't you?"

This remark drew a sharp breath from the Lord of Beirut, but he let his son answer. "No. I did not. My lord."

"Come now. There's no need to lie. If we intended to hold you to account, we would never have let you get out of Sicilian waters, but don't insult our intelligence with a denial when we can produce multiple witnesses."

"To what, my lord?" Balian countered with a quick glance at his father.

"To the murder of two sailors just moments before your ship fled in the dark of night." The Emperor was staring at him with narrowed eyes and lips clamped together.

"It is possible that two sailors were killed in a brawl of some sort, but I was below in my cabin during the incident," Balian answered, holding his breath unconsciously, "The captain of my vessel gave orders to cast off with two members of the crew still absent. Whether they were the victims or the perpetrators of a murder I cannot say; I was led to believe they were just deserters. I had nothing to do with whatever happened on the quay, and I'm willing to swear to the truth of that statement on any holy relic you choose—or to face you or your champion in judicial combat!" He added emphatically, letting out his breath in a rush of indignation.

"No." The Emperor remarked calmly as if he had lost interest in the subject. "That won't be necessary. Here's the course I've been waiting for: the subtleties."

The Emperor again turned his attention to the feast as imperial servants trooped in with platters of sweets held high over their heads. The sweets were brightly painted marzipan in various shapes, and many of the guests, including King Henry, strained to get a better look at them.

Balian was still simmering with fury and had no interest in "subtleties." He glanced across the room, looking for Novare. He should warn him of the Emperor's interest in the incident on the quay of Palermo, he thought, and his heart missed a beat. Behind the servants with the platters were imperial soldiers—and unlike the guests, these men were armored and armed.

Balian nudged Baldwin and then slipped behind the Emperor's chair to touch his father on the shoulder. When his father glanced up at him, he pointed with his chin. Beirut turned in his chair and froze. Balian saw his father's hands close tightly around his eating knife, and then very slowly and deliberately release it. He pulled his hands back into his lap and drew a deep breath. With his eyes and a subtle jerk of his head, he gestured for Balian to resume his duties.

Balian slipped back to the other side of the imperial chair, but on the way, he touched Karpas on the elbow. Karpas was bent over the carving table with his back to the room and had missed the new arrivals. At the sight of them, he growled deep in his throat, and his eyes became predatory.

Meanwhile, around the hall, other men were noticing them too. A strained silence slowly spread out from those who had noticed to those that had not. When King Henry saw the armed men, his eyes widened in alarm, and he looked anxiously to Beirut and Caesarea; they were too far away for him to consult, however. Miserably, he looked for someone else he trusted, but he was flanked by strangers. His growing distress expressed itself in fidgeting.

Gradually but inexorably the whole hall went silent. The Emperor, evidently pleased by this, turned to the Lord of Beirut and in a voice intended to carry to the corners of the hall and into history opened, "Sir John." That was an insult in itself. All talk of "dearest and honored uncle" had disappeared. In a tone hard as steel, the Emperor announced, "We have two demands of you. You will do them agreeably and well—if you know what is wise."

"Speak your pleasure, sire," Beirut answered no less loudly than the Emperor, although he, in contrast to the Emperor, still made an effort to clothe his words in a polite tone. "I will willingly do whatever I deem just—or what honest men so deem."

Balian was close enough to see the Emperor's eyes narrow at this answer, and the force with which he continued underlined his displeasure. "First, you will render to me all the revenues that the bailliage of Cyprus brought you and your brother before you, for it is mine according to the usages of Germany." Balian heard his brother Baldwin catch his breath behind him and had the satisfaction of thinking he had warned them this was coming.

But the Emperor wasn't finished. He continued, "Second, you will surrender to me the city of Beirut, for you do not have the right to hold it."

Balian glanced at Baldwin and their eyes met; Baldwin nodded once in acknowledgment that Balian had, after all, been right.

Meanwhile, their father was answering in a steady tone that betrayed neither surprise nor alarm. "Sire, I can only believe you jest and make sport of me. Or," he glanced significantly toward Barlais and his friends sitting at one of the lower tables, "it may be that certain evil men have suggested these demands." Then with increasing precision and forcefulness, he continued, "But I'm sure that as God wills, you are so *good* and *wise* a lord that you will *not* believe slander of *small* men."

The Emperor reached up to hold his head and intoned for his audience and posterity, "By this head which many times has worn a crown, we will accomplish our will in these two things, or you shall be our prisoner."

Balian had the impression that the Emperor had anticipated Beirut's refusal to comply—and was pleased by it. But he had not, Balian thought, anticipated Beirut's response to a threat of arrest when unarmed and surrounded by the Emperor's men-at-arms.

Beirut rose slowly to his feet—an affront that left the Emperor gaping—and announced with dignity. "I have and hold Beirut as my rightful fief, for it was given to me by Queen Isabella, my sister, the daughter of King Amalric, and her lord husband, King Aimery. It was given to me in exchange for the Constableship of Jerusalem at a time when it had been so badly destroyed that the Temple and the Hospital and all the barons of Syria had refused it. I fortified it and maintained it by my own resources and with the alms of many pious pilgrims. If you contend I hold it illegally, then furnish your proofs to the High Court of Jerusalem!" His speech ended with a slight crescendo that elicited calls of "Hear! Hear!" from many of the knights present in the hall. Balian saw the Emperor flinch at this public response.

Meanwhile, Beirut continued, "Regarding the revenues of Cyprus, I have had none and my brother who was regent before me had nothing but the trouble and labor of government, while Queen Alice, the widow of King Hugh and our niece, had the revenues. She disposed of them at her will. I will willingly furnish you proof of both the laws and customs and the accounts of the last ten years—before the High Court of Cyprus." He paused and, looking down at the Emperor, concluded, "More I will *not* do—not for fear of arrest or death—unless the High Courts have rendered judgement and required me to do so." Balian had never been so proud of his father.

The Emperor, however, was visibly furious. He rose to his feet, but, being shorter, still had to look up at Beirut. "We were warned that your words are exceedingly sweet and that you are a master of clever arguments, but we will show you that your wit and subtlety will avail you naught against our might!"

This was exactly what Balian had feared, and yet, he was almost relieved to have the threat out in the open. It discredited a king, much less an emperor, to dismiss law and justice in favor of the use of force.

As Balian expected, his father was equally unimpressed by the threat. "Sire, you say you have long ago heard mention of my polite words. Well, I have also long heard of your *deeds*. When you sent for me, my council warned me with one voice that you would do what you have done. I will tell you what I told them: I would rather suffer imprisonment or death than have it said that a chance to regain the Holy Land was squandered by my fear of you! If Our Lord Jesus Christ, who suffered for us, wishes my fate to be imprisonment and death, then I thank Him, so long as the cause of Jerusalem is not imperiled." He nodded once to the whole room and then sat down.

The Emperor was so enraged that his face was nearly purple. Balian could see his throat contracting spasmodically, whether from gulping for air or swallowing down his words, he did not know. He looked like he was about to explode, and the men-at-arms put their hands on their hilts awaiting the order to seize the Lord of Beirut.

The Archbishops of Palermo, Capua, and Nicosia, evidently expecting the same order, jumped up with a common desire to prevent that from happening. "Your Excellency!" and "Sire!" they called out as they burst up from their respective places. Seeing that Capua was nearer, Nicosia and Palermo let him take the lead. Capua rushed onto the dais to kneel before the Emperor. "Your Excellency! Do not succumb to anger! Think before you speak! We have come East on a great mission. We all serve Jesus Christ our Lord! This is no time to let disputes among ourselves endanger our greater cause."

"We are the Holy Roman Emperor! We represent Christ here on earth!" Frederick snarled back between clenched teeth.

The Archbishop of Nicosia blanched at so much hubris and admonished, "You forget His Holiness the Pope!"

"His Holiness be damned!" Frederick barked back.

"Your Excellency!" Capua admonished. "Curb your tongue for the sake of us all!"

"We will not be silenced or thwarted in this!" Frederick insisted, starting to raise his voice again.

"You jeopardize our entire undertaking!" Capua warned. "Don't forget, His Holiness is only waiting for you to fail. If you do, it will be child's play convincing your vassals that you wear the crown in error—an excommunicate, punished by God, for his intransigence. You will lose legitimacy and your enemies will exploit the situation."

The longer the Archbishop spoke, the redder Frederick became. Balian, still standing close by the back of his chair, could hear his breathing. Finally, from between clenched teeth, the Emperor spat out. "What do you suggest, Capua? Accept this insubordination! This rebellion by one so lowly!"

"Your Excellency," the Archbishop of Nicosia spoke up, "the Lord of Beirut has promised to serve you in this great expedition, and he has agreed to give account for both the revenues as well as his claim to Beirut. Hold him to his word." As he said this, the Archbishop glanced toward Beirut, who nodded shortly in agreement.

"Do you take me for a fool?" Frederick squawked back like an outraged crow. "The moment he leaves this room, he will turn against me!"

"Then demand hostages for his compliance."

Balian saw the Emperor start and then relax slightly. That was bad. He sensed it in his gut but there was nothing he could do to stop whatever would come next.

Frederick stood and lifted his hands for silence. The hall was loud from myriad arguments as men defended their respective side in the dispute. At the Emperor's gesture, the men across the room fell uneasily silent.

"Is there any man here who would stand surety for the Lord of Beirut?" The Emperor sneered. Balian had the impression he expected no one to stand up since it would have given him an excuse to declare that Beirut's word worthless.

Instead, nearly every Cypriot knight in the room jumped to his feet. The clamor was overwhelming. It gave Balian a moment of satisfaction—particularly because he could see the Emperor's discomfort.

"Twenty!" The emperor barked. "Take twenty of them!" Then he spun about and pointed with the index fingers of both hands at Balian and Baldwin respectively. "Starting with these two!"

Balian was grabbed roughly from behind by one of the Emperor's men and to his horror felt the sting of steel in his lower back. Whoever had hold of him also wielded a naked blade sharp enough to pierce all the abundant layers of clothing he was wearing. The blade, furthermore, pressed into his flesh right over his kidneys in a clear message; the man was waiting—hoping!—for an excuse to press it hard and deep into his vital organs. Baldwin too had been crushed in an embrace from an imperial sergeant, who held his neck in the crook of his elbow and a dagger to his back as well. Balian saw his father blanch and jump to his feet, while behind him he heard cutlery shatter and wood crashing as, apparently, Karpas or Walter of Caesarea made an attempt to rescue them.

The Emperor turned to see what had happened and his expression of satisfaction indicated that Karpas and Caesarea were as immobilized as Balian and Baldwin. With a smile, he called past Balian's shoulder toward the carving table, "I'll have your sons too, Karpas!"

Then turning back to Beirut, the Emperor remarked in what passed again for a civil, indeed friendly, tone. "Dearest uncle, I know well that our beloved cousin Sir Balian is your very *heart*. I know, therefore, that so long as I have *him*, I have *you*!" He dropped his voice to add, "by the balls!" Then lifting his voice to be heard more widely he added, "I promise, I will give him *special* treatment."

"By God," Beirut spoke for the entire room, his eyes meeting those of his eldest son. "I commit my sons unto you, my lord, and trust in Him that you will hold and guard them honorably, that you will neither cause them *nor suffer them to receive* any harm, villainy, or outrage. I trust that you will restore them to me when I come before the High Court of Jerusalem to prove my right."

"But *of course*, dearest uncle," Frederick answered with a smile that made Balian's stomach turn-over with fear. "They shall be enriched and honored, as God wills."

Chapter Thirteen

The Justice of the Emperor

Limassol, Kingdom of Cyprus
July 22, 1228

BEIRUT MADE IT BACK TO THE large encampment outside the walls of Limassol in a daze.

He later remembered getting woodenly to his feet, turning his back on his sons, and walking out of the great hall, but not how he got out of the palace. He remembered finding himself in the huge courtyard amidst pandemonium. Men were shouting for horses and squires, calling to friends and relatives to verify their presence, and repeatedly asking the names of the hostages. Someone brought up his horse, while Balian's squire Rob kept asking in bewilderment and increasing alarm, "Where's Sir Balian?"

Beirut found himself riding through the darkened streets of Limassol with Johnny and Hugh flanking him. They were no comfort. When he glanced at them, he saw only Balian and Baldwin gazing back. And if they looked away, he felt an icy cold hand clench his heart. How could he have walked out on his sons?

Balian. "Your heart," the Emperor had called him. Was it that obvious? He tried to treat them equally. Indeed, he had always been harder on Balian, expected and demanded more of him. Baldwin and Hugh, much less Johnny and Guy, were indulged; never Balian. But the Emperor was right. Balian was his firstborn, his heir, his favorite.

His father, Beirut reminded himself, had begged a favor of his worst enemy and—alone and unarmed—ridden through Saracen-held territory to save his two sons from danger. While he, Beirut lectured himself in a daze, delivered his sons into the hands of a treacherous and heartless enemy.

Not in the heat of battle either! Not by mistake or miscalculation. No. Balian had warned him. Balian had begged him not to go.

He will never forgive me, Beirut thought to himself. Nor should he. I took him into the trap. I handed him over to an untrustworthy autocrat. And then walked away. How could I do that? How could I forsake him?

"My lord!" The man-at-arms looked at him with eyes wide with concern. "We weren't expecting you so soon. Is something wrong?" When Beirut only stared in answer, the innocent man thought he had been rebuked for impertinence. "Sorry, my lord. Didn't mean to pry. I'll take your horse, my lord."

Beirut was simply disoriented—until he realized they had reached his traveling tent. Because the Holy Roman Emperor and his large entourage of archbishops, scholars, and scribes had commandeered all accommodation in Limassol town, whether fine or filthy, the Cypriots were camped outside the town walls.

His horse was tugging at the reins, impatient for a graze in the paddock, but his brother-in-law drew up beside him and stopped him. "John! I don't think we should dismount—or not for long. We should take the whole army back to Nicosia, if not to St. Hilarion and Buffavento—sooner rather than later."

"I'm not so sure about that!" Karpas boomed out in a loud and angry voice.

Beirut looked from Caesarea to Karpas and registered that there were decisions to be made. Decisions that other men expected him to make. He nodded numbly and swung his leg over the cantle to drop down. "Let us call the bannerets and bishops together to discuss the situation."

It didn't take long for the lords and knights to assemble. They had all been at the banquet and followed him out—except for the hostages. Beirut asked urgently for the names of the hostages, his sense of guilt almost making him nauseous. He was relieved to learn that in the confusion his men had deftly substituted younger knights, all volunteers, for the men of real power and stature. The fact that there had been no scuffling and no general chaos gave credence to the assurances that the hostages stayed willingly. They would not be here in such force if there had been any altercations in the great hall when they walked out.

Still, Beirut shook his head and announced, "I am honored, my lords, noble sirs, honored and deeply humbled by what has happened. You warned me. I did not heed you, and now... I honestly—" With a start, Beirut looked around in alarm. "Where is the King?"

After a stunned silence, Caesarea admitted, "He did not follow us out, John. I'm not sure if he didn't understand what was happening or if the Emperor's minions laid hands on him. I couldn't see what happened exactly."

"Oh, that slimy bastard Demetrius of Salonica detained him," one of the knights called out. "Held him by the arm right forcefully. If it had been anyone other than a fellow king, we could have intervened. As it was king to king, no one could call Salonica's clasp lèse majesté, while none of *us* could touch *him* without invoking the same charge. Bastard!"

"God help us all!" Beirut crossed himself.

"Don't underestimate Henry. He's not anyone's puppet. The Emperor will find that out soon enough if he tries to turn Henry against you," Caesarea predicted.

"I'm not concerned for myself," Beirut answered testily. "I am simply appalled that I have been the instrument of delivering my dearest sovereign into the hands of an unscrupulous autocrat. Forgive me, my lords, sirs. I am still in shock."

"Well, I have a suggestion!" Karpas spoke up in a booming voice. "Let's strike while they're still lolling about like cats in cream—*thinking* they have the best of us. That ass Hohenstaufen is so puffed up with his own importance—"

"Did you hear him call himself 'God's representative on earth!'" The Archbishop of Nicosia asked the pavilion at large, stunned by such an attitude in a mere secular monarch.

While several people, particularly the suffragan bishops, expressed outrage and started to talk about this, Karpas cut them off. "First things first! The point is that the Hohenstaufen thinks he's some sort of semi-divine Roman Emperor and that we all live in terror of him."

This produced a loud shout of defiance. The younger men, Beirut noted, were getting seriously riled up. That was not good.

Karpas had to shout to be heard over the angry declarations of fearlessness and courage that had little to do with the cause and a great deal to do with young fighting men feeding off each other's bragging. "So let's exploit it!"

"What?"

"Let's exploit the Hohenstaufen's conceit! If my lord of Beirut goes back to the palace begging to make peace, the Emperor will buy it hook, line and sinker!"

Beirut stiffened in visible distaste. The next second, however, he was gazing mentally into his sons' faces again and wondering if this was indeed what he must do. Meanwhile, however, the suggestion had unleashed such an uproar that Beirut thought they could probably be heard all the way back to the palace in Limassol. It was, he admitted, heartening that the Cypriot lords, bishops, and knights stood so solidly behind him. If there were Cypriot knights who believed he should submit to the Emperor's demands without a judgment of the High

Court, they were not in this tent, and from the number of men present, they could not have numbered more than 100.

Karpas meanwhile was shouting down the commotion. "Hear me out! On the way here Sir Walter," he nodded toward the younger Caesarea, "and I came up with a plan. We'll go with my lord of Beirut and dutifully hand over our long swords, but we'll have daggers in our hose and when the Emperor steps forward to give my lord of Beirut the kiss of peace, we'll take him from either side. Together we should be able to slay him quite easily."

Beirut was so shocked by the suggestion, he literally could not find any words and gaped at Karpas as the blunt baron continued enthusiastically, "Then, while the imperial men run around like chickens with their heads off, our men can rush in and free our cousins."

"Stop!" The elder Caesarea cut him off at last, Beirut joining in belatedly.

Karpas glared at them.

"It won't work! It will land you both on the gallows!" Caesarea focused angrily to his son rather than Karpas.

"And, more important," Beirut added into the silence, "in hell. We are not assassins! Do you understand me? Nor are we *traitors*. I do *not* challenge the Emperor's rights as overlord of Cyprus. I am only insisting on the rule of law, which includes the right of *all* men to defend themselves before their peers against accusations from *any* source."

Beirut's eyes swept across the room. The young men's blood was up and they grumbled and muttered in protest, but the older men were nodding.

Karpas made one last attempt. "But the Hohenstaufen—"

This time Beirut cut him off. "Do not speak of murder again, or I will personally strike you down!" He lifted his hand as if ready to deliver a backhand stroke to Karpas' already badly battered and scarred face. "If you kill the Emperor, you turn him into a martyr, and all the wrongs he has done us will be forgotten! He is our lord, and we must fight him *not* with unlawful force, but with the force of the law."

"And the brains we have in our head, John," Caesarea spoke up. "He's got your sons, Karpas' sons, and sixteen other brave young men in his clutches—not to mention the King. We would do well to take possession of something *he* needs and wants, or we'll have a very weak negotiating position indeed."

Beirut felt a thousand years old. His father had been called the "great negotiator" because he had snatched concessions from enemies that seemed to hold all the cards. Beirut knew he would never be as great a diplomat as his father had been, but he had learned a thing or two. He nodded to Caesarea. "You're right, my lord. My lord of Karpas." He turned on Sir Anceau. "May I request that you return with your men and secure the castle of Kantara? Ensure it is ready to withstand both siege and assault."

Karpas was still frowning over the rebuff of his assassination suggestion, but he growled consent.

"My lord of Caesarea, can you take charge of the royal castle at Buffavento?"

"Yes, of course."

"I will myself see to St. Hilarion," Beirut announced, "but first we should withdraw as a body to Nicosia."

To his surprise, a cheer went up from the Cypriot knights and nobles. He wasn't entirely sure what it was they were cheering. Retreat? Or was it action? Did they see this as an act of defiance? Or of self-defense? Beirut didn't know, but he was glad to have something to do that required keeping his eyes open. Whenever he closed them he saw Balian staring back at him in shock, horror, and reproach.

Limassol, Kingdom of Cyprus
July 24, 1228

Balian was no stranger to pain. He had broken his leg horsing around with Baldwin at the age of seven, and he'd taken his fair share of hard falls in the lists thereafter. He knew what it was to feel a stab of pain so sharp it took his breath away. He knew what it was to feel nauseous from sustained pain. He knew what it was to be temporarily crippled, and what it was to be unable to sleep for pain. But he had known nothing to compare with this.

In the past, the moment the pain started he also knew that everything humanly possible would be done to make it stop. Treatment might be accompanied by scolding or advice, and it might temporarily increase the pain, but it was forthcoming and well-intentioned nevertheless. At a very minimum, there would be a painkiller and the ability to adjust his position to ease the pain.

Now there was neither. The pillory ensured that any attempt to ease the pain in one limb only increased it in another. His back, permanently bent, felt broken in two places, and every move in any direction sent sharp pains up his spine.

Surely this was hell, and certainly, there were demons here as well.

Invisible though they were because his eyes were swollen shut, he heard them. They spoke in Barlais' voice, laughing, threatening and mocking. "So how do you like the pillory, Ibelin? Find it a fit place for a knight? Not exactly the high table, is it? Yet you're lucky, you know. I wouldn't *let* them display you in public—not like your uncle did me." Barlais voice was like the hiss of a snake full of venom.

Balian would have liked to remind Barlais that he'd tried to kill a man, while Balian had done nothing at all. He was merely a hostage for his father, but his mouth was too dry for speech.

Barlais moved closer and cooed like a dove. "No, no public display for our pretty Lover-Boy because too many stupid girls might have taken pity on the pretty, little boy," Barlais explained his actions.

Balian sensed the blow before it hit him, but the pillory gave him no means to avoid Barlais' fist any more than his questions.

"Aren't you pretty now, Lover-Boy?" Another blow cracked against his cheek, flinging his head to one side and wrenching the rest of his body against the wood and metal of the pillory.

"Oh, what lovely lips you have," Barlais whispered, "the girls surely love the taste of blood!" His fist punched Balian's mouth, breaking all the crusts formed from yesterday's beating so the blood gushed down and seeped into his teeth.

"And such big balls too!" The knee snapped up between his legs, and Balian howled in pain despite his fierce desire not to give Barlais that satisfaction.

Barlais laughed. "Maybe they won't be much use in the future, but that will make a lot of men sleep easier for their daughters, won't it?"

Barlais' breath blew into Balian's ear. "Makes it harder to seduce an heiress though, doesn't it? If you've got nothing left to excite her with." The next blow fell on his buttocks, making him rear up against the pillory and he heard something crack in his neck.

"God help me!" he screamed, but the words just echoed and echoed in the emptiness.

The faint sound of voices reached his consciousness. He stirred, causing sharp pains to set off a spasm of involuntary writhing, but no gasp escaped his lips. They were swollen too much to let out any greater sound than guttural moans. He tried to open his eyes, but they were still swollen shut.

Yet familiar as it all was, things were slowly getting worse.

The blood from his lips was as dry as the rest of his mouth. He had no spittle left, or urine either. The latter being perhaps the only positive feature of his present condition.

A man could live only four days without water, he remembered learning as a little boy. It was surely nearly that long already? As far as he could tell, this would continue until he slid from this earthly hell into the one beyond the grave.

"Look, I know he's a surly and stubborn fool," his brother's voice sounded normal as if they were in the palace of Beirut, "but you don't really want to give our father an excuse to rise up in rebellion, your Excellency. At least give my brother something to drink. He's had nothing all day."

"Nice try!" Balian registered.

"Did you say, 'we shouldn't give the Lord of Beirut an excuse to rebel'?" To Balian's amazement, the words were delivered in the Emperor's own sarcastic voice. Before his brother could answer, it continued tartly, "He obviously didn't need an *excuse* to do that! Your *rebel* father has already taken the knights and sergeants of Cyprus to Nicosia. We have been told he is also securing the inland castles."

Balian smiled at that mentally, proud that his father had stood up to this tyrant and offered resistance. He hated his inability to open his eyes, much less spit on this bastard in imperial disguise.

"You *do* understand," the Emperor continued in a pedantic tone, "that with his rebellion, your lives are forfeit. You were held to secure your father's good behavior, but he clearly considered your lives less important than his ill-gotten fortune and titles. If we choose to let you live, it is an act of imperial mercy."

Mentally, Balian spat in contempt, but his body was inert, held in place by the pillory and the pain it caused.

"Your father, of course, risks losing both his ill-gotten fortune *and* his two first-born sons," The Holy Roman Emperor continued in a smug voice. "We've sent for the Teutonic Knights under their marshal Gunther von Falkenhayn. They'll be able to reduce these castles of yours in a day or two, and then we will teach your father a lesson in fealty."

Ah, what you don't know, Balian thought with a smile that could not reach his blood encrusted and swollen lips.

Baldwin, on the other hand, agreed readily with a "certainly" before adding, "But mopping up could take time. Does your excellency really want to be bogged down in a long drawn out war, when you could be in Syria regaining Jerusalem?"

The Emperor didn't deign to answer. Instead, he remarked, suddenly much closer, "Oh! Don't we look *pretty* now, little boy?" A hand hit Balian in the lower back, making him stiffen involuntarily, a move that thrust his neck sharply up against the upper bar of the pillory. The pain was so sharp that the cry forced out of his throat ripped open the scabs holding his lips together. Blood gushed anew and he heard his brother gasp.

"Yes," the Emperor said, his head turned away, apparently to address Baldwin. "You are at our mercy. Utterly and completely."

"Your Excellency," Baldwin whispered, and Balian felt sorry for him.

"You can be our subject or our enemy," the Emperor lectured Baldwin. "One or the other. If you do not recognize our authority, you are traitors. We do not forget or forgive disloyalty." He paused, and Balian felt the Emperor's eyes running over his body. "Disgusting isn't he? Stinking of his own waste, unable to move, or speak. Where is all your arrogance now, little boy?" The Emperor mocked. "Think the girls would still find you attractive? Hah!" The Emperor burst out laughing, and Balian registered irrelevantly that the Emperor was jealous of his good looks and conscious of his own lack of sexual appeal. No doubt that was why he needed to surround himself with harem slaves.

"If any lady could see him now, your magnificence," Baldwin spoke out of the distance, "they would certainly be repulsed—by what *you* have condoned."

The Emperor sucked in his breath and took a step away.

"Think about it, your magnificent excellency, the ever-victorious wearer of so many crowns, God's representative on earth! Think how it makes you look mighty and powerful to torment a youth locked in a pillory for the crimes you *allege* his *father* committed!"

Shut up, Baldwin! Balian screamed silently, certain that his brother would soon be sharing his fate. He heard the crack and gasp, but Baldwin was an Ibelin. "Hit me again, your Excellency! It makes you so much more regal and imperial to beat pilloried prisoners!"

"We will have our revenge, you pitiable fool! Both of you! We'll keep you both alive just long enough to see your father *hang*—before we throw *you,* bound hand and foot, to the sharks!"

Paradhisi, Kingdom of Cyprus
July 25, 1228

A rare summer storm had riled up the sea, and waves rushed into the cove at Paradhisi to crash against the beach with white-frothing fury. Eschiva sank onto the thin ridge of rolled stones that collected at the top of the sandy beach and clutched her knees. Since her marriage to Gerard de Montaigu, she had been virtually imprisoned her on this small manor, an estate she had inherited from her mother Burgundia de Lusignan. Gerard (and his all-powerful uncles) had chosen it among all her estates as the most "suitable" place for her to remain secluded while her husband joined the other knights and nobles of Cyprus on crusade with the Holy Roman Emperor.

Although located in a beautiful setting on the south coast of the island, it was very isolated, and furthermore had been the venue of a horrible incident. Thirty years ago, the Lady of Lusignan, Eschiva's grandmother, and her younger children had been kidnapped from the beach here by the infamous Greek pirate Kanekes.

As Eschiva stared into the wind and watched the waves breaking, she was glad of the occasional drop of blown spume, or even tiny bits of sand and seaweed that the wind threw at her. There was something perversely liberating about sitting here on the edge of the sea at the very spot her mother had been carried away by pirates. It was a foolish thought, but Eschiva wished that a pirate galley would appear to take her away from everything.

It wasn't just the physical duties of marriage that she wanted to escape. Consummation, she had decided, was like a bad bout of stomach sickness that made you vomit. It was intensely unpleasant, but then you could wash out your mouth (or other parts of your body as appropriate) and fall asleep knowing that in the morning things were better.

Only they weren't. After six weeks of marriage, Eschiva knew things were never going to get better. Gerard didn't want them to. She was nothing but a means to an end for him. She brought him lands that had troops and income with which he could pursue his sacred "crusade"—a crusade that had nothing to do with Jerusalem, and everything to do with cleansing his own soul of some sin he would never tell her about. She was not going to be like Yolanda, she told herself, tying herself in knots, and wearing herself out to please someone who could never be pleased. She could never please Gerard, no woman could, because Gerard did not want to be married at all. *He* wanted to be a monk like his uncles. It was his uncles who, having renounced the function themselves, required him to secure the dynasty through marriage and children.

The smell of fish and the flapping and flutter of black skirts drew her attention to Papas Theodoros, the Greek priest from the village. He was standing beside her on the beach in his sandaled feet. She smiled up at him wearily, and he sank down to sit cross-legged beside her, looking out to sea.

After a few minutes of comforting silence, Eschiva remarked, her chin still on her knees and her eyes still looking out to sea, "I should confess."

Papas Theodoros nodded and muttered, "In the name of the Father, the Son, and the Holy Ghost."

"I was very glad to see my lord husband depart," Eschiva told him. "I hope he does not come again for a long time—or that he never returns at all."

"A terrible sin!" The Papas avowed. "For penance, you must eat dinner with us tonight. Mama has made *spanakopita*. You will like it. Was there anything else?"

"If I did not get pregnant last night. He will be back because the crusade has been delayed."

"Then I'm sure you *did* become pregnant—until he is safely overseas, when, to your great disappointment, you will discover that you are not pregnant after all. No?"

"Do you mean I should lie to my lord husband?" she asked with a mischievous smile over her shoulder.

"You are young and inexperienced. It is easy to make a mistake in these things, I think. Come! We'll have a glass of wine before dinner." He stood up again and offered her his thick, calloused hand.

Eschiva took it gratefully. The Greek priest and the fisherman Costas Drakakis with his family were her lifeline, the only things keeping her sane in her lonely new world as an unwanted married woman.

The wine was homemade from grapes that grew here on the property, and they drank it in pottery mugs mixed with cool water from the well. Despite the stiff breeze, Eschiva preferred sitting on the terrace to retreating into the dingy, smoke-filled kitchen for the meal. Thus, they were still here an hour later when the clear sound of a horse cantering up the road reached them through the trees.

The sound of hooves was rare enough to stop conversation as they all turned to see who it might be. "I do hope it isn't Gerard," Eschiva muttered.

"Alone?" Yiota answered rhetorically. Gerard traveled with a small cavalcade as was appropriate for a man of substance and title.

"Maybe he sent a message back of some sort?"

The horse pulled up before the house and they could hear voices but not what was said. Then the horse was led away at a walk and a figure started through the darkness. It was a man. Slender with fair hair. He wore hose and high boots under a surcoat that fluttered in the wind. The colors of the day had faded too much for Eschiva to make out his coat-of-arms. As he came nearer, she realized he wore none; the surcoat was embroidered with little suns rather than a particular device. He was obviously a Frank, but in the dusk, Eschiva did not recognize him.

"My lady?" A young, male voice asked as it came to the edge of the terrace.

"I am Lady Eschiva de Montbéliard," Eschiva admitted, shoving her wine aside and sitting straighter, unconsciously straightening her barbette and embroidered circlet. "Are you looking for me?"

The youth stepped closer and the lantern light lit his face enough for Eschiva to start a little in recognition. She had seen that face before, but where?

"My name is Robert de Maumeni. I serve Sir Balian, the Lord of Beirut's eldest son."

"Rob!" Eschiva jumped up in delight. "Of course! I thought I recognized you, I just couldn't place you! Come, sit down! Have you ridden far? There's some food left, isn't there, Yiota?" She called to the kitchen where Yiota and her mother were already starting to clean up.

"Have some wine," Papas added, pushing a pottery cup and the jug in the youth's direction.

The youth did not respond to the friendly gestures but stood awkwardly on the edge of the light. "Lady Eschiva? Have you heard what has happened?"

"Not really. I'm very isolated here. Won't you sit down and tell me?"

He seemed reluctant, but he took a seat on the wooden bench opposite Eschiva, and with a nod of thanks accepted the pottery mug of wine. Before he took a sip, however, he reached inside his gambeson and pulled out a letter. "This is from Bella. The Lord of Beirut has sent her to St. Hilarion under heavy escort. Otherwise, she says, she would have come herself. We're both very worried about Sir Balian."

"Why? What has happened to him?" Eschiva asked in surprise. The boy's tone was sober enough, but only now as she registered the fact that he was here by himself did she start to become alarmed.

"He is being held hostage by the Emperor," Rob reported. "Didn't anyone tell you?" He looked at the others around the table, but it was clear that these simple people were unlikely to know the news from court. So he continued, "I stayed behind after the Ibelins and the other Cypriot barons withdrew to Nicosia. I was able to bribe one of the Hospitaller sculleries—"

"What do the Hospitallers have to do with this?" Eschiva asked confused.

"Oh, I forgot. It seems that when the Emperor heard all the shouting from our camp—or it was reported to him—he took fright. He fled from the royal palace to take refuge in the Hospitaller commandery—and he took the hostages with him. Only the others are free to move about the commandery and take their meals with the brothers. Only Sirs Balian and Baldwin are being kept in the dungeon."

"Sirs Balian *and* Baldwin?" Eschiva asked. "But why? What is this about?"

"The Emperor accused my lord of Beirut of embezzling from the treasury of Cyprus and demanded that he surrender Beirut."

"What does Beirut have to do with the Cypriot treasury?" Eschiva was more confused than ever.

Rob shrugged. "I don't know. Nobody does. It's crazy. My lord rightly said he'd defend himself before the respective High Courts, but the Emperor threatened to have him arrested then and there."

"When and where was this?" Eschiva wanted to know.

"It was five days ago in Limassol," Rob told Eschiva about the banquet and how the Cypriots had all been told to come unarmed, but the Emperor's men had been armed to the teeth and had surrounded them.

"How did the Lord of Beirut escape?"

"He—he" Rob shrugged in embarrassment, "he just stood up and walked out—leaving Sirs Balian and Baldwin at the Emperor's mercy." Rob's misery was evident. He didn't like speaking ill of his overlord, but he clearly did not approve of what the Lord of Beirut had done. "Now, he's pulled the entire Cypriot army back to Nicosia, and he's fortifying and supplying the mountain castles, but I'm afraid for Sir Balian. I thought—Bella thought—that maybe you could help." His eyes pleaded with her out of the near darkness and he had not yet touched the wine.

"How?" Eschiva asked baffled. She felt completely helpless.

"Bella thought that you could ask to see your cousin the king or the Master of the Hospital since he is your uncle by marriage. If we just had some assurance that Sir Balian, and Sir Baldwin of course, aren't being harmed in any way, we could…" He lost courage and just stared at her expectantly.

The whole incident seemed surreal to Eschiva. How could Sir Balian be in danger? He was so strong and vigorous and fearless. It was impossible he was the Emperor's prisoner. But if he was—the thought sent a shiver down her spine. What if the Emperor had found out about Sir Balian's role in her escape? Was that the real reason he'd been taken hostage? But then why Sir Baldwin too?

"Please at least *try* to help, Lady Eschiva," Rob broke into her thoughts. "The scullery claims no food has been sent to the prisoners since their arrival, and they arrived badly beaten."

"Rob, I *want* to help, but I don't even have a horse! I have no way of getting to Limassol, much less—"

"We can take the fishing boat," Costas spoke up, turning to toss an additional remark at his father in Greek, who grunted in reply. "We'd have to tack out a ways, but if this wind holds we could run before it almost all the way. If we set off tonight, we could reach Limassol by tomorrow noon."

Rob looked sharply at the fishermen and then back at Eschiva. "Please! Sir Balian helped you when you needed it."

"I don't know what my husband will do if he finds out!" Eschiva pointed out, as fear and excitement seized her in equal measure.

"Sir Balian didn't ask what his father might do to him for helping you—or the Emperor. You asked for his help, and he gave it to you. Unconditionally."

"You're right, Rob. He did. Do you really think we could make Limassol by tomorrow noon?" She turned to Costas and Yiota.

"If we leave within the hour and the wind holds," Yiota answered. "Papas! Help my father with the boat, I'll help Lady Eschiva pack. You'll need to look your best for the king," Yiota told her mistress firmly.

Rob perked up. "Will you really do it, my lady? Will you go to the king?"

"Yes, I'll start with the king," Eschiva resolved, energy flooding her veins, as excitement and determination banished her fears. "He can hardly refuse to see me." Eschiva had made up her mind. The sense of taking control of her destiny was invigorating. It defeated her depression. Gerard be damned! If he didn't like her asking mercy for a good and honorable man, he was neither good nor honorable himself.

"I'll set out at once—well at dawn," Rob modified, "and return to Limassol. As soon as I reach Limassol, I'll ask for you at the Royal Palace."

"I'll try to stay with the Hospitaller sisters," Eschiva countered. "They may have more information."

"That's good!" Rob brightened even more.

"And, of course, I'll ask to see dear *Uncle* Guerin," Eschiva added with a smile.

Limassol, Kingdom of Cyprus
July 27, 1228

Eschiva's courage came and went in waves. It was on the ebb as she approached the royal palace in a dress that was damp and salt-stained in places despite Yiota's best efforts. Of course, she'd worn an every-day gown for the journey and her wedding dress had been carefully folded into an oilskin bag and tucked up in a shelf under the foredeck. Things had been alright as long as they were running before the wind, but they had to jibe once to enter Limassol harbor and a wave had swept over their stern and washed right into forepeak. It had drenched them all and seeped through the fastenings of the oilskin to partially soak the gown.

As soon as they tied up at the dock, Yiota had hustled Eschiva to a bath-house. Here, the attendants had washed the salt off her and out of her hair and massaged her with lavender oil that obliterated the last traces of fish smell. They had re-braided her hair and hidden it under silk veils still damp from being freshly washed. Her stockings too had been washed while she was bathed and oiled, but the Dowager Queen's beautiful gown was too heavy and too elaborately embroidered for a quick wash. All they could do was sponge away the worst of the salt stains and press it a little to make it respectable.

Now, with Yiota trailing her like a dutiful maid, Eschiva approached the royal palace. With relief, she saw that the sentries wore Lusignan arms rather than those of the Emperor. The sergeant-in-charge referred her request for an audience with the king to an older official without a blink of skepticism. The latter, who likewise wore a Lusignan crest on the breast of his robes, appeared willing to believe she was who she said she was. Ordering Yiota to wait in the hall, he escorted Eschiva up interior stairs around the inner courtyard and along a cool corridor paved with bright tiles. "Is the King expecting you?" the official asked as their heels clacked on the tiles.

"No, sir. I did not have a chance to send word of my visit in advance," Eschiva admitted.

He made a sound in his throat that might have meant anything. They stopped in front of tall double-doors guarded by two men-at-arms with Lusignan badges. The official nodded to them and they opened the doors simultaneously.

Beyond was a spacious chamber with a high, rib-vaulted ceiling and four batteries of double-light windows. The ceiling was painted like the morning sky with clouds and birds upon it, and the ribs were gilded. The walls were hung with light, silk tapestries that billowed gently as the open door created a draft. The floor was of glazed tiles, spotlessly clean. Eschiva took it all in while looking for the King.

Instead of the boy king, a man with a grey mane of hair wearing red robes adorned with the black eagle of the Holy Roman Empire stood abruptly. His face was drawn into a frown as he came toward her in apparent alarm. "What is the meaning of this? No one was announced!" he admonished sharply.

The man beside her bowed deeply. "Madame de Montagu arrived unexpectedly," he answered.

At that moment, movement in one of the windows drew Eschiva's attention to King Henry at last. He twisted around and gazed at her with big, questioning eyes.

Spontaneously, Eschiva opened her arms and called out, "Cousin Henry!"

With a bounce, Henry jumped down the steps from the window seat and ran across the room to fling himself into her arms exuberantly. Only after her arms closed around him did he whisper in her ear, "What's your name? I've forgotten"

"Eschiva, your Aunt Burgundia's daughter," Eschiva whispered back.

"Cousin Eschiva!" he exclaimed in a loud, happy voice. "It's been *much too* long since I saw you! Come! Come! You have to tell me all about your wedding!" He had Eschiva by the hand and was leading her toward the window seat, but then, as if noticing him for the first time, he addressed the Imperial dignitary with a dismissive gesture. "This is a family reunion," Henry declared, switching to his "regal" voice. "We don't need you. Leave us!"

Eschiva thought she saw a smile flit over the face of the Lusignan official, but he bowed quickly to cover his expression, while the Imperial dignitary fumed visibly.

"Go on!" King Henry insisted. "Go get something to eat! You've been here all day."

"I am not hungry, my lord, but if you wish me to send for something—"

"No. Just go away! We want to be alone with our cousin Eschiva! She's hardly going to do us any harm, and the guards are right outside."

After this, the Imperial official had no choice but to bow and withdraw.

As soon as the door banged shut, Henry hissed to Eschiva, "That's one of the Emperor's watchdogs! He's supposedly a great mathematician, but he's probably got his ear to the door at this very minute. Come!" He pulled her to the window seat and made her sit down opposite him. "You were at the banquet after the trial!" he announced. "I remember the dress. You were with Sir Balian, my lord of Beirut's son and heir."

Eschiva caught her breath. That evening belonged to a different world a lifetime ago. Or, rather, it had been the happiest moment of her life. "Yes, I was," she admitted. Should she raise the issue of Sir Balian's possible mistreatment now? Since he had raised Sir Balian's name, surely it would not seem odd?

But the opportunity had already passed. Henry was following his own thoughts. "Lady Yvonne told me you went with Queen Yolanda to Sicily and lived for three years in the Emperor's court."

"Yes," Eschiva admitted.

"So you must know him well. Do you like him?" Henry asked directly.

Eschiva held her breath for a moment, trying to think of a diplomatic answer, but Henry's blue eyes seemed to demand honesty. "No," she admitted softly, shaking her head. "I didn't like the way he treated our Queen Yolanda, his wife."

"I'm *glad* you don't like him!" Henry announced. Then he lowered his voice, and leaned forward, his hand shielding his mouth in the direction of the door, and whispered, "I don't like him either! He's pompous and all puffed up with his own importance. You know, he told me he was 'the best-educated monarch on earth,' but he doesn't speak a word of Greek! All he speaks is that bastard

Latin they speak on Sicily, real Latin, French, and Arabic. He doesn't even speak German despite being a German Emperor. I speak all those languages too, except that stupid Sicilian dialect, and I speak Greek too," he pointed out proudly.

Eschiva smiled. "I hope you told him that."

Henry frowned. "He doesn't listen to me. He treats me like a child. Everyone tells me I have to defer to him because he's my overlord, but, you know, *our* grandfather captured Cyprus *without* any help from the Holy Roman Emperor. I don't understand why he did homage to him."

"I think at the time it had to do with getting a crown," Eschiva admitted.

"But the Kings of Jerusalem aren't part of the Holy Roman Empire," Henry pointed out. "They just crowned themselves. Why didn't our grandfather do that?"

"I don't know. He died before I was born."

"But your mother was much older than my father. She must have known him better. Didn't she tell you anything about our grandfather?" Henry pressed her.

"My mother told me lots of things about him—that he was a handsome man who liked to tease her." Eschiva scraped together all her memories of her grandfather King Aimery. "He had a wry sense of humor, she said, and sometimes he seemed very stern, but he usually had a twinkle in his eye and soon gave in and laughed with her. She said when she was captured by the pirates that she never doubted he would rescue them, although our grandmother, she said, despaired and almost died in captivity."

"But why did he do homage to the Holy Roman Emperor?" Henry persisted.

"Our grandfather always resented that his younger brother had worn the crown of Jerusalem. I suppose that made him want a crown," she speculated.

"I would rather *not* be king than do homage to someone who *didn't* help me in any way," Henry told her emphatically.

Eschiva nodded understanding, and Henry changed the subject. "Your mother married Walter de Montbéliard."

"Yes," Eschiva agreed. "But he died when I was two and I never knew him. That was long before you were born."

"But his sister, Lady Alys, was Lord Philip's wife," Henry continued.

"Exactly," Eschiva agreed, glad to have something she could talk about to build more rapport. "I visited her on the eve of my marriage."

"Is she alright?" Henry asked earnestly.

"She seemed to be doing well under the circumstances. She had to get me ready for my wedding in a hurry, which she did with great competence."

"The Emperor is trying to convince me that Lord Philip was evil. He says Lord Philip only *pretended* to be good to me while stealing from me behind my back. Do you think that?"

"It doesn't sound very likely to me," Eschiva admitted, loyal to her Aunt—and the Ibelins—even if she didn't have a clue about the facts of the case.

"I'm sure it's not true!" Henry's indignation was so intense that he forgot to keep his voice down.

Eschiva put her finger to her lips and gestured toward the door with her head.

Henry drew a deep breath and lowered his voice as he asked, "Did you know Lord Philip bought all the animals for my menagerie?"

Eschiva shook her head.

"He sometimes had to go to all sorts of trouble to get them here, and once, the crocodiles nearly killed one of their keepers, and another time they got out of the pond and ate all the peacocks. We had to get a dozen new peacocks." Henry giggled at the memory, and Eschiva smiled with him.

Then he sobered. "I don't believe the Emperor. I think *he's* trying to manipulate me. Lord Philip, Lord Walter, and Lord John always *explained* things to me. They told me what choices I had, and told me why things were the way they were. The Emperor talks down to me as if I were *stupid*!" His voice became loud again with indignation.

Eschiva put her finger to her lips and wondered again if it was time to broach the subject of Sir Balian.

Henry didn't give her a chance. "And now Lord John and Lord Walter are in rebellion. The Emperor says they have rebelled against *me* and I must crush them, but they haven't rebelled against *me* at all! They have rebelled against *him*."

Eschiva nodded, and Henry sat up straighter to ask her. "That's the way you see it too?"

"That's *exactly* the way I see it," she assured her king. "But there is something else that worries me."

"What?"

"Sirs Balian and Baldwin, the Lord of Beirut's sons."

"They're two of the hostages," Henry noted.

"Have you visited them?" Eschiva asked.

"No—why? Have you news from them?" Henry asked surprised.

"Their sister is very worried about them. She fears they might be ill-treated."

"The Emperor *swore* he would do them no harm," King Henry told her frowning.

Eschiva felt her blood start to rush with agitation. Things had been going so well. She had not expected hesitation or doubts at this stage. "Don't forget that the Emperor swore to King John de Brienne that he could remain King of Jerusalem after his daughter's marriage."

Henry nodded, still frowning. "You're right. The Emperor is a liar, and I don't think he knows what honor is. But what can I do?"

"Henry," Eschiva took a deep breath, "you're the king. You can demand to see Beirut's sons."

"Imperial guards took them away. I'm not sure they would obey me."

"But I've heard they were taken to the Hospitaller Commandery."

"Yes. You want me to go there and ask to see them?"

"It would be a great comfort to his family if you could report that no harm has come to them, that they are being treated *properly*." Eschiva had rehearsed that phrase a thousand times on the way here.

Henry nodded. "I can do that. What time is it? Should we go now?"

"Yes," Eschiva agreed with a rush of relief. "Yes, we should go at once—just in case they aren't being treated as they should."

Chapter Fourteen

Teutonic Knights
to the Rescue

Nicosia, Kingdom of Cyprus
August 1228

THE GARDENS AT THE ARCHBISHOP'S PALACE in Nicosia were somewhat
smaller than the gardens of the royal palace, but they were exquisitely laid out
along crushed marble paths, shaded by pines and planes trees at strategic points,
and watered by a network of underground pipes that bubbled up into fountains
at three places. Birds twittered in the cypress trees, crickets chirped from the
pines, and bees hummed around the lavender. Potted hibiscus bushes provided
flashes of color. The sunlight glinted off the water of the fountains, and the
gurgling provided a gentle counterpoint to the breeze rustling the palms.

Guerin de Montaigu wearing the full, ecclesiastical regalia of a Hospitaller
Master was conferring with his brothers. Pedro was dressed equally formally in
the robes of the Templar Master, and their younger brother Eustace was dressed
in the jewel-studded robes of an archbishop. The three brothers were expecting
the arrival of the Marshal of the Deutsche Orden, the Teutonic Knights, at any
moment and were passing the time by strolling in the garden.

Guerin took the opportunity to describe to his brothers the deplorable state
in which he had found Sir Balian d'Ibelin. "Apparently he had not been given
water for almost two days. He could neither walk nor speak when my men
released him from the pillory. He had also been badly beaten by Sir Amaury
Barlais, I was told. His eyes were swollen shut, his lips blood encrusted. He had

dried blood all over his chin and throat, and bruises on his face and neck. I was shocked beyond words," Guerin noted in a low voice.

"What about his brother?" Pedro asked.

"He was treated somewhat better. He was not denied water and he was less severely beaten. He had only one black eye and bruises around his neck and chin."

"Perhaps Sir Balian had been more impudent and given Barlais cause to beat him?" Eustace asked with a cocked eyebrow.

"Eustace! What are you saying?" Guerin replied indignantly. "Both young men are standing hostage for their father! Neither of them has even been accused, much less found guilty, of any crime whatsoever! They are not common criminals receiving justice, but honorable and noble youth! Not to mention that the Emperor publicly promised no harm would come to them. Such treatment exposes him as an outright liar—a man utterly lacking honor and chivalry!"

"Too true!" Eustace hastened to agree. "And if you had heard him declare he was God's representative on earth!"

Pedro had heard about that many times before and waved his brother the archbishop silent to ask his other brother. "Do you think Beirut's sons will recover?"

"They are young and fit. I think they will recover, although Sir Balian is certain to have scars on his wrists and ankles for life. The pillory cut right to the bone in a couple of places! More dangerous, of course, would be any damage to his spine. I'm told he was in excruciating pain for days, and while that seems to have eased somewhat, it is too soon to know if he has slipped disks or cracked vertebrae as a result of this appalling treatment."

Pedro shook his head at this and noted, "I worry what will happen when Beirut finds out what was done to his sons. Did you send him word?"

"No," Guerin admitted. "I felt justified in interceding. After all, the King demanded it, and they were being held in my commandery. But sending word to Beirut might have been interpreted as going a step too far. We must retain our neutrality in this clash between the Emperor and the Cypriot barons."

"Indeed," Pedro agreed.

The Archbishop re-entered the conversation, speaking in a doubtful tone as he noted, "Wise as it was for you to intercede on the behalf of the young Ibelins, Guerin, I am less comfortable with the role played by our nephew's wife. We know she was exceedingly fond of Sir Balian before her marriage. It disturbs me somewhat that she was so energetic in bringing his situation to the attention of the king."

"If she had not, they might have died!" Guerin responded in outrage. "It was a very near thing as it was. I applaud her courage and compassion both!"

"But how did she find out? What are her ties to Sir Balian?" Eustace asked suspiciously.

"I don't know what you are implying, Eustace," Guerin again came to Eschiva's defense.

"Gerard reported to us that she bled profusely on the wedding night; she came to her marriage a pure and virgin bride and has not seen Sir Balian since. Any infatuation she may have felt for a dashing young knight as a maiden is now nothing but a childish memory, obscured, I'm sure, by the passion she must feel for her husband since she has known the full wonder of physical union. Furthermore, King Henry told us that it was Isabella d'Ibelin, with whom Eschiva was very close, who asked her to intercede on behalf of both Sir Balian and Sir Baldwin. Since Mademoiselle d'Ibelin has sought refuge at St. Hilarion with the rest of her father's followers, it makes perfect sense for her to seek the assistance of someone still at liberty, such as Eschiva."

"Or it may have been Beirut himself, who thought of using her. Don't underestimate the old fox," Pedro noted.

The Archbishop of Nicosia nodded, but his face remained clouded. "Her confessor reports to me that she is strange. She is very thick with the Greek fisherman and his family, and he suspects her of confessing to the Greek priest more than himself." The Templar Master's eyebrows twitched, and his brother from the Hospital pointed out solemnly, "Every Christian has the right to choose his own confessor, Eustace. You should not presume to impose one."

The Archbishop frowned in annoyance and added. "Maybe so, but she has moved into the old house and spends all her time writing and painting."

"Ah," Guerin smiled, "she told me about that. She learned copying and illuminating from the canons of the Holy Sepulcher and confided her desire to copy out and illustrate the psalms as a gift for Gerard. I was pleased by such a pious endeavor and encouraged her in it. I sent her parchment from our own stores. She sent me samples of her work, a lovely page with the Lord's Prayer on it, in thanks. She is a gifted illuminator."

Eustace did not look convinced but before he could say anything, Pedro indicated a young priest who was hurrying toward them flushed with excitement. "I think our guest has arrived," he commented.

"My lord archbishop! My lords! The Germans have just ridden into the courtyard!"

"Good," Eustace said. "Fetch my miter." Turning to his brothers he informed them, "We'll receive them in my audience chamber. Come this way." The Archbishop led his brothers out of the garden by way of a small door almost hidden in the shrubbery. This opened into a narrow, windowless stairwell that led up to the floor above and gave access to the private rooms of the Archbishop's palace. From here they made their way to the large representational rooms at the front of the building, sliding into the audience chamber by a door at the back of the dais. Eustace seated himself in his tall, high-backed chair, arranging his robes carefully around him. A young priest appeared with his miter, which he set carefully upon his head. His brothers took up positions flanking him just as, from the far end of the chamber, the sound of stomping feet reached them.

A moment later five men burst into the room. The man leading was stocky with hair so blond it was almost white around a bright red scalp. The beard was likewise white-blond under a bright red face with a peeling nose. The Marshal of the Teutonic Knights had evidently not yet adjusted to the Mediterranean sun. He was flanked and followed by four giants that towered over him—although the Germans might not have seemed so tall if they had not been led by their undersized marshal. These knights wore their coifs up over their heads, obscuring their tonsures, and their beards were lost under the aventails fastened across their chins.

The Templar Master bristled inwardly as he noted the Teutonic Marshal wore the gold crosses of Jerusalem beneath the silver-edged, black Latin cross of the Deutsche Ritter Orden. He considered the insignia an unjustified affectation given the fact the junior order had not made its appearance in the Holy Land until after Jerusalem was lost. The fact that the privilege to wear the crosses of Jerusalem had been granted by King John of Brienne nine years ago did not make matters any better for the Templar; Brienne too was a parvenu in his mind.

The Teutonic Marshal came to a halt some six feet short of the dais and inclined his head. "My lords."

"Welcome to Cyprus, Marshal von Falkenhayn," Eustace answered for all three of them.

"I would have preferred to make my acquaintance with the island after capturing Jerusalem," the German replied bluntly. "I had not expected to be called from Acre to put down an unseemly rebellion!"

"This altercation between the Emperor and the Cypriot nobility is indeed regrettable," the Archbishop of Nicosia agreed.

The Teutonic Marshal frowned darkly. "I call it more than regrettable, my lord; I call it treason. Indeed, it is blasphemy as it endangers our Holy mission to retake Jerusalem."

Pedro growled behind Eustace's chair, muttering, "He conveniently ignores the law, doesn't he?"

Eustace, however, ignored his brother and responded to the German in a conciliatory tone. "We all agree, I think, that it is in the interests of Christendom to put an end to this dispute."

"Which is why we are here. My brothers and I have come to crush the rebellion and take the leaders captive. I hereby request the support of our brothers-in-Christ, the Knights of the Hospital and the Knights Templar." His eyes had already left the Archbishop to shift between the Masters of the other two militant orders.

"The Hospital will not take sides in this dispute," Guerin answered immediately and firmly.

"Take sides?" Gunther von Falkenhayn asked, raising his eyebrows and curling his lips in a sneer. "What sides are there? On one side are God and the Emperor, on the other, rebellious felons! Does your order also not take sides between murderers and their intended victims? Between Christians and Saracens?" he sneered.

"I will not lower myself to answer such a question. As for God and the Emperor being on the same side, that is debatable, given his excommunicated status. The Lord of Beirut certainly has the law on his side—and the loyalty of four-fifths of the lords and knights of Cyprus. That should give you pause."

"And the Temple?" Falkenhayn dismissed Guerin and the Hospitallers.

"The Knights Templar are prohibited from fighting fellow Christians. Nor do we recognize the leadership of a man expelled from the Holy Communion of Christianity by His Holiness the Pope."

Falkenhayn again raised his eyebrows. "I see. So both of you are going to sit here on your—" he stopped himself, smiled, and with a little bow revised his phraseology to "comfortable, cushioned seats while the German knights alone defend Christendom and deal with these rebels?"

"We will not interfere in these secular matters," Pedro affirmed, but added, "yet I am curious about how do you intend to 'crush' these 'rebels,' as you call them?"

"They have already fled before us," Falkenhayn answered with a dismissive gesture of his hand. "They have abandoned Nicosia. We will run them to earth wherever they are. I doubt they will put up much resistance. They appear fundamentally cowards with, I dare say, a guilty conscience, as well."

"I see," Pedro noted with a glance to Guerin. "Would it change your opinion if I told you the reason the Lord of Beirut withdrew from Nicosia was to avoid Christian bloodshed?"

"The best way to avoid Christian bloodshed would be for that traitor to surrender to the Emperor his stolen treasure and his illegally held lordship of Beirut along with his miserable person."

"But it has not been proven before a court of law that he has a treasure, much less a stolen one, nor that he holds Beirut illegally—since it was granted to him by his sister and a king who loved him dearly."

"I'm not here to quibble with you, my lord. If Beirut cares even a little about Jerusalem, he will surrender his person, his treasure, and his city. The rights of it can be looked into afterward if the Emperor is so inclined. Meanwhile, we can all get on with this crusade."

"And if he doesn't surrender?"

"Then we will take him prisoner and deliver him."

Pedro nodded and Guerin and Eustace looked over at him curiously. "I would like to witness this arrest—if you don't mind. Would you have any objection to me accompanying you? I promise to bring only a squire and two knights with me." Guerin and Eustace looked at their brother even more astonished but did not question him out loud.

"It would be our pleasure to show you how the Deutsche Ritter Order conducts operations," Gunther von Falkenhayn replied proudly. "We will depart first thing tomorrow. If you wish to accompany us, report to my tent no later than sunrise."

Pedro bowed his head. "I will be there," he assured them.

The German returned the gesture, followed by a brief nod to the Archbishop and Hospitaller. Then he spun about on his heels to exit between his own men, who did an about-face as he passed so that they all marched out together in a compact unit. "Impressive," Eustace commented.

"We'll see," Pedro replied grimly.

Nicosia, Kingdom of Cyprus
August 1228

"Ulli, come quick! The Master has sent for you!"

"What? Me? Why?" Ullrich von Alvensleben had not fully adjusted to life as a Templar. He had joined the Order fourteen months earlier in his native Halberstadt, and after surviving the first nine months in Temple-hof on the frontier of the Mark Brandenburg, he had been selected to join a troop of Templars bound for the Holy Land. They had traveled overland as far as Marseilles and there taken ship for Cyprus, the total journey consuming more than three months. He had been on Cyprus for just under six weeks and he still found the climate oppressive, the food strange, and the natives bewildering. Somehow, he had always imaged the Holy Land would be like the Mark Brandenburg in summer; he was unsettled by being surrounded by the treacherous sea, strange vegetation and people he could not understand. Fortunately, the official language of the Order was Latin, which he spoke well, and his French was rapidly improving because most of his brother-knights at the Commandery of Nicosia spoke that language among themselves.

Gebhard von Salder, who had just called to him, was the exception because he was the other German here. Gebhard had been in the Holy Land for two years, and he had taken Ullrich under his wing. Indeed, they had formed an immediate friendship based on their shared heritage. Both Salders and Alvenslebens were staunch supporters of the Welf emperors, which made them bitter enemies of the Hohenstaufen.

Ullrich ran across the cobbled courtyard in response to Gebhard's summons and asked breathlessly, "Have I done something wrong?" Even as he spoke he was trying to figure out what he could have done to incur the displeasure of not just his own commander but the Master himself. Ullrich was the first to admit that he was not the perfect Templar. He liked both his food and his sleep too much, but his worst fault was a passion for good horses. He hated being assigned less energetic hacks and had a slightly guilty conscience for trying to persuade the Sergeant in charge of the stables into giving him one of the new stallions.

"How would I know if you have done something wrong?" Gebhard answered with a twitch of his eyebrows. "Your guilty conscience is for your confessor, not me. Now hurry." As he spoke, the older Templar started pounding up the stone stairs that led up the side of the perimeter wall to the wall walk—and the wooden footbridge that gave access to the second floor of the commandery tower. The ground floor which contained the armory and store was accessible from the inside only.

Their iron-clad feet clunked on the wooden bridge and then chinked on the flagstones of the tower. They entered one of two parallel vaulted chambers that served the brothers as a refectory and a chapter house respectively. From the refectory, they climbed by a spiral, corner stairway to the next floor composed of two more vaulted chambers set at right-angles to the chambers below. These were the chapel and the residence of the commander respectively. The latter was divided by wooden partitions into an office/audience chamber, and a bedchamber.

The Commander of the Temple at Nicosia was seated at a table with the Master. Alerted by the sound of men emerging from the stairs and crossing the chapel, he was looking straight at Salder and Alvensleben as they entered. Before they could even bow, he gestured them forward. "These are the men I was telling you about," he told the Master.

Ullrich stood as straight as he could, conscious that he could never stand taller than five foot four inches no matter what he did, and he kept his eyes focused on a spot on the wall behind the Master—which didn't prevent him from noting the man had black hair sprinkled with white, black eyes, and a solemn expression.

The Master stood and came around the table to stand directly before the two knights. "You are?" he asked in Latin.

"Gebhard von Salder, my lord."

"Ullrich von Alvensleben."

"Subjects of the Holy Roman Emperor?"

"Templars, my lord!" Salder replied firmly.

"We serve only Christ by following the orders of our superiors."

The Master nodded and glanced toward Alvensleben.

"The Hohenstaufen is a usurper, my lord."

That brought a scowl from his commander but a slightly more positive twitch from the Master's lips. "Tomorrow, starting at the crack of dawn, I will accompany the Teutonics as they set out in pursuit of the Ibelins. I promised to come with just two knights. I want men who speak German fluently and can mingle freely with the Teutonics, which is why I have selected you. I expect you to befriend the Teutonics, win their confidence, and listen closely to what they have to say. When we return here, I will expect you to report to me at length. Understood?"

"Yes, my lord!" They answered in unison.

The Master gestured for them to go.

Befriending the Teutonics was easier said than done, Ullrich thought to himself, as the sun climbed up the sky. They had set out at first light in a long, disciplined column, riding two abreast. Except for a joint "Pater Noster" before setting their horses in motion, the Teutonics maintained strict silence.

Of course, Ulrich reflected, the Templars did the same when patrolling in enemy territory and the like, but they were still in the Christian kingdom of Cyprus. While he didn't pretend to understand this dispute between the Cypriot barons and the Holy Roman Emperor, he certainly didn't feel threatened. As far as he could see, it was a dispute over titles and treasure that had nothing to do with the Templars—or the Teutonics either.

Before noon, they left the central plain behind and ascended the narrow but steep mountain range that, Ullrich had been told, ran along the northern coast of Cyprus for about forty miles. Since he had landed at Limassol, he had never been up, much less over, these mountains. They were nothing like the Alps, of course, much lower and not snow-capped, yet they were crowned with some jagged peaks of naked stone. These ran along the top of the range like a vicious spine or comb, and the closer one came to them the more dramatic the sheer sides of the rocks appeared.

Just after noon, they turned off the main paved road that led through the pass to the coastal city of Kyrenia and dismounted for a break. The men spread out to relieve themselves in the ample shrubbery. Then skins of water were passed around, both for washing hands and drinking, followed by a priest reading a short prayer before rations were shared out. At last, the Teutonics formed groups of five to six to share two loaves of bread, a round of cheese and a hard sausage. At a nod from the Master, Salder and Alvensleben each chose a different group and asked to join.

The Teutonics graciously accepted them each, and Ullrich found himself with five Teutonics who introduced themselves politely. By their names, three of the men were from Bavaria, one from Saxony, and one from the Rhineland. One asked Ullrich where Alvensleben was and he explained it was near Halberstadt. They nodded. Then one asked, "Why did you join a French order rather than us?"

"The Templars aren't French," Ullrich answered, trying not to sound defensive. "They were founded in Jerusalem. Jerusalem belongs to us all."

He was answered by a snort from one of the men.

"The current Master is from Spain," Ullrich pointed out reasonably. "And we've had English and Flemish Masters."

"But no one from the Empire," one of the Teutonics pointed out.

"Well, someone has to be the first," Ullrich countered with a smile and a shrug that was so disarming that they all broke out laughing.

With that, the ice was broken, and everyone seemed to be talking at once—getting in as many questions as possible before the "rule of silence" descended over them again. Most of the questions, fired rapidly and eagerly at Ullrich, had to do with the Holy Land—the weather, the food, the numbers of Templars and Hospitallers deployed for this crusade, and whether Ullrich had been to the castles in Palestine, whether he fought the Saracens yet, and the like.

Given his inexperience, Ullrich was relieved when the order came to mount up, and the questions were cut short. Ullrich unhobbled his horse, tightened the girth, and remounted. He took his place, riding directly behind his Master, who rode beside Gunther von Falkenhayn.

The dirt path they were on was just wide enough for two, so the Masters rode side-by-side, and Ullrich and Gebhard rode in single file behind Master Pedro with a Teutonic Knight beside each of them. The trail wound its way through the rugged landscape, gradually climbing toward the backside of the vicious spine of the mountain. It frequently skirted giant outcrops of limestone and dense stands of trees. Gorse, thorn and stunted pines clung to the ever-steeper slope on their right. The men and horses, although silent, made enough noise to frighten birds of prey into the air, where they circled silently, looking critically down on the pairs of horses stretching out for half a mile.

After riding well over an hour, Gunther von Falkenhayn broke the silence. "Are you sure this is the way to St. Hilarion?" he asked Montaigu with a frown.

"Very," the Templar answered with supreme confidence. Adding, "To be precise, it is the only way to St. Hilarion on horse. Indeed," Master Pedro lifted his arm and pointed toward the jagged peaks rearing up ahead of them yet still several miles off. "If you look hard, you can make out the chapel and the barracks of the middle ward."

Falkenhayn and Ullrich looked where the Templar Master was pointing and saw nothing. Falkenhayn frowned at the Templar but didn't dare challenge him.

Master Pedro assured him, "You'll see better as we get closer."

Ullrich like the Teutonic Marshal kept searching the mountain peaks ahead for some sign of a castle, but he couldn't find anything that looked like walls, ramparts, and battlements. He twisted around in his saddle with a questioning look for Gebhard, who just grinned at him.

They must have ridden another half hour before, with an exclamation of "Donnerwetter!" the Teutonic Marshal drew up sharply and sat gaping at the landscape ahead. The limestone had at last resolved itself into a chain of crenelated towers nestled into the very crest of the rock. The jagged spine rose to two peaks, separated by a pine-filled gorge, and on each of the peaks reared a tower replete with arrow-slits, battlements, and banners. From the nearest of these peaks, a wall cascaded down a sixty-degree slope of the mountain to a lower wall that curled around the foot of the cliffs boasting a chain of towers. From this far away, the walls looked tiny, but the dots of light that indicated men, whose helmets were reflecting the light of the sun, set things in proportion. The walls were at least 35 feet high and supported by towers even higher. Yet the top of the highest wall did not reach the foot of the bedrock on which the chain of upper towers had been built. Ullrich did a quick calculation and estimated that the sheer rock cliff crowned by the castle itself was more than 160 feet high. With the towers added, that was 200 feet from the base of the rock to the fighting platforms. Not only was it physically impossible for a man to climb such a precipice, it would be impossible to fire missiles that high either. From the base of the rock, arrows would have been shot at an angle so vertical they would come back down on the heads of the men firing them; from farther away they would simply shatter themselves on the rock cliffs.

"It will only take you a couple of days to reduce these castles, wasn't that what you said?" Master Pedro gloated.

Falkenhayn glowered and nudged his horse into motion again. As they continued along the path, the castle only became more impressive. There was a powerful barbican protecting the gate on the lower wall, but it was irrelevant. Capture of the lower gate and outer wall only brought an attacker onto a steep, rugged slope on which a substantial number of horses and cattle grazed. This led to the foot of the cliffs where they were still 160 feet below the castle. It would be pointless to try to tunnel through bedrock; not only would that be time-consuming and expensive it would not undermine the buildings so far overhead.

"What about the other side, the north?" Falkenhayn growled.

"The drop is both steeper and greater on the north," Master Pedro replied. "Not even a goat track can come close. The forest is very dense as well. As you see, at least to the south there's a broad shoulder on which besieging armies are wont to camp."

"There can be no water up there," Falkenhayn snapped, his eyes scanning the line of buildings, some square some round, some wider, some narrower, that perched upon the contours of the mountain crest. The higher up the slope the larger the windows became, until, the largest building below the two peaks with the towers smiled down from large, gracious windows with delicate tracery that haughtily proclaimed complete immunity to attack.

"The mountain gets a great deal of rain in the winter and the water is collected from all the rooftops and funneled through a network of drains to gigantic cisterns that are carved under the castle. The castle has been known to run low on supplies, never water. Knowing that, of course, Beirut has been provisioning the castle for the last two weeks. It is said to have sufficient grain, oil, and wine to feed the current garrison for twelve months—not to mention all those cattle on the hill that will provide plenty of beef."

The Teutonic Marshal looked furiously at his Templar companion, and his face was red as much from pent-up fury as sunburn.

They were, meanwhile, close enough to see the banners of Ibelin flapping from the flag-poles on the barbican and other towers. The bright yellow banners stood out sharply against the blue sky, the red crosses curled and straightened on the wind like living beasts.

It struck Ullrich that they were the same red crosses that the Templars wore, the mark of martyrdom. Maybe Falkenhayn thought the same thing because his eyes narrowed as his gaze shifted between the banners of Ibelin to the Templar Master and his two German Templar knights.

"The Ibelins," Master Pedro remarked in a mild voice, his solemn face looking almost saintly, "were defending Jerusalem more than half a century before the Deutsche Ritter-Orden was founded."

Falkenhayn growled something under his breath and spurred forward to ride along the base of the outer wall. When he came to the corner where the wall turned to go up the slope to the base of the upper towers, his horse stumbled and almost fell. As it scrambled to find its footing, it set off a tiny avalanche of stones that rattled down the slope behind him. Falkenhayn turned and rode back to the other end of the wall. This ended at the sheer rock face on which not so much as a thorn could grow. He drew the reins and looked up the face of the rock, squinting into the sun.

Meanwhile, his knights and sergeants collected on the comparatively level shoulder of land opposite the barbican and awaited orders. They took good care to stay out of range of the archers they could see manning the walls. Ullrich could hear the men counting and comparing estimates. "At least fifty archers, I'd say."

"Fifty? More like a hundred! Look at the towers, they have men in the interior as well as on the battlements."

"Just how many men does this Ibelin have?"

"More than 400 knights backed him at Limassol, they say."

"But they've dispersed, some to other castles."

"Yeah, so maybe only 100 knights, 200 sergeants, another 200 turcopoles, and 500 men-at-arms, not counting squires, grooms, and other servants."

Ullrich asked Gebhard in a low voice, "Has the castle ever fallen to assault?"

"Not in a quarter millennia."

Falkenhayn was back. He barked at the Templars, "What of the other castles? Kantara and Buffavento?"

"Kantara is similar, Buffavento worse—or better depending on your point of view. It is impregnable," The Templar reported with a shrug. Falkenhayn glared in answer, provoking Montaigu to suggest, "Please don't take my word for it. Go see for yourself."

Falkenhayn started barking orders in German. They would camp for the night here, but he had already seen enough to know that he was not going to be able to storm this castle, much less capture it in a few days.

Chapter Fifteen
A False Truce

Royal Palace at Nicosia,
Kingdom of Cyprus
September 1228

KING HENRY WAS IN HIS MENAGERIE. It had always been one of his favorite places, but since the arrival of the Holy Roman Emperor, he spent more time here than usual. His Sicilian watchdogs didn't like the stink of the big cats and made disgusted faces, preferring to stay outside in the garden when Henry visited the cats. Henry didn't like the smell either, but he found that the longer he stayed the less he noticed it, and so, whenever he wanted to escape the company of the various imperial officials the Emperor imposed on him, he came and conversed with the lion.

"We're in the same situation," Henry explained, looking into the unblinking, golden eyes of the lion. "You can't run free and be with your friends, and neither can I. But at least you don't have to listen to lectures all day long," Henry added. The Emperor insisted that King Henry needed more "education" and had assigned him instructors, particularly for the natural sciences and mathematics. That was bad enough, Henry felt, but what he really resented was that whenever the "the wonder of the world," Frederick Hohenstaufen, spoke with him, the latter spent most of the time telling Henry how evil and insidious his former friends were.

"Maybe Lord Philip did keep some of my revenues for himself," Henry told the lion, who yawned at him, letting out a puff of bad-smelling breath. "But it isn't as if I went without anything I needed or wanted," Henry pointed out.

The lion slowly pulled his hind feet under him and pushed himself upright. He sauntered over to the bars of his cage and looked more intently at Henry, who was sitting on the floor outside the cage with his back against the wall.

"Nor is the Emperor a particularly good king," Henry informed the attentive lion. "If he was, then people wouldn't keep rebelling against him. First, he drove the Lord of Beirut into rebellion by threatening to take away Beirut, and now all of Apulia is in revolt. Apulia," Henry explained to the lion, "are the lands in Southern Italy that belong to the Kingdom of Sicily. For weeks now, messengers arrive practically every day reporting on yet another city that has either fallen or just gone over to the Pope without a fight. And you know the best of it?" Henry asked the lion, who decided to sink down on his belly again but continued to stare at Henry. "The Pope's armies are led by King John of Jerusalem! Queen Yolanda's father. I wish my cousin Eschiva were here so we could talk about it," Henry admitted. The lion was not the best conversationalist.

Since he had no other companion he trusted however, Henry soon resumed his monologue. "I overheard Herman von Salza, that's the Master of the Teutonic Knights, who recently arrived from Acre, say that if Frederick wanted a kingdom to return to, he needed to take Jerusalem fast and return to Sicily. Frederick insisted he had to 'crush' the Ibelins first. Salza tried to convince him that this war on fellow Christians only played into the hands of the Pope, and warned him he might win Cyprus only at the price of losing Sicily. Then he told the Emperor, 'Take Jerusalem and you'll be the hero of Christendom. After that, you can do whatever you like to the Ibelins and their friends.'"

Henry paused, thinking about that. "I hope that's not true because I don't see why he should be able to take away people's lands and titles just because he doesn't like them. Beirut's father defended Jerusalem against Saladin, you know. If it wasn't for him, many more Christians would have been enslaved. And Beirut himself made a prosperous city out of Beirut that was a ruin before. The Emperor shouldn't interfere in affairs here. He doesn't understand anything about the Holy Land and those of us who were born here."

The lion yawned again and blinked at Henry slowly.

"I don't really think he can do Lord John and Lord Walter any harm," Henry told the lion a little uncertainly. "They hold the royal castles, and if you'd ever seen them you'd know they are impregnable." Henry stumbled over this word that he had only recently learned from Gunther von Falkenhayn. Then he brightened and confided to the lion, "Best of all, if Frederick goes to Syria to recapture Jerusalem, then I'll be rid of him! The first thing I'm going to do is ride to St. Hilarion to see my sisters, and then I'm going to visit Lady Yvonne and Lady Eschiva. In fact, I think I'll hold a tournament and have a banquet with lots of music and dancing." Henry was warming to the theme of being master of his own house again.

The lion tentatively reached one of his big paws out between the bars of the cage as if offering it to Henry. The fur looked wonderfully soft, and the paw was relaxed and looked gentle. It was almost as if the lion was offering him friendship. Henry wanted to reach out and touch that paw, but the lion-keeper had warned him never, never, never to try to touch the lion. He claimed the lion was still wild at heart and only looking for an opportunity to take his revenge upon his captors.

Still, Henry didn't *feel* any hostility emanating from the lion. The lion seemed to understand and sympathize with him. So Henry looked left and right to see if the lion-keeper was anywhere about. He *appeared* to be alone, but Henry knew from experience that the lion-keeper liked to keep out of sight yet within hearing. "Hello?" Henry called out to see if he got a reaction.

Although no one answered, he heard voices outside—angry, agitated voices.

Now what? Henry thought, pushing himself to his feet in anticipation of something unpleasant.

A moment later one of his Sicilian watchdogs burst in, grimacing at the smell and visibly holding his breath. "My lord! Come at once! The Emperor wishes to speak with you."

Henry nodded and followed the Sicilian dignitary into the fresh-smelling air of the garden (it *did* smell a lot better out here), but he refused to rush. In fact, he intentionally dawdled as the Sicilian became more and more agitated. Henry was enjoying himself. The man clearly wanted to give him a smack on his backside or a cuff to his head, as you would a lazy page boy, but Henry was consciously enjoying being exempt from such treatment. He was a crowned and anointed king and no Sicilian nobleman had the right to lay a hand on him. So he kicked at the marble stones in the path with his shoes and stopped to squeeze the figs to see if they were ripe or not.

Eventually, they reached the covered stairs leading back up to the royal apartments, and he slowly mounted them. Inside, Henry could at once sense that something was happening. The whole palace seemed strangely animated. Servants were running rather than walking, voices carried from several rooms they passed on their way along the corridor to the antechamber to his apartment. As they entered, Henry found the Emperor surrounded by a dozen men. Herman von Salza was one of them, of course, but more surprisingly the Masters of the Hospital and the Temple were also there—the dour Montaigu brothers that Yvonne had made fun of at the banquet. Sir Amaury Barlais, the "weasel," was standing right beside the Emperor as he so often did nowadays, as were the

Emperor's "pet archbishops" Berard of Palermo and James of Capua. To Henry's surprise, however, the two baillies of Jerusalem were also present. These were Eudes de Montbéliard and the Lord of Sidon.

Henry knew that Montbéliard was the Lady Eschiva's brother, but they were completely different. Eschiva was his friend, while her brother, who had visited several times over the last couple of months, never paid any attention to him at all. Instead, Montbéliard fawned on the Emperor, but he seemed nervous too. Anxious to please—and anxious to get away again. Henry had heard Frederick Hohenstaufen mutter, "silly little man" after he left once. Henry didn't know why the barons had elected him baillie, or why the emperor retained him.

Sidon was different. He was an energetic man in his mid-thirties with an aura of self-confidence. He was also a nephew of the Lord of Beirut, the son of his older sister Helvis and the old Lord of Sidon. He had been elected baillie of Jerusalem by the barons after the death of Yolanda.

"Ah, there you are at last!" The Emperor greeted the King of Cyprus.

Henry pressed his lips together. The Emperor never addressed him respectfully unless he was making a point in front of others.

Blind to Henry's resentment, the Hohenstaufen continued, slapping the table around which they were standing, "We have here the terms of an agreement with Beirut and his pack of rebels! We need you to sign it." The Emperor pointed to the end of the document and indicated a pen standing ready along with ink and a pot of molten red wax and the royal seals.

Henry's chin went up. "Not until I have heard the terms of the agreement!"

"Alright. Montaigu, Sidon, Montbéliard? Do one of you want to read the agreement to the King. It is in Latin."

"I'm perfectly capable of understanding Latin," Henry replied, fuming.

"I know you are," Guerin de Montaigu answered with a smile and a wink, reminding Henry of their joint action to rescue Sirs Balian and Baldwin from the dungeon. "And I'm sure you will like the first point of the agreement as well," he continued, "because it says that the Emperor will restore to the Lord of Beirut both his sons—safe and sound in body and limb." He switched to Latin to read the exact language of the agreement, then paused to politely ask the King if he should continue.

Henry nodded, and the Hospitaller Master read out the remaining terms: 2) that the Emperor would keep the peace with the Lord of Beirut and all his followers and they in exchange would join the Emperor's expedition to Syria to regain Jerusalem at their own expense, 3) that neither party would bear malice against the other for what had passed between them, 4) that no action would be taken against the Lord of Beirut without a verdict from the respective High Court, 5) the lords of Cyprus would swear fealty to the Emperor as overlord of Cyprus—"

"That's because," Frederick Hohenstaufen interrupted to lecture Henry, "they flat out *refused* to recognize *us* as regent! They said your *mother* was your regent."

"That's right," Henry retorted, staring at the Emperor and daring him to hit him for his impudence. "My mother is *regent* and appointed Lord Philip my baillie, and all my barons swore to recognize him as such until I came of age. Only he died before I came of age, but that doesn't change the fact that *she is* my regent. She just prefers to live in Antioch with her new husband and appoint baillies to rule for me."

"*We* are your overlord," the Emperor answered in a voice that made his minions stiffen with discomfort. "Should *we* choose not to act as your baillie personally, then *we* and *we alone* have the right to appoint someone else—"

"It is moot arguing this now," Herman von Salza spoke up diplomatically. "Beirut and his party will not under any circumstances recognize your excellency as baillie of Cyprus. These are the best terms we could get for now." He pointed at the document on the table. Salza, Henry noted, was almost the opposite of his marshal Falkenhayn. He was tall, thin and elegant, whereas Falkenhayn was stocky and short.

"May I continue reading?" the Hospitaller Master asked with raised eyebrows.

The Emperor gestured irritably for him to continue, but stood sulking beside the table as he did so.

"And finally, my lord," Guerin de Montaigu told King Henry, "the Lord of Beirut and his supporters agree to surrender the royal castles that they hold in your name to you, so that *you* may appoint castellans of your choosing, while they proceed with all their men to Syria to fight for Christ."

"Oh!" Henry was surprised by that provision—and pleased. If he could appoint the castellans, then they would really be in *his* power, and then he would be impregnable. He liked that word! "That's good!" he announced.

"Then you will sign?" The Hospitaller Master asked him with raised eyebrows.

"Yes, of course. Where?" Henry stepped to the table and looked down at the document written by a clerk in elegant and regular calligraphy. Picking up the pen, he dipped it in ink and, with a flourish he had practiced, affixed his name at the place indicated.

"There are three copies," Guerin explained, "so sign here and here as well."

Henry dutifully did, then he put down the quill, stepped back and looked at the assembled adults with a satisfied expression.

The three Masters looked decidedly relieved. Guerin de Montaigu even had a smile for him, noting, "Soon Sirs Balian and Baldwin will be reunited with their father and brothers."

Henry saw Sir Amaury Barlais frown at that, but the Emperor hissed at him. Sidon and Montbéliard bowed to King Henry and excused themselves, saying they would prepare to return to Syria at once, while the Templar Master rolled up the documents. He handed one to Herman von Salza with the words, "See this is filed in the Imperial archives." The second he gave his brother to place in the royal archives of Cyprus, and the third he kept to take to the Lord of Beirut. A moment later the three Masters had also left.

The Emperor, with his two archbishops, King Henry and Sir Amaury Barlais were alone. The Emperor turned on King Henry and announced in a tone that brooked no contradiction. "You will be coming with me to Syria."

Henry was taken completely by surprise. Not only did that mean he would neither be rid of the interfering senior monarch nor able to do what he liked, but it also meant he would be part in a military campaign. It was not usual for eleven-year-olds to go to war, even if they were kings. Henry recognized instantly that this was not an honor of any kind, but a means of retaining control over his person—and preventing him from taking possession of his castles. The Holy Roman Emperor was surrendering the Lord of Beirut's sons in exchange for an even more valuable hostage: his king. Suddenly King Henry of Cyprus felt small, helpless and frightened.

Famagusta, September 1228

The Genoese and Venetians had offered their fleets to transport the Cypriot army to the Syrian mainland and had collected their ships at Famagusta. It had been agreed that the Emperor's fleet would rendezvous with them there, bringing the Cypriot hostages on the Emperor's ship from Limassol. The hostages would be released to their relatives at Famagusta before the Emperor continued to Tyre and from there to Acre.

Although Famagusta had grown from a haphazard pirate's base into a small city in the thirty years of Lusignan rule, it was still overwhelmed by the thousands of men that converged on it to embark for this crusade. The inns and taverns were overflowing, while all the private residences had taken in relatives and friends, leaving the bulk of the Cypriot forces to camp outside the city walls. The harbor was equally congested, with ships moored three or more deep.

Under the circumstances, the Lord of Beirut gave the order that any contingent of men that was complete and ready to embark should go on board the outermost ships and proceed directly to Acre. This was where the Christian forces were assembling for the assault on Jerusalem. Many of the independent knights holding money fiefs from the crown, as well as marshals of Syrian barons bringing knights, sergeants and archers from Cyprus to join their lords on the mainland all departed for Acre incrementally.

The Lord of Beirut's Cypriot force, composed of 44 knights, 138 sergeants, and 325 archers, in contrast, awaited the rendezvous with the Emperor and the return of the hostages before embarking. Caesarea and Karpas remained with Beirut both to demonstrate their solidarity and out of concern that the Emperor might yet break his word and attempt to arrest the Lord of Beirut.

Beirut and his allies were camped outside of Famagusta on the broad plain before the ruins of the ancient city of Salamis. It was well watered by several small streams, and the horses had good grazing land, but it offered no good view of Famagusta harbor. As a result, the news that the Emperor's galley had been sighted reached them rather late, and they tacked-up their horses in a flurry of excitement.

When they were about to set off in a small cavalcade, Beirut noticed his sons Hugh and Johnny were with him. He furiously ordered them to remain behind. "You won't go near the Emperor until your older brothers are back safe!" he told them shortly, signaling Philip of Novare to come up beside him instead.

Novare was honored. He gestured in turn to Sir Balian's squire Rob to ride with him. Rob was leading Balian's destrier, the latter beautifully groomed and decked out in his finest panoply. Baldwin's squire was also in the party with Baldwin's destrier, while the Lord of Karpas, provocatively, rode the stallion he had won from Sir Amaury Barlais in the judicial duel.

By the time they entered through the northern gate of the city, the entire population seemed to know what was happening. People came out into the streets or crowded onto the rooftops and balconies to get a glimpse of the Lord of Beirut as he rode to meet the Emperor.

Beirut looked splendid in exquisite armor that fit him like a second skin. A surcoat of marigold silk with the crosses of Ibelin strewn across it like drops of blood fluttered in the light wind. The trapper of his horse, although made of a heavier fabric was just as bright a yellow and the red crosses on it were large and vivid. The banner of Ibelin was carried by a squire riding at the flank of his entourage.

As the Ibelin party approached the harbor, the spectators were so numerous that they clogged the streets, and Beirut and his men could hardly force their way through. Eventually, the street opened onto the quay and they had a clear view of the Emperor's large war-galley, painted red and black with red sails furled on the massive black booms. The Imperial eagle flapped lazily from the masthead and a gaggle of dignitaries in long, fur-trimmed robes hovered on the afterdeck around the pompously dressed Emperor.

In the waist of the ship, the hostages stood in a sorry cluster. They were still wearing the clothes they had worn at the infamous banquet, and their hair and beards were untrimmed. Beirut's eyes narrowed and he scanned the group twice, but he could not find his sons. He made a head count: eighteen. He caught his breath and drew rein. "Where are my boys?" The question was directed at Caesarea, who rode to his right.

Caesarea had come to the same conclusion: Sirs Balian and Baldwin were not among the men on deck. They looked at one another.

From the raised stern-castle of the ship the sound of giggling wafted over to them, and they both looked back in time to see a lovely, dark-skinned girl yanked back inside one of the windows. The watertight, wooden cover was shut so abruptly that the thud made the horses start, and still the shouting in angry Arabic reached their ears.

Beirut blanched as he registered this must have been one of the women of Frederick's infamous harem. The thought that a Christian monarch would keep slave girls like this offended him deeply.

Then a commotion near the forecastle drew his attention away from the imprisoned girls, even as he made a mental apology to his niece Eschiva for not believing her. A group of men emerged from the forward hatch onto the deck. A couple sailors came first, followed by men-at-arms in imperial livery. The latter were dragging and shoving two men in their midst. These men were tall, thin and dressed in what appeared to be the habits of Hospitaller lay brothers. They wore no hose, and their naked feet were in wooden clogs. Their hair was shaggy and their faces bearded. It took the Lord of Beirut a full second before he was certain that they were indeed his once proud sons.

Beirut felt his blood boil and his back stiffened enough to make his stallion fret. How often had he chided his sons, Balian in particular, for being vain? How often had he accused him of being a "dandy" and a "fop" because of his love of bright-colored silks, cloth of gold, and jewel-studded belts? How often had he chastised him for "excessive" attention to his outward appearance? Yet, this was far worse, Beirut conceded with inner shame, swearing to himself that he would never again criticize his son for dressing like the nobleman he was.

His sons had not seen him yet, their attention was directed toward the

Emperor and the crowd on the afterdeck. This gave Beirut a chance to assess their physical state before confronting their emotions. Baldwin looked considerably better than Balian, whose lips were cracked and swollen and whose eyes were sunken in dark eye sockets. Worse, when the men-at-arms started punishing them toward the afterdeck, Beirut saw Balian stagger and tense. His brother caught him by the arm, and the look on Baldwin's face said more than a thousand words. Baldwin looked *concerned* about his rival Balian and that suggested a serious state of affairs. Meanwhile, Balian had recovered and started forward with a set face. His expression, intended to disguise the pain he was in, was a grimace so unsuited to his usually debonair demeanor that it only underlined it.

The Emperor too turned to watch the emergence of the hostages, giving Beirut a chance to watch his face as well. The Emperor was gloating. There was no other word for it. He was smiling not for the audience, but from profound satisfaction at the sight of Ibelin's proud sons dressed like peasants and in obvious pain.

Beirut clicked to his horse and started forward, distracting the Emperor from the hostages. Beirut saw the look of triumph in his eyes before he hid his expression behind his "friendly" look. Beirut was not deceived. He never would be again, he promised himself. Yet his first priority was regaining control of his sons.

He jumped down from his horse, handed off the reins, and mounted the gangway in an easy fluid motion. Caesarea and Karpas scrambled to stay close on his heels. As he dropped onto the main deck he made eye contact with Balian and then Baldwin. The reproach, anger, and hatred he had feared to meet in their eyes were not there. There was not even bewilderment or incomprehension, only relief and, amazingly, respect. Baldwin nodded to him, as if in encouragement, while Balian tried to smile.

Beirut did not stop to speak to them. Instead, he turned away to mount the ladder up to the afterdeck. Here he approached the Emperor's party and went down on one knee in a gesture of homage.

The Emperor bent and raised him up, kissing him on each cheek before intoning in a voice that to Beirut's ears was sheer sarcasm, "What a joy to see you again, my lord! We rejoice to be united at last in this great enterprise for our Lord Jesus Christ. But, first, let us restore to you the hostages you left in our keeping. Here they are, whole and well, just as we promised!" Behind him, one of his Archbishops smiled benignly as if he didn't know what had been done to the hostages, as if he didn't know he served an excommunicate like a lapdog.

Sirs Balian and Baldwin had been brought onto the afterdeck in their father's wake and were shoved to stand at his elbow. The smell of them made Beirut's stomach turn over—not in revulsion but fury. He turned again to look at them up close, and his first impression was reinforced. Whatever the Emperor had done—or ordered or condoned others to do – he had not broken them. Beirut nodded to them, and they nodded back almost imperceptibly. All three Ibelins understood instinctively that this was no time for a great display of emotion. Anything that revealed how happy they were to be reunited would only make them more vulnerable and delight their watching enemies.

When the Emperor realized that there was to be no noisy reunion, he announced in a syrupy voice, "We must confess, however, we are so very, very sorry to see dear cousin Balian leave. In fact, now that he is happily no longer our hostage, we would most heartily welcome him into our household as a knight." He paused, smiling at Balian, who—to Beirut's relief—held his tongue, but smiled back at him with undisguised contempt. The emperor, unable to provoke a response from his victim, continued, "We would welcome your younger son John as our own body squire even *more* happily. It is a position that we award only to the highest and most *beloved* of our subjects. Both Balian and John would be richly rewarded for their service to me, we assure you."

"I would be *delighted* to serve you, my lord!" Balian burst out before his father had recovered from the shock of such a brazen request, and even as he opened his mouth to protest and decline, his son continued in a voice that was anything but polite. "I am sure, however, that in your *infinite* generosity you will first grant us the great *favor* of a little time together. If nothing else, it will allow me to prepare my dear little brother for his duties to you. We will join your household in Acre. Now, however, I *crave* your indulgence to return with my father to his camp." The words, so laden with humility were belied by the sarcastic tone of voice and the look in Balian's eyes.

Christ almighty, Beirut noted mentally, his hatred is enough to set the air on fire! I must help him tame it. To the Emperor, he added his voice to Balian's, requesting the Emperor's leave to withdraw and reinforcing, "We will join you with our full force at Acre."

"Excellent! Excellent!" The Emperor declared dismissing them with a wave and a smile. "We particularly look forward to your company, Sir Balian, and" turning to Beirut with a mocking smile, he added, "and to becoming acquainted with your young son and namesake John."

Beirut just bowed his head, then turned to depart. Beirut noted the way Baldwin helped his brother down the ladder to the main deck.

By the time they had stepped off the gangway, Rob's and Baldwin's squires had brought their destriers forward. Baldwin let go of his brother's elbow, kicked off his clogs and, putting his bare foot in the stirrup, swung himself up into his saddle with enthusiasm bordering on bravado. Balian took up his reins, but then seemed to freeze.

Rob, noticing the unexpected pause, assured him, "It's alright, sir. I've got the off stirrup." He was dutifully leaning his weight on the off stirrup to keep the saddle from twisting the horse's back as the knight put his weight on the near stirrup.

Balian didn't answer. He just stood beside his stallion's shoulder with the reins in his left hand.

"Balian?" Beirut asked, coming up behind him.

Balian shook his head inarticulately, drew a deep breath and tried to lift his left foot, only to gasp and grab onto his horse to hold himself upright. The surprised stallion threw up his head with a snort and stepped backward. Balian gasped and clung harder. His knuckles were white, his face a rigid mask.

Jesus God, Beirut thought, as he put his hand on his son's shoulder, and Rob tried to calm the unnerved stallion. At that moment, he was so horrified by the realization of how much pain his son was in that he didn't even care that this spectacle was taking place before a thousand eyes, including the Emperor's.

Then abruptly, Karpas pushed his way forward leading Barlais' horse. "Here!"

Beirut and Balian looked toward him bewildered. Barlais' horse was even larger than Balian's own. Karpas, however, gave the horse a little tap on his shoulder and his knees folded under him so he knelt before Balian, the stirrup at ground level.

Balian did not hesitate. Like his brother, he kicked off the clogs and put his bare foot in the stirrup, swung his right over the cantle, and took hold of the pommel as Karpas, with another tap, signaled for the horse to stand upright again.

Barlais meanwhile rushed to the railing of the ship to glare in fury at his beloved destrier forced into the service of his worst enemies.

Balian had no sympathy for him anymore. He spun the horse on haunches and rode directly at Barlais to hiss at him. "I will repay you a *thousand* fold what you did to me!" Then he nudged the stallion in the ribs so abruptly that the stallion started, skid on the cobbles, then recovered and trotted away.

Beirut rode back to his camp with his freed sons beside him, but they did not speak. Nor was the mood one of rejoicing, as he had expected. Although Baldwin smiled at him more than once, Balian had withdrawn within himself. He appeared to be brooding.

At last, they reached the camp. At the sight of Beirut flanked by his sons, the knights, soldiers, and archers began to cheer—until they got a better look at the two hostages. Then the cheers died on their lips and they looked at one another and started shaking their heads and muttering. Hugh and Johnny came spurring forward to greet their brothers, but their welcomes turned into exclamations of "Oh, my God!" and "Jesus! What did he do to you?"

"Later!" Their father told them, and they dutifully fell silent as they turned their horses to fall in beside their brothers, sobered.

At Beirut's large tent, they drew up and started to dismount. Balian hesitated, staring at the ground for a long time while Rob, his father, brothers, and Novare waited. Finally, he took a deep breath and swung his right leg forward over the pommel to drop down on the ground. As he landed, he gasped in pain and his legs gave way under him. He went down on his knees, and at once a dozen hands reached out to help. He took one without looking at who it was and grasped it so hard to pull himself upright that Johnny whelped in pain before turning to stare at his father in horror.

Beirut bade Novare bring the physician to his tent at once.

Novare agreed readily, turning his horse over to his squire as he hastened to find the Ibelin's physician Joscelyn d'Auber.

Meanwhile, Beirut gently pushed his younger sons aside and put his arm around Balian and guided him to the tent. Balian paused to find Karpas in the crowd behind his father. "Thank you, Sir Anseau. I don't know what I would have done without your horse."

"*Your* horse now, Balian," Karpas told him without a moment's hesitation. "He's called Damon, and he doesn't like me much. He remembers me trying to kill his rider in the judicial combat and holds it against me, but I'm sure you'll be able to win him over."

"But—thank you!" Balian appeared almost overwhelmed. "I owe you a great deal, my lord," he continued, and his father had the impression he was about to break down as he stammered. "I—"

"Don't worry!" Karpas cut him off with a grin. "I'll keep track and charge interest!" His quip and laugh dissipated the awkwardness and drew a weak but grateful smile from Balian.

Beirut gave Karpas a nod of thanks too, then asked the others of his party, all of whom were still staring in shock, to give him time alone with his sons. They withdrew with a murmur of well-wishes, while Beirut guided his eldest son into his tent, and Baldwin held open the flap for both of them.

Beirut led Balian to his own cushioned chair and had him sit down.

"I'm sorry, Father," Balian whispered.

Beirut just put a hand on his shoulder, then looked over his own. "Hugh, Johnny, bring us all wine."

The younger youths sprang to obey as Beirut directed his attention to Baldwin next. "Are you alright? Come. Sit down." He gestured to the only other chair in the room.

Baldwin accepted the invitation to sit, but insisted, "I'm fine, Father. They treated me better than Balian from the start." He cast a glance at his older brother, and Balian answered with a look that Beirut intercepted. He had the strong feeling Balian had just wordlessly asked Baldwin not to tell something.

Beirut immediately announced, "I want to know everything—*everything*—they did to you from the moment I abandoned you in the great hall. And then I want to know why you just volunteered not only yourself but Johnny to serve in that—" Beirut bit his tongue but then said it anyway "—that monster's household."

Balian took a deep breath and put his hand on his father's arm. When Beirut looked at him, he said slowly and deliberately, "Because, Father, he has the King."

"What do you mean?" Beirut asked irritated.

"I mean he has taken King Henry with him on this expedition, in his own ship, watched day and night by his minions."

Beirut stared at his son in disbelief. "That can't be! King Henry's only eleven years old!"

"I know. And the only way we can *try* to help him—and possibly remind him that we are *not* his enemies—is if one or the other of us are in the imperial household. Johnny is closest in age to Henry, and as a squire of the body might even be able to worm his way into a position where he can share Henry's chamber and meals. As for me, if I'm in the household, I'll at least have some idea of what is happening. I can *try* to protect them both—assuming I can regain enough strength to wield a sword ever again," he added with a surge of bitterness.

Beirut spun about to look at Johnny, who was bringing four brass goblets from one of the carved chests.

"What is it?" Johnny asked.

"The Emperor offered you a place in his household, as his squire, and your *brother* accepted for you—without my consent, so it is *not* yet decided. I will make my excuses to the Emperor and bear the consequences. I am not inclined to put any son of mine at his non-existent mercy ever again."

"Father, listen to me," Balian interceded.

Beirut had sworn on the night of the infamous banquet that he would never again disregard anything Balian told him. Against his instincts, he bit his tongue and waited for his son to continue.

"If not for King Henry, I am not sure I would be alive today." Balian paused to let the words sink in before explaining, "The Emperor threatened to throw us, bound hand and foot, to the sharks—after watching you hang."

"He's not exaggerating, Father," Baldwin hastened to support his brother. "The Emperor argued that your rebellion gave him the right to execute us. Although he promised to keep us alive long enough to watch you hang, I'm not sure Balian would have lasted. He was without water for almost two days. If King Henry hadn't gone to the Hospitaller Master and insisted on visiting us, it might have been longer. Master de Montaigu was appalled to discover the condition we were in and personally took us under the protection of the Hospital. He ensured that Balian was taken to the Hospital infirmary and received treatment there."

Beirut absorbed this with no visible display of emotion on his face—only fingers that could not stay still. First, they went to cover his mouth and chin, then fell to his chest and clasped his cross. He looked from his eldest to his second son uneasily.

Behind him, Hugh spoke up for the first time. "It was Rob who went to the Hospital and found out from the lay-brothers that you were being kept apart from the other hostages. He was the one who guessed you were being mistreated."

Beirut at once smiled over his shoulder at his third son and agreed. "Yes, that's true. While the rest of us withdrew immediately to Nicosia, Rob stayed behind to find out what had happened to you. I don't know how he got an audience with the King, but he must have gotten a message to him somehow." Beirut paused and added, "I never, never thought a Christian monarch could treat innocent hostages like criminals. Please forgive me for being so... naïve."

Balian almost laughed at that, and he reached out to his father. "I was never prouder of you than when you stood up to him and walked out, taking most of the Cypriot barons and knights with you." Then he added in a voice smoldering with hatred, "I would rather *die*, than watch you grovel at his feet."

"Balian speaks for me as well, Father," Baldwin joined in earnestly.

Beirut looked from one to the other, noting that the Lord had brought good even out of this terrible situation because the brothers had clearly buried their differences and found the love and respect for one another they should have as brothers. Still, he shook his head and asked, "How did it come to this? That we are subjects of a man without honor or Christian charity?"

"That fool Brienne was too damn eager for his daughter to wear an imperial crown, that's how! He's certainly lived to regret it," Baldwin retorted

Balian nodded agreement, adding, "But the way I see it, our *real* king is Henry, and he is now in acute danger. Not that the Emperor wants to humiliate him as he did us, but he does want to rob him of his inheritance by turning him into a puppet. He will certainly try to turn him against us. The fact that King Henry interceded on our behalf proves that the Emperor has not yet succeeded, but how much longer can we expect an eleven-year-old to hold out? Especially now that he is cut off from his own household?"

Beirut shook his head to indicate he did not know what to think, then turned to look at his son Johnny. "What do you think? Would you be willing to serve as a squire to the Holy Roman Emperor after what he did to your brothers?"

Johnny looked from Balian to Baldwin and then faced his father with his chin at an impudent angle as he declared, "I'm an Ibelin too, you know? If Balian and Baldwin can survive as the Emperor's prisoners, I'm sure I can survive as his squire."

Baldwin grinned at him and declared, "Well said, Johnny!"

"I will protect him with my life, Father," Balian swore, but the very solemnity with which he said it and the dark circles around his eyes made his father shudder.

"I don't doubt that you would *try*, Balian, but the sight of you does not inspire me with confidence! Rather, the Emperor might manage to kill you *both!*"

"For what it's worth, Father, I don't think he *will* kill us. Not now, not after he's signed the agreement with you. He wants to take Jerusalem first and to do that he needs to keep the Cypriot troops with him. If he harmed either me or Johnny, he knows you would withdraw your support. You've made that clear to him. Besides, did you see his face when I accepted his offer? He did not expect me to accept. He only made it because he wanted to see me quail and cower in horror. He does not know what to make of either—any—" he smiled at Baldwin and Johnny "—of us. He is used to men who grovel before him, and all his victories have been too easy up to now."

Beirut nodded, but his face remained clouded. While he shared Balian's assessment of the Emperor, he was acutely uncomfortable at the thought of putting Balian and Johnny in the Emperor's claws again. There had to be some other way to protect the King—and remind him that the Ibelins were his friends, not his enemies.

Hugh took one of the goblets Johnny was still holding, filled it from the carafe of wine he had brought, and handed it to his father. Beirut shook his head and indicated he should give it to his brother Balian first. The next goblet went to Baldwin and only then did Beirut accept one for himself. He sipped it slowly before, with a deep breath he announced, "Perhaps it is best for you to stay in the Emperor's household, Balian. Such a position would keep you out of the forefront of battle."

"Exactly. In my present state, I'd only be a liability to you there." He sounded bitter.

Beirut laid a hand on his shoulder again, reasoning, "Master d'Auber is a skilled *medicus*. I trust he will be able to restore you to your full strength. First, however, you both need to get out of those stinking and humiliating clothes. I'll have a bath made up for you at once, and send for the barber as well. We've brought your armor and wardrobe with us, and once you are suitably clean and attired, we'll celebrate with our good friends and vassals, who have all stood by us so staunchly these past four weeks. Johnny, go fetch the squires."

By the time the banquet was over, Balian wanted only to lie down, yet he dreaded it too. The pain in his back got worse some nights, though not others. He couldn't figure out what made the difference but presumed he sometimes remained too long in one position or twisted his back in his sleep. He was grateful that no one made a fuss when he asked to withdraw to the far side of the internal partition that separated the sleeping space from the larger room with the table where the meal continued.

Using only the light coming through the curtain from the room beyond, Rob helped Balian out of his clothes and into one of the beds, assuring him that there was both water and wine on the little fold-down table beside the canvas bed and that he would be within hearing just beyond the curtain.

"Rob, wait!"

"Sir?"

"My brother Hugh says you were the one who went to the King. I owe you my life."

Rob shifted from one foot to the other. "I—well—I mean, you know I couldn't go to the King myself. When Lady Bella learned from Sir Philip de Novare that you and Baldwin were being held hostage, she sent word to me that I should go to Lady Eschiva de Montbéliard. She's the King's cousin, see, and Bella thought she would be able to get an audience."

"You went to Lady Eschiva?" Balian asked amazed. "What did she say?"

"She took a fishing boat that very night and sailed to Limassol. By the time I arrived, the Master of the Hospital had already taken you under his protection, so I rode to Nicosia with the good news."

"She took a fishing boat?" Balian asked in approving wonder. "Where on earth did she find a fishing boat?"

"Her manor at Paradhisi is on the shore and there was a Greek fisherman in her household," Rob explained.

"Lady Eschiva is full of surprises!" Balian commented in obvious approval. He felt his interest in her growing again. Bella had tried to warn him off, saying he was playing with her emotions and that it was unfair and unkind. Yet, he wasn't playing. He was genuinely attracted to her. "How did she look?"

"What do you mean? It was dark and I—you know me, sir. I don't pay that much attention to feminine dress and—"

Balian laughed at his discomfort and then reached out to stop him from being offended. "What I meant was: did she look happy in her new life as Madam de Montaigu?"

Rob shrugged uncomfortably again. "I don't know, but why was she with her Greek servants at the shore rather than in the main house?"

Balian nodded, smiling slightly. "You see, you are more perceptive than you pretend. I *do* owe you my life, Rob—and apparently Bella, and Lady Eschiva, and the King, and the Master of the Hospital…. That's a lot of people to be indebted to—not to mention the Lord of Karpas and my father. I don't think I'm ever going to get out of debt."

"You know you don't owe me anything, sir. I'm just so glad I could find a way to help, even if it was only being a messenger."

"I owe you my life, Rob, and I won't forget it. Now, I'll try to sleep."

"Master d'Auber says you can put a pinch of this—but only a pinch—in wine to help you sleep if you need it." Rob showed him a little wooden bowl with a powder of some sort in it.

Balian nodded with a sense of unfathomable relief, not at the thought of taking a painkiller but the knowledge that he was indeed back among people who wanted to ease his pain and assure his recovery.

It was only after the other barons and knights had departed, the lanterns were blown out, and his sons and squires had all bedded down that Beirut went to check on Balian. He took a single candle and stood for a long time looking down at him. He seemed to be sleeping soundly, one bare foot hanging out and his shoulders exposed. The haircut and shave had done much to make him look less miserable, yet it also highlighted the extent to which his face had sunk upon his bones and the depth and darkness of the circles under his eyes. Only now, with his face relaxed in sleep, did he almost look like himself again.

Master d'Auber had reported to Beirut that he did not think any bones had been fractured. He suggested that with massages, heat treatments, and poultices Balian would be restored to full health and strength. "It's important not to rush things," he had warned. "A fall on the tiltyard, for example, could leave him crippled for life." The physician knew of what he spoke: he himself had been partially crippled by a bad fall while still a youth.

Beirut promised to pass that message to Balian and resolved that under no circumstances would he allow Balian to go into combat against the Saracens. Not yet.

Balian stirred in his sleep, gasped in pain and woke with a start.

Beirut dropped onto his heels and asked urgently. "Are you alright? Can I help in any way?"

"I just need to turn over," Balian muttered. "Can you give me your hand?"

Beirut put the candle down on the floor beside him, held out his hand and braced himself. Balian grasped it and, grimacing, adjusted his position enough to relax again. "Thank you, Father. Don't worry about me."

"I don't," Beirut lied. "But I want you to know that I do not trust this 'peace' that the Emperor has signed with us. I have learned my lesson. I will never trust him again."

"No, but we will pretend to for the sake of Jerusalem."

"Yes. We will." Beirut smiled to himself in the darkness. He did not deserve his sons, and yet their very existence seemed a sign of God's grace and favor. As long as his sons were with him, he knew God was too.

Chapter Sixteen
Winds of Change

Acre, Kingdom of Jerusalem
October 1228

ACRE SURPRISED KING HENRY. NEVER HAVING left Cyprus before, he had never seen a port in which Arab dhows were as numerous as Christian dromonds, where Arabic, Syriac, Italian, and French overwhelmed the sound of Greek—or where so many people were crowded together. Acre was so filled with humanity that it was never silent. Even in his chamber at the royal palace, Henry never quite had a sense of peace and quiet.

The Emperor, of course, had occupied the royal suite, and Henry had been given a room that looked out over the busy street leading to Holy Cross Gate. His Sicilian watchdogs, Masters Michael and Benjamin, occupied the adjacent rooms, and one of the Emperor's servants, Gormond, had been assigned to look after him and slept in a pallet at the foot of his bed.

Gormond, fortunately, had a weakness for wine and bawdy houses, both of which were offered in profusion in Acre. While the business of taking homage from all the Syrian nobility and negotiating with the Templars, Hospitallers, and Patriarch of Jerusalem for a joint campaign against the Saracens was occupying the efforts of Henry's higher-born watchdogs, Gormond was indulging himself. Henry was left to his own devices much more than he remembered in his whole life.

If only he'd been bold enough to just walk out of the palace and explore the city at his feet? From the balcony of his room, he could see all sorts of things he would have *liked* to explore. There were camel caravans, for a start; they entered through the gate and swayed their way down the length of the street to turn right about a hundred yards to his left. Where did they go? There was also a minaret visible on the far side of the city wall. Henry had never been in a mosque and he would have liked to see what one looked like both inside and out. Or there were the massive crenelated towers of the Temple visible on the far side of the city.

The Templar headquarters sat right on the shore, guarding the entrance to the harbor and it was the largest and best fortified urban fortress Henry had ever seen. He'd wanted to visit it from the moment he saw it from the deck of the Emperor's galley, but the Emperor had immediately squashed Henry's request. "The Templars are not to be trusted!" he'd snapped.

Trusted with what? Henry wanted to know. There could surely be no doubt about their devotion to Christ and The Holy Land, while their legendary honesty made them the preferred bankers of kings and popes. So in what way weren't they trustworthy? Henry could have asked Lord Philip or Lord Walter that question, but he didn't dare question the Emperor or his men. They made him feel stupid when he asked questions.

Henry sat on the floor of his balcony with his legs straddling one of the posts upholding the railing and his feet dangling. One of his Sicilian watchdogs had told him not to go out onto the balcony at all, reminding him that King Henry of Jerusalem had fallen to his death from a balcony of this very palace. Henry, however, figured that *that* Henry must have been very fat to make a balcony collapse.

He resumed his observation of the city below. Some important lord appeared to be approaching the gate from the far side because people were shouting, gesturing and converging on the gate in excited anticipation. Cheering could be heard from the suburbs beyond the gate too. Henry sat up straighter, but that still didn't give him a good view of the gate. So he pulled himself to his feet and leaned over the railing. Sure enough, horses were starting to emerge from the gate and a cheer went up from the people lining the streets. Hats were thrown into the air, and women waved their scarves. It was the Lord of Beirut!

Henry started waving wildly, and shouted, "Lord John! Lord John!" But his high-pitched voice didn't carry very far. The Lord of Beirut didn't look up and didn't see him. He was too busy acknowledging the cheers of the common people of Acre. Henry watched the way he rode slowly down the street, stopping frequently to reach down and give his hand to men who stepped up beside his horse. Henry had heard that Lord John was popular in his own city of Beirut, but he not expected him to be particularly popular here. This enthusiastic reception surprised him—and said a lot about Beirut.

Beirut's party of a score of knights and twice that many squires and sergeants turned into the street that led toward the Hospitaller HQ. The imposing towers of this large complex were also easily visible from Henry's window and much closer than the Templar HQ. Henry hadn't been allowed to visit it either. In fact, they hadn't let him out of the palace at all except to go to Mass at the Holy Cross Cathedral across the street. He sighed with frustration.

It didn't help that he was getting hungry. Maybe he should try to find the kitchens? At home in Nicosia, he not only knew his way to the kitchens, all the staff at the palace knew who he was and were happy to help him. Here he was more likely to be mistaken for a wayward page-boy and given a kick than anything else, he thought dolefully.

Listless and feeling sorry for himself, Henry wandered around his chamber. His tutors had given him a dozen mathematics exercises he was supposed to complete and return to them for correction, but he didn't want to. He didn't want to read the stupid book they had given him either. It was about logic, but it wasn't at all logical—just gobbly-goop.

A knock on the door made him start and look over guiltily. "Who is it?" he asked petulantly.

The door opened without an answer, and the man that looked in was young, dark, handsome and vaguely familiar, but Henry couldn't place him at first. Then it hit him. "Sir Balian!" he exclaimed in genuine surprise and enthusiasm as he ran to him. "You're all right! You've recovered!"

Balian seemed surprised by the King's enthusiasm, but he opened his arms with a laugh and accepted the king's hug. Henry looked up at him. "You *are* all right now, aren't you?" Henry had been horrified by what he'd found in the Hospitaller dungeon—and so had Master Guerin, who had quickly shooed the boy king out. As a result, Henry had not gotten a good a look at Sir Balian. He had seen only enough to realize he hung in the pillory as if he were dead, his jaw and neck covered with blood, and his eyes swollen shut.

"Right as rain," Sir Balian answered cheerfully, "and I've brought my brother Johnny with me."

"Oh!" Henry had been so excited to see Sir Balian looking so well, he hadn't noticed there was anyone else in the door.

"May we come in?" Sir Balian asked.

"Of course!" Henry backed up, letting his two visitors into his chamber. Sir Balian closed the door behind them. "Did you arrive with your father?" Henry was already putting things together. "I saw him arrive from my balcony and I waved and called to him, but he didn't see me. There were so many other people all crowding around. Why is your father so popular here?"

"That's a long story," Sir Balian answered. "First, Johnny has something to give you."

At this cue, Johnny threw back the linen towel over the basket he was carrying to reveal a floppy-eared puppy, who at once sat up and looked around with bright, curious eyes.

"OH!" Henry's delight was immeasurable. He reached out both hands and pulled the puppy into his arms. "He's wonderful! Does he have a name? Is he really for me? Do you think I can keep him?" Henry at once looked over his shoulder at the doors to the adjoining rooms.

"Of course you can keep him," Sir Balian answered. "Why shouldn't you? You're the King of Cyprus. But you'll have to feed him and clean up after him."

"Of course, of course!" Henry put his head on the puppy's head and let the dog lick his face, but already the little dog was squirming to get down. Henry happily put him on the floor and watched in delight as the puppy started exploring, his tail-less hind-quarters wagging from side to side. Then he remembered himself and looked at his two visitors. "Thank you! Thank you *so* much! I've been so lonely."

"Well, we've both joined the Emperor's household now," Sir Balian announced, shoving up his sleeves to reveal the scars on his wrists from the pillory as he spoke. It was a calculated gesture, Henry sensed, although he wasn't sure what it meant exactly.

Sir Balian continued, "I'll be with the knights, of course, but Johnny is to be squire to the Emperor, so he'll be just down the hall from you. Furthermore, Johnny knows where to find me, and we've developed a code which will let me know if you want to see me without any of the Emperor's men knowing. We can also speak Greek with one another whenever the Emperor's men are around."

"Oh, yes!" Henry got into the spirit of keeping secrets from the Emperor instantly. "That's a good idea. And could you take me out and show me Acre?" he asked next.

Sir Balian started but then shrugged. "I don't see why not." He looked around the room. "Are you alone?"

"I'm not supposed to be, but Gormond slipped out to visit some whore and told me to do my lessons while he was away. He wants to be here when the real watchdogs come back so that they think he's wonderfully diligent. That's why he always goes out as soon as they leave and then slips back just before he expects them to return. I was just wishing I had the courage to go out into the city on my own. Have you been to the Temple? I saw it when we sailed in and it looks awesome!" Henry hadn't felt free to talk in a long time and it was all flooding out.

"It would be better if we avoided places you could be recognized," Johnny spoke up for the first time. "Let's go down to the port instead—or to the weapons market. My father says you can get swords and daggers from Damascus there."

"Is there a pastry shop nearby?" Henry asked back. "I'm starving."

"Yeah, there are lots of bakeries and cook-shops between here and the harbor."

"I think I'm already superfluous," Sir Balian noted with satisfaction. "So I will leave." He started for the door, then stopped and turned back. "I'm serious, my lord king. If you need anything, send Johnny to me. Johnny, don't stay out too long. It would be better if the Emperor didn't find out what you were up to."

"No, of course not, but he's gone to see the Patriarch and that will take hours," Johnny replied confidently with a wave of his hand.

"Maybe. Be careful," Balian warned.

"Trust me, Balian," Johnny answered with a touch of annoyance creeping into his voice. "I know what I'm doing. I've had lots of practice escaping from you, Hugh and Baldwin."

Balian had to laugh at that, and with a nod to King Henry, he slipped back out the door.

Acre, December 1228

The bells were ringing for nones on the Monday after the Third Sunday in Advent, and Cecilia was losing hope that Maurizio would be home for Christmas. He hadn't actually promised her that, of course, but he had suggested it was possible 'if all went well.' And things had started out very well indeed.

After departing the second day after their wedding, Maurizio had caught an exceptionally good wind and sailed to Rhodes in less than a week. There, he had entrusted a ship bound the other way with his first letter to Cecilia. She had read it at least a thousand times and bought a beautiful box inlaid with ivory and mother-of-pearl to keep it (and the expected subsequent letters) in.

The second letter arrived little more than a fortnight later and was sent from Crete by the same method. This letter was less adoring and more businesslike, as her husband explained he was dashing it off so he could catch the tide and make use of the winds that still held good.

There had been a long silence after that while Cecilia became worried and anxious and her father admonished her many times to be patient. "A seaman's wife does not mope about and fret because she hears no news for a month or more!" he had told her sternly.

At last, on the very last day of August, a letter arrived from Bonifacio on Corsica. Maurizio wrote a long, long letter full of his longing for her and his excitement at the good progress he had made. Shortly afterward, came a short note dated Palma de Majorca. There followed another long gap, but in October one of the last pilgrim ships had arrived from Portugal with a precious letter from Maurizio. He had passed through the Straits of Gibraltar before the end of July and expected pleasant weather in the notorious Bay of Biscay. All was going perfectly. He expected to be in London by mid-August. "It will take me no more than a week to sell off the cargo and take new goods on board. I should set sail for the return voyage by St. Vincent."

But then the letters stopped. As her father explained, having gone so far, Maurizio could expect to return himself faster than anyone he encountered bound for the Holy Land—especially since there were hardly any ships that made the voyage around the Iberian Peninsula at all.

Despite what her father said about it being wiser to winter in London and return when the risks were less, Cecilia had spent days studying the maps in the reception hall of the Palace of the Genoese. She had calculated and recalculated the journey, using the dates of Maurizio's letters. She had convinced herself he should be here by now. No matter what her father said, she knew that Maurizio longed to be with her as much as she with him. He would go mad if he had to spend a winter idle in London. It was cold and grey and rainy there, Maurizio wrote, and the food was bad, the women stodgy and ugly, he said.

So on this Monday after the last Sunday in Advent, she ended her prayers with the usual one for Maurizio's safe and prompt return. Standing, she wound her scarves around her head proudly because they symbolized her marriage to Maurizio, and descended to the main hall to join her father at breakfast.

Her father sat as always in the beautifully carved armchair in the center of the high table on the dais. For some reason, he did not hear her coming. Rather than turn to smile at her as he usually did, he remained sunken in thought. She caught a glimpse of him unprepared and unguarded, and a shudder ran down her spine: her father looked very old and very unhappy.

"Papa!" Cecilia exclaimed as she ran toward him. "Is something wrong?" Reaching his chair, she stood beside him and searched his beloved face.

He forced a smile. "Of course not, of course not, child. Sit. Have your breakfast. I have some business to attend to, but don't worry your pretty little head about *business*." He shoved the heavy chair back and stood. As he passed Cecilia, he kissed the top of her head and stroked her cheek. "My angel," he whispered.

"Papa, you're so sad! What has happened? There's no bad news of Maurizio is there?"

"Of course not, of course not," he waved her concern aside a second time, but the smile he gave her was more a twisted grimace than a real smile. "It's just business," he insisted. "Nothing to concern you." He kissed her again, but she could feel his thoughts were elsewhere. She wanted to ask more, but she had been raised to be obedient and dutiful. It was not her place to question her father, so she sat down

Giovanni descended to the ground floor where his large, corner shop manned by three employees faced the busy junction of two important streets. He made a cursory inspection of the nearly empty sacks of saffron, cinnamon, cumin, almonds, and pistachios. His stock was running very low. Not good just before Christmas when sales were always best. He'd miscalculated a little when he'd sent so many wares with Maurizio. All would be well, of course, if Maurizio returned, but there were rumors.

Giovanni took a cloak that hung beside the courtyard door and exited. It was a cool, damp day with rain squalls coming in off the Mediterranean and gusting through the narrow streets. A gust rattled the shutters on the sides of the buildings and chased bits of rubbish along the gutters. The beggars had taken shelter in the doors of the many churches, and no one was about that had no need to be out of doors.

Giovanni made his way to the Palace of the Genoese. This was the large building constructed around a central courtyard and occupying a city block. The ground floor consisted primarily of storerooms, where the poorer members of the community who could not afford their own warehouses could rent space by the square yard. On the top floor, it had apartments that were rented out to Genoese who were transient rather than resident in Acre. But the first floor was composed of the offices, archives, council chamber, audience chamber, and festival hall for the community. It was half again as high as the floors above and below, with beautiful rib-vaulted ceilings, tall pointed windows, marble floors and wall-panels of mosaics or marble inlay. It was here behind the audience chamber that Signor di Sanuto, the Consul of the Genoese, had his offices.

Since the previous Friday, rumors had been circulating that the *Rose of Acre* had been lost a sea with all hands. Giovanni had been stopped in the street by one man asking if he'd heard the news, and the household steward had likewise reported to his master that he'd heard men talking about the wreck of the *Rose of Acre* when at the market. Giovanni had sent his personal servant down to the harbor to see what he could learn, and the man had returned with the news that the loss of the *Rose of Acre* was indeed being talked about in the dockside taverns.

Giovanni did not like to believe rumors, but when you heard the same thing from so many sources, it was hard to deny the possibility. Yet it was a possibility he could not—or refused—to fully grasp. Lost. A complete loss. With all hands. It would mean his ruin. His absolute and complete ruin—and it would break his little Cecilia's heart. He couldn't bear to think about it. Such a loss. He had to track down the source of the rumor.

There were already men waiting in the Consul's ante-chamber. In great agitation, they were discussing the latest rumors about the charters the Emperor had given to the Pisans. "He's virtually given them Arsur!" One man protested.

"Isn't Arsur still abandoned?"

"That's just it! It's been deserted ever since Saladin raised the defenses in 1187, but it used to be one-third ours! Now the Emperor has just handed it over to the Pisans."

"But the Lord of Beirut technically holds it by right of his wife, doesn't he? Surely only he can make grants."

"Legally, maybe, but that doesn't seem to interest the Holy Roman Emperor! Look how he tried to take Athlit from the Templars! He thinks he can dispose over the Kingdom of Jerusalem as he does over Sicily—like a despot!"

Sanuto's secretary emerged out of the inner chamber and gestured for Gabrieli to follow him into the office. Giovanni was grateful for that. He couldn't bear waiting any longer.

"Ah, Giovanni, my dear friend! Have a seat." Sanuto jumped to his feet and came around his desk with outstretched hands. "I'm so sorry! So terribly sorry! Indeed, words fail me. Who can forget how beautiful and in love they looked at their wedding! What a charming couple. And your dear Cecilia still so young, not yet sixteen is she?"

Giovanni staggered and would have fallen if Sanuto had not caught him. "Here, here. Have a seat," Sanuto urged again, sending the secretary to fetch water and wine.

"Then it's true?" Giovanni gasped out, his chest constricting about his heart so sharply that it hurt to breathe, and he could hardly speak.

"There can be no doubt, I fear. Young Paulo di Ferrario arrived on Friday from Limassol reporting that the wreck had washed up on the west shore of Cyprus a week ago. There were a couple of crates of wool and other wares from the Baltic still in the hold, but not a soul aboard. At first, they hoped one or another of the boats might turn up, but they never did." He paused as Giovanni grasped his heart, his eyes seeming to pop out of his face. "I presume this was a serious financial blow to you," Sanuto concluded.

"I'm ruined—" Giovanni gasped out. "Ruined."

"You have the house, of course, you could—"

Giovanni shook his head and rasped out "The Templars. Mortgaged—"

The servant arrived with the glass of water, but Giovanni couldn't swallow. He spat the water out and crumpled forward. The pain in his chest was unbearable. He could no longer make sense out of what was being said around him. The world was spinning, Cecilia's radiant face, Maurizio's confident smile, the hardnosed Templar banker, his creditors, Cecilia. Dearest, sweetest Cecilia. He couldn't face her. He couldn't bear to tell her Maurizio was dead, that she was a pauper, without a roof over her head. He couldn't.

The servants hadn't been paid in months, so they stole whatever they could before the Templars arrived to take possession of the house. The wine in the cellars was repossessed by the wine-merchant who hadn't been paid either. The larger items of furniture that the servants didn't drag out were impounded by officials of the court to be auctioned off to pay off Giovanni's debts. Within three days, Cecilia had not even a bed to sleep upon and they were threatening to dump her father in a pauper's grave.

Cecilia sold her wedding gown to pay for a coffin, funeral, and tombstone. Yet it was a very modest funeral and a very simple gravestone even so. A used dress, even one of cloth-of-gold, did not bring a high price when the merchants knew the seller was desperate, young and utterly ignorant of its real value.

Cecilia dyed every other shift, gown, surcoat and scarf black. Her gloves and shoes were black, too, when she followed her father's simple pine coffin to the grave in the pouring rain. Beside the priest, the gravedigger, and her father's dog she was alone. Neither the servants nor her father's creditors and former business partners dared to show up after robbing her blind.

As they tossed the dirt on top of her father's coffin, Cecilia didn't know what was worse: the earth smothering her father or the water that had suffocated her Maurizio. Was it better to be eaten by worms or fish? At least a priest could say prayers for her father's soul, but she could pay for no further masses. Not for him or for Maurizio. Dear Maurizio. My Maurizio.

"You mustn't stand out here in the rain any longer, child." The voice came from behind her, and when Cecilia turned she was so stiff it hurt to move.

Signor di Sanuto stood wrapped in a hooded cloak. He took her by the elbow and led her away from the grave. "I know you have nowhere to go, child.

I am taking you home with me. You can help our nanny look after the grand-children."

"I—I don't know—much—about children," Cecilia stammered out. She had never had younger siblings, and, for all Maurizio's virility, her womb had not quickened after their two blissful days of lovemaking.

"It comes naturally to all women," Sanuto told her patting her arm. "Now come along. We're both cold and wet enough already.

Chapter Seventeen

Dealing with the Enemy

Jaffa, Kingdom of Jerusalem
Early January 1229

THE EMIR FAHR ED-DIN HAD BROUGHT the Emperor a Syrian falcon as a "small token" of his regard, and the Emperor had invited him to a lavish feast in response. That was only natural, of course, particularly since, as Balian learned from the other knights of the Emperor's household, Fahr ed-Din had visited Sicily a couple years earlier. The Emperor and the Emir had become good friends, the others assured him, hunting together at a variety of the Emperor's hunting lodges and exchanging books. "They share a common interest in mathematics, biology, and astrology," Master Michael had told Henry, adding, "They are both very cultured and educated."

"As if no one else was!" Henry reported angrily to Balian, remembering how cultivated and well-read his beloved regent Lord Philip had been.

But it appeared true that the two men understood one another well, Balian conceded, watching from his position at the lower end of the hall with the Emperor's other household knights. From here nearly the whole length of the hall separated him from the principals on the dais, which made it impossible to see expressions, much less hear any words. Still, he could read gestures. By the way these two men frequently put their heads together and laughed simultaneously, they were good friends. Yes, Balian thought, narrowing his eyes, the Emperor and the Emir were thick as thieves—yet it was unlikely to be only a shared love of falconry, mathematics, and astrology.

He reached for his brass goblet and sipped at the wine without taking his eyes off the Emperor and the Emir. That he was reclining on satin cushions and eating Arab delicacies while watching the leader of the crusade laugh together with a leading emir of the Sultan of Cairo was only one of the many oddities of this so-called crusade, Balian thought cynically.

As on Cyprus, the Holy Roman Emperor had been far more interested in receiving the homage of the Syrian barons than in the liberation of Jerusalem— just as Balian had warned his brothers six months ago. The Emperor had even demanded the homage of the Prince of Antioch—a principality older than the Kingdom of Jerusalem and always independent. That was either evidence of the Emperor's gross ignorance of his deceased wife's kingdom or voracious greed. The Prince of Antioch, of course, had abruptly become deathly ill, fled back to his independent principality, and there enjoyed a miraculous recovery.

Eventually, after wasting months in Acre, the Emperor with obvious reluctance ordered his army to follow in the footsteps of Richard the Lionheart and march down the coast to Jaffa. In Balian's opinion, the very fact that he could think of nothing original underlined his lack of strategic competence.

Fortunately for the men marching with him, al-Kamil, the current Sultan of Egypt, was no Saladin either. On the contrary, al-Kamil had long been more interested in fighting his brother al-Mu'azzam, the Sultan of Damascus, than in jihad. Furthermore, his brother's recent death had greatly improved his chances of seizing Syria since his brother's successor was still a young boy. As a result, al-Kamil was diligently besieging his nephew in Damascus at the moment, while expressing his contempt for the Franks by ignoring the crusaders altogether. Balian supposed that, from al-Kamil's perspective, fighting crusaders was an irritant. So instead of the constant attacks that Richard of England's troops had suffered on their march from Acre to Jaffa, the army of Holy Roman Emperor had sauntered down the coast undisturbed.

When al-Kamil realized that the crusaders intended to seize Jaffa, he chose strategic retreat over confrontation. He pulled his garrison out entirely and warned the citizens to evacuate or face Christian rule. The bulk of the population chose the former, leaving behind Jews, Samaritans, and the owners of establishments that profited from armies regardless of nationality or religion. The Christians had re-established control over a city still largely in-tact with fully functioning baths, inns, taverns, and brothels. Only the churches had been sadly neglected, trashed or turned into mosques.

How different it had been thirty-six years ago! Balian's father had shown him the gate by which the King of England had forced his way into the city with just a handful of men to rescue the garrison. Balian wished intensely that he had been with that lionhearted King of England rather than the Muslim-friendly Hohenstaufen!

Balian's impatience, however, was kept in check by his physical weakness. He would sleep through most nights—only to wake feeling crippled with stiffness. Once he got out of bed, it took him five to ten minutes before the pains receded enough for him to disguise his discomfort and move normally. He could ride without undue pain and dismount normally, but still allowed Damon to kneel for him to mount. He had started exercises on foot with his sword and shield, but only with Rob, who was acutely conscious of the need to avoid a new injury. Rob parried Balian's blows but did not risk attacking.

At first many of the Emperor's household knights had mocked him for avoiding jousts and other games at arms. They spoke German or Sicilian among themselves, but he saw their sneers and heard their laughter following him. He had responded by demonstratively showing his scars whenever he sat down with them for a meal. The sight silenced them at once. Ashamed of what their lord had done, they looked away and left as soon as possible. He had also once indulged in a shameless demonstration of horsemanship that left them all gaping.

Recognizing that Damon was exceptionally intelligent and loyal from his dramatic defense of Barlais in the judicial combat, Balian had consciously courted the horse's affection. By consistently bringing carrots, riding and then hand-grazing him, he had built up a strong relationship with the stallion. Then he had spent hours every day developing Damon's responsiveness to his legs and shifts in weight alone. He now could ride with his arms outstretched while Damon literally danced under him, changing gait, direction, and moving laterally in response to the nearly invisible commands from his rider. After showing off to the Emperor's knights, they had stopped disparaging his skill at arms—at least to his face.

Yet while the Emperor's knights no longer openly scorned him, they had not befriended him either. Perhaps that was because he had given them no invitation. He did not want their friendship. They were the Emperor's men, and he, regardless of his official position, was the Emperor's sworn enemy. They all sensed it.

Johnny had been cleverer, Balian reflected. Johnny had ingratiated himself not only with King Henry (who followed him around like a puppy when he got the chance), he had managed to hoodwink the Emperor himself. The Emperor openly favored Johnny, calling him the "only good Ibelin" or "my loyal Ibelin." He frequently asked Johnny to serve him at table—without any of the insulting mannerisms he had used with Balian and Baldwin. He also gave Johnny various marks of his favor, from pieces of clothing and equipment to, most recently, the revenues of the South Italian city of Foggia. Johnny claimed the Emperor was trying to talk him into returning to Sicily with him once the crusade was over.

"Over?" Balian had protested in irritation. "We haven't even started yet!"

Meanwhile, tensions *within* the crusader camp were mounting. Balian was not alone in resenting the leisurely pace and evident lack of a strategic plan that characterized the Holy Roman Emperor's "crusade"—though he was almost alone in thinking the whole crusade was a ruse in the first place. Gerard de Montaigu was almost going mad with impatience, and his uncles, particularly the Templar Master, were increasingly acerbic in their criticism of the Emperor. As for the secular lords, they fumed and argued and complained, debating a thousand different strategies—while the Emperor entertained his Saracen friends in the lavish style of their own culture.

Balian smelled a rat amidst the luxurious wall-hangings and the silk-covered cushions, the Egyptian carpets and spicy Arab food. Not that he disliked Arab food. There were several excellent Arab cook-shops in Beirut that his brothers and he often patronized, but it still stank to see the Emperor adopt a totally Saracen lifestyle.

Then he had to laugh at himself because it was the adaptation of many aspects of Saracen lifestyle that made many crusaders view the natives of Outremer as "soft," "decadent" or "corrupt." It was true that his own family were happy to wear the long flowing, cotton robes of the natives when they were at their ease and in private. True, too, that they frequented the bathhouses, where they were happy to be rubbed down with scented oils, and they had adopted the glass oil-lamps common to the region. But lying down to eat had never taken hold among the Franks of Outremer, much less the form of entertainment Fredrick was now offering.

The dancing girls were very thinly clad, their bellies visible through sheer scarves, and they were bedecked with strings of beads that swung and bounced in response to their lithe motions. They played castanets with their hands, and bells jingled on their ankles. In the center were two nubile girls, who stood barefoot on two large balls and deftly rolled these with their feet while clapping with their hands, swaying their hips and singing in high, almost monotone wails.

"What's the matter with you, Ibelin?" The voice of one of his companions snapped him out of his thoughts.

"What do you mean, Sir Adelbert?" Balian asked back, instantly defensive.

"I thought you were a notorious seducer? Why the sour face when looking at such delectable samples of female flesh?" His companions broke into wine-induced laughter at the remark—or perhaps at Balian's evident discomfiture.

"I prefer willing partners," Balian snapped back, boiling inwardly.

"You think any of *those* would be unwilling?" They guffawed in near hysterical amusement. One of the German knights slapped his hand on the table in time with his loud "ha, ha, ha!" while Sir Adelbert laughed so hard tears trickled from the corners of his eyes and he had to wipe them away with the back of his hand.

Balian waited until the laughter died away before answering. "Those, good sirs, are *slaves*. What choice do slaves have? I would not demean myself by taking advantage of such pitiable creatures. Excuse me!" He pulled his feet under him and pushed himself up off the floor to stalk out of the hall into the adjacent corridor.

As the door clunked shut behind him, shutting off the noise of the Saracen singing and music and the babble of voice, he could hear the church bells from across the city ringing for the Feast of the Epiphany—or at least trying to. During the more than 30 years of Muslim rule, the church bells of Jaffa had been silenced. Indeed, most bells had been melted down or put to some other purpose. What clanged now were improvised bells, brought down from Acre or found in disuse. Many were damaged or had jury-rigged clappers. The effect was hardly harmonious, let alone joyous.

Then the bells, cacophonous as they had been, fell silent, and the mood was even more depressing. Balian thought he could hear the sound of surf pounding on the ledge offshore. According to legend, it was on that ledge that the Ethiopian princess Andromeda had been chained until she was rescued by Perseus riding the winged horse Pegasus. Balian imagined being chained to the rock and rescued by Lady Eschiva in a fishing boat. He pictured her standing at the tiller with the waves breaking over the bow. The image made him smile for a moment.

Then sobering, Balian regretted he had not yet had a chance to thank her for her intercession with the king. He had encountered her husband on multiple occasions. Gerard de Montaigu was never good company, but Balian felt Gerard had been pointedly cold and curt. Either he knew about Eschiva's role in Balian's release and disapproved, or he still begrudged them their innocent flirting at that long-ago banquet in Nicosia. Balian opted to let sleeping dogs lie and entrusted Bella with the task of expressing his gratitude to Eschiva.

Balian supposed he thought so much about Eschiva because he had lost all appetite for women of easy virtue since his humiliation at the hands of Barlais and the Emperor. His sleep was too often ruined by nightmares in which he was leprous or otherwise so badly scarred that women turned away from him in revulsion. He heard Barlais deriding him for cracked and worthless balls, and then the Emperor mocking him for being repulsive to women. Sometimes when he thrashed himself awake, it took long seconds before he realized he was still whole and not permanently disfigured.

Maybe he should go into town to find his father and brothers? They were with the army, of course, but they kept their distance from the Emperor and his household as much as possible. Still, there was no reason why they couldn't meet, Balian reasoned. He longed for the company of his brothers, even Baldwin, and would have liked to listen to his father tell again the story of how the Lionheart with just a handful of men shamed the Sultan Saladin by challenging the entire Saracen army to combat with him, or how his grandfather came to the Lionheart's relief. And then there was Ibelin, only a few miles to the south. Maybe, if they were just going to while away the time here he could ask his father to take him to Ibelin.

Balian had only just convinced himself that he should go in search of his father and brothers when Johnny burst out of the stairwell ahead of him. "Balian! I've been looking all over for you!"

"Well met, Johnny! I was just about to go in search of our father. Do you want to come with me?"

"I can't. You've got to come quick. Henry has sent for you."

Balian started. Over the last months, he had seen Henry often enough and they had exchanged nods and sometimes even winks. More often, Johnny had reported that Henry was fine—disrespectful to his watchdogs, sullen and unresponsive to the Emperor, and delighted with his puppy. Johnny and Henry were fast friends, although Johnny complained that he was still "such a child." At thirteen, Johnny thought himself very much more mature than his eleven-year-old king.

"What's wrong?" Balian asked in alarm.

"I don't know. He just burst in on me and insisted I must bring you to him at once." Johnny underlined the need to hurry by grabbing Balian's arm.

Balian did not resist. He followed his younger brother willingly but puzzled about what could have upset Henry while the Emperor was so preoccupied with his guest.

King Henry pounced on him the moment he came through the door, slamming it behind the two Ibelins and bursting out in a flood of agitated Greek. "He's betrayed us! All of us! I mean all Christians! He's negotiating with al-Kamil. Well, not *negotiating* so much as crawling on his belly begging for concessions! He doesn't intend to fight for Jerusalem at all!"

"Slow down, my lord," Balian urged, putting his hand on the boy king's arm. "That was too much for me at once. Start at the beginning."

"Oh, but you can't believe it!" King Henry was still extremely agitated, and he fell back into the more familiar French. "My dog Harry had to go out, so I snuck down the stairs to the garden behind the citadel, and while Harry was doing his business I noticed there were two men standing in the shadow of the cypress trees. They were murmuring to one another in Arabic. At first, I thought they might be assassins, but then I realized they were just two men from Fahr ed-Din's entourage. They were arguing in Arabic, I assumed about something immaterial—until I heard what they were saying! One said that al-Kamil had no further need of the Emperor and regretted ever writing to him and offering him Jerusalem in the first place. The other laughed and said it was easy to offer Jerusalem as long as he did not hold it, but now that he controlled the city he was more reluctant to let it go. Then the first said something about the Emperor being like spilt honey—sticking to everything, cloyingly sweet. The other man answered back that he was more like a woman, promising favors while begging for treats and arguing that he's not asking much, 'just a half-ruined city of no particular value'—that's what he said, Sir Balian, I swear it. Talking of Jerusalem!" King Henry was outraged.

"Well, it *is* fairly worthless to them," Sir Balian conceded.

"But he was quoting the *Emperor*!" King Henry protested, with the frustration of an eleven-year-old who feels adults aren't taking him seriously enough. "Don't you see what this means?" he demanded indignantly. "The Emperor has been negotiating since *before* he even came out here! He *never* intended to liberate Jerusalem—or not by force of arms. He's been *begging* al-Kamil to give it to him instead."

Balian nodded. "That explains pretty much everything—wasting time on Cyprus trying to subdue our father, the long months in Acre without any action, the slow pace of the advance, even the fact that al-Kamil has left us in peace the whole time—not to mention the ridiculous banquet going on right now. They've been at this diplomatic game all along."

"But isn't this terrible?" Henry asked incredulously and baffled by Balian's calm tone.

"That depends on the deal they strike, my lord. Don't forget that King Richard too tried to negotiate a settlement from the moment he got here. Every king prefers to win what he wants without bloodshed—if he can. In the end, even the Lionheart had to make the best deal he could over the negotiating table."

Henry stared at him frowning. He'd forgotten that Balian's grandfather had negotiated the Lionheart's peace with Saladin.

"The difference is that Richard first made Salah ad-Din respect him," Balian continued. "He beat him soundly at Arsuf and humiliated him entirely right here in Jaffa. So Salah ad-Din was forced to make concessions. The Emperor, on the other hand, hasn't even risked a battle and certainly hasn't won one. So why should al-Kamil respect him? Furthermore, he has precious little to offer al-Kamil. I can't see why the Sultan would surrender anything to a man who is no threat to him." Balian paused and the youth looked at him dismayed.

Balian forced himself to smile and added, "But perhaps there is some way we can turn this to our advantage. Thank you for bringing me this intelligence, my lord. I will go to my father and see what he has to say." Balian bowed deeply to his king and departed. He felt no satisfaction at having been proved right. He would so much rather have been proved wrong, but no matter how he looked at it, he came to the same conclusion: Jerusalem was beyond grasp.

Jaffa, Late January 1229

Frederick Hohenstaufen dismissed his clerks. Only after the door clunked shut did he cross to the table on which lay a book on falconry, a "gift" from Fahr ed-Din. The "gift" had been delivered in full view of the court with appropriate, obsequious bows, and Frederick had pretended only nominal interest in it and then ordered a servant to bring it to his chamber while proceeding to the elaborate feast as if the feast, not the book, interested him. But Fahr ed-Din had long ago promised him that the Sultan's answer would come in exactly this form.

Opening the book, he took a sharp fruit knife and cut open the inside back cover to remove a folded slip of thin paper. His eyes raced over the pleasantries expressing "humble devotion" and "infinite respect" then praising Allah and his prophet until he found the content.

Yes! The Holy Roman Emperor almost shouted with joy. Al-Kamil had agreed at last! Impressed by the Emperor's brilliance and his knowledge, al-Kamil agreed that he would allow the Christians to control Jerusalem for the duration of a truce on certain conditions.

Who cared about conditions? Frederick tossed the paper back down on his desk and breathed deeply in relief. He had done it! The world would again gaze in wonder at him. Stupor Mundi—the wonder of the world! And none would be more astounded—and confounded—than that worm in the Vatican! How Frederick wished he could be there to see the Pope's face when he heard the news. He would very likely have an apoplectic fit! With the Grace of God, he would die of it too! The idiot on the papal throne had excommunicated the one leader destined to restore Jerusalem to Christian rule! Now the whole world would see what a fool the so-called Pope was and turn away from him to bow down in admiration and awe to the Liberator of Jerusalem! Frederick, by the Grace of God, Holy Roman Emperor, King of Sicily, King of Germany, *King of Jerusalem!*

Frederick Hohenstaufen was pacing about his room, energized with the sense of triumph. He would be revered for all eternity! They would build monuments to him across Christendom. His image would gaze down from elevated places in every cathedral—including St. Peter's in Rome! The Wonder of the World. The Liberator of Jerusalem. He would crown himself Holy Roman Emperor again in the Church of the Holy Sepulcher itself! He would make them all bow down to him—including that ass Pedro de Montaigu, who had been harassing him to capture Jerusalem by force of arms.

Idiot!

And not just Montaigu. They were *all* idiots! Why shed Christian blood for something they could get handed to them on a platter? They had the minds of insects! The sensitivity of rabid dogs. Blood was all they understood. Not one of them had the subtlety he possessed. Not one of the understood diplomacy and the use of one's mind and tongue rather than the sword.

Except perhaps Beirut. Frederick stopped his exhilarated pacing and scowled. Beirut was too clever by half. He was a slippery, far too subtle man, who hid behind a façade of uprightness! Despicable man!

It still rankled that he had extracted his sons along with a promise of no repercussions. That agreement had given Beirut everything he wanted. The castles weren't his to hold in the first place, and he'd been planning to support the crusade anyway. It was truly a terrible humiliation.

But who would remember it after this triumph? No one, the Hohenstaufen told himself, resuming his excited wandering around his chamber. The bloodless liberation of Jerusalem would overshadow all the petty squabbles with the Ibelins. It would obliterate them from the historical record altogether!

Frederick Hohenstaufen stopped in his tracks. Why be content with their posthumous elimination? He had vowed before the assembled lords of Cyprus that he would force Beirut to surrender his city and his treasure—and he had done neither. He couldn't let Beirut get away with that. Now that he had no need of the Ibelins, their troops or their allies, he had no reason to respect the agreement. The entire Cypriot contingent could go home or drop dead for all he cared. Jerusalem would still be his. So why not strike a killing blow at the traitors before a living soul knew what was afoot?

Frederick Hohenstaufen paused to think about that for another moment, but he could find nothing wrong with the idea whatsoever. So who best to carry it out? Again he thought briefly, and then opening the door to his chamber ordered the guard to fetch Stephan, Count of Cotron.

The Sicilian count was familiar with affairs here in Outremer, having made a trip in 1225. He also commanded a strong contingent of troops from the mainland of the Kingdom of Sicily, from Apulia. They were good, loyal troops. These imperial troops would easily seize the Cypriot castles from the hands of King Henry's men—all old and worthless anyway, since Beirut brought the energetic and competent Cypriot knights on crusade with him. The fact that Beirut had brought his best men with him underlined his naivety. It was a mistake only dolts would make, Frederick noted with contempt. So once the Imperial troops had control of the castles, they could spread terror among Ibelin's vassals and friends—including the Montaigus, with their insufferable attitude of moral superiority! A little burning, plunder and—men would be men—rape would do much to intimidate the Ibelins, Montaigus, and their friends.

Furthermore, with the Cypriot fighting men here in Syria, it should be child's play to destroy the Ibelin's power base on Cyprus. It would also put the fear of God into their women and children—those that survived that was. And after learning the price of defying the Wonder of the World, no one would dare raise a word of protest when he finally arrested the Lord of Beirut himself and put him in a dungeon never to see the light of day again.

Chapter Eighteen
The Emperor's Peace

Kingdom of Cyprus
February 1229

THE NEWS THAT "LANGOBARDS," IMPERIAL TROOPS, had come to Cyprus reached Paradhisi indirectly at first. While out fishing, Yiota's father sighted a fleet of ships flying the Emperor's banners making for Limassol. Local farmers returning from market reported that "thousands" of troops had disembarked. A traveling peddler had heard that the Emperor had sent troops to take control of the royal castles. One of Karpas' squires asking hospitality for the night reported that the Imperial governor was threatening "anyone who sided with Beirut."

But should they believe an excitable young squire? And what did it have to do with Gerard de Montaigu's household?

Then Eschiva's clerk and confessor, Father Umbertus, received a letter from his superior and mentor, the Archbishop of Nicosia. He had alarming news: the Holy Roman Emperor had "sent Italian thugs to rifle through his archives and accounts." Allegations of corruption had been voiced. Hints of arrest were liberally tossed about by the Emperor's minions. "Be on the alert!" the Archbishop warned his nephew's little household, and not a moment too soon.

The very next day a troop of eight Apulian men-at-arms arrived at Paradhisi and demanded to see the steward. The steward was asked to show proof that the estate belonged to Gerard de Montaigu. When he answered it was part of Eschiva de Montbéliard's dower, inherited from her Lusignan mother, they seemed surprised and temporarily confused. They rode away, but not before they had trampled down half the kitchen-garden by careless handling of their horses. They had also helped themselves to a keg of ale and stole a cured ham and half the sausages, the cook reported in outrage.

Although that was hardly a catastrophe, Eschiva was unnerved by the incident. What right did the Emperor have to poke his nose in the titles of Cypriot fiefs? No overlord had the right to meddle in the feudal arrangements of his vassals.

On the other hand, for the first time since her marriage, she found herself sharing an opinion with Nana Flora, her husband's former nanny who now looked after his son from his first marriage, Pedrino. Nana Flora was a severe, humorless woman. With Gerard's full support, she had from the start taken over Eschiva's little household ordering things to her liking and intimidating the staff. It was largely to escape her constant criticism and bossing that Eschiva spent so much of her time with the Drakakis and her painting. "Those were evil men!" The ancient nanny declared with narrowed eyes and her hands on her hips.

"Yes," Eschiva agreed, relieved about any bridge between herself and her husband's "infallible" nurse.

Nana Flora looked at her critically and announced, "You must write to Gerard at once. He must know about this. Tell him he must send knights to protect us."

Eschiva found that reaction excessive and she had no desire to write Gerard for any reason. He had not seen fit to write to her once since his departure for Syria either. All the news she had of the crusade came from Bella, who fortunately was a prolific writer.

Bella had also stopped at Paradhisi on her way to Famagusta to take a ship for Beirut in the wake of her father and brothers. She had conveyed Balian's thanks, stressing that he might have been permanently crippled without Eschiva's intervention. "You can count on Balian's gratitude," Bella had assured Eschiva solemnly. "I haven't been able to talk to him since his release, but I know him. He's generous to a fault, and he never forgets a favor or a debt."

Eschiva had protested she didn't want a reward, only his well-being. Bella had nodded in reply. "I understand, but I wouldn't want you to think he is ungrateful just because he cannot thank you himself." Then she had assured Eschiva that she had "a home" in Beirut whenever she wanted it and promised to keep in touch.

Bella had been true to her word with a letter almost weekly since her arrival in Beirut. She had by this means provided Eschiva with regular updates on the progress, or lack thereof, of the crusade. Bella always included snippets of gossip in her letters too, such as Antioch's sudden illness and miraculous recovery, or Johnny's elevation to "Lord of Foggia."

Nana Flora knew that Eschiva wrote letters regularly and sent them by courier to Famagusta, but being illiterate herself she had no clue that the letters went to Isabella d'Ibelin rather than Gerard de Montaigu. Not wanting to shatter this very fragile truce between them, however, Eschiva nodded and promised to write Gerard. Besides, on second thought, there could be little harm in warning him of the Emperor's interest. His uncle the Archbishop of Nicosia was alarmed, after all.

Indeed, the very next day yet another outraged message came from the worthy Archbishop. The Archbishop now reported that the Holy Roman Emperor was a traitor to Christ. He did not provide details, but he reported that there had been some kind of confrontation between the Montaigus and the Emperor. Apparently, not only the two Masters but Gerard himself had been involved. According to his uncle, Gerard "covered himself with pious glory" while simultaneously earning the undying hatred of the Emperor.

Eschiva was desperately curious about what could have triggered this confrontation since she did not know her husband well enough to imagine it. All she knew was his fanatical devotion to liberating Jerusalem and atoning for his mysterious and unnamed sins in the Church of the Holy Sepulcher. Nevertheless, in light of this, she thought that the Emperor's interest in their estate might indeed be important intelligence. On the other hand, Gerard might dismiss it as feminine hysteria and reproach her for bothering him with domestic matters of no consequence when he had "real" issues to deal with. Then again, if she *didn't* write to him, and Nana Flora reported that she had told her to, he would certainly accuse her of not caring about the welfare of his son. Pedrino was a sickly boy, subject to frequent seizures of some kind. Nana Flora had dismissed Eschiva's early attempts to help, telling her she knew 'nothing' and that she 'made things worse.' After that Eschiva had lost interest in the boy. What did she want with anything that was Gerard's? What she wanted was to be rid of Nana Flora, Pedrino and—most of all—Gerard himself.

Eschiva signed, called for Father Umbertus, and asked what he thought she should do. "We must inform your husband of what has happened at once," he advised. "I do not like the way the wind is blowing. When I visited the Hospital yesterday they were extremely agitated and no one wanted to take the time to talk to me. Men were riding out in various directions, whether with orders or on reconnaissance I couldn't tell. When I caught a glimpse of the commander, he was frowning darkly as he rode away with an escort of a half dozen knights. He didn't even acknowledge me. I will take this message to Lord Gerard myself."

"Surely we could give it to the captain of a Hospitaller ship on its way to Syria?" Eschiva had always entrusted her letters to Bella to the ships of one of the militant orders that regularly plied between Cyprus and Syria with dispatches, reinforcements, and supplies. The discretion and reliability of the military orders was above question.

Father Umbertus sighed deeply. "I think not, my lady. My lord of Nicosia has important messages for his brothers, verbal messages, he asked me to deliver. I was about to tell you."

Eschiva felt outmaneuvered and manipulated. Clearly much more was going on here than anyone was willing to tell her.

"You need not fear for your soul," Father Umbertus intoned a little maliciously. "Papas Theodoros can hear your confession in my absence and also read Mass." He smiled cynically as he spoke, suggesting he knew perfectly well that she already confessed more to the Greek Papas than to him anyway.

"Yes, of course," Eschiva answered readily, refusing to be drawn into that discussion, "but can you tell me more about what is going on?"

"I'm afraid not, Madam, but I'm sure you'll be safe here."

He left later that same day, and as darkness fell Eschiva was left with an uneasy sense of lurking danger. It was inchoate yet so tangible that Pedrino was squalling and fidgeting more than ever. Nana Flora, although pleased by the departure of the priest with a promise to tell Gerard everything, was still enough on edge to take her temper out on the kitchen staff. Eschiva fled to the Drakakis household in their house by the sea. Instead of the warm reception she had expected, she found the family in an agitated uproar.

"Fire!" Costas called out to her, seeing her first.

"What? Where?"

"We saw it from the boat. Fire on the mountains!"

Yiota joined them, looking more worried than Eschiva had ever seen her. "We've had plenty of rain this winter, and no storms. The fire couldn't have started on its own, it must have been set."

Eschiva felt a chill run down her spine even as she protested. "Perhaps a stove was left untended or a goat knocked over an oil lamp."

"A fire could have started like that, but not spread so far," Yiota insisted.

"Where is it?" Eschiva asked.

"We think it's the sugar plantation of the Lord of Karpas, Sir Anceau de Brie."

Eschiva shuddered and wondered if Yvonne was safe. At least she had the castle of Kantara to retreat to.

Eschiva had only just managed to fall asleep when she was torn from her sleep by a violent knocking on the door. "Madame! Madame! Come quick!" Yiota shouted.

Eschiva fumbled to put her feet into shoes and drag a robe over her night-dress. She wound a veil around her head and pulled open the door. "What is it?"

"Hurry! Hurry!" Yiota gestured toward the courtyard, and Eschiva realized that it was lit up. For a heartbeat, she thought it had been set on fire, but then she realized it was just torches and lanterns. Agitated voices were carried on the evening breeze.

The steward intercepted her at the bottom of the stairs. He too was in his nightshirt, his greying hair in disarray. His legs were bare, but he had girted a sword around his hips. "My lady! The Lady Alys, Lord Philip's widow, and her two children just arrived. They only barely escaped the Emperor's men."

Before he could say more, Eschiva caught sight of her Aunt Alys with her daughter Maria clinging to her fiercely. She called out. "Tante Alys! What has happened?"

Aunt Alys turned toward her niece, and Eschiva was stunned by the look on her face. She seemed aged and haggard. "They slaughtered my men!" she announced without preamble. "Just burst in and started slaughtering them! We barely escaped by a back door and ran through the woods to the next village. Behind us, they set Levkara on fire. We could hear the horses screaming and the cattle bellowing. The peasants hid us in a goat shed and then got us to Agios Mamas by night. The monks loaned us donkeys to get to the Temple at Limassol, but the brothers said we were not safe there! Can you imagine that? They said they feared an attack at any moment. The *Knights Templar* said they were them-selves under attack from the Emperor! All they were willing to do was lend us horses. We've been traveling for four days now, and you are our last hope."

Her daughter was crying, and young Jacques stood beside his mother trying to look brave but only managing to look shaken and tense at twelve years of age.

Eschiva moved forward to put her arms around her aunt, enclosing the little girl at the same time. "Of course you are welcome, Tante Alys!" Eschiva assured her aunt. "Come in. Let me find you some clean clothes." She smelled very strongly of goat. "When was the last time you had anything to eat?"

"Thank you, thank you. Come, Maria." Aunt Alys shooed her daughter ahead of her toward the front door of the manor house, but even as she did so she told Eschiva bluntly. "We are not safe here. This is no more a castle than Levkara was. Nor is there a castle we can make for. The Emperor has control of all the castles—including Kantara! Poor Yvonne is trapped inside the Lady Tower while Italian mercenaries plunder the castle around her! At least that's what the Templars said, and they should know. They say the Emperor controls all the royal castles, but it's the men at Kantara that endanger us most! They are sure to come here sooner or later. We need to leave Cyprus altogether."

"But what's going on? What does the Emperor have against us?"

"Are you blind and deaf?" Alys de Montbéliard was too exhausted and had gone through too much to mince words. "The Emperor declared war on the Ibelins at the banquet in Limassol. Lord John managed to checkmate him by seizing the castles, and then word arrived that Sicily had been attacked by the Pope's troops forcing the Emperor's hand. He made peace with John to get him out of the castles, but he never intended to keep his word. I don't know why John fell for it! Indeed, I don't understand why men are so *blind* when they think 'honor' is involved. What does the 'Wonder of the World' care about honor? His word? His sworn signature? He's still Holy Roman Emperor! A man who breaks his oath to the Pope isn't going to honor his oath to a mere Lord of Beirut! Wouldn't you think that after what the Emperor did to his sons, John would have known better than to ever trust him again?" Eschiva realized that Alys was pouring out her anger on the Lord of Beirut for his lack of foresight when in fact she hadn't seen this coming either. None of them were prepared for this. They had all thought the "incident" was over.

"Sit down, Tante Alys," Eschiva urged, pulling out a chair and stroking her aunt's shoulder to try to calm her down.

Alys was in no mood to calm down. "The Templars say the Emperor has tried to seize Castle Pilgrim from the Templars. They claim the Emperor planned to turn it over to the Teutonic Knights. He acts as if *he* had built it, defended it, and manned it. As if it were *his* to give to whomever he liked. You can imagine the Templar reaction!"

Eschiva nodded, but at the moment she was not terribly interested in the Templar's fight with the Holy Roman Emperor. "The Emperor is grasping. I tried to tell everyone that. But I don't much care about the Templar—"

"Don't you understand anything, child?" Aunt Alys interrupted in exasperation. "Pedro de Montaigu, the Templar Master, is your husband's uncle! Apparently, he has nearly come to blows with the German Emperor! Gerard, I understand, backed his uncle most vociferously, leaving the Emperor in no doubt about where your husband stands in this power struggle. There is only one place we will be safe." She told Eschiva bluntly. "We must get to Beirut."

The word immediately conjured up images of the powerful castle on the hill over the harbor—and the splendid gardens, the fountains, the marble steps and halls. Bella was there, and—"But we need a ship," Eschiva protested, fighting away thoughts of the man who had offered her protection and refuge the last time she had been forced to flee from the Emperor of the Romans.

"You took a ship from here to Limassol," Aunt Alys pointed out.

"A fishing boat," Eschiva corrected. "I'm not sure it's large enough or seaworthy enough to take us all the way to Beirut."

Her Aunt grasped her wrist and looked her straight in the eye. "Eschiva. This is a matter of life or death. The Emperor—or at any rate his Sicilian bloodhounds—is making war *on* women and children. He knows damn well our fighting men aren't here to protect us because they are in front of his nose! He sent his Sicilian troops to terrorize us *because* he knows we are defenseless. We don't have any choice. At least I don't. I don't intend to let *my* children fall into his hands. I will get my children to safety in Beirut, whether you choose to come with me or not."

Eschiva looked at her own household that hovered in a circle around her. The steward shook his head in agreement, muttering, "I fear Lady Alys is right, my lady. We cannot defend you with the few men we have. None of us are fighting men. If the Hospitallers will not take us in…." His voice faded away.

"You must get Gerard's son to safety!" Nana Flora ordered, her eyes ablaze and her lips a thin line of anger as if she expected resistance. No one else had anything to say.

Eschiva sent one of the grooms to fetch Yiota's father and brother. They must have been waiting nearby because they appeared almost at once, and Eschiva put the proposal to them. Could they take her aunt with her two children, herself, Nana Flora, and little Pedrino to Beirut in the boat?

"Beirut?" Costas asked in shock, looking to his father. He shook his head. "Impossible, my lady."

Aunt Alys took over, explaining the situation in a flood of angry Greek, but the fishermen stood their ground. Their boat was not seaworthy enough to get them across the open sea to Beirut.

Yiota spoke up, "What about Vasili's new boat?" she asked.

Her father frowned but weighted his head from side to side before deciding. "Maybe. It's ten feet longer and built to go farther offshore."

"Tell him he will be well-rewarded," Aunt Alys told the fisherman firmly. "Tell him the Lord of Beirut will give him ten bezants in gold if he brings us safety in Beirut."

The Mediterranean is treacherous. It smiles even in winter, blue and glistening in a light breeze—until a storm blows up out of apparently nowhere. The winter storms are notorious and have swallowed many a ship whole, leaving not a trace much less a living soul behind. Or they leave the carcass of the lifeless ship broken on some rocky shore like the beautiful Genoese *Rose of Acre*.

They were more than two-thirds of their way to their destination when the storm struck. Vasili sent the women and children into the forepeak, cramped as it was, and he handed all sails except a tiny triangle. Thereafter, he tried to keep the little vessel headed into the wind with the strength of his own and his sons' arms on the tiller.

The little boat was tossed about like a cork. It bounced, pitched, rolled and yawed on the waves so violently and unpredictably that none of the passengers could keep food in their stomachs. Pedrino wailed and Lady Alys' children clung to her, tears of terror streaming down their faces. Water broke over the bows, splashed down from the collisions with the waves on all sides, and soon nothing on board was dry much less warm.

Eschiva was generally a good sailor and she had withstood several storms on her outward journey to Brindisi, but that had been in a proper three-masted ship, not a fishing boat. From this perspective, the waves towered so high over them that they blocked out the rest of the world. Yet even when the boat rose onto the crests there was no comfort. The sea stretched to infinity in all directions under a low, grey sky. Soon the boat was rushing down the slope of the swells again. The waves came crashing into the boat, frothing and raging as before.

Vasili and his sons looked grim. Eschiva saw one of the boys clutch the cross on his breast more than once. Behind her, Nana Flora was praying in a monotone too, but Aunt Alys was grimly silent. Although she was shivering and her teeth chattered, Eschiva focused on Vasili and his sons fighting the tiller.

At some point, Pedrino cried himself to sleep. Eventually, Aunt Alys' children also nodded off, while Nana Flora continued chanting prayers. Eschiva looked to Aunt Alys. "Yes," came the answer to the unasked question. "It is better to drown here by the Grace of God than to fall into the hands of Frederick Hohenstaufen."

But although the storm blew itself out by the next morning, it became clear that they were still not out of danger. The little fishing vessel had survived, but not the provisions or the barrel of water that had been made fast aft.

Pedrino was thankfully still asleep in Nana Flora's arms. She held him to her breast and whispered to him, stroking his face with great tenderness as tears of concern ran down her face. Aunt Alys' children were less restrained. Maria kept whining that she was hungry and thirsty, provoking her brother into hitting her and telling her to shut up. Aunt Alys told them both to stop fussing and pray for assistance instead.

At about noon, Vasili called her in a raw voice and announced that he and his sons needed to rest. No one argued with that, but it meant they were adrift God-knew-where with nothing to eat and no water.

As the afternoon wore on, Eschiva began to think it would have been better to be drowned than to suffer this slow and increasingly unbearable agony of thirst. She was stiff in every muscle, bruised in multiple places, her face and hands were encrusted with salt. Her body was wrapped in cold, wet clothes that ensured she could not warm up. Her head was splitting, whether from thirst or some injury, she no longer knew.

She looked around at the endless, unsettled sea and saw only the depths of hell waiting below the surface. She looked up toward the heavens, but rather than light there were only low, grey clouds. They became a mirror reflecting her life back at her.

She did not like what she saw. While she might tell herself that her mother and Yolanda had loved her, they were dead. Her brother and husband, her closest surviving kin, clearly did not. When death finally came, she thought, no one would mourn her except, maybe, the Drakakis family, Papas Theodoros—and Bella. She did not flatter herself that Balian would mourn her. He might say something nice to Bella, but his thoughts would move on, his eye would focus on the next pretty face.

That had to be a reflection on her own worth. The Emperor had summarized her: cold, boring and plain.

All she had ever done in life was run away from it—unless she counted going to King Henry about Sirs Balian and Baldwin. Yes, she reflected. That had been a good deed, but against that deed was this evil one: dragging Vasili and his sons to their death in a futile attempt to reach Beirut.

So on balance, what justified her survival? Why should God save her from her own folly?

For her paintings? Self-indulgent sketching while other women were mothers or looked after children like Nana Flora did. If God thought her work was of any value, he would not have brought her here.

Jacques woke up and wanted to know why they didn't set sail. His mother told him it was still too dangerous. He didn't want to believe it. "We can't just drift!" he protested. "We might never reach land, or—worse—end up the hands of the Saracens! We'll be sold as slaves!"

No one had an answer for him.

By nightfall, the wind had settled enough for Vasili to risk setting sail. This at first lifted everyone's spirits—until they discovered that they were taking on water. The fisherman and his sons took turns at the tiller, while the other two bailed with the instruments left to them: a couple of pottery mugs. When one of these broke, Vasili exploded with so much rage that he dashed the second mug as well. The women jumped in terror as the shards sprang at them.

"Why did you do that?" Aunt Alys shouted furiously, wiping blood from Jacques' face, where a piece of broken pottery had grazed him.

"Because we are all going to die!" The fisherman answered her furiously. "Because we are sinking and will all drown before we can possibly reach land! Me and my greed! I knew this would happen! I knew it! At this time of year, the sea is never calm for long! I knew this was madness! God has punished me for my greed!" Then he collapsed into the bottom of the boat and started weeping helplessly. His sons stared at him for several minutes, and then, without a word, they got up to hand sail so that they would sink more slowly.

When day broke again the boat was barely afloat. They had abandoned the forepeak altogether. Within it, now waterlogged beyond rescue, were all Eschiva's paintings, the work of nine months. They didn't matter anymore. As they huddled together near the stern, Eschiva felt as if she were already dead. The others too appeared far too miserable to speak or cry. Nana Flora clutched Pedrino in her arms with a fierce, almost mad, protectiveness, turning her back on the others, but the rest were gripped by the listlessness of despair.

The combination of hunger, thirst, exhaustion, and hopelessness dulled their ears and eyes. The galley was almost upon them before they noticed it.

It was one of Vasili's sons who saw it first. He half jumped up, lost his balance and crashed down on his father. The latter yelped in pain and reproach, but his brother started shouting and waving furiously. Aunt Alys and Jacques joined in frantically. Eschiva just watched.

The galley ignored them and continued on its way at a purposeful pace, all forty oars thrashing the water in near perfect unison. More from habit than interest, Eschiva noted that it was flying the banner of Venice.

A shout reached them very faintly them from across the water. The oars of the galley lifted simultaneously out of the water and hung motionless in the air dripping water. The galley continued to glide forward, silently moving farther away. Yet there was a commotion on the afterdeck and then, with a great flourish, the oars along the far side started moving while the near side oars sank into the water to help pivot the ship about. Their stroke as the galley approached the wreck was slow. Men ran to the foredeck and lined the rail, waving and jabbering to one another.

There were no questions asked. The Law of Sea recognized them as "sailors in distress." At the sight of women and three children, however, the Venetian sailors erupted into a flurry of alarm and concern. Blankets were soon handed down, and large water skins were lowered along with mugs and sweets for the children to suck on. A bosun's chair was rigged on the foot of the boom and swung out over the wreck. The sailor in it signaled for Nana Flora to give him Pedrino, but she shook her head and clung to him more fiercely.

Aunt Alys had no nerves or patience for this nonsense. "Stop being a fool. Hand the boy over!"

When Nana Flora still refused, Eschiva urged. "Come! The sooner he gets some water and warm clothes, the better it will be for him." As she spoke, she reached out and her hand touched the infant.

Eschiva screamed in horror. "Pedrino is dead! He's *dead.*"

The Venetian sailor shouted back to the ship and then gestured to Alys' daughter. The girl didn't have to be asked twice. She reached up eagerly and let the sailor take her to safety, followed by Jacques. The rest of them, including Nana Flora, still clutching the corpse of little Pedrino, clambered awkwardly into the tender and were rowed across to the galley to climb up the netting thrown over the side.

Eschiva remembered none of it. All she could grasp was that Pedrino was stone *cold* dead. He had been dead for hours, maybe even a day. She had lost all her work, and Pedrino was dead. Her own survival made no sense to her.

Chapter Nineteen
The God of Love

Acre, Kingdom of Jerusalem
Early March 1229

"Johnny!" Balian called to his brother just before the latter disappeared through the door behind the dais toward the royal apartments. "I need to speak to you."

"Now?" Johnny countered. "The Emperor plans to set out for Jerusalem at the end of the week, and between now and then I have to—"

"Now!" His elder brother told him, adding more gently, "It will only take a minute."

Johnny made an exasperated face, then glanced over his shoulder toward the solar before jumping down from the dais to join his brother at the far end of the hall. "What is it?"

"I need to go to Beirut. Will you be alright?"

"Of course I'll be alright. I'm the Lord of Foggia, remember? Has the Emperor given you leave?"

"I haven't asked," Balian answered, his face hard and his eyes glinting defiance, "and I don't intend to."

"Did Father send for you?" Johnny asked next. "I thought he was planning to stay here in Acre?"

"He is. Bella was the one who sent for me."

"Bella? Since when do you take orders from Bella?"

"I don't, but, unlike you, I have a tiny pinch of chivalry in my soul, and I am glad to assist fair ladies, particularly when they request my help."

"Bella? Fair? Besides, what kind of help could *she* possibly need?"

"None of your business, since she didn't ask you. Now, you're sure you and King Henry will be alright while I'm away?"

"Better than you will be when the Emperor finds out you've taken off without his permission!" Johnny made a gesture of something flying off into the air.

"He probably won't even notice, but if he should happen to ask where I am, tell him I'm attending to my own affairs, now that the crusade is over and my vows have been fulfilled."

"They have? I thought we had to pray at the Holy Sepulcher?"

"Under interdict?" Balian countered.

"What?"

"The Patriarch of Jerusalem has threatened to put the entire city of Jerusalem under interdict if an excommunicate sets foot in it."

"What?" Johnny gasped. "Are you serious?" He was flabbergasted.

"You need to stick your nose outside the Emperor's camp more often, Johnny. This 'treaty' the Emperor has signed stinks worse than a sow's ass. It only lasts ten years for a start—after which point in time the Saracens will immediately take control of Jerusalem again because the treaty denies us the right to fortify it! Indeed, it denies us the right to fortify any of our major border fortresses—not to mention leaving the Temple Mount in Muslim hands—you can imagine how that went down with the Knights Templar! It also prohibits us from taking offensive action against the Saracens in any *other* theater, so we can't attack Egypt. And if that's not enough, think about this: it is a personal treaty between the Emperor and al-Kamil. It is not binding on other Saracen leaders, most notably the Sultan of Damascus, who happens to think—with every legal justification—he is the legitimate Saracen ruler of Jerusalem. In short, the Emperor's 'treaty' isn't worth the paper it's written on, and would be better used to wipe his ass!"

"Balian!" Johnny was genuinely shocked to hear his usually gallant older brother use such crude language. "What does Father say?"

"The same thing—only more politely. The Templars are ready to explode. The Hospitallers are, for once, siding with the Templars. And the Lords of Outremer are refusing to accompany the Emperor to Jerusalem. I really don't think he'll miss me," Balian concluded cynically.

Johnny was stunned. All he'd heard in the Emperor's household was what a "genius" the Emperor was to win a "bloodless victory." Everyone had raved about Jerusalem being "restored." No one had mentioned it was only for ten years—or that the Sultan of Damascus, not being bound by the treaty, might take it from them before then. "Does King Henry know?" he asked lamely.

"Not unless you told him."

"Couldn't *you* do that?" Johnny suggested. "You seem to know the terms of the treaty, and I've only heard them for the first time. I think he should know."

Balian had to admit his brother was right about that. "Alright. I'll tell him before I leave. Is he in his chamber?"

"No, he's out walking Harry in the garden."

Balian nodded, already glancing back toward the stairs down to the garden. "I'll find him," he agreed confidently, but then turned back to his brother and asked uncertainly, "The Emperor won't blame you for anything I do, will he?"

"It's a little late to ask since you obviously plan to do whatever it is anyway," Johnny grumbled.

Balian caught his arm and looked him deep in the eye. "*Will* you be alright?"

Reassured that his brother did care, Johnny rolled his eyes and declared. "Go away, Balian. I'm thirteen—not a baby. I'll be fine."

Balian still didn't let him go and continued to look at him intently.

Johnny grew serious too. "Really, Bal. I'll be fine. As you said, the Emperor probably won't even notice, and if he does I'll tell him I'm not my brother's keeper and haven't a clue what you're up to. I'm the tame Ibelin, remember?"

Balian gave Johnny a hug so short and sudden that Johnny didn't even have a chance to protest before it was over. Then Balian was gone, pounding down the spiral stairs that led to the garden.

Beirut, Early March 1229

Balian and Rob rode hard, following the coastal road. They shunned Tyre and were able to spend the night in Ghaziye. The following day they covered the last 30 miles to reach Beirut as the bells were ringing Vespers. They were hungry, dusty, thirsty and sore, but Balian was both glad to be home and anxious to speak with his sister.

The horses stretched out their necks and strained up the final slope to the barbican. Here the drawbridge over the fosse had already been lifted and the gates were barred, but Balian called up to the sergeant on the ramparts by name. At once, with surprised shouting, the drawbridge was lowered and the gates re-opened to admit them. Balian and Rob rode through the dog-legged barbican to emerge in the outer ward just as the Sergeant emerged from the back of the inside tower.

"What are you doing here, my lord?" the Sergeant asked astonished. "I had no word—"

"No worries. It was a spontaneous decision."

"Is your Lord Father—"

"No, it's just me and Rob."

Knight and squire continued toward the stables, and Balian told Rob he could leave their horses to the capable care of the castle grooms. "You must be as famished as I am."

"Hungrier, really," Rob muttered. "I'm still growing, remember?"

Balian laughed and clapped him on the shoulder. "Do you want to go straight to the kitchen?"

"If you don't mind, sir?"

"No, I don't mind," Balian assured him. With only a small garrison left in Beirut, the household would be eating in the ground floor kitchen hall rather than the formal hall on the floor above, but Balian assumed his sister and Lady Eschiva would take their evening meal in the solar. They would certainly be there after the meal.

Rob nodded his thanks and ducked into the corridor leading to the kitchen block. Alone, Balian mounted the interior spiral stairway that led up to the lower hall. Little light penetrated to the stairs from the outside and there were no torches lit, so Balian advanced more by feel than sight. With each step, he felt his weariness give way to nervous anticipation. He had thought about Eschiva in far too many ways these past months, and very shortly he would meet her again. Bella said she would welcome him. Self-consciously, Balian ran his hand through his hair to comb out any tangles created by the wind.

He came out of the stairwell into the lower hall. This was lit only by the luminous but fading sky over the ocean. Coming from the deeper gloom of the stairwell, Balian could make out the tables folded against the walls, the benches beside them. He crossed to the screens with their spiral pillars holding up the arched doorways that separated the lower and upper hall. He passed through the central archway and entered the chamber where the fountain gurgled sooth-ingly in the center of the room. His heels clicked on the marble as he crossed the chamber heading for the dais and the solar beyond, but on second thought diverted to the fountain. He bent and dipped his hands into the cool water, then wiped his face clean. He repeated the gesture twice before shaking out his hands and drying them on the skirt of his surcoat.

He mounted the dais and faced the closed door to the solar. His hand closed over the cool metal of the handle and then he stopped himself. They weren't expecting him, he thought. He shouldn't just barge in on them. He raised his hand and knocked instead.

There was no answer.

He knocked again.

Still no answer.

He pushed the handle down and slowly pushed the door open to find himself alone in an unlit and unheated chamber. That was odd. Where could they possibly be? Confused, he considered continuing into the corridor, which gave access to the private family apartments, but his hunger got the better of him. He returned the way he'd come, feeling vaguely betrayed. He'd been riding hard for two days in answer to a summons from Bella and now she wasn't even here.

"Balian!" Bella burst into the upper hall from the garden stairs. "I saw Rob in the courtyard. I was over at the chapel for vespers. I wasn't at all sure you'd come!" She crossed the room to him and caught his hands in hers, clutching them as she told him earnestly, "You are such a dear! I honestly don't deserve a brother like you."

Balian made a bow to her that was only half-mocking. "At your service, my lady."

"Oh, Balian, come!" She pulled him toward the window seat flanking one of the tall windows facing the sea. "We must talk," she told him, still breathless from hurrying up the stairs.

Balian looked at her bemused. The only girl in a brood of boys, Bella was both one of them and special. She could tease and take teasing as well as any of her brothers, yet she was better than the rest of them. Balian recognized that she had a genuine calling to the Church—as long as you didn't think of the Church as a place of pure contemplation and prayer. He thought she'd be best suited to the Hospitallers.

"I need your help, Balian," Bella admitted candidly.

"In what way?"

"It's Lady Eschiva." Bella sighed. "She's such a lovely soul, but she's been so alone in the world. She's lost everyone she loved: her mother and Yolanda. She hardly knows her brother and he certainly cares nothing for her." Bella's tone was indignant.

Balian smiled and quipped, "Well, you *have* been spoiled by *your* brothers."

"Balian, I'm serious!" Bella answered frowning. "He used her for his own political ends by marrying her to a man who never wanted to be married at all. Gerard de Montaigu would rather be a priest. His uncles forced him into the marriage, and Gerard has treated Eschiva terribly. I don't want to go into details. You have to believe me."

Balian nodded. He did trust Bella's judgment; he just didn't understand what it had to do with him.

Bella continued, "Since her mother's death, she has learned to be self-suf-ficient. She has built invisible walls to protect herself, and she creates her own world through her artwork. In Sicily, she used her art to protect both Yolanda and herself from the reality of the Hohenstaufen's indifference. On Cyprus, she was working on copying out the psalms and illustrating them—allegedly as a gift to her husband, but more to protect herself from him." Bella interrupted herself to ask, "You know she is a gifted illuminator?"

Balian nodded, remembering the page covered with whimsical and lively creatures set in letters he had found tucked in his grandmother's copy of the Odyssey.

"When I visited her on Cyprus," Bella continued, "she talked of finding ways to annul the marriage. She thought if she could avoid giving Montaigu an heir, he would lose patience and be happy to get rid of her."

"I'm not sure I should be hearing these intimate details of another man's marriage," Balian noted uncomfortably.

"Oh, don't be so male," Bella dismissed. "Listen. Last fall she was unhappy in her marriage but fundamentally *sound*. Do you know what I mean? She had her head screwed on properly and her faith in God intact. She was looking rationally for ways out of her situation while working on other things that made her happy like the manuscript of psalms. She was also fighting back against that malicious old woman that Gerard had imposed on her, and she was evading the confessor the Archbishop of Nicosia had forced on her. She was *fighting* for herself—just as she fought against the Holy Roman Emperor."

Balian nodded slowly. That was what he had liked about her from the start, that she had the courage and determination to shape her own destiny.

"But something happened on this voyage," Bella told him. "I mean, Aunt Alys told me about the ordeal they all endured on the fishing boat. First, a storm that nearly overwhelmed them, then a day without food or water, as the boat drifted and ever so slowly sank. Montaigu's little boy died sometime during this voyage, and none of the others noticed because the boy's nanny wouldn't let them near him. Eschiva only realized he was dead when she tried to hand him to their rescuers and he was stone cold. She had a dreadful shock."

Balian murmured a sincere, "Poor Eschiva."

"And, yet, she should have recovered—as she did from the assault of the sailors at Andria. Eschiva's so strong, and she wasn't close to the boy because the nanny never let her near him. His death shouldn't have unbalanced her like this."

"What do you mean 'imbalanced'?" Balian asked cautiously.

"She's lost her natural optimism, her self-confidence, her *faith*. She has withdrawn into herself, and I haven't been able to reach her since. It's as if she's in a daze or a trance. She goes through the motions of living. She is preparing to join Montaigu in Acre because he ordered her to be there in time to travel to Jerusalem with the Holy Roman Emperor. But she is *dead* inside."

"And what do you expect me to do?" Balian asked.

"Reach her!" Bella answered with desperate frustration. "Bring her out of the spiritual grave she has dug for herself. Shatter her self-hatred—because that is what has made her feel she deserves whatever Montaigu does to her. She says things like 'I'm nothing.' Or 'My feelings don't matter.' It's not self-pity. It's deeper than that. It's much more destructive."

Balian respected Bella's intuition. She understood people. At least most of the time. It was a gift she'd had since she was very little. But this time he wasn't sure. "And why do you think I might be able to help?"

"Oh, Balian!" Bella threw up her hands. "As if you didn't know! She's head over heels in love with you. If you would show her just a little attention, affection. If you would make her feel loved—"

"That's exactly what you told me NOT to do last time we were together," Balian snapped.

"But that was different," Bella protested. "That was before her marriage, before this horrible ordeal. She needs you now."

"Bella, let me be sure I understand: Are you asking me to commit a mortal sin?"

"I don't remember you thinking about your immortal soul when you seduced Denise—"

"That was three years ago, for God's sake! I've grown up since then. A lot!" Balian's tone was blistering, and Bella reached out to calm him.

He shook her off and jumped up to pace across to the fountain. Bella could feel his fury across the space between him, and she was bewildered. She had not expected his resistance. She had thought…. she nervously played with the end of her braid.

Balian's fingers played with the surface of the water as it spilled over the edge of the wide marble bowl. The gurgling of the water was soothing; the water cooled his blood a little. After a bit, he took a deep breath and announced, "I will *not* play with her, Bella. She deserves better than that. She deserves *love*."

"Yes, Balian," Bella agreed contritely. "I'm sorry. I just thought…."

Balian let the words hang in the large, empty room for a moment and then prompted, "What? What did you think?"

Bella hardly dared say it and the words came out in a near whisper: "You haven't been the same since you were tortured by the Emperor."

Balian caught his breath and turned sharply to look at his sister.

"You're so brittle, Balian. So tense and twisted with hatred."

"I have every reason to hate that bastard!"

"I know," Bella conceded contritely.

Balian didn't acknowledge her answer but snarled instead. "And if I seem *twisted* to you it's because my back still hurts so damned much that I can't *be* the knight I should and want to be!"

"I'm sorry!" Bella gasped out, tears brimming in her eyes as silence fell between them again.

It seemed to stretch into eternity. As Bella watched her once sweet-tempered older brother smoldering in the darkness, the tears escaped and started down her face, but she didn't dare say anything.

Finally, Balian broke the silence to announce in a brusque voice. "I need something to eat."

"Of course," Bella agreed, hastening to assure him, "I told the cook to heat up some of the meat pies we had at mid-day. I'm sure they're ready for you." She slipped off the window seat and hesitantly joined her brother by the fountain. She did not dare touch him. She was still too bewildered by his anger.

He looked down at her with an expression she could not read, but almost suspicious.

"I'm sorry, Balian. Really I am. I didn't mean to insult you. I sincerely thought that you and Eschiva might be able to help one another. Maybe it was a stupid idea, but I meant well. Really, I did. I just wanted to help you both…."

Balian could see the marks of her tears and he took pity on her. He pulled her into his nearest arm and assured her, "It's alright, Kitten. I know you don't have a mean bone in your whole body, but you are a little out of your depth when it comes to love between men and women. Now, let's go down to the kitchen before I get so hungry I take a bite out of your shoulder. It looks very delectable, you know, soft and juicy."

Bella swatted at him, but she was biting back sobs. He kept his arm around her as he led them back toward the spiral stairs to the kitchen.

The fire was dying. Eschiva registered that she ought to put another log on it, but that would mean getting up and taking a log from the basket beside the fireplace. The light had gone with the daylight too, but she could not be bothered with lamps or candles. The darkness was fine, even if it made it impossible to stitch. She looked down at her lap. She had been working on embroidering the cuffs of a shirt when there was still enough light to work on it, but what was the point? The person it was intended for would never wear it. Never even see it. Maybe that was why her hands had fallen idle hours ago.

As if she had slept, she could not remember her thoughts. They were like a bottomless pit of darkness in which she spun slowly, revisiting the same things again and again and again.

Pedrino was there, of course. A child she had never tried to befriend much less love. And his mother. She found herself wondering more and more what she had been like. And Gerard, her husband of nearly nine months, yet a man she didn't know at all. He appeared to her most frequently with a face full of anger or contempt. Poor Nana Flora was there too. Her eyes were empty of the superiority now. They had gone blank. All she did was pray. She blamed herself—and she feared Gerard. As did Eschiva.

Poor Pedrino. What sort of life had he had? She had failed him. She had never tried to befriend him, to know him, to love him. She had preferred her own world, her paintings. It was hardly any wonder that God had destroyed them all. She had favored her artificial world over the world He created. She had preferred her *own* creations to *His*.

Had there been a knock at the door?

She twisted around to look but then shook her head. Bella was at her prayers by now. She never came at this time. She turned back to stare at the dying fire. The room was getting chilly, but what was the point of stoking the fire. She should go to bed instead.

There it was again! A noise from the door, as if it had shut. She twisted again and started. It was closed, but a man was standing in front of it. They stared at one another as if they were strangers.

After what seemed like an eternity, he said. "I came to thank you for my life."

Eschiva shook her head. "It was the King. King Henry and Master de Montaigu."

He moved closer to her, stopping two feet away. "They would have done nothing if you had not asked them to."

"I was just the messenger, Bella's messenger. Thank her."

"I have. But I wanted to thank you too." He sank onto his heels and they were eye to eye. "Are you alright?" he asked softly.

"Yes, of course. Why shouldn't I be?"

"Sitting alone in the dark." His voice was almost inaudible. His eyes never left hers.

"I was stitching," Eschiva answered, nervously stroking the silk across her lap.

"In the dark?"

"I—just—I don't know."

"May I put a log on the fire?"

"Yes, of course."

He stood, moved to the fireplace, took a poker and scraped the embers together before placing a large log strategically across them. He took the bellows leaning beside the fireplace and pumped them until flames sprang up around the log. He took a lamp from the mantel and held the wick in the flames until it caught fire. He returned to Eschiva. The lamp lit up the silk over her knees. "What are you working on?" he asked and reached out his free hand to get a better look.

"It's just a shirt," Eschiva answered, acutely embarrassed.

"Yellow with red crosses on the cuffs?" He lifted his eyebrows.

Eschiva stared down at it so self-consciously that she couldn't even answer. The blood flooded her head and turned even her ears dark.

"It must be for my brother Johnny. He's everyone's darling."

"No, of course not!" she protested, looking up at him. "It was for—"

Their eyes met and she realized he was teasing her. He was smiling very faintly. He set the lamp down on the table beside her and reached out with the back of his hand to very gently touch her hot cheek. "I hope it was for me. I would be honored to wear it."

"Yes," she managed to whisper. "Yes, it was for you."

"I am ashamed. I have brought you nothing."

"You're here," Eschiva mouthed soundlessly.

Balian nodded. "Yes, and I would like to stay with you a while. May I sit with you for a moment?"

Eschiva nodded and looked around for a chair, but he sank down at her knee and looked up at her with a faint smile. "Tell me about all that has happened since we parted," he urged.

"But that was—before my marriage," Eschiva gasped out.

"Then tell me about your marriage," he suggested softly, without taking his eyes from her face.

"I can't!" Eschiva protested. She was inwardly reliving the degradation of the marriage bed and she pulled away from Balian, mortified by the whole sordid business. She did not want him imagining her like an animal.

"Then tell me about Paradhisi," he changed the subject gently, his hand touching her elbow as if in comfort but so very softly that she wasn't sure he had really touched her at all.

"Paradhisi is where my mother was kidnapped by pirates—" Eschiva started, still indignant that she had been sent there, even if she had come to like the manor more than expected.

"I know. My father was serving your grandfather as a squire when the incident happened. He told me about it. He greatly admired the Norse captain that tried to rescue your mother and grandmother and died in the attempt."

"There was a rescue attempt?" Eschiva had never heard that.

"On the high seas. Didn't anyone tell you?"

"No," Eschiva shook her head baffled.

"I'll tell you another time," Balian offered, "Tonight I want to hear about *your* Paradhisi."

Eschiva shrugged, not knowing what he wanted. "It's very pretty and there are two houses. I moved into the old house because Gerard's son cried all night—" She caught herself. Pedrino was dead. A shudder went through her as she remembered how he had felt, cold and stiff, reproachful and accusing.

Balian's hand, soft and firm, was on her arm. "There was nothing you could do for him, Eschiva. You nearly died yourself."

"But I deserve to die!" she cried out, unable to keep the thought trapped inside her any longer.

"No!" Balian responded sharply, grabbing her arm and shaking it. "No, Eschiva!" he said again, more gently, but his words broke through the cold and the darkness. She stared at him, wanting him to continue, desperate to believe what he was telling her. "You don't *deserve* to die. You are a precious and beautiful soul, rare and unique, and you have hardly been given a chance to live! *You do not deserve to die*." He said the words very softly yet very intently. "How can you possibly think you know better than Christ, who saved you from the storm and the sun?"

Eschiva shrugged, but she was struggling with tears. "Because, because, I never really tried to love Pedrino—I preferred my painting. Pedrino—he was just an innocent infant. God wanted me to love him, but because he was Gerard's son—I didn't want to have anything to do with him. I didn't—don't—want to be married to Gerard at all!" She broke down and started sobbing.

Balian stood and put his hand on her shoulder. That was all. He didn't try to take her into his arms, or to kiss her. He just stood beside her with his warm, firm hand on her shoulder until she had control of herself again. Embarrassed by her outburst, she dabbed at her face with the silk shirt, *his* silk shirt, and still hiccupping whispered, "I'm sorry. I shouldn't have said that."

"Why not, if it's true?" Balian countered, adding, "Bella doesn't think your marriage to Gerard is valid since neither of you consented of your free will."

"I know," Eschiva admitted, trying to smile. "She is a dear, dear friend. I think she is the only friend I have in the whole world. But what difference does Bella's opinion make? The most powerful churchmen in Outremer were witnesses to my wedding and are the ones who want it most."

"I'm sorry that you don't think of me as your friend," Balian answered.

Eschiva gasped slightly and looked up at him. A friend? *Just* a friend? What else should he be? Their eyes met, and after a moment he asked, "So how do you plan to survive?"

"I don't know," Eschiva admitted. "In Paradhisi I had my paints and Master Geurin of the Hospital had sent me a whole crate of parchment. I was working on copying and illustrating a book of psalms, but I lost everything when the boat sank—my pens and inks, the book of psalms and all the pages and pages of work. I have nothing left. Not a single illustration. I left everything I'd drawn on Sicily behind when I fled the harem, which was why I insisted on taking my work with me on the fishing boat. I couldn't bear to lose everything again—but that's exactly what happened."

"It must be like losing a child," Balian murmured, catching Eschiva by surprise.

No one had ever understood that before: that when she created her figures in ink they were precious and unique and, in a way, a part of her. "Thank you!" she whispered in gratitude, but tears were starting down her face again as she confessed, "but—but I think God wanted to show me how vain my painting is. That's why he destroyed it all."

"No," Balian answered simply. Then he elaborated, "No more than a child's life is vain simply because it is snuffed out. The Lord giveth and the Lord taketh away. We don't know why. All we can do is rejoice at what he gives." He leaned down and kissed her on her forehead with the lightness of a butterfly, and with one hand he stroked the side of her head in a gesture that seemed almost one of admiration.

"Balian?" she whispered, afraid of her own courage.

"Yes?"

"Why are you here? What brought you?"

He drew away from her, going toward the fire. He stood looking at it for what seemed like a long time to Eschiva, and when he spoke it was so softly that she could hardly hear. "Since they told me you were the one behind my release, I have thought of no other woman."

Eschiva caught her breath, and he turned around sharply to look her in the eye. "Does that offend you?" he asked.

She shook her head very slowly.

"Then I may stay a little longer? May I just sit here at your feet?"

"You don't need to sit at my feet!" Eschiva protested, jumping up in distress. The shirt she had been working on fell to the floor forgotten. "Bring a chair."

"But I'd rather sit at your feet," Balian countered, returning to face her. They stood for a moment, gazing into each other's eyes, and then he put his arms around her shoulders and pulled her firmly against his chest. "Or stand like this."

Eschiva had no resistance. Nothing had ever felt better in her whole life than Balian's arms around her. He was warm and strong. She felt both cherished and protected. She surrendered utterly and tried to savor the moment, unable to imagine what would come next.

Balian bent and kissed the top of her head. Then he sank down onto the rug in front of the fire, pulling her down with him. He picked up the forgotten shirt and draped it over the arm of the chair. Then he propped his back against the legs of her chair, his legs stretched out in front of him, crossed at the ankles. She sat beside him, her legs bent to the side, and very tentatively leaned against his chest. At once his arm slipped around her waist to hold her closer. "I was afraid, you know," he remarked to the fire, "that you might not want to see me."

"What on earth could have made you think that?" Eschiva asked, genuinely baffled.

He pushed back the sleeves of his shirt and stared at the scars.

Eschiva reached out with the fingers of her left hand and gently stroked them. "Bella told me about them. That was the idea behind the shirt. The red crosses of martyrdom on your wrists."

Balian laughed out loud, but held her closer and kissed the top of her head to reassure her he was not laughing *at* her. "I'm the least likely martyr on God's earth, but I would love to wear that shirt in front of the Emperor because he would know exactly what you meant. May I unbraid your hair? I'd like to see it loose. Just once."

Eschiva sat up straighter and reached for the ribbon at the tip. As she pulled the ties to release it, Balian's fingers slipped up the back of her neck and started to shake her hair free. The feel of his hands curling in her hair and gently tugging at her scalp sent warm shivers down her spine, and she realized her breathing had become strained. Still, she made no move to stop him. Why should she? Whatever he did, it could not end in the disgusting grunting, sweating and brutal pummeling of her insides that constituted the sin of fornication, or adultery in her case.

"You have beautiful hair," Balian murmured as his fingers combed it out around her shoulders.

Eschiva, although frightened by her own audacity, whispered, "So do you."

Balian kissed her for that, on the lips.

Eschiva surrendered to the unfamiliar sensations this produced. This was what a woman was supposed to feel, she thought to herself. This was what love between a man and a woman was about. Not the other. His kisses were not demanding or domineering or smothering or choking. They were playful and tantalizing, sweet-tasting and utterly relaxing. She felt as if she were drifting away on air. She was sorry when he stopped.

He pulled back to readjust his position. The legs of the chair were obviously becoming uncomfortable. He looked around, spotted some cushions, and stood to fetch them. As he settled back down on the floor, the cushions at his back, he crossed his legs and pulled her down to lie with her head in the bowl of his legs.

"If I killed Montaigu, would you marry me?"

"Balian!" She sat bolt upright. "Don't talk like that! Don't even think about it! I don't want you to kill anyone. Much less for me. What made you say such a thing?" She was horrified, and her heart was beating wildly.

"I want you, that's all." He shrugged. "And there's no other way to have you, is there? I would not want to endanger your immortal soul."

"Balian! You can't avoid one sin by committing another."

Balian nodded absently and admitted, "I know. But I *do* want you." He glanced down at his lap.

Eschiva drew away. "I'm sorry. I—I've been—inconsiderate. I'm sorry." She got her feet under her and stood up. "I can't." She was trembling all over although she didn't know why.

Balian also got back to his feet. Their eyes locked again. He nodded. "I know, but I hope you don't blame me for wanting what I can't have."

"No," she assured him. "Of course not."

They stood looking at one another, Eschiva's thoughts and feelings in a confusion too great to sort out.

Balian reached out and slowly ran his fingers through her hair again before he announced gently, "It's time for me to go then, but tomorrow I'd like to take you for a ride up onto Mount Lebanon. We can take lunch with us."

"Please!" Eschiva felt her heart lurch both in joy at the prospect and in disappointment that he was going.

He bent and whispered in her ear, "Good night, my love, and sweet dreams." His breath in her ear as he spoke made her writhe as if her nerves were set on fire, but before she knew what was happening he was gone. The door fell shut behind him and she was alone in her chamber. The fire was dying and the lamp had already gone out. Had he really been here at all or had she fantasized the whole episode?

She shook her head to clear it and slowly started to smile. She no longer wanted to die. She no longer felt worthless. She was looking forward to tomorrow.

Eschiva dressed for riding, hoping it wasn't too obvious, and then tiptoed down to the kitchen, afraid that she had hallucinated both Balian and his offer. But even before she reached the kitchen she could feel the energy emanating from it. There was more noise than ever—clatter and clunking, chatter and laughter—and the smells were mouthwatering. She supposed it was because the lord's heir was home, and he needed a "proper" meal. Yet the laughter betrayed that this was a service of affection, not duty.

She was even more surprised when she hesitantly stepped down into the vast, vaulted kitchen cut out of bedrock to find that not only was Bella there collecting the daily alms for the poor, but Balian himself peering over the cook's shoulder as if to make sure he did his job right. "More sugar," she heard him order just before her presence was observed and Balian turned to look at her.

His face lit up, and she turned warm all over.

He crossed the kitchen to take her hand and raise it to his lips. "My lady. I'm just making sure we have an adequate picnic for our ride. Sit down in the hall, and we'll have breakfast in a moment."

She dutifully returned to the servant's hall, which was already filling with the household. One of the kitchen staff entered with a bowl of steaming porridge, which he thumped down on the table. At once, everyone crowded around with their own pottery bowl and held it out for a portion. They washed the porridge down with water or ale, depending on inclination, and soaked up the last remnants with yesterday's bread. Balian ate standing up, and then excused himself to see to the horses. In leaving, he told Eschiva to join him in the stables when she was ready. "But don't linger too long. I want to take you to one of my favorite places and it's a three hours ride away."

"Are you coming with us, Bella?" Eschiva asked, unsure what answer she wanted.

"No, I have too much to do. Today's the day I go to the Orphanage of St. Martha, and the children would be miserable if I didn't show up with a basket full of tarts. Don't worry. My brother will take good care of you, and for propriety's sake Betrada, my mother's maid, will join you." She indicated a well-padded woman with a round face bound by a wimple, who was eating hastily.

"Don't want to starve on the way up the mountain!" she announced to Eschiva in a booming voice.

Bella leaned in to speak directly into Eschiva's ear. "If Balian tries anything you don't want, just shout. Betrada beat his backside often enough as a little boy to have no compunction about doing it now either!"

Eschiva laughed without thinking, and Bella smiled at her. "What a wonderful sound!" Only then did Eschiva realize she had not laughed since her flight from Cyprus.

At the stables, Balian and Rob had four horses lined up and were tacking them. At the sight of Eschiva and Betrada, Balian came over and led Eschiva to a dappled, grey mare with a dark face and legs, who looked curiously over her shoulder. "This," he told Eschiva as they approached, "is Mamush."

"Mamush?"

"Yes. She's from our own stud and she's very gentle with lovely smooth gaits. She's no longer in her prime, I admit. She was my mother's favorite palfrey, but she'd grown fat and lazy since her death. Still, she's game to follow the other horses. I think you'll like her."

Eschiva was delighted. As a child, she had been proud of her riding, but she since going to the convent at the age of ten she'd hardly ridden at all and had lost her skills. A gentle mare was just what she needed, and it was thoughtful of Balian to select a suitable mount. Meanwhile, Betrada happily mounted a greying and scarred gelding that had obviously seen better days but was sturdy enough to carry the heavy woman. What surprised Eschiva was that while Rob mounted on a very elegant black stallion, Balian swung into the saddle of a tall but ugly chestnut with a blaze on his face that came below his eyes. Indeed his eyes were light in color, making him an exceptionally ugly horse by most standards.

"Do you recognize him?" Balian asked as he drew up beside her.

"No, how could I? I've never seen him before," Eschiva answered.

"You did, actually, at the judicial combat between Barlais and Karpas. He was covered with a trapper from his ears to his fetlocks, however."

"You mean he's Sir Amaury's destrier? The one who defended him when he was knocked down?" She could hardly believe it.

"The very same. He's called Damon."

"He's a destrier, then."

"That's the way Sir Amaury used him, but I'd hate to risk his life in combat. We've become very fond of one another." Balian reached down and patted the horse's neck, while the latter snorted conversationally. "He's also quite fond of Mamush." He added with a smile and then asked if Eschiva was ready.

They first descended into Beirut town, where they wound through the narrow streets for about a quarter hour. Eschiva noted that most townspeople recognized Balian and greeted him with a smile and a wave. In return, he wished them well, or asked about wives and children, adding asides to Eschiva as they rode on.

They left Beirut by the eastern gate and took up a trot through the surrounding orchards and fields until the road started to climb steeply. Here they fell back into a walk as the horses labored up the slope. As they looked back down toward the coast, Eschiva was struck by how beautiful it was. It was the end of the rainy season, and the coastal plain was green, while the sea beyond was swathed in a veil of pale blue haze.

Balian took the opportunity to point out the sights along the coast as they came into view. He had a story about each—their history, or legends associated with them, or just his own or his brother's adventures there. It struck Eschiva that this was a beautiful place to grow up—and that Balian and his brothers had been much freer than she remembered her childhood.

Soon, however, the sun started burning down on them, and the horses were sweating. Eschiva sweated too and dropped the upper flap of her gauze veils over her face to protect it from sunburn. She was not unhappy when the road slipped into a forest of tall pines, which offered shade. Here they passed several trains of mules and donkeys loaded with kindling gathered in the forest for sale in the city. An old woman, bent double from a life of toil, was on her way to market with a sack full of mushrooms.

By mid-morning, they reached a crossroads at a spring-fed fountain. They all dismounted for a drink of water and to let the horses drink from a long trough. The paved area around the fountain was crowded, including a small camel caravan with Bedouin drivers, but commanded by a Seljuk merchant. The latter wore very beautiful silk robes and a turban with a peacock feather held in place by a large pearl. He recognized in Balian a lord, and at once tried to strike up a conversation with frequent glances in Eschiva's direction. She was glad she had the gauze lowered over her face and sipped the water by bowing her head and slipping the cup under the protective covering rather than lifting her veil.

"This treaty is an insult to both our faiths!" the merchant was quick to tell Balian. "It is neither fish nor fowl. My lord Nasir Daoud is furious! He has vowed to retake Jerusalem and slaughter every infidel he finds there—no matter what his uncle has promised in his truce."

Eschiva started at the words, but Balian reacted with what she thought was remarkable calm, simply shrugging and remarking, "We will defend ourselves as necessary, but I agree the treaty is an insult."

"Have you met this so-called Emperor?" The merchant was eager to know. Balian laughed darkly and muttered, "far too intimately."

The merchant either didn't hear or didn't believe him. Instead, he continued proudly, "A friend of mine met him. He said he is fat, balding and short-sighted. My friend said he wouldn't fetch 200 pieces of silver on a slave market!"

Balian laughed at that.

"Why do you follow such an unworthy man?" The merchant wanted to know.

"I don't," was Balian's blunt answer. "This Emperor will soon sail away and we will find better leaders."

Eschiva sympathized but wondered if it had been a wise thing to say. The merchant would surely tell everyone he met that the Christians were divided. But then they probably already knew that, she supposed.

The merchant glanced again in her direction, apparently still hoping for a glimpse of her face.

Balian deftly thanked him for a pleasant conversation, then slipped between them, leading Mamush forward and holding the off-stirrup as Eschiva remounted. He remounted himself and they continued on their journey. "Is this treaty really as bad as he said?" Eschiva asked.

"Worse," Balian answered tersely. His expression was so forbidding that Eschiva did not dare pursue the conversation. To divert him, she asked instead where the other fork in the road led, and how far they were from the border. Balian relaxed and started talking again.

An hour later they reached a village clustered around a monastery with spectacular views both back to the coast and down into the valley to the east. In front of the monastery was a paved square with a spring that disgorged water into a long trough through bonze lion heads. They dismounted and let the horses drink, while Balian rang the monastery bell. A few moments later a Maronite monk opened the door, and Balian bowed his head politely before explaining in Arabic that they had come for a picnic but wished to pray in the church first.

The monk looked skeptically toward Eschiva and Betrada, but Balian slipped something into his hand and he nodded and backed up. "Just five minutes!" he warned.

Balian signaled for Eschiva to come, while Betrada waved him off, saying she'd been often enough in the past. Rob too opted to stay with the horses.

They entered the cool darkness of the entryway, and the monk shooed them along an equally dim corridor to a narthex. At once the flooring changed from flagstone to mosaics, and Balian tapped his foot on them to draw Eschiva's attention. She caught her breath as she realized at once that these were Roman. As they passed into the nave of the church, the mosaics changed again. These were older and depicted a series of sea monsters in a vivid blue sea. A whale devoured a man. A giant octopus pulled a ship, from which men were leaping, down into the depths. As they approached the wooden screens that separated them from the altar in this Orthodox church, Balian went down on one knee bowing his head humbly and crossing himself. Eschiva followed his lead instantly. As she finished, Balian reached out his hand as if to help push himself back to his feet, but his finger pointed. Eschiva followed the finger and realized that between them was a mosaic depicting a galley with a man tied to the mast and surrounded by female figures with wings. Ulysses and the sirens!

Eschiva glanced at Balian, but he was dutifully crossing himself and getting to his feet. He bowed toward the altar and backed up two steps slowly. Again, Eschiva followed his example and realized that to her feet were other scenes from the Odyssey. Trying to see as much as possible without appearing to, Eschiva reached the narthex to find the monk gesturing for her to hurry. "Time to go! Time to go!" he insisted.

A minute later they were back in the sunshine of the square before the monastery.

"They're beautiful! And totally inappropriate for a church!" Eschiva exclaimed as soon as she dared.

"My father believes it was a Temple to Athena, who was Ulysses' protector, which the early Christians converted into a church," Balian explained, adding with a laugh, "I fear the monks know I'm more interested in the art than the prayer."

"Thank you, Sir Balian! They were worth the long ride."

"I'm glad you liked them. Not everyone appreciates them," he noted with a disgusted look toward his squire.

"I'm starving," was Rob's answer, "and I unloaded everything while you 'prayed.'"

He had indeed spread out a linen cloth on a patch of grass beside the square. It was weighed down with wooden bowls in which he had already placed cheese, sausages, meat pies, oranges, and raisins. As Balian and Eschiva sank down on the edge of the linen, Bertrada brought them some cushions, and Rob poured wine into bronze goblets enameled with Ibelin crosses.

Balian lifted his goblet to Eschiva. "My lady," was all he said, but the words seemed laden with meaning. Or was she just imagining it?

She lifted her goblet in return, unsure what the response should be, but he didn't seem to expect one.

Instead, he unsheathed his knife, cut a hard sausage in two and peeled off the outer skin before slicing it for Eschiva. "Those mosaics," he remarked as he offered her the salami, "were made by artists living more than a thousand years ago, yet they still bring pleasure to people. Isn't that wonderful?"

"Yes, it is!" Eschiva agreed.

Balian next cut the hard cheese into squares while Rob sawed the bread into slices and placed the latter in a basket. As he offered Eschiva the cheese, he added, "And the mosaics remind me of your paintings. They too will live long after we all are dead. That is a wonderful thing, Eschiva. A wonderful gift. Promise me you won't stop."

"What do you mean?"

"I know that you have lost a great deal, that no two paintings can ever be the same." How did he know that? Eschiva wondered. "But promise me that you will resume your painting as soon as you are settled. The canons of the Holy Sepulcher have a school of illumination in Acre, you know?"

"Yes," Eschiva squeaked out, her throat tight with emotion. "I—I studied there during my last year at St. Anne's."

"Then promise me you will go to them and ask to take up your studies again—or just offer to help them. They will not turn you away."

Eschiva was left speechless. The thought of going back to the Illumination School was a wonderful one. They had so many books, so many examples, and the canons were masters. It was something to look forward to. Yet—she caught herself. Wasn't it just an escape from reality? Wasn't she just running away—again?

"Creation is never a sin," Balian spoke into her thoughts as if he could read her mind. "It is an imitation of the divine."

Eschiva turned to gaze at Balian in baffled wonder. And then the moment of revelation passed. Betrada started talking about what it had been like here two decades earlier, and Rob told stories of adventures with Balian. They all ate together companionably as if there were no Gerard de Montaigu anywhere on earth, and no Emperor either. It was just the four of them on an ordinary "family" outing.

When they finished their meal, Balian went across to Damon with a handful of raisins that the horse happily devoured. Eschiva watched as he hand-fed the horse with one hand while stroking his neck with the other. "You *are* very fond of him," Eschiva remarked, coming to stand beside him.

"Yes," Balian admitted. "He is intelligent and loyal. Loyalty is a thousand times more valuable than beauty. But loyalty must be reciprocal or it is slavery."

He washed his hands in the fountain trough, then returned to peel an orange for Eschiva. "We'll need to set out on the return soon," he remarked as if that weren't like a death sentence, then touched the side of her face very gently. "Don't look so sad, Eschiva. Not yet. We still have half a day together."

She nodded absently and tried to smile. Inside, she wanted to cry in despair or scream in protest. It wasn't fair that they had only a half a day! But yesterday at this time she'd had nothing at all. Now she wanted to live. She even wanted to paint.

He washed off the orange juice and, with Rob's help, re-tacked the horses. They mounted and rode back the way they'd come, but now all the sights had been pointed out, all the memories shared, the conversation and laughter that had accompanied them on the ascent sank with the sun and their descent.

They reached Beirut at dusk when the bells were ringing vespers. Entering the outer ward, they encountered Bella on her way to church, and she smiled and waved. "Did you enjoy your ride?"

"It was beautiful," Eschiva admitted, adding, "One of the most beautiful days of my life." She was fighting tears. If she had thought the indifference of despair was terrible, this acute pain of impending loss was worse. No, she corrected herself, she was richer than ever because she would always have the memory.

"I'm so glad!" Bella answered. "Go ahead to the solar. I'll meet you there as soon as Mass is over. Tante Alys is back. She's most anxious to see you both."

Dinner was terrible. Aunt Alys kept casting Balian reproachful and Eschiva shocked glances. Betrada tried to keep the conversation going, saying what a pleasure it had been to visit the monastery again, and Bella chattered about the orphanage and the last minute preparations for Eschiva's departure. Neither Balian nor Eschiva spoke more than a dozen words.

As they rose from dinner, Aunt Alys pointedly requested Balian's assistance. "I want to move the chest in my room, and I'm much too weak." It was an all too transparent effort to keep him from escorting Eschiva to her chamber. He dutifully obliged without the slightest protest.

Eschiva returned to her chamber and looked at her packed bags filled with the gifts Bella had yet again given her. She felt as if she were preparing for her execution.

She did not want to return to Gerard. She never wanted to set eyes on him again, much less lie with him and let him invade her body. But she knew she would. She could not run away from her marriage as she had run away from the Emperor's harem. She had nowhere to go. Her brother would only send her back, and even Bella and Balian could not shelter her here against her lawful husband. No matter what Bella said about not believing her marriage was valid, it was very much legal.

The darkness deepened and Eschiva waited. She was sure Balian would come, even though she wasn't sure what she would do when he did. She still felt an intense reluctance to besmirch and soil the memories of the last 24 hours with the sordid business of sex. Yet she was equally afraid that if she turned him away again he might be angry. The rules of courtly love entitled her to reject him, but what did life have to do with courtly love?

The stars had come out and she was very stiff from the ride. She could only hobble across the room toward the fireplace to light a lamp from the embers and stoke it a little. From the corner of her eye, she registered that something wasn't right. Then she noticed that something was on the floor near the door. Even as she approached, her heart sank. It was a folded piece of paper.

She picked it up. It was folded in thirds and secured with hardened wax bearing the imprint of Ibelin. Her heart sank to her belly as she lowered herself onto the nearest chest and broke open the seal. There was a second piece of paper folded inside and it floated to the floor. When she bent to retrieve it she recognized with amazement that it was covered with her own illustrations. For a moment she was totally baffled—until she recognized the ships and fish she had made while traveling home on Balian's ship. She must have tucked them inside the *Odyssey*, which she had duly returned to the Lord of Beirut, forgetting all about them. But Balian had found them and returned them to her. "It must have been like losing a child" echoed in her brain. It made tears come to her eyes even before she turned to his message.

"Mi dons," he opened. Mi dons? That was the way a knight addressed his lady—the lady to whom he pledged his service and fidelity. It was the highest courtesy possible.

> *It is better I do not torment you with my presence. I do not wish to harm or pain you in any way, and even if I believe that I could bring you joy, what value is that if the pain it brings afterwards is all the greater?*
>
> *I would give you comfort if I could, but I know not how—beyond the inadequate comfort of a kiss, an embrace.*
>
> *I would free you of your sorrow if I could, but I know not how without murder.*
>
> *I would offer you the protection of my arms if I could, but what good are my weak arms against the law, the Church?*
>
> *All I can offer you is my heart, though I know not what good it is.*
>
> *A heart alone can do nothing but love in silence. I offer you my love. In silence.*
>
> *Balian d'Ibelin II*

Eschiva burst into tears and clutched the letter to her heart. In her mind, she kept saying, "I love you! I love you!" but she dared not open her mouth and say it aloud. In silence. My love. In silence.

Chapter Twenty
Emperor in Jerusalem

Jerusalem
March 18, 1229

THE CHURCH OF THE HOLY SEPULCHER, Frederick thought, was a dingy, sorry church of uninspired architecture. He had seen much grander cathedrals in Aachen and Cologne, not to mention his own Monreale. Admittedly, the sculptures were quite good, particularly some of the capitals, and the effigy of King Baldwin III, but otherwise it was all comparatively mundane.

Frederick turned his attention back to the altar where the Imperial crown of the Holy Roman Empire lay waiting for him. Since the Patriarch had placed Jerusalem under interdict, neither he nor any of the other bishops of Outremer were present, but that hardly bothered Frederick; his four Sicilian Archbishops were still with him, tame as lapdogs. Likewise, the lords of Outremer were absent, but Frederick was positively relieved not to have the brooding Lord of Beirut and his bevy of hangers-on spoiling the scene. A bunch of sycophants! It was refreshing to be surrounded by honest pilgrims, even if they were mostly semi-morons awestruck by the idea of walking on the same paving stones as Christ. As if these *were* the same paving stones! Stupid idiots, actually.

As for the Templars and Hospitallers, they too had remained in Acre whining and muttering about this and that, but the good Herman von Salza was here with his splendid knights of the *Deutsche Ritter-Orden*. These German knights truly looked stronger, taller and purer than the members of the older militant orders with their mix of Spaniards, Italians, French and English, Frederick told himself.

The moment had come. The Archbishop of Palermo nodded to him. Frederick reached out and grasped the crown of Germany and Lombardy. He held it up high for all to see and then ceremoniously placed it upon his brow. It was highly satisfying that there was no pope giving it to him this time. No sanctimonious implications of subordination to the See of Rome. With this gesture he made visible the reality: that he was Holy Roman Emperor by right and by the Will of God—not the Pope.

Frederick had ensured that there were strips of velvet inside the crown so that it sat nice and snug. He turned to face down the length of the church as the crowd broke into the *Te Deum*. Thankfully, his household had managed to fill the church, even if it meant letting quite a few of the common pilgrims in.

As the organ fell silent and the voices faded away, Herman von Salza stepped forward to read Frederick's prepared speech. Salza had a fine voice and, pedestrian as the architecture was, the church had very good acoustics. Salza, reading the text Frederick had himself prepared, noted that "the feared Caesar, the Great Roman Emperor, the Ever Victorious, the Ever Illustrious, the Sublime Frederick, son of Henry, Son of Frederick," had taken the cross at Aachen thirteen years ago, renewed his vows in Rome eight years ago, and that he had now stood before them in the Holiest Church of Christendom—the Church of the Holy Sepulcher—having fulfilled his vow. Frederick (through Salza) acknowledged papal opposition to his crusade, but he "pleaded" (Salza read the word splendidly with great pathos in his voice) for "reconciliation" (I'll make the bastard kneel before me and beg for it! Frederick promised himself) now that the crusade had come to such a gloriously successful conclusion. (Gregory will eat his own puke when he finds out about this! Fredrick couldn't suppress a faint smile at the thought.)

Salza's voice turned dark and threatening as he referred to the "flagrant opposition" of "forces in the Holy Land" that *ought* to have supported the Holy Roman Emperor on his sacred and devout mission to liberate Jerusalem. For, Salza read on, the Emperor was here in the service of God. He was here as God's vicar on earth to do God's will. (And anyone who opposes me thereby opposes God, you bloody, insubordinate bastards!)

As Salza concluded the speech, his knights spontaneously broke into cheers. (Just as they had been instructed to do.) The cheers were quickly picked up by the gullible pilgrims at the back of the church, who could be counted on to imitate their betters in everything. So it was between the rows of cheering admirers that Frederick exited the Church, passed by the tombs of his predecessors and out into the brilliant sunshine of the courtyard.

Unfortunately, the bells had been removed from the bell tower by the Muslims during their 42 years of occupation, so there was no ringing of bells as there had been at his coronations. The silence reminded Frederick that he hadn't heard the muezzins call to prayer during the night or this morning either. Catching sight of the qadi of Nablus, Shams ad-Din, whom al-Kamil had assigned as his host during this two-day visit to Jerusalem, Frederick beckoned the Muslim cleric to his side.

The qadi was a venerable old man with considerable diplomatic experience in the service of al-Kamil. He bowed deeply to the Christian monarch now parading in his full regalia with the Imperial crown on his head. "Oh, qadi," Fredrick asked as the man waited attentively, "why did the muezzins not give the call to prayer in the normal way last night?"

"This humble slave prevented them out of respect for Your Majesty."

"But our chief aim in passing the night in Jerusalem was to hear the call to prayer given by the muezzins," Frederick answered with a smile at the dumbfounded expression on the Muslim scholar's face. "And now," Frederick added, "we wish you to lead us to the Dome of the Rock, as we are as keen to see that great mosque as to see this old church."

The Muslim cleric bowed deeply to indicate compliance.

Obviously, Frederick did not intend to walk that far, so he mounted his magnificently caparisoned stallion in the street. The Imperial cavalcade then moved off at a stately pace, winding through streets inhabited by Jews and Muslims more than Christians. The former watched the cavalcade warily, aware that they had been sold by a man they did not consider their master to "the devil" himself, but unwilling to abandon their goods and chattels.

At the entrance to the Temple Mount, Frederick and his escort of Teutonic and Imperial knights dismounted again and passed through the gate. Here Frederick waited for the qadi of Nablus to catch up with him while gazing up at the great, golden dome. When the Muslim cleric rejoined him, Frederick noted, "It is a beautiful structure—far more magnificent than the Church of the Holy Sepulcher. Is it true that that madman Balian d'Ibelin stripped the gold from it during the last siege?"

The qadi bowed deeply. "It is true, your majesty. He is said to have used the gold to pay the mercenaries that defended the city against the forces of Salah ad-Din."

"Barbarian!" Frederick dismissed Beirut's father with contempt.

The qadi gestured for Frederick to proceed, and they mounted the steps and crossed the wide paved platform in the direction of the great mosque. Frederick kept nodding in approval as his eyes swept over the mosaics of the exterior. Then his eyes fell on a marble plaque. He paused to read it, deciphering the Arabic out loud. "*The Great Sultan Salah ad-Din, may Allah's blessing be upon him, purified this city of the polytheists.* Ah ha!" Frederick turned to grin at the embarrassed qadi. "So who were the polytheists?"

The poor Muslim scholar opened his mouth and closed it again, bowing deeply in embarrassment as Frederick burst out laughing. He passed into the interior of the mosque with the qadi trailing unhappily in his wake. Fredrick looked about as any tourist would, noting the interior decorations with approval before wandering over to the "rock" itself. This was protected by an iron fence and screen. "What's this for?" he asked over his shoulder to the qadi. "Something to keep out the pigs?" He jovially referred to the Christians by another name popular among Muslims.

The qadi looked as if he wanted to sink into the foundations, while Frederick again laughed heartily at his own joke.

His tour of the Dome of the Rock complete, Frederick proceeded toward the al-Aqsa mosque—that large complex that had served as Templar headquarters and which the greedy bastards valued more than the rest of Jerusalem put together. Ahead of him a throng of pilgrims of the poorer sort were already gathered, oblivious to the fact that the Holy Roman Emperor had arrived by the other gate to the Temple Mount. They were shuffling forward to pass through the narrow entrance guarded by some Mamlukes.

The Mamlukes looked angry and disgusted, Frederick noted, and he imagined they thoroughly disapproved of the terms of the Treaty that gave Christian pilgrims the right to set foot on the Temple Mount at all. The terms were restrictive, but they did grant those in Frederick's army the right to visit all the "holy" sites—even if Fredrick couldn't see what was "holy" about the Knights Templar's former headquarters.

Shaking his head in disgust, his eyes fell on a priest clutching a copy of the Bible in his hand. Frederick instantly lost his temper. "You tactless idiot!" he called out.

At once all the pilgrims turned to stare in astonishment. At the sight of the Holy Roman Emperor still wearing the Imperial crown and robes, they fell to their knees in awe.

Fredrick waded into the crowd, grabbed the stupid priest by his arm and yanked him to his feet. "How dare you come in here with a Bible? Don't you realize this is a sacred Muslim site! You are here as a guest only! You have no business carrying a Bible with you! Get out! Out!" The Emperor shoved his knee into the priest's backside to lend his words greater force, and the man stumbled over his own robes as he staggered forward. "Go!" Frederick shouted after him, and the man started running, with a backward look at Frederick as if the Emperor was mad.

Turning to his host, Frederick intoned, "We apologize for the tactless stupidity of our subjects, o qadi."

The qadi of Nablus bowed deeply in reply, but he failed to disguise his intense disapproval.

The Temple at Acre
April 24, 1229

The Montaigus were meeting in the Templar Master's private quarters at the Commandery of Acre. These were located in the comfortable, northwest tower of the complex, which offered splendid views out to sea. The white limestone walls were, in accordance with Templar austerity, naked of tapestries, tiles, and marbles. Likewise, the floors were bare of carpets, rugs or matting. The only adornment was a lifelike crucifix almost a yard tall with an ivory Christ of exceptional beauty and craftsmanship, a gift from the King of Portugal.

"We have a Turcopole," Pedro de Montaigu was explaining to his brother Guerin and his nephew Gerard, "who we infiltrated into al-Kamil's Mamlukes almost ten years ago. The man is now 24 and has begged to be allowed to return to his duties with the Temple, but he's invaluable to us where he is."

Guerin nodded in sympathy. "I can imagine, but at some point, you must show Christian charity. A devout Christian living the life of a Mamluke is cut off from all the sacraments. He cannot confess his sins, and if he dies unconfessed he is damned. You do not have the right to ask that of any man indefinitely."

"Yes, yes, yes," Pedro answered a fraction peeved. "But at the moment, as I said, he is invaluable. Among other things he was able to report on the reaction of his comrades and master to the Emperor's sojourn in Jerusalem."

"Yes?" Guerin asked.

"Disgust! Pure disgust! They cannot comprehend how a man can be so disrespectful of his own faith. They see him as a 'pure materialist,' our spy reports. They said he behaves as if Christianity were a 'mere game.' Their opinion of him has reached a new ebb—and with it their contempt for *us* for following such a hypocrite."

"Beirut reported much the same thing," Guerin answered nodding. "He said his son ran into a Seljuk merchant, who asked why any man of honor would follow such an 'unworthy' man. That, I think, sums it up very nicely. An unworthy man."

"Who thinks he's 'God's vicar'—not to mention 'the wonder of the world!'"

His brother snapped back. "*Stupor Mundi*, indeed! We are all speechless with astonishment at how a Christian monarch can be so disrespectful of Our Lord, His Sacrifice for our sake, and His Resurrection!" Pedro was simmering with agitation as he spoke. He turned on his nephew. "And you, Gerard? You insisted on going to Jerusalem despite the interdict. What did you see?"

Gerard clutched his silver cross in his right hand. "You know I had to go. I had to pray in the Holy Sepulcher. I had vowed to do so." His tone was belligerent, defensive and raw all at once. His eyes were sunken in his face; his skin was lined and sagging. He looked much older than his 35 years.

His uncles were tired of arguing with him, and Guerin spoke for both of them. "We didn't call you here to reproach you, but to hear any intelligence you might have."

Gerard looked sullen and resentful. "What should I have seen?" he asked back. "It was a city filled with people who hate us—Jews stand behind every shop counter, the money-lenders practically in the courtyard of the Holy Sepulcher! Muslim brothel owners assault you on every corner. It is a city that *should* be holy but which has been turned into Babylon! They have silenced the bells, put camels in the convents, and piss in the Stations of the Cross! It is—a travesty." His anger broke and he dropped his face in his hands.

His uncles stared at him. Gerard was a deep disappointment to them both. He was too obsessed with his own soul to be of great use to them. Even his wedding had brought them little value as Eudes de Montbeliard had proved a poor ally, too weak and spineless to stand up to the Hohenstaufen, and his sister had proved barren.

After a moment, Guerin took pity on him. "It is indeed a sad state of affairs, and you are still grieving for your little son, although we knew he was not long for this world. How is your poor, young wife doing? She survived the ordeal without damage?"

"As far as I can see. She has said nothing about it. Indeed, she says very little at all. She spends most of her days with the Canons of the Holy Sepulcher."

"They will bring her solace, and prayer will bring her peace, whether it quickens her womb or not," Pedro concluded.

"I am not sure she is praying. She returns with ink-stained fingers and tells me she is helping in the scriptorium." Gerard sounded resentful.

Guerin at once took Eschiva's side. "It is a great compliment that the Canons of the Holy Sepulcher wish her assistance, Gerard. It confirms what I thought myself: she has a great talent. A gift at illustrating the Word of Our Lord is a gift from God. It is something to cherish, admire and foster."

"Of course," Gerard agreed unconvincingly, adding, "now that the Count of

Cotron had withdrawn from Cyprus, however, and King Henry will be returning to his kingdom, I have ordered her to return there. Things are too unsettled
here and I do not trust this truce. Uncle Eustace has promised to provide her
accommodation in his palace in Nicosia. Nana Flora has decided to take the veil
here."

His uncles looked mildly surprised. "And yourself?"

"I wish to visit the Jordan, the Church of the Nativity, the Church of the
Annunciation, and return again to Jerusalem at a more propitious time—when
the Emperor is not there."

They nodded but did not seem particularly approving, much less understanding.

"I must see to my soul," Gerard insisted petulantly. "There is nothing more
I can do for you."

A heavy pounding on the door startled the three men. Pedro called out
sharply, "Who is it and what do you want?"

"My lord! My lord!" A breathless voice shouted through the wooden door.
"One of our sergeants has been shot as he tried to exit by the main gate!"

Pedro cursed under his breath, sprang to his feet and plunged out of the
door, leaving his brother and nephew behind. He pounded down the stairs as
fast as possible until, reaching the courtyard, he paused to look about. Just inside
the main gate, a crowd had gathered. Pedro plunged in to find at the center a
sergeant with a crossbow bolt in his shoulder. A brother from the infirmary was
already with him and a stretcher was being organized. Pedro leaned over him
and asked, "Did you see who shot you?"

The man shook his head, and gasped out, "I'm sorry, my lord." He grimaced
with pain and clamped his teeth together to keep from groaning.

Pedro patted him on the other shoulder to indicate it was no matter and
nodded for the others to remove him to the infirmary. Then he lifted his voice
and bellowed toward the barbican, "Bar the gates."

"Done, my lord!"

Montaigu next looked around and spotted a knight who had evidently run
over at the commotion but had no particular role in treating the injured man.
"Ring the alarm!" he ordered.

The knight sprang to obey, running as fast as he could across the courtyard
toward the chapel. Meanwhile, Guerin and Gerard had caught up with Pedro.

"Who would dare shoot a Templar in the heart of Acre?" Gerard asked
incensed.

The older Montaigus ignored him. Guerin announced, "I must return to
my brothers! I'll take the underground passage. Gerard come with me!" Pedro

nodded, and Guerin, with Gerard on his heels, headed for the tower from which an underground passage led from the Temple to the port.

Pedro meanwhile ordered men to secure the two postern gates that both opened on streets to the north of the Templar compound. He had barely finished giving these orders when from beyond the east-facing main gate came the sound of trumpets and then the clatter of hooves. Pedro turned toward the main gate, his eyes narrowed as he held his breath, but the gates had indeed been secured. A rapid patter of thuds on the wooden doors recorded a volley of crossbows followed by louder thumps as men evidently threw axes or spears, but the heavy gates hardly reverberated under the assault.

"Should we return fire, my lord?" a voice called from the battlements of the barbican.

"Not yet!" Montaigu shouted, but he hurried to the foot of the barbican tower and started up the stairs as fast as he could, holding the skirts of his robe in one fist to keep from tripping over them. He was annoyed he was not in armor, but could not take time to change.

As he emerged into the guardroom, the alarm bell was ringing at last. He snapped his fingers at the first sergeant he saw and demanded his helmet from him. He was about to start up the steps to the ramparts when the man stopped him and offered his hauberk as well. Montaigu didn't hesitate. He pulled the chainmail over his robes. His shoulders were much narrower than the sergeant's and the chainmail sagged on him, but the rings still offered protection.

When he reached the ramparts, he looked briefly down into the courtyard to make sure men were responding to the alarm. Men were tumbling out of every nook and cranny of the extensive buildings around the inner courtyard, pulling on their helmets or buckling swords on the run. Satisfied, he turned toward the outer wall. Here the Officer of the Watch and a half dozen sergeants were pressed against the inside of the parapet and peering cautiously through the crenels.

"Can you see who they are?" Montaigu asked.

"Not really, my lord—not the archers anyway. The men who rode up to try the gate appear to have been Teutonics. In their white robes, we almost mistook them for some of our own men!"

Yes, Montaigu registered, that was *another* reason to resent the fact that the Pope had granted them the right to wear robes so similar to the Templars. The knight was looking at him expectantly. "Why, my lord—"

"The Teutonics are the Emperor's lap dogs!" Montaigu snapped in answer. "Was it Salza who led the attack?"

"No, my lord. I think it was Falkenhayn."

"Ah, here are the archers!" Montaigu stepped aside to let a half-dozen archers, Templar sergeants, responding to the alarm, take up their assigned positions. Turning to the senior sergeant among them, Montaigu ordered, "Don't let anyone within fifty feet of the gate! Fire warning shots first, but shoot to kill if they persist."

"Yes, my lord!"

Montaigu had learned all he needed to. He descended to the floor below, returned the borrowed helm and hauberk to the sergeant, and made his way back to his chamber. By now his ten companions, likewise responding to the alarm, had collected outside his chamber ready to for his orders or to escort him wherever he went. He nodded acknowledgment and signaled for his squire to help him change into armor. He also sent one of his companions to call the Officers of the Temple together in the Chapter House.

Within an hour they had verified that they had enough provisions to withstand a six months siege or more. Frederick didn't have time to sit out such a long siege, however, because the Kingdom of Sicily had been invaded by the army of John de Brienne. The Templars concluded that he would be forced to attempt an assault.

None of the senior Templar officers questioned that the Temple at Acre could withstand an assault. It had been built according to the most advanced principles of military architecture with overlapping fields of fire covering every approach, and high walls backed by interlinking wall-walks to enable the rapid reinforcement of any salient under pressure. The barbican was dog-legged, all the spiral stairs twisted counter-clockwise to ensure the defenders had the advantage, and arrow-slits pierced the walls at regular intervals even facing the interior courtyard to ensure that any enemy that made it inside was still vulnerable. The *ability* to defend the Temple wasn't the issue.

The problem was entirely one of public relations. How could the Knights Templar kill—and be seen to kill—their fellow Christians?

"We need to find out what is being said in the streets of Acre. Are people with us or the Emperor?" the Marshal suggested.

Montaigu agreed, but he was reluctant to send a single Templar into the streets of Acre. A Templar on his own could too easily be arrested and tortured. After all, if a man did not hesitate to torture the sons of a prominent nobleman held as honorable hostages, what wouldn't he do to an anonymous brother of the Temple? Especially after effectively declaring war on them?

"Do we know if every brother is safe inside the Temple?" Montaigu asked, ashamed he had not asked sooner.

"There has been a roll call, my lord," the Commander of Acre answered promptly. "Absent are two lay-brothers from the kitchen, who had gone to the market to buy fresh vegetables; one sergeant smith sent to fetch a cargo of horse-shoe nails due in from Beirut; he took a lay carter with him; Father Ernesius, who wished to visit the Scriptorium of the Holy Sepulcher about the Hymnal we ordered; and Brother Ullrich, who volunteered to escort him."

"So, two lay brothers, one sergeant, one servant, one knight and the good Father Ernesius are all missing?"

"I wouldn't say missing, my lord. They were all excused."

"Of course. Nevertheless, they are not here, and we cannot know where they are or what will befall them in the city."

Acre
April 24, 1229

Ulli had volunteered to accompany Father Ernesius to the Scriptorium because it was located in the suburb of Montmusard very near the weekly horse market. Ulli was always on the lookout for good horseflesh and even if he couldn't *buy* without permission from the Marshal of the Temple and funds released by the Treasurer, Ulli rationalized that it never hurt to *look* at what was available on the market.

He escorted the severely short-sighted Father Ernesius to the large waiting room at the front of the Scriptorium. Here lay-people came to see samples of the work done by the Holy Canons and commission work. While Father Ernesius was greeted warmly by the canons and led down the steps to the cloister from which the workrooms of the Scriptorium opened, Brother Ullrich pretended intense interest in one of the books on display until he was sure Father Ernesius was out of hearing. Then he slipped quickly back into the street and headed for the horse market.

This was held twice weekly in the open area behind the deep dry moat that separated Montmusard from Acre proper. Both Arab and European horses, those freshly imported in the large horse transports of the Italian city-states, were sold here. Saracen horse-dealers brought their horses in long trains, and tied them up on rails, while the Western horse-dealers generally kept their horses in small paddocks. Here they milled about in various degrees of unease. Mares and stallions were, of course, strictly separated, but that contributed to a considerable amount of whinnying and agitation when the stallions were led past the mares' paddocks or vice versa. There was also a small ring where prospective buyers could ride briefly, and this also attracted crowds of idle bystanders.

Ulli went straight for the stallions' paddocks near the landward wall. He was looking for a horse like the one he had been forced to surrender on entering the Order: a horse that was powerful and had real endurance but didn't shy at every bird or rabbit. In his opinion, high-strung horses were greatly over-rated. He wanted a horse that was solid and reliable, not flighty and scatterbrained.

Last week, he'd noticed that an Armenian horse-dealer had several horses that looked promising. He was anxious to get a second look at them. There was a large crowd of secular knights clustered around a Saracen horse-dealer just in front of the paddock he was seeking out. The Saracen apparently had some yearlings that were attracting attention. Ulli started to weave his way between the others, muttering a soft "*Verzeihung, verzeihung,*" as he went. Out the other side of the crowd, he was pleased to see the Armenian had no customers at the moment.

Ulli called a greeting and the man came over at once, bowing and smiling in welcome. Ulli asked about one of the horses, and the Armenian went to fetch him, taking a halter so he could lead the horse back.

No sooner had the dealer moved off into the paddock than Ulli felt men step up close behind him. In fact, they surrounded him and pressed him against the paddock fence. "*Verzeihung!*" One of them hissed out in a sneering tone. "*Verzeihung!*"

Ulli was not tall and all these men, a half dozen of them it seemed, were four to six inches taller than him. They were also all in armor.

"Did I understand correctly?" One of the knights opened, continuing in German. "We have here a *German* in the robes of the traitorous Templars?"

Ullrich could feel the hostility and it made his breathing come a little shorter, but he stood his ground. "I'm Ullrich von Alvensleben and I'm a true servant of Christ—which is more than I can say about the likes of you!"

One of the men thrust a knee into his groin so fast and so hard that Ulli didn't stand a chance of defending himself. He crumpled up with a short groan, and already the next blow and the one after were raining down on him. The three men closest to him were using the hilts of their swords mercilessly. At the sight of so much concentrated violence, the Armenian horse-dealer backed off in terror—shouting for the watch at the top of his lungs

Ulli's assailants were shouting "Templar traitor!" and "Templar bastard!" as they pummeled him to his knees. Kneeling, he tried to cross his arms before his face to protect his head, but one of the blows broke his right wrist. He howled in agony and shrank back farther, falling against the upright pillar of the paddock fence. The next blow snapped his lower left arm, and Ulli screamed in pain again. He tried to crawl under the fence, but one of the men grabbed his ankles and dragged him back. They started kicking his ribs, his kidneys.

Hooves landed beside his head and dust blinded him. Someone screamed, and it wasn't him.

"Stay out of this, Ibelin!" a voice shouted.

"You're under arrest, Sir Adelbert!" was the answer.

"What the hell?"

"Seize them! All five of them! Don't even try, Sir Bodo!"

The moment the hooves arrived, the assault had stopped, but Ulli squirmed his way as best he could to the comparative safety of the paddock. Only then did he twist around to see what was happening. A handsome young man on an ugly chestnut horse was holding his sword pointed at the throat of one of the five assailants, who was holding both hands in the air in evident surrender. The horse formed a barrier between Ulli and the other men, but he could see a second man on a horse had drawn his sword as well, apparently in support of the first. As Ulli watched, sergeants of the watch clamped hold of all five men, wrenching the swords out of their hands.

Not that they didn't struggle, except for the man with a sword at this throat, but the moment they did, the crowd pounced on them. Even the Saracen horse-dealer joined in with apparent enthusiasm. Soon the assailants were being kicked and spat upon with so much increasing violence that the young man who had rescued Ulli called them to order. "Enough! They're under arrest!" To the city watch, he ordered, "Get them to the city jail before any more of the Emperor's men or the Teutonics find out what happened!"

"Don't think you can get away with this, Sir Balian!" one of the men shouted at him as the watch started to hustle him away.

The young man rode his horse closer and spat on the man who had spoken. "Oh, but I can! You're in *Acre,* not Aachen!"

Then he spun his horse around and jumped down in a fluid motion to bend over Ulli. "How badly are you hurt, Sir Brother?"

Ulli managed to gasp, "My wrist and arm!"

The young man looked at both limbs but covered as they were in chainmail it was impossible to see anything more than that Ulli held them before himself helplessly. "I'll get you to the Hospital. It's nearer—"

"No, I need to—the Scriptorium. My brother—Father—" Ulli had just remembered he was supposed to be escorting Father Ernesius. He was going to get into trouble for coming here.

The young knight slipped his hands under Ulli's armpits to help him to his feet without touching his arms, but at once his companion jumped down with a "Wait! *I'll* do that."

"I can manage!" Ulli's rescuer answered irritably, but already the knight's smaller, more compact companion was on Ulli's other side. Together they helped him to his feet as gently as possible.

Once Ulli was standing, his rescuer told him firmly, "I'm taking you to the Hospital. If you need me to get a message to the Scriptorium, I will do that next. First, we go to the Hospital."

Ulli didn't have the strength to fight. The pain was blinding and numbing both. He surrendered to the care of his rescuer, and this was not inconsequential. Without giving orders, he seemed to attract helpers. Someone had found a lady's litter and this was converted quickly into a stretcher. Someone else brought Ulli water to drink, and another brought wine, while the second knight wiped away some of the blood streaming from his nose and the gashes to his head. In a crowd, they moved forward.

Ulli couldn't concentrate for the pain, but he started to catch phrases: "laid siege to the Temple," "no one can get in or out," "shot at least one man dead," "bringing up siege engines." He was beginning to grasp that he was only a tiny piece of a much larger puzzle, but he still couldn't figure it out.

At the Hospitaller complex, the brothers were on high alert, but after several agitated voices explained who their victim was, the brothers at the gate agreed to send for a senior officer. When this man arrived, Ulli heard his rescuer raise his voice to declare, "Knights from the Emperor's household set upon this Templar without warning or cause. He has been badly injured."

"What did you have to do with this, Sir Balian?"

"I interceded before they actually *killed* him and ordered the arrest of his assailants."

"On whose authority?" But it appeared to be a rhetorical question because at the same time the door was opened and several Hospitallers came to help Ulli out of the litter and inside. Only Sir Balian was allowed in with the patient. He turned to his friend with the request, "Get word to my father at once, Philip!"

"If he doesn't already know! Not much happens in Acre that doesn't get to his ears as fast as lightning—least of all when it involves you!"

"Well, then tell him where I am, will you?"

"Of course."

Inside the Hospital, Ulli was escorted, limping because of the pain in his side, by two Hospitaller brothers toward the hospital ward. The officer and Sir Balian followed them. Ulli heard the Hospitaller ask, "What is this was all about? Why would the Emperor's men attack a Templar without reason?"

"The Emperor accuses the Templar Master and Patriarch of planning to violate his truce and take troops to Jerusalem to fortify it. My father was warned that the Emperor planned to kidnap the Templar Master and take him back to Palermo in chains to ensure the 'good behavior' of the Templars."

"Do you think that credible?" the Hospitaller asked skeptically.

"Let's put it this way. My father does not go anywhere without an armed entourage of six knights, and he won't let me ride with him or enter the Emperor's presence at the same time he does. He wants to be sure that whatever happens, one or the other of us is at liberty to rally our vassals and men. Meanwhile, the Temple has been cordoned off by the Teutonic Knights and anyone trying to enter or leave is shot at."

"What?"

"He speaks the truth," these words came from a man who emerged out of apparently nowhere.

"My lord!" the Hospitaller officer and Sir Balian exclaimed in unison.

"And what are you doing here, Sir Balian?"

"That Templar was set upon by five of the Emperor's knights and severely mishandled before I could intervene. He needs medical attention."

"He will receive it. Brother Honorius, give the orders to secure all access points to the compound and man the walls. Then send for all senior officers to meet me in the Chapter House at once."

The officer bowed to his Master and withdrew. Meanwhile, Ulli and his escort had reached the door to the ward. Ulli cautiously stepped down into the long, well-lit hall, and the Hospitaller brothers directed him toward a bay with an empty pallet. Ulli eased himself down onto the pallet but hastened to warn the nursing brothers, "my right wrist is broken and my left arm, and I must get a message to my brother—"

"No worries on that score. I said I'd take care of it," Sir Balian stepped forward with a reassuring smile. "Who should I seek and who should I say has sent the message?"

"You must find Father Ernesius. He's at the Scriptorium of the Canons of the Holy Sepulcher. I—I was to escort him there and back because he is nearly blind and quite frail. I—if it's true—what you are saying about the Temple being cordoned off—"

"It's true," the elderly man beside Sir Balian assured him, and Ulli realized that he was confronting none other than the Master of the Hospital.

"I don't understand," Ulli admitted, feeling nauseous from both pain and sheer confusion.

"It is not easy to understand how a so-called Christian monarch can attack the Poor Knights of the Temple of Solomon," the Hospitaller replied, "but whiter heads than yours will have to work on the solution." He smiled at Ulli as he spoke. "Now drink that potion my brothers are giving you and lie down for a bit. We will need to remove your armor and shirt to set your bones."

"Your name, sir, so I can tell Father Ernesius what happened?" Sir Balian insisted before Ulli became completely consumed with his own pain.

"Brother Ullrich von Alvensleben—and thank you, sir! I think they would have killed me if you had not come along."

"It was my pleasure, Sir Ullrich. In fact, I was rather hoping that ass Sir Adelbert would give me a legitimate excuse to run him through."

"Sir Balian! Don't talk like that! Your father—" The Hospitaller Master was shocked.

"I know, I know. My father would never talk like that, but I am neither my father nor grandfather. I am who I am, my lord."

"And God Bless you for it!" Ullrich called after him as Sir Balian bowed deeply to the Hospitaller Master and withdrew.

Scriptorium of the Canons of the Holy Sepulcher, Acre
April 24, 1229

Father Ernesius sat comfortably in the wooden pew-like seat behind the writing pulpit. Bright sunlight streamed from the arched window beside him onto the paper held in place by two wooden rulers screwed into place. His face seemed to reflect the light as he smiled in contentment. "You have a gift, my child," he told Eschiva nodding. "It would be wasted on anything as simple as a book of psalms for private use. My Order has long wanted to commission a complete copy of Archbishop William of Tyre's *History of Deeds Done Beyond the Sea*. We can hire an ordinary copyist for the text, but I would like you to do the illustrations. What do you think?"

Eschiva caught her breath, and then she started mentally thanking Christ. Thank you, thank you, thank you! And Balian, who had sent her here. She had never dared to dream of a commission—much less from an institution as prestigious and powerful as the Knights Templar! Nor had she dared to think of a project as complex as a full history of Outremer. The Lord giveth and the Lord taketh away. All we can do is be joyful when he gives.

Thinking her silence was hesitation, Father Ernesius continued earnestly, "look here." He pointed to one of her sample figures. "Most monks, being sedentary creatures, have little affinity for horses. They make them much too rigid and all similar to one another. You, on the other hand, have one throwing up his head, and the other trying to snatch some grass—so charmingly realistic!"

Eschiva blushed with pleasure. "Thank you, Father."

"Not that there aren't things you still have to learn," he warned, a twinkle in his eye. "Your saints all have the same face, I fear."

Eschiva had to laugh at that because it was true, and Father Ernesius laughed with her.

"You should try to change the expression of your humans as much as you do that of your animals."

"Yes, Father, I will try. Will you come next week to—oh." She broke off.

"What is it?"

"My husband wants me to return to Cyprus with King Henry. I'm not sure when he will leave, but I've been told it will be soon. I'm not sure I'll still be here next week."

Father Ernesius said nothing. All the joy had vanished from Eschiva's face, and he could feel how rigid she had become. After a long pause, he asked softly, "Do you think it would do any good if I asked him to let you stay on to continue your studies here?"

Eschiva shook her head sharply. "No."

"And if the Master asked him?" Father Ernesius pressed her.

She still shook her head, but a little less decisively. The Templar Master was Gerard's uncle and he sometimes seemed to dance to the Templar's tune.

"Hm." The Templar priest drew a deep breath and noticed that the sunlight had shifted significantly. It reached only some of the illustrations, slanting sharply to the left as the sun moved. "I fear I have stayed too long again. Poor Brother Ullrich will be going mad with boredom! But before I go there is a favor I wish to ask of you."

"Anything at all, Father!" Eschiva promised, thinking her debt to him could never be repaid.

"Two weeks ago you mentioned that you did not have a woman to wait on you. You said in Cyprus one of the Greeks looked after you, but since your flight, you have had only the inadequate service of your landlady's daughter."

"Who, of course, will stay in Acre when I leave," Eschiva admitted.

"So you still have need of a woman?" Father Ernesius concluded hopefully.

"I do, yes, do you know of someone suitable?"

Father Ernesius sighed deeply. "Men, even rich and powerful men, sometimes cannot resist temptation. A penniless widow of impeccable reputation, hardly more than a child really, was given refuge by one of her father's closest friends—only to discover that the man—I will not say who it was—wanted her favors in exchange. She fled to the sisters of St. Anne, and they came to me with reproaches because, you see, it was my brothers who foreclosed on her home and left her with no place to go in the first place. I'm sure she would be a very devoted servant to you if you would give her a chance."

"Of course father, I would be happy to. You can have her come to my lodgings tomorrow."

Father Ernesius smiled broadly. "Thank you, my dear! That is a great burden off my mind. I will tell the Sisters of St. Anne on my way back to the Temple. Now, I must be off." He stood up, noting each of his aching muscles after sitting so long in one position.

Eschiva rose with him. "I'll see you to the waiting room," she offered, knowing that his eyesight was so poor that he often didn't see the random steps created to accommodate the uneven terrain underneath. Holding Father Ernesius firmly by the elbow, she paced herself to his slower, smaller steps. Together, they exited the scriptorium, walked around the cloister, and mounted the three steps up into the waiting room.

Unlike the hushed awe that usually reigned here, they found the room abuzz with conversation and dramatically gesturing people. "But how could he do such a thing? By what right?" one priest demanded, while another protested, "the Saracens will fall on us from behind!" Another said, "This is a diabolic joke: The Holy Roman Emperor attacking the Knights Templar!"

"Not just the Templars! The Emperor's men tried to arrest the Patriarch himself! He barely managed to escape inside his palace!"

"The Patriarch's palace? But that's not a fortress! He won't be safe there."

"My father's men have taken up positions in front of it," a voice said, and Eschiva felt as if she'd been struck by lightning. *He* was here!

She turned in the direction of his voice, while around him the clerics called down blessings on the Lord of Beirut. He was partially obscured by the men clustered around him. Still, his forehead rose above theirs, his dark hair falling over it. Even as she watched, he lifted his head to shake the hair out of his eyes, and their eyes locked. He had not expected to find her here, and the sight of her paralyzed him for a second. Then he started toward her.

"What is going on? What has happened?" Father Ernesius asked bewildered and agitated beside her.

"Father Ernesius?" Sir Balian asked as he approached, although his eyes left Eschiva only for the briefest moment.

"Yes, yes, and who are you?"

"Sir Balian d'Ibelin at your service, father. Sir Brother Ullrich von Allvensleben asked me to bring you word of his misfortune."

"Brother Ullrich?" Father Ernesius asked alarmed, looking around the room nervously. His poor eyesight did not enable him to distinguish faces, only figures, so he looked for the white surcoat of a Templar and realized there was none here. "Has something befallen him?"

"I happened to be at the horse market earlier this morning when I saw five of the Emperor's household knights close in on a lone Templar and start attacking him without the slightest provocation. I went to his assistance as quickly as I could, but they had already succeeded in breaking one of his wrists and a forearm as well. As soon as the watch had arrested the assailants, I escorted Sir Brother Ullrich to the Hospital so his injuries could be treated."

"But—what—I don't understand," Father Ernesius stammered.

"The Emperor has cordoned off the Temple and his archers shoot anyone who tries to leave or enter. I fear, after what happened to Sir Brother Ullrich, you should not risk going into the streets without protection. Indeed, you are probably safest right here."

"Of course," the Abbot, who had come to see what the commotion was about, confirmed at once. "You must stay with us, Father Ernesius."

"But if my brothers are in danger, my place is with them!" the Templar priest protested.

"Of course, but no one can enter without being shot. You will have to stay with us at least until darkness, and even then the risk is too great—I would not want your death on my conscience. Come! Let us retire to my study to discuss this situation." The abbot had Father Ernesius by the arm.

Eschiva squeezed his arm with a whispered, "Go with the abbot, Father. At least until we understand what is happening."

Father Ernesius responded by demanding, "Promise you won't leave Acre without seeing me one more time and please interview the widow I was telling you about."

"I will do my best, Father."

Then the abbot led Ernesius away and they were alone in the crowded room—conscious that at any second the world around them could break in on them. All Eschiva could do was *think* over and over again as she stared at Balian: *I love you! You saved my life. You've given me back a future.* She could only *hope* that he could read her thoughts from her eyes.

Balian bowed deeply. "My lady. Are you alone here? If so, you should not return through the streets unescorted. The city is in an uproar."

Eschiva's heart thrilled at the thought of him taking her home, but already a kindly Venetian merchant was declaring that his litter was waiting outside with an escort of six men-at-arms. "I'll see Madame de Montaigu safely to her husband's lodgings," he assured Balian.

"If that would not be too much of an inconvenience," Balian answered smoothly, bowing his head to the kindly, interfering Italian.

No, no, no! Eschiva screamed mentally. I don't want to be crushed in a litter with this fat merchant. I want to ride in the front of your saddle with your arms around me.

"Not at all, not at all. Come with me, my dear."

Rob burst into the waiting room. "My lord! Your father has sent for you! The Emperor's men have started beating-up the friars spreading the news of the siege of the Patriarch's palace! Frederick's also deployed siege engines that are bombarding the Temple!"

The news set off an explosion of commentary. Balian had time only to turn directly to Eschiva and plead, "My lady, I *beg* you to stay here—with the Canons of the Holy Sepulcher! It is not safe to be on the streets of Acre. Not as a Montaigu."

"On your advice, sir, I will. Please explain to my husband where I am," she spoke carefully for the crowd.

He took her hand and raised it to his lips in a swift gesture that was quite unnecessary for the roles they were playing, yet vital to them both. It was less than two seconds of contact, but it was enough. He kissed her hand, and she gripped him for dear life—for an instant.

Then he was gone.

Chapter Twenty-One

Farewell to Acre

Acre
April 30, 1229

CECILIA HAD NEVER GONE OUT INTO the streets alone until the day she fled to St. Anne's. As long as her father lived, she had not been allowed to set foot outside her house without a maid and at least one groom or footman in attendance. On the day of her father's funeral, she'd had no servants, but she had been accompanied by the hired pallbearers. After she had been given "refuge" by Signor Sanuto, she had not left the house except to go to Mass with the rest of the household. Only after Signor Sanuto had trapped her in the stairwell and nearly forced himself upon her had she found the courage to flee. But that had entailed running only a handful of blocks to the familiar place where she had been a day-student for seven years of her life.

Now, she was being told to go to a stranger's house. Cecilia found that prospect very daunting, but she had no choice. The Sisters of St. Anne made it clear that, penniless as she was, she could not remain as a boarder, and since it was not certain her husband was dead she could not take the veil either. She had to find employment. This was her last hope. She was very frightened.

To be sure, the violence that had seized Acre for five days was over. The Emperor had stopped his attacks on the Templar Headquarters as suddenly as he had begun them. It was rumored that he was preparing to depart Outremer altogether within a day or two. An uneasy calm had descended on the city, but no one seemed to trust the peace entirely. Many shops, Cecilia noted, were shuttered, particularly the jewelers and bookshops, the silk merchants and embroiderers, anyone with something valuable. Open were the bakeries and fruit stands, the vegetable, egg and cheese shops. They had fresh produce that rotted if they remained closed and, judging by the crowds around them, many households were short of these kinds of goods.

The apothecary beside the Gabrielli shop and residence was open, too. The Gabrielli house and proud corner shop, in contrast, were locked and barred as they had been ever since the Templars seized the property. It brought tears to Cecilia's eyes because it seemed vindictive. The Templars had no *use* for her father's home much less his shop. They had seized control of the properties merely out of principle—because they were the owners. They had thrown her out, not because they had a better use for the house, but because it was their right to do so.

She turned her face away from her former home and focused on following the instructions given her. She had to go another block and then turn to the right before she reached St. Lawrence, and instead make her way toward the port until she saw the campanile. Then she had to turn right again and look for a sign depicting a glass goblet marking a glass shop.

After turning the second corner, she came upon a pair of dogs growling viciously as they fought over something. In terror, she leapt back with an audible gasp. She was afraid of all dogs, much less mangy street dogs like these. Her obvious fear, however, attracted the attention of some young men loitering on the other side of the street. One called out to her. "Hey, signora! Afraid of a couple of dogs? Come here and I'll comfort you!" The youths burst out laughing. Then another pursed his lips and made loud kissing sounds in her direction.

Cecilia was sure they spoke with a Pisan accent, which only increased her distress. They were sure to ravish her if she let them get near her, but the dogs might tear her apart alive! She was on the brink of fleeing back to the safety of St. Anne's when the dogs, who were only playing, abruptly broke off their game and bounded down the street with upright wagging tails. In relief, Cecilia continued down the street to the shop described. Here she entered hastily so the Pisans could no longer follow her even with their eyes.

Inside she asked for Madame de Montaigu, and one of the sales clerks showed her to the interior stairs and pointed up. "The Montaigus are renting the whole second floor," he told her.

Cecilia collected her skirts and mounted the stairs as new fears beset her. Her entire life had been encompassed by the Genoese Commune of Acre. Her only exposure beyond the Commune had been her fellow students at St. Anne. Among the girls, there had been, in addition to eight Genoese, a half-dozen Venetians and even two Pisans, as well as a dozen daughters of the nobility.

The latter were mostly boarders, however, and tended to keep a little apart. Her contact with noblewomen had been very limited indeed.

The sisters of St. Anne had not been able to tell her anything about her prospective employer beyond the fact that she had need of a "waiting woman." Cecilia did not know whether to expect someone old or young, married or widowed, much less fat, thin, kindly or cruel.

She pulled herself together and knocked on the door. When there was no response, her instinct was to go back downstairs and say no one was home. Then she thought of the Pisans and the dogs, and she knocked again, much harder. A moment later the door was opened by a young man. "Yes?" he demanded.

Cecilia swallowed in terror. She was alone in a dim corridor, just as when Signor Sanuto had pushed her up against the wall and started fumbling with her breasts. This young man, whoever he might be, was much less trustworthy than the Consul of the Genoese Commune. He was young and—she forced herself to speak even as she glanced toward the stairs and her escape route. "I—I was sent—by the sisters of St. Anne—to—Madame de Montaigu."

The young man looked over his shoulder and called, "Madame? Are you expecting someone?"

From the far room, a woman emerged. She was not much older than Cecilia herself and dressed modestly for a noblewoman. Her face was encased in a barbette of saffron-colored silk, and her gown was a copper-colored silk-linen hybrid fabric trimmed with yellow embroidery. She smiled at the sight of Cecilia and gestured for her to come in. "Are you from St. Anne's?" she asked.

Cecilia curtsied. "Yes, Madame. I—"

"Wonderful, that's where I went to school too," Madame de Montaigu announced. "Come, let's sit here." She indicated a cramped window seat in the narrow dormer of the room. "We are packing to depart so there's nowhere else to sit I'm afraid."

Cecilia was both reassured by Madame de Montaigu's tone and alarmed by the news that she was leaving, "But I was told you needed a waiting woman, Madame," she protested, her fear making her voice breathy.

"Yes, that's true," Madame de Montaigu admitted, looking at her hard, "one willing to come with me to Cyprus."

"Cyprus?" Cecilia was horrified, but only for a second. Cyprus was where the *Rose of Acre* had gone aground. Maybe she would find someone there who could tell her more about Maurizio's end. And even if not, she would still be safer there. Signore Sanuto *ruled* Acre, and he would never admit he had done something wrong. The Abbess had already warned Cecilia that his wife was insinuating that Cecilia had tried to seduce her husband. She did it to discredit Cecilia and shield her husband from any accusations Cecilia made. She preferred to tolerate her husband's actions instead of risk damage to her husband's reputation. In short, in Acre she had no future, but Cyprus would give her a new beginning.

"We will be leaving tomorrow with the King," Madame de Montaigue continued. "Would you be willing to come and is that enough time to pack your things?"

"Yes, Madame, I would be happy to come. I was just surprised. As for my things, I have nothing more than what you see before you," Cecilia answered, opening her hands. "My father died in debt, and everything he owned was taken by his creditors. My husband lost everything he owned including his life in a shipwreck. I had to sell my wedding gown to pay for my father's funeral. I can leave at once if you so wish."

"You are a widow," Madame de Montaigu stated, her eyes watching Cecilia intelligently. "Your husband is buried here?"

Tears welled instantly in Cecilia's eyes as she shook her head, "No, Madame. My husband died at sea. He has no grave."

"I am sorry to hear that," Madame de Montaigu sounded sincere. "Then if you are willing to come, I am happy to have you. My name is Eschiva, Eschiva de Montbeliard, now married to Gerard de Montaigu. And you?"

"I was born Cecilia Gabrielli, Madame, perhaps you knew my father's spice shop? The one on the corner of South Street and St. Joseph's?"

"Beside the Golden Lion apothecary?"

"Yes, that's the one, Madame. My husband was Maurizio di Domenico—" she had not even finished the name before Eschiva caught her breath.

"You are Captain di Domenico's bride?"

"Yes, Madame. Did you know him?" Cecilia asked hopefully. Anyone who had known Maurizio offered her a means of keeping his memory alive.

"He commanded the ship that brought me home from Andria almost a year ago! A gallant man and a fine seaman. He was so excited to be returning to his wedding and his bride!"

Cecilia flushed and whispered, "Thank you, Madame," adding intensely, "He was my whole life."

"And he's dead?" Eschiva asked surprised. "When? How? He was so full of life!"

"His ship, the *Rose of Acre*, was wrecked on the homeward journey. I'm told the wreck washed up on the coast of Cyprus."

"The *Rose of Acre*? Yes, everyone talked about that. But—but that's not the ship he brought me home from Andria in. That was the—"

"No, it was her maiden voyage, Madame, unless you count the outward voyage to London. Before that, he commanded one of his uncle's ships, but the *Rose of Acre* was his own ship."

"Cecilia, I'm so sorry!"

Cecilia felt the tears constrict her throat and even as she tried to swallow them back they gushed down her face. Eschiva was the first person to express sympathy over Maurizio's death. Everyone else had been too busy telling her that her father had died hopelessly in debt. As Eschiva pulled Cecilia into her arms, Cecilia vowed to herself she would be Eschiva's slave forever. At least she had known and liked Maurizio and she was kind.

Acre
May 1, 1229

"Do you always travel with five trunks?" Balian complained to his friend Philip de Novare. The latter was returning to Cyprus and Balian had offered to help him with his luggage. His ulterior motive was to catch a last glimpse of Eschiva, maybe a moment to say goodbye.

"Of course not! My things wouldn't fill even a single trunk, but your father loaded me down with the rest of this stuff."

"Five trunks worth? What is it?" Balian started eyeing the trucks with more interest now.

"Not a treasure—though you might think that from how heavy they are. It's mostly documents and accounts, evidence that your uncle and he meticulously handed over the revenues of Cyprus to Queen Alice. He wants to be able to refute the Emperor's charges of embezzlement before the High Court of Cyprus."

Balian snorted. "The Emperor doesn't give a damn about evidence—or the opinion of the High Court either. You'd think my father would have learned that by now."

"The Emperor may not care about the opinion of the High Court, but your *father* does. He believes in the Rule of Law."

Balian sighed and nodded then turned to the task at hand. He'd brought a cart and he signaled the driver over. "Can you manage to load these on your own?"

The man tried to lift one, grunted, and stepped back shaking his head.

"Go round up a couple of strong men. Tell them we'll tip well," Balian ordered and turned back to Novare. "Where's Andre? Did he go ahead with your horses?"

"Yes. Rob was giving him a hand with them."

"Of course," Balian agreed. Their squires were good friends. Rob would miss Andre.

The carter returned with two burly men. They nodded respectfully toward the two knights and then set to work manhandling the five trunks onto the back of the cart with considerable grunting and cursing. When everything was loaded, Balian tipped them as promised before mounting Damon and offering Philip a hand up. Philip handed the leather bag with his lute up to Balian first with an automatic, "Be careful! It's fragile."

Balian hung the lute bag from the hook on his pommel designed for his great helm. Riding double, Philip behind Balian, they set out with the cart following behind.

Novare's lodgings were close to the Ibelin palace that sat on the shore just north of the Templar HQ. As they turned right into the street leading to one of the posterns of the Temple, Novare remarked, "Did you hear what Templar casualties were when all was said and done?" As far as anyone could see, the Emperor had achieved nothing with his attack on the Temple beyond the increased hostility and mistrust of the lords and people of Outremer—not to mention the Temple.

"I was told they had no dead, but there were injured, including poor Sir Ullrich. There was also considerable damage to the gates and one corner tower lost some of the battlements."

They were by now in the shadow of the urban fortress and both men looked up to survey the damage to the façade for themselves. There were scattered indentations in the quarried stones where missiles from the Emperor's siege engines had shattered the face of the stone, causing a layer to crumble and fall. The rubble of spent ammunition and slivers of broken stone littered the cobbles in front of them. Damon could pick his way through easily, but the cart had more trouble. They had to ask some of the street urchins to clear the rubble out of the way.

After passing St. Anne's they entered the Pisan quarter. Many of the Pisan merchants maintained independent shops with storerooms behind and residences on the upper stories. The shop-fronts opened onto the street, offering everything from imported pottery to weaponry from Toledo and Sicily. There were also a number of taverns and, grouped around a public oven, a number of cook shops offered ready-made food to passers-by. Because the Pisans sided with the Emperor, however, Ibelin and Novare kept moving as rapidly as the cart allowed, alert for any kind of trouble.

They emerged just behind the massive Court of the Chain, the customs house of Acre. This was already a beehive of activity. From the courtyard came the sound of crowds of people arguing and haggling in a variety of languages. Men from all the corners of the earth, wearing the turbans and sandals of the east or the hoods and closed footwear of the west, moved in and out industriously. Pickpockets and litter-bearers, porters and pimps clustered near the entrances shouting out their services and looking for customers. Novare and Ibelin skirted around the three-story, stone structure to reach the quay of the inner harbor.

Here, although the harbor was clogged with various ships from dhows to dromonds, only two galleys lay alongside the quay. The larger was a black-and-red galley flying the Holy Roman Emperor's standard from the masthead. Immediately behind it, a smaller galley painted a gayer blue and gold flew the standard of the King of Cyprus. Both ships had gangways run out onto the quay and bustled with activity in preparation for sailing. Sailors were busy on deck clearing the running rigging, while the oarsmen were receiving a ration of water. Barrels of water and wine were being rolled up the gangway onto the main deck or secured before the forecastle. At the foot of the gangway, several other carts were off-loading, and a score of men stood about either giving directions or watching critically.

As they approached the King of Cyprus' ship, Ibelin drew up sharply.

"What is it?" Novare asked from behind.

"That's Barlais!" Balian hissed back.

Novare leaned to one side to get a better look and followed his friend's gaze. "And Cheneché," Novare added, seeing the second man as well.

"And Gibelet, of course. I don't think they go anywhere alone anymore," Balian concluded, adding, "I don't like this."

"And I don't like those Langobard archers lounging around on the deck either," Novare countered, nodding toward the galley itself.

Balian's eyes shifted back to the deck of the ship and rapidly counted a score of archers loitering on deck watching the sailors work. Mercenaries.

"We should have known there was some trick behind the Emperor's apparent willingness to allow King Henry to return to Cyprus!" Balian declared, inwardly cursing himself. His father and he had been afraid that the Emperor would try to take King Henry and Johnny back to Sicily with him. To their surprise, Johnny had sent word that the Emperor had authorized King Henry to return to his kingdom, while inviting Johnny to return with him to Sicily. "I'll make you Lord of Foggia if you come," he'd sweetened the offer. According to Johnny, King Henry had come to his rescue by saying he did not want to be separated from Johnny, and the Emperor had shrugged and said, "Go with your king for now. You can always join me later."

"I don't think you should board that ship, Novare!" Balian told his friend, putting a restraining hand on Novare's arm.

"Don't be ridiculous, Bal. If King Henry is going aboard this ship with all those Langobards and the likes of Barlais, then that's all the *more* reason that I should go too." With these words, Novare vaulted down from Damon and reached up to remove his lute from Balian's saddle. Then he gestured for the carter to get in line for off-loading the trunks.

Balian hung back, watching warily.

Novare approached the men still at the foot of the gangway and bowed to them gallantly. The men, startled, returned his bow and then exchanged pleasantries. After a few minutes, they nodded to Novare and one after the other boarded the galley. While all that was happening, Rob and Andre appeared on deck. Seeing Novare on the quay, they crossed back to the shore. Andre took charge of the lute, and Rob organized the loading of the trunks, while Novare returned to Balian.

"Balian, I understand how you feel about Barlais—"

"Actually, I don't think you *do* understand!" Balian snapped back. "You have *no* idea what it is to be clamped in a pillory, unable to move your arms or legs, and *then* have someone start punching and insulting you!"

"I'm sorry," Philip replied steadily. "You're right. I don't understand that. But what I wanted to say is that as much as Barlais hates you and your father, he's quite civil—almost friendly—to me. He is witty and intelligent, can be a good companion and he's very loyal to his friends. This might be the perfect opportunity for me get on his good side and talk sense to him. You know your father would like nothing better than for there to be peace between you."

"My father is a hopeless idealist," Balian countered in exasperation. "Barlais cannot be won over with reason. We've tried that twice already!"

"There's no harm in trying again," Novare insisted.

Balian didn't have an argument against such sentimental nonsense; all his inner alarms were screaming at him again, and he knew that—as before—no one was going to listen to him.

"Look, the crossing will give me a chance get re-acquainted with Johnny and the King—not to mention your lady love!" Novare had just caught sight of Eschiva and he meant the remark as a joke. To him, Eschiva was still just the plain maiden he'd rescued a year ago in Andria, not to mention another man's wife. He had no idea that Balian, after a career of conquests, had fallen seriously in love for the first time in his life.

Balian snapped his head toward the ship again and saw Eschiva on the afterdeck. She was dressed for the voyage in a practical linen gown, but she'd wrapped her head in blue-silk veils and wore a bright blue cloak with dark embroidered edging. She was searching the quay for something or someone. Balian left Philip standing and rode to the edge of the quay opposite Eschiva. She saw him at last and her face lit up.

Damon, however, balked at getting too close to the edge of the quay. Water was slapping between the stonework and the side of the ship because small waves, driven by a stiff breeze, had unsettled the harbor. The splashes burst upwards frightening the horse. Balian had to jump down to go to the edge of the quay. It put him so far below Eschiva that, even when he reached as high as possible and she leaned over the railing and stretched out her hand, their fingers barely touched.

"I was hoping to catch sight of you, my lady!" Balian called up to Eschiva. "Sir Philip is returning to Cyprus aboard your vessel. If you need *anything*, you can go to him. You can write to me, by way of him as well. He will not betray us."

"But you'll be coming soon, you said," Eschiva reminded him.

"As soon as I can. I fear—" he broke himself off. What was the point of making her worry her? Of telling her he was certain Barlais' presence on Cyprus boded ill for the Ibelins. Indeed, if Barlais had charge of King Henry, God alone knew what would happen next. Trying to disguise his anxiety, he told her, "Things are too unsettled yet."

As if to underline his point, shouting was coming from the city. It was loud enough to make him raise his voice more than he would have liked. But he had to say it. "Never doubt my love, Eschiva! Whether I am near you or not, it will not be diminished!"

Eschiva nodded, and although she tried to smile, her eyes were sad. She too had to raise her voice to be heard above the uproar that appeared to be coming nearer by the minute. "Please tell Father Ernesius I have hired the widow he recommended, and that I have not forgotten his offer. Tell him, my husband has forbidden it, but I—"

The shouting was so loud that she broke off and looked in the direction of the city in alarm. Balian glanced first in that direction and then back at the ship where one of the ship's officers was gesturing furiously for Philip to come aboard. Other sailors leapt nimbly over the side of the ship to start casting off. Rob hastened to go ashore, with a last hug for Andre.

Turning back to Eschiva Balian asked surprised, "Is King Henry already aboard?"

"Yes, and Johnny."

"They seem to be preparing to cast off."

Eschiva nodded, her face tense.

The shouting from the street opening onto the quay was not just growing, it was threatening. Damon was dancing in nervousness, casting frequent looks at his rider, as if urging him to remount so they could flee together. Novare rushed to fling his arms around Balian in goodbye. "Take care of yourself, Bal. And don't linger too long in Beirut!"

"Go with God, Philip, but be on your guard!"

Novare ran for the gangway and sprang onto it even as two sailors started to pull it inboard. Already the bow of King Henry's galley was nosing out into the harbor as the oars were run out.

Balian swung up into Damon's saddle as the stallion turned away from the ship nervously. The horse was seeking an escape route away from the still approaching shouting and hooting. Balian hauled on Damon's reins in a rare test of will and strength with the otherwise obedient stallion. Damon was starting to lift his forefeet off the cobbles and threw his head up to evade the bit. It took two hands to haul him down again, and when he finally got the horse back under control of sorts, the galley was fifty feet away. Balian only managed a single wave to Eschiva, and then had to take hold of the reins more firmly again.

"Calm down!" he growled at Damon, confused by the horse's skittishness—until he realized that the air smelled foul, as if he were beside a charnel house. Of course, it was the Street of Butchers that emptied onto the quay here, but he'd ridden down that street hundreds of times and it had never smelled like this. He glanced toward the head of the street again. Out of the narrow entrance rode an apparition that made his heart miss a beat.

For a moment, he thought a corpse or some sort of devil was riding toward him. Then he realized it was a man covered with entrails and offal and riding a horse stained red with blood and trailing intestines. The horse's eyes were wide with horror and he would surely have bolted had not two men walked on either side of him, holding the bridle firmly.

"Christ in Heaven!" Balian gasped as he recognized first his father and then Eschiva's brother as the men holding the horse under control. Only then did he grasp that the man all but obscured by the innards of slaughtered beasts was none other than the Holy Roman Emperor.

A large liver quivered tenaciously atop his ruined velvet hat. Blood from

God-knew-what had stained half his face. Intestines and bowels were draped haphazardly over his shoulders, and a cow's kidney had landed in his lap.

Frederick Hohenstauffen was so rigid with rage that he seemed made of stone. He sat immobile in the saddle, ignoring the stench and the blood and the filth as Montbéliard and Beirut with difficulty guided the horse to the gangway of the Imperial galley. The Imperial officials were running about in near hysterical distress. The archers gaped, the sailors suppressed their instinct to laugh, the servants ran about looking for water and fresh robes, while Frederick's household officials rushed to welcome him.

Balian gave up trying to convince Damon to approach such an appalling visage stinking of death. He jumped down and let go of the reins altogether. Damon at once trotted to the far end of the quay but loyally waited there while Balian went on foot to join his father.

He reached him just as the Lord of Beirut helped the Emperor up onto the gangway, handing him off to one of the Imperial officials, who rushed forward to take the Emperor's elbow and guide him aboard the ship. He moved like a zombie: his face still a rigid mask of frozen fury. He held his arms stiffly away from his sides so the gore dripped off him, and he slapped his feet down on the wooden planks to shake off the entrails that still clung to them.

Orders were shouted for the ship to cast off. When it didn't happen fast enough, an officer grabbed an ax and hacked through the hawsers. The ship instantly veered into the harbor.

"Go with God, my lord!" Beirut shouted to the Emperor's back.

The Emperor spun about and the look he leveled at Beirut was one of sheer hatred. It was, Balian registered, a hatred *magnified* by the fact that the Hohenstaufen now owed Beirut for rescuing him from the people of Acre.

Beirut lifted his voice to be heard across the increasing distance as the oars started to pull in earnest. "Who have you named baillie of Jerusalem?"

"Sidon and Werner von Egisheim!" came the answer.

"Who?" Monbéliard asked at once, obviously offended that he had been slighted.

"Sidon and Egisheim," Beirut repeated in a low voice.

"Why them? What have they done to deserve it? Why not me? And you? This is all my sister's fault! He still hasn't forgiven her for running away."

"If you think that, Monbéliard, you're a bigger fool than I thought!" Balian snorted. "Can't you see this is about more than petty, personal quarrels?"

Beirut looked over at his son, noticing him for the first time, and with a smile, he noted, "Well said, Balian. This is indeed about much more than personal quarrels."

"What happened?" Balian asked his father in return.

"What the Emperor refused to believe was possible: the people of Acre expressed their opinion of him to his face."

Balian burst out laughing.

His father tried not to join in, but he couldn't help himself from grinning as he noted, "One has to give them credit for planning. They must have been saving up their offal for days! They dumped buckets of the stuff from the balconies and rooftops along the whole route. They had remarkably good aim." Then, unable to contain himself any longer Beirut guffawed.

Balian joined him. It was good to be able to laugh again. It was especially good to *share* a laugh with his father.

Beirut got control of himself first but still smiling explained, "I rushed down as soon as I heard what was happening and ran into Monbéliard here, who was on his way to the port anyway. By the time I arrived, the people had had more than enough time to make their point. And *that* is what pleases me, Balian. The Emperor always blamed us, the Ibelins, and the Patriarch, and the Temple for not 'understanding' him, for not 'supporting' him, for not 'appreciating his genius.' But it wasn't *us*. It was the people of Outremer, the *ordinary* people of Outremer, who were most honest. While the rest of us tried to find common ground, to explain our points of view, to win the Emperor with reason, they found a way to tell him what they thought without dissembling *or* violence. It is a lesson he will not ever be able to forget."

"No," Balian agreed. "And I wouldn't have missed seeing it for the world." He paused before adding more soberly, "Although I dare say there will be consequences."

"No doubt," his father conceded, "and we will have to face them when they come, but at least neither you nor Johnny are in his clutches anymore."

Balian guessed that this accounted for at least half his father's good humor: the thought that Johnny was no longer in the power of Frederick Hohenstaufen. He hated to shatter his father's good mood by mentioning Barlais, but he also knew his father would be angry with him if he didn't. Still, he hesitated before finally remarking cautiously, "Did you know that King Henry was accompanied to Cyprus by Barlais, Cheneché, and Gibelet?"

"What?" Beirut gasped. He'd been watching the Emperor's ship clear the harbor entrance and now spun back to stare at his eldest son.

"Yes. They boarded the King's ship just before Novare did."

They stared at one another. Then Beirut shook his head. "That is not good news, but Barlais is not an anointed king, much less a crowned emperor. Nor is he my liege's overlord. I don't give a tinker's damn if the Emperor names him baillie of Cyprus or not—as we must assume he has or will. The *Emperor* has no right to appoint baillies of Cyprus *at all*, not as long as Queen Alice lives. So, we will pay no heed to him."

"Maybe one of us should go to Cyprus. We need to assess how much damage was done by Cotron, and prevent Barlais from preying on our vassals and tenants," Balian suggested hopefully.

His father nodded. "Yes, you're right. But not just yet. I want to have a little time with you. Time we have not had this past year. I want to ensure all is well in Beirut. I want to be sure Bella is alright. We need time together as a family." As he spoke, Beirut put his arm over his heir's shoulders and pressed him close.

Balian didn't have the heart to protest or contradict. He and his father had fought far too often in the past. He did not want to fight with him now. And he knew his father would not approve of his devotion to another man's wife. Eschiva would have to wait a little, but he promised himself he *would* find a way to get to Cyprus—and Eschiva—soon.

Part IV

The Right of Self-Defense

Chapter Twenty-Two
Cyprus under the New Regime

Nicosia
Late-May, 1229

"HENRY?" JOHNNY SAT UP IN BED and felt frantically for his king. The latter should have been sleeping beside him, but he was alone and the sheets were cold.

"Henry?" Johnny pulled open the bed-curtains and peered out into the room beyond. Moonlight and a cool breeze were pouring through the arches of a double-light window. The moonlight made the polished marble pillar separating the arches appear almost luminous. The moonlight also fell on the spiral and polygon patterns of the mosaic floor and stretched nearly to the empty fireplace where a bed had been made up for the King's dog, Harry.

"Henry, what's the matter?" Johnny had located his king at last. He was clutching his knees as he sat hunched under the hood of the fireplace *behind* his dog's bed.

Henry didn't answer.

Johnny flung back the covers and pushed the curtains aside to go to his friend. Like the king, he was dressed only in a night-shirt that hung loosely to mid-calf. "What's the matter? Is something wrong with Harry?" He looked down at the dog as he came to stand before the dog's basket. But Harry was sleeping peacefully, indeed blissfully, his ears flopping over the edge of the basket and his paws relaxed as he breathed evenly.

Johnny went down on his heels to be at Henry's level and peered at him. The moonlight was sufficient for him to see the king's face was streaked with tears. "What is it, Henry?"

"I don't want to get married," Henry burst out.

Johnny could understand that. Who wanted to be married at twelve to a complete stranger? The Emperor had chosen Alice de Montferrat, but the girl was still in Greece or Bulgaria or somewhere, so neither of them had ever laid eyes on her. It didn't help that she was said to be five or six years older than her bridegroom. Yet Henry was supposed to marry her by proxy on the morrow.

"Can we sit somewhere more comfortable to discuss this?" Johnny asked practicably; he had goosebumps from the night air.

Henry seemed to consider this for a moment before, with a deep sigh, he let go of his knees and squirmed his way past his sleeping dog to come out from under the fireplace hood. Johnny indicated the comfortable cushions of the window seat and handed Henry the blanket from the foot of their bed in passing, before going to fetch wine and water from a sideboard. When he came back, Henry had snuggled himself into a corner of the window seat with his feet under him and the blanket almost burying him. With a demonstrative sigh of annoyance, Johnny set the pitchers on the window sill, then went back for mugs and a second blanket for himself.

When he was himself settled opposite Henry, clutching a blanket around his shoulders for warmth, he asked more pointedly, "What happened this evening?"

Henry shook his head and frowned and then murmured something Johnny could not understand.

"What?" Johnny insisted.

"I told Barlais I didn't want to marry Alice!" Henry burst out angrily, still not meeting Johnny's eye.

"And?"

"And he said I had to anyway!" Henry snapped.

Johnny could have guessed that much. Henry might be a master at saying "No" and stamping his foot and throwing a tantrum, but the adults always had their way in the end and they both knew that. "Surely you knew he would say that? He promised the Emperor he would see the marriage celebrated 'at once.' He wants to prove to the Emperor that he's reliable."

"He wants more than that!" Henry spat out.

"What do you mean?"

"He's ruining my kingdom! He's turning my people against me! Haven't you heard what people are saying?"

Of course, Johnny had heard—he'd been the one bringing the gossip in from the kitchens, stables, markets, baths, and taverns. Henry wasn't allowed out of the palace unless Barlais, Cheneché or Gibelet was with him, and they always took at least six Langobard archers with them, not to mention heralds and squires and grooms. In short, the King couldn't move among his people freely, only ceremonially with trumpet fanfares and the like. Johnny, on the other hand, was barely tolerated by Barlais and found it quite easy to slip down the back stairs of the palace to the kitchens or stables and from there into the streets of Nicosia. He spoke both Greek and Arabic, the languages of the common people, as well as Latin and French, and he had no trouble overhearing conversations and sensing the tenor of feelings swirling in the streets of Henry's capital. People were very angry.

For all that, Johnny instinctively sensed that Henry's behavior now was only marginally related to righteous indignation over the baillies appointed by the Emperor to rule his kingdom for him. Just before sailing for Sicily, Frederick Hohenstaufen had sold the bailliage of Cyprus until Henry came of age to five men: Amaury Barlais, Gauvain de Cheneché, Hugh de Gibelet, Grimbert de Bethsan, and William de Rivet. The first three men had been hostile to his father and uncle for as long as he could remember. Without knowing what had upset Henry, however, all he could do was answer his words. So he pointed out, "People are angry with the baillies, Henry. They bought their offices by promising to pay the Emperor 10,000 marks and they have to raise that money somehow. Everyone knows you have nothing to do with the new taxes."

"Barlais is evil!" Henry flung at Johnny from behind his blanket barricade. "Have you forgotten what he did to your brothers?"

"It was the Emperor who took them hostage." Johnny countered.

"And Barlais who tormented and beat them!" Henry countered, adding with the exasperation of a twelve-year-old, "You don't understand! The Emperor has no feelings except when it comes to his imperial dignity. He's not human really—just a bunch of ideas. All mind with no heart. He only keeps a harem to make him *seem* more virile, not because he really *wants* all those women. But Barlais is different. He's—*evil*!" Henry's tone, which had been almost normal while talking about the Emperor, turned strained when he took the name Barlais into his mouth. Henry buried his face in his blanket, and Johnny *knew* something terrible had happened between them.

Johnny was a little frightened because he sensed that Henry needed his help, but he didn't know what to do exactly. After thinking about it a minute, he realized that if he'd been found crying in a fireplace by any of his older brothers, Baldwin would have scolded him about acting like a "cowardly cur," and Hugh would have teased him to try to cheer him up, but Balian would have pulled him out and put his arms around him and *then* asked him what the trouble was.

Taking a deep breath, Johnny crossed to Henry's side of the window seat, opened up his arms and pulled Henry inside his own blanket. Henry at once turned his face into Johnny's chest and started sobbing. "I'm so scared, Johnny. I'm so scared of him!"

"Christ in heaven, what did he do to you?"

Henry shook his head. "I can't talk about it. It was terrible. Please, Johnny, don't ever leave me alone with him again. Ever. Please."

That was a huge promise. Much too big for Johnny. How could he promise something like that when all Barlais had to do was order him out of the room? What was he, a fourteen-year-old boy, supposed to do? "Henry, I'll try, but I think my father needs to come here—I mean *soon!*"

"How can he?" Henry asked back exasperated. "The Emperor made the baillies swear they would *never* let your father or brothers back on the island. He ordered them to dispossess your whole family of all their fiefs on Cyprus. *Surely* you knew that was why Frederick kept insisting you come to Sicily to become Lord of Foggia? He wanted to give you something because you won't inherit anything here in Outremer."

Johnny hadn't realized this at all. He looked so dumbfounded, that Henry felt compelled to continue. "Frederick's determined to *crush* your whole family— well, except you. He can't forgive your father for standing up to him and then making him back down. He says your father offended his majesty and so must be brought low. He said he wants to be sure no one even remembers the name Ibelin a hundred years from now," Henry explained.

Johnny shivered. He had not realized the Emperor's resentment ran that deep. Balian had warned them, of course, but no one had wanted to believe him.

"You're all I've got, Johnny!" Henry broke into his thoughts. "Please promise you won't leave me."

"I won't leave you. Not voluntarily," Johnny dutifully assured his young king. "They'll have to use *force* to separate us," he promised, trying to sound brave and confident.

Inside his head, however, he knew that "they" had all the weapons, and it would be child's play to separate them and keep them apart. All Barlais had to do was snap his fingers and a dozen mercenaries jumped to obey. What could he possibly do to stop them? Nothing.

Johnny shuddered despite the blanket shielding him from the cold. He was afraid, and he wanted his father and brothers. It didn't matter what Henry said, he would write his father about what was happening. He had a right to know and he would surely do something to stop it. After all, he couldn't just allow the baillies to take away his properties on Cyprus. Could he?

Nicosia
Mid-June, 1229

Novare viewed the summons to the royal palace as a good sign. He'd gotten along very well with Cheneché during the short passage from Acre to Limassol. They had agreed that Philip should try to mediate between the Ibelins and the baillies—when the time was right. Cheneché had explained quite reasonably that the baillies first had to convince the Emperor he could rely on them before they risked alienating him with overtures to the Ibelins. Cheneché pointed out that if Barlais and the others didn't have Frederick's confidence, the Emperor might name one of his Sicilian dogs baillie, instead of a Cypriot.

"You've got to believe me," Cheneché had urged Philip in a low voice over their 9th or 10th glass of wine. "We don't mean Beirut any harm. Barlais is satisfied with being baillie. It's all he's ever wanted. If Beirut will accept him as baillie, he won't take any further action to seize his properties on Cyprus. But first, we need to consolidate our position. Only after we're secure, can we risk breaking with the Emperor and treating with Beirut."

It had all made sense at the time, and Cheneché and the others had even agreed to swear by the blood of Christ to do Novare no harm—whether he succeeded in his reconciliation efforts or not. With this, Novare had agreed to wait until he was summoned. He had, however, sent a message to Beirut outlining his intentions and receiving the Lord of Beirut's blessings.

As the weeks went by without that summons, however, Novare had started to get a little uneasy. His mood was not aided by the fact that the baillies seemed overzealous in their execution of the Emperor's will. They'd married the king by proxy to Alix of Montferrat within a week of the Emperor's departure. They had then proceeded to remove the royal constables from the all the castles and replace them with their own retainers. Most recently, tax increases had been levied, and when these provoked protests, the rioters had been ruthlessly beaten and arrested by the Emperor's mercenaries. Everything suggested that power had gone to their heads.

Their behavior made it all the more urgent for peace to be established between the baillies and the Ibelins so that Beirut could return to Cyprus. Beirut understood government. He knew it was a contract with the people, not a license to exploit. Novare was increasingly convinced that Barlais didn't understand that. Yet, he was also sure Beirut wouldn't set foot on Cyprus – or let any of his sons do so – until he had solid assurances from the baillies that he would not face arrest. Novare hoped that he would be able to secure a promise of immunity for Beirut from the baillies at his next meeting with them.

To his disappointment, however, he found that he was not the only man who had been summoned to the royal palace. On the contrary, there were scores of knights already there when he arrived, and more kept arriving. The stables were already full, and he had to send Andre with their horses to a public livery. Alone, he started up the wide formal stairs that curled around the front court-yard along with a half dozen other men heading the same way. They spoke with barely suppressed anger about this or the other outrage. One man complained that the Langobards had seized wine from his cellars without payment. Another said they'd arrested a miller for allegedly using false weights without consulting his lord: "Just hauled him off, without any due process!" A third man claimed Langobards had beaten up a cobbler for making a derogatory remark about the Emperor.

"They've been extorting money from the Franciscans and Dominicans as well."

"Well, that won't yield much!" someone scoffed. "They should go after the Benedictines instead."

"That's not the point! It's extortion!"

"Have you heard that the Emperor has expropriated all the properties of the Templars in his kingdom of Sicily?"

"Where did you hear that?"

"Ah, Novare! There you are at last! We've been waiting for you," Cheneché called and waved from the gallery.

Scandalized by this friendly greeting from one of the baillies, the others parted to let Novare through. Their conversations stilled, and their faces were abruptly rigid. As Cheneché threw his arm over Novare's shoulders and led Novare deeper into the palace, the others gazed at him resentfully. He thought he heard someone mutter "traitor" behind his back as Chenéché swept him into the audience chamber. No worries, Novare told himself, he'd soon prove them wrong.

In the main audience hall, the King sat on a throne that was too big for him with Barlais seated immediately to his left and Gibelet to his right. The other baillies had chairs on either side. King Henry, Novare noted, did not look terribly happy. He had made himself as small as possible inside his oversized throne, and he wore a sullen expression. His feet swung nervously, clunking against the wood of the carved panel below the seat.

Novare tried to catch his eye. When Henry saw him, Novare winked and then gave him a deep, dramatic bow. "My lord king! Philip of Novare at your service."

Henry sat up a little straighter and something that might have been a smile flitted across his face, but then he looked nervously toward Barlais.

Barlais was leaning in the other direction and whispering with Gibelet. The latter was a man almost as small as Barlais himself with a face that looked like it had been pinched by a giant. Novare always thought of him as a monkey. Cheneché drew Barlais attention, and at the sight of Novare, he declared with apparent enthusiasm, "Ah, there you are at last! We want you to go first."

"What do you mean first?" Novare asked back confused.

"You're all here to swear an oath to us as the baillies of Cyprus until King Henry comes of age. We want you to go first. We *especially* want you to go first."

It might have been an honor of some sort, but it was not what they had agreed. "My lords, ah," Novare looked around at the room already crowded with knights and getting fuller by the moment. He saw the men who had been on the stairs with him. They were glaring at him resentfully. He turned back to the dais. Cheneché had taken his seat alongside his companions. He smiled at Novare, but it was no longer a friendly, comradely smile; it was mockingly triumphant. "Good sir," Novare addressed Barlais, "I beg, speak with me apart, you and your four companions."

"God help us! Look at all the men here!" Barlais retorted irritably. "We don't have time to speak to each of you individually. We have much to do, and if we take counsel with one and all, nothing would ever get done. You are here to take the oath to your baillies. It's time to start and you are to go first."

Novare felt trapped. A sensation reinforced by the realization that Langobards literally lined the room controlling every door, while men in Barlais' livery had shouldered their way forward to surround him. This was like that horrible banquet in Limassol all over again, Novare registered with a sense of déjà vu.

"Come, what's the problem?" Barlais demanded.

With a gesture for Barlais to be patient, Cheneché interceded, "My dear friend, Sir Philip, if you swear your homage to us we will do more for you than those whom you have served up to now. We will give you a fief for yourself and your unborn heirs." He paused significantly before adding with a smile and a wink, "*and* we will pay all your debts."

Damn him! No, damn me! Novare corrected. During that long night drinking with Cheneché, he had somehow ended up talking about his gambling debts. They were huge, and he didn't dare go to Beirut about them because

Beirut sternly condemned gambling. But Novare just couldn't stop. The cards seemed to have a magical attraction for him. And Cheneché knew it. He was grinning triumphantly.

Damn them all! Novare knew he had weaknesses for women, wine, and cards, but weaknesses of that sort were human failings. Treason was something else again. He might gamble and sin with women of easy virtue and, yes, he had serious debts, but he was still a man of honor.

But he would not be able to call himself that if he betrayed Beirut, and with him Balian.

Novare took a deep breath and lifted his chin to answer. "I'm happy that—in the hearing of so many men—you offer me so much. You do me a great honor. I'm most grateful. But, with deep regret," he gave them his best bow, "I cannot swear to you because I am already sworn to Queen Alice. I cannot swear to you without breaking my oath to her."

"Stop lying! No one gives a damn about the ever-absent Alice of Champagne! The only reason you won't swear is that you won't go against the Lord of Beirut!" Barlais' face was contorted with hatred as he spat out the name "Beirut."

He really does look like a weasel, Novare thought irrelevantly. Then he took a deep breath and stood as tall as his five feet, four inches allowed to proudly and loudly proclaim, "Against the Lord of Beirut I will never be, God help me, for I love him and his children better than any others in the world." He was consciously playing for the audience and had not anticipated what followed.

Sir Hugh de Gibelet jumped to his feet to demand rhetorically of the room, "Did you hear that? He is loyal to the Emperor's enemy! He should be hanged!"

"You're a hothead, Sir Hugh! Your wise father Sir Bertrand would have known better than to call for blood just because a man is true to his word!" Novare tried to shame the young Gibelet.

The other baillies, however, had already taken up the call. Rivet and his "friend" Cheneché were shouting, "Take him!" and "Hang him at once!" Trying to rile up the entire audience—unfortunately with some success, as opportunists from across the room joined in.

Novare had never thought the mood of a crowd could change so quickly. Most of the men had arrived here hostile to the baillies. Now they were shouting for his blood just to placate them. It was a chilling lesson in human inconstancy. Novare had to act fast. He flung himself on his knees, shouting to King Henry, "My lord king! These men are oath breakers! They swore to me on the blood of Christ that if I failed to make peace between them and my lord of Beirut that they would do me no harm!"

"You lie!" Cheneché shouted louder than anyone because he was the one who had proposed and formulated this oath.

Novare looked to King Henry, but the twelve-year-old just looked down and hunched up his shoulders. Things were getting very dangerous. Trying another tactic, Novare sprang to his feet and flung his glove at Cheneché's feet. "I'll prove I do not lie before the High Court and God!" Sensing the surprise of the baillies, Novare upped the ante. "I'll fight any of you, my body against yours, to prove the truth of what I say."

The baillies recoiled, but now their retainers started to press forward, offering to fight for them. These men were landless knights, household knights, the kind of men who made a living by the strength of their arms. They were confident that they could win no matter what. Novare wasn't exactly Richard the Lionheart.

Despite feeling increasingly panicked, Novare steadfastly shook his head and swatted their gloves aside. "I will fight any of the five baillies and only them. *They* are the men who are foresworn if they do not let me depart from here unharmed!"

"Take him!" Barlais snarled, pounding his fist on the table.

This time Novare was seized by a dozen hands. Someone ripped his sword from its sheath before he could grasp the hilt. Another snatched his dagger and a third yanked the buckle of the belt itself, so it fell to the floor with a clunk. A monster of a man yanked Novare's elbows behind his back, and another man pointed a naked sword at his throat.

Barlais jerked his head toward one of the doors, and in a large gaggle, Barlais' knights shoved Novare in that direction. He cast one last look at King Henry, but the twelve-year-old had crumpled up and was hiding his face in his hands. He didn't want to see what was going to happen to Novare.

"Beloved Balian." The words stood on the page staring at Eschiva. In fact, they had been staring at her so long she had been able to turn both "b"s into elaborate images: butterflies lifting up from bright flowers and bees circling above a hive respectively.

It wasn't that she didn't have anything to say to Balian. She had far too much. But how much should she commit to paper? How much dare she share at all?

She still felt unworthy of his love. Was it credible that a woman called "cold, boring and plain" by other men could win the heart of one of the noblest, wealthiest, and best-loved young knights of Outremer?

No.

Yet he *said* he loved her. And not as a means to seduce her either. When he'd the chance, he'd walked away instead. Rather than taking advantage of her vulnerability, he called her *"mi dons."* He had restored her sense of self-worth by returning to her some of her lost illustrations, a gesture that showed how much he valued them (by saving them) and how much he understood what they meant to her (by returning them). He'd given her hope by urging her to go to the canons of the Holy Sepulcher, where she had found not only support but a commission from the Templars. He'd restored to her a sense of independence by giving her his mother's horse so she could regain the mobility and freedom of movement taken from her by being tied to litters. Most of all, he'd restored her desire to live.

She wanted to live just for the chance to see *him* again, to speak to him and hear his voice, to maybe touch his hand, or feel it on her cheek.

It didn't matter that she could not imagine how they could be together. It didn't matter that she *feared* a situation where he might indeed seek consummation of his love. All that mattered was that he was out there, and *he* cared whether she lived or died.

She had not understood love before. She had been only ten when her mother died and a mother's love was so natural that she had not rightly cherished it before it was gone. Eudes had never inspired strong feelings. Yolanda had been her best friend. She had shared her pain and wanted the best for her, but Yolanda had been struggling to survive her own disappointment and insecurity. Eschiva had been the one giving comfort. Yolanda was in no position to lift up Eschiva from her own disappointment and doubts.

Yet through this love for Balian, Eschiva was conscious of glimpsing a first, faint flicker of what divine love must be. If the love of one small, imperfect man could make a person want to live and create and laugh and share joy with the whole world, then anyone who truly felt God's love would be empowered to overcome anything at all. That, Eschiva reasoned, was what inspired the saints. It was a tiny insight into the spiritual world that she had lacked before. For that, too, she thanked Balian.

She could hear him laughing. He did not see himself as in any way saintly. And indeed he was not. Yet the joy he gave her was a reflection of something greater than himself. Eschiva was sure of that.

Only she couldn't put that into words, much less write it down on paper. It would sound silly, pompous, or just plain juvenile.

So, should she write about people and events, instead of feelings? Should she tell him about Cecilia and the death of Captain di Domenico? Or about the taxes the baillies had raised? Or the unrest? Or even the rumors that the baillies were just waiting for an Ibelin, any Ibelin, to return so they could arrest him and throw him in a dungeon? Should she report that the Preceptor of the Hospitaller Commandery in Nicosia, Sir Guillaume de Teneres, had come to the Archbishop of Nicosia last night to report that no less than five women with their children had sought refuge with the Hospital because they feared for their safety?

The Archbishop had tut-tutted about how lawless the Langobards were, and the Hospitaller had snapped back, "This has nothing to do with lawlessness! The Langobards are following orders, and the men giving those orders are *targeting* the estates of knights serving with Beirut! Every single one of these women is vulnerable because her husband went with Beirut on crusade."

"Yes, yes," the Archbishop had conceded. "But once their husbands return, things will settle down."

"What makes you think that? The way I see it, these attacks are *intended* to provoke Beirut's vassals into returning to Cyprus—only so the baillies can do them harm."

"That doesn't make sense," the Archbishop had protested. "Why should the baillies want to harm honest knights?"

"To get their greedy hands on their land, of course!" The commander retorted in exasperation with the Archbishop's naivety. Then, curbing his temper, he had continued, "My lord archbishop, these so-called baillies *bought* Cyprus from the Holy Roman Emperor for their own gain. They intend to enrich themselves and they are targeting men the Emperor dislikes because they know they can get away with outright theft, and the law be damned, just as long as they steal from the Emperor's enemies rather than his friends. Barlais and Cheneché have their eyes on the Ibelin properties, and the others hope to gobble up the scraps."

"Have you informed your Master, my brother, of your suspicions?"

"Of course! But he is more concerned about the Emperor's confiscation of *Hospitaller* properties in the Kingdom of Sicily and across the Holy Roman Empire. Cyprus is an insignificant sideshow for him at the moment. You, on the other hand, are not under attack from the Baltic to Palermo. On the contrary, you are the leading cleric on this island. You represent the *Pope* on this island. I would have expected you to use your moral authority to oppose the predations of these five thieves."

"What do you expect me to do?" The Archbishop had sounded scandalized. "Excommunicate them?"

"That would be a good start!"

"No, that is out of the question," the Archbishop answered dismissively.

"Why?"

"It is inappropriate. A man cannot be excommunicated for things he has not yet done. These are just suspicions, allegations, speculation."

The Hospitaller had not replied and soon afterward he had gone, but his words chilled and frightened Eschiva.

Is that what she should write to her beloved Balian? That she was afraid? God forbid! He might then feel he had to come to her, and thereby put himself in danger!

But she should certainly tell him that the wives of his father's knights felt threatened, that the Commander of the Hospital on Cyprus believed the baillies intended to enrich themselves at his father's expense. She *must* tell him that the Ibelins were at risk of arrest or worse if any one of them dared set foot on Cyprus. She must warn Balian. She would never forgive herself if he came to Cyprus, perhaps because of her, and was arrested and abused.

She dipped her pen in ink and began to write:

Beloved Balian, I write this message to you in health and safety, but concerned by—"

She must not call them "rumors." The Commander of the Hospital did not spread rumors.

"...reports that the baillies are intent on dispossessing you and—"

The sound of the door opening startled her so much that she blotted the page and turned sharply to see who dared enter without knocking.

It was Cecilia, and she looked flushed and breathless. Her barbette was askew. "My lady! My lady!" She stammered. "This is for you!" From the folds of her skirts, she extracted a folded piece of paper and held it out to Eschiva.

Eschiva's heart missed a beat. Was Balian on Cyprus already? Who else would want to send her a message through her waiting-woman? She took the square of paper. It was unsealed. But perhaps he could not risk an Ibelin seal? Particularly not on a message to her. She unfolded the paper in a rush, only to stare at writing that was ragged and poorly formed. It was not Balian's hand, of that she was sure, and her heart sank a little. Then she forced herself to read.

"Warn Novare not to go home. They will kill him. HR"

That was all. She frowned, not understanding any of it. Where was Novare, if not at home? And who was HR? Then she started. Henricus Rex! The message was from King Henry. "Who gave you this?" She turned on Cecilia.

"That good-looking squire that was with King Henry on the ship," Cecilia admitted.

Johnny! "How did he find you? Did he say anything when he gave you this?"

"He pounced on me when I returned from my errands." Cecilia had gone into town to buy more quills for Eschiva. "He must have been waiting by the door. He thrust that into my hand and said it was 'very urgent.' He said something about Sir Philip being arrested and put in the pillory, but then about him being released, but that it was all a trick. Then he ran away, saying he was in trouble already and was sure to get a flogging." Cecilia's eyes were wide with fear and she spoke in a frightened whisper.

"Get me my veils and riding gloves. Then go to the stables and have Zach saddle Mamush at once."

"Surely you aren't going out into the city, Madame! The people are all riled up about something. There were loud crowds collected in front of the royal palace shouting things. I don't know what it was about, but they were angry."

"Sir Philip of Novare is in danger, and the King himself has asked that I get word to him."

"But, Madame! It's not safe in the streets—not for a lady."

"You don't need to come with me, Cecilia. Just go to the stables and tell Zach to get Mamush ready." Zacharius was the groom Eschiva had engaged to look after Mamush after arriving in Cyprus. He was from a local family and had been very keen to look after a noblewoman's horse, clearly envisaging a great future serving in more "exciting" positions when her lord husband finally arrived. Eschiva was certain Zach would be more than happy to escort her—even if he had to borrow one of the archbishop's cart horses.

"It's not about me, Madame!" Cecilia insisted. "I'll go anywhere you do. I just don't think *you* should go out there! You can't tell what will happen when the rabble gets angry like that. In Acre there was a riot about bread prices once, and a friend of my father was thrown out of her litter and almost raped!"

"Celia, I'll tell you the story later, but I owe Sir Philip my life. Nothing could prevent me from trying to help him now. I only hope I do not come too late."

Chapter Twenty-Three
Of Family, Friends, and Foes

Beirut
Mid-June, 1229

"I DON'T THINK YOU SHOULD DO that, sir!" Rob told Balian urgently, holding his knight back by the arm with a strength no longer juvenile.

Rob would be ready for knighthood soon, Balian registered, and he'd have to find a new squire. He didn't look forward to that. For now, however, he had his brother to deal with. "I can't let Baldwin dismiss me as if I were old bones or a monk!" he told his squire emphatically.

"Yes, you can," Rob countered steadily. "Let him treat you like you're a fragile old lady for all I care! It won't change the fact that you're your father's heir."

"That's not the point! I feel fine and it's time to show Baldwin, and everyone else who happens to be watching, that I *am* fine." Balian glanced at the large crowd of spectators that always collected around the lists below the citadel of Beirut. There was at least a score of his father's knights with their squires, the Lord of Karpas, of course, his cousin of Caesarea, and Hugh and Baldwin both, with their youngest brother Guy getting underfoot in his eagerness to help. On top of that, there was the usual crowd of idle or errant apprentices, sailors, peddlers, journeymen, and beggars, all attracted by the entertainment offered by knights testing their strength and skills against one another on powerful, high strung horses. On a fine day like this, all that was missing were the heralds, trumpets, and pageantry.

"You may *feel* fine," Rob countered, "but the doctor warned you not to risk a fall."

"That was almost a year ago. I can't spend the rest of my life avoiding risks. That's not how a man wins the respect of other men, much less retains his inheritance. If I can't take my place with my father and brothers in defense of the Holy Land, then I don't *deserve* to inherit Beirut."

"Yes, and for the defense of the Holy Land, Sir, you would be justified in taking risks," Rob answered firmly. "But this has nothing to do with defending the Holy Land. This is nothing but sport."

"This is training for war. If I don't get back into shape *here*, I won't be *able* to take on the Saracens."

"Whether we like it or not, we actually have a ten-year truce with the Turks," Rob pointed out.

"If you believe they'll respect that, you're more naïve than I thought!" Balian scoffed.

Rob refused to be provoked. "With all due respect, sir, this has nothing to do with training and everything to do with showing Sir Baldwin up!"

Balian burst out laughing and flung his arm around his squire's shoulders. "All right, Rob. You win. It does. And I'm going to do it." Then dropping his arm, Balian turned toward the lists and raised his voice to shout across the tiltyard to Baldwin. "Get a fresh horse, Baldwin! You're not done yet!"

Baldwin had just successfully defeated all comers and had been about to withdraw from the lists in self-satisfied triumph "for the honor of Ibelin"—as if he were the heir.

"What?" Baldwin twisted around in the saddle and looked over his shoulder in surprise.

Balian ducked under the railing and walked to the center of the tiltyard, calling as he came, "Do you want a formal challenge?"

Baldwin turned and trotted back toward his brother. As he reached him, he leaned his elbow on the pommel of his saddle and bent down to speak in a low voice. "Balian, are you sure?"

"Yes! You're too full of yourself. You need to be cut back down to a sufferable size."

"Ha, ha. Look, I don't want to hurt you, but in front of all these people, I'm not going to just roll off to make *you* look good. If you insist on jousting with me, it will be for real."

"I know." Balian met his eyes.

"And you want to go through with this?"

Balian smiled with his mouth, but his eyes were earnest.

"Mount up then, but don't say I didn't warn you!" Baldwin turned his horse around and shouted to his squire to tack up his reserve stallion. Balian meanwhile returned to Rob, who was still on the far side frowning.

"What's this? Insubordination?" Balian asked, only half in jest.

"No, you didn't tell me *which* horse you wanted, sir," Rob answered sullenly.

"Damon."

Rob nodded, relieved at that. Balian had said more than once that he wouldn't risk the intelligent and affectionate horse in battle, but this wasn't real battle nor even a melee. The chances were far better that the horse would remain uninjured than the rider.

By the time Rob returned with a saddled Damon, Hugh was with Balian trying all the same arguments Rob had already used to get him to withdraw, adding "Baldwin's really good. He's not as easy to unseat as he was a year ago. He's been getting better, while you've been getting—"

"I know. Soft. I appreciate your concern, Hugh, but I'm going to joust."

Balian gathered up his reins, pointed his left foot in the near stirrup and swung himself up into the saddle. Rob, with a deep sigh, dutifully handed up his quilted cap and the heavy, full helm. Balian left the latter in his lap for a moment, while he tied the tight-fitting cap under his chin. Then he pulled up the chainmail hood of his hauberk over the cap and stretched the aventail over his chin to tie it closed with a leather thong over his left ear. Finally, he set the heavy helmet on his head. The rolls of leather inside the helmet held it snuggly in place. Satisfied, Balian nodded and indicated with his hand the end of the lists opposite his brother. "Bring me a lance over there."

Rob nodded, and Balian turned Damon in the opposite direction to trot him back and forth to warm him up. Damon was a tournament stallion, and he'd been denied them far too long. He was already so excited, he kept half-rearing up. He was sweating too, and soon he started snorting at Balian impatiently. Balian reached down and patted his neck. "Good boy. Just calm down a bit." Damon couldn't have calmed down even if he'd wanted to.

Baldwin was back with a fresh stallion. Balian knew the horse well because he came, like most of their horses, from the Ibelin stud. Growing up, the boys had all learned to ride on the older horses, particularly their father's retired destriers. They had been schooled by their father's marshal, Eskinder, and by Beirut himself, switching horses during their early years to learn how to master various types of problems and personalities. Only as squires they had been allowed to select one horse as their own, a horse that often served later in life as a palfrey. At their knighting, they were each allowed to select two more stallions.

Despite their rivalry, horses had been one of the few things Balian and Baldwin had never fought over. Baldwin liked horses that were strong-willed and stubborn; Balian preferred willing and intelligent horses like Damon. The horse Baldwin now rode was a powerful, flashy white stallion, the kind of horse that made the spectators ooh and ahh (as they were all doing), but he also fought his rider and didn't always do what was asked.

Damon looked rather slight, and, with his oversized blaze and blue eyes, a bit ragged by comparison. Balian saw people looking over at him almost pityingly. If people hadn't known he was the heir to Beirut and riding this horse by choice, they would have thought he was some poor knight with a second class mount.

At last Baldwin signaled he was ready and Balian signaled back. They took up their positions at either end of the lists, and Rob handed Balian a lance with an audible sigh.

Balian couched the lance and lowered his head so he could clearly see the length of the tiltyard through the horizontal slit in the helmet. Now, when the noise around was dampened by the arming cap, chainmail, padding and iron helmet, he could hear his thoughts and feelings: he was terrified.

He looked down the length of the tiltyard and his head was full of memories of falls. Bad falls. Falls that hurt like hell. Falls that left him bruised. Falls that left him limping. Falls that left him winded. Falls that knocked him unconscious. And he remembered the doctor saying, "a bad fall could cripple you for life."

Balian was terrified of being a cripple. Those early weeks after being released from the pillory had given him a hint of what it might be like to be crippled. But it might also be much worse.

The earth was trembling as Baldwin gathered speed, and in his eagerness to be gone Damon was leaping up on his hindlegs, nearly rearing. Balian could not delay any longer. He let the stallion have his head and concentrated on his opponent, the tip of his lance and his shield.

The collision was jolting and splinters flew in all directions, but both riders remained in the saddle and a cheer went up from the spectators. They reached the opposite ends of the lists and took the next lance handed up to them by their opponent's squire.

Turning around, Damon didn't give Balian a chance to hold him back. Ears flat on his head he was streaking down the lists again with a vengeance. Balian dropped the reins altogether and concentrated on the actual clash of arms. With his legs and weight, however, he coaxed Damon a little to the right, drawing his brother's lance tip with him and making it harder for a clean and direct blow. The trick worked because Baldwin didn't have enough control of his destrier to follow with his horse. Instead, he leaned farther out of his saddle, and still couldn't land a direct hit. His lance slipped and scratched along the surface of Balian's shield rather than shattering.

Unfortunately, although Damon responded sensitively and slipped back closer at the last moment, Balian was out of practice and also missed the mark. His lance only glanced off Baldwin's shield.

Each with lances intact, they turned again and started down the lists for a third run.

Suddenly, a female voice was calling, "Balian, don't! Stop! Stop!" It penetrated all the padding over his ears only faintly, yet so intensely that it disrupted his concentration. He missed the center of Baldwin's shield by a hand's breadth and so failed to smash his brother to the back of his saddle, dissipating some of his brother's strength.

Instead, with the full weight of man, horse and armor moving at a combined speed of close to fifty miles an hour, Baldwin's lance hit him on the upper third of his shield. That was higher than normal and it unbalanced Balian. He felt himself start to fall backward while Damon continued to pelt down the tiltyard, oblivious to his rider's danger. Balian grabbed for the pommel of the saddle and gripped Damon with his legs. He didn't want to fall! Not at this speed!

Already there was daylight between himself and the saddle. For a split second he saw the sand rushing past, and then he hit the ground so hard that his helmet clanged and he blacked out. Yet, even as he lost his vision, he rolled and with his hand he shoved the helmet up and off so he could see and breathe again. He pulled his feet back under himself, pushed himself up and staggered a couple of steps before Hugh, Bella, and Rob converged on him in various states of fright.

Balian was grinning. "I'm alright!" he shouted at them. "I'm fine!"

Baldwin was looming over him, his stallion flinging lather in all directions as he fought the bit. "Balian! Are you hurt?"

Before Balian could answer, Damon galloped up, head down and ears flat. He thrust himself between Baldwin and Balian and started viciously lashing out at Baldwin's stallion. With a loud whinny of outrage, the white stallion fought back. Hugh and Rob grabbed Bella roughly and yanked her out of danger. While Baldwin struggled to get control of his mount, Balian threw an arm over Damon's neck to pull him back. "Calm down! Calm down! Come here!" He got hold of Damon's reins and pulled him away from the other stallion, stroking his neck and calming him with his voice.

Baldwin drew up six feet away, his horse still fretting and snorting, and shouted to his brother again, "Are you alright?"

Grinning over Damon's saddle, Balian called back. "I'm fine! Well done! I'll get you tomorrow!"

"Balian, no!" Bella rushed back to his side and flung her arms around him protectively. "You don't have to do this! You don't have to prove anything!" Then lifting her voice to be heard by Baldwin she added reproachfully, "And you shouldn't be provoking him!"

Baldwin raised his hands in a gesture of innocence. "He challenged me, Bella! I tried to warn him, but he insisted."

"He's telling the truth, Bella," Balian assured his sister. He bent and kissed the top of her head, and handed Damon's reins off to Rob. "And you don't need to worry, little sister. I'm fine. I really am."

He was, in fact, more than fine; he was elated. He'd fallen and had not hurt himself at all. He had rolled right back onto his feet, and as he flexed his shoulders, he could feel nothing more than bruises and muscular pain. He laughed as he tossed Guy, who had scampered up, his helmet, punched Hugh in the shoulder, and then laid his arm around Bella's shoulders and started to lead her off the tiltyard in the direction of the postern gate back into the city. He had vanquished his terror of a fall.

The spectators, sensing that the entertainment was over for the day, started to disperse. They were chattering excitedly among themselves, analyzing the techniques and discussing Baldwin's success. Not a few cast Balian strange looks; a defeated knight was not supposed to look so pleased with himself and happy.

Balian noted a particularly elegant Italian with peacock feathers held to his floppy satin hat by a large pearl brooch looking at him particularly keenly. The stranger stopped several people and pointed in Balian's direction. Everyone he stopped nodded and pointed at Balian again. Finally, the young man approached Balian and with a flourish removed his hat to bow deeply before him. "My lord Balian d'Ibelin?" He still sounded somewhat uncertain.

Balian supposed he didn't cut an impressive figure at the moment—covered in sand and horse-shit. "Yes," he confirmed as he drew up to face the man squarely. "I'm Sir Balian d'Ibelin. Are you looking for me?"

The Italian righted himself. "My name is Paulo di Ferrario." The name rang a bell, but Balian could not place it. "I am captain of the *San Valentino*." Like all sailors, he seemed to expect people to recognize his ship, but Balian had not heard of her before. Furthermore, the young man seemed rather immature to be a captain, while his clothing was bright and foppish. The word "popinjay" in his father's voice echoed in Balian's memory, and Balian was amused to find himself disapproving of another for his own former faults. The young Italian, sensing

Balian's confusion, added, "My father, Hugh, is the Consul of the Genoese on Cyprus."

"Ah." Balian nodded. That explained everything; the Genoese Consul was an extremely wealthy and influential man. Balian had had no dealings with him directly, but he had heard his father talk about the man. His father thought highly of the elder Ferrario. "And you were looking for me?" Balian wanted to get back to the citadel, bathe and change out of his dirty, stinking and sweat-soaked clothes.

"I was charged with the delivery of these three messages to you." Ferrario made another elaborate bow, and then with a flourish produced three sealed documents from his doublet pocket and held them out to Balian.

Balian's heart missed a beat. Eschiva! But his heart fell as fast as it had leapt. The largest, heaviest document was addressed in a strong, masculine hand that was obviously not Eschiva's writing. Flipping it over he saw the seal of Novare and, with an inward sigh, put it to the bottom of the pile. The second letter wasn't from Eschiva either; it was addressed to his father and sealed with an Ibelin ring. He presumed it was from his brother Johnny. The third letter, at last, was addressed in the beautiful letters of his artistic Eschiva. With relief, he hastily tucked the letter into the inside pocket of his surcoat, where it lay against his heart.

Bella watched him spirit it away without comment, but Hugh and Guy instantly clamored for an explanation. "What was that? Why did you do that?"

"None of your business."

"Ah ha," Hugh concluded knowingly. "From a lady then."

"What lady?" Guy wanted to know.

Balian did not answer, but that was answer enough. Instead, he turned to Ferrario to ask, "What do I owe you, sir?"

Behind him, Hugh remarked, "I hope she's not the type to go tattling to our father."

"You owe me nothing, my lord, except to remember my name, my ship, and my family. We are ardent supporters of the Ibelins. You can count on us."

"Paulo di Ferrario of the *San Valentino*," Balian answered. "We thank you."

The Genoese bowed yet again. Then he nodded to Balian's brothers, made an extra bow to Bella, and at last withdrew.

"What a puffed-up little parrot!" Hugh scoffed when the Italian was out of hearing. "It will be a cold day in hell before the Ibelins have need of the likes of that dandy!"

"I wouldn't be so sure," Balian countered enigmatically.

"Who are the letters from?" Guy asked.

Balian looked at them again. "This one is from Johnny, and this one's from Novare."

"It's really thick. What could he have to say that would take so much paper?" Guy complained.

"Let's see." Balian slipped his finger under the upper flap to break the seal and unfolded the letter. At the sight of it, he laughed. "It's all in verse! Dear Philip."

"What's funny about verse?" Bella demanded indignantly. "At least he *tries* to express himself more elegantly than the likes of you! Let me see!"

"No, he is writing specifically to me," Balian answered, holding the letter out of Bella's reach to read out loud:

More than a hundred thousand greetings, fair sire, and compeer, who is now a brother new...

Balian's voice fell silent as his eyes raced ahead and he started frowning. Abruptly he burst out, "Christ on the Cross!"

"Don't swear, Balian!" Bella reproved him automatically.

Balian just gripped her arm. "Bella! Listen to this!

Fair speech and plea for justice won me no respite;
For all I said, they judged me without law or right.
Within the pillory, the traitors chained me tight,
And then they sought to slay me treacherously by night;
But I was warned by one, who cares not whom it might
Displease, who gave me loyal counsel in my plight.

"What's that supposed to mean?" Guy asked impatiently.

"Novare's been arrested?" Hugh asked more intelligently. "What for? Did they finally catch up with him for those sailors in Palermo or for his gambling debts?"

"No, it says here for refusing to take an oath to the five baillies of Cyprus. He claims Barlais is bringing misery to Cyprus and plans to enslave us all. He says he fears for our house and urges action. Listen to this," Balian skipped over several stanzas to read:

The uncle of your father, my fair lord Baldwin
To no man living bent his head nor bowed his chin;
And if to five unworthy scoundrels you give in,
That God who punished and destroyed Cain for his sin,
May he destroy and punish you, unless you win.

"Ah ha," Hugh commented. "So he's gotten himself into trouble and wants us to come get him out of it."

"We better see what Johnny says," Bella urged.

"Then we'll need to go find father. It is addressed to him."

"He was in the library when Tancred burst in with the news that you were preparing to joust with Baldwin. I left him there to try to stop you."

"Let's see if he's still there."

Together the Ibelin children made their way up from the lists behind the citadel, back into the city of Beirut by a postern and up the steep winding path to the barbican. Here they had a splendid view back down to the city and the harbor, where a Hospitaller galley, flying the black and white banner of the Order, was maneuvering alongside the quay. They didn't stop to watch, however, but continued their climb, first up from the outer to the inner ward, then up the stairs to the great hall, along the wall-walk to the North Tower, and there up the winding interior stairs of this tower.

The North Tower, although a part of the defensive perimeter of the castle, stood directly over the sea and was comparatively invulnerable. It was primarily a watchtower, as from its crenelated roof it was possible to see both ships and caravans approaching from the north while still many miles away. From the arrow-slits at various levels, it was also possible to defend the postern gate facing north.

The Lord of Beirut had located his library here because it could be lit from all the directions of the heavens, yet it was far removed from the bustle of the castle, making it a place of complete peace, quiet and refuge. It was also easily sealed off so that the treasures inside did not "find feet" (as Beirut liked to word it). Last but not least, it was spacious enough to house his extensive library. Beirut had over 100 books, including the books he had inherited from his mother.

The chamber had stained-glass windows that could be opened to let in more light or fresh air as desired. The window seats were paneled with marble and softened with Saracen silk cushions. It had a parquet floor, and the walls were covered with bookshelves, but the ceiling had been painted with a night sky showing the constellations. The Ibelin children had all learned to identify the constellations here. From the center hung a bronze chandelier with holders for six candles.

The door opened long before the Ibelin children reached the landing, and their father stood framed in the door looking bemused. "With the amount of noise you lot make, you'd think the Saracens were breaking down the gates!"

"Not the Saracens, perhaps, but the baillies—" Balian started to answer.

"Did you just take a fall in the lists?" His father interrupted to ask, noticing with alarm the dirt on his surcoat.

"Yes, but only because Bella called out my name at exactly the wrong time, distracting me."

"Balian! That's not fair! I was only trying to stop you from taking such a stupid risk!" Bella defended herself indignantly.

"Your intentions were the best, as always, little sister, but the results were less admirable."

"You would appear to be none the worse for the tumble," Beirut observed dryly with his eyes focused sharply on his firstborn.

"I am indeed none the worse for it, but that's not why we're here. Novare has sent me a very long letter alleging the five baillies are behaving like tyrants and, furthermore, are intent on disinheriting us. He himself was arrested and put in the pillory for refusing to take an oath to the baillies."

Beirut's eyes narrowed slightly as he listened to Balian, and Balian felt compelled to add, "Yes, father. I know Philip can be melodramatic and embellish things somewhat, but we've also got a letter from Johnny."

"Why didn't you say so! Come in. Sit down." Beirut backed up into his library and seated himself behind his beautifully carved desk, while his children spread out across the window seats and made themselves comfortable. Beirut broke the seal with his knife and started to read out loud.

Dearest Father,

I hope this letter finds you and all my brothers and Bella well.

I fear I don't have any good news. Since the Emperor left, Barlais has become terrible. He's raised a lot of taxes and people are rioting. Recently, he summoned all the knights and made them swear fealty to him and his co-regents, and anyone who refused was arrested. They put Sir Philip of Novare in the pillory and only released him after a whole day. He was told to go home and return the next day to face charges, but King Henry over-heard Barlais say they couldn't let him stand trial because he would bring arguments that would embolden others to reject their rule. So Barlais gave orders to have Novare killed. Henry managed to get a message to him not to go home, so he escaped to the Hospital. When Barlais' men broke into his house, they killed one of his servants and stabbed his bed a dozen times or more before they noticed it was empty."

Guy laughed at that, but his father and brothers hushed him. Beirut resumed reading, his face clouded by a frown:

Henry says that the Emperor gave orders to the baillies to expropriate all our lands on Cyprus and prevent you from ever setting foot on the island again.

"That's outrageous! By what right—" Hugh erupted in agitation. His father silenced him with a gesture and the words, "There is more."

Henry says Barlais plans to keep our lands for himself and give the lands of our vassals, clients, and supporters to the other baillies. He says the Emperor wanted to give me Foggia because I won't inherit anything in Outremer—

"That means the Emperor is still intent on taking Beirut from us as well!" Hugh pointed out perceptively. His father and elder brother nodded calmly because they had never doubted this.

"Let me read to the end before we discuss things," Beirut admonished.

I don't know what Barlais did to him, but Henry is afraid of him. He used to talk back to the Emperor, but he just tries to stay out of Barlais' sight. He's begged me not to leave him alone with Barlais, but if Barlais orders his men to remove me, there's nothing I can do."

"Would Barlais really lay a hand on his anointed king?" Hugh asked in shock. "Why? What has poor Henry every done?"

"Henry can have done nothing, but Barlais has long been bitter about the fact that Henry's father never knighted his," Beirut explained, astonishing his sons with his insight. "I fear he may want to get his revenge on Henry. Let me finish reading."

I don't know what to do or what you would want me to do. I wish you could come, but Henry says you'd be killed the minute you set foot on the island—or as soon as Barlais' men find you. He says they'll kill any Ibelins that dare to return to Cyprus. But we can't just let them take everything away from us, can we? There must be something you can do, and please tell me what you want me to do.

Your loving, respectful and obedient son,
John

Beirut folded the letter back together again and then lifted his head to look at his firstborn. "Balian? What do you have to say to that?"

"Johnny's neither a coward nor a liar. Nor is he easily shaken. If he's asking us to come—because he is—then the situation must be very bad indeed." As he spoke, Eschiva's letter seemed to be burning his chest. Balian was afraid for her, and he longed to read the message she'd sent him, but he did not dare so much as touch the place on his surcoat over the letter—not in the presence of his father. He did not want to draw attention to it. He would have to wait until he was alone to read it.

"Yes, I agree. But 'returning' to Cyprus under these circumstances would mean open confrontation—armed confrontation—with the men the Holy Roman Emperor named as his representatives. You *do* understand that?"

"Yes, I do," Balian assured him, adding testily. "I'm not a fool."

"No one is implying you are," his father answered steadily, "I simply want to be sure we are all speaking of the same things. I want no mistake about what we are discussing here." He then turned to his third son. "Hugh?"

"Johnny's right. We can't allow these so-called baillies to just steal our inheritance! We won that land with damn-near forty years of loyal service to the Cypriot crown. Aimery de Lusignan would never have gained control of Cyprus in the first place if our grandfather had not put him there!"

"Bella?" Beirut looked next at his daughter, his face softening as it nearly always did at the sight of her.

"I'm afraid for King Henry, Father. He's completely at the mercy of Barlais and his men. If he's already afraid, then what will happen to him if no one stops them from abusing power?"

"Guy?" Guy opened his mouth to give his opinion, but before he could say anything his father continued. "I want you to go find Baldwin and bring him to the solar so we can discuss this with him."

"Don't you want to know my opinion?" Guy complained.

While his elder brothers remarked almost in unison, "Not particularly," his father smiled and said, "All right. Tell me."

"I think we should go and chase that bastard Barlais right off Cyprus and into the sea!"

"Thank you. That was a very enlightening. Now, will you go find your brother Baldwin?"

Guy sighed and then jumped down from his window seat and started down the stairs at a run. Behind him, his elder brothers got to their feet, but for a moment Beirut remained sitting. Lovingly, he stroked the open page of the book he had been reading before his children burst in on him. Sadly, he closed the *Book of the King*, which had been commissioned by King Aimery de Lusignan to record the laws of the Kingdom of Jerusalem based on the testimony of reputable men after the court records had been lost in the wake of Hattin.

Finally, with a sigh, Beirut stood. Catching sight of Balian he remarked, "May I request that you change into something clean, fresh and respectable before you rejoin me in the solar?"

"Yes, of course, Father," Balian answered readily. He felt Eschiva's letter against his heart begging to be read.

In his room, Balian called for Rob, and, getting no answer, he shot the bolt to the door to ensure he was completely alone. He removed Eschiva's letter, laid it carefully upon a chest, unbuckled his sword and pulled his surcoat off over his head. His hauberk, sweat-soaked gambeson and shirt were tossed aside, and half-naked he sat down in the breeze from his window to break open Eschiva's seal.

Unlike Novare and Johnny, Eschiva was sparing of words. Her message consisted of a polychrome image showing a castle surrounded by wolves, one of which was being ridden by a weasel with a shield bearing Barlais' arms. Inside the castle a cat dressed in boots, hauberk and covered by a blue and yellow surcoat, similar to what Novare liked to wear, stood on his hind feet, brandishing a sword defiantly. Behind the cat, a score of mice wearing wimples and dresses and holding baby mice in their arms huddled together in fear. Below the picture was a single phrase:

"Beloved Balian, we fear for our lives. Please help if you can—without too much risk to yourself."

The plea made him spring to his feet and start pacing the room. Then realizing that he had no time to spare, he pulled off his boots and hose, found a pitcher of water and poured the contents into a bowl so he could sponge away the sweat and dirt of the tilt-yard. Before he finished, Rob returned and was surprised to find the door bolted.

"Balian?"

Balian crossed the room to unlock the door, and Rob burst in exclaiming in agitation, "A Hospitaller ship just put in with news from Cyprus! Two knights came to report that they're harboring more than 100 people, mostly women, and children, in the Hospital at Nicosia and others in their houses at Limassol and Famagusta. Apparently, Novare's in the Hospital too. He recruited archers to reinforce the Hospitallers, but the Hospitallers say the situation is untenable—that they'll run out of food—"

"Does my father know?" Balian asked anxiously.

"He does now. The Hospitaller was taken up to the solar to report to him."

"Help me dress! I need to join them!"

By the time Balian rejoined his father in the solar, the entire castle was in an uproar and a Hospitaller, sunburned and sweating from his climb up from the port, sat at the center of attention. Someone had brought him chilled water in a large pewter goblet that he held in his left hand while gesturing with his right. "Novare took command of the volunteer archers," he was saying as Balian joined them, "and we were able to drive off the Langobards. The Hospital in Nicosia is well built for defense, my lord. I do not doubt we can hold it, but with so many women, children and civilian archers now crowded inside there is a serious risk of dysentery and, ultimately, hunger. Sir Philip has undertaken to dig a second well to help with sanitation, but we cannot hold out indefinitely. We must be relieved, or we will be forced to surrender."

"Are you expecting relief from your brothers?" Beirut asked, and Balian had to bite his tongue not to protest. From Novare and Johnny's letters, it was clear that the baillies were targeting the Ibelins. This was their battle, not that of the Hospital.

"We can expect no support, my lord. Our Master has gone to complain to the Pope about the Emperor's expropriation of our lands throughout his territories, and the sudden loss of reinforcements and revenues place a strain on the resources of all our houses here in Outremer. Furthermore, it is not our intention to take sides in any dispute between the secular powers on Cyprus. We offer protection to the weak, out of Christian charity, but my Order will undertake no offensive action."

"What are these women afraid of exactly?" Baldwin wanted to know.

"They have been made to feel unsafe in their own homes. The Langobards apparently show up at all times of the day and night and make demands. First, it's just wine and food, then it's horses, then it's outright extortion—pay us or we'll take what we want and have our sport with you and your daughters as well."

Balian caught his breath so loudly that everyone looked over at him. "We can't allow mercenaries to terrorize honest women!" He burst out.

"Thinking of anyone particular, Balian?" Baldwin asked in jest.

"Of course not!" Balian lashed back defensively. "The good Sir Hospitaller said nearly one hundred women have sought refuge!"

"Indeed," Beirut intervened before his sons could start fighting. "But I'm still somewhat unsure what the Hospital's intentions are." He looked pointedly at the Hospitaller.

"The best we can do is to try to negotiate generous terms for the women in our care, but I'm not confident that any terms would be respected if there is no one to enforce them."

"In short, you have come here in the expectation that *I* might come to the relief of your house?" Beirut pressed him.

"They are the wives, mothers, and daughters of men serving with you, my lord," The Hospitaller explained. "The Langobards aren't simply flexing their muscles; they are targeting the tenants, vassals, and clients of Ibelin."

Beirut took a deep breath, looked at each of his sons in turn, but then he turned pointedly to the Hospitaller again. "To come to the relief of Cyprus, I will need ships. Is the Hospital willing and able to provide them?"

The Hospitaller looked decidedly embarrassed now. "Ah, I was not given explicit instructions with respect to that, my lord, but, ah, I don't think that would be, well, compatible with neutrality in this dispute. If you see what I mean, my lord?"

"The Consul of Genoa on Cyprus offered his assistance," Balian hastened to inform his father. Beirut looked over sharply, and their eyes met. "It was his son who brought the letters from Novare and Johnny. He said we could count on Genoese support," Balian assured his father.

That made sense. Genoa was a bitter opponent of the Hohenstaufen's overweening policies on the Italian peninsula—particularly since Pisa was a staunch supporter of the Hohenstaufen. They were also the dominant trading commune in Beirut itself and knew the Ibelins well. Beirut turned to Baldwin. "Do you oppose taking action?"

"Not at all. Why would you think that?"

Beirut did not answer, he simply turned to Balian and ordered, "Fetch me my father's sword."

Balian was startled. His grandfather's sword hung in his father's bedroom, a constant reminder of him and his legacy. They all knew the story of the sword. Their grandfather had broken out of the encirclement at Hattin and led some 3,000 Frankish troops to Tyre, but his wife and children had been trapped in Jerusalem. He had gone to Saladin and obtained a safe-conduct to ride to Jerusalem and remove his family before the impending siege. The conditions of the safe conduct were that he go unarmed and stay only one night. On his arrival in Jerusalem, however, the people begged him to remain and organize their defense. The situation was desperate because all fighting men had mustered and gone to their death or capture at the Battle of Hattin. Jerusalem was flooded with women and children. Balian's namesake had agreed to remain and command the defense, but since he had come to the city without his arms, an armorer of the city undertook to forge him a new sword. In the pommel of this sword, he set an enamel disk with the arms of Jerusalem on one side, and a similar disk with the arms of Ibelin on the other. On the blade itself, inlaid in bronze, were the words: *Defender of Jerusalem.*

Balian went to fetch the sword, and as he took it from its hook, he could not resist pulling the blade out far enough to read the inscription. Then, succumbing to temptation, he pulled the sword out completely and weighed it in his hand. He had been provided with the best weapons money could buy and yet—there was something special about this sword. Reluctantly, he returned it to its sheath and carried it down to the solar.

He found his father and brothers on their feet impatiently awaiting him. Beirut held out his hand, and Balian handed over the sword. Although he was not dressed in armor but rather a long flowing kaftan with beautiful embroidery at the neckline and hemline, Beirut girded Defender of Jerusalem around his hips. Next, he snapped his fingers at Hugh, the only one still in armor, and demanded, "Your gauntlets." Hugh obeyed without question, and Beirut slipped the leather and chainmail mitten over his right hand. Only then did he lead them from the solar onto the dais of the Great Hall.

The hall was full of people, and the appearance of Beirut with his three adult sons flanking him created an immediate hubbub. Men surged toward the dais and the Lord of Karpas' voice boomed out. "My lady is trapped in the inner tower of Kantara surrounded by mercenaries who have plundered, slaughtered and raped my servants. I demand immediate action!"

"Karpas is not alone! My seventy-year-old mother was driven from her home. Just thrown out and forced to flee with what she could carry on a couple of mules!" another man called out.

"I have two daughters on Cyprus, my lord, and God knows I must now fear for their honor and lives!" someone else shouted.

"We can't just wait here, while the Langobards attack our families and plunder our homes!"

Beirut held up his naked left hand for silence. "My lords, sirs! Sir Gautier of the Knights Hospitaller reports that these are not acts of lawlessness, but rather have been ordered by the baillies of Cyprus—"

"They aren't legally baillies at all!" Karpas reminded them furiously.

"They are the Emperor's lackeys," someone seconded Karpas.

Beirut held up his hand for silence again. "Legal or not, they hold the King in their hands and they control the resources of the royal domain. They are cloaked in the trappings of legitimate power. If we take up arms against them, we will be labeled rebels—"

"Rebels against tyranny are liberators!" Karpas roared.

"No matter what we are called," Beirut raised his voice to be heard over the excited babbling spreading across the hall, "No matter what we are called—*or how we view ourselves*—we will bring civil war and bloodshed."

That silenced them. But only for a moment. Then Karpas growled, "There already *is* civil war, Beirut! A civil war waged against helpless and defenseless women and children! I *will* free my lady—alone and with my bare hands if necessary. I will *not* stand aside and watch greedy bastards steal what is rightfully mine and abuse my lady in the process!"

His words were greeted with a cheer of approval.

Beirut gestured for silence, and when the room was hushed with restless anticipation, he announced simply, "You will not be alone, my lord of Karpas." Drawing *Defender of Jerusalem* dramatically, he held it up by the naked blade in his gauntleted hand, the hilt pointing upwards so the sword formed a cross. "By this sword my father used to defend Jerusalem from Saladin, I swear that I will free Cyprus of the tyranny of false governors and their foreign mercenaries—or die in the attempt!"

Across the hall, men followed his example. They drew their swords and swore upon them to deliver Cyprus or die in the attempt. Balian could not suppress admiration at his father's masterful orchestration of this response.

Before the shouting had died down, Beirut turned to Balian and remarked soberly. "You better be right about the Genoese." Then he stepped off the dais and started to mingle with his men, accepting their personal assurances of support and thanking them as he moved through the crowd.

Chapter Twenty-Four
Return of the Ibelins

Gastria, Cyprus
July 10, 1229

BALIAN COULDN'T SLEEP. HE COULD NEITHER get comfortable in the narrow bunk nor filter out the myriad sounds of a ship at sea. The hull groaned, the waves rushed along the outside planking, the rigging banged against the mast, the booms creaked, and the sails flapped when the wind died. At the eight bells marking the end of the middle watch, he took his shirt, gambeson, and hose from the hook beside him, dropped down from the bunk, and grabbed his boots. Then he stepped carefully over or around the rows of sleeping men to the ladder leading up on deck.

As he poked his head out, Balian saw that the sky was greying from the east. He hauled himself up until he sat on the top step of the ladder and here he pulled on his red hose, attached them to his braies and then hauled on his suede boots before pulling his shirt over his naked torso and covering it with his gambeson. The gambeson was red, quilted suede leather, studded with small, brass crosses at the corners of the diamond-shaped quilting. Without his squire, he couldn't tie the laces on his sleeves and so left them hanging open. He ran his fingers through his hair to comb it crudely and then stood up on deck.

The wind that had been brisk throughout much of the night had died away. The sails had gone slack and the rigging banged loudly against the mast in answer to the roll of the ship. Glancing aft, Balian saw Captain Paulo di Ferrario looking toward the large galley off their starboard bow, the *Citta Sancta*, apparently awaiting a signal.

The *Citta Sancta* was the largest and newest of the Ferrario fleet. It was leading a little flotilla of six galleys, and it flew the pennant of the Lord of Beirut from its masthead. The other three ships were Balian's own *San Valentino*, a ship beyond his father's with his uncle of Caesarea, and a ship to larboard of the *San Valentino* with the Lord of Karpas. Together these four ships carried some 2000 men, over 300 of which were knights. Behind them were two modern horse transports with nearly 800 horses.

Balian squinted at the murky grey beyond the bow. It was hard to distinguish sea from sky. Whether that was because of the poor light of pre-dawn or a sea mist, he wasn't sure. What he knew was that he was nervous. Somewhere in that grey mass was Cyprus, but not the pleasant, fertile and peaceful Cyprus of his childhood and youth. Not his uncle Philip's Cyprus. Up ahead was an island held by Barlais, his supporters, and a thousand imperial mercenaries. A hostile Cyprus.

Balian noted that some of the Turcopoles had emerged onto the forepeak and were likewise looking about. His father had entrusted him with the command of their entire Turcopole contingent of 200 mounted archers, while his father would command their own and other Cypriot knights, Karpas the infantry, and Caesarea his knights and other volunteers from Syria.

Most of the Turcopoles were drawn from Beirut, with much smaller contingents from Caesarea and Arsur. They fought out of loyalty to the Ibelins and Caesarea rather than in their own interests. Many of them had never been to Cyprus before. They did not know the terrain nor did they speak Greek. Balian was acutely aware that both these factors posed significant challenges. He was also acutely aware that his command was a great honor, a great opportunity to earn credit—or disrepute.

He decided he should go forward to chat with the Turcopoles who were already awake. Just as he descended into the waist of the ship to make his way forward, however, a signal was run up on the mast of *Citta Sancta* and Captain Ferrario sang out an order. The crew, silent and still until now, came to life around him.

Balian found himself jostled aside by a man. Balian looked over annoyed, despite the mumbled apology, and the man's face jarred a memory. "Captain di Domenico?"

The sailor stopped but did not turn around. Instead, he snapped, "He's dead!"

But the voice only reinforced the image. Balian grabbed the sailor's arm and spun him around. "Maurizio!"

The sailor met his gaze. "I lost my ship, my cargo, and two-thirds of my crew. I'm not a captain anymore, just a common sailor, and we have to hand sail. Let me go!"

"You have a bride in Acre!" Balian countered. "I was told she was the fairest maid in all of Outremer."

"She's better off a widow! She can remarry. She can find new joy and fortune. God has punished me for my hubris. Let me go!"

The great booms were being hauled in over the deck and due to the lack of wind, they swayed as the ship rolled on the long swell. Balian and Maurizio were at risk of being knocked off their feet by the booms, and Balian acknowledged that this was no time to talk. He let Maurizio go, promising himself to talk to him later, and continued forward.

On the foredeck, he found the Captain of Turcopoles, Sir Solomon Arrabi. The Arrabi family had been in the service of the Ibelins for a hundred years, and although Sir Solomon had been knighted by Balian's father years ago, he was still a Maronite Christian and his first language was Arabic. Sir Solomon had been born in Ibelin in the same year as the Lord of Beirut, and he had made the dangerous journey from Ibelin to Jerusalem after the disastrous Battle of Hattin. He had been there during the siege and still had vivid memories of it. Sometimes, if he'd had enough to drink, he could be cajoled into telling them.

At the sight of Balian, he smiled sympathetically. "Having trouble sleeping, my lord?"

"To be honest, yes," Balian confessed, returning the older man's smile. "Whatever this day brings, it will be decisive."

The Maronite crossed himself. "We are in God's hands, and He has always favored the Ibelins. Besides, our cause is just. You need not fear."

"I hope I am as brave as the next man, Sir Solomon, but I do not want to fail my father in any way."

Sir Solomon nodded and looked over at the *Citta Sancta* before remarking, "Your father told me he wants us to secure the quay to enable the safe offloading of the horses."

"*If* we have to force a landing. My father hopes we will be allowed to land peacefully. That's why we're landing at Gastria. It is a Templar port and the Templars are neutral," Balian reminded him.

"And the Templars will not oppose us, thank God. But will they prevent Barlais' men or the imperial mercenaries from doing so? How can they do that and yet remain neutral?"

Balian nodded acknowledgment of the risks; he shared Arrabi's doubts.

Behind them, the sun was lifting itself out of the sea, a giant orange orb.

"I think I'll go wake up the men," Sir Solomon declared. "Breakfast never hurts before a fight."

Balian nodded and dropped back down to the main deck to make his way aft. He was surprised to discover another knight on the quarterdeck. The knights of this expedition had been spread over all four ships and housed in the stern accommodations of each, while the infantry and Turcopoles were housed in the holds and forecastles. The arrangement ensured that each ship had a commander and a combination of troops that would enable them to fight as an independent unit if any ship became separated from the rest.

Thinking it would be rude not to acknowledge the other knight, Balian wandered over and received a shock when he realized it was Sir Gerard de Montaigu. Although hardly an Ibelin vassal or client, Sir Gerard had joined the expedition. Why he had shipped on Balian's vessel rather than one of the others, Balian did not know.

Having approached, it would have been insulting to suddenly back away, so Balian forced himself to put on a good face. "Sir Gerard, I don't believe my father had a chance to thank you for your support. We greatly appreciate you joining us on this expedition. All the more, since you are not one of our vassals."

The Spaniard turned to look at Balian without a ghost of a smile. "Frederick Hohenstaufen is an instrument of the devil—as his ungodly attack on the Templars proved. No good can come of his rule in Outremer. We must resist it by all means at our disposal." *Even if it means fighting with the likes of you,* Montaigu appeared to be saying, although the latter words were left unsaid.

"We thank you," Balian repeated, bowing his head to the older man. But then the devil got into him, and he found himself remarking, "You must be concerned about your lady wife. Have you any news of her lately?"

"My wife is a flighty woman lacking faith and common sense."

Balian bristled at the insult to Eschiva. He had rarely met a young woman less "flighty" than Eschiva, and without thinking he rushed to her defense. "Your lady is a courageous woman, sir. I would *not* call her flighty."

"Oh? Do you know her so well then?" Montaigu asked sharply, his eyes narrowed.

Balian could have kicked himself. He beat a hasty retreat and lied without a qualm of conscience. "I hardly know her at all, sir. Indeed, I don't believe I've exchanged a single word with her in a year or more, certainly not since she became your lady. Yet her escape from the Emperor's harem was a daring deed. Surely you agree? Seeing how you detest the Emperor, you must admit she would have been mad to remain in the Emperor's harem after the death of Queen Yolanda?"

"She should have requested her brother's assistance, not run out into the dark of night to jump aboard the first ship in the harbor!"

"We are cousins, sir!" Balian reminded him pointedly. "She sought the protection and assistance of a cousin. There is nothing dishonorable—or 'flighty'—about that."

Montaigu did not answer directly. He stared at Balian for a moment, and then remarked in a dismissive tone, "Whatever the case in Andria, my lady behaved foolishly in Nicosia. She was perfectly safe with my Uncle the Archbishop of Nicosia, but instead of staying there, she rushed off to the Hospital at the first wild rumors. She is now trapped there with hundreds of others in cramped and unsanitary conditions. I have no sympathy since she brought this upon herself."

Balian had a hundred answers to that, but he bit his tongue. He bowed stiffly. "If you will excuse me, sir. I will go below and arm."

Montaigu returned the bow, and Balian felt his eyes boring into his back as he turned and crossed the deck to the ladder leading below deck.

By now several of the other men and Balian's squire Rob had woken and were struggling to dress themselves in the confined quarters. Balian made his way over to Rob and asked him to tie the sleeves of his shirt and gambeson before helping him into his hauberk and surcoat.

"Do you want your chausses, sir?"

"No, we'll be fighting on foot—at least initially."

Rob nodded, but he looked nervous. Balian smiled and cuffed him lightly to cheer him up. "Don't worry so much. I'll make sure the Turcopoles leave some Langobards for you to kill. Where's your hauberk?" The squire bent and grabbed it, and Balian helped him into it.

Meanwhile, with considerable shouting and clunking, the oars were run out. Soon the galley was moving forward in purposeful, short surges. Shortly afterward, the cook dropped down among the knights and squires and started to distribute biscuits. The knights washed down the dry sea biscuits with water or wine from their own canteens and finished dressing amidst friendly jostling and jesting.

A shout reached the common cabin from overhead that sent Balian scampering up the ladder with his cervellière in the crook of his arm. His sword banged against the sides of the hatch as he scrambled out. As he reached the deck, the young Genoese captain gave him a nod and pointed over bows. "We've made landfall, sir." Adding, with obvious pride. "We're dead on course. We'll be in Gastria within the hour."

Any hope that they would receive a neutral reception shattered when the first volley of crossbow bolts landed on the foredeck of the *Citta Sancta*. Beirut had been standing at the very bow, easily distinguishable by his gilded surcoat and the sword at his hip. When the arrows clattered down on the deck, everyone dived for cover, and Balian had a heart-stopping moment when he thought his father had been felled. Then he saw his father gesture everyone back off the foredeck.

Instantly, Balian turned to shout to Captain Ferrario. "Take us in as fast as you can!" Then he turned to Sir Solomon, who was in the waist behind the Turcopoles lining the port side of the ship, three deep. "Return fire!"

As the *San Valentino* surged ahead of the *Citta Sancta* the Turcopoles opened fire.

The volley of arrows that hit the *Citta Sancta* had come from a lookout tower on a promontory, but the Turcopoles ignored the handful of mercenaries in the tower and focused on the men on the quay itself. Many of these were just common sailors and longshoremen, who had not yet gotten word of what was going on. With a great deal of alarmed shouting, they abandoned whatever they were doing and rushed for the shelter of the buildings in panic.

The confusion was increased when troops of crossbowmen jogged onto the quay at the double. Balian guessed that the men on the tower had been able to identify the banners of the approaching ships some 20 or 25 minutes earlier. They had sent word to the imperial troops in the town, and these had maybe ten or fifteen minutes to arm. They were only now deploying. The problem, obviously, was that the crossbows these men carried were considerably more powerful and deadly than the lighter weapons of the Ibelin Turcopoles. The Ibelin advantage was numbers—but only after they had disembarked.

"Don't give them time to take up positions!" Balian shouted down to Sir Solomon.

The older knight didn't bother acknowledging the order. He had already divided his men into two units. As soon as the first echelon had fired, they went down on one knee to reload and clear the field of fire for the second echelon. In this manner, they kept up a steady stream of fire so intense that the mercenaries, with considerable shouting and gesturing, took cover behind their shields. As the distance closed with each stroke of the oars, the imperial troops fell back to the shelter of the harbor side buildings.

With a flurry of shouting and considerable clatter, the oars were shipped and the galley clunked against the side of the quay so hard that every man standing staggered.

Balian clung to the forward railing. He calculated they had only 30 seconds before the imperial mercenaries would place themselves indoors and windows ready to return fire. He drew his sword and sprang over the railing of the ship to land four feet below on the quay. The jarring up his legs was enough to be felt all the way to his teeth. He clenched the latter and started running for the largest building lining the quay, presumably the customs house. Many of the mercenaries had taken refuge inside it. He was followed by all the other knights and squires from his ship, roughly 100 men, and about a third the Turcopoles.

The open doorway to the customs house was looming, no more than fifteen yards away. A Langobard stepped into the doorway with a cocked crossbow in his hands and lifted it so he looked down the sights straight at Balian. He was perfectly calm, confident that his weapon would kill long before Balian's sword could come into play. Balian jumped sideways, but the tip of the bolt followed him. Just as the mercenary's finger touched the trigger, an arrow pierced his throat. With a shout of surprise, he dropped down on his knees. His aim disrupted, the bolt shot past its target.

Balian leapt over the man, drowning now in his own blood, as he entered into the customs house. Out of the darkness, men sprang on him from seemingly all sides. He couldn't properly see his opponents. He was fighting by instinct, countering anything that approached him. But with each second, he was joined by other knights and his Turcopoles. As his eyes adjusted to the dark, it became easier to find the enemy, and the knights quickly gained the advantage. Their opponents were imperial archers, who could not bring their weapons to bear in a melee in confined space. They were fighting with daggers and short swords. Within less than ten minutes, Balian and his knights had cleared the ground floor of the customs house. The quay, however, was far from secure because other mercenaries occupied the floor above and other buildings.

Pointing to the stairs, Balian led to the next floor. The windows were lined by mercenaries firing at the Ibelin ships in the harbor. Balian and his knights spread out and approached as quietly as possible—until something gave them away. Suddenly the mercenaries sensed what was happening and spun about to shoot back into the room. One of Balian's knights went down with a loud crash and another staggered with a gasp as he clutched his arm, pierced by a bolt. The rest rushed forward and overwhelmed the mercenaries.

Gaining the window, Balian looked out to see what was going on. In the harbor, his father and Caesarea's ships were hovering out of range, but Karpas' ship had veered away from the harbor entrance altogether and was fast disappearing behind the seawall—headed for the land. Balian surmised that he was going to try to beach the ship—and pay a fortune to the Genoese for it!— in order to take Gastria from landward. That could take as much as thirty or forty minutes—assuming he met no resistance. In the meantime, the remainder of the Ibelin Turcopoles were being pinned down in the *San Valentino* by the crossbow fire coming from the two adjacent buildings.

"We need to clear the warehouses on either side of us," he announced, turning to one of his father's knights. "Sir Amalric, take half the men with you. The rest come with me."

The knights divided themselves into two roughly equal groups, but the Turcopoles remained with Balian. He led them out the back of the customs house, and along the alley behind the warehouse. Here they found a large number of workers, mostly Greeks, cowering among the casks of wine and barrels of olive oil. At the sight of men with drawn and bloody swords, they started to run away with warning shouts to their comrades. Balian called out to them in Greek, "You have nothing to fear! We're only after imperial mercenaries!"

"There are fifty of them in there! In the warehouse!" one of the men paused to say. Another added, "And ten of Barlais' knights are at the courthouse!" He pointed deeper into the little town.

Balian couldn't remember where the courthouse of Gastria was, but it was to the west, while the Templar commandery sat on the eastern edge of the harbor. He looked back toward the Templar fortress. It sat still and silent as if utterly abandoned, while the dramatic fight for Gastria harbor unfolded at its feet. Hypocritical bastards, Balian thought to himself; hadn't the Ibelins supported the Templars when they were under attack from the Emperor?

But this was no time to think about that. He had to focus on clearing the imperial troops out of the warehouse so his father and uncle's ships could come alongside and disembark their men. While the warning about Imperial knights was valuable he was reluctant to reduce his fighting force to set up a defense against them. He turned to the Greeks to ask, "Can you set up sentries to warn us if the knights are approaching?"

Although most of the Greek workers just shook their heads or slipped away, a handful of men came forward warily. One of them asked, "Who are you?"

"Balian d'Ibelin."

"Is the Lord of Beirut back?" another asked hopefully.

"He's in the harbor. If we can clear the quay of opposition, he'll be able to land with 2,000 men."

"Then you're going to get rid of the Emperor's baillies and free King Henry?"

"We're going to try."

"Here! Come with me! They've bolted all the doors, but I can take you to the cellar entrance."

As they passed the rear doors to the warehouse, one of the knights tried to open them, but the Greeks were right; all were barred from the inside. The

Greek longshoreman led them to a side alley where a stone ramp angled down beside the warehouse. "The wine needs to be stored cool," the longshoreman explained. "It's easier to roll it than carry it down."

At the foot of the ramp, they found a door that was, thankfully, not barred. Opening it, they slipped into a dark, dank and cool cellar filled with wine casks. The only light came from the open door. The far corners were cast in complete shadow. Balian's heart was hammering in his chest. The smells and chill reminded him of the Hospitaller dungeon, the three days in the stocks. What if the Greeks were luring them in here only to lock them inside?

Behind him, someone put his fear into words as one of the Turcopoles asked in alarmed Arabic where they were being taken.

"There are the stairs to the floor above." The Greek pointed. Against the back of the cellar were rickety-looking wooden stairs.

"Go and see if the door is open," Balian ordered the longshoreman, pausing to let his men cluster around him. There was safety in numbers.

As he watched, the Greek carefully climbed up the stairs and cautiously tried the door. He opened it only a crack, proving it was not locked, but then closed it again and looked at Balian expectantly.

Balian nodded. He crossed to the stairs and mounted them, leaving his men clustered at the foot. When he came beside the Greek longshoreman, the man whispered, "The Langobards are in there."

Balian cracked the door as quietly as possible and looked through the slit. He could only see one window around which five of the Langobards stood, taking turns firing and loading. Between the Langobards at the far window facing the quay and the door from the cellar where he stood were barrels of olive oil grouped by consignment. They provided much better cover than any shield—provided one kept down and silent.

Closing the door quietly again, he turned to his own men and signaled for some of the Turcopoles to come up the stairs. He let the senior sergeant look through the door, and then they agreed in low whispers that the sergeant would take his Turcopoles into the room. They would line up behind the casks of oil, and then open fire on the Langobards all at once.

The Turcopoles, an arrow fitted in the strings of their bows, slipped out of the door one at a time. Moving slowly and crouching behind the barrels, they spread themselves out across the room. Through the slit in the door, Balian kept his eye on the reaction of the Langobards, while his knights joined him uneasily on the stairs. The Langobards seemed agitated by something that was going on outside and were not paying attention to what was going on behind them.

With a shout, the Turcopole sergeant ordered his men to fire. A volley of arrows exploded in the confines of the warehouse. While here and there the arrows ricocheted off the stone walls, most arrows found flesh, provoking an eruption of curses, screams, and grunts. Only one of the Langobards managed to turn around and return fire before he crashed down under three arrows. Balian was already in the room and he ran forward with his knights to finish off any of the mercenaries who had survived.

The shouts and screams, however, had alerted the Langobards on the floor above and two appeared at the head of the stairs and tried to shoot into the room. They were answered by the Turcopoles. One of the Langobards fell dramatically into the room with a sickening thud while the other rolled halfway down the stairs, head down, dripping blood. Overhead, footsteps and voices warned them that many Langobards remained alive.

"The cranes!" a longshoreman whispered.

"What?"

"The cranes on the dock. They go up to pulleys on the roof. We can lift some of your men up to shoot into the room. If you attack from the stairs and the windows at the same time you'll overwhelm them."

Balian wasn't convinced, but they had to try. As he stepped outside onto the quay, the Turcopoles still on the *San Valentino* cheered. Balian turned to silence them. Meanwhile, the longshoreman untied the halyard of two of the cranes from the side of the building and lowered the hooks. Turcopoles found a couple of empty pallets used for hauling crates and barrels to the upper floor of the warehouse. Three Turcopoles climbed aboard each pallet and took up positions kneeling, their arrows already cocked and pointed at the building. A half dozen squires grabbed the end of each rope and started pulling the pallets up, hand over hand. Balian meanwhile led the knights back inside and started cautiously up the stairs, his sword drawn and shield at the ready.

Just as the men on the first pallet reached the base of the window, a Langobard leaned out and fired at point-blank range. One of the Turcoples was flung backward by the force of the bolt and fell out of the pallet to crack and splatter on the stone quay below. His two colleagues, however, returned fire so rapidly that the Langobard likewise fell from the window with a drawn-out scream to land beside his victim. Meanwhile, the three Turcopoles from the second pallet opened fire into the room as Balian and his knights poured into the chamber from the stairs.

Three crossbow bolts crashed into Balian's shield, one piercing right through it to prick but not penetrate his chainmail. Another whizzed by the side of his head so closely he felt the wind. An inch more to the right and he would have been dead. But the Turcopoles in both windows had reloaded and were shooting into the room as the knights advanced. In five minutes, it was over.

Balian stepped over the corpses heaped next to one of the windows and looked out to see what was going on in the harbor. His father's ship had already gone alongside the quay ahead of the *San Valentino*, and Caesarea's ship was gliding to a position ahead of it. The horse transports, too, had come deep into the harbor.

"Knights! Knights!" The shouting came from behind him—in Greek. Barlais' knights!

Balian spun around and ran to the far side of the room. Sure enough, what looked like two dozen mounted and armored men were advancing toward the quay. That was bad enough, but in the distance were at least that many knights again. This was much more than the ten knights the Greeks had warned them about. Furthermore, these men were in full armor with great helms protecting their faces, *and* they carried lances. They would create havoc and kill dozens of men if they rode down the quay just as the men, much less the horses, were disembarking.

Balian ran back to the front of the warehouse and started shouting into the street. "Knights! Barlais' knights are approaching! From the west!" He pointed to the place where the street intersected with the quay.

Not waiting to see if his father understood, he turned and drove his knights back down the stairs and out onto the quay. They spread out across the quay, kneeling behind their shields facing the direction from which Barlais' knights must soon appear. Behind them, Balian could hear agitated shouts of "Hurry up! Over the side! Reinforce Lord Balian!"

Barlais' knights broke out of the side street already at a trot. Their horses slid and scrambled somewhat on the cobbles, but their riders soon collected them and, shouting, spurred them forward. They had only some twenty feet to gain speed, but they came on with their lances pointed downward at the kneeling men. The Turcopoles were firing rapidly, but against the armored knights, their weapons were inadequate. Balian and his knights had no lances to discourage the horses. In five seconds, they were overrun.

A hoof went right through Balian's shield as a horse crashed over him, knocking him backward. He thrust upward with his sword in the same instant. Horse blood and guts gushed over him. The beast staggered and stumbled forward to fall just behind him. The next horse veered sharply away from the horror presented by his comrade, and that saved Balian from being trampled. His shield ruined, and the cobbles drenched in blood and guts, Balian struggled to regain his feet. He kept slipping and falling. Around him horses were screaming, men shouting and weapons clashed. A sense of panic started to envelop him. From his position kneeling on the bloody cobbles, he had lost all sense of the larger picture.

Then suddenly a man had hold of his elbow and offered him a hand. "Here!" Balian looked up at his father in amazement.

"They're all dead, Balian. Karpas attacked from the rear just as they tried to ride over you."

Balian dragged himself to his feet by clutching his father's arm and looked around. The quay was carpeted with equine and human corpses and beyond several knights were milling about.

"Where did Karpas get the horses?" Balian asked in amazement.

"He insisted on taking a dozen on his galley. I protested, but we must be grateful that he did," Beirut answered.

At that moment Karpas himself trotted over, shoving his great helm up and off, to reveal his bright red, sweating face. He was grinning. "Alright, Sir Balian?"

"Yes, thanks to you, my lord!" Balian answered.

Karpas shrugged. "You cleared out the archers. All I did was finish off the knights."

"Is the rest of the town secured?" Beirut asked Karpas.

Karpas nodded. "If there are any Langobards left alive they're laying low and waiting for an opportunity to escape. I saw Greeks hanging one of the men they caught, and another two were just hacked to pieces. I don't think they were very popular."

Beirut gave a short laugh and then turned to his son with a smile. "I'm sorry, Balian, but dressed in horse guts you remind me too much of our dear friend Frederick Hohenstaufen. Let's get you cleaned up. Gastria, at least, is ours." As he spoke, he glanced toward the Templar fortress still brooding over the harbor from the east. It remained eerily silent, but from the highest tower, the Baucent dipped once—as if in salute.

Royal Palace in Nicosia
Early Morning July 11, 1229

The hammering on his door made Henry sit bolt upright in bed and grab for Johnny at the same time.

"Wake up, my lord king! Wake up!" The voice beyond the door was that of Sir Grimbert Bethsan, one of the five baillies.

At the foot of the bed, Gormond stirred with a groggy groan before calling out, "What? What's going on?" He'd been deep in his cups the night before and was clearly disoriented.

Johnny, wide awake beside his king, called out more sharply, "What do you want in the middle of the night, Sir Grimbert?"

"Get dressed at once! Both of you! We're leaving Nicosia!"

"Why?" Henry whispered in alarm, and Johnny shouted the question at the door for him.

"You'll find out soon enough! I'll be back in ten minutes and you better be ready by then, or I'll take you just as you are, even if you're still in your night-shirts and barefoot!"

Johnny was already out of bed. "Gormond!" He angrily shook the servant. "Help the king!" he ordered, while he grabbed his own braies to start dressing.

Harry, the king's dog, jumped up confused and excited. He stood with wagging hind end looking from one human to the other. The humans ignored him.

Gormond, still apparently half-drunk, staggered about trying to find the king's clothes while Johnny got himself dressed in a hurry so he too could help Henry.

"Why are you excited rather than frightened," Henry asked observantly, his eyes fixed on his friend.

Johnny shrugged in embarrassment. "I don't know, it's just…"

"What?"

"It might be my father."

"Your father?"

"Maybe he's come to rescue us."

Henry perked up at once. "Really? Do you think he might come?"

Johnny nodded firmly, but already Bethsan was back. "Are you ready?" he shouted through the door, banging on it again.

Gormond was at last awake enough to open the door. Bethsan was fully armored, and he mustered the boys critically. Noting the king was still barefoot, he ordered Gormond and Johnny to help the king into his shoes, adding, "Use the garderobe too. All of you. We may not stop for hours after we leave here."

"Where are we going, Sir Grimbert?" Henry asked.

"You'll find out. Go on." He nodded at the doorway to the garderobe.

Henry went, followed by Johnny and Gormond. When the later re-emerged,

Sir Grimbert herded the boys out of the door in front of him, but he kicked Harry back when the loyal dog tried to follow his master.

"Don't do that!" Harry protested furiously.

"We have a long journey. He won't be able to keep up."

"I'll carry him if I have to!" Henry countered.

"Don't be childish!" Bethsan snapped.

"There's nothing childish about a man taking his dog with him on a journey!" Johnny defended Henry.

"You call that cur a dog? It looks more like a lady's lap-cover!" Bethsan countered dismissively, but he made no further attempt to stop Harry from coming along. Instead, he started striding down the hall purposefully.

Henry bent to pat Harry for the rude kick he'd received rather than following the baillie. "Good boy," he told the dog.

Bethsan spun about and grabbed Henry under the arm to drag him along the corridor with a growl. "Forget the damn dog! You're coming with me now."

Johnny snatched Harry's leash as he went out the door and clipped it on the dog's collar, then ran after Sir Grimbert and his king.

In the courtyard, a score of horses was being led out of the stables. The riding horses were already saddled, but paniers were being strapped on packhorses, and various bags were being loaded onto them. Johnny caught sight of Barlais standing in one corner and giving orders to some of the palace staff. He was frowning angrily, his lips drawn in a tight, thin line. As he turned back toward the courtyard and caught sight of Johnny, his expression became vicious. "I should put you in the stocks like we did your bastard brothers," he shouted across the courtyard, "you son of traitorous whoreson!"

His father had come! Johnny registered with a surge of excitement. His sense of pride and triumph, however, was tempered by fear. Johnny felt Barlais' hatred across the breadth of the courtyard, and the sheer force of it unsettled him. What had the Ibelins ever done to Barlais to make him hate them so? Even if he had just grievances against Uncle Philip and his father, what had Balian, Baldwin or Hugh—much less Johnny himself—ever done to him?

"Don't blame the boy," Bethsan advised Barlais in a firm voice. "There's nothing to be gained from harming him."

Barlais hissed back inaudibly, and Johnny did not feel very reassured. Sir Grimbert, however, briefly laid a hand on his shoulder and murmured, "Don't worry. I won't let him hurt you. Now mount up."

Johnny hastened to do so. Wherever they were going, Johnny was relieved that Bethsan was to be their escort while Barlais stayed behind.

Bethsan helped Henry mount and then swung up into his own saddle. A moment later Barlais was beside his cousin's stirrup. "Come back as soon as you've delivered the king to St. Hilarion!" Barlais ordered his co-regent.

"St. Hilarion?" Henry asked.

"Yes, we're taking you to safety. You'll be with your sisters there," Sir Grimbert promised.

"While *we*," Barlais added, turning a hate-filled look at Johnny, "will *exterminate* the entire Ibelin family except for your friend Johnny here." Looking directly at Johnny he added, "I'll let you come back to clean your father's and brothers' corpses for the grave! Maybe seeing their bodies gutted, mutilated and drained of blood will teach you that you aren't anything special anymore! I'm going to stomp out your house and crush it under my heel like a scorpion!" He sprayed Johnny with saliva as he spat out this threat, and then ground his heel into the cobbles of the courtyard.

Johnny would have liked to be defiant and say something like, "You'll have to defeat them first!" But he was far too frightened. All he did was nod, swallowing nervously despite himself.

Hospitaller Commandery, Nicosia
July 13, 1229

"Sir Philip? Brother Commander Guillaume requests that you join him on the roof of the keep," The Hospitaller sergeant informed Novare respectfully.

Sir Philip jumped up. His nerves had been deteriorating for weeks. His initial arrest had been so sudden, he had hardly had time to become afraid. His escape from Barlais' planned murder had likewise been so fortuitous that it was only after his rescue that he came to realize how very close he had been to death. One of his servants had died defending his empty house, while his bed, he had been told, had been stabbed more than a dozen times before the assassins realized it was empty. The thought still sent a shiver down his spine.

In the first week here at the Commandery of the Hospital, Novare had busied himself organizing the refugees, digging a second well, establishing a duty roster for the civilian volunteers that had come to aid them, and, of course, drafting his message to his friend Balian. Even the second week had not been so nerve-wracking. It was obvious that it would take three to four days for his letter to reach Beirut, another three or four days for the Lord of Beirut to take counsel with his vassals and family. Starting more than two weeks ago, however, Novare had expected an answer—daily.

Each day in which no answer came had increased the tension a fraction. Each evening he'd found it harder to sleep. Each night he'd woken in the darkness, with his thoughts chasing each other in circles. What if Beirut didn't come? What if he came and was defeated? What if Barlais laid siege to the Hospital Commandery? What if the Hospitaller Commander received orders to turn Novare over to Barlais? What if…

Novare followed the Hospitaller sergeant with the impatience of the nervous. His nerves were not calmed by the sound of shouting coming from the streets. As they made their way up the stairs, Novare tried to get an idea of what was going on outside by peering through each arrow-slit they passed. They were moving too fast for him to make sense of the glimpses he caught.

On the roof of the crenelated "keep," Novare found Sir Guillaume de Teneres, the Commander of the Hospital on Cyprus. He was flanked by two of his knights and a sergeant. All were looking out over the crenulated roof into the city. From here, the noise was more distant and more defused.

Novare crossed the distance to the Hospitallers. "You sent for me, Sir Guillaume?"

"Ah, there you are," Sir Guillaume answered. As Novare joined him behind the parapet, he pointed to the large crowd in the street below them. Novare looked intently, trying to make sense of what was happening. There were about a dozen Imperial mercenaries who were shouting at people and gesturing. Most of the people, however, were apparently civilians without any kind of livery. They were milling about rather pointlessly… or some of them were. Others were starting to form up into rough clusters. The Langobards appeared to be inspecting the weapons and protective clothing of the latter.

"They've called up the militia," Sir Guillaume commented.

"The baillies?" Novare asked—and then felt stupid as Sir Guillaume asked back "Who else?"

"Do we know why?" Novare asked next.

"Not 100%, but rumors are flying thick and fast that the Ibelins have landed at Gastria with between 100 and 10,000 men."

"That's a rather large range," Novare observed.

The Hospitaller smiled and shrugged. "Such are rumors. Our most reliable sources—or should I say the rumors that sound most reasonable—is that the Ibelins have a couple thousand men at most, while the baillies have pulled together a force close to 10,000 strong."

"Counting that rabble down there?"

"Exactly. The local militia is not likely to stand and fight for the baillies. Their own knights and sergeants combined with the Imperial mercenaries, on the other hand, are strongly committed to confronting the Ibelins. The Archbishop of Nicosia is determined to ride out this morning to make peace between the parties. I and my brother from the Temple will join him in that attempt, but, I confess, I am doubtful of the outcome. Beirut sent word that he intended no violence and that he and his men came only to reclaim their own lands and rights. The baillies responded by calling upon all able-bodied men of the kingdom to take up arms against them. Not a promising start to reconciliation."

After a pause for Novare to absorb this news, Sir Guillaume continued, "I'm leaving now to join the Archbishop. I just thought you would want to know—and spread the word among the ladies."

Novare nodded absently, muttering, "God be with you," while his attention remained focused on the men still mustering in the street below. He was mentally trying to calculate just how many men Beirut could reasonably have brought with him, but he didn't like the answer he came up with. More than 250 knights seemed unlikely, and maybe that many Turcopoles, and double both in infantry. Compared to what the baillies could bring to bear if they issued the *arrière ban* it was much too little. The Ibelins were going to be facing forces at least twice, possibly thrice, their own, no matter how Novare calculated.

"And your husband is with the Ibelins?" Cecilia asked cautiously. She had served Eschiva for less than three months, and although she was devoted to her mistress and felt at ease with her, Eschiva's husband remained a mystery. Eschiva almost never spoke of him at all.

When they had lodged with the Archbishop, Eschiva had been focused on her illumination and Cecilia had not wanted to pry. They had talked mostly about books, enjoying access to the Archbishop's library and shopping together for paints, inks, parchment, papyrus, and quills. Since their flight to the Hospital, however, Eschiva's focus had turned to needlework as the women tried to support their hosts as best they could, repairing the robes and surcoats of the brothers, the sheets of the infirmary, and even making bandages. Eschiva had set herself the task of repairing a much-damaged alter cloth, and Cecilia had helped her with that.

The news of the landing of the Ibelins, however, had agitated Eschiva. She had pricked herself several times and made mistakes that she needed to tear out again. At last, she gave up all pretense of sewing, set the altar cloth aside and started pacing the sacristy.

"My husband?" Eschiva asked, startled out of her thoughts. "Did you say something about my husband?"

"Yes. You seem so upset. I asked if you thought he might be with the Ibelins."

"I doubt it. He is not affiliated with them in any way."

"Oh, I see," Cecilia answered, more bewildered than ever.

"The Ibelins are my cousins," Eschiva tried to explain. "Remember how I told you about fleeing the Emperor's harem?"

Cecilia nodded vigorously. She loved the story. It had been such a grand adventure! So much more interesting than her secluded life in her father's house. She had been cosseted and confined, almost as much as the harem slaves.

"Remember how I returned aboard your husband's ship?"

Cecilia nodded more vigorously still. That had been the most magical part of the story—that it included her beloved Maurizio, and that he had told Eschiva that he wanted to marry his bride on Calypso's island. If only they had! If only they had been imprisoned there forever together.

"Maurizo's ship had been charted by my cousin Sir Balian, the Lord of Beirut's eldest son."

"Oh!" Cecilia exclaimed with new interest. "The one who seduced the daughter of his father's steward?" At home in Acre, gossip about the nobility had been a favorite pastime of the Genoese women—almost as popular as gossip about their own community.

"Yes," Eschiva conceded rather wearily. She was almost as tired of hearing about this as Balian was. Could no one forget a youthful indiscretion at that age of eighteen? "But that was long before we met," she told Cecilia firmly. "I have never known him to be otherwise than honorable and chivalrous."

Cecilia nodded hastily, reading her lady's mood correctly: Sir Balian was, for whatever reason, special to her.

"Furthermore," Eschiva tried to explain, "the Lord of Beirut received me courteously and generously, while his daughter and I soon became fast friends. It was Bella d'Ibelin more than anyone who helped me overcome my grief for Queen Yolanda."

"But surely no lady is with this army?" Cecilia asked, uncomprehending.

"No, of course not, but it would break Bella's heart to lose any one of her brothers, much less her father."

Cecilia nodded contritely. "Of course!" she agreed, and yet…. She looked again at her lady. There was much more to this than Eschiva was telling her. She just didn't know how to ask about it. "Are you afraid this war will delay your husband's return?"

Eschiva smiled faintly. "You have been an excellent companion, Cecilia.

You've made my life so much more pleasant and have cheered me almost as much as Bella did." She paused. "I would *like* to trust you completely."

"Please do, my lady!" Cecilia begged. Life had turned so interesting since she had escaped Saluto and joined Eschiva. She had discovered not only Cyprus, but a new world of illumination, politics and, well, knights in shining armor. But the most important aspect of her new life was having a friend, and friends did not have secrets from one another.

Eschiva lowered her voice and stepped closer to Cecilia, touching her forearm very lightly as she explained. "Unlike you and Maurizio, my husband Gerard and I did not *want* to marry one another and, frankly, do not like one another. I would not be at all upset if I never saw him ever again as long as I live."

Cecilia gazed at her, surprised but not shocked. All her childhood friends from St. Anne's had married men of their parents' choosing without much say in the matter. Some of those marriages had worked out, but some had not. Cecilia had been acutely aware of how lucky she had been to marry the man she adored most in the world. She had felt so blessed, as if all the saints of heaven had smiled down on her—until, of course, he was taken away.

"It must seem very cruel of God," Eschiva spoke into her thoughts, "that he took away your Maurizio and left me with Gerard."

Cecilia looked down at her hands and dared not answer. She was ashamed of how often she cried out bitterly to Christ, demanding to know why he had taken Maurizio and her father, why he had left her in the clutches of Sanuto, indeed, why he hated her?

She heard Eschiva sigh. "Soon I may share your feelings, Cecilia, because the soul I love most in the world—though he is neither my husband nor my lover—may be called to God within the next 24 hours. And the worst of it, Cecilia, is that if he dies it will be because I begged him to come help us. I am the reason he is in danger, and, if God is as cruel to me as he was to you, I could be the cause of his injury—or death."

Twenty-Five
The Battle of Nicosia

Nicosia, Cyprus
July 14, 1229

"What is that stupid crest Barlais has on his helmet?" Balian asked his squire irritably as he took up his position at the head of the Ibelin Turcopoles. Rob had worked diligently to clean Balian's surcoat and gambeson of horse blood from Gastria; from a distance, it was impossible to see the stains and hasty repairs. The exposed chainmail on his arms, legs and the coif gleamed, and the silk of both his surcoat and his horse's trapper fluttered in the strong west wind. However, because the Lord of Beirut scoffed at such "ostentation," none of the Ibelins wore crests on their great helms. Once their faces were hidden by their great helms, they could be identified only by the red crosses on their marigold surcoats and trappers, or the Ibelin banner carried on a squire's upright lance. Beside Balian, Rob held the banner on his lance and it streamed out in the fresh west breeze, proudly displaying the splayed, red cross on a marigold field.

"All five of the baillies are wearing them," Rob answered his lord's question. "It's supposed to symbolize their authority. Probably some sort of Imperial device."

Balian nodded acknowledgment with an inward grimace. Belonging to the fourth generation of Ibelin to fight in Outremer, Balian had been raised on the legends of his forefathers fighting against overwhelming odds. But *they* had been fighting Saracens, men who wore lighter-weight armor, rode fleeter but smaller and less powerful horses and used more delicate swords. Today he, along with his father, brothers, cousins, and followers, faced an army led by knights equipped at least as well as they were themselves. Barlais might be small and Gibelet a lightweight, but Cheneché, Rivet, and particularly Sir Grimbert de Bethsan were strong men with solid reputations at arms. Furthermore, the baillies were outfitted with the best that money could buy: chainmail that encased their limbs from toe to fingertip and head. The latter were further protected by not only the cervellière over their skulls but the heavy "great-helms" that completely encased the head and face.

The baillies were supported by hundreds of knights, all of them nearly as well equipped as the baillies—or the Ibelins—themselves. Perhaps most intimidating, while the Cypriot infantry was a sorry lot, the Imperial mercenaries formed a solid block of highly disciplined and well-trained troops.

Beirut had given Sir Anceau, Lord of Karpas, the dubious honor of "neutralizing" the mercenary Langobards, while tasking Balian, as commander of the Turcopoles, to take on the Cypriot levees. The Lord of Beirut, his sons Baldwin and Hugh, and the Lord of Caesarea, meanwhile formed the center of the Ibelin line, directly opposite the five baillies; the leaders on both sides were supported and surrounded by their respective household knights and vassals.

The nearly 300 knights under the Ibelin banner were concentrated at the center of their host directly opposite the roughly 500 knights of the baillies. The Langobards had taken up a position on a slight rise to the right of the enemy cavalry, and the Turcopoles and Cypriot infantry clustered on the left wing of the baillies' host, blocking the road to Nicosia. The two hosts were separated by an open, plowed field roughly 150 yards wide.

After watching the enemy deploy, Beirut made his own dispositions. He tasked Balian with first clearing the road to Nicosia by putting the Cypriot infantry and Turcopoles to flight, and then circling around behind the baillies to cut off their retreat toward the mountains. "What we don't want," Beirut reminded his commanders solemnly, "is for the baillies to flee to the mountain castles. We must try to pin them down and defeat them here and now. Otherwise, this war could drag on forever—to everyone's impoverishment. It is tragic enough that we are about to face our fellow Christians in mortal combat; I do not wish to see this conflict prolonged a day more than necessary."

"Amen!" Caesarea answered, echoed soberly by the others.

Balian agreed with those sentiments but he was struggling with conflicting feelings nonetheless. On the one hand, his father had entrusted him with a strategically vital task. On the other hand, it meant he was not confronting their enemies head-on. His father, he suspected, was still protecting him, trying to keep him from the point of greatest danger. His father, he thought, was afraid that the clash with other knights might be too much for his tortured body.

Balian did not want to be protected; he wanted to prove he was ready to take on their enemies. He wanted, deep down in his visceral and uncivilized core, to personally smite Barlais down. He wanted—to hell with 'turning the other cheek'— to personally bash his hilt into Barlais' head, neck, and throat for each and every one of the blows Barlais had inflicted while he'd stood helplessly in the stocks.

Instead, he was to face the Cypriot levees and Turcopoles. These men were not his enemies. They were not the men who had challenged Uncle Philip's authority, not the men who had tried to seize power illegally. These were not the men who tried to murder honest knights in ambushes, nor the men who had taxed exorbitantly and terrorized women and children. They were not the men who had whispered poison about the Ibelins into the Holy Roman Emperor's ear, nor the men who had ensured he and Baldwin were mishandled as hostages. The Cypriots were nothing but frightened men called up to defend something they did not want in the first place.

"Sir Solomon!" Balian gently nudged his bay stallion Gebremariam with a spurred heel behind the girth and faced his deputy. "We don't really want to kill the Cypriots if we can avoid it, just put them to flight."

Sir Solomon nodded.

"At the signal, we'll charge them, but order the men to fire high or low, enough to impress upon them our numbers, but not enough to do much damage."

Sir Solomon grunted and countered. "We'll have to kill a few to make them see the error of their ways."

"Fair enough," Balian agreed. "I'm certainly not going to be able to soften my first lance thrust, but make sure the men understand that our objective is to put them to flight, not slaughter them. Once they break, I don't want a massacre."

Sir Solomon nodded and trotted along the line of his mounted archers to deliver the orders. Balian watched him, trying to judge the reaction of the Turcopoles, but he was soon distracted by a shout from his right. The Langobards had opened fire and Karpas' infantry immediately crouched down behind their shields. With the infantry pinned down, the enemy center burst out of their position, their banners streaming from their upright lances.

Beirut answered by lowering his lance and spurring forward. Sirs Baldwin and Hugh flanked him, so close at his stirrups they were like a single, twelve-legged horse. Ibelin's knights, on the other hand, spread out a little to take on individual opponents among the knights storming toward them. Caesarea with his son and knights formed the second fist of cavalry.

For a moment the sheer beauty of two strong hosts of gaily outfitted chivalry sprinting towards each other in the morning sunlight paralyzed Balian. The horses were racing each other with stretched-out necks and laid back ears, their curried coats gleaming in the sunlight. Surcoats and trappers fluttered, banners streamed, and sunlight glinted on helmets and lance tips. Here and there the sun caught on the bands of metal reinforcing the vertical front and horizontal eye-pieces of the helms; an ephemeral cross of golden light would flash then fade. Nothing yet was soiled with dust, mud, or blood. Nothing yet was shattered, severed or gutted. The only sound was the thundering of hooves, not the cries of dying men or wounded horses.

Balian looked away, hauled his helmet over his cervellière, and shouted to his men to take up their weapons. A second later, with a simple call of "Now," he asked Gebremariam for a canter from a standstill. As the eager destrier sprinted forward, willingly gaining speed, Balian lowered his head so he had the Cypriot infantry, kneeling behind their shields, in the rectangular sights of his great helm. As his stallion plunged over the plowed field, devouring the distance with his powerful strikes, Balian lowered his lance. Left and right of him, the Turcopoles were firing their bows. Their arrows landed both around and amidst the enemy infantry.

Soon the Cypriots were screaming advice or orders at one another. Balian sensed a softening of the line even before the first collision, but the Cypriots did not actually break and run.

Balian's lance went through an infantry shield, and the man behind it screamed in pain. Balian had no time to note if the wound was mortal. He pulled the lance up and reused it, this time with a downward thrust that went deep into a man's shoulder. As the man fell forward, the lance tip broke off, still embedded in the victim. Dropping his hold of the butt-end, Balian drew his sword and started to slash it down on men who had converged on him. Gebremariam was defending himself with his teeth and his front-hooves well enough for most of the foot-soldiers to stay clear of the front of him. Instead, they concentrated on his sides. Balian swung his sword from one side to the other and back again. The sword easily cleaved through the kettle-helms of the infantry, and, with one backhand stroke, he decapitated a man with a pike who threatened Gebremariam's haunches. Meanwhile, several archers stood up and tried to shoot at him from a half-dozen yards away, but they were almost instantly pierced by multiple arrows shot by Balian's Turcopoles.

These vicious deaths at the front of the infantry line undermined the morale of the men behind. Somewhere at the back, unseen by Balian, a man ran away. Once the first man fled, it was easier for the second and third. The infantry started to unravel.

Balian could feel the resistance give. As he nudged Gebremariam forward with his knees and calves, he found he advanced against mush rather than resistance. Soon, men were streaming back toward Nicosia. Some were so frantic that the stronger knocked aside the weaker, and the faster overtook the slower. Around Balian, men were no longer attacking but cowering behind shields to avoid the bite of his sword. The Turcopoles surged up around him. Only a few were still firing. Most had arrows fitted in their bows but held them.

Balian glanced toward the main battlefield on his right. The beauty of a few minutes earlier had been shattered. There was nothing but chaos. The hosts were so completely intermingled that the entire field was nothing but a writhing mass of humans and horses. It resembled a barrel full of fishes viciously trying to tear each other apart. Horses were rearing up, whinnying frantically as they twisted and turned around each other. Men were hacking, slashing, thrusting and hammering with their weapons. With each hoof fall, the parched soil of the field was stirred up further. Like morning mist, the dust was rising upwards and obscuring the legs of horses and riders. They started to look as if they floated upon the dirty air, as if they were swimming in smoke.

A shout drew Balian's attention back to his own sector. Sir Solomon was pointing, and he realized that Cypriots were starting to reform farther up the road. There was a stone wall on either side of the road, some sort of property boundary; the Cypriots were spreading out behind it. Furious at himself for not anticipating this, Balian spurred forward roaring, "Bloody bastards!"

They plunged down the road, scattering the men still fleeing. Balian had to lift his shield to deflect arrows coming toward him. Blinded by his own shield, he had to trust Gebremariam to keep on course for the gap in the wall.

Beside him, some of the Turcopoles leaned low over the necks of their horses and charged directly at the wall. They were wearing only leather or quilted armor and they had trained as much for rapid reconnaissance as combat. A half-dozen of them cleared the wall (although two of the horses refused, dumping one rider), and within seconds they were killing the Cypriots from the rear.

For a second time, Cypriot morale broke and men started running away again. Balian ordered Sir Solomon and half the Turcopoles to kill or take the surrender of the Cypriots still defending the wall, and with the rest, he set off in pursuit. His objective was to scatter these men as widely as possible to make it impossible for them to regroup. To this end, he ordered his Turcopoles to spread out, chasing after every cluster of men that tried to cut across the open countryside. He continued down the road, overtaking men and frightening them into the ditches until he had passed the man who had run farthest. Then he turned around and started back up the road, collecting his men to him as he did so. Rob was still beside him, the Ibelin banner on his upright and unused lance.

At the stone wall, Balian drew up to give Gebremariam a breather and to take stock of the situation. On the main battlefield, the dust continued to rise, obscuring all but the heads of the horses and the heads and torsos of the riders. His father's banner was still upright, but he could not find Caesarea's. That wasn't good, but might simply be the dust. More significantly, it looked as if Gibelet's banner was moving northwards. That was exactly what his father had feared. He'd known that if things got too hot, the baillies would try to slip away so they could entrench themselves in the impregnable castles of St. Hilarion, Buffavento and Kantara.

"There!" He pointed to Sir Solomon as the older knight trotted over. "Gibelet is trying to escape to the north." Glancing at his still greatly dispersed troop of Turcopoles, Balian thought some had taken the notion of pursuit to extremes—at least that was how it seemed now that he needed them back.

Turning to Rob, who had come up beside him and removed his helmet to get a drink of water, Balian ordered, "Sound recall!" Rob hastily replaced his canteen and took the horn tied to his pommel and put it to his lips. While he sounded the recall, Balian removed his own helmet, laid it on his lap, and uncorked his canteen to drink deeply while he had the chance.

As he replaced the cork in his canteen, his eyes scanned the panorama. His Turcopoles were converging on him, and the Cypriots showed no sign of reforming. However, now it looked as if Cheneché's banner was also moving away from the battle, toward the east. He might be making for Kantara.

"Come on! Hurry!" Balian shouted while signaling angrily to some of the men still straggling in. He pulled his helmet back on his head. Pointing across an open field, he indicated their next objective: beyond the dust-choked battle-field lay the east-west road that followed the base of the mountain range.

Beirut could hardly swallow. His eyes were streaming tears. His lungs tried to repel the dust dragged in by his heavy breaths. Beirut could only cling to the pommel until the coughing ended, grateful that for the moment no one was pressing in on him.

Yet the battle was far over. A little farther afield, men were still struggling with one another. The clang of weapons, the shouts and whinnies and screams still reached him. They were just, for the moment, a little farther away than they had been moments before.

Early in the battle, Beirut had been separated from his sons. He'd seen Hugh veer left to intercept a man with a lance aimed at his father, while Baldwin had been brought to a screeching halt by a knight whose attack flung Baldwin's favorite white stallion onto his haunches.

As his breathing eased, Beirut looked around to find himself entirely alone. He could see neither his sons nor his brother-in-law nor any of his household knights. What he did see was a man with an open-faced helmet bearing down on him from the left with a barbed mace in his hand. Beirut had the utmost respect for such a weapon, particularly when at the end of a stout, two-foot pole wielded by a man with a grim, determined expression. Beirut thought he had seen the man somewhere before but couldn't place him. Nor did it matter in face of his hostile intentions.

Man and horse were nearly upon him. The rider stood in his stirrups and raised his arm over his head to better smash his weapon down on the crown of Beirut's head. At this range, Beirut could see blood and remnants of brain between the vicious spikes. Neither his helm nor cervellière would offer him protection against those spikes.

Beirut had only seconds to prevent the blow. Everything depended on perfect timing and aim. He kept his horse still with his legs and steady pressure on the reins in his left hand. He had been sitting with his sword still in his right hand, his forearm resting on the pommel. Just before the blow fell, he straightened, twisted at the waist and swung his sword forward into his attacker's exposed face. The sword point found the other man's open mouth as he screamed a curse and cut straight through the back of his skull to jar against the inside of the helmet.

In the same instant, however, the attacking horse pushed Beirut's stallion staggering sideways. Both horses broke under their riders, as they tumbled into a ditch neither horses nor riders had seen in the swirling dust. Beirut was flung from the saddle clear over the corpse of his dead opponent and landed heavily on his back. The wind was knocked from his lungs and his vision dimmed. He tried to lift himself, but the world only tilted about him and then faded into blackness.

"He's alive! Come quick!" The shouts so close brought Beirut back into the world. Someone had removed his great helm, and his head was cushioned in someone's lap. He was surrounded by strangers, but by the way, they were taking care of him he knew they were his men—sergeants in linen aketons and gambesons with kettle-helms on their head.

"Are you injured, my lord?" The sergeant leaning over him asked anxiously.

"I don't think so. Just winded," Beirut answered honestly.

"Then you must get up, my lord! We need to get to shelter! Quick!"

Still dizzy and dazed, Beirut took the offered hand and was grateful for the sergeant's strength in pulling him to his feet. Standing, he tried to orient himself. Just a couple yards to his right lay the body of his destrier, his neck broken by the horse that had fallen on top of him. The latter was still alive but had broken both front legs and was flailing about in agony. His rider's corpse lay watering the plowed field with his blood. To his other side, a dozen archers had set up a protective barrier of shields. Beyond them, some fourteen or fifteen knights wearing the devices of the baillies were milling about casting glances in Beirut's direction.

At the sight of Beirut staggering to his feet, the knights started shouting to one another and within seconds had started to form up for a charge. The sergeants who had helped him to his feet, however, were already half-dragging, half-shoving him toward a walled enclosure emerging from the settling dust.

The wall was about four feet high, much too high to leap or even climb over in his dazed and winded state. There was a gate, however, and to Beirut's wonder, it gave way before them. He and the sergeants fell into the courtyard of what turned out to be a church. The archers who had been covering them fired a last volley and then made a dash for the door as well. The last of the sergeants slammed the gate shut and bolted it behind him.

Beirut looked about himself, trying to assess whether this was a sanctuary or a trap. There appeared only one way in, the gate through which they'd entered, which meant they had no escape. However, the side of the church was cracked and someone had started to build scaffolding to repair it. Staves of wood were laying in a heap. "Grab those and point them over the top of the wall!" Beirut ordered the sergeants, just as the charge of pursuing knights broke on the walls of the enclosure and surged around it looking for a second entrance.

Although the score of sergeants with him quickly improvised platforms so the archers could fire over the wall, the latter were rapidly running out of ammunition. Furthermore, some of the pursuing knights still had lances, and they started to use these like pikes, stabbing with them over the wall at the archers. For the moment, these tactics proved ineffective, but Beirut was acutely aware that they were surrounded in a small enclosure without water, food, or additional weapons. A moment later he heard a distinctive chink come from the beyond the wall, and he realized that baillies' knights were using their swords, daggers, and axes to smash the plaster and break open the stone wall itself. It was just a matter of time before they broke in and slaughtered them all.

The order to stop the baillies from reaching the castles had seemed reasonable enough when given, but Balian and his lightly armed Turcopoles soon found themselves facing heavily armored knights. These broke out of the cloud of dust in groups of four or five. If Balian charged them, they simply changed direction and broke through the line of Turcopoles to his left or right. The Turcopole's arrows were useless against the armored knights unless at a range that these men knew well enough to avoid. Balian felt helpless and frustrated. His only solace was that, so far, none of the fleeing knights had been one of the remaining three baillies. These were evidently still engaged in the core battle that remained shrouded in dust.

Meanwhile, the sun had reached its zenith and the air was heavy with heat as well as dust. Balian paused to drink his canteen to the dregs; the water was hot. Rob shouted to him and pointed. Coming out of the dust cloud was a large cluster of knights. As they emerged into the cleaner air, Balian made out the trappers of several of their vassals and then, the dirty marigold with red crosses of Ibelin itself. His brothers Baldwin and Hugh were riding straight toward him. Balian turned to trot towards them. As they met, they all shouted the same question at one another: "Where's Father?"

"We thought you were he!" Hugh answered, pointing to the banner fluttering from Rob's lance.

"That's why we brought as many knights as we could!" Baldwin explained. As it sank in that he'd only joined up with Balian and the Turcopoles he exclaimed, "Jesus God!" and wrenched his exhausted stallion around to look back at the battlefield still lost in dust.

More and more of the Ibelin knights were rallying around Balian's standard, riding up alone or in twos or threes. They cantered out of the dust and then slowed to a trot until they joined the others clustered around the three Ibelin brothers. Clearly, Beirut's standard was down, and Caesarea's too.

Although Cheneché and Gibelet had both fled the field, Barlais, Bethsan, and Rivet were evidently still fighting bitterly. Balian would never understand why they were so loyal to the weasel, but they had proved they were many times before this and were doing so again today. Whether his father was killed, injured or simply hard-pressed, Balian concluded he had to engage the baillies immediately. He had here over two score of knights, many still with their squires. This force, although small, would be able to deliver a powerful punch at this late stage in the battle.

"Take a moment to drink!" Balian called out to the knights collecting around him, before turning to his brothers to ask when and where they had last seen their father. The answers were worthless.

The knights around Balian removed their helmets to drink. Several dismounted to relieve themselves, while others tightened loosened girths, made hasty repairs to broken reins or simply removed their gauntlets to wipe sweat from their hands on the skirts of their surcoats.

Balian gave them time. No matter how desperate the situation, they would be more effective for quenching their thirst and catching their breath first—particularly the horses, all of whom were drooping with exhaustion and encrusted in dust. Meanwhile, he was trying to see something—anything—that might indicate where Barlais was. If his father was down, whether injured or killed, it was Barlais' fault. Balian was determined to take his revenge.

As the last man who had dismounted hauled himself back into the saddle, Balian raised his voice to be heard by all of them. "We'll attack from the north in the hope that we can drive them south—away from the castles. Better that they flee to Famagusta or Lanarka to take ship never to return! Ready?"

The men around him muttered, "Aye" or nodded as they pulled their helmets back on. Only Baldwin quibbled with his brother's leadership, asking, "Wouldn't it be better to attack from the east?"

"No," Balian answered sharply, irritated by Baldwin questioning him at a time like this. He pulled his own helmet over his head and took the last lance Rob had with him into his hand. Then he guided his horse through the other knights to lead them at a trot to a point more or less due north of the on-going battle.

As he turned toward the battlefield, he asked Gebremariam for a canter and lowered his lance. The men around him shouted "Ibelin! Ibelin!" and likewise pressed their weary horses into a canter for a final charge.

Gebremariam was far from finished. The whinnies of other stallions and the clang of weapons awakened his defensive instincts. Balian could feel him tensing in anticipation.

Then they plunged into the dust and instantly the atmosphere changed. Because the dust blocked out the sun, it was like being in a heavy sea-fog. Balian could feel the heat overhead, yet see at most ten feet ahead. He was shocked by the number of corpses, both human and equine, littering the field. The dead and dying made it impossible to ride in a straight line. Gebremariam had to dodge the bodies, leaping now left and now right, changing legs on the fly with dexterity, but foiling Balian's ability to pick a target and bear down on him.

Despite that, Balian rapidly recognized that they were fast approaching a gaggle of knights besieging a small cluster of men fighting desperately on foot. The knights on foot were defending themselves behind the bodies of their horses and their comrades. With a flicker of horror, Balian recognized his cousin Walter among the men fighting on foot. The jolt of recognition made him close his legs, and Gebremariam, insulted and angry, lunged forward. Balian thrust his lance between the shoulder blades of a knight trying to kill his cousin and then flung aside the butt to grab his sword and drive it down on the head of another assailant.

Yet, it was not so much the effectiveness of his arms as the shock of an Ibelin counterattack that shattered the resolve of the baillies' men. As the men beleaguering the younger Caesarea and his companions registered that some forty knights under the Ibelin banner had just returned to the fight, they broke and ran. Balian caught a glimpse of Barlais hauling his horse around and hammering the poor beast with his spurred heels. He was at least ten feet away, almost obscured by the dust, but Balian was absolutely certain it was Barlais in his ridiculous crest and his gold-trimmed helmet.

Instantly, Balian was after him. Barlais was flailing his horse and screaming curses. His standard-bearer clung to his flank and a handful of his knights rushed to surround him protectively. Balian's pursuit was hampered by the corpses between them. As Gebremariam shied sideways, Balian for a second lost his seat and was within a fraction of falling to the ground. He looked down onto the broken and blood-soaked body of his uncle of Caesarea, and his heart twisted. Grimly gripping Gebremariam's mane, he pulled himself upright again and dug his spurs into the stallion's flanks. In those precious seconds, Barlais had increased his lead and was lost from sight.

Balian could only charge blindly in the direction Barlais had disappeared. Around him, other men were fleeing, shouting to one another to disengage, to retreat. Spreading the word with the ring of panic was the repeated shout of "Ibelin! Ibelin!" His own knights were shouting the same word with triumph.

Guided more by instinct than intellect, and driven forward by emotion rather than reason, Balian pursued the indistinct shadows that he believed to be Barlais and his knights. He had no sense of direction anymore, nor time. One minute Barlais seemed almost within grasp, the next to be escaping. Quite abruptly Balian felt a blast of wind. It was cooling and it parted the dust enough for him to clearly see his quarry—an enticing twenty feet ahead of him.

Balian demanded more speed of Gebremariam. The stallion protested by bucking angrily instead. That gave Barlais another five feet. Worse, his standard-bearer peeled away and turned to face Balian. Balian closed with him at full tilt, his sword raised and ready for a downward stroke at the vulnerable juncture of head and shoulder.

Their horses collided, Gebremariam at a furious gallop. Balian brought his sword down swift, hard and deep. Only at that moment, at close range, did Balian register that Barlais' standard-bearer was a massively built man on a horse a hand taller than Gebremariam. Together they formed an immovable object. Even as Balian's sword cut through the sinews of his opponent's neck, Gebremariam with a sharp, shocked whiney staggered, lost his balance and went crashing down onto his left side. Balian felt the horse rolling left and kicked his foot free of the stirrup to fling himself to the right. Then as his knee hit the soft dirt of the plowed field, he staggered upright, his sword still in his hand.

Barlais' standard-bearer was still in the saddle, but swaying dangerously as his horse spun about to follow the others escaping eastward. Barlais had not even slowed down. Balian was left helpless in the dust kicked up by his horse's heels.

Other Ibelin knights surged up around Balian. Hugh was there, anxiously asking if Balian was alright. Baldwin was shouting, "They're making for Nicosia! Cut them off!"

But it was hopeless. The road to Nicosia was open, and Ibelin's knights and horses were utterly exhausted. They were swaying on their feet, dripping sweat if not blood. They had won the battle, but by no means the war. The baillies had all managed to survive to fight another day.

It was mid-afternoon before a squire found Balian and excitedly announced they had found his father alive and uninjured. Balian at once grabbed Rob's horse, Gebremariam being too badly bruised and a little lame from his fall, and galloped to the churchyard. He found not just his father and the score of sergeants and archers who had defended him, but also the Lord of Karpas. The latter was covered with cuts and bruises, and his hands were so strained from combat that he could no longer flex them. His horse was in even worse condition.

Balian flung himself down from Rob's horse and embraced his father. "Thank God you're alive!"

"I was well defended," Beirut answered with a nod to Sir Anceau and the archers. "These good sergeants found me unconscious after my horse landed in a ditch."

"After your father cut a man's head in half!" one of the archers called out proudly.

Beirut gave the archer a brief smile and nod. "They brought me here just in time before fifteen of Barlais' knights set upon us. We were soon out of arrows and had nothing but building staves to defend ourselves. You can see there," he pointed out the badly damaged wall, "how they were breaking down the wall. When my lord of Karpas arrived at a gallop, he took on all fifteen knights at once!" His admiration for the Lord of Karpas was obvious.

Sir Anceau answered with a grin, tossing to Balian, "I couldn't have held them much longer. It was your timely arrival with a strong body of knights behind you that made them break off and run for it."

"Yes," his father agreed. "That was decisive. You'll have to tell me where you got so many knights!"

"They rallied to my banner, since yours was down," Balian explained with a shrug. "But we feared you were killed, my lord! Prisoners told us Barlais and Cheneché each detailed twelve of their knights to kill you." Balian was outraged by this and his voice so raw with rage that Beirut laid a hand on his shoulder to calm him.

"They failed, Balian, that is the important thing."

"It's not honorable!" Balian countered. "A nobleman doesn't set *two dozen* men on a single knight! No *knight* should let *other* men fight his battles! It's cowardly—"

"You're right, Balian," Beirut interrupted him in a calming voice. "You're right and you're the better man, but Barlais is what he is, and we will have to face him again—unless you bring me the good news that he is dead?"

"No," Balian admitted, his face hardening with bitterness. "I failed. I almost caught up to him, but my horse fell when I struck down his standard bearer."

Beirut caught his breath and searched his son's face. "You're alright?"

"I've taken worse falls," Balian answered honestly.

At that moment, Baldwin rode up on his reserve horse and likewise vaulted down to embrace his father. "Thank God you are alright, Father!" he echoed Balian's greeting. "We heard Barlais detailed a dozen knights to kill you!"

"Yes, I survived thanks to these good sergeants and Sir Anceau," Beirut repeated before commenting perceptively, "You do not look like a man bringing good news. Tell me the worst."

Baldwin glanced at Balian, who shook his head to say he had not reported yet. Baldwin took a deep breath. "We have sustained serious losses."

Beirut nodded, looking back at the field where the dust had settled sufficiently to see that it was carpeted with corpses. "Go on."

"We're still collecting the dead," Baldwin continued cautiously, "but I'm going to guess we lost half or more of the horses we brought. The Turcopoles lost almost none of theirs, but the destriers have been decimated. We will not be able to undertake any mounted operation of scale until we have found replacements."

"What are you trying *not* to tell me, Baldwin?"

Baldwin took another deep breath and again glanced at Balian, this time reproachfully, as if he thought his elder brother should have broken the news. "It's Uncle Walter."

Beirut waited, looked from one son to the other, but they both looked down. "Are you saying he is dead?"

They nodded in unison.

Beirut dropped to his knees as if someone had pushed him. Then he bent his head, closed his eyes and crossed himself. As he prayed silently, his sons slowly got to their knees beside him, and Sir Anceau likewise eased himself down. The sergeants bowed their heads respectfully.

Only after several minutes did Beirut put his hand on Balian's shoulder and push himself back onto his feet. He turned to help Sir Anceau up, and then faced his sons. "His son?"

"We arrived in time to extricate him," Baldwin answered. "He and the remaining knights of Caesarea were all unhorsed and fighting on foot around Uncle Walter's corpse. Barlais was leading the attack, but we took them from behind and they broke. That's when Balian took after Barlais and nearly caught him, but after Barlais' standard-bearer broke Balian's pursuit, they escaped. Or most of them did. We've taken maybe two score prisoners, and they left at least as many dead on the field as we did. Maybe more."

"I presume Hugh is well or you two wouldn't be here talking to me so normally?" Beirut asked cautiously, looking from one son to the other.

"Yes, he's fine. That is, he took a sword thrust to his upper arm late in the battle, but it's been cleaned and bound. He should recover," Balian answered.

"What else should I know?" Beirut asked looking from one to the other.

Baldwin looked at Balian and then announced, "All five baillies survived. As far as we can tell, they made first for Nicosia but did not stop there. We assume that they will try to reach the castles and barricade themselves there while sending to the Emperor for help."

Beirut nodded. He expected nothing different. They had risked a battle here and paid a high price for half a victory. The war as not over. It had only begun.

Chapter Twenty-Six
Aftershocks of a Battle

Nicosia, Cyprus
July 14, 1229

IT WAS SHORTLY BEFORE NOON WHEN the first deserters started running through the streets of Nicosia. The men were clearly panicked and ashamed. They kept their heads down, eyes averted, and scuttled along the side-streets, seeking refuge with friends and relatives. They pounded angrily on doors or scrambled over walls to hide away, to get out of sight.

They were followed by the walking wounded, clusters of men holding each other up. Many of these came straight to the Hospital expecting treatment. The Hospitaller brothers set up an emergency ward to deal with them, and Novare offered to help so that he could learn more about the battle they had escaped. The Hospitaller physician politely but pointedly told him to get out of the way.

Several of the women intercepted Novare as he came out of the improvised emergency ward to see what he'd learned, but he could only shake his head. "They're saying the Ibelins have won a decisive victory, but early deserters can't be trusted. They generally make up facts to justify their behavior."

The women turned away anxiously speculating among themselves, while Novare climbed back to the roof of the keep to watch for more indications of what had happened.

After a lull of several hours, a new commotion filled the streets. This time it was horsemen, knights, who were hurrying through the streets. They were too tired to canter, their trappers were torn and dust-encrusted, and stained with sweat and blood. The riders too were the worse for wear and battle-weary. Many had dented, scratched and torn armor. Several were nursing wounds, but none stopped at the Hospital. They pressed on through the town. Although Novare was not able to positively identify any of these knights as Barlais, Cheneché or one of the other baillies, he saw men with Barlais' colors and no one with Ibelin arms. He started to believe the Ibelins had indeed achieved a victory.

There followed another lull. The streets went deathly still as the inhabitants awaited what would happen next. Anyone who had been out to do errands rapidly returned home. Those who had opened their workshops closed and barred them. The church bells rang vespers, but no one followed their call to Mass.

Novare paced the rooftop of the keep, stopping every few seconds to peer toward the south. The longer he had to wait, the more his imagination produced horrible scenarios of an Ibelin victory at the price of Balian or Beirut's life. Or what if both of them had been killed?

Finally, movement at the head of the street leading south caught his eye. Sure enough, a horse emerged, and then another three with more crowding behind them. The lead horse wore a red and yellow trapper, an Ibelin supporter, but it was unadorned with crosses, so Novare assumed he was just a household knight. Then he realized that the rider's surcoat bore the crosses of Ibelin, so maybe…?

Novare squinted and tried to get a better look at the rider. The knight had removed his great helm and it hung from the pommel of his saddle. Yet, while his face under his cervellière was framed by his chainmail coif, he was searching the buildings beside the street cautiously, anticipating possible ambushes, rather than looking up. As soon as the street widened out, mounted archers surged up to protect the lead rider with arrows notched in their bows—and Novare sighed with relief: the leading knight was one of the Ibelins, although he couldn't know yet which one.

Then again, it didn't really matter, Novare decided. He would know what had happened to the rest. Novare started running down the stairs with the intention of catching up with him and finding out. By the time he reached the foot of the stairs, however, the riders were already demanding admittance to the Hospital. Novare ran out shouting, "It's the Ibelins," but he was ignored in the general excitement as the gates were flung open.

The women and children who had taken refuge in the Hospitaller commandery rushed out into the courtyard to surround the riders. Several children recognized their fathers and started screaming in high-pitched excitement. One of the older women fainted at the sight of her son with his face sliced open to the bone and his eye missing. Soon the knights had dismounted amidst their families and well-wishers, all but lost in the jubilating crowd.

Novare had to push his way through the others to reach Balian, but as the latter caught sight of him, he smiled broadly. A moment later, the friends embraced heartily. "I've never been so glad to see that good-looking face of yours in my whole life!" Novare admitted, too relieved to dissemble. "Is your father alright?"

"He's alive and well, by the grace of God, but we took heavy losses. The Lord of Caesarea was killed outright along with nearly sixty others. Losses of horses were even higher." As he spoke, Balian was searching the crowd around him, evidently not focused on Novare.

Novare tried to keep his attention. "And the baillies? Did you kill or capture all of them?"

"No. That's just it. Not one. They all escaped. We presume they fled to the mountain castles. Have you word?" For a moment, Balian focused on Novare, but Novare could only shake his head, and immediately Balian's attention wandered again.

"Who are you looking for?" Novare demanded. As the man who had alerted the Ibelins of the situation on Cyprus and asked for their support, he considered himself the most important person currently lodging at the Hospital in Nicosia. "If you were hoping to find the King here, I'm sorry to disappoint you. He's already at St. Hilarion."

"Yes, the Archbishop of Nicosia told us that when he tried to negotiate a peaceful resolution of our differences," Balian admitted, his eyes still scanning the crowd, a slight frown on his face.

"Just who *are* you looking for then?" Novare asked irritably.

"My cousin Eschiva, the Lady of Montaigu."

"Lady Eschiva?" Novare knew she had taken refuge here—she'd had to after bringing him word of Barlais' treachery. He'd had little to do with her, however. She'd kept out of sight for the most part, doing women's things with the others.

"Yes, do you know where she is?" Balian asked.

"Not a clue."

"I must speak to her—if possible alone."

"What? Honestly, Balian! This is no time to be—"

But Balian had finally caught sight of Eschiva and started in her direction without letting Novare finish. Novare looked towards her, trying to see what Balian did. She was standing on the far side of the courtyard on the steps leading up to the chapel. Her blonde hair cascaded down her back from her prim white hat held in place by a pale-blue, silk barbette. She was clutching a dark-blue mantle around her shoulders, although the day was still warm despite the fading light and late hour. She appeared to have emerged from the chapel and was alone on the steps, gazing at the commotion in the courtyard as if she could not comprehend it. Suddenly, she caught sight of Balian pushing his way through the crowd towards her. Her expression was transformed by a smile, and her whole face glowed with an inner light—the way saint's images sometimes did. In that instant, even Novare found her beautiful.

He also registered: she's head-over-heels in love with Balian.

Novare shook his head in disapproval. She'd be wax in Balian's expert hands and he'd have no trouble getting between her sheets, he thought to himself, but then what? She was not only a married woman, she was married to an *Archbishop's* nephew—and they were cousins.

Balian bounded up the stairs, and Eschiva reached out both hands to him as her eyes devoured his face. He took her hands in his own and stopped two steps below her, returning her gaze. She looked so beautiful that he could only stare—until he became conscious that he stank, that he hadn't shaved in three days or brushed his teeth in five, not to mention that dried blood lined his fingernails. "Forgive me, *mi dons*, I'm in no fit state to touch you," he murmured. Yet he did not let go of her hands. Rather, he bent to kiss them, still clutching them in his own.

"I was so afraid, Balian," she gasped out, still so overwhelmed with emotion that she could hardly raise her voice above a whisper. "I was so afraid that I might *never* lay eyes on you again. *Never* touch you again. *Never* have a chance to tell you how much I love you…" Her voice drifted off, but her eyes continued to caress him.

He straightened and took the next step so they were eye to eye. His voice dropped to a murmur. "I have news for you," he warned.

Eschiva held her breath and waited, fear in her eyes. "Not your father or brothers?" she asked anxiously. Adding, "I have prayed for *all* of you!"

"We are all well. Though Hugh was slightly wounded toward the end. I bring, instead, word of your husband."

"Gerard? Is he here? On Cyprus? I thought he remained with my brother in Acre." In her voice was so much distress, even fear, that it wrenched Balian's heart.

"No, he chose to join us, seeing the baillies as an extension of Emperor Frederick, who he hates."

"Then he is not far behind you," Eschiva concluded, looking toward the entrance nervously. The thought that Sir Gerard might arrive any moment quenched the inner flame that had made her so beautiful. Her face suddenly seemed haggard, and her body sagged like a house on a broken foundation.

Balian was horrified by the transformation and reached out to her, calling her attention back to himself. "Eschiva!"

She looked at him with blue eyes swimming in tears.

"Sir Gerard, your husband, is dead."

Eschiva's eyes widened in shock. "What?" she gasped.

"We found him pinned under his horse. We have no idea how long he lay like that. Possibly, he would have survived his wounds otherwise, but the battle was raging. It was not until after Barlais fled that we could scour the field for our dead and wounded. When we found him, it was too late. He had bled to death."

Eschiva stared at Balian. Her expression was utterly stunned, as if she could not grasp what he was saying.

Balian whispered, "This changes everything, my love. Everything."

"Balian," she murmured, still in shock.

"I know. You'll have to play the grieving widow for a little bit. I will respect that. But you are free. *We* are free." He squeezed her hands. "I must go, but I will return after we have secured Nicosia. Will you stay here or return to the Archbishop's palace?"

"I don't know… You're *sure* Gerard is dead?"

"I helped extricate the body from beneath his horse. There can be no doubt."

When Eschiva made no reply but continued to look dazed he asked anxiously: "Are you all right?"

Eschiva seemed to shake herself out of her daze to admit, "I am stunned. I was so afraid. If you had not come yourself, I might not have believed you were alive, much less unharmed." Her hands tightened around his. "I must thank God—and pray for Gerard's soul."

"And I must go," Balian repeated. "If you need something—anything—send for me!" he urged.

"God be with you, Balian, as is my heart. Always."

"Mi dons!" He dipped his knee to her and disengaged his hands.

Plunging back into the general confusion, he made his way to his horse and remounted. The other knights followed his example and with hugs and kisses for wives, children and parents, disengaged from their families. As they turned to depart, Balian cast one last glance over his shoulder. Eschiva was still standing where he'd left her, her eyes following him, and she lifted her hand in farewell. He nodded in response and then rode out into the street.

Castle of St. Hilarion, Cyprus
July 15, 1229

King Henry liked St. Hilarion. It sat high amidst the peaks of the narrow mountain range that ran along the northern coast of his kingdom and offered spectacular views in all directions. Originally built by the Byzantines, his father and grandfather had invested huge sums in modernizing it. They had started building a luxurious palace, still unfinished, at the very top of the mountain, where the castle was so inaccessible that all pretense of defensive purpose could be abandoned. Here the windows were tall and glazed to allow the inhabitants to enjoy the splendid views. Furthermore, up here at fifteen hundred feet above sea level, the air was cooler and the breezes fresh. Indeed, in winter the infamous Mediterranean gales buffeted the walls and howled through the unfinished buildings like furious ghosts. Sometimes it even snowed. That made it an uncomfortable winter residence, but in the heat of summer, like now, it was an ideal retreat.

Henry had happy memories of spending summers here with Lord Philip. They would leave Nicosia early in the morning, and by mid-morning they would be toiling in the oppressive heat, sweating and thirsty. Then the castle would come into view, but still hours away, so they'd trudge on, getting hotter and dirtier, the horses straining. Bit by bit, they would get closer and the air would become cooler. The smell of pines would start to blot out the smell of their sweating bodies. Finally, they would reach the barbican, and with a great fanfare, the watch would announce the arrival of the king. The gates would be flung open and the entire castle staff would be lined-up to greet him. They would bow, and the castellan would come forward to offer Henry the keys to the castle—and his smiling wife would hold up a large, silver goblet filled with lemon sherbet sweetened with honey. Henry had loved coming to St. Hilarion.

Of course, Barlais had replaced the castellan, who was considered loyal to the Ibelins, and Henry's arrival with Sir Grimbert de Bethsan several days ago had taken the garrison by surprise. There had been no fanfare, no cheering staff, no sherbet. It didn't help that the men here were Langobard mercenaries in the service of the Holy Roman Emperor. Henry wasn't sure they knew he was the king or, if they did, they didn't much care. He wasn't *their* king.

Still, Henry reflected as he jumped and skipped his way down the long chain of steps from the upper to the middle ward of the castle, it was because they didn't take him very seriously that he had so much freedom. Nobody seemed to care where he was or what he was doing since Sir Grimbert had ridden back to Nicosia the same day he'd dropped Henry and Johnny here.

His sisters cared, Henry modified that, but they were girls and preferred reading or playing chess in the sunny great hall of the palace in the upper ward. Henry was already tired of their fussing over him. They'd insisted on cutting his hair and were outraged by the state of his boots (too worn down) and shirts (too threadbare at the cuffs). At least they liked Harry, he reminded himself with an inward sigh. In fact, they had adopted him completely, combing his hair and putting ribbons in it to keep it out of his eyes—until Harry scratched them off vigorously with his hind legs. They had also totally spoiled him with sweets. Harry was mercenary enough to hang around them for the handouts. Henry, in disgust, had left him with them.

Henry reached the broad rooftop of the garrison quarters in the middle ward. This was flat and crenelated so that it could be used as a fighting platform if an enemy ever got this far, something Henry found unimaginable. Still, there were a couple of Langobard sentries, who looked over at Henry without much interest and continued their conversation.

Henry was trying to find Johnny. Sometime after breakfast, Johnny had disappeared. Henry could tell that Johnny was even more bored by his sisters' conversation than he was himself. He also knew that Johnny was desperate for news of his father and brothers. So, not finding him here in the middle ward, Henry continued across the long, narrow courtyard, past the large castle church built by the Greeks, and through the passage that led to the south side of the mountain. Here he followed a steep and narrow passage past a guard tower and a middle gate. After that he continued down a steep path with irregular steps toward the cluster of buildings that guarded the outer wall and provided stabling for the horses.

There seemed to be a lot of people clustered down there already, Henry noticed, frowning unconsciously. It was only mid-morning, and it took most of the day to ride from Nicosia, so he hadn't been expecting any messengers until later. After a second look, he concluded that whatever was going on, it wasn't just a messenger. There were too many horses milling around in front of the barbican. Not just horses either. There were men too, and they were in armor—ragged, tattered and dirty armor.

Henry caught his breath and stood still so he could focus on what was happening. There were at least a hundred men and horses in front of the barbican, but they weren't attacking. On the contrary, they were being admitted through the gate a couple at a time. That was what caused the others to mill around outside; they were waiting their turn to enter. But if the garrison was letting them in, Henry realized, then they could only be the baillies' men.

Worse!

In horror, Henry recognized Sir Amaury Barlais himself emerging from the back of the barbican. As Henry watched, he turned his limping horse over to one of the castle grooms.

Henry didn't wait to see any more. He turned on heel and ran back up the hill as fast as he could. He didn't slow down in the darkness of the middle gate but plunged headlong through the passage past the church. By the time he reached the middle ward, he was panting heavily and his feet were dragging enough so that he stubbed his toes and stumbled on the uneven cobbles. Yet he kept running, turning away from the steps to the upper ward. He ducked inside a door and started up a flight of stairs built in the thickness of the wall, his breath echoing loudly in the narrow stairwell.

One flight up, he darted out another door and found himself in a large, loge hanging off the back of the cliff. The loge was perfectly square with a rib-vaulted, stone ceiling. Three sides were pierced by broad arches facing north, east and south.

In Lord Philip's time, Lady Alys had loved it here. She'd bring her ladies, a troubadour or lute player, her needlework or a book to read, and she would spend the whole day here because the crosswinds kept the loge comfortably cool. Henry had often joined her here, particularly when he was too little to tag along behind Lord Philip most of the day.

But Henry had never known Barlais to come here, and his lady was still in Syria. Henry thought—or rather hoped—that Barlais didn't know this loge existed. If he stayed here, Henry told himself, maybe Barlais would never find him. But even as he articulated the thought, he knew it was illusory. Barlais would send his men out to find him, and they would look everywhere in the castle until they *did* find him.

Henry went to each of the windows in turn and looked out, trying to find a way to climb down from here. There had to be some way to escape.

But the loge clung like a barnacle to the back of the castle and the masonry dropped straight-down for thirty-five or forty feet to stand on a ridge of jagged limestone stabbing upwards from a forest of stunted and gnarled pine-trees. Henry recognized he'd need a stout rope at least fifty feet long to lower himself from here to the rugged rocks below. And then what? There was no obvious trail from there. He was more likely to break a leg.

Henry turned back to face the door by which he'd entered. He returned and closed it firmly, but it could only be bolted from the other side. He could for the moment only barricade it with several wooden benches. This he did. Then seating himself on the outermost, he turned to look out toward the mountain range in the direction of Kyrenia and Karpas. He'd been told that you could see signals from Buffavento from here, but he couldn't even find the castle in the distant purple haze.

Besides, Buffavento was also held by a man loyal to the Emperor. All the castles, which *should* have been his according to the treaty Frederick had signed with the Lord of Beirut, had been taken from him. The baillies had put their own men into them instead. Henry had been ignored. Duped. Just like the Lord of Beirut. The Emperor, Henry reflected, had never intended to respect any aspect of the treaty. He'd only signed it—falsely—to make the Lord of Beirut surrender the castles to him.

Well, at least he *had* released Sirs Balian and Baldwin, Henry reminded himself, swinging his legs so that the bench tilted and then clunked back down rhythmically. The Emperor must have had his reasons, Henry supposed. He was a calculating man, untrustworthy and conceited.

But not *evil*. Not like Barlais.

Henry started pounding his fist on the bench beside him in fury. He hated Barlais! He never wanted to see him again! But Barlais was here—with a hundred knights.

Terror made Henry's spine stiff and his bowels loose. He was trapped in St. Hilarion with Barlais!

Henry jumped up and ran to the far window again. There *had* to be some way he could get out!

A knock at the door made him spin around with a gasp. The door opened and banged into his barricade of benches.

"Henry! It's me! Johnny!" His friend's voice came around the edge of the door.

Henry ran over and pulled the benches away just enough for Johnny to slip through. Then he slammed the door shut, shoved the benches back in place, and faced Johnny defiantly.

"What's this all about?" Johnny asked with a look of annoyance. "This is no time to be playing games! Barlais, Bethsan, and Gibelet have just arrived with what's left of their army. My father routed them! They had to spend the night at the foot—" Johnny cut himself off as he registered he wasn't telling Henry anything he didn't already know. "Henry, you can't barricade yourself in here. You've got no food or water, and it wouldn't take men-at-arms more than thirty seconds to push those benches aside."

"Well?" Henry retorted sharply. "Do you have a better idea?"

"Barlais isn't going to harm you."

"Yes, he is!" Henry screamed at Johnny with so much pent-up terror, fury, and frustration that the older boy instinctively took a step backward. "I've told you before!" Henry moderated his voice, but the intensity of his feelings was still blistering.

"You asked me not to leave you alone with him—"

"Well, why do you think I asked you to do that?" Henry flung back. "Do you think I would ask that if he didn't—didn't *hurt* me!"

"Henry...." Johnny gaped at his king

His look made Henry ashamed of shouting at him, ashamed of *everything*. He turned his back on Johnny and stalked to the far side of the loge. He stared at the masonry, and with his hand, he traced the joints between the stones. He felt Johnny come up behind him, but he refused to turn around. He couldn't face him.

"What has he done to you?" Johnny asked softly.

Henry vigorously shook his head. "I can't tell you. It's too—" He shrugged helplessly. Then fearing that Johnny wouldn't believe him if he didn't say more, he added, "But it hurts, Johnny! I hurts like *hell*, and if anyone finds out, Barlais says I'll never be able to be king. The church will revile me—"

"Henry?" Johnny gripped his shoulder and slowly turned him around. Henry kept his head down to avoid his eye. His whole body was hot with the memories, and his innards were twisting up inside him.

"Has he forced you to—to commit unnatural acts?" Johnny asked in a low but steady voice.

Henry couldn't answer. He just stood silently yet cringing inside and swallowing down rising nausea. The memories made him what to puke.

"When?" Johnny demanded.

"The first time was when I was just little. When Barlais came with the letter from my mother naming him baillie," Henry admitted.

"Has he done it since?" Johnny asked.

"The night you found me in the fireplace," Henry muttered.

"Any other times?"

"Once, when he came to tell me I would not be going with the Emperor to Sicily but coming here—with him. Three times altogether." The humiliation made Henry hunch his shoulders and try to squirm away from Johnny. "Promise you won't tell anyone," he pleaded. "Please, promise...."

"Henry! He's committed high treason, not to mention a mortal sin!" Johnny protested.

"But if you say anything, I'll never be king!" Henry remonstrated desperately. Being king was all that Henry had. His *mother* had delivered him to Barlais. Lord Philip, who had rescued him, was dead, and with Lady Alys in exile—

"You are *already* king, Henry!" Johnny countered. "You've been crowned and anointed. No one can change that. If he's laid a hand on you in an improper, unnatural way, then he should be castrated, quartered, and burned alive! Henry, he's a monster!"

Henry was grateful for Johnny's support. It made him feel better, but he still shook his head. "Don't you understand? We're his prisoners! Unless you know a way to escape from here?" Henry added hopefully, looking again toward the windows with their beautiful views of apparently endless opportunity.

Johnny looked out the windows and his expression was eloquent; he didn't know a way out either. Then Johnny took a deep breath and looked at Henry with more determination. "Look, Henry. My father has just routed Barlais' army. I overheard men saying that all the baillies survived, but they divided up so they could hold the castles of Kantara, Kyrenia, Buffavento, and St. Hilarion. My father isn't going to let them do that. He's going besiege the castles and he's going to get us out of here!"

"Has this castle ever fallen to assault or siege?" Henry asked back, his lips turned down in sullen anger.

"No, but my father—"

"Is the one who stocked the cellars with two years' worth of food," Henry pointed out bitterly.

"We can destroy some of it, you and I. We can put mice in among the grain or—I don't know right now, but we can find ways to make sure it won't last that long. Besides, my father will probably be able to talk Barlais into surrender. Have you forgotten my grandfather talked Saladin into letting the Christians surrender Jerusalem *after* he'd already breached the walls?"

"That was Saladin, not Barlais," Henry told him pointedly.

"Henry. You're our king! My father's not going to leave you in Barlais' clutches forever. Or me either. He's going to get us out. I don't know how, but I trust him. He's defeated Barlais in open battle. He'll take this castle too."

"And in the meantime Barlais buggers me!" Henry snarled furiously as tears of frustration, fear and self-pity flooded his eyes and started down his cheeks. He turned angrily away, wiping the treasonous tears away with the palm of his hand.

Johnny wrapped his arms around his king. "I swear to God, Henry! He'll have to kill me first! I will stay with you! St. George give me strength! I won't let him touch you like that! I won't. I'll scream and wake the whole garrison if I have to!"

Henry wanted to believe him. He could sense Johnny's determination. But they were both still children, helpless children.

July 18, 1229
Nicosia

Eschiva got stiffly up from her knees. She could not pray forever. Gerard was under the ground. His funeral had been attended by the Lord of Beirut, his three adult sons, and over a hundred other knights, as well as the leading merchants of the Genoese community, his uncles the Archbishop of Nicosia and the Bishop of Limassol, and representatives of both the Templars and Hospitallers. All in all, there had been almost as many people as for the Lord of Caesarea's funeral, which had been held only hours before.

The funeral had been followed by a banquet hosted by the Archbishop of Nicosia at the archiepiscopal palace. There, Eschiva had received the condolences of what seemed like all of Cyprus, including Balian, but the latter had tactfully kept his distance after a formal bow and expression of his sincere "sympathy." Over the meal, the Archbishop had given a long speech praising his nephew's piety and dedication to Christ and the Holy Land. The Bishop of Limassol had eulogized his sobriety and humility as examples to all Christian knights. Even the Lord of Beirut spoke shortly about Gerard's great sacrifice, despite having no close affiliation with the Ibelins or the others victimized by the baillies.

Although Beirut's speech had been honest and fair, Gerard's clerical uncles had created an image of a paragon of virtue that Eschiva could not square with the man she had known. In consequence, Eschiva found their speeches almost nauseating, and certainly tedious. Fortunately, "grieving" widows were exempted from making speeches.

When it became too intolerable, Eschiva had excused herself to come to the Archbishop's private chapel. The need to pray had become overwhelming as she listened to the clerics praising Gerard while watching from behind her veil Balian with his brothers. Eschiva had bargained with God for Balian's life and limbs. She had promised Him that in exchange for Balian's survival she would be a good wife to Gerard. When she first saw him alive and well, she had thanked God, but also prepared herself for the horror of returning to Gerard—and his bed.

But Gerard was dead. It made no sense to her. How could God give her both Balian *and* absolve her in the most perfect way of her duty to Gerard? It was as if Bella was right: as if God did not recognize her marriage to Gerard as valid. She had been married to Gerard in the eyes of the Archbishop of Nicosia, and the Bishop of Limassol, and the Masters of the Temple and Hospital, but not, it seemed, in the eyes of God.

And that meant that she was, as Balian had said, free. Utterly and completely free. The magnitude of Grace was almost overwhelming. She felt the need to thank God, but also to beg him to help her face the ultimate challenge of freedom. Because, of course, it was when humans were free to do as they pleased that they were most likely to displease God.

The chapel was dark now, and the vestry priest was coughing and fussing about irritably to indicate that the Archbishop would soon come to celebrate compline. Eschiva dipped her knee in the direction of the Eucharist candle, whispered a last prayer of thanks and an inarticulate plea for help, and withdrew. She took a lamp to guide her down the corridor to her chamber and let herself inside.

Cecilia at once jumped up and rushed to receive her. "Where have you been, Madame? I was worried about you!"

"Whatever for?" Eschiva answered with a faint smile. She had never in her life been so free of fear, not since her mother died and she had found herself an orphan with no one left in the world but a distant and vaguely unpleasant brother.

Cecilia weighed her head from side to side and nervously twisted her wedding band around her finger. "I—I—please don't be angry with me, madame, maybe I'm just a silly girl full of fantasies, but I—I—don't like the Archbishop."

Eschiva laughed. "I'm not terribly fond of the Archbishop either, Cecilia. But what is there to fear?"

Cecilia only looked more uncomfortable than ever. She fussed with her sleeves, pulling them down over her hands, and then pushed at the little hat tied to her head with a bright red barbette. "Signor Sanuto is also a venerable gentleman, my lady, but that didn't stop him from trying to put his hand up my skirt or grabbing my breasts whenever he could trap me."

Eschiva stared at her.

"That's why I fled to Saint Anne's, Madame. If I'd stayed in his house, I know he would have forced himself on me. He wasn't even ashamed of himself, madame, and when I tried to complain to his wife, she told me I was 'leading him on' and threatened to throw me out. But I *wasn't*, Madame. Truly I wasn't."

Eschiva believed Cecilia and nodded.

Cecilia changed the subject. "What are your plans now, Madame? Do you want to return to Acre and your brother's household?"

"No. Certainly not," Eschiva declared decisively. "I inherited large estates here in Cyprus from my mother, Burgundia de Lusignan. The Montaigus 'solicitously' assumed the management of them after my marriage, but I intend to take control of them myself. I will demand an accounting of all my properties, and I think it is time to visit each and every one. Zach will be happy to escort us."

"Oh!" Cecilia brightened at once. "That sounds very exciting!" Then she paused, put her hand to her lips, and asked timidly, "But, well, mightn't it be dangerous? I mean the baillies still hold half the island. At least that's what I heard."

The reaction, Eschiva thought, was very typical of Cecilia. She had an adventurous spirit, but it had been so slapped down and imprisoned by her protective father that she had learned to curb her desires. She always checked her enthusiasm before anyone else told her off.

Eschiva patiently explained to Cecilia, "The baillies are trapped in the mountain castles and Kyrenia, where they are surrounded and besieged by the Ibelins. We will avoid going too near the sieges." Mentally she added, however, that that did not exclude visiting a manor, if she had one, near St. Hilarion. Balian had managed to mention he was bound for the siege of St. Hilarion during his brief moment with her at the banquet.

Cecilia, encouraged, brightened instantly. "So we can still travel? That will be fun!"

Eschiva laughed. "I'm not sure how *fun* it will be, Cecilia. It will probably be quite exhausting, and we may find ourselves sleeping in all sorts of unexpected places since most of my estates have been neglected during my minority. I doubt any of them have accommodations fit for ladies. We may well have to sleep fully clothed on pallets in halls, and wash in cold water much of the time. Not to mention stopping at local inns and monasteries along the way and eating local food."

"I think that sounds wonderful, Madame! Maurizio used to tell me about traveling—all the strange and exotic places he'd been to. I so wanted to travel with him!"

"Yes, well traveling by sea is considerably more comfortable than what we will be doing. And as for exotic, we won't be leaving Cyprus."

"Madame?" Cecilia's voice had changed, and she was measuring Eschiva thoughtfully.

"Yes?"

"What about Sir Balian?" Cecilia didn't dare look at her directly as she asked this, but she looked at her sidelong with a tentative smile on her face—a smile waiting to burst into something more radiant.

"What about him?" Eschiva asked back with a pretense of innocence.

"He—he seems—or you seemed—it was *his* life that you feared for, was it not?" Cecilia asked puzzled.

Eschiva nodded and conceded, "Yes, it was. Ever since he rescued me from Frederick Hohenstaufen, we have been deep friends. There is no one on earth that I love more than Sir Balian."

Cecilia brightened. "Will you marry him now that you are a widow?"

Eschiva shook her head. "I cannot see the future, Cecilia. I think Sir Balian may want that, but I cannot be sure. We are cousins, after all, related within the prohibited degrees. Marriage would require a papal dispensation."

"Oh." Cecilia was clearly disappointed. "But you—you seem different. I mean, I know your mourning for your husband is only formal, but—if you don't know for sure about Sir Balian – what makes you so optimistic?"

"Is it that obvious?" Eschiva quipped back. "I must be sure to wear my veils over my face!"

"But, what *is* it, Madame?"

"I'm free. For the first time in my life, I am really and truly free. I am no one's daughter, sister, or wife. I am master of my own destiny. Unlike you, Cecilia, I am a rich widow. I don't yet know exactly what my income is, but I soon will. Tomorrow, I will ask the Archbishop to return control of my estates to me. There's no reason why he should deny me what is mine, now that Gerard is dead and buried."

Eschiva was wrong. The Archbishop of Nicosia was outraged to learn she wanted to take immediate control of her estates. "But you're still a child!" he protested with a look of astonishment.

"I'm eighteen—six years beyond the age of consent," Eschiva answered simply.

"My dear, you have no idea how complicated these things are. You have no experience."

"How can I gain experience if I am not given a chance?" Eschiva countered.

"You can't possibly learn everything at once."

"I don't expect to learn everything at once, Uncle, but I expect to start learning immediately. The best thing would be for you to have one of your clerks show me the accounts of my estates today."

"I doubt that can be arranged. I have many other things to do. Don't rush into these things. You need time to grieve. We can talk about this again in a month or two." He made a vaguely dismissive gesture with his hand and seemed to expect Eschiva to submissively withdraw.

Eschiva was in no mood for that. She did not want to stay with the Archbishop a day longer than necessary. She wanted to start her own life. She spoke as patiently as possible. "I *do* understand that you are very busy, Uncle. That is why I wish to relieve you of the great burden of looking after my affairs. It was a great imposition, and if Gerard had not been so busy with the crusade, I'm sure he would have taken control of my estates himself. That would have given me the opportunity to learn things from him. As it is, however, we must make the best of things. If you have no one who can show me the accounts, then just hand them over to me, along with all the ready cash collected at St. Johns, and I will hire a professional bookkeeper to assist me."

"There! That shows just how naïve you are! You can't trust a hired man to look after your affairs! You would be robbed blind!"

"I'm astonished to hear a prince of the church suggest that morality is a function of wealth. Christ, I believe, said that His kingdom belonged to the poor and also that it was more difficult for the rich than for the poor to find Grace."

"You are too uneducated to understand scripture and are making silly, facile conclusions based on superficial knowledge."

Eschiva was starting to get angry. She might not have the same education as the Archbishop, but she had been tutored at home and attended convent school for five years. Not just any school, either. the Sisters of St. Anne's had an excellent reputation because the Abbess, Evangeline de Montfort, was a highly respected scholar in her own right. She had written several admired commentaries on the gospels. Eschiva's skills as a copier and illuminator had been discovered by the Abbess when she copied some of these same texts. Her further education in illumination had been at the hands of the Canons of the Holy Sepulcher; there really was no better school than that in all Christendom, Eschiva thought. She was indignant to think the Archbishop assumed that she copied without thinking.

But even as her anger boiled up, she reminded herself that his opinion of her was immaterial. His control of her estates and income, not his opinion, was the issue. "My lord archbishop," she spoke as pointedly as possible, hoping she did sound too tart, "whether you like, respect or approve of how I manage my estates or not, they are *mine*, and I am legally entitled to take control of them. You, on the other hand, have no rights to them whatsoever. Do you want me to raise this with the High Court?"

The Archbishop bristled visibly, and snapped back, "The High Court cannot meet until the issue of who is rightfully baillie of Cyprus has been resolved."

"Then I will go directly to the Lord of Beirut," Eschiva declared, meeting his eye defiantly.

The Archbishop's eyes and lips narrowed. "If you *insist*, I could have one of my clerks show you the books for one of your estates—Paradhisi, for example. That way you can learn things on a small scale, incrementally, without taking on the burden for your entire inheritance."

"I don't want to return to Paradhisi," Eschiva told him firmly. "Not until I've seen *all* my estates and can make a decision on where I *want* to live."

"We chose Paradhisi for you for very good reasons. I can assure you it is the best place for you to live."

Eschiva again had to get a grip on her rising temper. She knew that anger would get her nowhere. She took a deep breath and declared as forcefully as possible without being impolite. "My lord archbishop, at the time you chose Paradhisi I was a young bride whom we all hoped was pregnant, and my husband was about to embark on the crusade. My circumstances have changed. I intend to visit all my estates, and decide for myself where I wish to live."

"You don't seem to comprehend the basics." The Archbishop's tone was as sharp as her own. "Your estates are scattered all across the island! You can't just go and see them all in an afternoon. It will take you weeks to see everything— months if you stop to actually *learn* anything about the various estates."

"All the more reason for me to visit them all and start as soon as possible."

"You are being irrational," the archbishop dismissed her.

Eschiva got to her feet, fighting down the desire to scream at him. She managed not to scream, but she raised her voice as she avowed emphatically, "Rational or irrational, my lord, I *will* take control of my estates, and I *will* visit them! As soon as possible. I will go to my Lord of Beirut now to inform him of your irrational" she could not resist flinging the word back at him "—as well as illegal—refusal to turn over my revenues and account for your time as my agent. You can be sure that my cousin the King will also learn of your—"

"Sit down and stop throwing this silly temper tantrum! I'll have the books brought to you at once, but you'll hardly be able to understand them." As he spoke, the Archbishop reached for a bell and rang it. A moment later a priest appeared. "My nephew's widow wishes to see an accounting of the estates we have been managing for her. Please take her to the scriptorium and bring her the books, then send Father Ignatius to me so I can tell him about Lady Montaigu's wishes."

The priest bowed his head and turned to leave, indicating she should follow him. Eschiva likewise bowed her head to the archbishop. "Thank you, Uncle. I promise I will soon cease to be a burden for you."

The Archbishop snorted softly and dismissed her with an irritated gesture of his hand.

Chapter Twenty-Seven
The Invincible Heights

St. Hilarion, Cyprus
November 1229

SIEGES ARE INHERENTLY BORING—ESPECIALLY WHEN ON terrain that does not enable the deployment of siege-engines and where assaults are sheer suicide. After the offer to negotiate was rejected with rude insults by Barlais, the forces of Ibelin had contented themselves with sealing off access to and from St. Hilarion and settling down to wait for Barlais to change his mind.

Since they could not trigger a change of heart by persuasion or force of arms, they had to starve him out. Yet, it would be more than a year, they calculated, before the garrison would run out of food. As for water, the rains had started and the cisterns of St. Hilarion were filled more after each drenching shower.

For the besiegers, the arrival of the wet weather brought additional discomfort. Even the best tents eventually became saturated and started to drip inside. Meanwhile, the soil around the tents, stone-hard when baked in the summer sun, became a morass of mud between the outcroppings and thorns. The wood was too damp to burn properly, so a heavy layer of smoke hung over the camp making it hard to breathe. Clothes never dried either, so men lived in damp clothing and rusting armor. Most men had developed hacking coughs from colds or smoke inhalation or both. Meanwhile, the food became increasingly inedible. Bread and cheese were moldy and the hay outright rotten.

Under the circumstances, it was hardly surprising that the once proud Ibelin host of fifty knights, their squires, sixty Turcopoles and nearly a hundred archers had shrunk substantially. The Turcopoles had been released within a few weeks; mounted archers were of little value in a siege, and the Lord of Beirut was reluctant to pay their wages for standing about idle. Not long afterward, the Cypriot knights started requesting permission to depart. They needed to attend to their own affairs after being away on crusade in Syria for a year or more. One by one, they left to go to their estates and families. This left only the Syrians behind, a total of just 28 knights and their squires. As the siege dragged on into the rainy season, several of these also announced their intention to return home. By November only 23 knights remained at the siege of St. Hilarion, almost all bachelor knights without properties or families to look after.

This was when Sir Hugh's cough became so bad that Balian agreed he should return to Nicosia to get well. Sir Baldwin had promptly announced he'd take Hugh there and "check up on what else was happening." That had been ten days ago.

Meanwhile, desertions among the infantry were mounting. Rather than reporting to Balian and announcing their intention to depart, they simply slipped away in the night. Each morning muster saw fewer men line up. They were down to 46 sergeants. In short, their strength was little more than a third of what it had been in July, but it was, Balian thought, still sufficient to ensure Barlais could neither escape nor be reinforced.

When the youth Zachery arrived with a message from Lady Eschiva saying she was staying at her manor at Vouno, only a three-hour ride away, Balian decided to risk going to visit her. It helped that Rob had been knighted. Balian was now served by Eudes de la Fierté, who went by his second name, Lucas. The young son of one of Beirut's Cypriot vassals, Lucas was far too eager to please to question anything Balian did.

Novare, on the other hand, was instantly suspicious. "Where are you going? Both your brothers are already gone," Novare protested.

"I'm going to buy livestock. Some goats or sheep that we could slaughter periodically would do much for morale."

"Only if we can keep a fire going long enough to roast the meat," Novare countered.

"The rains will ease up sooner or later," Balian responded with a shrug. "It rarely rains continuously."

"It's been raining for three weeks already."

"All the more reason it's likely to stop soon."

"When will you be back?" Novare wanted to know next.

"Three or four days from now at the latest. You should be pleased that I'm leaving you in command. It is an honor."

Novare nodded absently, but he glanced over at Zachery with a frown, as if trying to figure out who he was. Fortunately, he did not associate him with Eschiva, or he might have protested.

Balian packed his toiletries and several changes of clothes. He rolled these together to carry behind his saddle. He ordered Lucas to bring his armor so he could clean it properly during their stay in dry quarters. He left his tent, furnishings, Gebremariam and his packhorse in Sir Robert's care.

Finally, having sent Zach ahead with the news that he was on his way, Balian left the siege camp about noon, riding Damon, with Lucas beside him on a stout palfrey. They rode back to the main Nicosia-Kyrenia road, followed it southwards for less than an hour then turned off heading east toward the royal fortress of Buffavento. Vouno was located at the foot of the escarpment on which Buffavento sat. By now heavy rain clouds were gathering over the mountains obscuring the peaks and the sky flickered in response to distant lightning.

Zach clattered into the courtyard at the little mountain manor of Vouno just as heavy drops started to splatter on the cobblestones. He jumped down from his bay gelding, flung the reins over his head, and led him into the stables before the rain started in earnest. Inside, he turned the reins over to a groom with a hasty, "look after Dodger, would you? I've got to get a message to my lady right away."

The groom didn't have much choice since Zach had already dashed out the door to dart across the courtyard and run up the exterior stairs to the hall. By now, lightning was flickering behind the mountains, and the growl of distant thunder followed at ever shorter intervals.

In the hall, the kitchen staff was setting up the tables and benches: a short table on the dais with three chairs behind it and a longer one down the center of the hall flanked by benches for the household. Zach took the wooden stairs that led up from behind the dais to the floor above and entered the square block built over the solar. This third-floor room had been partitioned into two by a wooden wall. The back room served as the private quarters of the castle steward, Sir Rohard, but Eschiva had converted the front room into her studio. Here, standing against the wall under the window facing south she had a desk for working, and on either side of the desk were chests with parchment and pigment, pens, inks, and brushes. At the other end of the room, Cecilia had set up a spinning wheel and hand loom. Between them, Sir Rohard kept a locked chest with the estate treasury and the account books.

Zach was breathless by the time he burst into this chamber, exclaiming as soon as he caught sight of Eschiva hunched over her work. "My lady! Sir Balian is on his way."

"What?" Eschiva was so startled she blotted the illustration she was working on—and didn't even notice. "Today?"

"Oh, that's wonderful!" Cecilia exclaimed, setting the basket of wool aside and jumping to her feet.

"Balian is coming *here*?" Eschiva asked back, still dazed. "In the middle of a storm?" A flash of lightning underlined her words, while the rain had started in earnest. It was pelting the glass of the north-facing window and hissing on the courtyard below.

"He told me to hurry because he needed only a half hour to get ready," Zach answered excitedly.

Cecilia clapped her hands in delight. "You see, Madame! He is an ardent lover! Not just words, but deeds as well."

Too true! Eschiva thought. She had not expected Balian to respond so *rapidly* to her suggestion that they meet. She had expected him to send a letter with a proposed date and time to meet. She had expected to have more time to prepare.

"Surely this is what you wanted, Madame?" Cecilia asked, bewildered by her lady's apparent paralysis.

"Yes, of course," Eschiva answered absently. "Zach, run down to the kitchen and tell them to hold dinner for another hour or so and find Sir Rohard. Ask him to come here." As Zach left, she turned to Cecilia and asked, "Where are we going to put him?"

Cecilia giggled in answer.

"Don't be silly!" Eschiva admonished, flushing a deep red, and turning back to put away her brushes. She fumbled with them as she realized that Balian might expect the same outcome of this encounter as Cecilia: he might think she had invited him here to share her bed. But it wasn't that simple.

A flash of lightning followed almost immediately by an angry clap of thunder reminded her that she didn't have time to put away her brushes and paints. There was too much else to do. She put a hand to her hair, wondering how she looked, and only then remembered she was dressed for painting in a simple linen gown with a cotton smock over it. The smock was soiled with ink and paint and oil. "I must change out of this filthy smock!" she exclaimed out loud. "Cecilia, come quick and help me change." But she was only halfway up the stairs to the floor above which housed her bedchamber when the sound of rain reminded her. "Oh, he'll be soaking wet and frozen when he gets here! We must start heating water for a bath! And he'll need a change of clothes!"

She reversed direction on the stairs so rapidly that Cecilia bumped into her. She returned to her studio, and was relieved to see the old steward limping into the room. "Sir Rohard! Did Zach tell you? Sir Balian d'Ibelin is on his way here. We must prepare for him. He'll be cold, wet and hungry. Do you think we could prepare a bath for him here?" She looked helplessly about the room that was in disarray with Cecilia's wool and her own work. "Or the solar?"

"My chamber would be best, my lady," Sir Rohard answered. He was a man in his mid-fifties who had been steward at Vouno ever since he'd been badly injured in a hunting accident. He had been widowed several years earlier and his children were grown and living their own lives.

"He'll want to stay the night in this weather. Where should we put him up?" Eschiva asked next, her thoughts still scattered as her heart raced.

The old knight raised his eyebrows and grumbled, "You know, Sir Balian has a terrible reputation. He is not a man of honor when it comes to ladies. The best place for him would be in the hall with the household." Reading Eschiva's appalled look, he modified his suggestions. "Or, if you *insist* on treating him more courteously, I would be happy to give up my chamber, and bed down here on a pallet." The words 'guarding your honor and reputation' was left unsaid but very much implied by his words.

"Yes, that would be good," Eschiva answered, putting off thoughts of what Balian might think of such an arrangement. "Can you see to the bath? I need to change."

"Yes, I'll see to the bath and find some fresh kaftans for him and his squire. Will he be traveling with a large escort?"

"I haven't a clue, sir," Eschiva answered honestly.

"We'll deal with it, my lady. Go prepare yourself."

Eschiva thanked him and again started up the stairs to her own chamber. She tore off the dirty smock as soon as she was through the door and kicked off her run-down house slippers as well.

In the months since Gerard's death, she had enjoyed her freedom—only to rapidly realize that freedom alone was cold comfort. It had been Balian's love that had awakened her spirit when it was all but lost at sea. His love had given her a reason to live, and his love had opened a crack of understanding for divine love. His appreciation for her painting made her value it again. It had been on his advice that she had gone to the canons of the Holy Sepulcher, and it was only because she had been there that the Templars had seen her work and commissioned it.

Yet, since Gerard's funeral, they had neither seen nor corresponded with one another, and she could not bear the silence a moment longer. Yes, the war was far from over, and Eschiva understood that defeating the baillies was of the utmost importance; she accepted that Balian had more important things on his mind than her. And yet...

"You should wear this, Madame," Cecilia broke into her thoughts. "It is your prettiest gown and very flattering." Cecilia held up a pale blue silk gown with narrow sleeves so long they bunched up at the wrists where they were tied with laces. "With this surcoat," she added, indicating a blue-and-purple parti-colored silk surcoat trimmed with wide bands of gold and turquoise embroidery.

"No, that's far too formal for an ordinary, rainy day. I'll wear the simple blue surcoat with the wide sleeves," Eschiva decided to Cecilia's disappointment.

After slipping the gown and surcoat over her head, Eschiva sat down at her dressing table, removed her hat and barbette, and took a comb to her long, blond hair. Cecilia came to help her. "Aren't you excited, Madame?"

"Of course I'm excited, Cecilia. I just don't know… I don't know."

"*What* don't you know, Madame?"

"I don't know what to expect. I felt like I would go mad not hearing from him for four months. I felt I needed to see him and talk to him. I felt I needed him—and yet…. I'm so afraid, Celia." She ended in a whisper.

"But you're free now, Madame! You can marry Sir Balian."

Marry Sir Balian? Is that what she wanted? Did she want to be married to *anyone*? Marriage had broken and killed Yolanda. It had brought her nearly as much misery. She didn't want to live on an allowance when she had substantial income. She didn't want to be told where she could live when she had almost two dozen manors. She didn't want to be told she could not accept work as an illuminator, as Gerard had done. She *certainly* didn't want to submit to the degradation of the marriage bed! The memories of the pain and humiliation made her shudder. The last thing she wanted was for her love for Balian to be degraded and defiled by the brutal and repugnant act of copulation.

But she wanted Balian. She wanted to be with him, near him, touch him, talk to him—and be held by him.

And he would certainly want consummation. He was famous for it. He had been chivalrous to renounce it while she was married and adultery endangered both their souls. But she couldn't expect him to renounce physical intimacy now. It was a sin he had committed far too often in the past already, a sin for which he readily found understanding absolution. Priests were men. Cecilia was certainly right that if he had responded to her invitation so ardently, then it was ardor that spurred him here. If she denied him, he would be angry. He might feel betrayed and misled. He might walk out on her and never speak to her again.

She couldn't bear that!

"You must wear the blue barbette and hat to match the gown," Cecilia broke into her thoughts

"Yes, Cecilia," Eschiva agreed. She wanted to look as beautiful as possible.

"And let me put rouge on your lips and cheeks, and just a little bit of kohl around your eyes. You have beautiful, big, blue eyes, but they need to stand out a little more."

Eschiva nodded again numbly. It didn't make sense. She didn't want to make love to Balian, yet she wanted him to love her. She didn't want physical intimacies, yet she wanted him to find her physically attractive. She was being irrational and inconsistent, but she just couldn't help herself. She wanted Balian to find her beautiful.

Cecilia worked with deft precision, fussing about like a little bird. Eschiva soon became impatient. "I'm sure that's good enough," she insisted.

"No, no! Just a little—"

A shout pierced to the inner sanctum of the tower, and Cecilia ran to look out of the window. "They've been sighted by the watch, Madame. Let me—"

"No, we must go down to greet them! Give me my hat and barbette!"

Cecilia set the hat on Eschiva's head and deftly wound the silk scarves of the barbette under Eschiva's chin and over the top of the hat so the ends hung a little down her back of her head. "You look lovely!" she concluded, stepping back. "I'm sure Sir Balian will be enchanted."

Just short of their destination, the clouds opened up and dumped water on Balian and Lucas with so much fury that they were nearly swept off the slope of the mountain. They had to jump down and lead their unnerved horses. By the time they reached Vouno, they might as well have plunged fully clothed into the ocean.

Even before they were in shouting distance, however, the gates swung open. As they entered the compact courtyard, figures rushed out from the surrounding low stone buildings to grab the bridles of their bedraggled horses. The manor staff promised to give the horses the best care and gestured emphatically toward the manor house. Here too the door already stood wide open, and Balian made a dash for it. He found the kitchen warmed by a thundering fire in the large open fireplace and lit by a dozen hanging lamps. Best of all, a beautiful young woman in neat, pressed clothes with a wide towel greeted him. "Here, my lord. Dry yourself with this and then follow me upstairs. Katie, come help my lord's squire!" she called into the kitchen.

At once one of the women working in the kitchen left off pounding a slab of meat, grabbed a towel drying before the kitchen fire and brought it to Lucas. Balian, meanwhile, handed off his drenched cloak and removed his surcoat and gambeson as well. He was dismayed to discover even his shirt was wet and the

thighs of his hose were completely soaked. He used the towel to daub both partially dry. Then with a nod to the beautiful young woman, who he presumed
was Eschiva's waiting-woman, he allowed himself to be taken up the internal
stone stairs leading to the great hall on the floor above.

As he mounted the steps, the hall came into view with a large fireplace
under a stone hood bearing the arms of Lusignan. The floor itself was paved
with terracotta tiles in a checkerboard pattern of brown and cream, but the dais
was wooden and carpeted. Here place settings were being laid on a linen table-
cloth, and Eschiva was herself lighting candles. When she caught sight of Balian
emerging from the stairway to the kitchen, her face lit up.

How in the world had anyone ever thought she wasn't beautiful? Balian
asked himself dazzled.

Eschiva left the dais to hurry toward him, reaching out her hands. "Thank
God you made it, Sir Balian!" Even as she spoke a flash of lightning was followed
so rapidly by a clap of thunder that it seemed to shake the very foundations of
the manor. The sound of rain overhead was nearly deafening, and the gurgling
of water running down the drains and splattering in the courtyard was a counterpoint to the drumming on the roof.

"Just in time," Balian admitted, remembering to turn and introduce. "This
is Lucas de la Fierté, the son of one of my father's Cypriot knights." Lucas bowed
to Lady Eschiva, his face brightly flushed by the heat after the cold air outside.

"Welcome, Lucas," Lady Eschiva greeted him with a smile. "We'll have you
out of those wet clothes and into something dry and warm in no time. And then
we'll all have a warm meal," she promised, adding, "When Zachary arrived with
the news you would be coming, I told the kitchen staff to delay dinner until
you arrived."

"Very kind, my lady. We're famished."

"But first come and get out of those wet clothes. Oh! I almost forgot to
introduce Cecilia! She is so much a part of my life now, I forgot you haven't
met her! Cecilia joined me in Acre the day before I sailed for Cyprus, but I can't
imagine life without her anymore."

Cecilia blushed and dipped a curtsey to Sir Balian, while Lucas turned
an even brighter red. Balian recognized his squire's discomfort and laughed to
himself, feeling so much more mature. Cecilia was a very pretty young woman,
but in Balian's eyes, she was plump and conventional compared to Eschiva.
Cecilia, Balian thought, was just a doll, while Eschiva was a woman—a woman
of character, courage, and a trace of mystery that came from always being able
to surprise him.

Eschiva led them across the hall to the stairwell at the juncture to the solar that led to the floor above. Here, a grey-haired knight stood stiffly. Eschiva introduced him as the steward Sir Rohard, and he bowed his head to Balian with a muttered, "Welcome to Vouno, Sir Balian. We are honored." Somehow he managed to make his words sound less than welcoming, and Balian suspected he didn't feel particularly honored either. He gestured for Balian to follow him up the stairs with a nod to Eschiva that she could—or did he mean should?—remain behind.

The stairwell was dark, and they moved at a slow pace due to Sir Rohard's limp (one knee didn't bend), but at the top, they were met by warmth, the soft light of a fire, and a steaming tub. Sir Rohard told Balian and Lucas to strip down right away, and Balian looked for a chair to sit on while he removed his boots. He found himself standing behind Eschiva's desk, and was immediately distracted by the sight of her work spread out on the little table.

"My lady has a commission from the Knights Templar," Sir Rohard explained from behind him.

Balian spun about to look at him. "The Templars commissioned her? That's wonderful! What is it?" He turned to look more closely at the illustration she was working on. The light was terrible due to the storm, but from what he could decipher, it looked like a battle scene.

"It is to be a new copy of Archbishop William of Tyre's history of *Deeds Done Beyond the Sea*."

"What rich material! Eschiva must be delighted!"

"Yes," Sir Rohard admitted uncertainly. "Yes, I think she is. She has been working very hard on the project ever since she arrived here."

"When was that?"

"Almost a month ago."

That surprised Balian. She had been this close for a whole month and hadn't let him know earlier? Why was that? Distracted by this thought, he sat down, removed his boots and hose, and then stood to step out of his braies and toss aside his shirt. Sir Rohard took advantage of the fact that his guest was stark naked to ask bluntly, "May I ask why you're here, Sir Balian?" His eyes bore into Balian from under his bushy, grey eyebrows.

"I'd like to buy some sheep or goats to take back for the men at the siege of St. Hilarion." Balian stuck to his alibi as he stepped over the edge of the tub into the hot water, wincing a little at the hot temperature. Adjusting, he sank down with a contented sigh, and then submerged completely, sloshing some water over the edge. As he came up, he combed his wet hair out of his face with his hands and reached for the soap. "This is the first time I've been warm in months," he announced, rubbing the soap at the back of his neck and then under his arms and between his legs.

Sir Rohard was not so easily distracted from his interrogation. "We have no livestock at Vouno, sir. The manor produces predominantly olives."

"No livestock?" Balian tried to sound surprised.

"No, just a couple of goats and three cows for milk and cheese. Surely you knew that before you came?"

"No, I didn't. Tell me more about Vouno," Balian ordered as he stood, took a towel to dry his face, and then stepped out of the tub to let Lucas bathe before the water cooled.

As he rubbed himself dry, Sir Rohard frowned unconsciously but answered the question proudly. "It was held by a Greek nobleman who chose to remain in Constantinople rather than take service with the Lusignan, so it fell to the crown. King Aimery bestowed it on his daughter at the time of her marriage to Walter de Montbéliard on the condition it remain part of her dower. That was when I was sent here, still a young man, to look after it for her. I'd ruined my knee, you see," he patted the side of his knee as he spoke. Then he continued, "Lady Burgundia left it to my lady Eschiva at her death, and it is part of her inheritance."

"And you've been here all that time?"

"Yes."

"Were you harassed by the Langobards this past winter?"

"No, not really. They came once, but they must have had orders to leave royal properties alone. As you may have noticed, the Lusignan arms are still over the entrance to the courtyard and in the hall. I took the precaution to fly the Lusignan standard from the tower and instructed the staff to say it was a Lusignan property. Which it is," he stressed.

"Well done," Balian praised while noting mentally that Sir Rohard was a Lusignan man. Better that than a man of Montaigu, but he was hostile nonetheless. Balian supposed he'd heard about that stupid incident with Denise and mistrusted Balian's intentions vis-à-vis his lady.

Meanwhile, Zach was offering him one of Sir Rohard's kaftans, but Balian opted for his own clothes, which had been kept dry inside his leather saddle roll. He chose a clean shirt, hose, gambeson and surcoat, the latter red with elaborate gold embroidery eight inches wide depicting dragons and lions fighting. His boots were too wet to put back on, however, so he accepted low shoes from Sir Rohard. As he girded his sword around his hips over the splendid surcoat, he faced the older knight directly. "Livestock is only part of the reason I'm here. I am also here to see Lady Eschiva."

"I see. And just what is Lady Eschiva to you?" Sir Rohard asked bluntly.

"My cousin!" Balian answered with a mischievous smile. It didn't disarm Sir Rohard.

The old knight looked up at the young nobleman three inches taller than himself, dressed in splendor he could not dream of imitating, and stood his ground. "She is my liege."

"And she is lucky to have such a steadfast and loyal vassal," Balian praised, but his voice had taken on just enough of an edge to remind the knight that he was the heir to the most powerful man in Cyprus.

Eschiva, Balian, Lucas, Cecilia and Sir Rohard had seats at the high table on the dais. Zach and Sir Rohard's squire took over the duties of carving and serving for the high table, while at the lower tables the tenants and servants happily helped themselves. This was a country manor, not a royal court, and the atmosphere was decidedly relaxed. Meanwhile, the thunderstorm moved on and the rain grew gradually softer until it tapered off altogether.

Balian was acutely aware of Eschiva's proximity. She smelled of lavender. Her hair cascaded down her back like spun gold. The silk of her veils and gown shimmered in the candlelight. But most endearing, Balian thought, were her hands: they were naked of rings, her wedding band already discarded, and they were graceful as she fingered her goblet. But they were also stained with ink. Balian wanted to take one in his and kiss it. Instead, conscious of Sir Rohard's hawkeyed observation, he remarked to Eschiva. "Sir Rohard tells me you have been commissioned by the Knights Templar to illuminate a new copy of Archbishop William of Tyre's history of Outremer."

"All thanks to you, Balian!" Eschiva replied looking at him with eyes brimming with gratitude.

"How's that?" he asked back puzzled.

"Don't you remember? On our picnic to Mt. Lebanon. You told me to go the canons of the Holy Sepulcher and to ask to continue my studies. It was there that Father Ernesius found me. Remember? He was there the day the Emperor attacked the Temple in Acre. He had just offered me this commission, only the Emperor's attack and then my departure for Cyprus gave me no time to tell you." She paused and added sourly, "Gerard was angry with me. He said it was inappropriate for a lady to take commissions like a common laborer. He said it degraded me. He objected to the smell of the paints and inks, and said they stained my hands as if I worked in a dye factory."

Balian laughed, caught her hand and took it to his lips. "They do—but for such good purpose. Your husband was a fool, and we both know it. You have a great gift. It would be an insult to God for you not to exercise it."

Eschiva's hand closed around his fiercely as she whispered almost inaudibly, "Thank you, Balian. That's the most beautiful thing you could have said!"

They gazed into one another's eyes until Sir Rohard loudly cleared his throat and announced, "Sir Balian tells me he is here to purchase livestock. I suggest taking him to Agios Ioannis tomorrow. They have large herds and should be willing to sell for the right price."

Balian shifted his gaze to Sir Rohard, but he pointedly did not release Eschiva's hand as he answered. "That is very kind of you, sir."

Eschiva, however, slipped her hand from his and reached for her goblet nervously. Balian turned his eyes to her. She seemed unnerved, but he didn't understand why. He looked beyond her to her waiting-woman questioningly, but Cecilia just smiled back radiantly.

"Signora," Balian addressed Cecilia, "I don't believe I caught your full name."

"Di Domenico, Sir Balian. My lady tells me that you knew my late husband Maurizio."

Balian started visibly. "Maurizio? You're Maurizio's bride?"

His tone made Cecilia start and pull back. "Why does that surprise you, sir? Do you think me unworthy?" Her happy smile had vanished, replaced by a wounded look.

"No, no, not at all," Balian hastened to assure her while trying to decide if he should say anything about his encounter with Maurizio on the *San Valentino*. After securing the port, he had looked for Maurizio, but the Genoese had already taken his wages and disappeared again. The officers and crew of the *San Valentino* had shrugged: sailors come and go. To Cecilia, he stammered out, "I was—you are every bit as beautiful as he said you were. He talked of little else on our voyage to Andria and back. He couldn't wait to return to you, to his wedding. I—I could hardly believe the news that his ship had wrecked. But I— heard his remains were never found. Are—are you sure he is dead?"

Tears filled Cecilia's eyes and she shook her head. "It is nearly a year since his ship wrecked. Surely he would have found me, had he lived. Unless—I sometimes fear—he might have fallen into the hands of Saracen slavers."

Balian nodded ambiguously, but assured Cecilia solemnly, "You have my deepest condolences, Signora di Domenico."

Cecilia nodded. "I cannot believe my loss either, Sir Balian, but I am fortunate to have found a home and friend in Lady Eschiva." She glanced at Eschiva with an expression of gratitude bordering on awe.

Balian nodded vigorously with a glance at Eschiva. He would, he thought, tell her about Maurizio and let her decide how to handle it. Eschiva, meanwhile, was telling about how Cecilia had brought her the letter from King Henry warning Philip of Novare not to return home. The conversation turned to the many events they had experienced separately before and after the Battle of Nicosia.

After dinner, they retired to the solar. Although the rain had all but ceased, the cloud cover was still dense and low, bringing an early dusk. They lit several lamps and stoked the fire back to life. The intimacy of the solar combined with the fall of night filled Eschiva with almost unbearable tension. When Balian had mounted the stairs from the kitchen to the hall, looking as much like a drowned rat as a famous knight, her heart had overflowed with warmth. At that moment, he had been her beloved in need of warmth and food. When he had returned dressed like a rich nobleman, she had felt transported to a romance. His looks, his touch, his appreciation of her art had transformed her into a heroine, a beautiful heroine. The conversation had bridged all gaps of absence. For the last two hours, they had been good friends, catching up, sharing experiences and feelings. Not for a moment had she felt threatened or unsure.

But now, when Balian asked Zach to show Lucas where they could unpack and Cecilia excused herself with a conspiratorial smile, she felt a wave of panic rise up from her heart. Fortunately, Sir Rohard stubbornly refused to follow Cecilia's example. Instead, he settled himself in an armchair and conspicuously poured himself a goblet of wine. Then he looked at Sir Balian provocatively.

Eschiva held her breath for a moment, but Balian with a smile reached over and poured a goblet for himself. He lifted it to the old knight. "Sir Rohard. Your health."

Sir Rohard responded warily, "And yours."

They drank and, before Balian could get out another word, Sir Rohard leaned back in his chair and demanded, "Tell me about the sieges. We are not well-informed here in Vouno."

"You heard, of course, that my father obtained the surrender of the Langobards holding Kyrenia?"

"I did hear that, yes."

"Kantara still holds out, and Sir Anseau was, last I heard, building a new siege engine to reduce the outer works."

"With his lady trapped inside?" Eschiva asked appalled. She had not seen much of Yvonne this last year, but the thought of being a hostage to the baillies while her husband prepared to batter down the walls around her made Eschiva shudder in sympathy.

"Yes. It is an awkward situation, to say the least," Balian answered levelly. "My father has gone to Kantara to see if he can convince Cheneché to surrender—or at least release the Lady of Karpas."

"And you command at St. Hilarion," Sir Rohard noted.

"Such as it is," Balian responded with a shrug. "Most of my knights and archers have better things to do than sit around in the rain waiting for Barlais to see reason." He glanced at the ceiling where the sound of water trickling down the gutters was still audible.

"So you are here," Sir Rohard observed pointedly.

"I am here," Balian agreed. Then with a glance at Eschiva he told Sir Rohard, "Not only am I here, but I wish to be alone with Lady Eschiva."

Eschiva caught her breath. No, she wanted to tell him. No, not now, not yet, not tonight. Let us talk first. We can go together to Agios Ioannis, or visit the orchards, or ride up to Buffavento. Let us talk alone—but not after dark in the soft surroundings of the solar. She wanted to say that, but no sound came out.

Instead, Balian forestalled Sir Rohard's protest by announcing, "Before you *impute* base motives to me and reproach me with the indiscretions of my youth, I will give you my word of honor that nothing will happen between Lady Eschiva and myself that discredits her or dishonors me."

That caught both Sir Rohard and Eschiva by surprise. Eschiva held her breath and Sir Rohard stared him in the eye for a long time. Then he got to his feet, the goblet still in his hand, and announced, "I will take you at your word, Sir Balian, despite your reputation, and the shame be on *your* head, not mine, if you do not keep your faith."

Balian also got to his feet and bowed his head slightly. The old knight stiffly made his way up the stairs to the chamber overhead. Balian waited, standing with his ears cocked until he heard the door to Sir Rohard's chamber click shut. Then he set his goblet down and crossed to Eschiva.

She waited, holding her breath. God help me, she thought, I am wax in his hands. I will do whatever he wants of me, but...

He went down on his heels, resting his elbows on the arms of her chair. "Mi dons, what do you think? Would a kiss discredit you or dishonor me?"

Eschiva answered by leaning forward and kissing him gently yet intently. It was a lovely, long kiss, and when Balian drew back he looked searchingly into Eschiva's face. "I am here at your command, mi dons, yet you seem nervous and unsure of yourself. Can you tell me why?"

"Because we need to *talk*—to come to an understanding about our love, our future," Eschiva answered in a rush as she let out her breath in relief. Then she remembered to add, "Thank you for coming, Balian—and for giving your word to Sir Rohard about—about not dishonoring me."

"Mi dons, I am at your service—and hurt that you took so long to send for me. But you are right, we need to talk—about us and our future."

Eschiva indicated the chair beside her that Cecilia had vacated, and when he sat down she reached out her hand to him. He took it and waited expectantly. She clutched his hand, as she mustered her thoughts and arguments. "When I was fifteen, Queen Yolanda asked me to go with her to the court of the Holy Roman Emperor. I was thrilled and excited. I thought a whole new world was opening to me. Instead, I found myself locked, literally, inside a harem. When I ran away from the harem, I thought my brother would marry me to an important lord, and I would have my own manors, income, and household. Instead, I found myself married to a man who despised me and confined to Paradhisi with little more control over my life than in the harem. When I fled with Aunt Alys…" she broke off.

"Go on," he urged her with a nod. He didn't seem as angry or impatient as she had feared.

Eschiva could barely whisper as she tried to put her deepest feelings into words. "When I fled to Beirut, I saw in the storm and the wreck the wrath of God, and I thought I should have died. When you came to me, you saved more than my life, Balian. You saved my soul. I had lost more than my paintings, I had lost myself."

"I know," Balian told her, squeezing her hand. "Bella told me."

Eschiva raised his hand to her lips, before continuing, "You brought warmth to my frozen heart, Balian, and light to the darkness. I only wanted to live to see you again, but when I learned you had landed with your father and brothers to confront the baillies, I realized that my appeal to you might be the cause of your death. So I promised God I would be a good wife to Gerard if only He would spare your life and limb."

Balian looked over at her and teased gently, "I need you praying for me more often."

Eschiva ignored him and continued, "When you came to the Hospital and told me Gerard was dead, I was—amazed. And then you said I was free."

"Yes."

"What did you mean by free?"

"That you are now free to marry again." He stood and came to stand before her chair. "To marry me," he clarified and bent to kiss her.

Eschiva surrendered, but as she felt her limbs becoming molten, panic reasserted itself. She pushed him away to admit, "I'm frightened."

"Of what?" Balian asked pulling back.

"Marriage."

"Ah," he replied ambiguously. "Can you be more specific?"

"It killed Yolanda and made me miserable!"

"I see." Balian answered seriously, adding, "And you think I am like Frederick Hohenstaufen? Gerard de Montaigu?" He was looking deep into her eyes, an expression of hurt lurking in his own.

"No! No, of course not!" Eschiva admitted. "You couldn't be more different."

"Then, what is it?"

She tried subterfuge next. "I don't think I'd make a good mother. I'm too selfish. I never really took an interest in Gerard's son. I was much more interested in the crusade and my painting and even the Drakakis family."

"I'm willing to take a chance. I think you will love your own children just as you love your art."

Angry at being forced to say it out loud, Eschiva burst out, "I'm not good at *making* babies either. I—"

Balian burst out laughing.

Wounded and confused, Eschiva drew as far back in the chair as possible. "I'm serious!" she protested, offended.

Balian reached out and stroked the side of her face with the back of his hand. "I know you are, Eschiva. And I understand—"

"How can you understand when you obviously like it so much?" she flung back at him furiously.

Balian answered by pulling her into his arms. She resisted at first, but not too strongly. After a second or two, she stopped struggling and dropped her head on his chest with a deep sigh of confused contentment. It felt good to be in his arms, if only it wouldn't lead to other intimacies.

He bent and kissed the top of her head. "I understand because it is the stupidity and brutality of other men that have paved the way for my own successes. I'm not the least surprised that Gerard de Montaigu didn't know how to please you. Trust me."

"You gave your word to Sir Rohard," she reminded him trying to pull out of his arms again, angry with herself for being so weak and at him for being duplicitous.

Balian held her firmly and spoke calmly. "Mi dons, you will grant me your favors when you are ready, and not a moment before—Sir Rohard or no Sir Rohard." When she said nothing he nudged her with a kiss on the side of her head and prompted, "Am I right?"

"And you will accept that? Even if I am your wife?" she asked warily. It was not really believable that he could accept a marriage without consummation. He was heir to Beirut. He would need heirs. No, it wasn't reasonable. Marriage was out of the question without consummation.

Yet, Balian seemed totally at ease. "Yes, mi dons. Whether you are my wife or not, you are still my lady. What choice do I have but to obey you?" A smile was curling his lips as he spoke and he tilted his head to get a better view of her face.

"Balian?" She drew back, forcing him to loosen his hold so she could look him in the face as another thought struck her. "You are very sure I will surrender, aren't you?"

"Very."

"How can you be so sure?"

"Because, mi dons, you are a passionate woman with great depths of feeling and inner fire—not to mention courage enough for a dozen men."

Eschiva didn't seem to know what to make of that answer, and Balian was evidently content to let her think about it. He kissed her again, gently and longingly, but then drew back and left her alone in the solar.

If the visit to Vouno had not fulfilled Balian's expectations, it had left him far from disappointed. It was, he reflected, Eschiva's unpredictability and her interest in things other than love and babies that intrigued him. Too many of his conquests had been obsessed with love. As a youth, their adoration for his body had been flattering; now he found it at best boring and at worst demeaning. The other girls had mostly been obsessed with his seed and bearing offspring with the blood of Ibelin in their veins. Denise had been a bit of both. She left a bitter taste in his mouth and made him wary of anyone with similar inclinations.

Eschiva, on the other hand, had captured his attention and admiration by her courage, her enthusiasm for the world around her, and her imagination, as evidenced by her evocative images. Eschiva had the courage of a man and the imagination of an artist. Her allure lay in that which made her different.

He laughed at himself, recognizing that Philip of Novare was right about one thing: the harder it was to win a woman, the more valuable she became. At some level, he was pleased that Eschiva had not wanted to take him to her bed—just yet. She called it fear, but it was self-respect too. Gerard de Montaigu had made physical love degrading to her, and she did not want to be degraded again. She was proud, his Eschiva, proud and independent.

Not all that surprising, Balian reasoned, she had the blood of kings in her veins—and the blood of Baldwin d'Ibelin. His great-uncle Baldwin, Eschiva's great-grandfather, had preferred to renounce the Barony of Ramla and Mirabel to doing homage to Guy de Lusignan. That was the kind of self-respect and refusal to submit to unworthy authority that had induced Eschiva to risk the wrath of the Holy Roman Emperor. It was what made her want to run her own estates now. She was proud and independent, and he was proud of her because of it.

And she had saved his life.

Whenever he remembered that he felt his heart miss a beat. He looked down at his wrists. They were covered by the sleeves of both his shirt and hauberk and by the leather of his gloves, but underneath were the scars, the humiliation, and the mockery of Barlais and the Emperor. Pretty boy. Loverboy. The worthless son of the great Lord of Beirut. The weak link in the chain that they could break in order to shatter his father's resistance.

Balian felt his hatred for Barlais and the Emperor flame up again. Sometimes he suppressed it. Sometimes he forgot it altogether. Yet it smoldered subconsciously—until something triggered a memory of his humiliation.

"Sir? What are all these horses doing here?" Lucas broke into Balian's thoughts, and he looked up sharply. They had been riding for roughly two hours since daybreak and had already left the main Nicosia-Kyrenia road. They were still roughly an hour from the siege camp below St. Hilarion. Around them were steep, rocky slopes, hardly suited to grazing goats, much fewer horses. Yet horses spread out on the mountain face on either side of them. That didn't make any sense.

Balian drew up to look more closely. The horses were unsaddled, of course, but many were trailing leads or wearing broken halters. Worse, several were limping and bleeding from gashes in their shoulders and chests.

"St. George! That's Gebremariam!" He had spotted his own young destrier, milling unhappily among the rocks and scrub brush with blood on his face and neck. Balian turned off the track and started to cut across the rocky hillside. Damon snorted in commentary, and Gebremariam looked over, his head raised and ears pointed as he recognized Damon's voice or scent. Then, from farther up the trail, men on foot came crashing through the underbrush. They were staggering with exhaustion and more undressed than dressed.

Balian instantly changed course, and dropped his hand to his hilt, calling to Lucas to stay back. As soon as he rejoined the path, he nudged Damon into a canter and crossed the distance in less than a minute. Even before he reached the men, however, he released his sword and sat back to slow Damon.

"My lord! They overwhelmed us! Fell on us in the middle of the night!"

"They've taken the camp!"

"And all our supplies!"

The men who called out to him were strangers, archers by their clothes, but further back, stumbling and limping on foot, were knights who had been with him at the siege. Balian tapped Damon's flanks and the stallion sprang forward along the trail towards the horseless knights. "What happened?" Balian demanded as he drew up before them.

"Gibelet and Bethsan! They sortied out in the middle of the night and took us all by surprise!"

"Where the hell is Novare?" Balian demanded, but without waiting for an answer he spun about and shouted to Lucas, "Bring me my helmet!"

As Lucas jogged up, Balian pulled his padded coif from his saddlebag, secured his aventail, and took his helmet from Lucas to hang it on the pommel hook of his own saddle. Then he twisted around to shout back at the infantry. "Bring the sound horses back to the camp!"

Turning to the knights, he said, "You damn well better know how to ride bareback because it seems you lost your saddles!"

"They came out of nowhere, my—"

"They came out of St. Hilarion, and if you'd had a proper watch they wouldn't have caught you with your braies down!"

My father is going to kill me, Balian was thinking. He's going to skin me alive and hang my guts from the nearest tree.

He saw more men farther up the trail and was so agitated that he kicked Damon, provoking an angry buck before the loyal horse bolted forward. The next cluster of men were squires, looking frightened, and mostly half-naked. They too babbled about being taken by surprise in the middle of the night. "They stole our supplies."

"That prolongs their ability to hold out and hope the emperor rescues them!" Balian explained irritably while praying inwardly that the attack was indeed intended only to replenish supplies. But what if the attack on their supplies had been only a diversion so that Barlais could escape?

His father would never forgive him.

Forget his father! He would never forgive himself!

"Get the horses and return to camp! FAST!" he shouted after the squires, and again took up a canter, pressing for more speed as his fears mounted.

When he passed additional clusters of shaken and panicked men, he didn't even slow down, only shouted at them. "Turn around, you cowardly curs! Get back to the camp!"

The closer he got to the camp, the greater was the chaos. The paddocks had been broken down, whether by escaping horses or Barlais' men was a moot point. The woodpile had toppled over, probably pushed. Wine barrels had rolled in all directions and lay here and there against rocks or trees, some still intact, others leaking wine into the countryside and filling the mountain air with the smells of a tavern. The tents of the knights had all collapsed, their ties cut, and here and there they had been trampled as well. The mess tent, in contrast, had been sliced open, and the contents dragged out. The tent beside the oven which had held their sacks of grain lay gutted, surrounded by trampled ground.

Looking beyond the camp, Balian saw the gates to St. Hilarion were still open and his blood ran cold. While some men were still rolling barrels towards the barbican and others were hauling carts laden with sacks of grain and amphora of oil inside, other men appeared to be issuing *out* of the castle. The attack on their supplies might have been only a probe of their defenses, a daring sortie to see if the besiegers were awake. When they were caught sleeping, Bethsan and Gibelet might have reported back to Barlais that the camp was in disarray, resistance chased away.

Balian narrowed his eyes trying to see better what was happening at the barbican. For the moment, only confusion reigned. Meanwhile, the sight of Sir Balian brought men from behind rocks, out of gullies, and even dropping down from trees. Sir Robert ran over to Balian, limping badly. "My lord, Gibelet and Bethsan—"

"I can see, damn it! Get the tack out from under the tent! All of you! Get your weapons! You're knights, not clowns!"

Everyone started running in different directions.

"Where the hell is Novare?"

"I'm here, Balian!" Novare's voice came from one of the trees, and Balian turned to watch him scramble down, still in his nightshirt. "They surprised us just two hours before dawn, when—"

"Save it for later!" Balian told him sharply. "The baillies are trying to escape! Get armed."

From behind him, the first of the knights and squires riding the bareback horses were coming into the camp. Balian turned on them. "Get them tacked up immediately! Lucas!"

"Yes, my lord?"

"Find me a lance!"

"Yes, sir!"

Balian glanced again toward the fortress, and his heart tried to leap out of his mouth. The chaos had resolved itself into a body of fully armed knights. "Sir Robert! Mount up on Gebremariam! He's not seriously injured!" Balian had seen that his stallion was cantering voluntarily beside some of the returning horses and despite the blood on his face, he was evidently not lame. "Lucas! Bring three lances!"

Whether it was Balian's orders or other men had also seen what he had seen, the efforts to find tack and get the returning horses saddled had become frantic.

Sir Robert had Gebremariam by the mane and by the time Lucas returned with three lances, he had hauled himself up into Balian's saddle. Seeing that at least three other knights had managed to get mounted as well, Balian shouted for them to follow him and started galloping up the slope toward the barbican.

Philip de Novare was not among them. He simply gaped in horror as Sir Balian with just five other mounted men charged a body of nearly thirty knights emerging from St. Hilarion. He would later write that Sir Balian, "had so few strong men that this battle was amazing."

Balian caught sight of Barlais. As usual, he was surrounded by taller knights on bigger horses—as if he were a king or emperor, who deserved to be protected by the lives of others. Balian gritted his teeth.

We should have hanged him for the attempted murder of Toringuel, Balian thought. We should have let Karpas kill him for claiming the bailliage! How many good men had already died because of Barlais? Uncle Walter was only one, but one of the best.

Damon had his ears flat on his head and his teeth bared as they charged. He was leaping up the incline, racing Gebremarian. Lucas' palfrey lagged behind, but other knights trying to join the charge from farther back were gaining on the leaders. Ahead, trumpets were blaring. Abruptly Barlais' knights spun about and made a dash for the still open gate.

"Cowards!" Balian screamed at the top of his voice, but no one could hear it as the sound was trapped inside his helmet.

As he reached the top of the incline, at the base of the barbican, the portcullis crashed down so close on the heels of the fleeing knights that horses screamed. The sound echoed for a second before the gates were flung shut. Balian's lance smashed and shattered on the wooden beams, and Damon reared up and spun about on his haunches to avoid colliding with the barrier.

Balian tore his helmet off his head and screamed at the top of his lungs, "Coward! Come out and fight, you bastard! Come out and face me, Barlais!"

Sir Robert, however, already had hold of his arm and was shouting at him to get out of range. "They have archers up there! Pull back!" He grabbed Damon's reins, and hauled the horse down the slope, as arrows splattered into the mud around them. The latter, fortunately, had been shot in haste without much effort to take aim.

They spent the rest of the day trying to clean up, put things back together, and take stock of their losses. There had been no casualties as such. Some of the horses, like Gebremariam, had been injured breaking out of their paddocks or during their flight in the dark, but none so seriously that he had to be put down. As for the men, they had some twisted ankles and sprained wrists from running, tripping or rolling to safety as they fled. Since there had been no armed resistance, however, there were no serious injuries among the men either.

The tactic used by the baillies had been to sneak out of the castle and silently but more or less simultaneously cut the ropes holding up the accommodation tents. This had left all the inhabitants trapped inside and struggling to get out while the raiders chased the horses away and plundered the supply tents. In the darkness, men had not easily grasped what was happening. Many had been utterly disoriented and half suffocated by the time they got out of their tents. They could hear men shouting and plundering, and many assumed that they were lone survivors after the others had been slaughtered. As they came out from under the tents, they had either fled down the path or hidden in the surrounding gullies and trees. Arms and armor, like tack, remained trapped under the tents, but not plundered or damaged.

The losses in supplies, on the other hand, were serious. Their stock of grain had been completely gutted. The stores of cooking oil, smoked meat, salt, sugar, dried fruits, lentils, and beans had been decimated. Although a few barrels of wine were retrieved in-tact, at least ¾ of their wine supplies had either been stolen or drained out of damaged casks.

Balian, numbed by the magnitude of the disaster, was trying to draw up a procurement list when an intangible wave of agitation swept over the camp. It was late afternoon and the sun hung very low in the western sky. He looked up alarmed and squinted toward the barbican, but nothing seemed to be moving there beyond the listlessly flapping banners of Barlais, Bethsan, and Gibelet.

Then with a sense of impending doom, Balian realized the commotion was coming from the opposite direction: the trail back to the Nicosia-Kyrenia road. Balian put down the quill he was using to scratch his list on a re-used parchment and stood to watch his father ride through the devastated camp.

The Lord of Beirut sat straight in his saddle, the arms of Ibelin on his surcoat and trapper. His face was impassive as he looked from side to side assessing the damage. He was accompanied by a dozen men, and all the horses were dusty, tired and sweated despite the chilly temperatures. They had ridden hard to get here before dark.

Beirut caught sight of his eldest son and directed his horse toward him. Balian just waited. Novare and Sir Robert, who had been working with him on drawing up the list of goods needed, likewise got to their feet.

Beirut drew up in front of his son. "I'm told," he opened without prelude, "that not one of my sons was in this camp when it was attacked. Is that true?"

"Yes, my lord."

"Why?"

"Hugh had a lung infection so I sent him to Nicosia to recover."

Beirut nodded and waited for more.

"Baldwin went with him. I don't know why, but he hasn't been back since. That was fourteen days ago."

"And you?"

"I was trying to secure livestock so we could have fresh meat. It will be arriving in the next day or two." At least that was true, Balian reflected, but he swallowed hard nevertheless. If his father found out about Eschiva...

"And who was in command?"

"Novare, my lord."

Beirut's gaze shifted immediately to Novare, but beyond a twitch of his eyebrows, he made no comment. Instead, Beirut wearily dismounted from his horse and said, "I wish to speak with you alone, Balian." He handed off his reins to Sir Robert, took Balian by the upper arm, and moved with him to a copse of pine trees.

Balian could hear his heart beating and wondered if his father could hear it too. Beirut, at last, came to a halt and turned to face his son. "I don't know what to say. I have seen your courage with my own eyes. When you went down on the quay at Gastria, I felt as if a horse was trampling in my own chest. You, more than anyone, won the Battle at Nicosia. Your uncle was killed, I was trapped, the men of Ibelin scattered, but you rallied them and delivered the decisive blow. Now, men tell me your lance is still embedded in the gate up there!" He pointed in the direction of the barbican.

Balian said nothing. The ax hadn't fallen yet.

"You have the courage of a lion, Balian, but where is your common sense? Where is your judgment? Where is your sense of responsibility? I thought you had matured in the last year, but when I see this," his father gestured toward the disarray around them, "I see a young man still guided more by his passion and his whims than his reason."

What could Balian say to that? Guilty as charged.

Yet Balian felt a surge of rebelliousness too. "Are you so sure battles," and hearts he added mentally, "can be won by reason, my lord?"

"Sieges can, yes."

Balian nodded and swallowed down the rebuke. "It won't happen again, my lord. I will stay here until either Barlais or I are dead."

"No, you won't. We will establish a roster of knights and sergeants, and you and your brothers will rotate the command. One of you will *always* be here in future, but the other two will have time to recuperate and attend to other business, just as the knights and archers will. I should have thought of it sooner. I take full responsibility for what happened here—but I hope you learned a valuable lesson." The look his father gave him was conciliatory. The lecture was over, and he was on the brink of a smile.

Balian hesitated, but then he accepted the olive branch and cracked a smile. "Yes, my lord."

Beirut flung his arm over Balian's shoulders and hugged him briefly. "It was my fault, Balian. Really it was. This is a miserable place to spend your time—especially when you're only 22."

Chapter Twenty-Eight
Amnesty

St. Hilarion, Cyprus
Easter Sunday, 1230

"THEY MUST HAVE SLAUGHTERED THAT POOR donkey," Lucas announced, ducking into his lord's tent as he came off watch.

It was Easter Sunday, April 7, 1230. The Archdeacon of Kyrenia had come to the camp on Good Friday accompanied by several priests and acolytes to read the Good Friday Mass, hear confessions and bless the men. The churchmen had stayed two nights at camp, and read the Easter service at dawn. Breaking their fast after celebrating Mass, the besiegers had enjoyed a plentiful feast including roast lamb garnished with mint-yogurt sauce bedded in boiled wild greens. By noon, however, the churchmen had departed, glad to be heading back for the comfort and cleanliness of the city.

The soldiers, on the other hand, were conscious that the camp was much more comfortable than it had been in winter. The weather was predominantly dry, the temperatures neither too hot nor too cold and the breezes gentle. Most important, the rotation had done wonders for morale. Many men had returned to the siege, now that they knew they would spend no more than a month at a time in camp. Balian had resumed command on Palm Sunday and with him were nearly 130 men, including 60 archers and 37 knights.

"There wasn't much meat left on the poor beast," Balian answered his squire. "He was slowly starving to death and maybe it was best to put him out of his misery."

"They killed him so they could have meat on Easter," Lucas answered morosely.

When Balian returned to the siege camp, he and Lucas had discovered that there were only two horses and a single donkey left in the paddock of the outer bailey of St. Hilarion. The garrison, it seemed, had been reduced to eating their beasts of burden. While this elated most of the besiegers because it indicated the situation inside St. Hilarion was becoming precarious, it had depressed Lucas because the squire loved animals. His love of horses made him particularly conscientious when it came to looking after Damon and Gebremariam, but Balian had noted that he took as much care of their pack-horses and was kind to donkeys and stray dogs as well.

"Barlais ate a donkey for Easter Sunday?" Novare asked cheerfully, stretching out his legs and loosening the belt over his well-stuffed belly. "That would make a great theme for a song!"

Novare had always been good at writing drinking ditties and his lengthy political poems had been entertaining, but of late he had taken to mocking the baillies and their men by writing songs about their plight and singing his compositions loudly outside the besieged castles. It had started at Kantara, where Novare, doing the rounds with Karpas before Christmas, had overheard men inside one of the semi-ruined towers lamenting their fate and cursing Barlais as a 'traitor.' He had quickly turned their remarks into a song. The reaction from the walls of Kantara had been vehement and violent, suggesting he had struck a raw nerve.

Since re-joining Balian at St. Hilarion, Novare had performed to an equally "enthusiastic" reception from the defenders of St. Hilarion. Now, laughing with delight at his own cleverness, he started throwing out rhyming couplets about "long-eared lambs" and an Easter feast that would "take until Pentecost to chew on."

"Lucas, why don't you take Gebremariam out for a short gallop? He could use the exercise," Balian suggested to his squire, seeing that Novare's humor was getting on the squire's nerves.

Lucas nodded and ducked back out of the tent.

"The boy is too sensitive," Novare remarked at once, "and you shouldn't coddle him or he'll never make much of a knight."

Balian shrugged. Thinking that Novare too was better suited to composing poems and singing songs than fighting, he remarked, "Not all of us are cut out for the brutal business of war."

Novare missed the subtle rebuke and returned enthusiastically to his poem about the long-eared lamb. Indeed, he jumped up and found his lute to start trying out melodies for the rapidly evolving lyrics. Balian decided to leave him to it and went out into the late afternoon to stretch his legs.

As often before, he walked first around the perimeter of the camp, checking on the sentries and making sure all was in order. Then he struck out to walk along the lower walls of St. Hilarion. This meant climbing up the steep slope of the hill while keeping out of range of the archers. He had to navigate rugged and treacherous ground where the underbrush disguised the contours of the land. At this time of year, however, the hills were covered with wildflowers too. Balian had counted no less than 23 different varieties before he lost track. The intermingling of white, yellow, blue, purple and red reminded him of Eschiva's paintings, and he longed to be with her.

Since their meeting in November, he had managed three trips to Vouno, but Baldwin had somehow found out about his visits and, getting revenge for Balian highlighting his dereliction of duty at the siege, made remarks over Christmas that inevitably provoked a parental rebuke. After Beirut's admonishments about hoping he had "learned his lesson," Balian had felt compelled to avow his honorable and utterly chaste relationship with his cousin.

The suspicions, however, remained. Because of his careless youth, he was not taken seriously. He remained, in everyone's eyes, the "lover boy" Barlais had mocked. Recognizing this, Balian was more determined than ever to prove them all wrong—to prove himself worthy of Eschiva. She was, after all, not only a king's grand-daughter but a woman of rare wisdom and virtue. The more they suspected him of base motives, the more determined Balian was to prove them wrong.

Meanwhile, Eschiva herself greeted him with more enthusiasm each time he came. His longing for her grew with each meeting, and the pain of separation increased with each parting. He felt trapped in a delectably complex dance of two steps forward and one back, sidesteps and pirouettes. Sometimes it felt like an exhausting dance of uncertain duration or outcome.

He reached the highest point of the wall, where it intersected with the sheer cliff, and paused to take in the breathtaking beauty of the view. The spine of the mountains stretched to the east, while to the west, the rocks reared upwards to the half-hidden towers and halls of the castle. In between, the slope clothed in wild-flowers tumbled to the camp with its striped tents and wiggling banners.

Balian squinted upwards and wondered how his brother Johnny and King Henry were faring. He assumed, he *had* to assume, that they were not suffering unduly from the shortages. Even Barlais must know that if harm came to the King or the King's sisters that he would have hell to pay. Yet, as Balian started down the slope again in the mellow light of late afternoon, he was chilled by fears of what Barlais might do to his younger brother. He only kept his worry about Johnny at bay by telling himself that Bethsan would not let anything happen to him. Bethsan had sided with Barlais because they were cousins, but he wasn't a dishonorable man, Balian told himself.

As he reached the foot of the hill where the wall turned west toward the barbican, he noticed that a large number of men seemed to be gathered on the walls. Balian paused and squinted toward them, trying to figure out why they had collected. Maybe they were finally going to sue for terms? Easter Sunday was surely the perfect day to abandon resistance for the chance of a new beginning?

Balian continued along the wall, heading toward the barbican, but his hopes of imminent surrender were disappointed. The crowd had gathered to hear Novare sing his latest composition. He was mounted on his palfrey, a large and docile stallion with easy gaits, but had dropped his reins to take his lute in his lap. He was singing at the top of his voice.

Balian shook his head in amusement and then tensed. From where he was, he could see that only half the men on the wall were watching Novare and making rude gestures in his direction. The others were watching something going on *inside* the bailey. Balian couldn't *see* what was happening, yet his soldier's instincts smelled a threat.

Without waiting to see what would happen, he ran for the camp. Lucas had just returned from his ride, and Balian shouted to him, "Don't untack! Give him to me!"

The surprised squire obeyed at once, but protested nevertheless, "I've ridden him quite hard, sir—"

"Not so hard that he can't do a bit more!" Balian answered swinging himself into the saddle, just as a shout went up from the watch on the perimeter of the camp.

"Sortie! Sortie!" the watch shouted.

The alarm sent other men dashing for their arms, while Balian pulled his coif up over his head and turned toward the barbican. Barlais men had swarmed out of the barbican on foot, their horses eaten or too weak to carry them. Balian noted furthermore that they must be running short of arrows because several were brandishing lances. The hoard of men rushed toward an astonished Novare, who held his lute rather than his reins in his hands. As Balian watched, the singer tried to save his lute before taking up the reins, and in that fatal moment, one of Barlais' men used a lance like a javelin. It fell on Novare's left, making his surprised horse spring sideways—right into the hands of men who had poured out of the postern. One of these men grabbed the reins and started to pull Novare toward the castle, a valuable hostage.

Balian put his heels to Gebremariam's flanks to try to overtake the kidnapper before Novare disappeared inside the castle walls. Another man, angrier at Novare's words, ran up and jabbed at Novare's chest with a lance at close range. Novare twisted away at the last second, but the force of the lance thrust shoved him off his horse. He crashed down, the lance still stuck in his arm.

Cheers erupted from the castle walls. "Your singer is dead! Your singer is dead! We've killed your singer!" they shouted, jumping up and down and waving their hands in the air triumphantly.

Balian was still five strides away, but the sound of Gebremariam's hooves warned Barlais' men that their moment of victory was transitory. They started running back for the safety of the castle walls, one still trying to drag Novare's horse with him. Balian directed Gebremariam at the man with the horse, his sword raised over his head. Instinct made the man look back and adrenaline made him run faster. Balian's sword slashed down, severing the reins to Novare's horse, but failed to connect with the fleeing knight.

Balian turned Gebremariam around and sprinted back to where Novare lay. He was stretched out on his side, blood from the embedded lance soaking his gambeson both front and back.

Balian jumped down, turned Gebremariam free, and fell on one knee beside his friend. "Philip?"

Novare groaned, stirred, and tried to right himself. "My lute!" he gasped out.

"Lie still," Balian advised, laying a hand on his shoulder.

Novare dropped his head back onto the dirt, but his breathing was heavy and he groaned before again gasping out, "My lute!"

"Don't worry about your lute," Balian advised as he looked more closely at the wound. The lance had gone right through Novare's arm and the tip pressed into the chainmail of his hauberk at the start of his ribcage, pinning his arm to his side. As gently as he could, Balian took hold of Novare's arm and lifted it to see how deeply the spear had gone into his chest. Novare gasped and cursed him, but the lance had not pierced the flesh of his side, nor broken any ribs. That was good.

Other men from the camp were starting to cluster around. Balian ordered two sergeants to bring him a saw and a stretcher and asked a knight to send his squire to Kyrenia for a surgeon.

Balian looked up from his friend to be sure there was no risk of another sortie, but a dozen Ibelin archers had taken up positions between Novare and the castle. They had shields protecting them and their bows at the ready. They would deter any new sorties, Balian concluded. Of course, they didn't stop stones being lobbed at them from the wall catapult, nor the cheering and jeering that continued unabated.

"You really managed to offend them this time," Balian joked to Novare, and the composer grimaced in appreciation.

Although Novare's chest had not been pierced, the bleeding from his arm was so profuse that Balian began to worry. He pushed his coif off the back of his head and removed his arming cap so he could wrap it around the lance to staunch the bleeding.

"Christ that hurts!" Novare protested, and then pleaded, "My lute, Balian. Find my lute." He was also starting to shake. Balian looked over his shoulder for someone with something they could use to wrap around Novare. One of the sergeants, reading his thoughts, undid the laces of his aketon and pulled it off over his head. Balian gently slipped it under Novare's arm and tucked it around his torso. His arming cap was already soaked with blood, however, and he was afraid to apply pressure to the wound as long as the lance was still embedded in Novare's flesh.

"We should put a tourniquet around his upper arm right under his armpit before he bleeds to death, sir," a grizzled older sergeant suggested knowingly.

Balian glanced up at him. "Can you do that?"

"Give me a belt or cord." The sergeant ordered generally as he knelt beside Novare from the other side.

The men with the stretcher trotted up, breathing hard, and a third man handed Balian the saw. As soon as the sergeant finished with the tourniquet, Balian started sawing the long shaft off the lance. Novare cried out in pain, reared up, and cursed him bitterly. The sergeant held Novare down with a gruff, "Lay still, sir. We need to shorten the shaft before we move you."

When the shaft had been reduced to just six inches sticking out of the wound, they lifted Novare onto the stretcher and returned to the camp. In Novare's tent, they transferred him to his bed and covered him with two blankets, while Novare's squire brought him wine laced with spurge flax powder. Although Novare was drenched in sweat and ghostly pale, he turned to Balian and again pleaded. "My lute, Balian. You've got to find my lute."

Balian almost protested, but then changed his mind. "I'll go find it now," he promised. Outside, he looked again toward the castle. It was a sharp, black silhouette against the red-orange sky of sunset. From their field kitchen came the scent of lamb stew steaming over the large cauldrons, and the horses were collected at the head of the paddocks to get their evening feed, snorting and snapping and kicking each other half-heartedly to ensure each got his share.

Novare's palfrey had joined the others, his tack still on, and Balian walked over. The leather sack in which Novare carried his lute was still slung from the pommel, and as Balian removed it and looked inside he found to his amazement that the instrument was intact.

"Here it is, Philip," he announced as he slipped back into the tent. "Safe and in one piece."

"Thank God!" Philip exclaimed, trying to sit up and then falling back again. "I've got the first two lines of my next song, Bal. '*I am wounded, yet my lips cannot close tight, about the traitor and his dreadful plight...*'"

"You're incorrigible!" Balian commented, not sure whether to laugh or cry for his friend.

St. Hilarion, Cyprus
Easter Sunday, 1230

Henry slipped into the stables and closed the door behind him. It was dark and spooky here. The ghosts of the horses they had killed haunted it. Henry could feel them looking at him from the empty stalls, their gentle, trusting eyes full of reproach. He had refused to eat the horse meat at first, protesting that they should have let the horses go free rather than eating them. "We don't *need* meat!" he had flung at Barlais angrily. "It's the middle of Lent!"

"Then don't eat it!" Barlais had snapped back, "but don't think I'm going to let you give any meat to that cur of yours! The meat is for humans only! From this moment forward, not a single piece of meat will be wasted on a stupid dog!"

"But Harry will starve without meat!" Henry had protested.

Barlais had shrugged, and Henry had looked to Bethsan, who sometimes seemed more sympathetic to his needs.

This time Sir Grimbert, however, had shaken his head doggedly. "I'm sorry my liege. I told you to leave the dog behind when we left Nicosia. I warned you a siege was no picnic. In our circumstances, we can't feed *any* useless mouths, much less a lapdog. As king, you should set a good example, not expect special privileges."

After that, Barlais had started talking about "puppy soup" whenever he caught sight of Harry. "Don't you think we should eat him today before he gets any thinner?" he would tease, or discuss what herbs they should use for garnishing the soup. Henry had tried to keep Harry out of Barlais' sight.

As the stables emptied and became vacant, Henry decided to hide Harry there, shut into the abandoned tack room. To Barlais he declared he had let Harry go, and when Barlais could not find Harry anywhere in the upper palace, he had stopped threatening. Johnny and Henry fed the dog with crusts of bread or anything else they could hide inside their shirts. But Harry was wasting away, weaker each day, and whenever he saw Henry he whined in misery.

So today Henry had capitulated. At their Easter Sunday meal, he had asked for a portion of meat. "What?" Barlais had asked. "Don't tell me you've had an epiphany?"

"Lent is over and I'm hungry," Henry had declared belligerently.

"You wouldn't still have that cur hidden somewhere, would you?" Barlais challenged.

"No! I'm just hungry," Henry insisted.

"Then eat up!" Barlais ordered, watching him closely.

Henry cut his portion of donkey meat into small squares, playing with the meat on his plate as long as possible, hoping Barlais would look the other way. He didn't. Henry had been forced to put the meat into his mouth and start chewing. He pretended to swallow and took another piece into his mouth and chewed some more. He took the third piece and his mouth was getting very full, but he still swallowed without swallowing. Finally, Barlais looked away, and Henry had snatched a napkin from the squire serving them and wiped his face with it—taking the pieces of meat out his mouth into his hand as he did so.

"What was that?" Barlais barked, turning back to glower at Henry suspiciously.

"I'm feeling queasy," Henry replied.

"I'm happy to eat your meat for you, if you don't want it," Barlais offered with a smile.

"Yes, eat the rest!" Henry told him. "I'm going to be sick!" He leapt up and ran out of the hall, the napkin clenched over his mouth as if he was about to puke, Johnny close on his heels.

They dashed down the steps from the hall, across the courtyard and continued along the narrow steps to the middle ward, past the garrison church where vespers was being read, and out the other side to run all the way down to the stables. The sight of the King with his friend was far too common to arouse suspicion or comment from the garrison. They were further distracted by their success in killing—or at least wounding—the Ibelin troubadour; Barlais had allowed them an extra ration of wine for that feat, and they were talking among themselves louder than usual.

But the stables were silent, except for the faint scratching and mewing that came from Harry on the far side of the tack room door. Henry crossed the darkness and lifted the latch to let himself into the tack room. Harry crawled to him on his belly and looked up at him with mournful eyes full of incomprehension. Henry went down on his knees and patted the dog's head energetically. "I've brought you an Easter present, Harry. Look!" He opened his napkin and offered the three, half-chewed pieces of meat to his dog.

Harry lapped them up in a split second and looked at Henry for more.

Johnny dropped to his heels beside his friend and opened his purse and poured out his entire portion of meat. "While Barlais was watching you, I got my whole portion into my purse," Johnny explained, proud of himself.

Harry devoured this as well and weakly flapped his tail in thanks while looking from one boy to the other hopefully. Henry bent and laid his head on Harry's head. "I'm sorry, Harry! That's all we managed, but this can't last forever. They've got—"

The door crashed against an empty feed bin so hard that Harry yelped and the boys started. "I knew it!" Barlais shouted, grabbing Henry by the arm and yanking him to his feet. "I knew it all along, you little cheat!"

"Calm yourself, Amaury! He's your king," Sir Grimbert warned. Both he and Sir Hugh de Gibelet were with Barlais.

"We're having puppy soup for breakfast!" Barlais retorted triumphantly, shoving Henry to one side and making a lunge for Harry. Henry grabbed Barlais by the back of his belt and yanked him back so fiercely that he lost his balance and they both fell to the floor.

"You're not going to kill Harry!" The twelve-year-old king screamed at the top of his voice. His fury overwhelmed him so completely that his voice broke. "I'm the King, and I won't let you kill my dog! Ever!" His voice was an octave lower than it had been a second early. He somehow got astride Barlais and started pummeling him with his fists. "He's my dog! I'll have *you* for breakfast before I allow you to kill my dog!"

"Henry!" Sir Grimbert tried to pull the boy off the man, but Henry's rage gave him superhuman strength.

"I'LL BREAK YOUR BALLS. YOU'LL NEVER HURT ME AGAIN!" Henry was roaring. "I'LL FUCK YOU WITH THE BUTT OF A LANCE, YOU BASTARD. I'LL MAKE YOU SCREAM FOR MERCY!"

Both Bethsan and Gibelet grabbed Henry from either side and hauled him backward off Barlais. Although Henry struggled to free himself, the two knights had him firmly under control.

Barlais scrambled to his feet and turned to face Henry. "We'll see who fucks who!" He snarled, his face red with fury. But when he raised his fist to hit Henry,

Sir Grimbert sent Barlais staggering backward with the heel of his hand thrust into Barlais' face. "That's enough, Amaury!" he ordered.

The cousins stared at one another. Henry's rage had subsided enough for him to be grateful that Sir Grimbert stood between him and Barlais. In Barlais' eyes was pure hatred, but Sir Grimbert was much bigger and stronger than Barlais.

Barlais' eyes shifted to Gibelet, looking for an ally, but the latter shook his head. "Grimbert's right, Amaury. We've had enough. You and your arrogance! If Frederick Hohenstaufen was going to aid us, his help would have been here by now. Meanwhile, when summer comes, how long do you think it will before dysentery strikes? It's time to seek terms."

"With Ibelin?" Barlais asked in outraged disbelief. "He'll never make terms! He wants to see me hang! He's always wanted to see me hang!"

"If that's what he wanted, he would have done it by now," Bethsan growled. He didn't move, but he glanced over his shoulder at Henry and with a jerk of his head said, "Get back to your chamber, my lord."

Henry didn't wait to be asked twice. He pushed past Gibelet and ran through the darkened stables to the outer ward. Here, he stopped and looked up at the star-studded sky as his breathing slowly returned to normal. He was both frightened and elated. He had *enjoyed* hitting Barlais. He had *enjoyed* hurting him. Part of him felt that he would never be frightened of him ever again. Certainly, he would *never* let him demean him again. He felt for the little knife Johnny had given him. Johnny had told him to use it if he had to, but he hadn't thought of it in the heat of the moment. And he hadn't needed it. He had *beaten* Barlais—with a little help from Sir Grimbert.

But the fear was there too, like a cold stone in the pit of his stomach. It was a fear of more than Barlais. It was a fear of something much bigger than that. He had freed himself of his fear of Barlais only to realize that Barlais wasn't the problem. The problem was that he was a boy king and his kingdom was being torn apart around him.

"Are you alright?" Johnny's voice reached to him out of the darkness.

Henry turned toward the sound and saw his friend separate himself from the wall and come toward him. Only now did Henry have time to register that Johnny had abandoned him in the stables. Angrily he confronted him, "Why did you leave me alone in there?"

"I thought I should get Harry to safety," Johnny answered in a solemn tone. "Harry! Where is he?"

Johnny looked away.

Henry grabbed his friend. "Johnny? What did you do with Harry?"

"He was starving to death. You know we couldn't have repeated what we did tonight, and even if we did, it wasn't enough!"

"What did you do to him?" Henry demanded again, raising his voice in alarm.

"Shhh!" Johnny hissed back.

"If you killed him, I'll never forgive you!" Henry told him bluntly. He had fought Barlais for Harry.

"I put him over the wall, Henry. I had to drop him about ten feet, but he survived. I heard him yelp and then the underbrush rustling."

Henry stared at his only friend in the world for several seconds and then turned his back on him and walked away. He was not going to cry. He wasn't a baby anymore. He had fought Barlais. But he would never forgive Johnny. This was the end of their friendship.

St. Hilarion, Cyprus
Easter Monday, 1230

Balian was woken by Lucas stubbing his toe on a chest and cursing softly. "How many times do you have to go out in the middle of the night?" he growled irritably at his squire.

"There's a dog in pain out there!" Lucas hissed back. "Can't you hear him?"

Balian rolled over and sat up, frowning in the darkness. Just when he was about to say "No" and tell his squire to go back to sleep, he heard it too: a faint whining sound. "It must be some stray," he dismissed it and lay back down again.

"That dog is in *pain*," Lucas responded indignantly.

"And? What if he is?"

"He might be caught in a trap or injured in some way."

"Lucas, your job is to look after me, not every stray dog that gets himself injured."

"I *do* look after you, sir," Lucas responded stubbornly, "but that doesn't mean I can't try to help that dog."

"Lucas, in case you haven't noticed, it is the middle of the night."

"Yes, sir, but I can't sleep with the sound of that dog begging for help."

"Try," Balian ordered.

For two or three seconds neither of them moved. Then Balian cursed and sat up again. "Alright. Bring me my boots."

Lucas eagerly complied. Balian was sleeping in his shirt and braies. He shoved his bare feet into his boots and grabbed a cloak. Together they ducked out of his tent into the crisp air of early dawn. The stars were only just starting to fade as the eastern sky lightened. Still, there was enough light for them to see the other tents sleeping under the dew of night. The horses nickered at the sight of men moving. The baker was up moving around the oven.

Lucas whispered, "This way, sir!"

With a sigh, Balian followed his squire and the sound of the dog. As this took them closer to the outer walls of St. Hilarion's lower bailey, he scanned the ramparts for some sign of life. There appeared to be a couple of sentries slowly shuffling along their sectors of the wall, but that was all.

"There he is!" Lucas called out in a loud whisper and ran forward. Sure enough, a long-eared, tailless dog was dragging himself through the underbrush. He was all skin and bones and he had a broken hind leg.

"Jesus, Mary, and Joseph!" Balian exclaimed. "That's Harry—the King's dog." He went down on his knee beside Harry, stroking the dog's head instinctively, but his gaze went back toward the castle.

"The King's dog?" Lucas asked, disbelieving.

"Yes, I gave Harry to him about eighteen months ago," Balian informed Lucas, looking again at the miserable bundle of bones before him. Harry was licking his hand in a plea for help. "Come on!" He bent and collected Harry into his arms. Even as the dog yelped in pain at the jostling of his broken hind leg, he tried to lick Balian's face in gratitude. Balian found himself talking to the dog. "It's alright, Harry. You're safe now. We'll set that leg and get you something to eat."

Lucas was content to follow behind Balian, asking only, "Should I wake the surgeon?"

A surgeon had arrived well after dark to attend to Novare. He had pushed the lance tip out the underside of his arm, then cauterized the wound to stop the bleeding. Because Novare was feverish, the surgeon had remained to keep an eye on him.

"I'm not sure the learned surgeon will help a dog," Balian reflected, "but I dare say he's more likely to do so if he's not woken prematurely. Look, Harry's half-starved. Let's get him something to eat and water. You can see the surgeon later."

Inside the tent, Balian sat down on one of his chests, Harry still in his arms, and Lucas brought first a bowl of water and then went in search of leftovers from yesterday's feast. Balian was left stroking the little dog and trying to imagine what King Henry was going through. Had he thrown the dog over the wall himself, or had someone else done it? Was there really so little food left that the King would let his beloved dog starve near to death?

He scratched Harry under his floppy ears and muttered to him. "I'm sure

Henry didn't want to hurt you, Harry." He curled his fingers in the dog's long hair over his shoulders and froze. There was something tucked under the collar.

Balian tugged it free. It was a wood-shaving, the type sometimes used in stables instead of straw bedding. He frowned. Something seemed to be scratched on it, but the lighting wasn't good enough to read. He would have to light a candle or lamp, but he didn't have the heart to disturb Harry, who was cuddling in his arms with so much relief that it almost unbearable.

Lucas returned with bread soaked in the leftovers of the lamb stew and a little bowl of bones and gristle. "The cook says not to give him too much all at once."

"Very wise," Balian agreed. "Can you hold him while I look at something?"

Lucas happily took Harry onto his lap and hand fed him, while Balian went to the door of his tent where the daylight was rapidly increasing. Something was scratched on the wood shaving but it was very hard to read. He turned the shaving this way and that. It said: something (which he couldn't read)—"am"—another unreadable scratch—"J."

Johnny! He felt his stomach turn over. Johnny had sent the message. Maybe he had even thrown Harry over the wall? Maybe he was trying to tell them Henry was as close to death as his beloved Harry! Maybe, maybe, maybe…. He tried again to read the other scratches but impatiently gave up. Whatever it said, Johnny was trying to get a message to them. He had to send word to his father immediately.

St. Hilarion, Cyprus
Easter Monday, 1230

"Not 'am,'" Hugh declared holding the wood shaving up and bending it slightly. "Amnesty."

"What?" Balian gasped.

"Yes. Very clearly," Hugh insisted, "Offer amnesty. J." Pleased with himself, Hugh handed the chip back to their father.

The Lord of Beirut had arrived by mid-afternoon with both of Balian's knighted brothers and his nephew Walter de Caesarea, who had assumed his father's titles since the latter's death at the Battle of Nicosia. He took the wood chip in his hands and looked at it, seeing at last what his third son had deciphered, and he nodded. "Hugh's right. It says 'Offer amnesty.'"

"Never!" was Balian's instant reaction.

Beirut looked up and asked sharply. "What if your brother's life is at stake?

If the King is in danger?" He paused and then cautioned in a gentler tone, "Never say never, Balian. We do not know yet what circumstances or incident induced Johnny to throw a poor, half-starving dog over the walls, and send us that message. We must take it very seriously."

Balian took a breath to protest that he *did* take it seriously, he just didn't think that was the same thing as giving Barlais immunity for all his crimes. Fortunately, before he could contradict his father, Baldwin spoke up to ask, "So what do we do now? Shouldn't *they* be the ones asking for terms? If we make the first approach, it will be interpreted as weakness."

Balian flashed a look of thanks to Baldwin for that. He knew the objection would carry more weight coming from his more rational younger brother.

Beirut took a deep breath and looked toward the castle. "They can see how strong we are."

"They may be hoping for the Emperor's help, though," Hugh pointed out. "As far as we can tell, Rivet made it to Armenia, and from there he may well have gotten word to the Holy Roman Emperor."

Beirut looked at his third son with an unreadable expression.

"We can't exclude the possibility that he will send Barlais aid, either," Balian pointed out.

"All the more reason to make peace with Barlais now," Beirut concluded.

"Offer terms, yes, but not amnesty—at least not for Barlais. If we offer Bethsan and that miserable sycophant Gibelet amnesty, maybe we can induce them to abandon Barlais," Balian suggested.

"And what would you have me do with Barlais?" Beirut asked intently.

"Hang him! He is a traitor many times over!"

"Not to mention he is responsible for my father's death," Walter of Caesarea spoke up for the first time.

Beirut looked to his nephew with sympathy. "I do understand you, Walter. And you too, Balian," he added, "but I can't help thinking Johnny knew something that made him write this—and use the King's dog as his messenger."

"So, I repeat," Baldwin spoke up again, "what do we do? I'm not going up to that gate with a white flag, and I wouldn't walk *through* it for all the gold in Constantinople!"

"I think," Beirut responded pensively. "I think we should request mediation from one of the military orders. The Hospitaller Commander, Brother William de Teneres, made a very good impression on me."

His sons and nephew nodded, if with varying degrees of enthusiasm.

St. Hilarion, Cyprus
May 1, 1230

It took over three weeks for Brother William de Teneres to conclude the terms of surrender. Barlais, Bethsan, and Gibelet retained not only their life and freedom but their fiefs and wealth as well. The only concession they made in exchange for surrender was to swear an oath never to take up arms against the Ibelins again.

When Balian dropped by Novare's tent to tell him it was time to take up the positions to receive the surrender, Novare vehemently refused. "He'll get no kiss of peace from me! He's a treacherous little weasel. He always has been. You can't honestly believe that he will keep his word?" he demanded of Balian incredulous.

"No!" Balian snapped irritably. "No, I don't trust him to keep his word, but my father is set on this. It doesn't help that Tenere reports Henry and Johnny appear to have had a falling out. Henry ignores Johnny in all meetings as if he didn't exist. My father fears Henry may have been turned against us all. If Henry has become fond of Barlais, then punishing him will only earn us the enmity of our King, he says."

"And because a twelve-year-old has been manipulated during his imprisonment, we're all supposed to go out there this morning and throw our arms around Barlais as if he were a long-lost cousin?" Novare demanded. "God knows, Henry will probably change his mind again once he's free. He's just a child!"

"He's about to turn thirteen actually," Balian countered wearily, adding, "In any case, he *is* our king."

"I'm staying right here in my tent!" Philip answered stubbornly.

Balian drew a deep breath and nodded. "Fine. No one can blame you. You're still recovering from your wound." He turned to leave Novare's tent and assume his place beside his father.

"Are *you* going to go out there?" Philip pressed him. "Are *you* going to give the kiss of peace to Barlais?"

"Whether Barlais can be trusted in the future or not, at least today we release our King and my brother from his clutches. That is worth a great deal."

"Giving him everything he wants is too high a price," Philip insisted. "Mark my words. You will regret this. As soon as I'm well enough to play my lute again, I'm going to write a song of warning."

"Do that. I'll be the one who asks you to sing it, but for now I will be the dutiful son and heir," he told his friend firmly. Balian was tired. Tired of fighting with his father and tired of being dismissed as emotional and irrational. Most importantly, he wanted his father's support in requesting a dispensation from the Pope to marry his cousin Eschiva. Obedience would bring him more than defiance.

As Balian left his friend's tent, the Ibelin host was already going into position with banners flying and trappers flapping in the spring breeze. They had pulled together over 250 knights and nearly a thousand archers for this moment, a display of strength and wealth that was intended, Balian knew, to impress upon Barlais and his companions that the Ibelins had the power to break them—whenever they wanted.

Unfortunately, Balian thought to himself, his father didn't want to break them. His father sincerely wanted reconciliation.

The barbican gates stood wide open, and men appeared to be milling around inside, preparing to come out. Balian could see his father and brothers mounting up in front of his father's tent. He needed to hurry up. In his own tent, Lucas was standing by with Damon dressed in his finest panoply: red-suede saddle with brass tacks, a red and yellow trapper, and a leather face guard with the Ibelin cross between his eyes.

As Balian went to mount, Harry darted out of his tent, his hindquarters swaying from side to side in excitement. The dog still had his off-hind leg in a splint, but he ran three-legged with the energy of the reborn. "I thought he should go with you, sir," Lucas explained. "Since he's the King's dog."

Balian bent to pet Harry once and then swung himself up into the saddle. He trotted over to join his father and brothers with Harry at Damon's heels. From the castle walls, a trumpet fanfare announced the official surrender was about to begin.

The sergeants who had been with Barlais emerged from the castle in neat ranks and then divided in two to create an aisle down which the knights came, also on foot. The knights each kneeled before the Lord of Beirut, bowed their heads in submission, and then joined the sergeants at the side. Finally, Barlais, Bethsan, and Gibelet appeared in the doorway of the barbican. Barlais looked bitter, Bethsan relieved and Gibelet wary.

As they advanced together, Baldwin asked in a low voice, "Where's the King?"

"With Teneres," Beirut answered. "Barlais insisted that the King not leave St. Hilarion until I received him in peace. He seemed to think I might yet go back on my word."

Because *he* would, Balian thought to himself, but held his tongue.

Meanwhile, Beirut dismounted and waited for the three men who had caused him so much pain, expense, and worry to advance to kneel before him. It was Bethsan who spoke for them in his gruff, deep voice. "We hereby surrender St. Hilarion, my lord."

"And do you swear never to take up arms against me, my sons or my kinsmen ever again?"

"We do," the three men said in unison. Beirut hesitated, unsure if Barlais had really sworn or not, so he insisted, "One at a time."

Bethsan and Gibelet swore readily. Barlais, still having trouble overcoming his hatred, hesitated but at last spat it out, "I swear."

"Then all is forgiven and forgotten," Beirut declared, and he raised Barlais up and kissed him on both cheeks, followed by Gibelet and Bethsan. Fortunately, before Balian was forced to kiss Barlais, King Henry emerged out of the barbican with his sisters, the Hospitaller commander and Johnny trailing him.

Balian had a shock at the sight of his King. Henry had grown inches, and his surcoat was too short for him. He wasn't only taller, he was also more poised. He had learned from childhood how to behave, of course, but this was more. Henry looked like he was more comfortable in his skin.

At the sight of Henry, Beirut promptly went down on one knee in homage, his sons following his example, and he declared solemnly yet with patent emotion, "My lord king! I cannot tell you what pleasure it gives me to see you alive and well!"

Henry's composure shattered. He broke into a wide smile and rushed forward, exclaiming, "My lord of Beirut! What took you so long? I've been waiting for this moment since the day I arrived!" He was only half jesting, and the reproach left Beirut speechless.

At that moment, Harry broke out from behind Balian and bounded on his three legs toward Henry, yelping with joy and jumping about with so much delight that he seemed sure to break another leg. He tried to jump high enough to lick Henry's face and danced around him with his entire high-quarters swaying back and forth.

When he saw his dog alive, Henry forgot his dignity. "Harry!" He dropped down to embrace his dog, enduring the licks all over his face as he hugged him and patted him in relief. There was nothing anyone could do but wait for the reunion to calm down a bit.

When Henry finally turned his attention back to the humans around him, he looked up at Balian and asked in wonder, "Where did you find him?"

"He was crawling toward the camp. My squire heard his pleas for help."

"And you recognized him?"

"Of course, I did! I was horrified that you had been compelled to expel him, but then I found Johnny's message and realized you were trying to get information to us."

"Message?" Henry looked puzzled, then looked sharply over his shoulder at Johnny. "You sent your father a message via Harry?"

"I didn't know how else to do it, and I thought it might save Harry from Barlais," Johnny explained.

Henry jumped up and ran to Balian, flinging his arms around him. "Thank you! Thank you for saving him! And for saving me! I never want to be left alone with that—" he bit his own tongue, as if remembering he was a king, but the look he flung at Barlais was eloquent enough. Then he shifted his gaze to Beirut without letting go of Balian. "And thank you too, my lord. I know it wasn't easy, or cheap, to besiege this castle for nine months. I know this war has been very costly to you. I—I was so sorry to hear Lord Walter had been killed." His eyes shifted to the young lord of Caesarea as he continued, "I want to visit his grave and say a Mass for him, and we must give thanks together for this peace. I want peace in my kingdom."

As he spoke, Henry drew back from Balian's embrace and transformed himself into a king again. He stiffened his shoulders and stood upright. Although he glanced at Johnny, he spoke to Beirut. "The Ibelins have been my best friends, first your brother Lord Philip and now you and your sons. I won't forget that when I come of age."

"Thank you, my lord," Beirut answered solemnly, echoed by his four sons.

Henry's mood remained solemn as he added with a frown hovering on his brow, "I will not forget what you have done for me, nor what I owe you, but I must tell you I am still afraid."

"Afraid?" Beirut was astonished. "Of what?"

"Of the Holy Roman Emperor," Henry answered without hesitation. "He is a vindictive man, obsessed with what he sees as his God-given greatness. He will never accept that mere barons have defied him, set aside the government he put in place, and freed me of his puppet-strings. He will strike back."

Epilogue

THE STORY OF THE IBELINS AND their fight against Frederick II continues in the next volume of this series *The Emperor Strikes Back: Frederick II's War against his Vassals*. The expected publication date of the next volume is 2019.

For more about the history behind this novel, see the historical notes below, visit my website (http://crusaderstates.com) or follow my blog (http://defendingcrusaderkingdoms.blogspot.com).

Meanwhile,

If you enjoyed this book,
please take a moment to write and post a review on
amazon.com, Barnes and Noble, or Goodreads.
Thank you!
Helena P. Schrader

ịistorical Notes

- The events in this book are largely based on an account written in the mid-13th century by Philip de Novare. The original history written by Novare has since been lost but was carefully reconstructed, using sources that incorporated various parts of his work, by the French historian Charles Kohler in 1913. Kohler's reconstruction of Novare's history was translated into English and annotated by John La Monte in 1936. It was published by Columbia University Press under the title *The Wars of Frederick II Against the Ibelins in Syria and Cyprus*.

- Novare was a prolific writer, most famous as a legal scholar and author of one of the legal treatises that made up the *Assises of Jerusalem*. He was also a poet and a philosopher, who wrote a work called *The Four Ages of Man*. He was born in Novara in Lombardy at an unknown date. La Monte suggests that he was born in the late 12th century based on the fact that, according to Novare's own account, he was a "page" in the service of a knight who participated in the siege of Damietta during 5th crusade (1218-1220). Yet while pages could be as young as seven (and an orphaned boy such as Novare might well have been even younger), it is hardly reasonable that he was over 18 and still a page. An age of 11, on the other hand, would fit perfectly with the activities he describes (reading to a sick knight) and has the advantage of making him a contemporary of Balian. This is, furthermore, consistent with the tone of his own writing—the fact that he speaks of John d'Ibelin (his patron) in tones of awe and respect, while speaking of Balian as his "compeer." It is

particularly significant to me that he wrote his appeal for help to Balian
and that he describes Balian rescuing him at the gates of St. Hilarion.
The bottom line is that we do not know his date of birth and making
him a close friend of Balian served the interests of the narrative best.

- While Novare's age is debatable, there is no doubt that he was a vassal
of the Ibelins and historians agree that he was biased in their favor.
Nevertheless, he was an eye-witness of many of the events described
in this book, and his account remains the only detailed contemporary
history of these events. As such, his book provides a lively, detailed and
authentic account of life in the crusader states of this period.

- According to Novare, after Barlais accused Torginguel of cheating in a
joust, he waylaid and nearly killed him the next day. The Lord of Beirut
had to "use force" to prevent his brother Philip from doing Barlais
harm, and immediately ordered his eldest son Balian to escort Barlais
"wherever he wished to go." Shortly afterward, Barlais left Cyprus and
sometime after that Beirut had him sought out and brought back to
Cyprus in order to enact a reconciliation. He made his brother Philip
forgive Barlais "completely" by threatening never to speak to him again
if he did not. Thereafter, Barlais pretended to "love" the Ibelins, particularly Sir Balian. I have chosen to condense events into a single episode
for the sake of brevity.

- Alice of Champagne's marriage to Antioch occurred after the incident
with Barlais and Torginguel; I have made reference to the marriage and
its implications in the chapter with Barlais and Toringuel for the sake
of keeping the narrative concise and coherent.

- Chronicles differ on the date at which the Count of Acerra was named
baillie by Frederick. Although most historians date his appointment
to a later point in time than I have chosen, it is indisputable that both
Sidon and Montbéliard sailed with Queen Yolanda, and I have found
no source that names another baillie who filled the gap between the
departure of these men and the appointment of Acerra. Since it is
improbable that the Kingdom was left without any regent for more
than two years, I chose to name Acerra (and so introduce him) as baillie
right from the moment of Sidon and Montbéliard's known departure
with Queen Yolanda.

- There is no historical evidence that Beirut's son Hugh was part of the large entourage of lords and knights who escorted Queen Yolanda to her marriage with Emperor Frederick—but there's also no reason why he couldn't have been. We know that Beirut did not go, but it would be plausible for him to send a younger son (who didn't attract much attention) so he had an eye on what was going on and could not be accused of boycotting the event. Most important, it provided a literary device for the details of what happened in Brindisi to reach Beirut.

- As the sister of the Eudes de Montbéliard, baillie of Jerusalem, Eschiva de Montbéliard would have been very suitable as a lady-in-waiting to the Queen of Jerusalem/Holy Roman Empress. There is, however, no historical evidence that she filled this role.

- Furthermore, there seems to be some question as to whether Eschiva was Eudes sister or cousin. She was unquestionably the daughter of Walter de Montbéliard and Burgundia de Lusignan and the granddaughter and cousin of a king. Yet more recent scholarship claims that Eudes (also known as Odo) was *not* the son but rather the *nephew* of Walter de Montbéliard. If this were so, it would explain why Eschiva was such a great heiress, but also made a complex relationship even more so. I opted for the older interpretation that Eudes and Eschiva were brother and sister.

- The coronation of Henry I of Cyprus at the instigation of the Ibelins occurred when he was eight years old. Henry was born May 3, 1217, which means the coronation took place either in the second half of 1225 or early 1226. I have opted for the later date so that the chapter about the affairs of Jerusalem (Yolanda's marriage to Frederick Hohenstaufen) is separate from the chapter about affairs in Cyprus (the dispute between the Ibelins and Barlais).

- Queen Yolanda died in Andria of complications resulting from the birth of her only surviving child, Conrad, on April 25, 1228. Most accounts carelessly give her age as sixteen, but she was not born until November 1212, and so was still fifteen at her death. She had given birth to a still-born child roughly a year earlier, at fourteen.

- Although most historians agree that Frederick II Hohenstaufen's alleged indifference to his wife Yolanda was probably papal propaganda that originated with her father, John of Brienne, the rumors circulated even in his lifetime. It is also historical fact that Frederick, like his Sicilian predecessors, maintained a harem full of slave girls. For the dramatic tension of this novel (which unapologetically takes the side of the Ibelins in their war with the Hohenstaufen), I felt it was legitimate to treat Brienne's accusations against Frederick as fact.

- Michael Scott and Moses ben Samuel are historical figures who played the roles ascribed to them. The two experiments described are attributed to Frederick II.

- The description of the Ibelin palace in Beirut is based on a firsthand account left by Wilbrand, Bishop of Oldenburg, who visited the palace in 1211/1212.

- The judicial combat between Amaury Barlais and Anseau de Brie took place in the fall of 1227, not the summer of 1228. Again, because it is far too important to understanding subsequent events to be left out, I moved it to the summer to include it in the narrative of the novel without more gaps or jumps.

- The number of ships which sailed with Frederick is unclear. Philip of Novare talks of a total of seventy ships, most of which had already proceeded to Acre. The Patriarch of Jerusalem Gerold speaks of forty, but it is unclear if these are the ships that went independently to Acre, or came with the emperor. Other sources (Boulle, p. 97) speak of 23 ships. If the latter were the ships with Frederick and forty had gone ahead to Acre, we would have a total of 63—which is what I have used for this novel.

- The number of troops on these ships is even less clear. Boulle estimates two to three hundred knights and maybe a thousand archers, while he claims the Emperor's traveling household of four (!) archbishops, scholars, clerks, falconers and, of course, his harem took up most of the space.

- The text of the Emperor's letter to the Lord of Beirut and Beirut's arguments for following the Emperor's summons despite opposition from his friends and council are taken directly from Novare's account of the wars between Frederick II and the Ibelins.

- Likewise, the gift of robes, the roles Balian and Baldwin played at the banquet and the verbal exchanges between Frederick II and the Lord of Beirut at the banquet are drawn from this same source—including the promise to do the hostages no harm. Novare's account is in some ways more dramatic because he describes how 3,000 of the Emperor's soldiers were slipped into the palace at Limassol secretly after dark the night before.

- Although there is no question that two of the Lord of Beirut's sons were held hostage and one of these was his eldest son, Balian, some sources suggest the other hostage was Hugh rather than Baldwin. Novare has Beirut personally hand them over to the Emperor, entrusting them to his good keeping.

- Novare reports that the Emperor had Beirut's sons "put in pillories, large and exceedingly cruel; there was a cross of iron to which they were bound so that they were able to move neither their arms nor their legs." He also reports that "Sir Amaury Barlais and his company were quartered in the house where the hostages were in prison. It was said that he did much foulness, which did fall directly upon them." There is no mention in Novare's account of intervention by the Hospital, much less Eschiva de Montbéliard—these are entirely my own invention, yet it seems obvious that since the Ibelin brothers were held by the Emperor for roughly two months, at some point their treatment became more humane or they would not have survived. Nevertheless, Novare reports that when the Emperor finally turned Beirut's sons over to him "they were so miserable that it was pitiful to behold them."

- According to Novare, after Beirut withdrew with his supporters to Nicosia, the Emperor sent to Syria calling "his army and many mercenaries to come to Cyprus." He lists the Prince of Antioch, the Lord of Gibelet, and the Lord of Sidon as coming to support the Emperor. Rather than introduce yet more barons, I decided to give the Teutonic Knights the role of supporting the Emperor's cause because historically they were staunch supporters of the Hohenstaufen.

- During Frederick's sojourn on Cyprus, the Prince of Antioch arrived to welcome Frederick to the Holy Land. Either upon hearing about what happened at the infamous banquet or simply because the Emperor demanded homage of him (which was completely unprecedented, as Antioch had never been subordinate to the Kings of Jerusalem), Antioch pretended illness and fled back to Antioch, where he experienced a "miraculous" recovery. Because so much else was going on in the novel when this occurred historically, I do not refer to it until later, implying it happened when the Emperor was in Acre rather than on Cyprus.

- Curiously, in the same paragraph cited above, where the miserable state of Sirs Balian and Baldwin is mentioned, Novare claims that the Emperor "received Sir Balian into his household and offered and gave him much; and [Balian]...served him willingly and amiably so that emperor was well pleased with him." That was just too much "peace, joy, and apple-pie" for me. I don't believe that someone who had been cruelly mishandled while a hostage would turn around and "happily" serve the man responsible for his mistreatment. The leading modern historian of Cyprus, Peter Edbury, agrees with me and suggests that Balian and Johnny were effectively still hostages, held by the Emperor against their will. What is certain is that both Balian and his younger brother Johnny served in the Emperor's household throughout the 6th Crusade. In looking for a way to reconcile the accounts of Novare and Edbury, it struck me that at the same time the hostages were released King Henry was effectively made Frederick's prisoner and taken on crusade. This made me think the Ibelins might have been concerned for his safety—and their standing with him – and so consented to the arrangement described.

- The news of Frederick II's excommunication apparently did not reach the Holy Land until the Emperor was already in Syria, and allegedly the military orders initially welcomed Frederick with great joy. To describe a flip-flop in feelings, however, seemed like an unnecessary complication, and I preferred to keep the storyline neater.

- According to Boulle, Frederick lived in a palace outside of Acre, but I have no other source for this and found it more convenient to let him stay in the royal palace in Acre.

- The Patriarch of Jerusalem reported with outrage to the Pope that Frederick gave meals for the Saracens with dancers etc., and Boulle suggests that these took place both before and after the actual truce was signed. It seemed appropriate to include one of these, and the storyline dictated the venue as Jaffa. The dancing girls on balls are specifically mentioned as something Frederick took back to Sicily with him, where they became a special attraction of his court there.

- Hard as it is to believe, Emperor Frederick II did turn around and blatantly break the agreement he had made with the Lord of Beirut within six months. He sent Stephan Count of Cotron to seize both the castles and lay waste to Ibelin properties and terrorize his supporters. He did this while Beirut was still serving under the Emperor's banner and while Beirut was protecting Frederick from the ire of the inhabitants. I have found no historian who can justify the Hohenstaufen's treachery; his admirers simply ignore it as they do most of his actions in the Holy Land beyond the "liberation" of Jerusalem.

- Philip of Novare reports, "John d'Ibelin—who later became count of Jaffa and who was a child at that time—with his sister and other gentlefolk fled in the heart of winter, and they encountered such bad weather they barely escaped drowning." (Novare, p. 89). John (who I have called Jacques in this novel to distinguish him from the other Johns—the Lord of Beirut and his fourth son) was the son of Philip d'Ibelin and Alys de Montbéliard, so it was probably his mother who organized this escape, and Eschiva de Montbéliard, as her niece, could well have been one of the "other gentlefolk" with her. Novare says they made landfall at Tortosa, but Beirut would have been a logical place for the Lord of Beirut's sister-in-law to seek refuge.

- Frederick's "crown wearing" ceremony, the content of the speech he wrote for Herman von Salza to read, his visit to the Dome of the Rock (which he admired), and his rebuke of the priest carrying a bible into the al-Aqsa mosque are all recorded in Arab chronicles. Likewise, the exchange with the qadi of Nablus about the muezzins is recorded in Arab sources—as is their disgust for a man who was so contemptuous of his own religion. The terms used to describe himself are taken from a letter he composed for a personal message to a Saracen friend.

- Frederick really did lay siege to the Temple in Acre for five full days. He also threatened the Patriarch of Jerusalem and had the friars that preached against him beaten up.

- Frederick was pelted with offal and rubbish as he walked through the Street of the Butchers to the port to embark on his return voyage. He was rescued by Beirut and Montbéliard. Frederick shouted the names of the baillies of Jerusalem from the deck of his ship.

- Frederick appointed five "baillies" of Cyprus. These were Amaury Barlais, Amaury de Bethsan, a cousin of Barlais, Hugh de Gibelet, William de Rivet and Gauvain de Cheneché. To avoid two Amaurys, I have altered Bethsan's first name to Grimbert—the name used by Novare to describe Bethsan in his poems.

- Frederick appointed the five baillies in exchange for the payment of ten thousand marks, effectively selling control of Cyprus. He also left an unnamed number of mercenaries with them to help them enforce their (Imperial) rule on Cyprus. King Henry was virtually their hostage.

- Novare's encounter with the baillies, in which they demanded that he swear an oath to them, offered to pay his debts, and then ordered his arrest is based on his own, firsthand account. He composed a lengthy message in verse that he sent to Balian d'Ibelin. The excerpts quoted in the text of the novel are direct quotes. The following text is the basis for my fictional account of King Henry and Eschiva warning him:

For all I said, they judged me without law or right.
Within the pillory, the traitors chained me tight.
And then they sought to slay me treacherously at night,
but I was warned by one, who cared not whom it might
displease, who gave me loyal counsel in my plight.

- The castles of St. Hilarion, Buffavento and Kyrenia were unquestionably royal castles, but Kantara is sometimes referred to as a baronial castle. In *The Last Crusader Kingdom*, I chose to make Kantara and Karpas the price of Sir Henri de Brie's adherence to the Lusignan cause, and I continue that tradition here. I wrote long ago, but have not published, a book about Sir Anseau de Brie in which his siege of Kantara is a pivotal event.

- The sortie out of St. Hilarion, while all three of Beirut's sons were away, is a historical event. According to Novare, "Sir Balian came at the news, recovered the camp, and, spurring up to the gate; he broke his lance on the iron of the wall gate; he had so few strong men that this battle was amazing...." (Novare, p. 106)

- Likewise, the incident at Easter when the garrison of St. Hilarion ate a donkey is told by Novare, who also describes being nearly captured and rescued by Balian. He claims he was, "hit one day by the point of a lance which pierced completely through his arm, all of the sleeve of his hauberk and the flesh so that the lance broke on his side and the broken piece remained with the iron in his arm." He relates that the men in the castle cheered triumphantly, thinking he was dead, while his enemies seized the reins of his horse, but "his lord succored him and rescued him most vigorously." (His lord being Balian.) He also brags that "The evening following he made two couplets in song and sang loudly," so that those in the castle knew he was well. (Novare, p. 106)

Glossary

Abaya: a black garment, worn by Islamic women, that completely covers the head and body in a single, flowing, unfitted fashion so that no contours or limbs can be seen. It leaves only the face, but not the neck, visible and is often supplemented with a mask or "veil" that covers the lower half of the face, leaving only a slit for the eyes between the top of the abaya (which covers the forehead) and the mask or veil across the lower half of the face.

Aketon: a padded and quilted garment, usually of linen, worn under or instead of chain mail.

Aventail (also camail): a flap of chain mail, attached to the coif, that could be secured by a leather thong to the browband to cover the lower part of the face.

Baillie: An official exercising the authority of a regent. The constitution of the Kingdoms of Jerusalem and Cyprus recognized the closest relative of a minor king as the "regent," but in cases where that regent was unwilling to assume the day-to-day burden of government (as in the case of Alice of Champagne) or was absent from the kingdom (as in the case of the later years of John de Brienne's reign, or throughout the period in which Hohenstaufens claimed the throne of Jerusalem) one or more baillie was appointed to exercise the power of the regent.

Battlement: a low wall built on the roof of a tower or other building in a castle, fortified manor, or church, with alternating higher segments for sheltering behind and lower segments for shooting from.

Buss: a large combination oared-and-sailed vessel that derived from Norse cargo (not raiding) vessels. They had substantial cargo capacity but were also swift and maneuverable.

Cantle: the raised part of a saddle behind the seat; in this period it was high and strong, made of wood, to help keep a knight in the saddle even after taking a blow from a lance.

Cervellière: an open-faced helmet that covered the skull like a close-fitting, brimless cap; usually worn over a chain-mail coif.

Chainmail (mail): flexible armor composed of interlinking riveted rings of metal. Each link passes through four others.

Chausses: mail leggings to protect a knight's legs in combat.

Coif: a chain-mail hood, either separate from or attached to the hauberk.

Conroi: a medieval cavalry formation in which the riders rode stirrup to stirrup in rows that enabled a maximum number of lances to come to bear, but also massed the power of the charge.

Crenel: the indentations or loopholes in the top of a battlement or wall.

Crenelate: the act of adding defensive battlements to a building.

Crest: a heraldic, cognitive device fixed atop a great helm, popular from the second half of the 13th century.

Crossbow: a horizontal bow spanned by mechanical means, such as a winch, or by a stirrup in which the bowman could use the full weight of his body.

Crupper: armor to protect a horse's rump.

Crusader: The term "crusader" per se was not used in the crusader era, but then nor was American English. In short, the language of this novel is not the language of the subjects in it. It is a modern novel about a past era. The medieval French and Latin terms for those fighting for the Holy Land varied. One common term was "armed pilgrims" (but they were often individuals and not necessarily part of an organized campaign), while another common form of referring to what we call crusaders was "those who took the cross" or "those wearing the cross"—which seem to be complicated ways of saying "crusader" without adding any new information. I have opted, therefore, to use the modern term "crusader," conscious that many will find it an anachronism.

Faranj: Arab term for crusaders and their descendants in Outremer.

Fief: land held on a hereditary basis from a lord in return for military service.

Fetlock: the lowest joint in a horse's leg.

Frank: the contemporary term used to describe Latin Christians (crusaders, pilgrims, and their descendants) in the Middle East, regardless of their country of origin. The Arab term "faranj" derived from this.

Damascening (also inlay): a process for decorating metal surfaces, usually silver or gold, onto iron or steel. It is a form of inlaying wherein grooves or channels are cut into the surface to be decorated and the softer metal, usually shaped first into a tiny wire, is hammered into them.

Destrier: a horse specially trained for mounted combat; a charger or warhorse.

Dromond: a large vessel with two to three lateen sails and two banks of oars. These vessels are built very strongly and were consequently slower than galleys, but offered more spacious accommodation.

Gambeson: a quilted doublet of cloth, often made of linen, but also of leather, worn by all classes either under or on top of a mailed shirt, or as a separate defense on its own.

Garderobe: a toilet, usually built on the exterior wall of a residence or fortification, which emptied into the surrounding ditch/moat.

Gauntlet (also gage): armor defenses for the hands in the form of a glove or mitten. Initially of chainmail, eventually of plate armor. Throwing down one's gauntlet or gage at the feet of another knight constituted a challenge to judicial combat.

Greek Fire: an incendiary developed by the Greeks and decisive in the defeat of the first Muslim attack on Constantinople in 678. It could not be extinguished by water and was usually delivered in grenade-sized pottery pots that broke on impact, spattering the viscous liquid substance. In sieges, larger pottery vessels could be delivered into a besieged city by catapult, but defenders could also use it to destroy siege engines. It was particularly effective against ships.

Hajj: the Muslim pilgrimage to Mecca, one of the five duties of a good Muslim.

Hauberk: a chain-mail shirt, either long- or short-sleeved, that in this period reached to just above the knee.

Iqta: a Seljuk institution similar to a fief in feudal Europe, but not hereditary. It was a gift from an overlord to a subject of land or other sources of revenue which could be retracted at any time at the whim of the overlord.

Jihad: Muslim holy war, usually interpreted as a war against non-believers to spread the faith of Islam.

Kettle helm: an open-faced helmet with a broad rim, common among infantry.

Lance: a cavalry weapon approximately fourteen feet long, made of wood and tipped with a steel head.

Melee: a form of tournament in which two teams of knights face off across a large natural landscape and fight in conditions very similar to real combat, across ditches, hedges, swamps, streams, and so on. These were very popular in the late twelfth century—and very dangerous, often resulting in injuries and even deaths to both men and horses.

Merlon: the solid part of a battlement or parapet between two openings or "crenels."

Outremer: A French term meaning "overseas," used to describe the crusader kingdoms (the Kingdom of Jerusalem, County of Tripoli, County of Edessa, and Principality of Antioch) established after the First Crusade in the Holy Land.

Pommel: 1) the raised portion in front of the seat of a saddle; 2) the round portion of a sword above the hand grip.

Palfrey: a riding horse.

Panoply: the complete equipment of a knight or soldier.

Parapet: A wall with crenelation built on a rampart or outer defensive work.

Quarrel: the arrow or bolt shot from a crossbow.

Quintain: a gibbet-like structure with a shield (or dummy carrying a shield) suspended from one arm and a bag of sand from the other, used to train for mounted combat.

Rampart: an earthen embankment surmounted by a parapet, encircling a castle or city as a defense against attack.

Scabbard (also **sheath**): the protective outer case of an edged weapon, particularly a sword or dagger.

Snecka: a warship or galley which was very swift and maneuverable but had only a single bank of oars and so low freeboard. These evolved from Viking raiding ships and carried square sails. By the late 12th century, some appear to have had battering rams.

Surcoat: the loose, flowing cloth garment worn over armor; in this period it was slit up the front and back for riding and hung to mid-calf. It could be sleeveless or have short, wide, elbow-length sleeves. It could be of cotton, linen, or silk and was often brightly dyed, woven, or embroidered with the wearer's coat of arms.

Tenant-in-chief: an individual holding land directly from the crown.

Turcopoles: troops drawn from the Orthodox Christian population of the crusader states. These were not, as is still mistakenly claimed, Muslim converts, nor were they the children of mixed marriages.

Vassal: an individual holding a fief (land) in exchange for military service.

Also by

Helena P. Schrader

A leper king,
    A landless knight,
        And the struggle for Jerusalem.

Book I in the Jerusalem Trilogy.

Balian, the younger son of a local baron, goes to Jerusalem to seek his fortune. Instead, he finds himself trapped into serving a young prince suffering from leprosy. The unexpected death of the King makes the leper boy King Baldwin IV of Jerusalem—and Balian's prospects begin to improve.

A divided kingdom,
    A united enemy
        And the struggle for Jerusalem

Book II of the Jerusalem Trilogy.

The Christian kingdom of Jerusalem is under siege. The charismatic Kurdish leader Salah ad-Din has united Shiite Egypt and Sunnite Syria and declared jihad against the Christian kingdom. While King Baldwin IV struggles to defend his kingdom from the external threat despite the increasing ravages of leprosy, the struggle for the succession threatens to tear the kingdom apart from the inside.

A lost kingdom,
    A lionhearted king,
        And the struggle for Jerusalem

Book III of the Jerusalem Trilogy.

Balian has survived the devastating defeat at Hattin and walked away a free man after the surrender of Jerusalem, but he is a baron of nothing in a kingdom that no longer exists. Haunted by the tens of thousands of Christians enslaved by the Saracens, he is determined to regain what has been lost. The arrival of a crusading army led by Richard the Lionheart offers hope—but also conflict, as natives and crusaders clash and French and English quarrel.

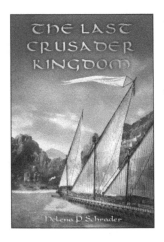

An armed insurrection,
    A military occupation,
        And the dawn of a dynasty.

John d'Ibelin, son of the legendary Balian, will one day defy the most powerful monarch on earth. But first, he must survive his apprenticeship as squire to a man determined to build a kingdom on an island ravaged by rebellion. The Greek insurgents have already driven the Knights Templar from the island, and now stand poised to destroy Richard the Lionheart's legacy in the Holy Land: a crusader kingdom on the island of Cyprus.

Learn more about the Crusader Kingdoms at: http://crusaderkingdoms.com

Or follow my blogs: http://defendingcrusaderkingdoms.blogspot.com and http://schradershistoricalfiction.blogspot.com to learn more about the historical background for this novel and progress on the next: *The Emperor Strikes Back.*